Praise for Tom Carson's
Daisy Buchanan's Daughter

"Tom Carson's new novel is simultaneously an epic sequel to *The Great Gatsby*, a tour-de-force meta-narrative of the last 90 years of American history, and a dazzling feat of old-fashioned storytelling. The octogenarian narrator of *Daisy Buchanan's Daughter* is by turns wistful, sarcastic, bemused, nostalgic, furious, and scathingly funny as she evokes—intimately, pungently, and in gorgeous detail—the best and worst century in human history (so far). **She is the first great literary character of the new millennium, and her all-encompassing story is some sort of crazy masterpiece.**"

    —James Hynes, author of *Next* and *The Lecturer's Tale*

"To the generations of Fitzgerald readers who wondered what became of Daisy Buchanan's daughter, Tom Carson has the answer. She grew up not careless, but witty, seductive, alarmingly intelligent, and possessed of supernal powers of observation. She lived nine decades that swerved to include everything from prewar depression, to war coverage, to Cold War power-jockeying and well beyond, with Broadway, Hollywood, and jet-set stopovers aplenty. She did it all with an eye that took in everything from the way her contemporaries were wearing their suits to what lies they told the public and each other. And she recorded it all in a playful, imaginative, and extremely funny narrative—and posted it online. Great dames of the 20th century, open your ranks: Pam Buchanan is part of the sisterhood."

    —Farran Smith Nehme, the Self-Styled Siren

"As brilliant as fireworks exploding over the Washington Monument, *Daisy Buchanan's Daughter* is that rarest of triumphs—a laugh-out-loud funny novel that's also dead serious. Conjuring an American landscape in which fictional characters seem as real as flesh-and-blood people, Tom Carson's unforgettable heroine escapes from *The Great Gatsby* to take us on a tour-de-force guided tour of the past century, from flipped-out flappers to Dubya's dream of the orgastic future. Here is history seen through the looking glass—delirious, diabolically witty, and absolutely unique."

    —John Powers, Critic at Large for NPR's *Fresh Air with Terry Gross* and author of *Sore Winners: American Idols, Patriotic Shoppers, and Other Strange Species in George Bush's America*

"Take a skippy, dizzy, dazzling joyride with a chick who cracks the East and West Eggs wide open. The old lady holding the gun and the keyboard may be Daisy Buchanan's daughter, but she's the stylish stepchild of Nabokov, blogging about what happened after Fitzgerald set down his pen. Her own wild adventures—literary, sexual, historical—anticipate a fateful phone call from one of the great villains of recent years. Pammie is the dame-iest of dames, and this is the rompiest of reads. Huzzah!"

—Susann Cokal, author of *Mirabilis* and *Breath and Bones*

"In this inventive and masterful novel, Tom Carson takes us inside the privileged post-Gatsby world of the iconic Buchanans, bringing to bear his exquisite and confident imagination as he presents the world of Daisy Buchanan's daughter—a world no less fraught and socially dangerous than the one in which Fitzgerald's characters roamed. Carson's skill with multiple voices brilliantly illuminates the kaleidoscopic sense of identity one invariably finds in a brittle milieu. The reader will be captivated."

—Thaisa Frank, author of *Heidegger's Glasses* and *A Brief History of Camouflage*

"Sprawling, clever, flamboyant, recklessly ambitious, *Daisy Buchanan's Daughter* takes gigantic risks and delivers gigantic rewards. There aren't many people writing novels like Tom Carson, but one may be all we need."

—Geoff Nicholson, author of *Bleeding London* and *Gravity's Volkswagen*

Daisy Buchanan's Daughter

Daisy Buchanan's Daughter

TOM CARSON

Paycock Press
Arlington, Virginia

This is a work of fiction. All of the characters and events portrayed in this novel are either products of the author's imagination or are used fictitiously.

Cover painting by Glenn Arthur
Design and copyediting by Nita Congress
Printed by Main Street Rag Publishing, Charlotte, NC

ISBN-10: 0-931181-34-8
ISBN-13: 978-0-931181-34-4

First Edition
Published in the USA

Paycock Press
3819 North 13th Street
Arlington, VA 22201
www.gargoylemagazine.com/books/paycock/paycock.htm

Visit www.daisysdaughter.com.

In memory of Alice, with love to her friends.

My deepest thanks to Richard Peabody—a man I'm proud to call "Big X"—and to designer/editor extraordinaire Nita Congress. A special thanks to Glenn Arthur for letting us use *Le Navigateur*.

For help of various kinds, I'm also grateful to Virginia Carson Young, Ron Perkowski, Saïdeh Pakravan, Arthur Shaffer and David Rowland, Ron Anteroinen, and Alberto and Victoria F. Gaitán.

"One thing that flatters me and Bill a lot is that Diana, who is normally shy with children, seems genuinely devoted to ours so we don't feel that it is a strain for her when we take them to Chantilly. Anne hangs on her words and follows her in from the garden helping to carry the great heaps of flowers, and stands adoringly passing them up as Diana creates one of her magical arrangements. 'Four delphiniums now, Anne, mix the pale blues with the darker. Thank you. Now a big bunch of roses. That's it. Always remember when doing a mixed bouquet to have clumps of the same flower together. Not one here, one there, that makes for an arty bouquet. Arty things are common, don't you agree?' 'Yes, Lady Diana...Is it a party, Lady Diana?' 'No, it isn't, and that is why we must take a lot of trouble...Suppose we put the white china unicorn on the middle of the table and make a wreath of white flowers for him to wear around his neck. Shall we go to pick the wild flowers?'"

—Susan Mary Alsop, *To Marietta from Paris, 1945–1960*

There was an old man of Khartoum
Who kept two black sheep in his room.
To remind him, he said,
Of two friends who were dead.
But he never would specify whom.

—quoted by Gene Smith in *When the Cheering Stopped: The Last Years of Woodrow Wilson*

Contents

Part One

1. Cadwaller's Gun

POSTED BY: *Pam*   As of now—6:22 a.m. on Tuesday, June 6, 2006, my eighty-sixth birthday—my full name is Pamela Buchanan Murphy Gerson Cadwaller. I'm waiting with some asperity for a telephone call from the President of the United States.

You know how his minions must've hounded poor Potus, congratulations to the likes of me not crisp in their relation to his game plan. "The old bag will never make it to ninety, Mr. P.!" they said. "And she did a lot of something or other back in the way-back-when."

True enough, I did. Google away. For the fuck of it I sometimes do myself, checking Pam's grip on cyberspatial immortality. Are you surprised this old bag knows how to surf the Web? Mine was the first female voice broadcast from Omaha Beach. Beyond its grassy bluffs, a lone Spandau still hammered as D-Day waned. I believe I can handle your toy.

That five-mile crescent was ours by then. The proof was that rations were being unloaded around us along with ammunition. I'd done Anzio, and I knew how that first case of Hershey bars meant victory. Just didn't expect what happened next, as the flicks of distant tracer fire making a tailor's dummy out of twilight had damned little resemblance to candles. Neither did the hulks of charred landing craft to gifts.

"Happy BIRTH-day, Miss Bu-chan-an—HAP-py birth-day to you." Heard in the States on my better-known colleague Edmond Whitling's radio report, the original recording is in the National Archives, crackling on earphones for school groups to whom such sonic chaff is now the Baskin-Robbins side of history. Listen close for Pam Buchanan, just turned twenty-four, saying faintly, "Thank you, boys! Thank you all very much."

I'm now a longtime Washingtonian by not only address but temperament. Encased in fat lunettes, the mimsy borogoves I call my glaucomedic eyes have watched those school groups spill out of the Archives many times into our summer's gobs of unhaulable heat. Then their no less Baskin-Robbinsy teacher calls out, "All right! Who's going to the Holocaust?" As lovely girlish arms stick up, I wonder if they've just heard my voice.

Sensational 1943 divorce from Murphy or no sensational 1943 divorce from Murphy, I'm sure none of those temporary survivors of Company A, 116th Infantry, 29th "Blue and Gray" Division, landed to be massacred at H Hour and left behind like dazed American barnacles on the Vierville sea wall by fresher troops' advance, knew me from Venus on the halftrack. All they were in a position to understand was that some lanky dame had crouched among them—"And *now* what?," their eyes said—yelping "Where you from, soldier?" and passing around dry Lucky Strikes. I may've been a sort of human Hershey bar with two almonds under the wrapper myself, maybe not the finest candy but definitely made in U.S.A.

Getting sung to on Omaha as bulldozers finished clearing the exit wasn't Pam's idea of "If they mean to have a war, let it begin here." But Eddie Whitling was no chump at contriving human interest for the home front. Hearing a grainy "Happy Birthday" sung in no longer wholly occupied France would tell the other Omaha—Nebraska's—that not only were our boys ashore but the day's costs hadn't damaged their humor. Spotting his opportunity in Company A's lack (I wonder why) of officers, he beguiled—since I don't want to use a stronger word—beguiled those weaponless and stunned late adolescents into singing to his pal Pamita.

"*Happy birthday, Miss Buchanan—happy birthday to you.*" In Pam's own D-Day piece, finished with a gin assist (I just hated those buzz bombs) in London two weeks later—"The Day the Tide Ran Red," *Regent's* magazine, June 28, 1944—I omitted that chorus in chafed fatigues around the perpendicular pronoun. There I am thanking them in the Archives' earphones like some lost stewardess on Clio Airways just the same. Then I inanely add, "Good luck to you tomorrow, boys!" On the recording, the grind of newly landed trucks blots out my most vivid *viva voce* memory: a teenage voice saying, "Tomorrow?"

Eventually, Eddie and I had a confused fight about his stunt. It was over a dinner of *omelettes à la rations K* near Notre Dame, in a Paris forced to depend—oh, but it was enough—on its pure Parisness for wonder. On an ocean of cheers, de Gaulle had just strolled up the Champs-Élysées, and Eddie grinned at my naive belief our friendship made him human. Nonetheless, when it comes to memorable birthday serenades, Potus will have his work cut out for him to compete.

POSTED BY: *Pam*   "She was some sort of stewardess for something called Clio Airways, Mr. President," they said. "She wrote some book called *Glory Be* and married some Ambassador. No, one of ours, not one of theirs. He's long dead and she's one of those old bags who roost on upper Connecticut Avenue like falcons. On the plus side, she used to be on some museum board with your mother."

I was for fact, the pearly bitch. Even then, she looked as if she launched herself each morning by smartly cracking a perfume bottle over her own jaw. Recruiting Pam thirty years ago for whatever District cultural chore stood in urgent need of pointless discussion must've been one of Callie Sherman's odder jokes, which if you know Callie is saying something.

"Just make the call, please, sir," they said. "We know it won't do much for your afflatus, Potus, but it's only a blip in your day. No, sir—we can't figure out why *he* cares either. It's the first time he's asked us a favor in forever."

Dear Bob. I don't really know my Senatorial benefactor well at all. Callie Sherman introduced me to him too, and later he surprised and touched me by adding Pam's name to the honored-guest roster for the dedication of the World War Two Memorial on the Mall. I gather he's forgiven me for what I brayed as that atrocity smacked my fat lunettes: "My God! Why didn't they tell us the *Germans* won?"

Even so, he's plainly never wrapped a brain with plenty of more bulging files in its cabinets around the fact that I'm a liberal Democrat. Or else he supposes the flattered senior citizen or *noblesse oblige* Washingtonian in me will make decorum win out. Oh, well, what the hell: his factotum *did* hang up without asking me what I think of this awful and unending war.

Bob doesn't know my bitter current name for the city we both love is Potusville. When his office phoned yesterday to give me a heads-up about the treat he'd laid on, I felt mildly pleased he'd remembered me, much less my birthday. Also mildly amused by his faith I'd be honored to get even this President's June 6 salutations and mildly annoyed at the prospect of having to take the damn call. Only when I let the Metro section of today's *WashPost* settle rugward, skating-seagull style, did I gather a decision I hadn't even known I was mulling had been made.

My only remorse is that Bob meant well and I'm fond of him. What I'm planning is a betrayal of his apparent, surprising affection for me. The White House won't be panting for his *next* request to give some upper Connecticut Avenue crone a holler, put it that way. And too bad, because is Potus ever going to get an earful!

The gun in my lap was Cadwaller's. It nestles near my most intimate memory of his cranium in younger, nuder days, during that expert diplomat's preferred (he swore!) stage of our lovemaking. Like so much about Hopsie, the pistol seemed mildly absurd until the night a thief brazenly broke, with an annunciatory crash whose declarativeness would've pleased Beethoven, into the Residence in Delhi. Then my brisk third husband reached behind a certain book on our shelves and it jumped into his hand as obediently as a phone receiver, his customary daytime armament.

Which sound is the one with which Potus is most unfamiliar? Because I'm only human, I'll laugh if you say "Beethoven," but the answer is a shot fired in anger. If I can find the nerve to fire it, mine will be.

"She's harmless enough, your brush-cutting majesty," they said. "What can she do to you? Even if she's a tiresome old bag and no Christian, she's too old to be a terrorist."

Hah. As I fetched the gun from the Paris footlocker, I began humming a tune I'd heard for the first time quite recently. Didn't get far, since I'm eighty-six and have the singing voice of an aardvark. But I wanted to please Panama, Cadwaller's unmet—by him, not me—great-granddaughter.

POSTED BY: *Pam*   Rightly or wrongly, I think I've got some standing as well as a stake in all this. That's not just because *Glory Be* was edged out for the '57 history Pulitzer only by Jack Kennedy's *Profiles in Courage*. At least I'd written mine myself, not that Jack laughed when I told him so.

Or that Richard Anson "Hopsie" Cadwaller was one of the finest envoys this country ever produced. Or that the interior décor of my digs at the externally nondescript Rochambeau Apartments, a pile of slag in wolverine gray whose juts and recessed windows probably looked eloquent when Coolidge was in, is actually pretty goddam, well, descript.

Panama Cadwaller is now sixteen. Her pirouetting and earplugged visits to "Gramela" always seduce her into examining bric-a-brac whose oddity must strike her as belonging to a forgotten *ancien régime* somewhere on Mars. Yet to Pam's fellow old District hands, my loot—"*Oh hé, oh hé, bibelot*," goes the corsair song of the U.S. Foreign Service—is instantly decodable as the spoor of diplomatic postings in the way-back-when.

Once visitors dogleg from foyer to living room, they're met by the African Adam and Eve, two whittled sentinels of mine whose unabashed dowsing rod (his) and genital pineapple (hers) vaunt fertility as a be-all and end-all. Also from the former Nagon is my small maquette of copper figurines pegged to a salver. Depicting a seated woman with arms outflung on a palanquin, it's been known to three generations of Hopsie's progeny as "The African Queen."

On the wall above is a silkscreened Ganesh, Pam having adopted the elephant-headed god as her mascot during Cadwaller's Ambassadorship to India. During her own time in Delhi, my dear friend Nan Finn was always a Hanuman gal instead. No other religion has gods that so invite affection and followers who don't feel insulted when that's all there is to it.

Signed by Hopsie, me, Andy Pond, Callie and Cy Sherman, and a couple of dimmer names, the framed menu is from Paris, where Cadwaller and I met in the Fifties. We'd been married two years by that La Coupole lunch, and I still remember how I dropped my oyster fork and the waitress crouched to retrieve and then replace it with a new one even though my dish was empty. Who knew whether the happy American lady would order another half dozen after she'd smiled her gratitude and wonder?

Beyond my Mac's screen as I input with rheumatic fingers and lunetted mimsies by my living room window, where dawn's cerise is already giving way to torched daffodils, Pam's trophy bookcase looks eager to chip in. With *Glory*

Be bookended by *Nothing Like a Dame* and *Lucky for the Sun*, my own trio of contributions to library sales crowns its top shelf.

Down at cat level, Brannigan Murphy's *Collected Plays*—from a minor academic press, and remaindered when I picked it up in a fit of post-marital loyalty—looks sheepishly bullheaded. In between, among others, are Cadwaller's photographer son Chris's *May or Mayn't*, eighty or so images of Paris barricades, rock-throwing students, and cops wreathed in tear gas during the '68 upheavals, and Chris's son Tim's *You Must Remember This: The Posthumous Career of World War Two.*

As the last of these is dedicated to me, I did my damndest. But culture criticism will never be this old bag's bag. Though musings on faith aren't either whether they're Catholic or pagan, I can't help being fonder of *The Mountain and the Stream*, my onetime guardian's collected letters from Nenuphar Monastery, and *The Pilgrim Lands at Malibu*, by possibly my favorite minor poet. The half dozen cookbooks by Dottie Crozdetti have made Andy Pond chortle more than once, since he knows better than anyone that Pam in a kitchen is Nixon at a beach resort.

Nearby, my Anzio Bobbsey twin Bill M.'s book of war cartoons and Nachum ben Zion's *Israel: One State, Two Nations* bicker in a friendly way over which one's inscription to Pam is warmer. Another old friend is a slim volume called *The Producer's Daughter*, subject of a review by Pamela Buchanan that caused some controversy at the old *Republic*'s offices back in '41. While I've never met or corresponded with its author, over the decades I've felt a sisterly affinity and gotten odd hints it's reciprocated.

Hung in the bathroom and visible in reflection in my daily medicine-cabinet mug shot is a gift from Tim Cadwaller: a one-sheet for Metro's 1949 flop *The Gal I Left Behind Me*. Most prized today thanks to the young actress whose button nose and luscious eyes swim out from under an overseas cap between two doll-sized men atop her shoulders—however negligible otherwise, it was Eve's first film—the poster is more cherished by Pam for less prominent reasons. Nestling in small type among its quartet of screenwriters, my name presciently nuzzles the "Gerson" in the credit underneath mine. Rotten movie, though, not that I've seen it since the first Glendale preview almost sixty years ago.

The most ancient and/or tattletale of my mementos, however, stay out of sight in Pam's catless and Christ knows sexless bedroom. They're in the foot-locker with my mother's effects that got sent two weeks too late to my old school in Chaillot. The damn thing sat for a decade in Chignonne's attic before wise-cracking Eddie Whitling and I pulled up in front of said school's vined façade in a jeep late on August 25, 1944. Augmented by my own marital trophies, Cad-waller's gun included since his death twenty years ago, the Paris footlocker's contents may not only explain my sense of having some standing as well as a stake in all this but provide a reductively psychological explanation for the origin of my anti-Potus animus.

POSTED BY: *Pam*   My mother was Daisy Fay Buchanan. Unknown now except to Jazz Age specialists, she was one of the nudest pearls in that era's champagne goblet until the scandal whose aftershocks, ultimately leading Mother and me to sail for Europe in confusion (hers and definitely mine), italicized my childhood.

As everyone knew once, she missed arrest or even grilling. Yet however indolent our moneyed neck of Long Island liked its police work to stay, three corpses had stunk up the joint. Plenty of rumors swirled around us, lapping even small Pammie's chubby-kneed legs.

One held Daisy'd been behind the wheel (true), the other and nastier that she'd fired the gun (not). Until my divorce from Brannigan Murphy became a more urgent source of social jitters—no new acquaintance ever quoted Pam's most notorious courtroom jape to my face, but dozens couldn't help reciting it with their eyes—the conversations I was least likely to enjoy were those that brought out who my mother was.

That stayed true for a few years after the proper tense became *had been*. Since dead Daisy's exit had been unforeseen, abrupt, and noisy, the less usual bang following her more customary whimper as she lay alone in her Brussels bedroom one all too Belgian day in the winter of '34, you'd think that might make strangers kinder but frequently it didn't.

Unexpectedly, one who broke the mold was Mencken. The only time I met him was in the press gallery at the 1940 Republican convention: twenty-year-old Pam had tagged along to Philadelphia with a political writer for the old *Republic* who turned out to know him slightly. He told me the Scandal hadn't been so *very* momentous back in the Twenties: "Really just a sort of anecdote."

So too, perhaps, will be her daughter's telephonic protest today. So too, no doubt, my life, my books. Its Amazon ranking "from these sellers" reliably roosting in seven figures, the long out-of-print *Glory Be*, quite the treekiller for Random House in Eisenhower's time, might as well be retitled *Glory Went*.

Despite the retitled movie version's belated cult appeal, *Nothing Like a Dame* (Holt, 1947), Pam's frothy account of knocking around as a gal war correspondent in the ETO—European Theater of Operations to you post-deluvians out there—isn't about to get reissued. Until Tim Cadwaller looked up the date of *South Pacific*'s premiere, even he thought I'd gotten the title from Rodgers and Hammerstein. Not that I'm bitter, of course.

Short version? "You're some dame," said Richard Rodgers as we ate breakfast together in '46. To which I replied, wearing nothing but his shirt at the time—I was one of that tireless adulterer's more fleeting conquests—"I am nothing like a dame." Then we looked at each other and I dashed back to my Brooklyn garret, stuffing his shirttails into my skirt, while he got poor blinkered Hammerstein on the phone. But I wrote a lot faster.

As for my third and final contribution to Gutenberg's funeral pyre, *Lucky for the Sun* couldn't have sunk faster back in '68 if it'd had Jimmy Hoffa's ankles chained to it. All in all, I'd rate myself about as minor as celebrities get. Even so, one reason my planned act of telephonic terrorism has already made me grin as I rattle away on my Mac—last year's Yuletide medusa, brought here with bows on and tentacles trailing by Cadwaller's son Chris—is the headache I'm sure to give the *WashPost*'s and *NYT*'s obit writers.

It's not hubris to assume mine is long prepared, only partly thanks to Mother. That's why I've just chuckled again through my *Popular Mechanics* dentition. Cause of death aside, most likely all my obit has left blank to plug in with a "TK"—trad newspaperese for "To come," I'm only guessing still in use—is who survives me in the final graf.

I also guarantee that in my case "Survivors TK" is a formality. The only reproducing Pam's done has been the result of anonymous paid sex with Xerox photocopying machines. Their genetic contribution to the bairns—my articles, of course—strikes me as unflattering but not decisive.

But a new opening graf or two or three, cobbled together in extremis? Even today, any family newspaper worth its endlessly passed salt won't reprint the unexpurgated Pam-quote that helped make my first divorce New York's most sensational of 1943. Figuring out a backflip from my obit's startling new lead to Pam's way-back-when will stump even those specialists in shovel-ready legerdemain. While I've seen it done and quite recently too, that doesn't mean it's easy.

At most or worst, the obit writers were prepared for one last marriage. Some groping union in my senescence, some phallic fallacy groggily probing my mess of dotage. Among other things, that's what I intend to deny them.

POSTED BY: *Pam*　　　The problem's that I know myself unreasonably well. Every brave act I'm said to have performed, marrying Murphy ever Manhattan's Exhibit A in the way-back-when, has been Pam's way of indulging a suspected greater cowardice.

You know, I couldn't have invaded the Philippines. That's despite the grumblings of *Regent's* editor that all us literary stage-door-Johnnies lining up theaters of war were obnoxiously wild for our sainted Europe. Roy bemoaned our selfishness in letting those muddy bastards in the Pacific die minus chic prose's unction.

A true bill it was too, from *Marseillaise*-humming, gustatorially concupiscent Joe Liebling on down. I was three years out of Barnard and I couldn't bring myself to buck my prejudices. Bugs, diseases, larvae, ordure, MacArthur: no cocktail shakers nearer than Sydney. Hell, I'd've *swum* to France.

Incidentally, my objection to Liebling, and I know having any puts me on the outs with settled taste, is that he *wrote* like a fat man. Nothing so disastrous to humanity that he couldn't adjudicate it as a meal. Gerson, my second husband, loathed him. But no matter.

I was about to launch into a splendid discussion of my cowardice. Look! There's the *WashPost*'s Metro section at my feet, done with its dotty brief imitation of a Chekhovian seagull. Considering I've just explained my intention to fire a gun whose bang will surely shock the shit, indeed we did and do talk that way, out of Potus—not that he'll otherwise be its target or in harm's way, since he's a couple of miles from here and I'm visibly alone in this room, without even a cat—you may be forgiven for wondering just what I'm hoping to *avoid* thereby.

In the glow of my plan's dawn thrill before I logged on, my answer would've been a heroic "Nothing!" Even though Pam's one appearance onstage, subbing for ailing Viper Leigh in *A Clock with Twisted Hands* on its opening night in 1941, got me clouted with the accurate verdict "no-talent" by the playwright (Murphy), I do have an actress in me, as Cadwaller may have known best of all. The truth is that self-devised heroics, or vainglory in a drool cup if my charm as a telephonic terrorist is utterly lost on you, are never exempt from the bubble-bubble-stew of multiple agendas.

Even as I fetched Cadwaller's gun and hummed Pam's aardvarky "La, la, la—la, la," I decided to suspect my own buried motive. I knew Andy Pond would and fat chance I'll ever let him be smarter than I am. Nicer, not smarter, is the trophy I've never competed for against Cadwaller's onetime Paris deputy. One proof Andy's got a monopoly on nicer is that he never complains when I hurt his feelings.

Hurt his feelings, though, this will. I don't know what kind of coverage my protest will get: my protest on behalf of bankrupt, never existed, but fondly remembered Clio Airways against this Administration's splatter of diarrhea over everything we stood for—flawed, lumbering, but gallant—in the way-back-when. But even if my act is ridiculed, Andy knows me.

He'll understand that to his old friend Pam, her idiosyncratic pistol shot had dignity. Unfortunately, as a trained analyst of mingled public and private motives—Hopsie always said Andy got it better than most—he'll also intuit the corollary. To wit, that I must've decided that remarrying at my age—and in my shape, since now I look and usually feel like a pretzel someone gave up on midway through unbraiding—did not.

Andy, if you pass up the vaudeville cue to murmur "Pam, a simple 'No' would have done fine," you'll disappoint me.

POSTED BY: *Pam*   Even under duress, I'd never have blurted out my reaction when Andy's hope of a December-January matchup first dangled its withered mistletoe. To wit, that it'd feel like marrying my favorite endtable, bought by the new Mrs. Cadwaller in Paris in '58 and presently doing marble-topped mail-catching duty in my apartment's foyer. I didn't even think it was an insult: when you've moved house as often as I have, you're fond of seeing the good old furniture turn up on the next continent. I can still see how he might not be delighted by the comparison.

Not that he'd take offense or anyway show it, since he's a gentleman. He was awfully good during Cadwaller's long dying. Then he made every practical decision—except for the site, my one fetish—about Hopsie's burial in the diplomatic section of Rock Creek Cemetery.

In the District, where pigeons have their pick of gesturing admirals ("What the hell is that, Gridley? Land? Explain yourself, sir"), mounted generals ("I've put in two quarters, and this thing *still* isn't moving"), and inquiring Founders ("This place is strange to me, Miss. Could you direct me to the Executive Mansion?"), that patch of moss near the Madeleine Lee memorial is the only monument to the "striped-pants boys," as the way-back-when's yahoos called them. There Cadwaller's ashes have rested compactly since 1986, and only many years later did Andy start to press his quiet suit.

Eventually, he got into it, put the ironing board away, chose a tie, and came over here. Sorry, but Andy does bring out my Perelman side. In truth, it may've been a decade since I've seen him in a tie. After his last posting in East Berlin, he adopted retirement's male uniform of old sports jacket, gray slacks, open-collared white shirts under V-necked red sweater—when the *sweater* is the splash of color, a man has calmly accepted aging—and ancient but lovingly tended loafers. In some leafy and unevenly sidewalked residential neighborhoods of the District, that outfit says *retired Foreign Service officer* the way antic frogging under coronation headgear would lead you to expect a chorus of "Sgt. Pepper's Lonely Hearts Club Band."

My junior by two birthdays, Andy has the fine head of a minor jurisprudential figure in a Siena mural, teeth from nature's catalogue rather than the *Popular Mechanics* manual my teenaged dentist uses—"And which Hardy Boy might *you* be?" I asked unkindly when he first examined my X-rays, and of course he'd never heard of them—and elegant long fingers he's fond of flexing and steepling. When a man's last surviving pride is his cuticles, he's no longer thinking of the world's approval but his coffin's.

Andy's also a lifelong bachelor, and as he's awfully easy on the eyes, that used to raise knowing eyebrows in our crowd. Then those brows' owners would learn better, in my case from Cadwaller. "He's had a girl at every post I've known about," my final husband set me—and you might say Andy—straight soon after I'd met his Paris No. 2. "He just likes women who won't complicate the rest of his life."

"And nothing ever comes of it?"

"I gather what I've just said didn't cover that for you," said Hopsie. "The Foreign Service is full of bores who've mistaken themselves for enigmas. Andy's the reverse."

True, since something about him so pleasantly forbids inquiry that half a century later I still don't know what Andrew C. Pond's middle initial stands for. He's a "Yes, and" conversationalist: "Yes, and then Rummy called it old Europe," he'll say to my latest Pamamiad over lunch with Nan Finn in Georgetown at Martin's or La Chaumière. "Yes, and did you see what Peggy Kristhammer wrote yesterday?" he'll chirp as he drives Pam to the Kennedy Center for another stinko production of lousy *La Traviata*.

Of course his "Yes, ands" always jump-start me. "Considering the intelligence of the average NRA member, I think they're doing the world a *favor* by leaving lots of loaded guns around for their children, don't you?" I'll say, craning my neck a bit awkwardly as he loads my despised wheelchair—"Just in case"— into his car's back seat before we set out on the long drive to another geezers' waltz past Bethesda Naval Hospital toward Maryland or past Arlington Cemetery into Virginia. And Andy will close the rear door and then mine, open the one on the driver's side, get in, smile, and say, "Yes, and don't forget little Mack McCork saying reconstruction will pay for itself. Rakh, rakh, rakh."

He's never outright proposed. At our age, getting down on one knee has its perils. Forcing Cadwaller's old ring past my rheumatic knuckle to slip on a new one would require passing up the minister so we can hire a surgeon. In recent months, though, the oblique equivalent—"Did I really just nearly sideswipe that messenger? Pam, I'm definitely not the driver I used to be. Wouldn't it be much easier if we were under the same roof?," etc.—has cropped up more and more often.

I do loathe this wheelchair, or perhaps I mean that I loathe being seen getting trundled along in it in public when Andy insists on sparing my shaky pins.
If I'm sitting in it now as I rattle away on my Mac, that isn't because Pam's too
dilapidated to manage the distances inside this apartment from the table beside
my living room window to the bathroom, the bookcases ranged along the interior wall next to the foyer, the bathroom behind my right shoulder, or the Paris
footlocker in the catless and sexless bedroom behind my left. I'm sitting in it
because sitting in it means I don't have to look at it.

POSTED BY: *Pam*   One reason I know Andy has marriage and not shacking up in mind is that he was so close to Cadwaller. While marrying Hopsie's
widow would earn him nothing but congratulations from Hopsie's ghost,
shacking up would put Andy at perennial risk of watching my third husband
tug his ear and mutter something mild but devastating about seemliness.
We've also been friends since Dick Nixon was in Vice-Presidential short
pants, and after half a century with chumhood as our Pondian bond, we both
know we'd need to formalize the transition.

No less familiar with the actuarial tables than I, Andy must realize I'd spend
precious few years as Mrs. Pond. Yet no doubt he figures I'd spend that or fewer
as what I am now, and it's true we get along. He has the quiet humor of acceptance; I have the brash humor of assertion. His hints never wander into our
bedroom arrangements, and I've got no idea whether he can or still wants to, as
they say, perform.

If he's merrily stocking up on Viagra, would even I have the right to disappoint him? So far as flying solo goes, you could call me Amelia, but Pam's last
session with a partner occurred the night of Clinton's first State of the Union
and was even less memorable. The C Street *grognard* in question had been Cadwaller's inept replacement heading up the Department's Policy Planning Staff,
and bluff Homer MacWhite turned out to be worse at imitating Hopsie in the
sack. Thirteen years later, the thought of Andy's and my wattled flesh attempting to commingle makes my pretzel-shaped half of it creep.

Better the pistol. My rendezvous isn't in Tenleytown but by phone past
the end of Connecticut. Past proud Dupont Circle—nobody's ever been sure

what it's proud of, but imprecision that stout-hearted has its Washingtonian pleasures—and the Mayflower Hotel. Past Farragut Square ("Damn it, Gridley! Have you gone deaf?") and the Army-Navy Club's amber heap.

Past Lafayette Square, where forty years ago we watched scattered out-of-town picketers swell over the seasons into crowds calling, "Hey, hey, LBJ! How many kids did you kill today?" The man they were taunting so hated that chant he could never bear to repeat it in full, and I should know: these mimsy borogoves once watched him try and fail in Shakespearean closeup. While I don't mean to bore you by sounding like a cranky, *neiges d'antan* sort of old lady, back then the White House switchboard had a lot more hop-to-it-iveness about getting Mrs. Cadwaller on the line.

Oh, yes, Potus: as Huck Finn would say, I been here before. And I wish your fucking switchboard would hop to it. What they don't seem to understand (and listen to me treating understanding as an operative value in Potusville; what a Yankee Doodley true believer I must be even today) is that forming and then hanging onto this resolve wasn't all that easy. I mean, glamor of the thing or no glamor of the thing. Yet all Bob's secretary could tell me was that the call would come sometime between now and sundown, whenever a window of opportunity beckoned in Potus's seething schedule.

And it's hard work. We have that apparently not self-evident truth from his own mouth, whose itchy lips, take it from the convive of plenty of hard drinkers, haven't stopped wondering what became of all that lovely bourbon. A nicer old bag than Pam would be flat on her withered ass with gratitude that he's promised to find time today to congratulate her on living long enough to see these atrocious sights.

Granted, my own side of the aisle is no Tennyson poem. Maybe our man last go-round looked good on paper, but that stuff's foldable and he was pretty much origami by Halloween. At least a few of us geezers saw the writing on the wall at Nan Finn's Christmas party the winter before.

Ever "the glorious girl" in Pam's shesaurus, Nan's someone I've known since her husband Ned was Cadwaller's DCM in Nagon. Half the decrepit Foreign Service retirees in the District shuffle up her Woodley Park front steps to attend Nan's annual "Deck the Halls with Frank Sinatra" Yuletide wingding, as her son once called it. Hard to believe the strange lad I used to hear yelping "Geron-imo" as he repetitiously reparachuted off a chair or a log in West Africa is now a fifty-year-old graphic artist whose bizarre comic books about what he calls the superpower diaspora have, from my limited sampling, a streak of obscenity.

His mother does her best to keep the median age south of eighty by includ-ing a few other relative youngsters besides her son. We generally congregate around them like moths around a crayon we've mistaken for a candle, including that year's charmer: a Snapple-cheeked, BlackBerry-checking female lobbyist who'd met our limberly deboned white knight and gotten an invite to sign on with his Presidential campaign. When her work and prospects got apologeti-cally divulged—after all, she knew we had neither—someone asked how she'd sized him up at her job interview.

She gave a wrinkle-free frown, that miracle of under-forty skin. "He's less telegenic in person," said she, sounding troubled.

So were we. Luckily, our faces are trained as well as wizened, so we managed to nod without looking noticeably more grotesque than we do anyway. Once she'd traded in our Dubuffet of duffers for our hostess's hors d'oeuvres, I put up my hand as if leading a tottering school group from Archives to Holocaust.

"Hell, I'm done," I drawled. "Anyone else need a ride to the glue factory?" Frail as a fork but sharp as its tines, Laurel Warren gave a two-fingered salute.

Forgive me, Andy. I don't really believe Potus will even be nonplussed by Pam's protest. Why should he be? I'm eighty-six and eminently 86'able. What's left of our dapper, boozy, questing, and imperfect generation is just marking time in the Clio Airways lounge as we wait to hear our separate boarding calls for Carole Lombard's plane. He's probably never heard of that lovely lost star either, but some parting gesture has to be made.

POSTED BY: *Pam*   When you're waiting for a phone call of the unnatural nature I'm waiting for and plan to end it the unnatural way I'm hoping to, said phone's actual ring is no ordinary event. Baggy heart lurching into bridge-work, feet moaning "Haven't we suffered enough?" from outdated habit as they smacked the rug, I seized Cadwaller's gun: *Yes!* Hello. This is Pamela Cadwaller."

"Believe me, I know," a tickled voice said. "Pam, are you expecting another call?"

Gun lowered, heart leakily loping back to business at the old stand. Feet in mild pain, rug's feelings unknown and frankly unconsidered, I tamed my fat lunettes: "Oh, Andy. It's you."

"I know that too." He's always peppier than I at this hour. "But if you're expecting another call, I can—"

"No, no! Just snoozing over the paper. Honestly, does anyone think David Broder's funny? He's the worst humor columnist I've ever read. Andy! How are you?"

"Oh, fine. More important, how are you? I realize we're seeing each other tonight, but I thought I'd check on the old birthday girl."

"Mf," I sniffed skeptically. At my age, you come to appreciate how written Hebrew has no vowels. "You didn't have anything better to do either, huh?"

"How could I?" said Andy, flipping the meaning to play the chivalry card.

"Andy, I'm not sure about tonight," I told him, making the pistol in my lap go do-si-do. Clearly, I miss pet ownership. Sit up! Wink, Cadwaller's gun. "I don't really feel up to it."

"If you did, I'd ask who the new tenant was. We're Methuselan, Pam. If we felt wonderful, what would we talk about? It's like what they used to say about the weather, only now"—never one to look a bon mot in the mouth, Andy chuckled—"the weather is inside us."

"That's exactly right and nothing I can do about it. Some get rained out."

"But you won't have to do anything. I'm handling the cooking. I've already shopped," he said, sounding caught between glee at having had a project and wistfulness it was behind him. "I've gotten the movies."

"Oh, God. Which?"

"*The Gal I Left Behind Me*, of course," Andy said, either ignoring or delighting in my unstifled groan of horror. "And *Meet Pamela*, which I bet you've never seen."

"No, but why would I want to? Didn't it come out and flop ages ago? Honestly, Andy. Since it's my birthday, you could at least have asked yourself what I'd enjoy."

"I did, but I can't perform miracles and we've already seen every Kirsten there is. Except *Interview with the Vampire,* but you never wanted to."

"Of course not. She was too, she was only a child back then. Realizing she was one would just force me to acknowledge even Kirsten has feet of clay." Less clay than veined pottery with toes, one of Pam's nudged the Metro section wallward. "Well, no bother! You watch whichever one you like. I'll probably just fall asleep and you can let yourself out."

"Pam! It's your birthday. Promise to stay awake through at least one."

"Why?"

"Oh, to help me pretend it's some sort of occasion," Andy said. "I *always* let myself out."

POSTED BY: *Pam*   If you're getting ready to weep for the lonely old bag roosting on upper Connecticut Avenue, I wouldn't blame you. I might laugh at you, though. Let me dash last year's Christmas-card list in your face.

By 2005's tally, Pam had one hundred and fifty-seven extant friends. I don't mean near strangers to whom she feels an inexplicable need to suck up. I mean chronologically protean faces in snapshots stretching over decades, mutually misremembered anecdotes, e-mails from California or India about politics, books, upcoming trips, and recent losses in the club. The next time they came to Washington or I got to California or India, they'd've been as glad to see me as I them.

Those are the people I *sent* cards to. Another eighty or ninety jokers I'd just as soon forgot I'm alive burdened the postman with what neither they nor he knew was junk mail. The reaper's gouges have whittled down both totals from their circa-1975 peak.

Closer to home are Nan Finn and Laurel Warren, with whom I can do the biddy bit at Martin's or La Chaumière anytime. We knock waiters around like ninepins as they wait for the heftier bowling ball of their tip: "More wine!" Plus Carol Sawyer, also from Nagon days, not that I'd eat with her alone. Fond of my fingers.

Plus Callie Sherman, though Callie doesn't get out much anymore. Ninety, blind, often turbaned (oh, please), occasionally dabbling in an unseen cigarette the way Tiberius in old age enjoyed the nips of little fish while swimming, she Receives.

Even so, I've got only one favorite endtable. One gent who not only will-ingly accompanies me to the Kennedy Center, Martin's, La Chaumière, the Folger, and Arena Stage but puts up with the late-blooming crush I'd never admit to even my fellow movie addict Nan Finn. I've literally disturbed young girls with my knowledge of Kirsten Dunst's career.

Mind, the day I see the closing credits of any of her pictures, even those Andy's Netflixed or Nextflicked for me multiple times, will be when I realize I've died and there is an afterlife. Then I'll be too resentful about the nonsense I've been put through to pay attention to the happy ending. Yet Andy loyally sat through *Bring It On* to the end so he could tell me, *in detail*, how Kirsten's cheer-leading team had fared after I dozed off during one green-pantied set of splits.

I sometimes wonder what I look like, schnozz buzzsawing at a Leaning Tower of Pisa angle and dentition gaping like I'm one of the freaks at Bomarzo—clearly, Italy figures somewhere in my idea of pleasant dreams—as Andy hangs in there in order to elucidate the last act's plot turns for Pam's sake. And to think he was our man at the Berlin Wall: the last, rotated home just before it came down for good. Maybe it taught him patience.

POSTED BY: *Pam*   In regular contact, if mostly in cyberspace and by phone since I gave up my visits to Amherst at Thanksgiving and New York anytime the latest ridiculous musical's reviews fooled me into thinking it was worth snoring through, are three generations of Cadwaller's progeny. The eldest is Hopsie's son by his first marriage, and I marvel that the alert adolescent who took Pam's hand as we strolled along the Seine is a grandfather. Even before his biological mother's death, Chris taught his son and later grandchildren to call me Gramela, giving me all the fame and none of the responsibility.

As does Panama—for now—Chris's son Tim adores me. Before he settled into his current job, he wanted to pitch a profile of Pam Buchanan, museum-quality war correspondent, to *Smithsonian* magazine.

The exhibit put the kibosh on that. "Absolutely not. I know you, young Mr. Cadwaller! I'll just be an excuse to fill it with tommyrot. You'll get moony over the liberation of Paris, and all I really remember is the horrible headache I got from all the diesel fumes."

"Then why don't you write it yourself? Not just the war, the whole thing."

"But I have. In *Nothing Like a Dame*, and—"

"Gramela, you always say yourself that was twaddle," Tim objected.

"Yes, and don't you understand that anything I tried to write this late in life would be too? By now I can hardly remember the difference between what happened and what you wish had. That's why I like your imagination better."

"Why?"

"Because it's uninformed. That's what imagination should be. When nothing's true, everything can be."

"It's not completely uninformed," grumbled the author of *You Must Remember This: The Posthumous Career of World War Two.*

"If you mean history books, no. But we didn't have them."

Soon afterward and what a mazurka I danced, Tim had a friend design the website I'm using now. It has lain fallow for two years. That's why he and his fellow Cadwallers are less likely than random strangers who won't care to stumble across these June 6 posts and try to stop me from carrying out my protest, since Tim and company gave up long ago on the idea I'd ever use it.

Among other things, I hated its name: daisysdaughter.com. My amateur psychoanalyst—see how I'm already contending with his projections?—is a sucker for not only the Jazz Age, something I don't remember hearing it called at the time any more than we called Jack's Administration Camelot, but the whole cavalcade from Depression to war to Ike to Jack to how many kids did you kill today. Around then Tim's own juvenile presence in front of TV sets starts making his Gramela's hoarded way-back-when less precious, less unique, less fucking magical. Not that reminiscing over Jimmy Carter's epic Presidency strikes me as Shazam time either.

I felt dismayed by the website's name for professional reasons as well. Since Tim's one himself, he ought to've known which bauble of identity any writer guards most fiercely: his or her byline. His clever notion of reducing me to nakedness also disguises me from whatever handful of readers still recognize it, since anyone romantic or idle enough to Google Pamela Buchanan, most likely to confirm she's dead, may not learn before scrolling gets tiresome that daisysdaughter.com is her blog.

I never cared in social life. I was Pamela Murphy when my divorce testimony knocked the latest Washington benefit performance by Winston Churchill's one-man rep troupe off New York tabloids' front pages in May of '43, I was Pammie Gerson to other industry wives in the creamily ceramic Cinerama of Beverly Hills. I was Pam Cadwaller to not only the *Foreign Service Journal* but Lyndon Johnson's White House operators. But all through my marital trolley transfers, *by Pamela Buchanan* was the war cry I exulted in.

For better or worse, I was Pamela Buchanan on the rollickingly corpse-free cover of *Nothing Like a Dame*, my eager-to-please account of the fun side of World War Two. Now long out of print and good riddance to all but Bill M.'s jacket art, whose affection for his Anzio Bobbsey twin glows painfully through my memories of the light-hearted hour I spent posing. Yet my silly first book did stay on the *NYT*'s bestseller list long enough to play ships in the night, Pam sinking to starboard as curly-haired Norman scrambled up portside, with *The Naked and the Dead*.

With pride that's lasted to this day, Pamela Buchanan could've kissed every one of the enthusiasts for our nation's birth pangs who bought *Glory Be* when it came out the year said nation was deciding for the second time whether it liked Ike or needed Adlai badly. One of the Paris footlocker's prizes is a laminated telegram—I'M JUST GLAD YOU AREN'T A POLITICIAN BEST WISHES JACK KENNEDY—I got the week my sloop skimmed past his ghost-skippered PT boat in sales.

Intermittence may be my byline's cross to bear. That's not the same as discontinuity. My last foray into print was an op-ed in the *Los Angeles Times* dated 6/6/2004 in the clippings file and begging the ninnies who run the show out there to spare the Ambassador Hotel from the wrecker's ball. You can see how they listened, too. It still meant something to me that the Pamela Buchanan who signed that piece could nod across a span of seventy years at Pamela Buchanan, the fourteen-year-old authoress—a term she then thought divine—of "Chanson d'automne."

My first and only stab at verse, which politely reached for a cotton swab and moved on, its wretched dozen lines were printed in the Fall 1934 edition of *Pink Rosebuds*, the literary magazine of Purcey's Girls Academy of St. Paul. From its title on, to call the thing derivative would be an insult to plagiarists everywhere.

Its one acute bit was a game of peekaboo with nonperpendicular pronouns, silly but not bad for a teenager.

Inanity wasn't the reason "Chanson d'automne" shattered my brief spell as a poetess, an even yummier-sounding word to my young ears. Winning me Professor Hormel's writhing plaudits along with my classmates' far more decisive mockery, my poemess was written in French.

Back then, I couldn't see what I'd done wrong. Collected by my new American guardian when the *Paris* docked in New York, I'd only recently been shipped back to my perplexing homeland. My mother's Belgian second husband had advertised his reluctance to see more than the back of *la petite Pamelle* in the wake of his Day-*zee*'s surprise exit from the breathing business.

On a more practical, Brussels-sprouting sort of note, Georges Flagon didn't care to keep paying my tuition at Mme Chignonne's. C'EST LA VIE, his cable sighed, and I doubt Tim Cadwaller realized the real pang of the name he'd picked out for my website. I never felt more like Daisy's daughter than in the first few months after she'd left me as the only surviving Fay or Buchanan on the face of the globe.

Used as I was to her ways by then, I couldn't help thinking she'd carried negligence a bullet too far. Hello, mother mine.

POSTED BY: *Pammie*   In my younger, less invulnerable years, I often wished my guardian hadn't told me what Daisy was alleged by no less an authority than herself to have wished for me at birth. He had so few even fugitively Pamcentric anecdotes in stock that I can't blame him for sharing that one when I kept whinging, and she didn't get her stupid wish. Or, depending on how you count, her fairy-tale three wishes.

No, Mother: your daughter never did get to be beautiful. Nor even stay so little once I shot up to a hoop-hunting five foot ten in the Midwest the year after you died. And I wasn't a fool. I made my way.

Early on, I learned or relearned how to be American, a skill you couldn't have imagined was one. By the age of twenty-one, I was doing something you never did: earn my living. And as a writer too, just what I once heard you bragging to the Lotus Eater in Provincetown you'd be.

No need to pretend you're jealous, though! We both know you'd have soon found a reason to be dismissive. Measuring my real career against your fanta-sized one, you'd've found Pammie's clumsy imitation, with my big feet and my ugly hair and my stupid tugs at your beaded dress in East Egg, wanting.

I made my way. Along the line, catching a bottle of shampoo—not cham-pagne—from a woman gnarled as oak and naked as the truth outside Riceville, Tennessee, I fell in love with my country. Once again, we're up against some-thing you'd have found puzzling, since you always did treat the U.S.A. as the caterer and not the bridegroom.

In a dopey way—and pun intended, mother mine—you pined for France. Your daughter saw it in an overseas cap and GI shoes, saw Paris liberated. Dachau too? Dachau too.

In ways Gerson and I forbade ourselves to articulate, it bothered my sec-ond husband that his shiksa wife had been the witness he hadn't to his fellow Jews' destruction and survival. Vowing nobody would call his patriotism a mask for a more personal—*personal!*—grudge, he spent 1941–45 in Culver City, supervising training films on the dangers of loose talk, defeatism, booby traps, and finally fraternization.

Pam had seen GIs chatting up Bavarian dollies a week after Dachau. So I had to tell him batting .750 wasn't so bad. Showing me around Metro, Gerson grinned: "Oh, we knew it was hopeless. But that actress got a contract faster than I could say '*Arbeit macht frei.*'" I winced for a reason he didn't learn for six months.

My first husband, incidentally—like yours, mother mine—was an anti-Semite. A Communist anti-Semite, guaranteeing he and Stalin would've gotten on famously. Stalin a bit more famous, but trust Murphy to find a grudge. A few months into my marriage to Gerson, puttering among the breakfast bagels and bacon in Beverly Hills, it did cross my mind that somewhere Bran, in his Mur-phine way, was seething that I'd never stop betraying him. Well, of course not! He was Brannigan Murphy, making that the whole planet's job. Stalin's included.

Yes, mother mine: for a while, your daughter basked in the voluptuous allure of Hollywood. That phrase was the lone one retained by a then sixty-plus Pam after Tim Cadwaller, hoping I wouldn't be too irked or bored, took me to a New York bar to hear a Texan songwriter he liked. The fellow's fondness for our pliable American idiom charmed me even as the organizing principle of his musical shuffles eluded the newly, now decisively old lady.

Not that Gerson was a voluptuary, far from it. In a trait he shared with many another decent man, *how* far could exasperate him. Having to be Gerson, Gerson, Gerson all the time left him surrounded by doors he couldn't be sure were locked from inside or out. I loved him for ignoring the invisible keys dancing all around the room.

Came Cadwaller, and you should know he and Gerson got on well from their first meeting. As dark date palms beyond the balcony gently mopped night's parquet, we had a lovely introductory dinner in Jerusalem. If Pam was the transom for their mutual respect, don't blame the old bag this website calls your daughter for thinking I can't have been all bad.

Physically, you should know, I survived the 20th century unscathed. The only exception is or was a small scar over my left eyebrow. For almost half a century I used to focus on it in my medicine-cabinet mug shot, trying to decide if it looked more like part of an *i* or part of an *r*. Then it got lost in wrinkles like everything else except the mimsy borogoves, fat-lunetted but still mine.

Cadwaller last, all three of the major men in my life met their end long ago. As did all three of yours, mother mine, though I hope you'll be pleased to hear my guardian made it to old age. I discount Georges Flagon, fate unknown.

All of Pam's, even Murphy, left me with gifts of the type I value most: tools. Because seeing one's own life as metaphor holds few attractions for me, I'll leave it to others to find symbolism in Cadwaller, the upright envoy, having been the one to leave me with this gun.

Why am I pretending you can hear me, mother mine? That illusion got kicked away by the authoress of "Chanson d'automne" in Roosevelt's first term. Soon after swearing she'd never write another goddam poemess again, she decided she didn't give a rap if some invisible old fool whose beard could use barbering was looking down from more than Sistine ceilings. Perhaps it's because I'm so near death myself, but to my incipiently Alzheimerish surprise—I knew they'd get me in the end—I pine for allies in the cyberspatial ether.

When the White House switchboard finds me, I need to be able to feel I speak for you. And—why not?—for Kirsten, too. Hell, she'll never know, any more than you will.

When the phone rings, I'll snatch up Cadwaller's gun from my ancient snatch. As Potus starts burbling birthday congratulations to an old bag he's never heard of, I'll interrupt. Yes, I will!

With what, mother mine? A litany of what he's done? By now he could've heard all that from millions. As countless readers of the Declaration of Independence have discovered with surprise and annoyance, particularized lists of offenses can get tiresome even in indictments written by Thomas Jefferson. Or else, mother mine, should I just say this?

"Yes, yes. I know who you are. Do you know who I am, Mr. President? I'm Daisy Buchanan's daughter. Their only child, the last of them. These days I roost on upper Connecticut Avenue like a falcon, and believe me: I've seen 'em come and I've seen 'em go down at your end. Oh, hell, Potus! We both know you're going to do whatever you like. I'm just an old lady without even a cat, and I can't stop you. But before you get on with it, I've got one question. Do you expect me, me, me, me! Do you really expect *me* to put up with this shit?"

At which point, at least if all has gone well—can my hand raise Cadwaller's gun in time? Will he have hung up by then?—I'll give a screech of fury. That will be my wordless last word before, right in Potus's ear, I blow the prettiest thing about me at fourteen—my attractively bejangled, hopeful brains—to goddam Clio come.

In this as in other things, you're a poor example to follow, mother mine. Your daughter's always feared she might mimic your big exit one day, though I now feel I've got no choice. Face it, an opportunity like this only comes once in a lifetime. It still makes me furious to know my emulation of your final act seventy-two years ago, nine months before "Chanson d'automne" appeared in *Pink Rosebuds*, will give Potusville's hyenas the easy out of saying self-destruction was in our genes.

Like mother, like daughter, they'll shrug. You bitch! You fat, drugged, forgotten, hopeless bitch.

As for my favorite young actress, no doubt they'll say I was just trying to impress her.

2. The Lotus Eater

POSTED BY: *Pam*   I'd just turned five when, I've been told, I watched my father's sudden death during a polo match on Long Island. Not the horse's fault, but it got a bullet behind one twitching ear just the same.

That suspended play temporarily. Cherished for the high marks he gave insensitivity, Kipling wasn't yet out of fashion in some circles. Yet the survivors' flask-rescrewing cries of "Let's win this one for Tom!" ended up inscribed only in mud. They'd all seen Father reaching across another rider's mount for the hook when his mallet tangled in the reins.

Yes, daisysdaughter.com readers: my hatred of Potus is partly Freudian. His prototype's contribution to the Paris footlocker is a scattering of snapshots whose scalloped edges date them as surely as Elizabethan ruffs. Here he is proudly carside, standing with balled fist in pocket at a garden party or chin out as he quizzes innocent but deadly horses.

Before pretzelhood, I also had the genetic custody of a gangly build I blessed for changing me from a Purcey's exotic to the tall girl who played basketball. Plus a jowl of which I was less enamored, its hammock of misleading sullenness only lifting when I smiled or laughed. Though I still do plenty of both, now it's just another county heard from in a face made of Clio Airways–carved newspaper crumples.

Then to mimsily borogoved now, my face's best foot forward has been my eyes, balanced between blue and stormy gray like twin Civil War memorials. And just as well, since my functions as a child were purely ocular. My mother's widowhood filled my retinas with a rich brocade, pattern mostly indecipherable, in which she figured mostly by omission.

She was a white back scampering in dresses that daringly exposed it from her helplessly disputative shoulderblades nearly to the spinal nub's Appomattox. When she returned in another taxi next morning or next Monday, a hand as hasty and vague as a postcard from a Beaux Arts ball would caress my forehead as if for luck. Whose unknown.

My early hope was that she was trotting off to Manhattan to see Daddy, who was only dead in Nassau County. That didn't outlast the night her cab led a convoy of peculiarly dressed people back from there and he wasn't one of them. I got scooted up the stairs as glasses swayed in hands detached from any identifiable owner, prefiguring the minor Dali canvas Daisy would later tire Georges Flagon into buying for her in a final token of her stint as a free spirit.

That transfer of Dali Buchanan from Manhattan to East Egg was a onetime affair. At home, where I was looked after by a succession of mighty-aproned Scandinavians all prone to clucking at me as if I were not one but several chickens, my mother's masterpiece was the Sleeping Daisy. At its pre-Raphaelite best, it was executed in daytime amid vomited dress shops and her sheets' blue typhoon behind a muslin screen's impersonation of blond twilight.

One hand would be curled as if guarding her soft breaths from monsters, a logical worry to me at six. The other was most often wrapped around an oblong velvet-covered pencase: a minor mystery, since no letters were ever mailed from our home. My mother's later attempts at fiction began with the purchase of a Smith-Corona manual typewriter, its carriage rearing over the keyboard's tadpoles as strictly as a nun's cowl. Twenty years later I clattered through *Nothing Like a Dame* on it, secularizing things considerably.

Then she'd go away again to Manhattan, miraculously restored to the Daisy I knew best: a stranger twitching taxiward with marcelled coif, bright eyes, and sequins that bragged their good fortune at mincing on such enfevered shanks. That's when I used to warble along to her anarchic bedroom and rifle her lace-leaking chiffonier for that pencase. At least when my latest nanny, peeled like a nippled onion field, was doing the Sleeping Scandinavian in her own unventilated quarters and I'd gotten tired of observing (and inhaling) the mysteries of Copenhagen.

I can't say whether Pammie's curiosity about my mother's pencase meant I was already a budding scribbler or simply jealous of any thingummy whose proximity my mother so clearly preferred to mine. As if there's any difference, writers everywhere will roar. I never found it, though, much less opened it up to gaze at its innards, and just as well. A pencase it wasn't.

POSTED BY: *Pam*   In the frisky days of her young widowhood, my mother's favorite saying was on the chilling side. "Beauty is as beauty does," she'd coo into the phone or—at her worst—to the uncomprehending Scandinavian, justifying her newest achieved or anticipated act of Daisyesque frivolity with affected hurt followed by an unaffected giggle.

The adjectives traded places by 1928, and she quit saying "Beauty is as beauty does" at all once she'd lost her looks. In my mother's mind, nothing that was or ever had been true of *her* could be a generality. By then, however, a little alarm bell was lodged in her daughter's brain.

Only on movie screens has the bliss stayed unalloyed. Otherwise, I was never to confront true loveliness in women—I mean the kind that's a painting that breathes, a Charles Ives concerto for face and voice, with lashes that dip as if tasting their own eyes' forbidden fruit before showing it to you like a one-armed bandit's jackpot—without intimations of terror at both what beauty had license to do and what the world apparently had license to do to it.

Once adolescent torments were done, I was relieved that my own case was no special cause for concern. By college I did have some assets, starting with my lanky frame's long legs. If I'd been younger when Sixties fashion produced its masterpiece, a miniskirt would've been my Jolly Roger. Beyond the gams, the Buchanan bod had its drawbacks, including a bosom whose bulge would've looked like the most minor of Indian raids on a map. My favorite description of my physique in the nude was Cadwaller's: "Friendly."

One of the minor blessings of being my age is that you've by and large quit noticing—all right, *assessing*—other women's looks too. So feeling the old fear and wonder creep into my bones whenever, either in person or her grandpa Chris's photographs, I see Panama Cadwaller laughing and cavorting wounds me, stuns me, makes me want to protest at life's reminder that the thing and the thing's perils aren't done.

Like her untamable hair and unlike the blue-gray whorls I've outed as the mimsy borogoves here on daisysdaughter.com, Hopsie's great-granddaughter's eyes are as dark as tributes to Goya. When I told her so, she batted them and teased me by pouting false ignorance: "Aw, Gramela! You mean the *beans*, right?" So far Panama's eyes are famous only to her relatives, of which I am one by marital proxy and geezery prerogative. But since she occasionally chatters of trying acting, they may yet end up suspended on billboards over some carnival wasteland or another.

I'm fairly sure now they're closed. It's only a little after seven a.m. on June 6, my second D-Day—my, I'm certainly *whizzing* through these posts, aren't I?— and her school in Manhattan's already out for the summer. Luxuriously free from now 'til fall, she probably isn't out of bed yet: her dark hair spangling a cool pillow like a messier sun turned black in the developing room, her hurled limbs turning sleep into one more athletic event where teenagers take the gold just by breathing.

June or no June, I'm astonished her dad lets her sleep in that outfit. What can you be thinking, Tim? Sleeveless ribbed undershirt hiked up nearly to ribcage by a restless fist. Innocent (well, let's pray) plum in panties I wouldn't have risked wearing on my wedding night to Abelard, let alone Murphy. In frontal view, the tiny red bow at waistband's center would've alarmed me less if it'd just been a mite nearer—honestly, would another inch be such a sacrifice?—her belly button. Are you awake yet, Panama?

No matter. Even asleep, you know your name at birth was *Pamela*, a tribute to me you improved on by refusing to be anybody's namesake. The mimsies were thrilled when I caught on it wasn't just baby talk: *"Panama!"* you insisted at three when grandpa Chris tried to correct you. Used to it himself, he worried you'd hurt the elderly, dentition-mulling (yes, the teeth were shot back in my seventies) guest's feelings.

Panama it has been since. That stubby act of defiance was what first let your Gramela imagine that—via some osmotic smearing of unguents, and spared the claptrap and forceps in between—I'd produced a great-granddaughter.

Your looks don't unnerve only me. In spite of my mimsial whimsies that you've somehow inherited the Buchanan gams, I played no biological role in creating them, and that your dad did baffles even Tim. Most people can't repress a blink when they learn that Panama's the spawn of his prosaic, too often ashily Dockered loins.

At forty-four, he's presentable enough. But he's tending to stoutness like his dad and showing signs of growing as sparse up on Mt. Noggin as his grandfather. Years of New York screening rooms, followed by computer sessions as he dredges up the deep thoughts about that month's slew of cinematic shallowness of *Qwert* magazine's "Man in the Dark," have given him a molelike mien augmented by a certain incredulity that in real life people can hear and respond to what he's saying. When he looks at you, Panama, his dilemma is that he often can't think of a thing to say.

You left him poleaxed even as a baby. As you skidded into adolescence, poor Tim's awe grew talons of paternal anxiety. When last you two came to Washington and he and I watched you scudding, hipboned and earplugged, around the FDR Memorial, he rolled only belatedly comical eyes my way: "For God's sake, Gramela! Pam, help me. What on earth am I going to *do*?"

He and I have different apprehensions. Grounded in his own experience, Tim's fear is that even on movie screens, let alone in Manhattan high schools, beauty like yours is an open invitation to the world to crash in, destructive and greedy. After all, if *he* can't help reacting as he does, what sorts of sewers must be flooding the brains of those less fettered by paternity? My fear is that beauty is a drug that ends up craving other drugs for company.

POSTED BY: *Pam*   Did I blame my mother for turning hophead? In my teens, definitely. She was off the stuff by then, but that age's vengeful motto is "Better late than never." A child's wishes are an adolescent's accusations, persisting well into maturity nowadays if Oprah's to be trusted. By middle age, they've reverted to wishes, now colored by sepia mournfulness rather than crimson (Oprah *isn't* to be trusted) urgency. When you've made it to my reef of the surf, far out past the warranty's three score and ten, even the wishes are the same weak shade of wash as everything else.

I do fault Dr. Nassau—not the name he's known by to history, which is none at all—for producing the mind's equivalent of Botox to "cure" her of hysteria. She'd watched Daddy's panicked mount hurl and then maul him as if he were a jackbooted beanbag with a Yale degree, a cheat's instincts at polo, and too much money to need to know much about much. Dead so young herself, my mother was always a naif around medicos—unlike her gnarled daughter, now on Ph.D. terms with doctors the age of the Hardy Boys.

Doc Nassau soon went back to Supernumerary Hospital, outflashed in the role of nemesis by an intruder ideally devised to carry the brunt of blame. Aside from a chestnut coiffure I wanted to own or possibly just pet, everything about her was ghastly. Let me introduce any daisysdaughter.com readers I may've acquired—no comments signaled yet when I homepage, but it's awfully early— to the Lotus Eater.

I knew the L.E., incidentally, well into Eisenhower days. Her hair oyster-shelled by then, she'd stare with dead fish eyes if Gerson and I happened to sit down on our New York visits in one of the Manhattan restaurants where she liked to hobnob. I'd get an arctic smile only once she'd established to her satisfaction that a) my husband still wasn't a millionaire, b) clothing shops in Beverly Hills still hadn't caught up to the latest from Milan and Paris, and c) I still hadn't grown or bought breasts whose Lollobrigittian magnificence might've flummoxed her. While I could fish her name out of the septic tank if I cared to, let her stay the Lotus Eater here.

She took up residence in our lives one breakfast too soon after my seventh birthday in June '27, still wearing the scoopbacked powder-blue number and Cuban heels she'd had on the evening before when I came upon her and my mother, brisk snap of a pencase closing as I entered Daisy's room, after their unexpectedly joint return from my future guardian's wedding in the city. In later years, he remembered Pammie as having been a flower girl, and I didn't tell him that by peopling the scene with loyalists his mind was trying to make up for his bride's contrary vamoose just four months later. He never tried *that* gold-ring stunt again.

That morning, the Lotus Eater was proud of herself for having woken up and discovered she was the Lotus Eater. Petulance, her kewpie face's at-rest expression, was experimenting with malicious tranquility as its fresh mask.

"Hello, sweetie!" said my mother, her smile coping as usual with the surprise that giving birth to me hadn't all been a dream. "Why, you two didn't get properly introduced last—yesterday. Darling, this is my young daughter, Pamela."

"Hullo, Pamela." It was plain the Lotus Eater would've gladly left it at that. Briefly, her face wondered why the Scandinavian didn't just toggle a light switch to pop me back into invisibility. Since that wasn't going to happen, she had to make a show of creating a relationship, and did by jiggling her plate oddly forward and back.

"Don't even think about stealing one of these sausage links, little girl," she said with a disturbing and unnatural attempt at making her keen features appear jolly. "That's death! I'm ravenous. I'll stab you in the heart with this knife!"

"I've eaten," I said stolidly. "And they're made from pigs, not lynxes."

"Why, of course you've eaten! You won't believe it, but I was a good little girl once too. I know they've got to get up early! Then quick as death, they're off to… school?" she asked my Scandinavian mother, by which I mean her glance invited either woman to take the job.

"It's summer vacation. I won't go back until the fall," I explained.

The L.E. had already gone back to deciding dead pigs were the best use for her mouth. "Where are you sending her, Daisy?" she asked, chewing.

POSTED BY: *Pamalyst*   Even without a White House cue—why don't they call?—I may be readier for the glue factory than I knew. Blinking at my Mac's screen, on which a word rhyming with "Lotus" has appeared more than once, Pam has realized the old synapses aren't what they used to be.

To be fair, the Beltway loons and goons I've just reclassified as Potus eaters—addicted as they are to jingoism's heroin—tricked me by behaving differently. Instead of nodding off, they're energized. Bolts of vitaminy special-effects lightning shoot from their fingers. Trumpets are wedged in their throats.

With one exception, they've got no traits at all in common with the sulky, quite pretty, and, to be fair, evidently troubled young woman my mother took on as a sort of experimental grown-up Pam—or so I was left to guess, taking what passed for optimism where I could—in the summer of 1927. Said exception is a staggering inability to imagine the planet exists for any other purposes but their own.

Potus himself is a creature of habit, no longer including the big one he kicked. Well, let's all keep our fingers crossed on that one, what do you say? As sobriety was his major accomplishment at forty, he treats it as evidence he's got the *cojones* to make big decisions, meanwhile staying cagey about just how much whiskey and cocaine went thataway in his youth. Since Jesus got the credit for weaning Potusville's answer to Tom Buchanan off the sauce—oh, the *ego* of these people!—he now guzzles God like Jim Beam.

So far as we know, otherwise his substance abuse is confined to his speeches. The Potus eaters, on the other hand, seem in no hurry to sanitize their polluted blood. That's why for six years the test of Pam's stamina has been my ability to go on reading the *WashPost* and *NYT*. I've spent time around junkies before.

Did I know it then, Panama? In the sense of information, no. At six or seven, adulthood *as such* describes itself to your perceptions as a state of being drugged. Odd reactions, puzzling apathies (look at the seagull, Mommy!), unprovoked laughter, secrets. I had no other ready image of motherhood to test against Daisy's, as Scandinavians plainly reproduced by some means all their own that skipped childhood and went straight to chafe-wristed and gargantuan middle age.

The new calculus the Lotus Eater's advent presented to Pam was that I'd obviously been right in guessing that having a child might be the overlooked cure for my mother's restlessness. I'd just as obviously been wrong to count on myself as the solution she'd spot rubbing my fat nose under her dainty one. Her evident loneliness—always the one adult condition any child has decent odds of correctly identifying—had been my main reason to hope one day she'd catch on I was here at hand.

As garbled as my understanding was, I still think Daisy might've reveled in maternity if she could've given birth to a daughter exactly her own age or perhaps a year older. Preferably one who was pretty and outgoing but not quite as alarming a beauty as Mom ("Just call me Daisy, darling!"), keeping the tacit sexual and social pecking order undisputed. Hell, I'm just glad I'm not bitter.

Yes, that's a joke. But I hate bitter people, always have. The Lotus Eater was so born to it that, so far as I could tell, she got bitter first and then set out to find a provocation.

POSTED BY: *Pam*   Many years later, as the auburn-laced ice cubes of a Georgetown November did their best to mimic stained glass in our living room's bay window—Church of the Late Great Society, I think: maybe

1965—Cadwaller was intrigued by my verbal sketch of his unmet Daisy-in-law's morphine crony. Peculiarly so, since he and I never spent much time discussing each other's antediluvia.

Besides, by then Daisy's daughter was a tall forty-five or so, sipping a Bloody Mary amid Sunday papers as a Redskins game hutted and jabbered from the den. My mother'd been pushing up repetitions of her first name for decades. What did it matter and who cared anymore?

Yet it turned out at halftime that Hopsie'd known the harsh Thirties residue of the Lotus Eater in Newport. Complete with youth's black toupee above white flannel trousers I can barely imagine him wearing, my future husband was disguised as a sailing instructor.

In his college and law-school years, Panama, your great-grandfather kept himself entertained and in pocket money by running over there summers to reteach drunken millionaires' wives boatmanship from his own people's merely genteel digs in Providence. During Franklin Pierce's unmemorable Presidency, the first Cadwaller was in whale oil, among the oddly hatted merchants scanning the horizon for the *Pequod's* return. Once his sons caught on Ahab was no businessman, the elder went into shipbuilding; Hopsie always said his bark was worse than his frigate. The younger—your great-grandfather's ancestor—opted for banking.

Sensibly aware his forebears' industriousness had left him privileged, my own Cadwaller was bored silly at the thought of a life spent making the beast with two greenbacks. Half a decade at a white-shoe New York law firm avidly dedicated to keeping said beast away from the taxman didn't excite him either. The aversion got turned crystalline by his three years—he was a pipe-smoking thirty-five when they ended—of skippering a corvette in the North Atlantic during the war. On a welcome break from hunting submarines, he was herding landing craft off Omaha Beach the same afternoon his war-correspondent wife traipsed ashore. After our wedding night, which predated our marriage by several months, we laughed about our nonexchanged glances across *that* crowded room.

Among other things. For certain men of Cadwaller's generation, the great test of their poise was retaining an air of virility while telling a woman to whom they were sexually drawn their undergraduate nickname at Harvard. My Hopsie brought it off without either batting an eye nor losing an ounce of manhood, which should've made my third guess my first.

"As in 'hopping down the bunny trail'?" I ventured.

"Nope."

"As in 'Please don't throw me in the briar patch'?"

He rubbed his now bald head. "That would have been more Princeton's sort of thing. Andover's, really."

"Cadwaller, do you want to tell me about the rabbits?"

He beamed delightedly. "Nope. But that doesn't mean there weren't any."

POSTED BY: *Pam*   Nope, Panama: the Lotus Eater's Thirties residue wasn't one of his cottontails. Your great-grandfather wasn't remotely interested. Besides, even though the former L.E.'s doltish husband stayed up in the attic, mucking around with his collection of vintage spyglasses—he'd clearly never trained one on his yard—somebody named Dicky was on the ground floor and came along on the sailing lesson.

"It seemed to be one of those off-and-on things that go on forever," Hopsie shrugged that auburn-and-ice-cube Sunday. "I doubt they even liked each other much, just had similar manners and didn't want to explain themselves to somebody new."

"That's her to the teeth," I said bitingly. "Doesn't that sound exactly like too many marriages?"

Your great-grandfather could always outfox me. "To me it sounds like all of them. Except for the liking part, which you'll agree makes a difference."

I'd just turned over the paper to exile her oyster-shelled photograph. "Trust me. Nobody could've liked her."

"Didn't your mother?"

"Hell, what did she know? She was on morphine."

"What did she really want, though?" he asked alertly, which didn't necessarily mean anything. A man who'd stood a few deck watches, he still had one ear posted to monitor halftime's scrimmage of commentators from the den. Dear bright-eyed dog having its whiskery belly ruffled on our sofa, were you Jubjub or Peanut?

Imagine, Panama: there was no such thing as the Super Bowl. On the other hand, Bloody Marys were well known to us aborigines. Must've invented them right after we killed the last dodo. Never had liked its stupid, accusing stare.

"More morphine. What else? And someone to fix with. I've told you. To my mother, *nothing* made sense except as a social situation."

"I meant the girlfriend. What was she after in all this?"

"She was awfully young," I said after a minor hesitation. "I doubt she knew."

"That's how I remember the sailing lesson going, but I'm asking *you*, darling. The perceptive one. What'd you make of it all?"

"I probably hated her much too much to make anything."

"Ah, well. There's a clue right there," he said, gesturing with his briar. Take it from me, Panama, there isn't a pipe smoker on the planet who can resist Sherlocking it up on occasion. Near the end of Cadwaller's long dying, I remember reading his favorite Holmes story to him: "A Scandal in Bohemia."

"How so?" I asked a mite peevishly. He *had* just called me the perceptive one.

"Maybe you sensed she was out to kidnap you. When she met me, she knew I'd get Pamela instead. Maybe that's why she tried to brain me with the oar that day."

"Oh, she didn't."

Since it was usually his wife who provided the slapstick in our three-decade-long conversation, he beamed. "I think it gave me my taste for danger."

A crunch of celery proved Cadwaller was being whimsical on just one Bloody Mary. I was mixing, and I usually forgot the celery sticks on the second round. I wondered if I should have another or straight vodka once he went back to the Redskins game. Back then I was a lot less used to reading the obituaries of people I'd known, although sometimes even now I still feel I'm not.

"Kidnap me for what? Believe me, she had loads more money than we did. Even then." I meant the now extinguished Buchanans, not the just lit (I'd turned on a lamp as the dog stopped glowing) Cadwallers.

"There are other kinds of ransom." The Sherlock routine was really starting to wear thin.

"Oh, she never paid any attention to me. To be honest, I imagine she was just looking for a harbor. Like most women," I added, since he'd know I was exempting myself and my surprising kindness to the Lotus Eater had annoyed me.

"Ah! They're back at it," my husband announced. "Have you seen my tobacco pouch? No, the yellow, not the leather. That one's empty. I think I'll switch to beer. Come on, Bandicoot! Let's go watch the home team finish fouling up this one, what d'you say?"

With a raucous meow, the creature I'd been petting—sorry, but I'm in a big hurry and memory does play tricks—arched its Siamese back. Alert enough to Cadwaller to be reacting to him all the same, it independently hopped off in a different direction. Nonetheless, my mother's pet back in the summer of 1927 had definitely been a dog.

POSTED BY: *Pam*   A nameless one, at least almost eighty years later. What I do remember is that the Lotus Eater sometimes seemed to get the pooch and me mixed up, although the different amounts of attention paid to us by our shared mistress should've tipped her off. Not being fussed over as I stubbily glared meant I was probably Pammie.

After that first lynx-eyed breakfast—my reassurance that she wasn't committing cannibalism had zoomed right by her, you'll recall—the Lotus Eater graduated to becoming a form of weather, her East Egg appearances as unpredictable as fog's fingers in Jack the Ripper's London. From my third-floor playroom, to which the Scandinavian with the special murmur of one uselessly instructed used to cart the toys I'd formerly had leave to scatter almost anywhere, I'd hear the L.E. skidding hither and yon downstairs with those odd squeaky little pulleys in her laughter.

Before the Scandinavian had shut my door behind her, I'd hear my mother's enchanted babble: "Darling! But we *mustn't*. What, so soon, again? Pammie, after all… No, no, no! I see we must. Well, when *I* say so, it's different. It is, nasty, and so there!"

I knew Daisy had just stuck out her tongue, that enamel-sentineled rose petal. "I *am* her mother, don't forget. Oh, what am I saying? Do. Did you tell the cab to wait?"

Then off they'd jitterbug again to Manhattan. Either less or more expensively so, depending on your point of view, once the L.E. began turning up in our driveway behind the wheel of a touring car as long as a Dreiser novel.

Pammie thought she'd seen a gray-backed chauffeur on the L.E.'s first visit, but he must've been imaginary. And too bad, since anticipating his return—what else did I have to keep me occupied?—the precocious reader that was me had named him Quint from *The Turn of the Screw*.

Once they'd rolled on, tiny and chic in the Dreiser, out of my playroom's window, I'd troop downstairs, occasionally tossing a ball or a doll ahead of me on the coal-mine canary principle but once again at liberty to do nothing wherever I liked. More than once, that rotten little dog and I ended up beyond the overgrown grass at our grounds' seaward end.

Not that I understood anything yet about the Scandal. Just had dim memories of a summer when my father'd been more volatile and head-tossing than usual, my future guardian even more observant. I still used to gaze across our private jug-jug of Long Island Sound at a boarded-up mansion, never reoccupied and soon torn down, from a wharf that had lost its lone green eye at night once my mother, widowed by then, gave up puzzling over the fusebox. Then the dog would bark.

POSTED BY: *Pam*   Deep into the night, my mother and the Lotus Eater would return, the Dreiser's headbeams now a U-boat firing torpedoes at the house. Contradicting the glow of curiosity in Cadwaller's pipe bowl, since I wasn't such a ninny as to misunderstand the submerged possibility piquing his interest, the L.E. always went to sleep in a separate room. Across the way from Pammie-after-all's, it was far down the hall from my mother's.

I used to hear the L.E. wandering back from there, wall-whiskbrooming and slow, after they'd spent a nightcap hour examining the pencase. Its hasp's clicks and evident fascination had led me by now to revisualize it as a sort of stereopticon. Cued by one of my mother's rare audible indiscretions ("Darling, don't be so greedy! He was mine first, you know. But if you're nice, I promise we'll get you one of your own") as I padded past the door, pretending the living room was going underwater and I had to rescue a dolly the Scandinavian had been too hefty to stoop for, I'd decided the two of them were arguing over pictures of the strange men, not to be redundant, they'd met in the city.

It was loneliest in the mornings. Until midday, the two of them stayed hidden like nesting dolls inside the columned bulge of East Egg grandeur where were tucked Pammie's increasingly fictional memories of having had a father. Still pointlessly braced to attention by summer's commanding officer, it now felt like my home only when they were gone and I was waiting for Quint.

Along around noon, the Scandinavian would start preparing lunch, grumblingly aware it might end up scrapped by the clock hands' Alphonse-Gaston routine, my mother's capricious palate, or a rush back to Manhattan. When our houseguests, must correct that plural, finally emerged, both Daisy and the L.E. often looked distinctly the worse for good weather.

On afternoons when serious recuperation was called for, they'd rest on our white lawn furniture. Vaguely clad, their bodies lolled on iron scrollwork like faked photographs of ectomorphs trying to rise skyward from skeletons. The Scandinavian's offerings of deviled eggs or mutually surprising—to the food too—tongue sandwiches took care of keeping body and soul in the identical bind.

"Why, Daisy! I think this one's yours," the L.E. exclaimed one day, peeping between two slices of bread. That alarmed me until my mother's horribly affectionate answer—"Share and share alike, darling"—proved her powers of speech were unimpaired.

My mother would often be frowning or trying to at a book, sometimes guessing right about posterity's opinion of the new. Even so, a vanished bookmark's tombstone of pallor on an otherwise yellowed page tells me she never got to the fifth episode of *Ulysses*. (How you talk, Pam! You're mired to this day in the ninth.) Her struggles to prove she could stay in the modernist swim from aboard her morphine raft left the Lotus Eater, no reader aside from speedometers and price tags, staring not through but into her own sunglasses, occasionally reaching out for a champagne glass that would startle her when it had fur and barked. Only then would Daisy's daughter be drafted as her interlocutor by default.

"Why, oh, there—Pamela. What is that racket—dear?" I remember her calling, her mouth seemingly attempting flight from the black warders covering her eyes by twisting itself into the incognito of a smile. As my mother decided the sun had dried that page and turned it, a dull thunk from my area had caught the L.E.'s restless ear. "Are you practicing polo?"

"It's a mallet, not a racket. And it's for croquet, not polo." Along with a weathered ball, I'd found it in—not on—our unmown lawn some days earlier. No need for wickets: the hunt after each whack kept me busy even when the dog got bored.

"Croquet's dull as death," that mouth lamented as the lenses flashed, twenty feet away. It was the pot calling the kettle tiresome, but she could hardly be expected to see the joke—not with all those fascinating thoughts about herself twisting and worming around inside her cranium's narcissistic seraglio. "You should play polo! Now there's a game. Gallop along, gallop along!"

Unnoticed by the Lotus Eater, my mother'd stopped reading. "I don't like horses," I said, unwilling to use the word *scared* in front of my rival.

As the L.E.'s long gone, I can admit on daisysdaughter.com that the flinch lasted well into adulthood. I wasn't to ride until Gerson and I went to Tahoe for our fifth anniversary. Even on mounts as tranquil as the slow-motion clouds overhead, we made unlikely cowpokes; Gerson looked as if he feared arrest for impersonating a Cossack. As for me, every pine was measuring the strictly provisional demise of a phobia I was sure a trot or even a loud snort or mane toss would bring back at gale force. We were both giddy when we got back to our cabin, knowing we'd make love.

Back to 1927. "Try it with the dog!" the L.E. shrieked with now unfeigned hilarity, the ever busy seraglio having worked its way out to her writhing lips. It was absurd, since SooSoo—what do you know, Mnemosyne?—stood barely higher than my knee. "Doggy polo, there's your sport. It's settled. One day you'll thank me, little—Pamela…"

My mother's swiveled stare by then was proof of just how calmly Hamlet takes to hefting Yorick's skull. Since reproach was impermissible—oh, no! Not with her dear Lotus Eater—she only looked disbelieving.

"Do you *mind?*" she finally said. And in my memory's most hateful, unforgivable footage of that summer, made amends for her strained tone with a conciliatory smile.

"Oh! Well, Daisy. I forgot," the Lotus Eater stammered, genuinely nonplussed. "And well—it *is* a game, you know, and scads of people play it. All the time. And well—you never liked him. You told me so. That's why I didn't think of—bother!—anything, really. Anything at all."

Couldn't stand either of them, suddenly. "Can I go back to my game now?"

POSTED BY: *Pam-Chen*   It must've been going on August when my mother decided to force us to be friends. The Scandinavian included, since you need four for mah-jongg. It tickles me that I spent years convinced "Pong!," "Chow!," "Chen-chen!," and "Mah-jongg!" were the only words my childhood nanny knew how to speak…of English.

We played in the kitchen, the best way to secure her participation. Wood-backed ivory tiles went click under a lamp meant to light meat or ice cream. The Lotus Eater's gin flask stood at her elbow like a prompter. Even with two cushions, Pamela had to stand on her chair's lower rung to crane for the far wall—the game's, not the kitchen's—when the Scandinavian was dealer. That made the collection of my initial thirteen tiles a stretch once the dice had told her where to break the fortress.

Naturally, I was delighted when the dice or multiple games appointed me dealer. Only long afterward did I realize my mother and the L.E. would never've been able to stay so calm during those long mah-jongg nights if the stock of morphine upstairs hadn't been lavish enough to hold them well into tomorrow, making a Dreisered dash into Manhattan to see their *other* dealer unnecessary.

Even so, I won't deny—and why should you, Pam, almost eighty years later?—that mah-jongg in our kitchen, with the clicking of the pencase or stereopticon's hasp held at bay by chen-chen, chow, and pong, is my happiest memory of that summer. It may be this old bag's happiest memory of the whole damned Nineteen-Twenties.

Yes, the tiles included dragons: red, white, green. But the black one—night—was barricaded by the kitchen's windows. They held off the giant squid's inky sieges even when, far out past our lawn, mute heat lighting, meteorology's answer to silent movies, flashed in the Sound.

You see, my mother's plan did work up to a point. Some games expose and inflame people's personalities; my playwright first husband always claimed poker nights in college (the Merchant Marine to interviewers) taught him how to dramatize character. The rules of others act to suspend temperament, again up to a point.

My mother, for instance, couldn't stop trying for all primes, all concealed, or some other overly strategized bonus, only to be forestalled time and again when one of the rest of us called "*Mah*-jongg!" at the first workaday combo of any old four triplets or chows and one pair. Even so, those Chinese women knew what they were doing. In steerage, in doss houses, and in Gold Rush brothels, they'd needed a pastime whose strictness would foster intimacy independent of liking.

War has the same effect. In 1944–45, it wasn't so much that Pamita didn't notice what a prick Eddie Whitling was as that the observation didn't strike her as relevant. His way with an MP or a map, his nose for indiscretion, and his ability to crack the first joke after a shell plowed into the next ridge or orchard were all more to the point. What I mean is that I used to honestly forget the woman saying "Pong!" and "Chen-chen!" to my left was the Lotus Eater.

It awes me to consider that sometimes she did too. With atypical foresight, my mother'd arranged things so that the L.E.'s usual kitchen seat meant I chowed from her. You can't help but make jokes when your rival's discards end up as the linchpins of the visible part of your hand.

"Oh, *Pamela!*" the mahj-disguised Lotus Eater used to wail, for once with no audible unease before she called me anything at all, when I'd chirp "*Chow!*" and reach for the Three Bamboo or One Dot she'd just called and laid down. "Why do I bother to keep the rest hidden? Here, here, why don't you have a look at my secrets? Just take from me whatever you need? I'll save you lots of time. Go on, go on!"

Levitating her tile rack for a surprisingly funny, two-fingered balancing act (she never handled the dog that well), she'd make the same odd forward-and-back motion she'd performed with her breakfast plate in June. Only now, as I suppose she may've meant it to the first time, it only made me—made us, even the Scandinavian—laugh.

Then I'd ponder my own tiles, discard a dragon, and my mother's lithe fingers would flash out like forest sprites: "That's mine. *Pong!* Why, Pammie, *thank* you."

"Oh, darn."

"Such a good little girl," Daisy would laugh as she set out her triplet and flashed her eyes at the L.E., her white throat sweetly bubbling with its old Dom Perignon from my pre-Scandal infancy. "I must've done something right—don't you think, darling?"

Panama, at that age I could've given myself over to mah-jongg the way Duchamp did to chess. I just wouldn't have had the inspiration to draw a mustache on the Mona Lisa first. Yet nothing, neither my yelps nor the Scandinavian's greasily crumbly potato pancakes—nor even the Lotus Eater's gin flask, which I'd gone from resenting as a silvery kibitzer to welcoming as an ally in keeping us all around that kitchen table forever—nothing could stop the newly exclusive slyness that'd steal over two of our four faces as the kitchen clock's hands neared convergence at the peak of their circular Alp. For half of our quartet, their arrows' function had gone from chronological to directional.

It's no fun for children to discover that the companionship of adults is always in some sense an imposture. Why don't they *always* want to be this way, you wonder? Even after, like all adults, I'd learned the myriad answers to that one, I did my best to feather the transitions.

I only had to learn how when Chris Cadwaller, sixteen and wary, visited Paris soon after I'd married his father. I was in my late thirties by then. That may've been my advantage over the L.E. and Daisy, since smart Chris and I were agreed there'd be no illusions Pam was still youthful herself.

Maybe it's just as well that your future Gramela never did talk him or the rest of you, or for that matter Hopsie, into trying mah-jongg. All that three generations of Cadwallers have taken from it is "Chen-chen!," the cry to the dealer to draw two final tiles and begin the next game. First Chris, then Tim—and now you, Panama—use it for everything from ending a phone call to changing the subject after an argument to starting a meal once everyone's served.

Chen-chen! If that's my Cadwaller legacy, I'm not complaining. You all treat it as hopeful. It's never "Goodbye," much less "Go to hell," but "Let's start the next game now." If it sounds ornerier as your Gramela mutters it, that's because my next game's my last. Having drawn Pam's thirteen and arranged them to suit my best chances of mahj-ing, I'm waiting on the White House switchboard to lay down its fourteenth.

"Chen-chen," I've just told the phone, your great-grandfather's gun in my lap. My determined dentition feels like a mouthful of dead Daisy's long lost wood and ivory (they weren't in the Paris footlocker, to my regret) mah-jongg tiles. "Chen-chen, *petit* Potus. Chen-chen."

POSTED BY: *Pam-Pam*   1927: Heat lightning, boiled smell of Copenhagen. Alphonse and Gaston climbing up their round Alp. "Last one?" said the Lotus Eater, tattooing her underlip with avid teeth. "Last one, agreed?"

Unable to predict their own impatience, she and my mother would never call the last hand until it was well underway. Pam was always denied the fool's reward of cherishing it from start to finish. It was rude of the L.E. in another way too, since she'd just konged—added a fourth matching tile to a triplet, forcing her to draw now from the dead wall—and that set her up for a high score if she won.

"Yes, darling. Of course. It will be. Pam-Pam's tired."

Like hell I was, Mother. But I didn't have much to work with. One chow, a potential triplet, and a bunch of tiles otherwise with less in common than bus passengers.

I drew an East Wind and hummed in dismay, knowing I had to keep it. No help to me, it was a risky discard when none of its three matching tiles was in sight. Choosing another from my rack and setting it down, I grumbled "Polly"—our private mahj name for One Bamboo. Unlike the other tiles in its suit, it showed not count-'em-and-weep bamboo poles but a bird of paradise.

My mother's hand was all concealed, a virtual scream she was angling for one of her would-be high-scoring masterpieces. She barely glanced at her new tile before she discarded it. "Polly want a Five Crack?" she said.

With two chows and two triplets in plain view, the Scandinavian had only one tap-tapping tile unexposed, so we knew she was just waiting on her pair. The North Wind she drew and gruntingly flipped for our benefit was no use to her. Or the rest of us, as she could see for herself: the other three North Winds were already face up in the discard rows that had lengthened until they nearly formed the square of a single-tiered fort inside the vanishing two-tiered one's outline.

Then the Lotus Eater drew. As if her new inability to concentrate—not with that morphine stereopticon calling to her and Daisy from its pencase upstairs—left her no choice but to mimic the Scandinavian's gesture, she put the tile down face up right away: "Six Dot," she said restlessly.

Once she heard herself *call* it, though, some hophead circuitry substituted the sound of her own voice for plain sight. Her hand fluttered: "Oh, no! I need it. Can…? Um, *chow!*" said the L.E. nonsensically. Making as if to retrieve her own discard, she gave the nitwit giggle—and nothing's more likely to offend a child—of someone who'd stopped taking the rules seriously.

Offended, my ass. I was appalled. "You can't chow yourself! And it's too late. We've all seen it. And anyway—*pong*." I reached out.

A boiled red hand superseded us both: "*Mah*-yongg." But she never knew I'd seen her naked, crouching with hands gripping white bedstead bars in her tumid room as she napped. That same red hand that had just seized the tile was at rest next to scrub brush whose crevasse hid Bering Sea herring. The last thing that would've occurred to me was that I had one too.

"Oh, dear. Look at this," said my mother, crestfallen enough to commit the mahj solecism—to Pam the stickler's eyes, at least—of displaying a losing combination. "I had all the dragons, hidden! And my own wind. I only needed the pair."

Except for the L.E., who was fidgeting now that she'd spilled the tiles back off her rack onto the table—but then, unlike me, she wouldn't be saying goodnight to my mother just yet, but "chen-chen"—our commiserations were genuine. It was a nearly miraculous hand. Or would've been if my prosaic Scandinavian nanny hadn't barged to victory with a common, low-scoring, practical two chows, two triplets, and pair.

Her only reward was to rebox the tiles. We never knew what became of her after she quit near the end of the summer, but I don't doubt that, unlike her employer, she lived to be a hundred.

POSTED BY: *Pam*   My recollection is that the scene that ended any chance of chowed or unchowed companionability between me and the L.E. took place the next morning. Be warned I spent eight years in Hollywood and a day and a half there will teach you glib dramaturgy if you're susceptible.

Whatever morning it was, I'm sure it was one of mid-August's drowsiest. My mother came downstairs just before midday, dressed for Manhattan but less soignée than usual. That meant she looked like a *lesser* Modigliani for a change.

She grew more jittery as a whole hour of August dithered by without the L.E. appearing. Then finally crazed enough to kiss my head out of nowhere, her delicate hands caging Pammie's stunned ears like white spiders, and act as if we did that all the time.

What I intuit in hindsight is that they'd used up the last of their M the night before. My mother was frantic to get back to Manhattan and score before the cravings grew strong enough to make madness look like an appealing alternative. And for that, she needed the L.E., not having driven a car since the Scandal.

She finally scooted me upstairs—a first—to wake her chauffeur. Another turn of the screw, and why hadn't I seen it sooner? Not Quint, whom I'd plainly imagined: Quintess. No jackboots or uniform, that was how I'd been fooled. The scariest phantasms are those in plain sight. Right then, I'd've sooner climbed onto a pony.

"Why can't you?" I complained. "She's your lousy friend." If that sounds comical, Panama, I'd better explain that back then people still knew lousy meant infested with lice. I might as well have said *fucking*.

Daisy was too nervous to rebuke me. "Because little girls are sweeter," she said, a non sequitur if I ever heard one. "Besides, you know [though I didn't] she doesn't like me walking in on her. I'm, oh!, much too noisy, you see. With my great big feet. Clump, clump!, like your father's," she improvised, using her hands to demonstrate. "I must've gotten them from him, I don't know. Oh, Pammie, please."

Just like her hands, my mother's feet, if you can't guess, were elfin. Mine were the boats, and genuinely my father's chromosomes having a laugh: one reason my growth spurt in teenhood was a relief. But her plea wasn't one I could've refused. Other than mah-jongg, this was the most important I'd been since my birthday in June, and I clumped up the stairs.

Across the hall from mine, the Lotus Eater's door was closed. My soft knock got me silence, my bad-dolly one did too. When I pushed, I was mildly surprised (but why?) that she didn't lock it. She was asleep in a grotto of shadows, one stalactite stocking hanging down from her bed's canopy.

From the sheet tugged around her slender frame to its unmistakably pent youthfulness even in exhaustion, she made the mountainous Scandinavian look like a member of a different gender altogether. Petite with more hips than bust, made to order for Twenties couture: thank God I was her age in the boxy, Rosalind Russellized, row-row-row-your-shoulders-girls Nineteen-Forties instead. Her back was to me as I came around her bed.

She was sucking her thumb. Its tip was nestled in her parted lips as if it had either lost hope upon finding teeth there or been reassured by their existence. On her bare other arm, flung out past the pillow, I could see a few of the same violet stains that blemished my mother's arms at the rare times they were exposed. That didn't surprise or upset me, since I knew they gave each other bites with the stereopticon.

What did surprise me was that her face, seen now for the first time without her jerkily wired mind's pulleys playing puppetmaster, seemed kind. Kind only to herself, I grant, but we've all got to start somewhere and she didn't know I was present. Anyhow, the revelation to Pam's puzzled eyes was that acting pleased with herself, which was how I saw the L.E., didn't necessarily mean she was being kind to herself.

Or that anyone else was, but I was here on a mission and unsure how to accomplish it. "Hello," I told the sleeping L.E. "Mommy says it's time to wake up."

Nothing. Breathing. Nothing. "You have to wake up," I explained to her. "Hey, it's time for school!"

I thought that might make her laugh the nice way she did during mahjongg, not the nasty one when nobody joined her. She didn't stir, and they must've shot up enough M to take care of a wounded platoon. So the adult Pam is in a position to estimate, having seen those syrettes stuck in enough dead men's blasted bodies as Eddie Whitling and I barreled on in our jeep toward Falaise or Bastogne.

I'm not sure I can explain what prompted me to do what I did next. A girl of seven's most attracted to what she misses most in herself. That chestnut bob's lustrous gloss and svelte motion had become the tangible representation to Pammie of everything I wasn't and couldn't be in either my mother's eyes or my own. For young girls, destiny's earliest prefiguration of giving birth to an idiot child is having hair nobody can do anything with.

Not your problem, Panama! You never do anything with yours either and no one would want you to. Even in adulthood, during most of which time I could afford to try driving any coiffeur to drink I cared to, mine stayed a gingery brindle mop, courtesy of the Buchanan side and resistant to gentling.

One of old age's few perks is that, cut short, it's turned unremarkable. The best even Hopsie could do was "Harvest moon, misty night in October," and at the time your great-grandfather was playing 20th-century Song of Solomon, gallantly lyricizing each part of me. *All* of them, and you shouldn't blush. I want you to know what the world can be like at its best, too.

Anyhow, I started stroking the Lotus Eater's hair. Played gliding Niagara with its silky fall, mussed and rechoreographed those docile bangs. "Wake up, wake up," I crooned in my mother's old singsong, not heard by me since I was a toddler.

Eventually, she woke up. She screamed as if I were a hairbrush on fire.

3. *Provincetown*

POSTED BY: *Pam*   After eighty-six years as a frequent flyer and sometime stewardess on Clio, I know how often bits of the way-back-when have vanished by the time searchers find Carole Lombard's plane's black box. No, Panama: don't go all Wiki in the knees. It didn't have one. On a tour to sell war bonds, that infectious actress got smacked into a mountain with twenty-two other people in 1942. I had a posthumous connection to one of her fellow passengers, which I'll explain on daisysdaughter.com if Cadwaller's gun hasn't been fired by then.

No competent social history of the Twenties omits the mah-jongg craze. Some tenured Tom Swift's mention that there was one won't bring back the slither between my fingers of wood-backed ivory as Pam chose to discard a white dragon, the gradients thermometerizing my nanny's arms, or the Lotus Eater's habit of keeping us waiting by applying full makeup before—chestnut-bobbed, kohl-eyed, and green-mouthed—she sat down to play in our monstrously boxy East Egg kitchen. For that you need Gramela: the mimsy borogoves' retinal photographs, the *autentico* prattle of Long Island Shakespeare eighty-odd years ago. Just invaluable, aren't I?

Even if I weren't licking these withered lips at the prospect of doing myself in with a shriek and a bang right after I hear "White House calling for Mrs. Cadwaller," I'll obviously never read a social history of the year we're living in now. Still, listen, Swift; your ancestor Jonathan would've. I don't want you to neglect the mimsies' most jarring sight of our national insanity in the jangled third spring of this awful and unending war.

For months now, a pack of tatterdemalion loons has been turning up outside Arlington Cemetery for military funerals. Jeering and catcalling, they hold up repulsively gloating signs as the thunderstruck mourners enter and exit.

I'd seen this on the local news. Then with greater disbelief I watched it crawl by in three dimensions as Andy Pond drove me to some geezers' waltz on the Virginia side of the river.

"My Gawd, Andy!" I squawked once I'd gotten mimsies, fat lunettes, and dentition back inside some sort of rational corral. "I'm so sorry. Can we turn around and go back to the District? You know what a forgetful old lady I am."

Turning us south toward Lyndon Johnson Memorial Grove, Andy simpered. "Oh, Pam! Did you leave your ACLU card at home *again*?"

"Yes, but how did you know?"

"I've heard that joke before."

"Andy, so what? Haven't you heard *all* of them?"

"Well, I hope not," Andy said.

Famous last words, don't you think? "You'd better," I told him as we swept past the now repaired Pentagon. "I've heard all of yours."

POSTED BY: *Pam*   Pam's consolation was that it was Memorial Day weekend. Only a week ago! That meant the Rolling Thunder boys were in town.

So long as they've got hairily aging Vietnam vets straddling them, I'll never let blatting motorbikes annoy me. By now their annual rumble, filling our streets with Steve McQueen's sons, is as Washingtonian as the Tidal Basin cherry blossoms that precede them. No doubt the cherry trees' unbottled messages to Thomas Jefferson will outlive Rolling Thunder's Chincoteaguean roar.

Is that sad or not? Can't decide, doesn't matter. It's no skin off my nose, as the leper said to the headwaiter. Unless dear Bob's pull with the White House is nil, I'll be dead as Dickens's doornail by sundown.

By my own hand, I think with a thrill the authoress of "Chanson d'automne" would have shared and may well have prompted. Then I ask myself: left or right? I usually pick up the phone with my right. Must try playing with Cadwaller's gun with my sinister.

Anyhow, some of the vets had made a cordon between the picketers and the cemetery's entrance. It won't be on audio at the Archives, but I'd like Pam's octogenarian voice to go on record here on daisysdaughter.com as saying, "Thank you, boys. Good luck to you tomorrow, boys."

Who were these protesters, you ask? Some callous pack of peacenik crazies, venting their hatred of this awful and unending war by scoffing at its dead? Oh, heavens, no, Professor Swift. They're demented homophobes. They show up at funerals to brag—the right word—that the coffins being shipped back home are fit punishment for America's tolerance of homosexuals.

"Oh, Jesus fucking Christ," I said to Andy once we'd seen those loonies in action. "Cripes! What's Denmark *coming* to?"

POSTED BY: *Pam*   From what I gather, Panama, your generation could not care less where love is found or which two sticks (or not) two people rub together to make fire. I just hope there's a recognizable U.S.A. around by the time you're in a position to call the shots, because the anti-fag outrage you and yours so merrily see as quaint is our other national pastime's final inning.

Not that I'm urging you to try experimenting with homosexuality's cunning, titillating, enjambed, and netherworldly distaff version, certainly not at your age. Your father may read this and I do want Tim to stay fond of me after I'm gone. Even without Cadwaller's gun in my lap, I know I won't live to see the end of the long haul that began on April 19, 1775. Decades before your birth, that was the date chosen by your Gramela to cap the final chapter of her now forgotten *Glory Be.*

I'm sure that looks like a shameless bid to boost my "Used and Collectible" sales on Amazon. Most likely that's because it is one, and I must say I wish I'd discovered the egocentric pleasures of having my own blog a bit sooner. But my point is that once you and yours are done, at least until the Martians or Venusians land and give us all new six-eyed, twenty-bellied scapegoats, there won't be anyone left in this country whom it's permissible to hate.

In my day and certainly in my circles, we weren't as benighted or obtuse as you and yours may think. I did successively attend Mme Chignonne's École des Filles in Paris, Purcey's Girls' Academy of St. Paul, and Barnard. While none of those XX-chromosomed environments was the triple-X smorgasbordello beloved of pornographers, one certainly knew with which instructors or head-mistresses a private conference might take on a never verbalized undertow of Charybdis.

Despite a pretty intractable aversion in my own case, I can even remember several bathetic pre–Pearl Harbor fumblings after I quit college with my Bank Street roommate, now dead. They led absolutely nowhere in my case, and in hers bore no more post–Pearl Harbor fruit than did her giggly ambitions for a Hollywood career. Thus was I vindicated in a *veni, vidi, vade retro* sort of way.

It must've been something in Manhattan's air or water. Years before I reached the scene, Murphy was embittered when *The Other Eye of the Newt,* his play about a spinster who couldn't admit why she'd stayed one—not an altogether easy work to defend, especially when your first word had to be "Comrades"—got blown to smithereens at the notes-and-sketches stage by Lillian Hellman's *The Children's Hour.* Lillian and Bran were violent rivals anyway, as the dilemma for Stalinists was that, not unlike their favorite ism's eponym, they all wanted to be the only one.

As for Hollywood in the Fifties, I well recall Gerson's chuffed return from a Rock Hudson script conference whose date Hudson had misremembered. My

husband had to wield his producer's pencil poolside amid male bathing beau-
ties clad in swim trunks barely masking the foliaged union of their muscular
legs' barkless tree trunks. "And he's so dull in his movies," Gerson marveled.
"Well, maybe that's why. Not much left over."

In all these years, Potus has succeeded in disarming me—what an entertaining phrase that is to input with Cadwaller's gun weighting my crotch!—in
disarming me just twice. The first "Gotcha, Pam" was a no doubt easily Google-
able photograph of the future Potus holding his twins right after their birth. For
once, his amazement at life's unruliness looks awed, not disgruntled. He's a few
million dazed new fathers compressed into one representative face: proof that
democracy as truth predated democracy as system.

The other time is more relevant here. Three Junes ago, his Yale reunion
was held at the White House. In that all-XY crowd, since there wouldn't be XX-
chromosomal Elis—Ellies?—until years after the Class of '68's most prominent
grad said goodbye to all that elitism, a patently female classmate approaches.
Why do I want her hair to be a one-eyed blonde waterfall, like Veronica Lake's?
Why do I see her sylphlike and radiant at fifty-plus, in long white gloves and a
shimmering off-the-shoulder gown—in daytime, yet? Oh, just because. I'm so
fucking old, indulge me.

"You knew me as Peter," says Veronica Yale.

"And now you've come back as yourself," says Potus, extending his hand.

Maybe they didn't read that in Alabama. I sure did in the *WashPost*'s Style
section, and gaped so wide I nearly had to shove my *Popular Mechanics* dentition
back in. I mean, my onetime acquaintance Jack Kennedy—met at a Waldorf-
Astoria luncheon when we were rivals for the Pulitzer, he was grinning as if
each tooth was one more of Dad's bank accounts even as his cool eyes demoted
them to his stake at billiards—couldn't have done it better. And wouldn't, not
with Bobby's bleak gaze keeping tabs on *how* considerate Jack was thinking of
getting. As for Ike or LBJ, both of whom I also knew—Eisenhower only in the
round at wartime press sessions, but Lyndon one on one—you can't picture
them inhabiting a universe where such encounters were possible.

Oddly, Dick Nixon, who going by my reception-line encounters before
Kissinger had Hopsie posted to India certainly knew what it was like to know

yourself as Richard, might've managed it. But would have bungled the line reading and flashed that sickly smile, hoping to broker an agreement that while we all try, no one's exempt from the world's little treacheries.

Anyhow, it's the only occasion I can recall of Potus embracing a value I hold dear, which you could call emotional elegance and I define as generosity combined with aplomb. If I hadn't known it before, Cadwaller showed me that kindness is often a form of quick-wittedness. I've met farm boys in foxholes who did it instinctively.

The *WashPost* didn't speculate on who'd kidnapped Potus and replaced him with somebody civilized, gracious, pleasant, and thoughtful that afternoon, but I say there's a mystery there. Maybe only I wondered: in the name of all that's fucked in heaven, why doesn't he want to *always* be that way?

POSTED BY: *Pam* Some of my thus far hypothetical readers here on tireless little daisysdaughter.com may be thinking I've lost the drift. Maundering, addled old harridan, etc. But before you consider patronizing me, may I remind you Pam's packing heat?

Anyhow, others, I trust, have got it. Years before the Holmesian glow of Hopsie's briar advertised his urbane best hunch, maybe even before the Paris footlocker gave up its secrets, I'd divined that the unpleasant young woman you know as the Lotus Eater must've had what society called Sapphic tendencies in coyer days and I've always privately labeled the Charybdis temptation.

Even with the L.E.'s genius for thwartedness—I mean the kind that goes on feeling thwarted from pure habit even after the desire has faded—I couldn't help but feel compassionate at the thought of her yen to rub four Charybdean nipples together centering on my mother. Daisy Fay, the belle of Louisville to half the khaki with officer's buttons stationed there in '17 and '18? Daisy *Buchanan*, the hypotenuse of Long Island's best-known recent XY-XX-XY love triangle? Even in Gramercy Park, site of the L.E.'s robber-baronial family townhouse, they must've heard about the Scandal.

My mother's brand of sophistication was essentially a way of keeping her innocence at liberty. Supposing her mind was even able to accommodate the notion that any such Charybdean lust was in play, she must've opted to put up with those occasional burning looks and odd tilts of the Lotus Eater's jaw for the sake of the companionship she craved not only in her heart but, more urgently, her veins. I still imagine it must've been touch and go for her during the week we spent in Provincetown: the only time that, with the budding pudding that was Pam exiled to a small brown vacationer-scarred ottoman in the front and only other room, she and the L.E. had no choice but to share a bed.

POSTED BY: *Pam*   The peculiar thing was that the L.E. had vanished from our orbit just days earlier, seemingly for good. So I gathered from my mother's hysterical return in the Dreiser—she'd *driven* it!—from one of their Manhattan jaunts with neither a Quint nor a Quintess. The Scandinavian took charge of trundling every last gloomy chapter of that endless car out of our driveway and back to Gramercy Park.

Came a precious intermission, which I spent as the baffled apple of my mother's uncertain eye. Just what Pammie had always wished would happen, only in my version she hadn't been red-nosed, constantly stanching or yielding to sudden tears, and gabbling nonsense I couldn't understand along with the silly kind she remembered I liked. Even so, I glowed to hear myself called "Darling," an endearment with only one addressee since the L.E.'s East Egg debut in June.

Though I still never got to see it open, she even fetched the pencase—no longer a stereopticon since the L.E.'s departure, the object inside it was once again vaguely a pen in my mind—down from her room, keeping it near her as a sort of amulet. Or potential Pamulet, even if my blood does run colder than its tepidly pretzeled norm when I think of the solution to her new loneliness that must've flitted once or twice through my mother's panicked mind.

As she clutched at straws she didn't fully grasp were her little daughter's arms, her problem was that her beauty was dependent on her selfishness. To have seen anyone other than herself as fully human would've told her she was losing her looks. Still, who else was there she could have considered getting hooked to keep her company, the Scandinavian? My mother may have been half out of her skull, but you could count on her to balk at the grotesque. At least I belonged to the same social class she did, making that crazed option more palatable.

Since it never crossed my mind there could be two of them, the mystery that didn't get explained until I first opened the Paris footlocker in August '44 was why the pencase's velvet was now midnight blue rather than the black I remembered. But I hadn't seen it since its contents had mutated into a stereopticon at the beginning of summer, the span of the Pleistocene Era at my budding-pudding age, and my mother didn't quite resemble herself either. I'd gotten more used than I'd realized to the Daisy whose behavior varied according to her proximity to the Lotus Eater, making it reliable in a way.

POSTED BY: *Pam*   Despite its confusions, don't blame me if I reveled in that intermission. It was a return to not only the months right after my father's death when it had been just her and me, but more magically to the by now half imaginary time when I'd been a toddler, Daddy was alive, and I remembered her paying much more attention to Pammie. At least when Tom Buchanan was in the house, attending to me was her only irreproachable task that didn't require his say-so and even he couldn't sulk about.

And yes, Panama: I've made that best-of-both-worlds crack many times. While my mother would never have voiced the thought, I'm not sure she didn't share it. At least when she wasn't preoccupied by the Lotus Eater's nonpresence (and please: however dislikable Daisy's morphine crony was, whatever quarrel over a man or even intrusion of the L.E.'s Charybdean tendencies had caused the break, have enough pity for my mother to grasp how frightened she'd have been at having to go back to shooting up alone), she seemed as happy as I was to revisit the lost days of my infancy. If the L.E. hadn't shown up on our doorstep under a week later, I think Daisy might've tried to take me all the way back into her womb.

"Pammie, darling!" she said one oven of an afternoon. No air conditioning even for richies back then, Panama. We sweltered democratically, privilege's perks confined to rising breezes from the Sound.

Brushing her eyes, she put aside the pencase, which she'd been clutching as she sniffled. My newest hypothesis was that it held some sort of miniature Daddy, which pleased me. Make what you will of the fact that I had no desire to open it.

"Yes?"

"Do you remember when you were a *very* little girl, and you and Mummy used to bathe together? Lovely, long, cool baths? Wouldn't that be perfect now?"

I pondered. "Should I tell Nanna to run one?"

"Oh, no! I'm sure she's napping. I think we can manage by ourselves, don't you?"

I did feel shy about it. For one thing, I *didn't* remember, not really. Plausible and pleasant was the closest my memory could come. For another, I was acutely conscious of my doughily pale small Pamcorpus: so unlike my mother's, somehow neither plausible nor pleasant, and unseen by anyone since the dawn of time. The Scandinavian, who normally bathed me, didn't count. Frequency aside, there was no difference between the red-elbowed way she scrubbed me and the way she washed our dog.

I stood in my summer frock, pudgy knees (you'd better believe they felt like an item of clothing), and strap shoes and watched the tub fill. Then my mother reappeared in a green silk wrap and bent to turn off the tap in the first domestic or practical gesture I suspect I'd ever seen her perform.

"Why, Pammie! Why aren't you in yet?"

That confused me. Insofar as my memory had managed to make infancy's prequels to our joint bath plausible and pleasant, it had sworn up and down that I'd been too young to dress or undress myself. Even now, the Scandinavian took charge of disrobing me, impatient with my illusion that I was a girl and not a package from the dry cleaners'. So far as I could and can recall, I'd never taken off my own clothes in front of anyone, and it had an unwelcome element of *decision*. So I hesitated.

"Oh, honestly, darling!" said my mother. "Did I really raise you?" [Short answer to that one, mother mine: no.] "For God's sake, it's just Daisy."

If nothing else, her scorn took away the unwelcome element of decision. All that was left was the familiar element—though not in this context—of clumsiness, of inadequacy, of wondering why nobody had ever seen fit to tell me the lousy rules of anything. Keep in mind, my mother had clavicles as delicate and in many contexts as expressive as wood creatures' eyes.

Not that more than the ends nearest her throat of those very odd bones was on display just now. It was evident she wasn't going to join me in the nude until I'd plunged my seven-year-old Pamcorpus into the tub.

So I shed strap shoes, Pamunderwear (odd priority, you may say, but I was most used to—and still, at seven, proudest of—pushing them down when tin-kling), summer dress, and chemise (chemise? *Mais bien sûr.* I was a rich girl, not a farm girl, and in August I counted those bitches lucky). Then I turned to the tub as if it were my porcelain and all but woofing St. Bernard.

After all, the bathroom's wall tiles *were* white as Alps. And as somehow professional, not that I'd seen one yet, as Swiss sanatoriums. Yet I must've hesitated again, briefly but fatally, over which leg to fork over the damn thing as she watched.

"Oh, no, dear!" Daisy said. "Your hair."

On behalf of any number of hard-working hairdressers in Manhattan, Hollywood, Paris, the District, and even New Delhi, I'd love to tell you I put hands to hips, faced her with seven-year-old brashness exposed from China to Peru, and said, "Yeah, you fucking junkie. What about my hair?" But that Pam—the one who's carried on a fair number of interesting conversations in the altogether over the years, the one with hips to put hands to, the one who drawls "fucking" the way Pepys writes "But I digress," the one who knew my mother was addicted to morphine—that Pam was a long way from existing.

"I'm sorry," I said instead in panic. Couldn't wait to learn what I'd apologized for (it's all *information* at that age). Though it was August, forgive me for remembering I was shivering.

"Can't let it get wet! That's death."

I cringed for two reasons. One was that "death" as an all-purpose comparison was an L.E.-ism and I'd thought we were shut of her. The other was that, as she tugged a ruffled and honey-colored bathing cap down over naked, hopping Pam's head, my mother—and until you follow this logic, you'll never understand Daisy Buchanan—said, "My! You are a bit roly-poly, aren't you?"

"But what about your hair, Mommie?" (Oh, please! Can I get in the tub now?)

"Oh, what I do I care?" she said. "What does anyone?"

After all that, the actual *bath* was a relief. Water was better to wear than nothing, and our tub, of course, was huge. Before the polo horse did its bit, Daddy'd been pretty doggone wealthy, and we were two years away from the Crash.

As for what Daisy Buchanan looked like when she slipped off her silk bath wrap and slid into the far end of the tub, I'm sorry. She was my mother and I'm not a pornographer. She had Those Things (had I suckled them? No information, but I must've drained both). She had That Thing, which I thought was too pretty and small for me to've come out of it. Briefly and discreetly, she'd had its hind twin's scything when she joined me in the tub.

She still had the smile that had made the Fay house in Louisville swarm with khaki and officer's buttons. She had Rorschach-blotty purple and yellow splashes of bruises from shooting up morphine all over her arms and legs.

She pushed a duck at me and giggled. She let me take off the honey-colored bathing cap and soak my head when I complained for the third time about how gunky it felt. She asked her daughter to look away when she stood up with water cascading and reached for her robe, and I did even though I regret it.

She called me "Pammie," not "darling," during most of the bath.

She never mentioned the Lotus Eater. She never touched me, not once, not even when we were both toweled. I'd never done towel turban before. She helped. That was as close as she came.

Not once. Other than that, for once I don't care about history. You bastards! Do you expect me to tell you what her snatch looked like? She was my mother.

POSTED BY: *Pam*   Foreshortened into troglodytism by the downcast view from my third-floor playroom, the Lotus Eater got out from behind the wheel of her Dreiser, and that was that. Intermission accomplished. She looked as ratty in her white dress of surrender as a Popsicle wrapper glued back onto the stick after the Popsicle's gone, but that couldn't have mattered less to my mother. Going by the murmurs that rose once I'd crept down to the second-floor landing—my mother's bright "All you want, darling! Whatever you want," the L.E.'s forlornly merry "*Quid pro quo vadis,* Daisy. Isn't that in Dante somewhere?"—I gathered all was forgiven. By whom and for what, I'll never know.

The L.E. drove away only an hour or two later, after a reconciled parting at the front door I'm sure Pam didn't witness. I have a vivid memory of toycotting it instead in the playroom, mauling two of my dollies' heads together as if I were trying to force them to swap faces and making disgusting "Shmek, shmek" noises which I must've been mimicking from the Scandinavian's mutters when at some point she shoved a third doll into the room. A stupid one I'd always hated, too close to me in size to be good for much; that was why I'd abandoned it on our pointlessly boatless wharf.

My memories of that night and the next morning are more muddled. I'm positive I remember an exhilarated Daisy prattling about what wonderful fun the Scandinavian, SooSoo the dog, and I were going to have during the whole week bothersome, bossy, blissfully flickering Mummy was away. Yet when I came down to breakfast, she was anticipating her Belgian second husband's line of business—Georges Flagon peddled safety equipment to small airports—by waving two squares of burnt toast around an otherwise vacant kitchen.

The toot of a hired car outside made her wildly eye me and then the now odorless, Scandinavian-less servant's quarters behind her. Then a cupboard, as if wondering how long she could responsibly trust Pamela to survive on a diet of dishcloths, dog food, or whatever it contained. Ironing board, Mother.

A second toot unlocked her feet and hurried me upstairs, where my mother began to toss random Pam-garb into a suitcase she'd rejected while slowly feeding her own wardrobe, Smee-style, to three much wider sets of crocodile jaws the night before. Her haste was complicated by her dashes to the window to semaphore our progress to a—what do you know, Miss Jessup?—gray-coated, jackbooted, quintessential (he was male, albeit Asian) chauffeur.

"We're going to the most wonderful place on Cape Cod," she told me as clothes flew. "You're going to meet all Mummy's bestest, most special friends! Oh, here's a lovely sort of little Russian blouse. Is it mine?"

"It's the sun dress I had on yesterday, Mother, and it's dirty. And too small." Taking it back from her dazed hands, I thought the Scandinavian might use it to wipe furniture or finally blow her great big nose in if we still had a Scandinavian. "How do you know where we're going is wonderful?"

"Because I've decided it will be! For everybody, and I'm always right. Yes, always! Wasn't I smart enough to pick you out from all those other little jellybeans when Daddy and I went to that great big expensive candy store on Fifth Avenue?"

"Is *she* coming?" No need to identify who *she* was, much as I might wish my mother hadn't unconsciously agreed.

"Why, of course! She's going to help me take care of you. Won't that be fun?"

"Then I don't want to go. I hate her," said the budding pudding that was Pam, with twin Civil War memorials for eyes. "She's a witch."

"Oh, sweetie, don't be silly. You're too young—don't know enough about anyone yet to really and truly hate them. And she isn't a witch! She doesn't look like one, does she? Isn't she pretty? Well, now, doesn't that just show you? She, oh, she just gets put under a spell sometimes—by her father, who's an awful, wicked, mysterious ogre in the mountains—and that makes her act like one. But she doesn't want to! That's the important thing. Please remember that, Pammie. Watch out for the people who want to. Won't you? For me?"

My mother's failure to become a writer was a failure of discipline, not imagination. Either on the page or in person, I've never been able to improvise like that. Not without a single nugget of reality to wrap my words around.

My face scraped a crushed Daisy-bosom's blossoms in surprise as she lifted me, apparently forgetful that I'd been three the last time she'd tried and was more of a handful now. Unable to maintain a rib grip, her hands scooted up under my armpits as the suitcase staggered toward my unexpectedly defrocked rump. I thought she was going to pack me in it and spare the Lotus Eater the sight of Pam until we got to Provincetown, but it turned out she only wanted me to sit on its lid.

POSTED BY: *Pam*   Of course it's peculiar to be getting ready to describe Provincetown to you, Panama. You know it better than your Gramela. You weren't born yet when a cousin of Cadwaller's with no children deeded her place on the Cape to your grandpa Chris and his wife Renée not long after Hopsie died.

I still wonder sometimes if that unmet Cadwaller relative was the mournful adolescent watching Daisy, the L.E., and Pammie wander through Provincetown from her chair on a now ruddily mobbed, bikini-throbbing, and thong-thronged porch that nonetheless looks familiar in your grandpa's photographs. That porch and the house behind it have featured in every summer of what you always amuse me by calling your *whole* life.

You're the age your grandfather was when I met him. In my memory, he goes in an eyeblink from a wiry sixteen-year-old I'm leading onto a *bateau-mouche* to a newly bearded nineteen-year-old snapping cross-legged pictures of his equally new French bride—today your placid, rotund grandmother—from the rug that then lay in our Paris living room, home now only to the Metro section and Pam's feet.

Chris was still an Agence France-Presse stringer when he first grew the scraggly fuzz that left us unsure at first if he was trying to look older or younger. Once *May or Mayn't*, his photographic documentation of the '68 Paris upheavals, got Amherst interested in putting him on the faculty—Hopsie and I both bemused by his impersonation of an academic, not to mention Amherst's of swinging with the times—he gradually added the belly, wire-rimmed glasses, and cheerfully glottal middle-aged voice that to this day makes it sound as if the piece of paper stuck in his throat has the most wonderful joke written on it. His zest for zany adult masks went on tickling us until we realized they connoted him. Before Cadwaller died, at least he got to see his son complete.

Even down here in Potusville, I'm aware Provincetown has evolved too, not only since my five-day visit in 1927 but over the decade and a half you've been alive to join your parents' jolly, sunburnt two weeks with Chris and Renée there every summer. I've certainly seen lots of pictures, supplemented lately by your Panamanic Margaret Meadisms on the phone about the local boys' club celebrating its XY-seeking-XY summer festival—though no girls' club celebrating an XX-seeking-XX one, I gather, at least from your long-distance descriptions—in that gay mecca, as I believe it's called. It must be a comfort to Tim to know you could saunter around starkers without being an object of more than ornithological curiosity to all but a few of the XY's in sight.

Then Chris comes on the line to report on his latest sighting of my onetime trapeze partner—hi, Norman! Bye, Norman—on the 1948 *NYT* bestseller list. In the near sixty years since *Nothing Like a Dame* was going down on one side of the gutter as *The Naked and the Dead* scooted up the other, he's certainly outdone your Gramela at productivity of every sort. Now a full-time Provincetonian, my fellow author gets around these days on two gnarled canes, so Chris told me last year. To which I retorted, "Thirty-odd books, nine children! What, *only* two canes?"

I never met him in '48 and surely won't remeet him now. Every year, you all (no, not Norman) pile on the phone to beg me to come to Provincetown, and every year I refuse. I steadfastly did so even back when I still got up to Amherst every turkey day and to Manhattan half a dozen times a year—so often that sometimes I'd come and go without seeing you. "Next time," we'd agree and usually make good on it.

No such thing now. No *next time* for anything I've done or haven't done, with the exasperatingly likely exception of having to hit "Save" once, twice, or three or four more times to heave Pam's lap and the rest of her up for the tiresome process that is peeing at my age—a chore whose one interesting novelty today is that each time I've had to set aside Cadwaller's gun, telling it not to worry and I'll be back soon. Trust me, Panama: you've got no idea how boring one's own ablutions get. You'll look back with wonder on the ballerina days when you just yanked 'em down, yanked 'em up, flushed in a flash, and raced back to the party.

Even if I weren't getting ready to knock myself off when the White House calls, I'm afraid I'd still have to decline your clan's invite to come up to Provincetown this year. Doesn't my Mac have oodles of downloads of Chris's pictures from previous Cadwaller-fests? Wasn't I there for five days in 1927? Aren't I reasonably observant? And isn't the rest just architecture?

My God! Pam, you senile imbecile. Maybe Dr. Johnson was right that the prospect of hanging concentrates the mind wonderfully, but what he left out is that the thing being concentrated on is the prospect of hanging. *When* do you all traditionally implore me to come to Provincetown, Panama?

On your unfailing group call to Gramela on my birthday. Oh, bloody hell.

POSTED BY: *Pamincetown*   Naked or not, I can't imagine what it'd be like to walk along Commercial Street today. Living up to its name must be a gaudy challenge. But in my day or my five of them, the fleecings of leisure took a distant back seat to practicality's mutton. There was food and, even under Prohibition, drink, for which my mother's friends blessed the wine-bibbing Portuguese fishermen whose forebears had added Catholic spires to Provincetown's sea-scoured skyline well before Teddy Roosevelt turned up, appropriately escorted by the skirts of seven battleships, to lay the cornerstone of the Pilgrim Monument. The booming salutes of the ships' guns blew out half the window glass in the harbor.

Yet even the rare restaurant with white tablecloths was roughly weathered. Whether olive-skinned or Whartonishly Yankeefied, culinary Provincetown still made it its business to fill customers' stomachs, not their eyes, and without emptying their wallets either. Poets, playwrights, painters, and critics had been congregating there for over a decade; if they hadn't, my mother wouldn't have known the place from Rangoon. They still saw themselves as the décor's fans, though, not its reason for being. Adults who see everything as the occasion for themselves make me shudder.

My mother would've been the last to understand that a seven-year-old child sometimes needs to. So during my five days, I was largely left to make all that up for myself: tugging the masted scrawl of scenery that broke blue infinity in half into a crescent that Pam-Hur's Roman chariot could scoot along in shy triumph to the sea's tame cheers, pressing my mother's and the L.E.'s ambling sack-dressed backs into unwitting service as a pair of stallions. Picking my way alone along the breakwater, which was new then, to act the Little Mermaid to blackened fishing smacks, obligingly yodeling dorymen, and the occasional white quiff of a skiff.

When all else failed, I made sand castles: no mere beach pastime to a child, but the atypically concrete representation of a year-round endeavor. If you ever find yourself at the Art Institute of Chicago, you'll naturally rush to *American Gothic* first. But not far from its place of honor, you'll find Pam depicted in the act.

Despite his recent rediscovery—busy, busy, Ph.D.s, how I wonder what you see—I'm no admirer of Eldritch Weaver (b. here, d. there, who cares). As a measure of his powers of observation, the sky's chartreuse makes me glad he was never a witness in a murder trial. In life, my mother's profile was an albino salad, not a slab, and her costume has idiotically been given more presence than her limbs. While I get no joy from knowing it, the Lotus Eater, 1927 edition,

was prettier than the gouached squash peering anxiously at Grant Wood's masterpiece in the next room.

That this is said to be the earliest American painting in which anyone is
wearing sunglasses gets no very awed ululations from me. Nonetheless, it may
be I'm most hostile to the painting—on behalf of my violet but recognizable
Pam-face, pale knees, and empty pail, included in the lower left-hand quadrant
for balance with the lone blue (never!) sail keeling seaward in the upper right—
because of its title: *Two American Women on the Beach, Provincetown, 1927.*

I'm sorry, Panama, because what you wrote on the back was funny:
"Eldritch Weaver, gay deceiver." But I didn't keep the postcard.

POSTED BY: *Pam*   My mother's Village friends were up on the Cape in
force. As promised, that gave me my first look since a younger Pam's quickly
shuttered glimpse of Daisy's lone attempt to Salvador Dali-ize East Egg, which
had cost us our first Scandinavian, at the people she and the Lotus Eater had
been madhatting it with in Lower Manhattan all summer. Minor painters,
minor poets, minor don't-get-the-wrong ideologues, they've all fallen out of
the history books except for an occasional letter in which they promise to
repay that five-spot to an eventually more famous friend. That the exception
turned out to be Eldritch Weaver just proves immortality is a game of American roulette in which only one chamber *isn't* loaded.

(No, don't be jealous, Cadwaller's gun. Despite being lighter and more
manageable than I worried you'd be before I lifted you from the Paris footlocker's still life of way-back-when rubbish, you're no figure of speech. You're every
bit as real as my eighty-six-year-old lap.)

Daisy and the L.E. got through five days on the Cape without hopping it
back to Manhattan to replenish their supply of M, haunting me with a belated
guess that someone in that rollicking crew of Village transplants was their dope
supplier. Sentimentally, I hope it wasn't St. Clair Sinclair—or was it Sinclair St.
Clair?—who was my favorite among those uncommonly promising future has-
beens. Big as a condor's idea of an egghead, he was likely after three glasses of
dago red to start calling himself Poët Chandon. One mollusky restaurant dinner, he made me giggle with an improvised rhyme, accompanied by eager and

then chastened demo, that I still think of when I'm having seafood and occasionally, in the right company, recite:

> *To eat an oyster*
> *You crack it foister.*
> *This part is moister!*
> *Oh, drat, I—loyst her.*

Judging from his brushwork, Eldritch Weaver would've spilled the morphine before pocketing the money, so he's out. But the face that leaps to mind as the best candidate, tricked out with all the right diabolic attributes, is trailing no name-tag. Nor is *face* strictly accurate as regards my definitive image of Morphisto. The back of a head, one alarmingly red ear, a wristwatch—still something of a badge of modernity then for men. Its Pam-seeking flash was having an angry argument with the sun.

One bulge of large male shoulder, one determined bare male heinie. Two dune-grinding knees above smart duck trousers turned into tangled accordions by his having rolled them up to his shins before yanking them down past his thighs. One oyster turned jellyfish underneath, who saw me.

Perhaps he wasn't the one who sold M to my mother. Gerson would say it's Hollywood carpentry taking over again, combining my terror of what I didn't quite know yet were drugs with my terror of what I didn't quite know yet was sex by blaming the same konging and chowing red dragon on both counts. The main reason I favor that anonymous, brawn-nuggeted, amorphously morphine-fleshed male for the dealer's job is that I happen to know the dope addict I caught him fucking, fucking, fucking, fucking behind a dune was a fucking dope addict.

POSTED BY: *Pam*   My guess, Panama, is that you wouldn't have been unduly perturbed if you'd been the one to come across the wristwatch and the jellyfish in flagrante. Agreed, I couldn't blame that pair if they'd been made restless, as I had, by St. Clair Sinclair's monologue down the beach. Defying the gulls in a striped bathing outfit that gave him a comedy bank robber's masked second nose below the waist, he was running down Eliot to praise cummings. Knowing neither man's work, I was under the impression he was comparing a prim hotel clerk who'd annoyed him to our local bootlegger, making my attention and then Pam-containing swimsuit wander.

Still, even at seven, goggling but not threatened, Panama Cadwaller would probably just've been Margaret Meadishly impressed by her discovery that men and women try to make the same unmanageable, awkward meals of each other in three dimensions that you'd seen them do countless times on cable. And put it out of your mind by nightfall, not seen it loom as sleep neared all through Chignonne's and then Purcey's. If so, well! I envy you. Being able to say "Bring it on" to everything as I hook my thumbs in my cut-offs' front belt loops would make me happy as a clam.

I know you giggled on the phone last summer. You were tickled that your salty Gramela had finally outed herself as repressed, despite all her fucking this and fucking that at meals and her crusty assessments of actresses' charms when we've watched TV together—though never Kirsten's, since that Dunst cap is one I only wear with Andy. And I'm sorry, kiddo, but you'd just turned fifteen. I couldn't help getting agitated by your grandpa's pictures of you during last year's Cadwaller-papered Provincetown romp.

In spite of boasting that it came from NEW YORK FUCKIN' CITY, the T-shirt you were wearing with a big scream of a Panamanic smile at the dinner table and in some of the beach shots was a relief. Under it, no doubt, you still had on the twin scraps of bikini top, pennants stolen from some lad's quite small toy sailboat, that earlier the same day were fighting for dear life to cling to the newly round breasts, as perfect as Christmas ornaments and so visibly tender that the mimsy borogoves were restrained only by Pam's fat lunettes from leaping half out of my head to protect them from harm, in the ravishing image of you with your arms raised to recascade your Goya-dark hair.

At least you're still wearing the cut-offs in that one, though God knows why you bothered. Above their useless but hookable belt loops, your teenage hips' turnstiles show off concavities to either side of the ovalized discus of muscle your bare navel bullseyes. While I hope they're just tricks of shadow, I fear I'm seeing delvable crevices where Panamanic skin meets no denim.

Mouse-click, and you stand with one shoulder hiked and its matching foot planted higher on a dune than the other. The femoral griffins whose twin

indents guard the inner tops of your thighs openly boast that here the leg business ends and something else happens. Between them, the silver-gray mottling
of the snippet of Lycra that alone holds the fort between you and complete
lower nudity damn near yells to the world that this part is moister.

I know Chris snaps away with a love of beauty that's most ardent once it
turns two-dimensional. I remember how he stupefied Amherst when his first
local show after joining the faculty included a dozen images of your future
grandmother nude, already ample but gorgeous as custard, and I got through
that in one piece. Having a fully dressed, quite matter-of-fact Renée strolling
beside me made the whole thing at once stylized and comical.

One reason your self-exposure is different is that it was on display in the
flesh not only to Chris but to anyone: male or female, oldster or teen, friend or
stranger. So I suppose I should just be grateful he spared me a view of how much
of what you sit on you were baring to all, Tim and sundry. At any rate, I've spent
a year praying that the quite comely tushy halved by no more than a thin string
of licorice in the background of one shot—its owner's head and torso casually
Black Dahlia-ized by the frame, since Chris's focus is Renée, ampler than ever in
a grandmotherly white one-piece—belongs to some anonymous, older, more
experienced, unimportant non-Panama.

Believe me, bikini girl: I loathe being the person this plaint has so helplessly
exposed. I despise it more than you can imagine. Set it down if you like to a no
longer tasty pretzel's envy, since when I look at those photos I feel on thin ice
claiming we belong to the same species. I know which of us Darwin would have
put his chips on to flower and prosper even when I was your age. (Good luck
finding the teenaged Pam's skull, archeologists. Purcey's Girls' Academy met the
wrecking ball in 1966. Posing as a women's prison, its exterior is preserved on film
behind the opening titles of Paspartu's unmemorable Thirties crime melodrama
The Fall Girl. Thank you for your attention to this utterly irrelevant matter.)

While I doubt he's likely to, even granting that with him you never know,
your grandpa Chris could tell you I'm neither shy nor easily flustered. He was
still a wiry sixteen when his new stepmother went to fetch aspirin from Hopsie's and my unlockable Paris bathroom. She left empty-handed with a mild "Oh,
forgive me" after being greeted by the sight of his gripped goslingam as it threat-

ened—you're welcome, Chris—to go Vesuvius at unclad visualizations not of underendowed, too brisk Pamela but hot, remote, *Paris Match*'ed Brigitte Bardot.

My standing vis-à-vis his real mom went up when my unruffled later hello and Hopsie's obliviousness told him that, to Pam's way of thinking, I hadn't *caught* him at anything. (Honestly, Chris: would I have told your father if I'd "caught" you playing with toy soldiers?) Almost thirty years later, seeing me emerge from another bathroom with a vial of Bayer, he gave an unannotated bark of friendly laughter, pleased that I'd finally gotten what I'd gone in for. That was near the end of Cadwaller's long dying, making us both sensitive to time's unsuspected symmetries.

Anyhow, the point is that the rant most of you have just scrolled past in your pained search for dialogue isn't particularly what I'm like. After many gloriously normal innings of the old buck and wing with one man or another over five or six decades, plenty of them happy or at least entertaining even before I met your great-grandfather, I'm disgusted by Pam's reawakened hysteria. She sounds more like a crazed and dotty spinster. Or worse, one of those pathetic women who had a single dotty fling in her youth and never had the courage or plain good sense to grasp that there are lots more fish in the sea.

Even if I weren't getting ready to kill myself, bikini girl, you can see how this might not make me such a grand addition to this year's Cape Cod reunion. I'd blow my cover as your uninhibited old Gramela in under an hour when I gave up on just mulishly shifting my dentition as you pranced by and started screaming at you to put some goddam clothes on. Then I'd go bucketing along the beach in my hated wheelchair, screaming at all the other bikini girls to cover themselves up before I went mad.

POSTED BY: *Pam*   Mind you, at seven, the budding pudding that was Pam could've built her sand castles all week without a stitch on and my mother wouldn't have been more than mistily the wiser. Not that I did, since I was a good little girl. Adaptable, too: I soon got used to my little bed on the ottoman, the tiny algae-perfumed kitchen, the bathroom whose weather-warped door was reluctant to close unless we tugged hard. "Oh, who *are* you people?" that door groaned every time one of us used it.

Like a good little girl, I trundled along on my two swimsuited legs with four-legged SooSoo after my mother and the L.E. as they straggled down to the beach from our dormouse of a rental. The scuffs and scruffs of the uncomprehending surf—it doesn't understand what *we're* talking about either, the reason you can't argue with it—muttered in near Scandinavian as it served up chipped light. I snatched back my hand from door handles arsonized by noon's blaze when the car took us to Truro or Wellfleet, learned in restaurants to chirp "scrod" and "quahog" as I'd once chirped "chen-chen," "chow," and "pong." Waited for Eldritch Weaver to spring me from his canvas jail, wandered from each crowded night's table of contents to its suddenly gnomic index in dense rooms where grownups roared, wine flowed, and the inevitable piano player had found a salt-warped upright.

If they meant to tire me out, it worked. When I was redeposited on the ottoman made up as Pam's bunk, the bedroom door closing on murmurs as SooSoo vainly scratched at it, I couldn't get through two pages of *The Patchwork Girl of Oz*—it wasn't all Henry James at seven, even for precocious me—before my eyes turned grainy. Exhaustion's deep sleep spared me all but the early stages of the gasps, sheet fights, and groans that signaled the onset of my mother's nightly nightmares, along with the less audible whimpers and protests of the L.E.'s less interesting ones.

Hophead or no hophead, my mother still had her fastidious side. Even at its wildest, her tossing and turning must have been unpleasantly quasi-coffined by the Lotus Eater's new penchant, discovered by me the morning an open door revealed a browned back—half a gluteus, too—between two rifts of bedclothes, for sleeping in the nude.

In daytime, the L.E. was often morose, perhaps because her nightly courtship had been frustrated yet again. Still, I have a hard time believing she'd have dared to try so much as a Charybdean cuddle, even in the "There, there" guise of femininity's so *transportable* gift of motherhood. The L.E. wouldn't have been convincing as a "There, there" type, and by all accounts was a dismal mother to the red-faced little crap factory she eventually coughed up.

And for my own mother's memory's sake, I won't tolerate—just won't!—my mind's unwelcome pencil sketches, all too reminiscent of something Nan

Finn's cartoonist son Sean would dream up, of a crafty Lotus Eater faking her own shot of M so as to have her red-mouthed, nudely bobbling, dottily idyllic, arse-hiked crouching way with her comatose bedmate's unwittingly acquiescent form. They're both dead now and I shall be shortly.

No doubt that unwelcome pencil sketch's true origin is the open-air sex act Pammie did witness, whose only pornographers were its participants. It may have happened behind the same dune you're standing on in that last pic, Panama, or at least one scooped from the identical Eve's rib of Cape Cod. Assuming you've never witnessed sex, I hope your eyes' loss of *their* virginity involves pleasanter performers.

Sinclair St. Clair is fading out behind me, foghorning in his striped bathing outfit that he for one will be Prufrocked if a wilted pleonast (wonderful word) like T.S. has anything to teach his e.e. Her profile now his exclusive concern, my mother's still posing for Eldritch Weaver. Pammie's sand castle in that painting—*Two American Women on the Beach, Provincetown, 1927*, delightfully credited "On loan from the Garment Foundation" the time I saw it in Chicago—is about to be washed away.

He was a wristwatch wagging a man, and the Lotus Eater was the one he was fucking, fucking, fucking, fucking. Inside the crook of his hefty arm, one barely rounded breast's flat peak gleamed, a coin from Ali Baba's cave. Her legs were swung up as if she were trying to hoist them onto the display hooks in a butcher shop.

Breathing like a sawmill, the L.E.'s mouth was slobbery, her wet lips yanked back from her wet teeth as if protesting they didn't even *know* anyone in that cemetery. Her eyes were open—some lay *he* must've been—even before she turned her head my way.

They grew confounded as the L.E. understood she was staring at someone other than herself, the true object of their delirious search. A blink turned me from generic Other into someone she could recognize.

Her mouth hadn't made the connection, went right on devouring sweat and air. What was making it twist and shudder had nothing to do with me. She didn't look away, though, and in the fractional eternity between the moment she placed me as Daisy's daughter and the one when I called "SooSoo! SooSoo!" and ran away, her crazed eyes had flashed an unmistakable message.

Good. But how, *good*, Lotus Eater? I mean, in what way? Good for the heaving refutation of a Charybdean charge I wouldn't be conceptually equipped to make for years? Good from pure cruelty, which would mean you hated as well as loathed me? (Loathing's social, hating's private. When we played loop-the-loop at New York restaurants in later years, my impression was that we agreed on that if not much else.) Or good because you thought I'd trot off on my pudgy seven-year-old legs to tell Daisy?

I didn't, then or ever. What Eldritch Weaver missed in my mother's profile that summer was that her smiles were starlings skimming sorrow's lake. I'd never have clipped those fluttering wings, no matter how furious I was for our sakes.

POSTED BY: *A Pamgrim*   In the Fifties, I put my memories of Provincetown to use in the opening chapter of *Glory Be*. No, bikini girl: not those memories! The as yet unwristwatched, un–Lotus Eaten dunes. The as yet un–Eldritch Weavered sea.

I had to imagine it icy, though, once I'd looked up likely temperatures for that time of year. November, 1620: three centuries shy of Pam's birth, a boat rows out from the *Mayflower*. Of that famous one hundred and two, sixteen soiled men were aboard.

In her Beverly Hills study, blond sun squaring a desk squaring a typescript as yet four pages long, Mrs. Gerson worked like the dickens to get that reek into their clothes. A blue pencil (we had dozens around the house) behind one ear as President Ike's wandering assessment of Dien Bien Phu relocated Oz in Kansas on the radio, I imagined grime oiled by sweat and then resealed by frozen mid-Atlantic rime. Almost seventy unlaundered days at sea.

They had the laundresses; only fresh water was hard to come by. What lousy sailors they'd been! Now birds by the thousands were on the wing.

The longboat grounds in the shallows. Cold as ice cream, but unfrozen, the sea swirls around patched boots and foul trousers. Now isn't the time for pronouncements: the hollers are practical as the boat is beached. Clattering oars join a wooden orgy: meet me in the bilge. Standish is swelling with a landsman's new scope of command.

Or could they really have been prating their dreadful, grim nonsense already? Whatever you think, it will sustain them. Horrid people, but they *got* here. The Pilgrims are ashore in America, and birds by the thousands are on the wing.

Shakespeare had been dead less time than Potus has been President. I searched the documents in vain for some original of the man I wanted to imagine undoing his too complicated trousers, grateful to piss at last with no deck's heave splashing half of it back at him. Their digestions harrowed by the Atlantic's slaps and rancid food's punches, I'm sure they were farting like Oldsmobiles.

Soon, coming across a stock of corn that's plainly been hidden—that is, by men, not nature—they'll steal or rather "confiscate" it. Whoever had that idea launched a great tradition. Looking back, one of them finally lets himself be frightened by the castled smallness of the smelly ship that brought them.

It doesn't matter a damn. England's way-back-when is over, and the great "Now" that begins ours is cawing around the bedraggled voyagers on the beach. Half resolute, half eager—is the secret of being a Pilgrim a refusal to recognize the difference?—they plod on toward the site of the Pilgrim Monument.

Obliviously, Miles Standish's eye rakes past the spot where seven-year-old Pammie's filling her pail with another wet tower. Intent on nourishment and their God's approval, maybe not even in that order, they can't see the radiant teenage girl rushing toward them and flaunting the answer to both. Thrusting out its bountiful Christmas ornaments, her T-shirt boasts that it's from NEW YORK FUCKIN' CITY.

Toward the end of "A Landing," I mention that they soon went back to their smelly toy ship and sailed on. Yet to the indignation of Midwestern, for some reason, reviewers most of all, I only mentioned the Mayflower Compact in my book's opening sentence: "An emergency agreement as to purpose stopped the malcontents from bolting once landfall was made."

God! Did I work on *that* son of a bitch, too. A, e-e-e-a-ee-e, o-o-o-o-o-o-o, a-a-a-a. I didn't say they'd name the place they did stay Plymouth. They hadn't known that at the time I let the *Mayflower* vanish into white space: "From any perspective except those of the passengers, it was soon again tiny."

By today's standards, I had to force things a bit to end on "tiny." No editor now would let that word arrangement stand. But I'm still very happy with "those." Unless "malcontents" counts, it was *Glory Be*'s first indication of multiplicity, my theme.

I cheated on one thing. On my research trips, I spent more time than I'd've otherwise cared to in Boston. Before I wrote the concluding chapter, I walked all over Lexington. But I didn't go back to Provincetown. My argument—which was with Pam, so I won—was that my distance would make it feel more like history.

POSTED BY: *Pam*　　Restlessly disguised as sea and night, the Pilgrims were on the march outside our rental's window as Pammie struggled to finish *The Patchwork Girl of Oz*. We've come to my final night in Provincetown, which wasn't supposed to be. I recall we had the rental until Monday.

We'd been to the movies. Or to something that resembled moving pictures at the mechanical level, but was otherwise as foreign to the budding pudding's eyes as Francis X. Bushman in *Ben Hur* had been reassuringly American. It was plainly out of the ordinary for Provincetown's lone movie palace, whose marquee promised a promisingly mustached Victor Muet opposite Tesla Morse in *Mixed Signals*. One of Euclid's scrambled comedies, it had been seen and giggled at by a now lost, Scandinavian-accompanied edition of me just weeks earlier.

My mother herself may have footed the bill for bohemia's one-night takeover of Commercial Street. Anyhow, I distinctly remember Sinclair St. Clair lofting a jug of wine as his broad rear crushed a seat not far from a usurped-looking, preemptively bored Eldritch Weaver. As for the first film we saw, the dates don't quite mesh when I Google. Nonetheless, sitting next to Dwight Macdonald at a MoMA screening in the Forties, my realization that I hadn't been surprised by what the straight razor was for convinced me this wasn't my first viewing.

The projectionist at my second was the man who'd made the movie. Known to us only as Dali's estranged collaborator, since the results of that particular hare-and-tortoise derby were the future's best-kept secret—of course it would've been Dali's name that excited my mother's friends when a smuggled copy of *Un Chien Andalou* showed up in Provincetown that summer—he was a lean exile with the exquisite manners of a man who knows that trying to explain who he *really* is, was, or will be is futile.

After hearing two words of my Spanish—and I had at least four more in the bullpen, too—he switched to strained English until we swooned into French. To Tim Cadwaller's incredulity, since to *Qwert's* Man in the Dark the biographical tidbit that I once met Luis Buñuel is the equivalent of learning I once swanned around with Zeus, I can't remember what we were mourning. Our shared Paris, most likely, then Nazi-occupied.

As for Dwight, over a decade later he ended up slamming *Glory Be* in the worst review it got, lambasting "Mrs. Gerson"—up yours too, McDonuck: it was *by Pamela Buchanan*, said so right on the cover—for her "sewing-club" vulgarization of W.C. Williams's *In the American Grain*. "It's a mug's game, this trick of disguising her theme's sentimentality with acid or hard-nosed details"—oh, well. He'd caught my hard nose red-handed there.

When next we saw each other, in Washington in the fall of '67, he hurried over like a Macy's Santa about to hoist me onto his lap without sitting down. Dwight had a way of greeting friends whose books he'd eviscerated as if they'd been in a bad car wreck. Genuinely glad to see us on our feet and talking again, he was oblivious to having caused our week in traction. That had been literature, not personalities. On the other hand, I did and still do prize my nice letter from Williams, who hadn't read my book but said he didn't care much who got what from who so long as the thing went on.

Not that I knew it, but the thing was unquestionably going on in Provincetown as I squirmed in my seat and St. Clair Sinclair passed wine over my head. A few hundred feet from the spot where the Pilgrims had dragged their stinking longboat ashore, staggering in freezing surf that rushed like emeralded ermine under a dull but cawing sky, two or three dozen people dressed in the Nineteen-Twenties' floppy notion of bohemian liniments sat in the dark, watching what almost certainly must've been the first American screening of Luis Buñuel's, forget Dali, *Un Chien Andalou*. While I've never been able to explain why, I think of that as the crystallizing moment when I unwittingly became the Pamela Buchanan I later knew best and favored most when her name marched along behind a two-letter flag: *by*.

Afterward, two American women on the beach, decorated by a little dog and a child who probably should've been kept home reading *The Patchwork*

Girl of Oz, strolled back to their cottage in a newly frameless dark. Surf was all around us, primarily by sight ahead and primarily as sound behind.

Guessing wrong about posterity, my mother and her friend were chatting with some difficulty about the other movie on that night's bill. Some German thing, Teutonic in the way that makes you wish they'd add some damn gin. "I thought the one who played the vamp was pretty," the Lotus Eater volunteered, or something equally inane.

Remember, these were the primitive early days of sound. So much so that both the movies we'd just seen, like the one advertised on the marquee—*Mixed Signals,* the comedy I'd giggled at only weeks earlier—had been silent. On the soundtrack, my mother's reply is maddeningly fuzzy.

Scratched by night-surf even then, it's since been further garbled by too many trips through Pam's projector. I'm still nearly positive she said "Sketch" just before stumbling, as she must've for her purse to end up konging her companion's arm in that misleadingly intimate way. Among the other possibilities, while I'd be the first to agree "wretch" fits the L.E., I can't see the provocation. Its vulgar soundalike would hardly have been a likely Daisyism.

Unless my mother was in a spectacularly bad humor with the Lotus Eater, which I doubt as the profile she turns to her lesser binary before stumbling glistens with a quick moonlit smile, "Fetch" would've been addressed to our dog. So no, no. "Sketch"—as in "Well, *you're* a sketch," an authentic 1920s-ism that would've been only mildly infra dig in my mother's crowd or crowds—is the strongest candidate by miles, a wry way of disputing her fellow female's opinion ("I thought the one who played the vamp was pretty good") of an actress whose performance my mother hadn't cared for.

Given not only its nonsensicality but Daisy's bum language skills even after she and her daughter had moved to Europe, *"Mèche,"* the French for wick or fuse—as both Sean Finn and Tim Cadwaller would know, a despairing or triumphant cry of *"La mèche est allumée!"* would mean "The fuse is lit," for instance—isn't even in contention. Still, I realize memory can play tricks. One proof is that I've just described the fuzzily soundtracked clip, in phosphorescent b&w thanks to night and sea rather than photography, that turns up most often by mistake—counting on its status as a memory to fool me into awarding it pride of place over authentic East Egg snapshots snapped by others—when I'm asked about my parentage.

POSTED BY: *Pam*   I was usually left undisturbed once their room's shut door had turned into a faintly outlined rectangle of light, except sometimes by my mother's bad dreams and the bed's squeaks as it tried to wake her. Though I'd never known her to be scared of the dark, in Provincetown she slept with the lamp on. But that night my eyes were cracked open first by the door's click, next by a padding rustle. In a nightgown, which unnerved me more than a naked L.E. would've (it was another *difference*, you see), the Lotus Eater was slipping into our bathroom. She had something oblong and vital to her in one hand.

When the light went on inside it, the outlined rectangle of light was thicker on one side: she hadn't managed to close its recalcitrant, weather-warped door all the way. Then came the click of a pencase's hasp, audibly more expensive than the light cord's abject one had been. Then the prosaic clank of a tuning fork trapped in a kitchen spoon's body as she dropped hers with a faint, surprisingly human "Drat." The impatient rasps must've been matches.

Always more helpful with the blue-pencil stuff than Murphy, Gerson objects to the melodrama of having that badly shut, weather-warped bathroom door swing open to reveal the Lotus Eater in the throes of shooting up. Even so, it did swing open sooner than it should've, by which I don't mean sooner than never. I never liked her, but starvation's just too horrible a way to go.

It swung open in time for me to see the silver syringe the L.E. hadn't yet restored to its case. Since I now know my mother's was the gold one, the distinctively reddish flash of the hypo the L.E. was holding, however long imprinted on my retinas, shows just how easily even a child whose functions were purely ocular could get things wrong. Unless the L.E. had *borrowed* the one she'd given Daisy, but that strikes me as unlikely.

How do I know my mother's was the gold one, Panama? How do I know it was a gift to her from the Lotus Eater and not the other way around? Simple. When I found them in the Paris footlocker on Liberation Day, opening the black and the midnight-blue cases and lighting a fresh Lucky Strike before I handled each for the first and only time, the gold syringe was the one with the—yes, get ready to blink: this was the Jazz Age, and they were both rich—engraved inscription.

Etched at the L.E.'s bidding by some bribable jeweler, its words were barely decipherable without a magnifying glass. Unless you had good reason, which Daisy Buchanan's daughter did, to be familiar with the old-fashioned lyric they quoted. No doubt a court might demand more conclusive proof of who was the would-be seductress and who was the prey—something like *To Daisy from your Lotus Eater, with love and hopelessly thwarted Charybdean lust.* But that wouldn't have fit, and I defy a single daisysdaughter.com reader I may have acquired this morning to see any ambiguity in the inscription Pam read, crouching in her correspondent's uniform as she lifted the surprisingly petite gold hypo to the light, shortly before sunset on August 25, 1944: *Give me your answer do.*

POSTED BY: *Pam*   Since the Lotus Eater had just slammed a Gulliver-sized dose of morphine into the delicate Lilliput of her arm, her assimilation of the information that the door was open, the bathroom light was still on, and Pammie was watching from the cottage's darkened front room was no match for her jellyfish leer the last time I'd caught her in flagrante. I was merely someone she'd forgotten about, not a startling pseudo-stranger staring as some wristwatch wagging a man or some man wearing a wristwatch fuck-fuck-fuck-fucked her. The only real news she had to absorb was that I wasn't asleep.

She just blinked a few times, muttered something in a fairly pathetic voice about me not knowing how lucky I was—presumably meaning I didn't have to *court* Daisy to have a relationship with her—and got rid of the silver syringe's reddish glint by putting it back in the case before she fumbled for the light cord. Then the bedroom door's faint outline of light widened on one side, grew a huge black tulip nodding on two stalks as the L.E. was briefly silhouetted by my mother's bedside lamp, and closed again.

After a while, I grew conscious that the insistent murmur of my mother's voice had stayed more protracted than its midnight norm. Unable to make out her words, I couldn't help hoping she was berating the L.E. for subjecting Pam to such a sight, or even—that *other* Gulliver, other Lilliput—sights.

That wasn't because I was even any too sure the Lotus Eater deserved castigation other than for breathing. Nobody'd told me what the rules were, and a child who lacks rules is a neglected blackboard, happy for any old chalk at all. Reproaching the L.E. would simply have meant I was Daisy's topic, a budding pudding worth salvaging from what I now saw I'd been intuiting for some time was chaos.

I never did find out which shore her voice's faint surf was scrabbling at. Or what eventually provoked it, having realized it was water, to break down in sobs. If only the L.E. hadn't been there—nightgowned, not nightgowned? Hands to recocked hips, arraying her pretty body's Ali Baba coins and Charybdean salt lick before my mother's, my *mother's*, blindly pained eyes?—I could have crept in and comforted her.

Morning. Pam's alone on the unpeopled beach. Through the screen door behind me, I can hear the two ends of a conversational ball of yarn getting tangled, but I've had it with knitting. They're the ones with the needles, not me. I'd never have gone back to the house if SooSoo hadn't taken it into her snowball head to sniff a jellyfish.

I'd never gotten on with my canine rival, any more than SooSoo and I liked the Lotus Eater when *she* turned up. A mutt the size and color of an off-white, ragged muff, our dog had been limping and whining—probably grazed by a car—near our front gate on Long Island for two days when she was adopted not long after Pam's now tiny papa (he was riding away) played his last polo match. My mother took a new widow's privilege by daring anyone, even our ur-Scandinavian, to complain at how she spoiled that trotting bit of angry fluff.

Even so, a stung nose is a stung nose, and ownership—however carelessly delegated—is ownership. A yelp of pain is a yelp of pain, and to a dog, a jellyfish is an incomprehensible accident. Bundling SooSoo in my arms like fifty furry, wiggling worms, I trotted back to our cottage for help.

SooSoo never got any, although—unlike me, I suppose—she recovered soon enough. Barging through the unlatched door, I heard my mother, my *mother*, begging for the L.E.'s mercy. What she was babbling made no sense, but the explanation for her voice's frantic despair was the sight of Daisy trying to stop a nightgowned Lotus Eater from smashing her in the face.

Or was she trying to rip her clothes off, have her way with her at last? Seems too Fu Manchu even for Murphy, but it didn't matter: their frenzied faces made almost any scenario possible. If my mother's grip on the L.E.'s wrist had been any less of a manacle, that clawing hand would have just *flown*.

"Let me!" the Lotus Eater raged. Then her wild eyes saw Pam staring unexpectedly at her in flagrante for the fairy-tale third time.

"*God!*" the L.E. screamed in frustration, and my fearful mother's white-knuckled grip was finally able to relax. Jerking her still tense arm away, the L.E. wheeled, working off her stymied aggression by making the bedroom door see stars—Victor Muet, Tesla Morse?—when she slammed it. If SooSoo hadn't already bounded out of my arms, that crash would've done it for sure.

"It's just—pain, that's all, sweetie," my mother tried to make excuses for the Lotus Eater's crazed behavior. "She'd, oh, burnt her arm on the coffeepot! And I was trying to make it better by putting on some salve. Now where did the jar roll off to? Help me look for it. But the big silly just thought it would hurt even more. Don't worry! She'll be all right."

"SooSoo isn't," dutiful Pam reported. "She got stung by a jellyfish."

"She did? Poor little woof-woof dear. Well, it's all. It's all. It's all just really just kind of a shambles, isn't it? At least *you're* all right. Oh, where's she gone?"

I was stupefied. "The bedroom."

As if I'd slapped her myself, my mother burst into tears. "Dog," she finally choked. "Oh, Pammie, I try so hard."

Then I started crying too, since I couldn't find a dog to fetch her. Nudging the screen door with that same nose, SooSoo'd had trotted back outside, where things were apparently safer: jellyfish yea, humans nay. As the Lotus Eater yanked drawers open, punished closets for existing, and hurled away shoes that didn't fit, my mother and I ended up on the vacationer-scarred ottoman that had been my bed, her lap Pam's pillow at last as I lay there lumpily sniffling with my face turned to her trim belly. Still crying herself, she did her best to soothe my unsmoothable hair.

The bedroom door's groan of "Enough" as it was reopened told me the L.E. was back in the room. I've never been prouder of my mother than I was when her hand on my Pam-hair didn't stop moving. Neither of them said a word before the screen door got its chance to creak "Good riddance," but I don't know whether they looked at each other or not. I was blinded by my mother's lap.

"Is she gone?" I finally asked, since the uncomfortable part of being comforted is usually the breathing problem.

"Yes, darling. She's gone."

"Forever," I insisted. My insights at seven could've held their own with Henry James, but my dialogue was pure L. Frank Baum. Every childhood's unbridgeable chasm.

"Yes, sweetie. It looks that way."

"She was mean to you, wasn't she." I can't account for my impulse coda: "Like Daddy."

Things I'd heard Daisy say since his death had left an aura of cruelty around his missing silhouette, but what paradoxically made it easier for the idea to take hold was Pam's belief that the cruelest thing he'd done to her was vanish. Maybe he'd been thoughtless in life too.

"Yes." Then: "No, not like Daddy. Like, oh—" and I was glad to hear my mother's old silvery, mocking laugh, even though her unfamiliarity with children's stories was never so well illustrated—"Little Red Riding Hood."

That was my cue to pull my head off her lap, since the smuggled-in subversion of the Grimms' tales is that the children are always explorers. For that much license, you'd risk the odd gingerbread house. Besides, one thing children can always do for their parents is *scout*.

"She left her clothes and suitcases all over everywhere. She took the car, though," I reported after an all-the-way trot around our cottage's exterior and a peek in the bedroom. I'd hoped to catch her being swallowed by a whale, but back to Gramercy Park would do.

My mother looked quizzical, the most reassuring expression I'd seen on her face in some time. "What, darling? Wait. Our driver, too?"

I hadn't known that would need amplifying, since I thought of them as a unit. You may've just read the single most illuminating detail regarding my material situation and my perception of it before we lost the Buchanan money in the Crash.

"Yes," I said. "Or ate him. Anyway, Wong's wong gone."

"Well, isn't *that* rich," my mother said. "Well, we'll show her! We don't need that lousy car. Do we, Pammie? We'll swim."

"To Long Island? Golly."

"No. Out to the first big ship we see. It'll stop for me, I promise."

POSTED BY: *Pam*   I swear to Christ, if it doesn't ring soon, I may end up just shooting the goddam telephone. Don't misunderstand, my daisysdaughter.com readers if any: this *has* been fun. Not that even one of you has seen fit to out yourself when I homepage. But the mimsies have taken a drubbing from my Mac's screen and my fingers are starting to cramp in rheumatism's version of Morse code.

I do need to be sure at least one of my hands will retain enough vim, control, and general can-do spirit to hoist and fire Cadwaller's gun once I've said "Yes, this is Mrs. Pamela Cadwaller" under what I don't doubt will be considerable strain. Even in the final months of Lyndon Johnson's Presidency, it wasn't as if the White House switchboard called me every fucking day, you know.

I only hope Potus gets me before the Cadwaller clan chimes in with its birthday greetings. Now that I've remembered their tradition of telephonically gathering to wish the batty wreck of Hopsie's old U.S.S. *Bonne Femme Pamela* many returns of June 6, it's driving me bughouse that I don't know whether the phone's first ring will be my summons to Valhalla or Hallmark.

Not, you'd better understand, that fifteen minutes of providing the mangy slice of toast for all of you to butter up has the remotest chance of shaking my dawn resolve. Uh-uh, Hopsie's brood. I can't think of a thing Chris, Tim (is he back from Cannes yet?), or even Panama could say to make me reconsider. It's just that when you read tomorrow's headlines, I hope you'll understand if your Gramela sounded a mite, oh, *distracted*.

At least you'll have the consolation of belated evidence my mental capacities were unimpaired. If you've ever known me at all or truly remember him, maybe you'll be moved to learn I used Cadwaller's gun. Maybe if you read this you'll understand why I could never go back to Provincetown, no matter how many times you asked. I'd still honestly rather get this over with not having had to cope with and fend off your jokes and warmth, your whoops of "Chen-chen!" to each other, your affection.

Sleep late, Panama. Oh, please sleep in, bikini girl: you know Chris and Tim won't make the call without you. Why, it's not even nine a.m.! Well into the White House's working day, but no hour at all for a teenager on vacation to get out of bed. No, not even in Manhattan, wondrous as it is. Sleep on, my rebellious and untrammeled namesake that was, exactly three score and ten years younger than me.

Doesn't the cool pillow feel nice where it's mashed against your cheek, snaring some of and yet ruled by that oceanic insurrection of Goya-black, untamable hair? You probably don't even know one reason we're fond of the sight of you sleeping is that now it's our only chance to study your newly bursting lips in their old role as the soft gates of breath's castle, not energetically hurled into action in the scream of a Panamanic grin or yelping on the phone. That's all lovely, dear. What it isn't is Platonic.

Besides, to get to the bathroom, you'll have to schlep down the hall past your dad's cubby. Poor Tim's been at work since dawn! I imagine about the last thing he wants to see is a vision of Goya-haired teen pulchritude saunter past, yawning and arching her new Christmas ornaments.

Underneath her T-shirt, they're unmistakably nippled as she reaches back to scratch her barely pantied plum. Then she mumbles, "Morning, Dad. Don't you ever stop working?" and vanishes in search of a toothbrush. It must be pure hell for even the most conscientious father when it's his own flesh and blood.

But me? I'm just old Gramela in Washington, far removed from the action by age and by now vestigial gender. Honestly, Panama, at the pretzel stage, you only notice in the tub; you'd better believe it's reluctant. I'm preoccupied by other things. Chiefly, getting ready to blow my brains out in a protest against this awful and unending war.

I have the strangest fantasy that if only for a moment, they'll be lovely: a pretty girl in her birthday suit exploding out of a birthday cake, just as she should've over seventy years ago but didn't. I may've put together one hell of an interesting life to distract me and everyone from *that* little corpse, but as a terrorist I grant I'm a late bloomer. Shall soon be a very late Bloomer indeed the minute the White House finds that teensy gap in Potus's schedule to honor an odd request from one of his own party's once baleful, now doleful elders.

Are you dog or cat, Cadwaller's gun? I've owned and loved both in my time. SooSoo, Jubjub, Peanut! See, they bark at me. Born in West Africa, Bandicoot, our hook-tailed Siamese, caught a mouse in Georgetown and then came on with us to India, dying with one paw stretched toward Jaipur in the land of Shere Khan. Do you know what, little gun? That wasn't long before I saw you leap into my husband's hand the night that amazingly brazen thief (we never caught him) broke into the Residence.

As for the noise you'll make when I pull the trigger, right in Potus's astonished hearing, I've always liked the old word *report*. Yes, little gun: you'll be Pamela Buchanan's last report.

Her first was called "Chanson d'automne." All too inevitably, my mawkish poemess was fourteen-year-old Pam's clumsy attempt to say goodbye to my mother—or maybe hello, but you know what sniffly twerps girls that age can be—after she shot herself in Brussels in 1934.

Not without venom, my fellow Purcey's alumnae, your classmate can boast it's taken me over seventy years to throw in the towel. But all right. I'll give you your fucking *Like mother, like daughter.* See the mess on the rug?

The mess on the rug? Pam, you idiot! Pamidiot. Why was I worrying about the Cadwallers? Far from here, they'll only read about my suicide. Unless I can think of a way of warning him off, Andy Pond—who has his own key, and lets himself in as well as out—will be the one who finds me.

Wearing his old sports jacket and ancient, carefully tended Florsheims—slacks too, unless Andy's *really* gunning for a birthday surprise—he'll whistle along the dowdy hall. In its cabbagey and kingly upper-Connecticut, *echt*-District way, the Rochambeau does have its Miss Havisham side.

Putting down the bag of groceries he's brought to cook my birthday dinner—yes, and those stupid Netflix or Nextflick DVDs of *The Gal I Left Behind Me* and *Meet Pamela*, too—he'll fish for his keys and open the door. The foyer will tell him nothing except that Kelquen's collar is still there.

In the foyer, so far as Andy knows, I'll still be alive. But once he doglegs into the living room, he'll see a crumpled pretzel and my splashed brains in their birthday suit at last. My mother didn't spare me much, but she did spare me that.

4. Hosts

POSTED BY: *Pamphibious*   Hello again, sweet sleepyhead. Along with any readers (show yourselves!) I may've attracted since dawn. It's now 9:15 a.m.

Believe me, sixty-two June 6ths ago—at least on British Double Summer Time, invented by the Brits for the duration: "Double Summer Time, and the living is easy," Eddie Whitling used to tunelessly croon—Omaha looked like a raving shambles by then. Not that we could see such a hell of a lot from miles offshore.

Three waves gone in, the landing craft jerking on that choppy sea like cockroaches crossing a Whistler painting. With disbelief, we'd watched the launching of the amphibious tanks: Shermans supported by canvas water wings, one of our team's secret weapons. They bloody well stayed one too, sinking faster than Thomas Wolfe's posthumous reputation almost as soon as they plopped off the ramps.

Their crews were inside, and the commanders of the tanks behind had seen those in front of them founder. Not one stopped. It was Omaha, and even one tank might've helped. We all knew by seven that the leading infantry was pinned to the shoreline like upholstery tacks.

Where, unlike Tom Hanks and his gutsy crew in a certain movie that shall go nameless, they didn't recover from the shock of slaughter to start killing Germans as enterprisingly as Winnie-the-Pooh's pal Tigger. Too incapacitated by what was going wrong everywhere around them to understand that any behavior of theirs could affect it, they went right on being upholstery tacks.

When the second and then third waves dumped their loads into this mess, the survivors took one disbelieving look around and became miserable upholstery tacks too. Even the incoming tide couldn't nudge them. Arguing with the water that was creeping around their bit of upholstery was as incomprehensible as arguing with the fusillade that had nailed them there.

With all its gore, the supreme fact the Movie That Shall Go Nameless never permits its audience to grasp is that the thing could have *failed*. Not only were Eddie Whitling and I sure we were onlookers to a disaster, we could tell that Gerhardt—he was the 29th's C.O., and his headquarters aboard the *Maloy* was to stay our box of the Navy's floating opera house until around noon—and his staff feared the same. Even from this far offshore, any idiot could see that no matter what was getting piled onto the beach, absolutely nothing was moving off it.

So the tanks kept rumbling off the ramps and sinking with all hands. In our sector, that was what the morning of D-Day was like.

I doubt anybody noticed, Panama, certainly not Timmy. At my last Amherst Thanksgiving, I'm sure a peculiar look came over your Gramela's face as the mimsies watched your little brother bang-bang his Playstationed way up a Spielbergized Omaha. I wouldn't have so much as cleared my throat for a queen's ransom, but still: there at the real one, even my *advice* unsought. Not that Timmy needed it, since he could and did just start over again at the shore-line.

POSTED BY: *Pam*   As a writer, I've often done the same. It tends to be our big advantage over infantrymen, which is why grasping I can't on my second D-Day has taken some getting used to. Once I hit "Post," it's gone and out there, bandersnatching all over cyberspace as frumiously as a Slinky toy. The Slinky toy, sent forth, can never be recalled.

On top of that, I haven't even been rereading this charabia before each heave-ho, much less reglancing at my previous posts. In the days when *by Pamela Buchanan* adorned the jackets of *Glory Be* and *Lucky for the Sun*, I was a far more intricately graceful stylist, not that too bloody many of you are likely to hit "Add to Shopping Cart" to confirm it.

When he still hoped to get me posting here, Tim Cadwaller told me blogging's standards aren't as strict, and *l'équipe* here at daisysdaughter.com is
grateful for the reprieve from jousting with *mots justes*. As for *l'équipe*'s full roster, maybe it's time you met Pink Thing and Gray Thing.

We switched names in my mid-sixties, when calling myself the Pink Thing
to my brain's Gray Thing began cutting no ice with mirrors. After the swap, the
new Pink Thing's first two cents were a reproachful whisper that I'd known it
was the real Pink Thing all along. Either way, we've been each other's best company and major amusement ever since.

Right now, Pink Thing's cursing the mimsy borogoves for having so carelessly scrutinized Tim's e-mail explaining this website's bag of tricks. Surfing
the Internet is old-hand stuff for me by now; *very* old-hand stuff, like pretty
much everything else these rheumatic fingers of mine are either capable of or
still interested in doing. But I've never generated Web content before and keep
being frustrated.

I've seen the websites linking, each to each; I don't think they will link to
me. (Joke, bikini girl. Google "Prufrock" if you're curious. Adieu, Sinclair St.
Clair.) I also don't know how to link to them and am in too much of a hurry to
even try, so you'll just have to trust me without any backup. It's Google this an'
Google that an' Wiki how's your soul, but it's thin red line of Pink Thing when
the blog begins to roll.

Sorry! My onetime pre–Pearl Harbor Bank Street roommate, now dead as
I may have mentioned, was very fond of burlesquing poetry. I must've acquired
the taste from her

POSTED BY: *Pam*   I've also got no way of putting images up, no great
regret to me regarding Eldritch Weaver's *Two American Women on the Beach,
Provincetown, 1927* but a real one in the case of the Paris footlocker's vintage
photos of my mother, father, and even the budding pudding that was Pam.
(INSERT gag shot of Pam trying to feed Nick Carraway–snapped Kodak to
her A drive, and you shouldn't think Gerson was a *complete* sobersides.) That's
why the only image you've seen here on daisysdaughter.com is the same old
picture of a Panamanic teenager with her arms garlanding a dentitioned cau-

liflower, taken not at J.D. Salinger's latest book signing but in this apartment twenty-one months ago and captioned *Panama and Gramela, 2004.*

Until Clio Airways first Lindberghized cyberspace, that was also the most recent addition on my blog, unknown to the *blogista* herself until my dawn logon. *Posted by: Tim C.*, it must've been your dad's last try at getting me interested before he realized I wasn't into his damned website.

Your Christmas ornaments were just a couple of new Easter bunnies then, under the impression my dowager's hump was lettuce. Your bray of glee wetted my ear. Finishing up *You Must Remember This: The Posthumous Career of World War Two*, he'd brought you along to see the FDR Memorial.

"Hell, I'm the unofficial one," I said. "Don't I rate lunch?" We went to Martin's.

Still, maybe it's just as well I can't do images. With the whole online lollapalooza at my disposal, I might start introducing every post with a different picture of Kirsten Dunst in *Bring It On.* Which would be entertaining but ridiculous, since of course everyone knows who she looks like.

What, rather. As for me, I've never owned a camera. Never wanted to interrupt or arrange life even that long when I was enjoying it, never saw the point in recording it when I wasn't. With a shelf of albums in her den that marches back in time nearly to Harry Truman's election, Nan Finn is the shutterbug in our gang of Foreign Service relics.

Andy and I last ate with Nan at Martin's in April. At least visually, may I point out with some dryness, the occasion was all but identical to the previous fifty, excepting Andy's bold *charcoal-gray* sweater and a few added bits of desiccation all around. She'd already waved a ninepin waiter over to snap the traditional facial triad when her familiar grope in her purse came up missing a camera.

The glorious girl looked as dismayed as Potus without a speechwriter, albeit more adorable. As I protected her with a cover story I found agreeable— "More wine!"—Andy smilingly squeezed her hand.

"I know it's a shame, Nan," he said with Pondian fondness. "I guess you'll just have to *remember* this one."

"I'll try, but how?" she laughed. "My God, at my age?" She still seems very young to me.

No matter, no matter! Should it turn out daisysdaughter.com hasn't snared a single reader, I'll never know. Even as I prepare to turn myself into a mess of pink and gray things on the rug in protest against this awful and unending war, I'm finding it exhilarating to be Pam in a medium new to me. If there's one thing I've had practice at, it's change.

To you, Panama, my fellow author or "author" Jack Kennedy is as remote as—my God, *Cleveland!*—was to me. Yet nobody was better at making fulsomeness sound jaunty. I liked his explanation when John Glenn became the first American to orbit in space: "This is a new ocean, and I believe America must sail upon it."

Cadwaller, look! Here's Pamela's sail.

POSTED BY: *Pam*   As I strain to match the Manhattan skyline you know today with the one I saw approaching on a blustery day in March of 1934, the major resemblance is obviously the lack of a World Trade Center. Wind is ramming clouds toward Illinois and Minnesota. In a buttoned blue coat from Mme Chignonne's, round-brimmed yellow hat, strap shoes, and, I swear, frilled socks, I'm straining at the bit to turn fourteen.

The magnetic prow of the *Paris*, pride of the French Line, is pulling the filaments of New York City into view for my deracinated inspection. The hat is multiply bobby-pinned to my hair, caught between a gingery brindle mop whose basic relation to headgear is puzzlement and a Circe breeze that wants to lure my chapeau to its doom.

In front of my forbidden—to me, too—and mysteriously macramé-ing crotch, a toy handbag (no money) is dutifully clasped in prayer-book position. What a sight I must've been.

Mark of my generation, bikini girl: for decades, we went on dressing for *airplane* trips. That was the thing to do, and well!, we were the ones doing it. One day in 1970—"April first or Halloween?" Andy Pond proposed, in full agreement about the year—we realized we were the only ones doing it. Footnote to history: Pamela Buchanan bought her first pair of adult sneakers at the age of fifty-one.

Under normal circumstances, I'd never've been allowed to cross the Atlantic unescorted, but normal circumstances these weren't. The *Paris*'s purser did draft an old biddy from Saratoga, luckless enough to have the cabin opposite mine and a real-life niece along for credentials, to pretend to be my duenna as she snored through gin rummy. My guardian had cabled Brussels that he could get to New York from the Midwest in time, but Europe was impossible. We'd just have to take the chance, and in the event, I was safer than a football at a tennis match. No jewel thieves on *that* crossing. Turned down the niece's offer of a cigarette behind the second funnel.

Soon to be outdone in fame by its French Line kid sister ship, the *Normandie*, to me the *Paris* had boasted every luxury I could expect from an ocean voyage except a mother. Still youthful enough to think it was *my* ship, designed to transport Pam and purposeless otherwise—it was practically true, since the great wedding-cake Atlantic tubs sailed barely one-third full in those Depression years—I cried in 1939 when I heard it had burned. And I admit it, thought of Agamemnon.

Customs, that perfectly named transition. *"Madam Was-elle, pass-a-port, plea*—oh, you're American?"

"Oui!" Pam brags. "Um, yes."

As a huge porter in blue serge heaved my trunk onto his skyscraped and skyscraping back, I unthinkingly jabbered, *"Mais que faites-vous? Que faites-vous?,"* undone above all by the recognition that, unlike Paris's ebony colonials, an American Negro wasn't exotic. Unlike a thirteen-year-old in a tilting blue coat, turning her jonquil-hatted head like a spinning top as I looked around in desperation for my guardian. I didn't have anything for the porter's *pourboire*.

He came up in the nick of time, gray-suited and gray-templed. "Pamela! I'm sorry. Wrong dock, red light, long story. I'd hardly have known you."

"How did you?" I blurted, since he seemed familiar with the way things worked here and I was eager to learn my native land's tricks.

"Fear and excitement. No, really, there just weren't that many unaccompanied girls the right age milling around. Taxi, please. Thank you—that's for you."

In the cab, he explained we had just a couple of hours before we took the long trip on the long train to Chicago. A bit elaborately, he envied me both Paris and the *Paris*: "I never did get over to Europe. And now it's—oh, too European, I suppose."

He told me we were passing the new Empire State Building. I peered with interest at all three of its glimpsable stories. As more yellow side streets flashed by like masonry learning to tell time, a sort of considerate second mouth that had been mulling its moment inside his visible one came forward.

"Pamela, I'm so terribly sorry. Your mother was…just lovely. That's all."

"I know she was." Nobody in the United States needed to hear how many pounds she'd packed on in Europe. They hadn't been pounds but kilos. It'd been Belgian weight—gloomy, rainy Brussels weight: not the Daisy they'd known's weight at all. Anyhow, it was off me.

My guardian was now worried—*et pour cause*, given Pam's hokey-pokey, still experimental, never-to-be-Daisylike form—that he'd slighted the daughter by praising the mother. "That's a very pretty coat you've got on, by the way."

"It's a uniform," I explained in surprise.

That reunited his outer and inner mouths, whose main point of contact had been thoughtfulness. They grinned at me as his eyes crinkled. Only my being female had been getting in the way of his remembering what it's like to be thirteen.

"Yep, I just keep making those mistakes," he said. "Of course, I ought to've saluted." I was devoted to him until the day he died.

POSTED BY: *Pamrod*   Call it bachelor awkwardness. In his shoes, one wouldn't, simply *wouldn't, ever,* pull back the curtains on a pubescent girl in a Pullman car's sleeping berth, no matter how awful her sobs. So my guardian couldn't give me much direct comfort when the strangeness of everything about being Pam and here overcame me on our journey.

Indirect comfort was another story. Like a black marketeer's, a hand offered a tepid but welcome glass of water, a hankie, a green apple, and—oh, serendipity!—one of Booth Tarkington's *Penrod* books. Wrong gender for me, but a dandy guide for any going-on-fourteen newcomer.

"All out of fashion, of course," he confided over a dining-car breakfast the next morning as overburdened black men in white coats came down the aisle as if shooting the train's rapids and the still reddish early sunlight made our cutlery flash taunts to vanished Injuns. "And maybe it wasn't like that in my real boyhood—I honestly can't remember now. Reading them reminds me of how

I used to at least think things were, before all the craziness between the war and the Crash."

"Mme Cassandre—at the school I, *was*, in—says there's going to be another war." Proud to be springing this European news on chugging, stubbly, inattentive Indiana (?), I picked up my butter knife. "'*Méfiez-vous de Hitler!*' she says, shaking her ruler like this. '*La prochaine fois, Napoléon sera de par là-bas.*' Of course, she's a *fanatic* anti-Bonapartist, but—"

"'Eet-lair'? Oh, Hitler. Well, who knows?"

"Cassandre! And '*la rue des Rosiers.*' That's what we call, called Rose Bauer. And—" But his mind was still on the Twenties.

"Listen, Pammie," he said, calling me that for the first time unless he had the summer of the Scandal. "Anytime you start thinking *everyone's* flush and it's all hunky-dory? Try to look past the crowd you're in. Things are pretty awful now, but at least even stupid people can't pretend they don't know."

"I'm sorry, Mr.—sorry. Nick," I said, flustered. I'd never been instructed to call an adult by first name, and in France for a girl my age to do so would've been no joke. I'd have been indicating he was a servant. "What don't we, they, don't know what?"

My guardian had forgotten I was under twenty-four hours off the boat and we'd mostly been passing through farm country. Not much in the unself-conscious landscape had been shrieking "Depression."

"There's always misery. If we'd remembered that during the Boom, maybe there'd be less of it today." Catching himself, he grew wry: "Said the Chicago ad man, polishing off his steak and eggs. Well, I'll have to leave our boy a whopping tip, that's all. Do you remember which he was?" And wryer still: "Is?"

POSTED BY: *Pam*   Some weeks of one's life wear seven-league boots. I still think it's preposterous that according to the calendar—they always testify for the police, prohibiting our memories from hopping getaway cars at will—only eight days had gone by since Pam, boarding at Le Havre, had grown undecided whether an empty starboard berth or an empty one portside was more likely to grow a corpse the second my eyes shut. So I'd gone back up on deck and watched the French coast turn into a soup bowl's rim, then soup.

Back when the *Paris* had parted ways with the dock, for there's always a thunderclap moment when *both* seem to be moving, the only Pamfetti to loose its streamers had been the scraps of a life I'd thought would have the grace to last until I understood it. Thanks to that, I'd had several reasons to decide I'd never been on an ocean liner—indeed, this one—before.

Primo, at going-on-fourteen—three months before the official handover, half that before I'd gambled I could start fibbing about it—one's seven-year-old self is the idiot cousin: unwelcome company at the start of a new adventure. Second, we'd been going the other way. Third, the corpse in the starboard bunk—or had it been the portside one?, I wondered yet again on my return to the cabin once the French coast turned into soup, deciding my best chance at sleep on the return trip was to switch our places—had been alive, gabbling and Gablering about ship's parties and the other Paris and asking Pammie, for the first time, how her fussed-with hair looked.

For my mother's sake, I've sometimes tried to picture her as the Daisy she either thought or hoped she could be in Europe, discussing the first four episodes of *Ulysses* with Joyce as her own novel magically wrote itself in the next room. *The Gold-Hatted Lover* was its most frequent title, and its chaos of beginnings made for pitiful reading when I fished the pages out of the Paris footlocker many years later. The truth is I can't imagine what would have become of us, especially after the Crash, if she hadn't met the Belgian on our New York–Le Havre crossing in October of '27, all of six weeks after we came back from Provincetown.

Name: Georges Flagon. Preferred sartorial color: Belgian brown, distinguished from French brown by a refusal to hint other options existed. Business: Flagon & Cie., Bruxelles-Leopoldville-Dakar, exporting windsocks, wheel chocks, and other safety equipment to small airports in out-of-the-way places. Major departure from a lifetime of never counting his chickens until plucked and beheaded, a bid for my mother's hand before we passed Iceland.

Georges had taken ship to America hunting much bigger game. (Wonderful expression, "taking ship"! I miss saying it more than doing it.) The compatriot of ours he'd been hoping to woo was the most famous man in the world that autumn; other than Chaplin, anyhow, but that Charlie was familiar. Charles Lindbergh had been unknown to anyone until his plane bumped to a halt at Le Bourget in May, and when I used to take visitors to the Smithsonian and see the *Spirit of St. Louis* suspended overhead, I'd privately goggle—while holy relics aren't my thing, there it *is*, you know—at its and its pilot's indirect role in shifting Pam's destiny.

Inept only as a person, Georges was an innovative businessman. Lucky Lindy's endorsement of his line of goods would have been the equivalent of Jesus of Nazareth talking up your carpentry kit, and my future stepfather spared no pains to make my mother understand that Lindbergh had considered the proposal seriously before changing hotels. I don't doubt it: the celebrated aviators of the Twenties and Thirties weren't daredevils but propagandists. Eager to proselytize for the new church of air travel—mail, passengers, bombing, they couldn't have cared less which miracle made converts—they'd have given any co-religionist a hearing.

Still, the promised second meeting never happened. Half the globe's population wanted a bite out of Lindbergh's day, and I gathered the head of Flagon & Cie. had been made to feel a bit Belgian about the whole thing. Once the *Paris* was bound for the Old World and all was definitely lost, the humiliation of retracing Lindbergh's route by means wingless and sinkable may have maddened my future stepfather into a resolution to obtain *some* American's endorsement of *something* Georges Flagon had to offer.

If not his company's useful products, perhaps his life? His view of the rue Rémi in Brussels, his taste for crepes and veterans' parades, his lonely postprandial cigar. At age thirty-six, he could've even been handsome if he'd only known how. Sharing space in a shuttered mahogany cabinet with Papa's colonial service revolver, a brown hand under glass commemorated his father's administrative excellence in the Congo circa 1898. It was peculiarly counterpointed now by Georges's own artificial foot, souvenir of the day hordes of spiked helmets flowed toward the spot to which newly mobilized Corporal Flagon had been rooted one day in 1914. Oh, hell, Panama—no *wonder* he felt incomplete.

"You mean we *aren't* going to Paris to live?" I asked my mother dumbfoundedly. After proposing we two take a turn around the deck, she'd moved to the railing on a beeline. So much for our Pam-and-Daisy romp among the lifeboats, merrily singing "Yes, We Have No Bananas."

"Not just yet." The wind taught her hair to scribble in soft Cyrillic as she turned. "Not now, that's all, big silly! I'm sure we'll all move there eventually."

If there's a more meaningless word than *eventually* to a seven-year-old, it's probably in Cyrillic too. To me, anything farther off than *soon* meant *never*, and right I was so far as my mother's hallucinatory relocation of Georges Flagon to a salon off one of Paris's *grands boulevards* was concerned. I wonder who lived there instead.

"But why not now?" I asked, wondering if that brown bit was the Isle of Wight, the Isle of Man, or giant seaweed.

"You know Mummy needs to write her book. That's going to be the only proof I ever existed, darling!" she said, smiling down at me. "And, well! I think it'll all just be much, much less trouble this way."

"Can't you write wherever?"

"Georges has a staff." As if that statement's starkness surprised even her, my mother went on, "And don't you think he's nice, in a sort of Belgian sort of way?"

"I couldn't care less!" I shouted. "Nobody told me it would matter."

"Well, it doesn't," she said, annoyed.

POSTED BY: *Pam*   The mystery was and is the extent of my mother's self-knowledge. Which was the cage, which was the bird—that's how you'd try to decode her decisions. Dubious any answer was final, you still felt confident the aviary was the right part of the zoo.

Panama, I'll never know whether she'd deluded herself a well-off Belgian husband would be the blindfolded orchestra she needed for her fluttering, reckless "Hello, Jim—hello, Pablo!" Charleston toward immortality. Or whether even that early she had intimations that *The Gold-Hatted Lover* was a kazoo made of tinsel. What I refuse to believe is that she'd boarded the *Paris* planning to troll for a man, since she'd scanned the passenger list in vain for any women she knew who were sailing unaccompanied. What may not need saying is that your Gramela would go all pretzelly with laughter at any suggestion Day-*zee* Flagon married for love.

Not that I saw overmuch of the happy couple once I was enrolled at Mme Chignonne's. My mother's choice of school for me puts her state of self-knowledge in play again, since I do like to think that at some level she trundled Pam off to Paris as a sort of delegated Daisy. It gave her an excuse to visit—not me, except technically, but an imaginary version of herself. As the Daisy who *would* live in Paris grew more fragile, she eventually (I was nine by then) came to cling to one who *had* lived in Paris. It wasn't her fault if people thought she'd been in Nassau County, Greenwich Village, Provincetown, or mid-Atlantic at the time.

The practical reason for scooting me out of the way was that my presence off the rue Rémi might've given Georges one reason too many to regret his marriage. His Day-*zee*'s lack of interest in producing another generation of Flagons was enough of a black tablecloth under the white one without a brindle-mopped daily reminder that she'd gotten docilely if not happily preggers—the post-1914 Georges Flagon wasn't my pick to brood on that missing "happily"—by his unknowable but evidently two-footed American predecessor. Polo would've been the tipoff there.

Marriages that start well and go bad at least alert both parties to the change. Marriages that are dismal from the wedding on can have a terrifying normality that pretty much keeps both parties chloroformed. There are even marriages that seem to be undertaken as a sort of suicide that doesn't actually kill you, a pretty wan definition of eating your cake and having it too but conceivably the reason I didn't wind up having to write my abysmal "Chanson d'automne" six years early.

Anyhow, some combination of the latter two was the situation off the rue Rémi. Feeling baffled by other people's obstinate denials of universal Flagon-ishness and nursing the lonely valor of the dull wasn't different enough from his bachelor life to stir Georges to rebellion. Fatefully, my mother discovered that being sluggish and depressed in Belgium let her indulge the same character trait that had made Daisy Fay the belle of Louisville and Daisy Buchanan a champagne pearl to postwar male New York: utter obliviousness to anyone else's desires. As for Pam, I blew any hope of a modus vivendi when I not only wandered into Georges's temporarily vacant study (strike one), but opened the mahogany cabinet (two), then asked him where the withered African hand had come from (three and out).

"At your age I knew better than to poke around in there," said my stepfather, massaging his knees. Of course that's because his father had *told* him not to, but to his helplessly Flagonish mind that meant all children everywhere had been.

"Oh, Georges, what does it matter?" sighed my mother. "Pammie's—eight, now? You can't blame her for being curious."

"*Pourquoi pas,* Day-zee? You aren't."

I suspect the bitterness there was on the convoluted side. Yet by no means was Georges a cruel man or even an unkind one. That his notions of kindness were entirely bound up with the way he thought people should treat *him* gets considerable backing from the New Testament. If only he hadn't been so literal-minded in how he put it into practice!

Brother, did I eat a lot of crepes. Telling him I didn't like them wouldn't have made him call me ungrateful. Unwilling to see a child deprive herself from sheer perversity of his own main pleasure *à table,* he'd have gone on patiently feeding them to me every day until I finally understood that, like any normal person, I did.

POSTED BY: *Peter Pan Am*   As the ultimate example of his inability to grasp that other people didn't share his predilections or biography—and therefore might have different reactions than his on exposure to them—let me describe one of our rare outings as a duo. Its being rare rather than inconceivable dates it to the summer of 1928. That was the year my mother spent six weeks in a Swiss sanatorium, from which we were soon to fetch her.

Yes, she'd entered her second marriage thinking she could go right on hitting the capital M key on her inner typewriter whenever the outer one's tadpoles unnerved her. And no, Georges Flagon wasn't about to let it continue. He'd largely resigned himself to the mania of strangers and people in news stories for playing carnival games that pretended they weren't him. Drug addiction in a woman who was at least nominally a Flagon was carrying the whole preposterous if evidently bizarrely satisfying affectation of non-Flagonism too far.

I knew his cue had been the calendar. Gaze at it, gaze at me, recognition that it was the maid's and the cook's day off. Slap of table: *"Pamelle! On y va."* Being Georges, he didn't say where we were going, but not because he wanted to surprise me—which he did and then some, since I had nightmares for years. It just never crossed his mind I wouldn't know.

Anyway, I always liked turning the corner onto the rue Rémi. Oh, maybe a more adult pair of eyes, demanding more *visible* bazaars, would've seen only monotony in each block's humdrum if confidently regulated panel of largely ornament-free prewar architecture, broken only by a very occasional larger vista for contrast. In attributing Pam's silent happiness to a child's overactive imagination, the peculiar thing is that those eyes' owners would've been patronizing rather than envying me.

Yet I didn't have much that was solid in my eight-year-old life, and the very reliability of that march of panels somehow simplified the world enough to let me conjecture adventures underway within. Hunts for treasure, delegations from mysterious Balkan countries, plans for a moon rocket or—same difference to me by now—a visit to America. Though Georges's hand in mine stayed earthbound, I was as diverted as Wendy in Peter Pan Am'ed flight.

Amid the tintinabulations of shop doorbells, a pleasant young man in a belted jacket would be out walking his snowy dog. As we passed a bar—or was it a fishmonger's, smelling of marlins, pike, and haddock?—a black and blue duffel bag of a man blustered at the broken stem and bowl of his pipe. Distracted but for that reason friendlier than any teacher at Chignonne's, the neighborhood savant fascinated Pam with the thinness of the bandy legs under his green coat.

Two bankers disguised as policemen—or was it the other way around?—raised their bowlers in tandem to a stripe-vested butler. A visiting Chinese student beamed a quick chen-chen. Her *gémissements* making the nearby pet store's parrots squawk, for the rue Rémi's major eccentricity was a fetish for exotic birds, a blade-nosed woman in a fur coat was upbraiding a foreign officer with a monocle. Her trilling voice turned her complaints into an aria from Gounod's *Faust*.

Of course, the rue Rémi held no magic for Georges. He'd been born here. "*Alors! Vous êtes, euh, heureuse, Pamelle?*" he asked, his voice creaking into conversation with Day-zee's child as tentatively as, no doubt, his prosthetic foot had first eased into a shoe. "*Tu sais que tu reverras ta mère bientôt.*"

While I'm sure he didn't mean it to, that made me feel chastened. I hadn't been thinking about my mother at all. If her three postcards from Switzerland had featured her face as opposed to mountain views—on one, with a flash of her old humor, a cross identifying "My Room" that decorated one window of a chalet was topped by another X on the white peak beyond it, marking "My Alp"—I might've been more convinced she was somewhere, not simply absent here. Our trip to retrieve her was a week away.

"Mais oui, bien sûr que je suis heureuse." In what connection my first year at Chignonne's could've have familiarized me with the French for "happy," I don't know. Maybe I'd overheard some other girls discuss their attitude toward having locked me in a closet, but the confirmation squared Georges's accounts with Day-zee. Duty done, he relapsed into silence.

A newly pent one, however. I could sense his mood change as we turned off the rue Rémi and onto a side street whose terminus wasn't the gabled mansion at the end of a drive I'd been subliminally expecting. A gray hospital stood there instead.

Since the only ill person I knew was my mother, I was mystified. Had the Switzerland postcards been a ruse, had she been ten minutes' walk away all along? Or was it that this was where she *would* have been if I'd thought of her oftener?

After ascending steps the hue of terns, we passed into an unlit lobby smelling of chemicals and dark as burnt stew. Murmuring, Georges produced a much-folded letter. The brisk thumb and forefinger of his unwithdrawn hand indicated he'd refold it himself when the uniformed *intendant* made as if to do so before passing it back.

Seeing me there at waist level, the *intendant* considered saying something. Then he grew eloquently resigned. What he'd read had set no conditions.

Someone else escorted us to a drab room furnished with a table and chairs. Were we going to have lunch here? As we waited, Georges grew expectant. Given my mother's refusal to uncork a squalling little demi-Flagon, the minutes we sat there were as close as I was ever to come to see him acting the maternity-ward papa-to-be.

The door opened, how I couldn't guess. Not unless the thing's bearer had had the stomach to one-arm the thing as he turned the knob. Two beefy hands set down a jar in which something boomerangy and mushily toenailed floated. A faded handwritten label (oh, yes, Pam, let's please read the label; the label deserves our exclusive attention) read *d'un obus. Liège. 5 août 1914*, along with a catalogue number.

"*Tu sais ce que c'est, Pamelle?*" His hands folded in front of it, Georges was unperturbed. So help me, I'm fairly sure he was smiling. His chin lifted as if pleased to introduce one business acquaintance to another: "*Eh bien, ça, c'est mon pied!*"

Understand, the urgency of denying my eyes' report that it was *a* foot had strained my concentration to its limit. So Georges's confession that it was *his* foot went straight from my unprepared ears to unprotected brain, where it's stayed in Pink Thing's archives to this day: a recording labeled *Bruxelles. 5 août 1928. I was eight. She was in Switzerland.*

Even though Pam was present, I can't really write "we." I'm not sure there's a pronoun that covers the situation. Even though various factors—e.g., my refusal to exist—made my timekeeping iffy, I don't think the séance lasted over ten minutes. In more than one sense, Georges wasn't looking at anything he hadn't seen before. His hands never unclasped, nor did he speak again. Too tunelessly for me to guess the song if any, I think he hummed once or twice.

Finally, he glanced up past the jar. "*C'est bien,*" he said with satisfaction. "*Vous pouvez l'emporter.*"

The beefy hands hadn't unclasped either. This was a specimen, Georges was known to them only as a veteran with a dispensation allowing him to visit his own foot. They couldn't take the chance that, left alone with his foot, he might smash the jar and try to reattach it. Now the beefy hands came forward and lifted the thing. Luckily, my memory is blessedly blank as it was seized and rose on scream-inducing details about bobbing, corns, state of pedicure, illusory soccer kick at my eyes' goalpost, and the like.

The like? I saw worse in the ETO. But except by cold during the Bulge, it hadn't been *preserved*, and certainly not for longer than I'd been alive. I'm grateful to this day the beefy hands made the jar disappear to parts unknown before we got up to leave. Otherwise, I'd've had to walk around it with my eyes glued to the thing, not knowing what it would do. That might've put me off ballet for life.

"*C'était aux premiers jours de la guerre,*" he told me as a miraculously unchanged outer world bowed with its granite tulle skirts. It was his lone comment before we regained the rue Rémi, whose characteristic duns and powder blues, toyshops, displayed diving suit, bright exotic birds, small Inca statuette, and white balloons—somehow somehow more voluble than the red ones I was used to in Paris—the war had left so poignantly immaculate.

He may've thought he needed to account even to Day-zee's daughter for what in retrospect must have seemed to medical students the absurdity of preserving a sample of what Krupp's new shells could do. During what historians call the Battle of the Frontiers, the medicos couldn't have guessed the Western Front would provide them with literally millions of such artifacts, all but interchangeable. Well, to everyone but Georges.

Yet he may have felt he creakily marched in veterans' parades as a fraud. With his ridiculously early maiming, he was a relic of when the Belgian infantry had gone to war in peaked caps. He'd known nothing of helmets, gas masks, barbed wire, *mitrailleuses*, trenches, and the rest of the apparatus that now defines World War One.

Invalided out to a French hospital, for there was only a coastal widget of Belgium left by that September, it may even have been as a volunteer that he and his artificial foot returned to limited duty. He helped to wheel out Spads and Nieuports on rustic airfields. Pilots needed to be able to run for them.

POSTED BY: *Pam*   That was in 1917, Panama. French troops took to baa-ing as they marched to the front. Mutinies flickered like grassfires, though there was no longer any grass, and trees, like farm animals, were only a memory. Like all wartime ground crews, Georges must've stayed out under the sky even in cold weather once the planes he'd been responsible for wheeling out were aloft. He was unwilling to be warmed by a stove or go back to the card game until his Spads and Nieuports tipped out of sight toward a dogfight.

At least among Barnard's livelier sophomores, nobody was less surprised than Pam when the Belgians and French crumpled in the face of the Hitler blitzkrieg. Nor could I force myself (I tried) to feel too reproachful when I learned, as I did somewhere—I never saw Georges again after he saw me off at the Brussels train station in 1934—that he'd been a *collabo*. He put Flagon & Cie.'s stocks at the Luftwaffe's disposal and its contacts abroad at the Abwehr's.

His compatriots probably didn't blame him. Business owners were in a special bind. Their only option would've been to shutter their companies and the Germans might not have permitted even that. I'm not endorsing his behavior by a long shot. Still, however you may judge Georges yourself, I can't accept that keeping the rue Rémi intact was an unworthy goal.

Naturally, my opinions are as anachronistic as your Gramela's childhood in what our dry, unhearing SecDef dismisses as old Europe. I don't suppose, Panama, that either he or Potus has ever watched a not especially interesting or likable man gaze at his own foot in formaldehyde fourteen years after losing it. But the reason Europeans know something I wish we could learn without finding out the way they did is that they don't go *away* to war.

POSTED BY: *Pam elle*   During the Occupation, Mme Chignonne's École des Filles was taken over by the Gestapo. I've won laughs with that line from L.A. to brightest Africa, but I was taken aback the first time Gerson and Gene Kelly chortled. I hadn't thought of it as a punchline. I was just noting my old school's most recent function as of August 25, 1944, the day Pam Buchanan scrambled out of a jeep to revisit.

Since the *Geheime Staatspolizei* had had its pick and those screams would've been screamed anyway, my main regret is that it was such a nice old building. All covered with vines, as they say, off a cul-de-sac in Chaillot called the rue Plan de Trochu. Since the Trocadéro as we know it didn't exist, that relic of the Exhibition of '37 was to baffle a certain gal in a jeep—one heard all too recently braying she knew this *arrondissement* blindfolded—as I gave our driver directions and Eddie flicked the flowers thrust at us near the Place de la Madeleine at random bits of Paris and Parisians.

Until recently, though—that damned Tour Montparnasse!—the genius of Paris was to know which temporary things to make permanent. And which not, like the flag Cassandre herself, more stooped but as vulpine, was bundling as I reached past our driver's shoulder to honk.

I wasn't sure if she'd recognize me. Should have known better, as I'd left only ten years ago under memorable circumstances. *"Madame!"* she called to Chignonne. *"C'est l'Américaine."*

"Ah, enfin! Elle est venue reprendre son colis" my old headmistress answered. She gave me the most fleeting of nods before a terrifyingly familiar jerk of her head produced a brisk summons. *"Venez!"*

"I can see why you wanted to come back, Pamita," Eddie told me. "Love like theirs doesn't bloom every day."

"Ta gueule," I said automatically. Eddie didn't know Cassandre and Chignonne. I'd never seen either one express affection for anyone or anything.

Nor did I feel any tenderness toward them, except possibly dating to the night I left school. Dealing with my situation had put them in peril of acting unlike themselves, which made me even more relieved to see them back to normal. You don't want to look up and catch one of Notre Dame's gargoyles practicing its golf swing.

I also had no idea what they were talking about. I'd taken my trunk with me to the Gare du Nord in February '34 and you've already glimpsed it being heaved up by a New York porter on daisysdaughter.com. What they meant was the Paris footlocker, which I hadn't known existed.

Reaching the rue Plan de Trochu from Brussels after I'd reached the States, it had stayed in a corner of the dorm's attic for a decade. Uninspected even by the Gestapo and just as well, since they might have thought my mother's pages of *The Gold-Hatted Lover* were in code. They'd have arrested Cassandre and Chignonne for harboring a spy.

As we climbed, I kept annoying Cassandre, who was groaning in French up ahead—and Eddie, moaning in American behind—by pausing on every landing. Yet I couldn't help it. Not only had I spent seven years here as a boarder, but this was a first for Pink Thing and Gray Thing alike. Starting with Provincetown, I'd never been *back* anywhere.

Recalled nearest the attic, the first year was the grimmest. Untutored in French, the budding pudding that was Pam had soon learned the language's ability to departicularize her by personalizing her nationality. It was especially stinging in the feminine case.

As Marie Antoinette had been *l'Autrichienne* to eighteenth-century Paris and the Empress Eugénie *l'Espagnole* in Second Empire salons, so Daisy's daughter—definitely the tin can in that progression—was *l'Américaine* to Mme Chignonne's. You could say I got off easy if you've ever heard a French epiglottis try to pin "Buchanan" two counts for three. Since the day of my enrollment I never had even once.

At that age you get your bearings through mimicry, leaving me out of luck as well as out of place. The only other Anglo name frisking around Chignonne's belonged to Molly Flanders-Fields, indecorous offspring—born August 1919, and let your fingers play calendar—of Marshal Foch's housekeeper and some Irish brass hat on Haig's Intelligence and Planning staff. Now there was a man with time on his hands.

But Molly was two forms ahead of me, raised in France and known as neither *l'Anglaise* nor even *l'Irlandaise*. Too engaging and quick with retorts and her nails for that. Her dorm monicker was *la Belle alliance*.

L'Américaine, on the other hand, was a figure of fun. A bumbling pudding in my blue, yellow-tabbed school frock, I clambered up the stairs and down the stairs, hiking the most of them on my shortest legs. We roomed by year, and one of the upper forms' perks was fewer flights to climb.

Since I'm in a hurry and "Chanson d'automne" looms, I won't avail myself of the chance to reprise my travails in detail. Let's just say imitations of me were miles more popular than I was. Greeted with laughter that stripped paint all the way to the attic when they realized I was a witness—one whose stunned stare usually proved two out of three details right, I'm afraid—the basic elements were wide eyes in a gibbering face, an open textbook imbecilically clutched upside down.

I wasted an hour and my pillowcase's most recent laundering trying to sort out what a wailed and batting *"Oeil! Coude et doigt, coude et doigt"* could mean syntactically. Joke about my clumsiness, some sort of plan for a group attack? Finally deduced it was "Hey! Cut it out"—my regression to English one helpless day.

The worst sensation wasn't loneliness or bewilderment, Panama. The novelty was to learn I was a cretin. Shouldn't I either have been advised of that or protected from knowing it at my birth?

Back in my lost world, I'd been precocious intellectually. Had even had a few hints it might be my ace in the hole. Now the silliest girl at Chignonne's outranked me and I couldn't call it injustice. She *did* know more than I did. What I knew that she didn't couldn't have been more irrelevant to us both if I'd been Iroquois.

Adding to the confusion, the religious instruction at Chignonne's was, of course, Catholic. Our daily catechism was overseen by Chignonne herself, who as an advocate of Christian mercy was on a par with a cook specializing in fish made of barbed wire. Mass each Sunday was the only time when our full blue-coated, jonquil-hatted regiment got marched all at once in the same direction to the same place, no gainsaying allowed from either Rose Bauer or a nominally Protestant *l'Américaine*.

To remind Chignonne or Cassandre I'd been baptized a Presbyterian, something I scarcely knew I knew anyhow, would've been like announcing my determination to attend class wearing nothing but a Stetson. As for Rose— school nickname, the vicious *la rue des Rosiers*, often shortened to *la rue*—she had her hands full protesting that her family didn't even *know* Léon Blum.

Google away, Panama. With a little persistence, you'll turn up that charming slogan of the French right in the Thirties: "Better Hitler than Blum." The rue des Rosiers was and is the heart of Paris's Jewish quarter.

If my mother's death included any sort of reprieve, it was that it happened the year *Pamelle* would've been confirmed. That might have roused even Daisy to catch on she'd had her hand off the steering wheel awhile.

You probably don't need me to tell you my religious education didn't take. At Chignonne's, it wasn't supposed to take. It was supposed to *be*, irrespective of what any of us made of it. To be raised in France, even as abortively as Pam was, is to experience Catholicism simply as a table society has laid: no leeway about the menu, no pretense that this has a blessed thing to do with one's own hunger pangs. If Jesus had been French, paintings of the Last Supper would isolate Judas by showing him using the wrong fork.

Anyhow, nobody gets away scot-free. My hunch is that Pink Thing and Gray Thing owe their birth in part to uncomfortable benches, incense, and droned but potent Latin ensnaring our bent heads in a lesser, undistinguished

Chaillot church. Its crabbed walls nonetheless ascended to a ceiling whose soot had been there under, or rather over, the Sun King.

Even in '44, dressed in fatigues and GI shoes, I didn't risk sauntering back in. Kept expecting a long arm in a surplice to reach out with a cry of "Got you at last."

POSTED BY: *Ram-Pam-Pam* The vine-covered old house off the rue Plan de Trochu was only where we dormed. What Mme Chignonne's taught best was urban topography. Mass wasn't our only expedition.

Each form's schedule took it to petrified classrooms in converted but still dusty ossuaries. They ranged from the rue Cognacq-Jay, where Pam would trudge past a church to be exited by Mrs. Cadwaller, with a peregrin, one day in 1958, to the Place Vendôme. One dwarfy double file of us often passed a more senior form's taller troop of blue topped by jonquils on that *douzaine*'s bobbing return—only twelve to a year at Mme Chignonne's—from the one we were headed to. No doubt our little parades through the Place de la Madeleine had charm in a watercolor, prewar sort of way.

Our teachers were all male if safely gelded by senescence and encased in the olfactory sarcophagus of the tobacco stench that seemed to have clung to their clothing since Gauloises was a term identifying living women. They materialize in Pink Thing's archives as sheepdogs whose masters were briefcases. Last new trick learned, a wait-and-see attitude toward the Commune.

I still recall some of their names. Fougasse, natural sciences; Hebdomadère, mathematics. Michelin-Michelet, geography and history; Rodolphe Charbovari, French language and literature. Whispered data exchange from Fro to To on the rue Cognacq-Jay: *"Attention! Hebdo est saoûl. Faites gaffe à vos culs, les septième!"*

Don't picture individual desks, Panama. Long benches at inclined tables with shallow slots along the top to rest our pens in, next to the inkpots we began each class by extracting from our *cartables* and noisily banging into scarred inkwells. Once we sat down, we weren't allowed to leave for *any* reason, ever. To have asked permission would've been to announce one was from Mars or worse. Two or three times a year, a face crowded and red as a crabapple quietly gasped, then turned eyeless and chasm-mouthed from shame as a pale puddle grew around her shoes.

Whoever she might be, her harshest punishment would be the instructor's refusal to acknowledge anything had happened. She just had to sit there, making her frog twitch for Fougasse or whispering *"Je crois. Tu crois. Il croit. Nous croyons. Vous croyez. Ils croient"* for Charbovari. Meanwhile, the rest of us waited to see which continent the puddle would resemble in its final form.

The sense of *sanctioned* public degradation was so powerful that, in the ultimate girls'-school tribute, those episodes were never mocked or reported to the other forms, no matter how hated the stinking one might be. It's a wonder we didn't all become urinary erotomanes.

Did it ever happen to me? Oh, Panama, please! Let's not go into it. Wasn't it bad enough that I was *l'Américaine?* Anyhow, it usually looked more like Australia.

Our form's left-handed girl, forced to write with her right, used to weep quietly every time her clumsy grip smeared her calligraphy's wet ink. Bad marks for penmanship canceled out good ones for grammar or spelling. Our pens had wooden nibs whose paint had a meditative taste, a meal that turned unpleasant in a hurry when an unguarded chomp got a paint-flecked splinter wedged between two teeth. When their metal styluses got too scratchy, we'd consecrate the bishop, in Chignonne slang, by fitting a fresh one to the waiting circlet of tin at the nib's plumper end. Not that non-Catholic Pam knew it her first year, but they did look like tiny metal miters.

Hearing the expression, Michelin-Michelet set us a composition on "Great French Churchmen." Our choices were Richelieu, Mazarin, and Talleyrand. French citizenship would've been useless then without hostility to something, and 'Lin-'Let was anticlerical.

Politically, all that Pink Thing's archives can add to newsreels of the late Twenties and early Thirties is that mine are in color. We were little girls and fairly pampered ones. When our mini-*défilés* got held up by massed coats and slogans, we accepted it as drivers do the sight of numbered strangers running a marathon.

Our *douzaines* of jonquil-hatted blue were certainly less trouble to our own supervisors, much less the authorities, than the gang at the boys' school just a block from our vine-covered dorm. That's where the rue Plan de Trochu became the rue Almereyda. Even Chignonne, who'd seen everything, was stunned into a violent *"Ah, non! Ah, non"* when she found a troop of us goggling through the dorm refectory's tall windows at their latest rebellion. One of the upper-form boys was climbing the steeply angled roof to plant a black flag at its peak.

To Chignonne, it was no joke at all: that was the Anarchist banner. At least to her, it wasn't so very long since they'd been chucking bombs at heads of state for real. She was in such a hurry to phone the police that she didn't dismiss us first.

She could've spared herself the trouble, though. A couple of *flics* in kepis and capes came into view almost instantly. Scrambling up the slate in their hobnailed boots, they each grabbed an arm and slitheringly led him down again after chucking his flag and its improvised pole to the roof's gutter.

As it teetered there, my friend Giselle Girondin squealed, *"Ooh, Pomme, regarde!"* Rising miraculously above the trees, a child's balloon had gotten its string entangled with the flag, and we watched in suspense as it tugged. Which would win?

To our disappointment, they parted ways and were soon both out of sight. One rose skyward, the other tipped streetward. Daringly, Giselle mimicked our headmistress.

"Zéro de conduite pour le ballon rouge!" she snapped, neck hoisted like a glare on stilts as she tapped one stiff palm against an open one. And got the same mark herself soon, since Chignonne had finished her phone call and was a black-clad guillotine with eyes right behind us.

If you've just coughed, my daisysdaughter.com readers if any, I believe I know why. My *friend* Giselle Girondin? Oh, yes. This was '32 or '33. The social calculus at any school is wanton cruelty mitigated by jadedness.

My translation into just another Chignonne's fixture was far more inevitable than Pam could've guessed the afternoon she realized the closet really was *locked*, and next that I wasn't yet certain of the French for "Help." By my third year, I was no longer "the Americaness," my favorite title as a Barnard freshman for my autobiography. However much my classmates' tone mimicked wet percussion, I was *Pamme, Pamelle,* or even, to Giselle Girondin, *Pomme.*

For part of '32 and all of '33, I was also *Ram-Pam-Pam*. For that I can thank a far more famous, infinitely less shy Americaness, not that we ever saw her shows or were supposed to play her records. But the many gifts to Paris from Josephine Baker's undulant hips and abundant smile included rechristening me. As in:

"Ram-Pam-Pam! What is it, all the fracas up there?"

"Oh and then. The littles of the Seventh saw a *flic* pursuing a thief in the Vendôme Place. They all pulled the tongue."

"Hold! That's truly efficient. Eh! But to the thief? Or to the *flic?*"

"Without doubt that depended of their politics. But what do you have? You have the air of a someoness one has slapped."

"Oh then shit. The Wastebasket Alliance [Molly Flanders-Fields wasn't *universally* popular] said to The Break-face [i.e., *Le casse-gueule:* Chignonnese for Cassandre] that it was me who put herself to laughing at the moment that Great Mutilated One [not school slang: *grands mutilés* was the official term for disfigured war veterans] with the crutches slipped at the Invalids. It wasn't me, it was the little Bemelmuh-muh-muh-*muh* [horrid simper]."

"I surmised that of myself. She becomes truly disgusting since the stupid appendicitis."

"Ah, ah! But you know very well that the Madam [not having a nickname was the most frightening certificate of Chignonne's authority] will not that believe of me! Even if I tell it her. Ah, no! No. Never in the world her little darling."

"We would have well done to simply let Mister the Tiger eat her."

"Agreed. But that's not all. Regard me this, Apple! What horror. *I am commencing to push out some breasts!* You know very well the uncle of whom I've to you spoken. He makes always some dirty cunteries, it him amuses. My God! Easter! It will be a torment."

"As is habitual, me, I remain here... But shut your shirt, finally, Gigi! I don't want to look at your tangerines, finally!"

POSTED BY: *Pam*   Skip the occasional reek of nubile piss in winter wool, impatience with Giselle's proudly displayed new *mandarines* (did you really think she'd been complaining?), or belatedly recognized literary rivalry. The proof of Pam's integration—I'm still tickled I picked Talleyrand, that genius of adaptivity—is that I stopped yearning for my mother to rescue me and then even to come visit.

She and Georges would train down from Brussels two or three times per year. That was just often enough to give her ever cloudier Paris a meteorological correlative in every season except summer, though Day-*zee*'s eyes increasingly seemed to be at sea to me—lingering somewhere in mid-Atlantic, unlike Pam's now propellerized blue-gray Lindbergh-Blériot twins. Still, the precious side of any *rencontre* we had in Europe was a reminder that here there were a few things only she and I knew. Not until I turned twelve did Ram-Pam-Pam start trying to tug her away from Mme Chignonne's as quickly as I could.

So far as any practical reason for her to hang around went, that was no problem. French schools followed the sausage-making principle by treating education as no sensible parent's business. To Cassandre and Chignonne, the meddling that goes on now would be as bizarre as a mother following her newly drafted son to boot camp.

Unaware that here I was *Pomme* and Ram-Pam-Pam, my mother would look uncertainly around two facing rows of metal beds. An intruder, she at least understood her opinion was moot.

Amateur archeologist of Daisy Fay that I am—is that a search known to all daughters, or only those with mothers as lovely as mine'd been called by fifty uniformed beaux in the balmy days before her first engagement?—I should probably've been mesmerized by how her puffy face brought out tricks of vivacity she hadn't had to summon up since Louisville. Showing lively interest without having opinions of anything had been the lure for swarms of khaki with officer's buttons. Instead, I twitched through those vague inspections. Ram-Pam-Pam dreaded what would happen if any of my schoolmates wandered in.

Nor was I much better when I got her past those vine-covered walls and out to the gate where Georges Flagon waited. My mother's idea of a celebratory treat was always a meal in a well-known restaurant. I'd try to get her out instead to the relative safety of the Luxembourg Gardens, the Tuileries, or—best of all—her and Georges's hotel room. Anywhere the odds of her making a fool of herself were reduced.

It wasn't that she behaved badly, Panama. As the years went on, her helpless presence in my life seemed to have less and less to do with any kind of behavior at all. Nor was I upset by the onetime sylph's Brussels-induced expansion into ever more capacious, less contoured coats, along with the low heels her porcine calves and swollen ankles now pleaded for. My mother had so much beauty to drown that for a long time gaining weight just seemed like her Belgian hobby, even if by the end—her hair dyed brown too—she did look like a stricken match girl peering out of a too large, fleshy Daisy mask.

Among other things, it was pleasant to reflect that now the Lotus Eater wouldn't recognize her. Besides, if forty kilos of flab paid the ransom for no trip back to Switzerland, it was worth every quiche. But I was mortified to stupefaction by—and on at least one occasion I don't think I'll share on daisysdaughter.com, actively cruel about—my mother's faltering, inept, gauche French.

POSTED BY: *Pam*   Switzerland was a spurious country, invented solely to give my mother's face placid backdrops. It was an enormous broken wine bottle, the upper shards streaked with snow. Their only job was to supply an open-air arena for the air you whooped down in big gulps. You were glad if somewhat terrified to be guzzling the pure elixir after nothing but shoddy imitations.

Pleased to be quasi-airborne once our toy train from Geneva had clambered up to the sanatorium, Georges even made an exceedingly rare joke, and about a generally taboo subject at that. As we climbed to the gate, he grunted that he found it agreeable to be someplace where *both* his ankles creaked. Yet with the as yet unnamed Pink Thing and Gray Thing's memories of his surviving foot's shell-blasted twin still so new and jarringly unique, as the fond ex-owner's weren't, I was too stunned to answer. No doubt my muteness inadvertently advised that pained man to give it another decade or two before his next try at humanizing himself with a wisecrack.

We stayed there just three crisply soaring, sharded white-on-blue days, waiting for my mother's final discharge. It seemed very Swiss to get us here first and judge her cured second; maybe they make good psychiatrists because the banking impulse runs deep. Pam was warned not to engage with any other patients, only some of whom were, like my mother, there for addiction. Plenty were lungers, as we used to call them when TB was still common enough to rate its own slang.

The problem was that others were mental cases. Nothing distinguished one pair of pajamas from another in the way that, say, Disneyland keeps Fantasyland and Tomorrowland's workers recognizably garbed. Surprised, Panama? Don't be: Gerson and I were guests at Anaheim on opening day. But as you may well have learned in Disneyland itself, an eight-year-old's control over what or whom she deals with is limited.

I was frightened when a woman with chopped hair, her mouth like San Simeon's letter slot after an earthquake, taloned my wrist in a braceleting grip. Her strange hawk's eyes roving, she insisted I was her Scottie—and after what I'd been through vis-à-vis SooSoo in the Summer of the Lotus Eater, being confused with someone's dog *again* was no joy. Her warder was all rushed politeness: "*Madame, madame!* Please, you know you don't belong here. What would your husband say to all this?"

Another woman was so pretty—San Simeon's letter slot *before* the earthquake, more or less—that I wondered what past, or whose, she could be expiating. She looked as if she belonged on the Riviera, not here. It turned out she was married to the one American doctor on staff, a weak charmer whose cheek was warmer than a medical man's probably should've been.

"Are you really all right, though?" an anxious Pam asked the first time my mother and I were alone. It must've been the afternoon Georges took the Belgian chocolates he'd chauvinistically brought from the rue Rémi and his favorite travel brochures to the sanatorium's small ward of *grands mutilés*.

"No," she cooed serenely, alarming me into a quick scan for white coats with large Swiss ears attached. Not yet Ram-Pam-Pam, I wanted her to come back with us—Georges handling Christmas brought on nightmares.

A breeze was teaching Daisy's hair to scribble in soft Etruscan. "Oh, no, darling, no, not at all! I'm just, all grown up—and that's better. 'All right, all right!' Why, that's just a silly thing to say about yourself, like claiming you can fly. Unless you've seen the whole world, why, you're just one, rabbit-hole, away! Georges wants so many things he's learned to do without, you know; he knows he doesn't have the right personality for them. I couldn't, couldn't be his rabbit-hole! Not when he's paying for everything, the doctors said. Oh, Pammie! I don't know why I bothered with—*anything.*"

POSTED BY: *Pam*   I hate to say it, bikini girl, but she was probably right. The most American thing about my mother was a hopeless inability to match the mirror's shards with the map's winks.

Only in East Egg could Tom Buchanan's widow fancy herself a budding writer and uninhabited, I mean hibited, free spirit, seizing on pockets of Manhattan and Cape Cod that simulated Europe's freedom in manageable—if you had money—miniature. She hadn't even set foot on the Continent when, out of some atavism of terror or habit or suspected inadequacy, she agreed to marry an unimaginative businessman. She might as well have stayed in New York.

She might have done better to stay in Louisville, ignorant of everything except all that had been so cautiously prepared there for her to know, more charming and less unnerved at being outdone by moneyed out-of-town visitors than most of the hatted *le tout Lou'vul* dames in the top tier of Churchill Downs on Derby day. Oh, Panama! Imagine being led in the ritual singing of "My Old Kentucky Home" by middle-aged, still frisky Daisy Ibsenhower, her lower lip mischievously drooping on one line to mimic the hilarious new singer named Elvis all three of her sons like. At their one meeting, a bit of a flustered and handbaggy thing in '59 when both their flights got delayed at O'Hare, she and Jacqueline Bouvier Nixon would've gotten on immensely well.

She might've died at seventy or so in one of those beatifically calm houses whose golden innards start to glow between nicely mussed trees at twilight, soon after watching the first moon landing and feeling wistfully pleased that *somebody* had done it. I'd never have existed, but you can't have everything.

Anyhow, within their brief, those Swiss doctors did what they said they'd do. So far as I know, my mother never shot M again with either a silver syringe or the gold one whose miniature inscription proved beyond any shadow of a doubt that it had been given to her by the Lotus Eater.

She drank her fair bit, true, ate enough for two or three Daisys, but that was all. She never said anything memorable to me after her remark on the sanatorium's breeze-blown plaza that "all right" means nothing until you know the whole world.

We spent her last few Augusts at the beach. Bray-Dunes, outside Dunkirk; Tati-sur-Mer, near Dieppe. I've sometimes thought the reason France made the Côte d'Azur its postcard for postwar seaside frolics was that the Channel coast's old e.e. cummings catalogue of names doglegging it down to Le Havre was too battered by history's linotype to successfully spell *vacances.*

Wearing a scarf to make her face less obese, my mother died not knowing Dunkirk would be the site of a famous evacuation. No Daisy appeared among those queues of Tommies, shyly asking if there was room for one more. Seated on a beach chair whose mint stripes vanished at her hips, tried to reassert themselves above her shoulders, and crushed the already shapeless back of her bell hat, she didn't know Dieppe would be the site of a famous failed commando raid. No Daisy stumbled off to stalag, wearing an all but shapeless overcoat, after her confused brief fight upon landing.

"Oh, no. *Auw, nawn, Pamelle!*" she calls. "Georges, tell her not to get on that sailboat. She doesn't even know the boy!"

"Why bother, Day-*zee*? There'll only be another in a minute." At the beach, Georges (socks and shoes the whole time, of course) is peculiarly confident, in his favorite proxy element at one remove. Kites, Blériot, the Wright Brothers. Its shadow passing over the future location of his hopefully craned face, the *Spirit of St. Louis* may've flown over this bit of coast.

Looking back at them at just-turned-thirteen, already in up to my waist, I'm surprised. I don't care about the *boy*; I care about the sailboat. For human company, I miss my friends at Chignonne's. But boys aren't human! They're part of nature.

"*Alors, on y va?*" Whoever he is (I could not care less; he had a scar), he's getting impatient.

"*Ouais, ouais. On y va.*" As I shimmy aboard, wet keester alerted to unsettlingly lopsided elastic by left knee's wild lunge and unwetted non-*mandarines* going squeak on the hot shininess like two comedy mice, I'm thinking *ouais, ouais* sounds like waves. As we push off, the striped tents on the beach—a dozen docile circus elephants, doing their one trick—begin to pad toward my mother and Georges's new seesaw. Leave her in sunlight if nothing else.

POSTED BY: *Pambulance*   It was a police *camion* in the form of weather: that black, that unlikely to find itself being quarreled with, sounding its klaxon of shrieking February cold. Pulled from her flashlit bed (Gestapo!), Pamela *Bou-qu'un-un* was hastened down a hall (Gestapo, Gestapo) by a bathrobe-caravelled Cassandre.

Behind the desk in Chignonne's sanctum, the headmistress was folding and refolding her glasses as if they were a letter in a language she suddenly disdained. As Cassandre brought me in, she put them on, needing *some* badge of office. Her black dress had been burned by the mob that threw that crocheted shawl around her. Her careful daytime bun had gone the way of Stavisky's bonds.

"*Pam'la! Ce que j'ai à vous dire n'est pas facile.*" I still wish she'd tried to make it easier, but soft soap wasn't her strong suit. "*Votre mère est morte.*"

Dead? I found my mouth, which had gone flying toward the window before discovering it was still attached to my face.

In French, "*Comment?*"—even gasped—can mean "how" as well as "what." Ever practical, Chignonne assumed I meant the first.

"*Je n'en sais rien. Et tu ne doit pas penser à cela, mon enfant.*"

In her lone symptom of distress aside from dropping her formally consolatory *vous* for the *tu* of everyday reprimands to her students' backtalk, she patted her desk for her ledger, which was locked up at night. Even Cassandre, on whose sharp face exhaustion cringed like unwelcome nudity, couldn't think of everything.

I already knew, though. (Clearly, so did they.) I didn't get to say goodbye even to Gigi, much less Chaillot's balloon salesmen or the *Zéro de conduite* boys on the rue Almereyda, and I can't guess what Ram-Pam-Pam's fellow Chignonne *mignonnes* were told the next day to explain my absence. If they learned the truth, I doubt they stood around scrubbing an eye with their fist as they all blubbered to Cassandre, "*Bou-hou-hou! Nous, on veut tous que notre mère se tue avec une balle dans la tête,* too."

As a taxi was summoned to rush Pam and her hastily packed trunk, its contents as ill assembled and bonkers as *The Gold-Hatted Lover*'s multiple Chapter Ones, to the Gare du Nord—my God, how they wanted me out of there!—I knew. As the driver nosed through rioters lurching back from the Place de la Concorde, all welts, bent fedoras, dark-mawed overcoats, headlit pale faces, and clutched bloody handkerchiefs around the cab's prow—Daladier's government quit the next day—I knew they'd tell me different, but I knew. As the night train to Brussels got underway, chuffing out of a Paris whose bone-cold cobblestones were in contention—for no one believed the official claim that one Serge Alexandre Stavisky, a swindler with highly compromisable friends in high places, had killed himself before he could be taken into custody—Pam knew she was heading to that deceit's minor mirror reverse in Belgium.

I knew why the coffin had to be closed. I knew it hadn't been gout. I knew why Georges's glares until he finally packed me off to America were rimmed with rage as well as suffering, as I was now the world's most unwelcome living reminder that, in Georges's view, his Day-*zee* had refused to Flagonize herself. Above all, I knew a withered brown hand from the Belgian Congo hadn't been the only object I'd seen in the mahogany cabinet that day.

It had taken a staggeringly unsuperstitious man to place his father's colonial service revolver next to that desiccated claw. They wouldn't let me into my mother's old room, but I could still smell the cordite.

POSTED BY: *Pomme* What I don't know is who found her, Panama. Remember, Georges had a staff. Since February 6, 1934, was a weekday—a Tuesday, if you're curious: we had Music on Tuesday in *quatrième* that year. By assignment, not choice, Pam played flute—he was probably at Flagon & Cie.

Knowing my mother as I do, I'm sure she didn't think of or care who came through the door. And I'm perversely grateful for that farewell fillip of obliviousness, since it's my best chance to avoid making *Like mother, like daughter* come true in every detail. But I still haven't solved the Andy problem.

Every time I mentally rehearse his entrance, he still comes into view (my God, Pamidiot! Whose?) from the foyer, toting a bag of groceries he's quite pleased with and DVDs from Netflix or Nextflick of *The Gal I Left Behind Me* and *Meet Pamela*. Every time, he sees a mess of pink and gray things on the rug. Even disregarding thoughtfulness, which I can't—after all, in a sense I'll still be his hostess, and old habits die hard—his ticker is no more what it used to be than mine.

Call him back, tell him to stay home? If you read my early-morning postings here on daisysdaughter.com, you remember how well attempting to cancel my little birthday dinner worked the first time. Besides, Andy's told me more than once that anytime my phone doesn't answer, he'll rush over in an octogenarian's careful version of a flash. He'd still be the first even if he showed up tomorrow or Thursday.

The confession that may and indeed should appall any unknown readers I've acquired, especially if you work for Domino's, is that I thought of one horrid way to ensure my discoverer would be anonymous. Said brainstorm bit the dust fast, done in first by logistics: I couldn't put Potus on hold while I quickly phoned up for a medium pizza with—no, don't like mushrooms, maybe anchovies? Anchovies. Yes, I'll leave the door unlocked. Then: "Hello, Potus? Sorry for the delay, but not for this." *Bang.*

It was done in next, I hope not *unreasonably* late, by recognizing the callousness my worry about Andy had tricked me into. Irreligious as I am, I do try to remember the words lettered on the storefront window of the first Catholic Worker house I laid eyes on during the Depression: "Whatever ye do unto the least of these my brethren, ye do unto Me." If a delivery boy doesn't qualify as the least of these my brethren on upper Connecticut Avenue, bikini girl, I don't know who would.

So *l'équipe* here at daisysdaughter.com is still mulling over that one, even as I wonder if I've left myself open in this latest batch of posts for Potusville's favorite way of demonizing any citizen who dissents from this awful and unending war. All those comings and goings in old Europe, all that untranslated French! Never mind that those times were ended by the former Daisy Buchanan's suicide. The vital news the folks out in Des Moines, Terre Haute, Eau Claire, French Lick, and Baton Rouge had better be alerted to is that her daughter's something fishily or froggily less than fully American.

Oh, really? Hey, cut it out. In an old house in Paris all covered with vines, Ram-Pam-Pam learned something about being American most Americans will never need to. I learned how strange it is to be one. It may be even stranger than it is lucky, which is saying something. *L'Américaine, c'est moi.*

It took some reacclimatizing, I grant that. So did my guardian, in a letter he may've never finished or mailed. No, I didn't go rooting around in his study: Georges Flagon's mahogany cabinet had cured me of that, and any thirteen-year-old's primary object of curiosity is herself. It just turned out that his home in Oak Park had a walled side garden, overhung not by an oak but an unexpected magnolia—a tree unknown in France, and none too damned common in Illinois either—which was his favorite place to read and write. And meditate, not to augur his future with a blunt auger on the magnolia.

On the first halfway balmy day of April, pliably two-sweatered but delighted by the sun's promise to be, if not a California orange, at least a pleasantly peeled Midwestern onion after its long winter as a chilly coin, he left me in the library. Where I stayed, at once floundering (there are only three *Penrod* books), baffled (Flaubert in translation is Garbo in burlap), and reassured.

Whatever else this was or was going to be about, I could see his prematurely gray head and sweatered cottage of shoulder through the leaded window, oh! any time I wanted. *Magnifique, l'Amérique.*

Even so, what makes April famously cruel—and really, of *all* people to indulge the pathetic fallacy, Mr. Eliot, right there in the first line too—is how quickly its sun's promising onion can be retransformed into a chilly coin. After a telephone call summoned him back inside, my guardian didn't return to his garden, and in fairness to Pam, I was *asked* to please fetch him his reading glasses.

In fairness to me, they were looking up from a page where my name appeared. Among the books on the table, my search for a substitute paperweight stumped me anew: what was epistemology, who was Virgil Michel? Cluelessly, I also guessed that Hope must've been among Lily's schoolmates. But no matter. Here's what I read:

> *or even had word from her in years, but her will gave me the guardianship of her daughter Pamela. Said daughter is now on the premises, looking wide-eyed and furtive at once. She's off soon to Purcey's Girls' Academy in St. Paul, which I—you know my vast experience in these matters!—have deemed the best of a bad lot.*
>
> *You'll recall our old friend Lily Highlow, of the house of mirth, who went there and to my (decorous) knowledge has never been arrested. Well, except for that odd Hope Diamond business, but we were all young once.*

*If you remember Daisy at all, the daughter is honestly a bit spooky. Speaks
perfect (as if I'd know) froggy, doesn't resemble mother in the least except a bit in
the old peepers and some of the archaic Twenties lingo, doesn't know Al Smith ran
for President or who Dorothy is. All in all, a perfect little Paree-sienne, and I ask
myself: how will I keep her down on the farm? But in time*

5. Scenes from American Life, Not All Mine

POSTED BY: *Pam*   Just in case I've lured a few helplessly creaming NRA
members to daisysdaughter.com by slyly mentioning that incredible orga-
nization in one of my dawn posts, glad to oblige. The gun in my lap's an
automatic. A 9mm Beretta, I believe, but Pink Thing's unclear tape recording of Hopsie's long-ago identification as he tucked it behind its traditional
marker on our bookshelf in no way reflects expertise or experience of my own
with this crap. Yes, I could Google to check, but as snappy excuses go, "Life's
too short" has grown on me this a.m.

Its lightness gratifies an old bag whose forearm muscles are rubber bands
made of tapioca that wrap balsa. The only other time I've handled Cadwaller's
compact little gun was when I exiled it to the Paris footlocker twenty years ago,
and I'll have to snatch it up from my ancient snatch in one hell of a dotty hurry
when the phone rings. It's certainly a far more manageable firearm than the
heavy Browning, a ring soldered to its butt for the leather lanyard beloved of
colonial administrators, my mother played lollipow with seventy-two years ago.
Then again, she was recumbent and only in her thirties, and I'm an octogenarian in a wheelchair—mitigating, admittedly only to my own satisfaction, all the
Like mother, like daughter Shinola in tomorrow's screaming headlines.

And yes, NRA: the safety's off. I may not remember much more of Cadwaller's one try at indoctrinating me about our family ordnance than I do of Tim's e-mail explaining how to manage my website, but I did look for and flip that little doohickey. I'm not about to risk the comedy of juggling phone, gun, fat lunettes, and burlesque dentition in panic as a certain voice starts wishing Mrs. Cadwaller a happy birthday. The fewer actions this old bag needs to perform at H Hour, the better.

If only I still had the luxury, bikini girl, of *exclusively* imagining your great-grandfather's gun barking its single report in Potus's telephonic hearing to spray my mess of pink and gray things on the rug! I'm afraid your old Gramela doesn't perform too well in the other images now shoving in to compete.

Where will they be coming from, I wonder? Have two or three SUVs with indigo windows already burst from the White House's South Gate, so often quietly entered and exited by Mrs. Cadwaller in Lyndon Johnson's day, to boil up Connecticut Avenue? Just in time, they're alerted to avoid Farragut Square by its statue's warning shout—"Gridlock!"—and encouraging cry in their red-eyed and fishtailing aftermath: "Don't fire until you see the mimsies of her borogoves." Or will they leap from NSA headquarters in Fort Meade, racing down through Maryland on the 295 until they smash into Rock Creek Park to come at me from the north?

Panama, Panama! What have I done? Pamidiot, Pamcretin, Pamfool. Call me old-fashioned, call me—all right, even I've got to clear my throat for this one—too modest. I thought I might win a few random readers piqued by either my plan or the prequels I hope illuminate it, and I don't mind tweaking the NRA's nose with one cyberspatial hand as I naughtily milk their cyberspatial dingus with the other. (Nobody tops an ancient widow for putting the lay back in Rabelaisian, boys. I once considered writing a somewhat Sebastian Knightly book called *The Lewd Pretzel*.) Why didn't I realize until now that spilling the beans on daisysdaughter.com could bring agents from half a dozen acronyms barreling, screeching, and locking and loading to the Rochambeau any second?

POSTED BY: *A harmless old lady (without even a cat)* Should these turn out to be the final words I input, I'd like it recognized that at no point have I threatened physical harm to anyone but myself. Not a bit! I'm contemplating a technically illegal act in Potus's auditory presence. The mess of pink and gray things when I'm done will belong to no one but Pam.

As an American, I'm revolted by anyone—anyone!—who fantasizes cocktail-party style about assassinations of actual political figures. Yet I suspect the distinction won't matter. Now that our government's the master of all it surveils, any website where the terms *Potus, gun,* and *terrorist* keep cropping up near the phrase *this awful and unending war* is a cinch to get me and my gat in dutch with the feds P.D.Q.

Remember, those are the movies of my youth. Since he's *Qwert* magazine's Man in the Dark, let's ask Panama's dad: Tim, shall I Cagney it out? Christ, if *anyone* deserves to buy the farm screaming "Top of the world, Ma!," you're reading her blog right now.

Pam's own hearing isn't good enough for me to count on hearing the SUVs snarl into a more ominous indigo-windowed pretzel down below. Thudding non-Andy footsteps in the hall will be my first warning, moments before a fist slams and the door shears. Here they are!

No, they won't surprise me: I won't be dottily shuffling myself and my walker out of my kitchen with a friendly smile as those heavily armed gents break in. When they do, I'll have had just enough time to pivot my damned chair to face the foyer.

Bring it on. Clapping left hand over weaker mimsy to steady my lunettes' right lens, I raise a forearm whose muscles are tapioca rubber bands wrapping balsa to aim Cadwaller's gun. Then I start firing, but my shots go wild—splintering the heads of the nude fertility statuettes I call the African Adam and Eve, giving silkscreened Ganesh a see-through new third eye, shattering the framed and signed menu from La Coupole, and wounding Tim Cadwaller's authorial feelings with a stray bullet's opinion of *You Must Remember This: The Posthumous Career of World War Two.*

That's my worst-case guess of how many times I'll have to pull the trigger before I'm pulp in a wheelchair that's gone spokes over Pamkettle. Gun chucked from my feeble grip like AARP's answer to the Loyalist soldier in Capa's famous photo, lunettes shattered to Potemkin come, slippered feet sticking up like they're auditioning for *Who Killed Cock Robin?* Not much in between those extremities except eighty-six varieties of Heinz, and *l'équipe* should probably explain that, unlike some sites, daisysdaughter.com doesn't take money for product placements. We do it for love and glory here.

Oh, Panama! You didn't think I was aiming at *them*, did you? For one thing, if I'd been trying to shoot it out for real, I sure as shit would've been keeping my wheelchair in motion as I fired, not only having learned a bit from our tanks' tactics once we finally got out of the bocage but maximizing Pam Cadwaller's superior knowledge of her living room's terrain. I was only shooting to make sure I'd be eighty-six varieties of Heinz in seconds.

Do you know what, though? I don't think I can do it. They're fellow Americans, performing what they think is their duty. I can't bear the thought of wounding or killing one by mistake. No, I'll toss Cadwaller's gun bedroomward as the door hits the floor. Then I'll shuffle obediently down the Rochambeau's dowdy hall.

You know, black isn't really my color, Captain Lyndie. Can I have a red hood instead? Sorry to keep repeating myself, but it's hard to make myself heard when I have this black one over my head. Also my vocabulary's obsolete and my dentition's back in the elevator. You remember.

Waterskiing? I loved waterskiing. Lake Tahoe. My second husband, fifth anniversary. We were across the lake from that noisy Corleone thing. Did I hear you wrong again, Captain Lyndie?

Oh, *boarding*! Yes, I've been to boarding school, Captain Lyndie. In an old house in Paris all covered with veins. I mean vines. Why do you ask? Where's that red hood you promised me?

You know I really hate this black one on me or anybody else. It's just not becoming.

Do you really want to see hooded, naked eighty-six-year-old me in that pyramid, Lyndie? *If they belong there, so do I.* Do you? Do you, do you, do you, do you, do you? Light a cigarette. Thumbs up!

Discounting my first marriage, where I think we all get some leeway, only once in my life have I felt capable of killing or trying to kill anyone. If anyone had handed your Gramela a weapon the day we liberated Dachau, I'd have shot, and shot, and shot until there wasn't a fucking guard left alive. That Holocaust deniers still try to make a scandal out of the fact that some of our boys did machine-gun a few dozen—Google "45th Infantry Division" and "Dachau" if you don't believe me—makes me want to quote none other than you, Panama: "Oh boo fucking hoo."

You never knew I'd heard you, commaless one. It was the last time I was up in Manhattan, and I was frankly getting a little bored with your dad's complaints about his book troubles; his ace copy editor and he were tussling over a *Dirty Dozen* interlude that struck her as overkill. So I excused myself on the pretext of seeing if anyone needed help in the kitchen—it speaks half a dozen volumes about Tim's acuteness outside screening rooms that he didn't realize this was equivalent to Custer asking for Sitting Bull's address—and there you were on the phone.

"Oh boo fucking hoo," you said with that special peering look people get when they can't see what's right in front of them. (It wasn't me: I was behind you, an old lady trapped between light and dark.) "So what if you think she's a dyke? So what if she *is* a dyke? So what if you are, or I am, or anybody else is? Who put you in charge of the salad bar?""

No, Panama: I don't really think they'll hood me. As I'll be visibly elderly, defenseless, and not Muslim, whichever agency gets the job of hauling Pam to the hoosegow or the nut ward is reasonably likely to play by some semblance of the old rules. That's why the Porlockian intruder whose interruption I'm most fearing is Chad Diebold.

Don't know who he is, you say? That's what you think. Chad is a spirit abroad in the land. The reason you don't know him is that he resorts to pseudonyms and disguises. He thinks he's Zorro and the Scarlet Pimpernel. He thinks the likes of me are Easter Island heads. He knows a few sheets of scrap paper in the Archives, preserved not far from twenty-four-year-old Pamela Buchanan's faint voice on school-group earphones, have faded to near illegibility.

Chad is the architect of Potusville. (Pierre L'Enfant, move over.) He thinks he's in charge of the salad bar, too. Not least because I know he'll outlast Potus's own term, I fear him more than I ever could Lyndie Gump. Given Chad's druthers, he'll send the memory of all of us stubborn Clio Airways frequent flyers right from Archives to Holocaust, and call the bonfire Old Glory in fireworks.

POSTED BY: *Pam*   Cadwaller said once that if Americans had invented the Olympics, leaping to conclusions would be the climactic event. In a very real sense, he thought of remarks like that as a form of bitching about his boss, but I forget which extraordinary popular delusion had wearied him. Was it the outcry over John Lennon's quip that the Beatles were more popular than Jesus?

Your grandpa if not you, Panama, will recall we didn't only take that as a mortal *(sic)* insult to the man from Galilee, though he seems to have recovered with his usual buoyancy. In a way only our compatriots could either devise or understand, it was an attack on our patriotism, which we peculiarly expected a Briton to share. Normally, I doubt unmusical Cadwaller would've given a damn: in one of his rare traits shared with Dick Nixon, Hopsie liked Richard Rodgers's *Victory at Sea*, or thought he should. But he had a meeting with Kim Hastings over at the Brits' brick heap on Mass Ave the same morning photos of Beatles LPs topping bonfires begrimed the *WashPost*'s front page. Among foreign friends, back in the days when we had 'em, what American diplomats dreaded most was the *teasing*.

Anyhow, I suspect one name in the letter from my guardian I quoted a few posts back is susceptible of a wildly wrong guess from my readers if any. My guardian wasn't amused by my ignorance of L. Frank Baum's Dorothy, with whom I was perfectly intimate even at half my young lifetime's remove from Pam's childhood library. If anything, having just passed by train through Midwestern farmlands to Chicago after seven years in Paris, I was newly conscious that Baum had made the whole Kansas-to-Oz transition, emotionally speaking, a mite easy.

To those of us reared on the Denslow and John R. Neill illustrations, accepting that she'll never again pry off the blubbery mask of Judy Garland hasn't been managed without a goodbye pang. Too old for such stuff by the time it came out—hell, I was too chic for *Gone with the Wind*—I never even saw the damn movie until the Fifties, on a set whose salt-and-pepper graininess made the ta-dah of Munchkinland fairly lame. But my guardian meant a different sort of voyager.

Even Andy Pond had trouble placing her over a pre-matinee lunch in the Kennedy Center's rooftop restaurant last fall. He'd looked keener and more knowledgeable when I'd mentioned Nick's eponymous ad agency, but one skill every diplomat acquires is an ability to quickly sort names he can tell he's expected to recognize from those he can feel confident he isn't. Spoken with the special timbre we reserve for names with an aura, "Dorothy Day" had him fumbling.

Automatically, he hummed a few bars of "Que Sera, Sera." Then stopped: "No, of course not. That's Doris. The evangelist, Los Angeles? Wasn't she always on the radio? Why on earth are we talking about her?"

"My God, Andy," I complained. "What is the use of you being nearly as old as I am if you can't remember anything? You're right! I *should* get a new cat. That was Aimee Simple—oh, hell—Semple McPherson. Say 'meow' now. Go on!"

Andy let his eyes glaze instead with distinctly secular happiness. "Do you know Chaplin boinked her once? That haunts me."

"It ought to've haunted him. He did get less funny, though."

"No, no. Think of the *spawn*, Pam! Charlie Semple McPherson. He'd have been President at six. We did dodge a few bullets back then, you know."

Spearing an asparagus, he hummed a bar or two of "Once in Love with Amy." We had tickets for Christine Baranski in *Mame* that afternoon, and musicals always put Andy in a generically musical mood.

"Where's Charley indeed," I said to shut him up. "But I, Andy, was speaking of Dorothy Day. A woman a million miles more obnoxious than I could ever hope to be."

Napkining, Andy held up his free hand. "Wait, wait, I've got it. The *Catholic Worker*, pacifism. Houses for vagrants and bums. Wasn't she still getting herself arrested in the Sixties? Wasn't she a nut?"

"If you were most Catholics, you'd have called her worse than that. She was the one who decided the Sermon on the Mount made Marxism redundant, and spent the next fifty years being a *perfect* pain in the hoo-ha about it. Thank Christ I wasn't churchy, I'd have wanted to strangle her."

"But you weren't and you aren't. I do know you, Pam, and you have no queen but Kirsten. Please tell me this isn't Talleyrand taking unction on his deathbed."

"No chance of that," I said, "but I did meet her once. Not Kirsten. Dorothy."

POSTED BY: *Pam*   It may sound bemusing that a man should have begun his withdrawal from the world by founding a small Chicago ad agency. Still, this was an older America and my guardian followed his own path.

In my pre-Scandal infancy, he'd tried out for a part as one of Wall Street's many real-life Harold Lloyds, though he hung off no clocks and later told me with a smile that the secret of the memorability of that image in *Safety Last* was that it was the Boom's unwitting version of Christ crucified. True, Harold just swung up into his sweetie's arms, but that was a very Twenties idea of heaven.

My guardian's own brief marriage had ended in disaster. Off she flew and down he stayed, as publicly as an avocado left on a doily. No one will ever know if his decision to quit New York was a moral decision disguised as a social one or the other way around, and to me—in a joke I hope he'd have liked—elucidating that is like firing a gun at angels' feet to make them dance faster on the head of a pin.

As for the ad agency, however incongruous it may look on the future Brother Nicholas's c.v., my hunch is that it was the bungled and therefore true beginning of his never finished journey to the priesthood. Men of the cloth are, after all, facilitators. Nobody blames them for *inventing* what the OT has to say about concubinage or oxen. Before the Crash darkened his penciled deprecations of the business world's heedlessness into swatches of van Gogh crows all over his world view, my guardian may've been groping toward a similar relationship to capitalism. Envisaging himself, let's say, as the sort of conscientious objector who'd perform clerical or transport duties, but balked at being a rifleman.

Anyhow, it was a good enough little agency, thanks to a scrupulousness that predated any notion of professions or vocations and the mild but steadfast humor he was never to lose, not even in a rope belt and sandals at Nenuphar. On the wall of his office, which he showed Pam soon after my arrival—"It's the old story of the seven blind men and the elephant, I suppose, but this is a bit of America"—a prosaic placard featured the first slogan he'd ever been hired to think up. It was for a laundry somewhere in Iowa: WE KEEP YOU CLEAN IN MUSCATINE.

As the published volume of his letters bears out, he'd begun even then to read the Christian apologists. But Chesterton didn't do it for him and neither did Lewis. He wanted a view that would accommodate the tectonic instabilities of the American earthquake.

He'd also started to correspond with fellow doubters who shared his concern that a chicken in every pot might turn out to be a parrot in every kettle. Which my guardian, no revolutionary, mistrusted only because parrots are inedible. He didn't want to see a bird that could both fly and talk mistaken for one that could do neither but could feed a family, his metaphor in Letter 13.

To my regret, *The Mountain and the Stream* (Vaughn Trapp and Co., 1971, a publisher primarily of hymnals; it's so out of print it makes my *Glory Be* look like *The Da Vinci Ultimatum*) includes no missive announcing a perfect little Paree-sienne's arrival in his one-man midst. For one thing, I might've found out to whom it was addressed: perhaps the "Father Francis," spoken of by him but never met by me, who was eventually his conduct to Nenuphar. Few letters that predate his entry into the monastery are included, however, and I believe his abbot edited the heck out of them.

By the time I showed up, the bread lines in Chicago streets stretched like a breathing stamp collection. Roosevelt was trying whatever he could, and my guardian was practicing tithing. "You're not seeing us at our best," he told me as we drove out to Oak Park past splotches of the unemployed, soup kitchens, Hoovervilles, movie palaces playing Myrna Loy in *When Ladies Meet,* and news vendors shrieking up Capone. "Well, maybe with some exceptions. Who knows?"

His agency had kept a firm grip on the ledge, making up for the lost business from failing department stores, granaries, and abattoirs with commissions from shoddy amusement parks, circuses, and dance marathons. While I don't know what they teach you in school, Panama, you shouldn't picture middle-class life simply evaporating during the Depression, then springing back just in time to welcome the boys home from Tarawa with every calico tablecloth and beaming, secretly murderous Beulah in place. I did go to a private school, and my guardian was no millionaire: just a man who went on respecting gentility's social values after he'd started rejecting its spiritual ones. By and large, the bourgeoisie to which I've never quite managed to stop belonging held its roost, just on a tree stripped of its leaves and frailer branches by a hurricane. Unofficial motto: "Whatever you do, don't look down."

My guardian felt helpless not to, but Communism had no appeal for him: "They aren't wrong, Pam. But they are misguided," he was to primly tell my avid Barnard incarnation. The first issue of *The Catholic Worker* might as well have been printed in Eureka, NY, when he bought it for the fabled penny in the spring of '33.

As I've already reported myself telling Andy Pond, more conventional Catholics were appalled at the madwoman's heresy. Her campaign to turn the Gospels into a how-to manual struck them as not only bizarre in theory—"That was then, and honestly! Should we go back to riding camels, too?" one especially snooty Purcey's senior sniffed one day, no doubt quoting straight from the parental fount, as she snuffed an illicit cigarette in the fourth-form loo—but dangerously socialistic in practice, no matter how strenuously Miss Day tried to pass off the resemblance as some sort of mixup at the paternity ward. A certain thoughtful Chicago ad executive, however, was sold.

"She made me understand that the purpose of thought was to provoke behavior," he writes in Letter 123 of *The Mountain and the Stream*. As someone who's never been sure what, exactly, *Madame Bovary* is bidding us to *do*, I have to dissent from that, but this is his pilgrimage and not mine.

Soon in contact with the *Worker*'s only begetter, by late fall he was scouting property for Chicago's first House of Hospitality, as the *Worker*'s free food-and-lodging edifices were officially known. "I don't remember needing to be *taught* to take showers," that same Purcey's senior said. That led un-Christian Pam to un-Christianly picture her gasping under a cold one, shielding her deeply uninteresting frigleaf and lively little badminton birdies from our thigh-whacking, bobble-bopping truncheons.

Yet I don't want my schoolgirl snits to distract from Nick's quest. For the rest of his life, even after they differed—after Pearl Harbor and before Hiroshima, like so many people, he had serious problems with her pacifism—there was only one *Dorothy* in my guardian's hesaurus.

You know what? The hell with it, Panama. Writers are born to seize on coincidences the rest of you find meaningless. Hello, old Scarecrow.

POSTED BY: *Pämchen in Uniform* It was to be over a year before I actually met her. (September 1935: Dorothy voyages to the Midwest to rally her troops. I suppose you *could* look it up.) Up to then, even as I defended the

Worker's only begetter from the dormant Tories in Purcey's dorms and lava-
tories, I can't say I'd thought about her much on my own hook. A half sawn
product of Chignonne's, I reacted to my guardian's awakened faith with a sort
of charmed bafflement that religion could be an internal matter, perplexing
and harassing intelligent people—of their own volition, too—as if it were an
emotion or a relationship.

As for Purcey's Girls' Academy of St. Paul, Minnesota, it was nondenominational in the brochure and Episcopalian in practice, my guardian having done his
best to guess dead Daisy's wishes on that front. Talk about through a glass darkly,
too. Too bad for Jesus that the all-girl student body was also all adolescent, caught
as if by motion-study photographs in various stages of pimples, surprise fuzz, col-
leen *collines* made of pale flesh, and hormonal moans—for Clark Gable, mostly,
but with Tyrone Power ready to assist the cowards—along with sneaked cigs, the
eternal hairstyle steeplechase (Pam a nonstarter there), rhetorical lewdness, and
one honest-to-gosh alkie: Sigourney Keota of Skunk River, Iowa, nearly expelled
after she threw up all over Longfellow and they found the white lightning. No
wonder the sermons in chapel had an unswervingly cautionary tilt.

We heard an awful lot about how our bodies were temples, prompting
Harmony Preston, who came from La Crosse and played it too, to hoot "Who
does *your* temple pray to?" as she sashayed back across the Quad one Sunday.
If wishes were visible, ten or twelve Gables, three or four Tyrones, two Robert Youngs, and one puckish Mickey Rooney—my God, was Sigourney *that*
sozzled?—would've materialized in the dorms at lights out. As for Pink Thing's
own solo jimmyings of the temple door—oh, don't go all blushy on me, bikini
girl! I'm sure you do the same, not that I imagine your dad wants to think about
that too much—they were usually provoked by mildly mournful alloys of
moments left unseen in the *Thin Man* series. I always did aim for sophisticated.

Spare me, boys. I'm well aware which Thirties flick any male readers daisys-
daughter.com may have are praying I'll reprise. *Mädchen in Uniform*, preferably
colorized, in Purceyish reenactment, yes? Even Cadwaller asked, so I know
you're all hopeless. Since *l'équipe* wants to be user-friendly, I'll do my best to
dredge something up, but I warn you it's not much. I personally found and find
it about as erotic as a month-old Spam sandwich.

Basketball practice, winter '36 or '37: Buchanan, gawky but determined forward, wrenches her shoulder. Miss Hormel, intramural coach and instructor in French—you *bet* she thought the world of me, folks—thinks a long soak in the tub with salts will do better at getting the kinks out than the nasty communal showers back in Radclyffe Hall. Fortunately, the teachers have private ones, waiting on their short white little Pekinese legs with their silver tongue-faucets panting.

My shoulder did hurt like the blazes; I accepted. What did I care? I can't remember if Hormel moused up the nerve to wash my Pamback or just stood in the open door, swapping blather for lather with diffident questions about Bawdyleer. While I don't mean to be cruel, I could've been *raging* to yield to the Charybdis temptation, just champing to get my strawberries soaped, and that accent would still have depressed me. Anyhow, she was furry, fifty, fat, squat, and fearful—you know, no great advertisement for Sappho's delights, any more than I was the gal to put more than the tall in Tallulah. At least the Lotus Eater had been pretty. End of pornographic sex scene.

She did ask why I no longer wrote poetry, dumbfounding me with her frank if unwitting admission she was too stupid to breathe. It'd taken me two years of hard work—basketball, sneaked cigs, *Thin Man* movies, Eleanor Roosevelt jokes—to exorcise the Pam, still only a half vivisected frog, who'd spent a whole wretched semester wiping off pie or worse in Purcey's halls after the appearance in *Pink Rosebuds* of "Chanson d'automne." My lesson learned, I'd gotten a hell of a lot better at being a fake Midwestern private-school girl than poor Hormel would ever be at passing for heterosexual on any continent.

"Because I'm rotten at it?" I wonderingly asked her tile wall. "Jeez, everybody ought to be counting their blessings I catch on fast. Don't you think, Miss Hormel?"

That wasn't too charitable of me, since she was the kind of teacher who got rattled when asked her opinion of anything. Her class handed down Greatness with no Hormelized mediating, and I'd once struck horror into her squat soul by idly saying Corneille bored me. All things considered, she didn't do badly, though.

"Well! Ahm, well. Ah, Pam. You weren't all that good at basketball when you went out for the team, but I didn't see you giving up on that."

"Sure, but come on. Look at me, Miss Hormel," I said, which was probably *really* unkind. "I'm the tallest girl in school except for Bellaire Petoskey from Wolverine, Michigan. There's 'good at,' Miss Hormel—then there's 'right for.' I started with a lot of 'right for.'"

"I thought you did at poetry too," she muttered, leaping like a lemming into the void of a judgment unconfirmed by the world's approbation.

Well, I'd pretty much had it. Decided, as if I'd had any doubt, this wasn't the tub for me. Fidgety little loon with her scalded-looking upper lip, her Bawdyleer.

I stood up. "Tell you what, Miss Hormel. I'll try again next time my mother dies."

POSTED BY: *Pam*   Fortunately, I do not own and have no wish to own a copy of the Fall 1934 edition of *Pink Rosebuds*. Though it took me a good decade, I've successfully expunged most of my poemess from Pink Thing's archives. During the rest of my time at Purcey's, I wrote for the yearbook, not our simpering lit mag. And in English, since I wasn't a fool.

To give you an idea of the flavor, the only line of "Chanson d'automne" I remember is *"dans les grands blés sanglotants."* Its bathos was most likely inspired, to use the utterly wrong word, by the landscape chugging by on my trips from Chicago to school and back. Farewell to my guardian at Dearborn station, then a snip of Illinois and a lot of Wisconsin before we came into Minneapolis six or seven lion-pelted, intermittently bovine hours later. From there, I'd hop into a taxi—the now familiar Negro porter wrestling my trunk—for the backward zip across the river to St. Paul.

Oh, Pam, you unspeakably privileged twat! Hop in by all means. Stroll past the railroad guards checking the Los Angeles–bound freights for jumpers. Feel curious at a purely war-whoop and firewater level about the alcoholic Chippewas for whom, alone among the puzzled hundreds trying to sweep streets with their shoes, the Depression hasn't changed things much. Earn your imaginary movie audience's contempt with your ignorance of the meaning of all the impressive historical scenery.

A fairly serious amateur of the American past in his spare time, Gerson couldn't abide that cheap vein of "We know better now" irony, and while I'm prejudiced, he was right. I was in my teens, fresh from seven years abroad. I had a very hard time believing any of this looked different from exactly how it was supposed to look in its role as a quondam backdrop to my life.

Panama, at that age, in my shoes, it's *all* Oz. My guardian's attempt to help put things right on Dorothy Day's yellow brick road, which I defended simply because anything he did was unimpeachable, struck me as one more fixture of this universe, not an effort to amend its rules. He was the one who gave me cab fare, presumably for dead Daisy's sake, to cross the river in style to my second-rate (cf. Hormel) private school.

Anyhow, I guarantee my image of *"les grands blés sanglotants"* had no socio-economic dimension, even if it does sound like the title in French translation of some lesser Steinbeck novel. The real epiphany of one train trip had nothing to do with either the "sobbing" wheat and rye or the Depression, and I claim it transcended both.

On a Pullman going south, Pam reads a discarded schedule. Goggling, she learns Muscatine's a *place*. Thinking of it as a product, like Crisco or Rice Krispies, I'd pictured Iowans frothing in it up to their sudsy necks after my guardian's sales job, happy to be keeping clean in Muscatine. That's what I should've written a poem about. I might have if "Chanson d'automne" hadn't cured me forever of trying.

My guardian often took a train north to visit me, since there was a Worker house in St. Paul whose bedding and cookware he'd had a hand in supplying. After celibately squiring me around on the Saturday, he'd stay over to volunteer on the Sunday, sharing the dispossesseds' lives as Dorothy wished. Then back to Chicago on Monday, determined to find urgency in the rhetorical pretense that Ypsilanti could use more Rice Krispies or only no Crisco stood between Toledo and joy. If you find that absurd, may I recommend Belgium? I promise you'll be happier there.

Naturally, once it got around he wasn't a relative, his twinkling, patient waits for Pam in the lobby of Nordhoff Hall—a man then in his forties, his gray hair closely cropped, hat to slackly draped thigh and jacket parted to announce his no longer trim waistline's second act, all finished off by his one Twenties souvenir, white shoes—were bound to excite comment. Girls will say anything about anyone but themselves.

"Get wise. What does he want with you, Buchanan?" said Cass Lake of Deer River, Minnesota. (Or was it Marion Swayzee of Kokomo, Illinois, Alma Franklin from the vicinity of Red Cloud, Nebraska? *Où sont mes vierges d'antan?*) "I bet he's just an old lech. One snowy night, he's going to—"

"He is not. And you don't know what you're talking about." Hormel was going to like this *composition*, or rather cum-paw-Z-shun. I could've done it in my sleep, probably had more than once. I slammed my book shut.

"A lech? Oh, but I say he is. They all are. Maybe he was the same lech you saw on Cape—"

"God! I can't stand that word. Can't you be stupid with more *variety*?" (If he ever reads this, Andy Pond may well call that quote "Dawn.")

"What, 'lech'? Ooh, Buchanan doesn't like to hear 'lech.' Lech, lech, lech, lech!"

Five foot ten of basketball player belted her tormentor's shoulder, which shouldn't have even made Cass blink—or was it big Sandy Hingham from near Chester, Montana? At Purcey's, we used to smack each other around like sumo wrestlers, only trimmer. But she rubbed her arm: "Ouch, Buchanan. I was teasing."

It's true, though. I did hate to hear women say "lech," common enough slang though it had been since my childhood. My guess is the aversion's source was my lonely bilingualism, since *lèche, lécher, lécheuse,* and so on meant something altogether different if no more, in some contexts, palatable. Since I was trying to be an uncomplicated American girl in my ersatz way, the distraction must've annoyed me.

POSTED BY: *Pam*   Having put in time among the grandees of Hollywood, Washington, D.C., and what used to be called the Third World, I'm responsibly placed to tell you this. To the last man or woman, the egotists who burst upon us with the news they've transcended their egotism have unknowingly only sublimated it. During the Great Depression, the Dorothy who found her Scarecrow in my guardian was an example to beat the band.

What I won't do is beam after that remark as if it's a grand slam that puts the troublemaker in her place, letting the rest of us go airily back to discussing the futility of everything. Sublimation is as sublimation does, and she got a lot of people fed.

Thanks to my presence in September of 1935 at Dorothy Day's lunch with my guardian, the future Brother Nicholas, I can also report a certain amount of comedy is involved in entertaining a saint. Don't think I'm speaking figuratively, as the Vatican has started to kick canonization down the road. She'll be only the third American woman with her own Catholic baseball card, and sometimes I wish I hadn't been fifteen the only time I met her. More often, I'm glad I was.

It was understood they weren't going to eat at the St. Paul Worker house itself. Dorothy had shared a thousand meals with her flock of capitalism's displaced, but under the pressure of a tour including radio talks, personal appearances to browbeat the well-heeled into forking over, and the continuance of her column in the *Worker* while she traveled—it was still "Day by Day" then, not "On Pilgrimage"—she could honestly use a break. Her brusque request to my guardian to find some decent place for lunch before she shot on to St. Cloud and Milledgeville without him tested even his acute sense of appropriateness just the same. In Dorothy's vocabulary, "decent" had enough potentially clashing meanings to make the Sphinx go crosseyed.

The future Brother Nicholas obviously couldn't take her to one of the posher places where, as dedicated in his job as guardian as he was in serving Dorothy, he treated me to non-Purcey meals on his visits. She'd've been on her feet before the appetizers, prowling for rich folk who looked Catholic and demanding that they open their wallets. He did want her to have a good meal, however, and after some hunting settled on a plausible-looking Italian place, one checked tablecloth and jacketed waiter up the scale from a workingman's café. It was all of a block from the former appliance store whose windows now proclaimed in hand-lettered white paint, *The Catholic Worker Hospitality House. All are welcome. Whatever ye do unto the least of these my brethren, ye do unto Me.*

Pam was surprised to be brought along. Though he was pleased anytime I asked about it, my guardian had never tried to get me involved in relief work. I'd never even gone to see him at either this Worker house or the one in Chicago where he spent most of his Sundays cooking for fifty. "Cooking for four, I can't do," he'd said once. "They know where to find you, after all. But fifty? I can just blend into the angry crowd."

My recollection is lunch was his only chance to see me this trip, since he was in St. Paul as Dorothy's facilitator and not Pam's guardian for a change. I only wish the old bachelor's concerns had included the odd fashion tip. So help me, I think I was wearing white gloves.

If his worry had been the ambiance, he'd wasted his time. I suspect Miss Day came into *everyplace* as if it were a train station in disguise.

"Dorothy! We're over here," my guardian called just before her unbraked momentum would've taken her into the kitchen for a word with the conductor. "Dorothy, this is my ward, Pa—"

"I probably shouldn't eat at all," she said rapidly, sitting down in a chair that had needed its wits about it to be in the right place at the right time. "I've just found out I'm speaking *tonight* in St. Cloud. Virgil talked the Lions into giving me my say, but I hate what all this does to my nerves. Nothing but butterflies in my stomach! Oh, well. I suppose I can't let them starve."

"No—they didn't know what they were getting into, either. But you speak in public all the time," my guardian said affectionately.

"The Light Brigade charged, too. What's your point? Oh God. Is this a menu or my schedule? Nick, am I due to speak to Neal Parmegian at eighty o'clock?"

She still had that Saracen nose you see in earlier photographs. In the later ones, the rest of her face seems to have crept gauntly forward to keep it company. She hadn't yet started doing her hair in the tightly wound braid whose resemblance to a crown of thorns might've struck you as hubris if it hadn't looked so practical. In the restaurant, she sat with her hands coiled around her elbows, turning her torso into a shell for her face to thrust forward from. I swear she kept kicking the table.

"Have we had any word about more beds for the Detroit Worker house? I'm sorry, but I didn't have time to find out myself."

"Six are on their way." My guardian looked pleased.

"Six? They're sleeping in the bathtubs! A whole factory closes, and you found me six beds? And smile? What are we here for?"

"To have lunch before your train goes." He said it so gently I wondered if she genuinely needed the reminder. "Six beds is six more, and let's face it, I'm not you. I can't perform miracles, Dorothy."

"I don't. But nothing in the Gospels says we aren't allowed to try."

Was I awed to be in her presence? While I'd love to say yes, the truth is the whole torrent of words had left me on the riverbank. At loose ends, I was wondering if I should tell my guardian what I'd discovered about the new draftsman at his agency on my last visit there that summer.

"What can I say? You've always known I don't have the stuff," he cheerfully told Miss Day. "It's been the same ever since Yale. I only got into religion in a failed bid to make myself popular."

"Hah! Did I tell you about one *wonderful* letter I got last year? Oh, it was sublime. Its author prayed God would give him the patience to endure my what was it, 'lunacy,' until the police shut us down for encouraging loafers, traitors, and—oh, yes!—'publicity-seeking psychotics.' My hunch is that last fine phrase was lobbed in my direction unless he meant Maurin. It was written by a priest."

Surprised—I shouldn't have been—I laughed. That obliged Miss Day to absorb my inclusion at the table: the white gloves, a frilled blouse I quite liked in real life, tulip skirt. Thrillingly grown-up stockings too, but I'm not going to indulge any male daisysdaughter.com readers I may have. For God's sake, back then we *all* wore garter belts! Under the impression they were practical.

"What sort of work do you do for us?" she asked as if she'd missed shaking hands with me among the volunteers at the Worker house.

"I'm in school," I said, stumped.

"I've been trying to introduce you, Dorothy. This is my ward, Pamela Buchanan. Daisy's daughter. Let up on her, will you, she's not even—"

"Catholic?" Miss Day guessed. [Wrongly, I think: my guess is Nick was about to say "sixteen."] "Yes, yes, I know: the excuses for doing nothing are endless. I do realize it's not your fault. I met your mother once or twice." With a swift smile, she tossed her face ceilingward: "Well, that certainly came out wrong! Oh, they're going to love me in St. Cloud tonight, Nick. At this rate?"

Pam was shy about asking, but in those days I read the way otters swim and I'd been mad for *The Emperor Jones*. "Miss Day, excuse me. Did you really know Eugene O'Neill?"

Message from a future edition of Pamela to a prior one: for Christ's sake, act on any curiosity you've got about O'Neill *now*. Once you've married Murphy, you'll learn he can't abide the name. One of several major differences between them is that O'Neill will have no idea they're rivals.

In the meantime, the detectable narrowing of Miss Day's eyes had mystified me. I didn't know she disliked being reminded of her free-and-easy bohemian youth—concerned, so she said, that young people would assail their parents with "If Dorothy Day did it, why can't I?" Then she decided to concede I was fifteen and therefore asking about a Great Man, not the one she'd drunk under the table in Village saloons.

"Oh, I knew all sorts of people then," she said not unkindly. "Gene was struggling for God in his own way, I think. Black Irish, you know—they always do it by insulting Him." I don't normally capitalize that *H*, Panama, but believe me, she did. "Why, does writing interest you?"

"She writes poetry," my guardian said proudly. After the effort he'd put into deciphering "Chanson d'automne" a year earlier, he wasn't about to admit he needn't have bothered. I shudder to think the copy of *Pink Rosebuds* the poetess fulsomely inscribed to him may still exist somewhere.

"Then you should talk your uncle into writing for the *Worker*," she told me. That not only promoted him with such certainty that he and I eyed each other as if we might as well enjoy our new connection but proved Dorothy Day was Dorothy Day without letup. "I was hectoring him to try half the way from Chicago. I think he'd have a gift."

"Oh, no," my guardian said. "One year, I wrote a series of *very* solemn and obvious editorials for the *Yale News*. The relief when we parted was mutual. Besides, I've been writing ads too long. Stringing together above eight words at a time would feel unnatural."

I knew that wasn't strictly true, since he'd once told me a bit awkwardly that he'd tried to set down his memories of my mother for my benefit after her death. Yet he didn't feel he'd captured her, so he said—my own hunch is the portrait came out more unsympathetic than was fit for her daughter to read—and ended up burning the thing.

If he was fibbing about destroying the manuscript, I'll never know. Nenuphar kept his effects when he died, and there can't have been many of those. As I'm not blood kin or in contact with Nick's surviving relatives, if any, I've got no access to them.

"Stuff and nonsense," Miss Day told him. "Or quite possibly vanity. Where do you think I'm going to write Monday's column? On the train to St. Cloud. Will it be artful? Of course not. Will it say things worth saying? All we can do is hope."

"Can I ask the subject?"

"Oh, Nick! Don't look at me that way. Or do, since I couldn't care less and it seems to give you a peculiar sort of agonized pleasure. Yes, I'm going to be writing about the tenant farmers' strike *again*. And yes, I'm going to tell the *Worker's* readers to send every penny they can spare to the union. They've got nothing, nothing! Isn't it bad enough I have to listen to Peter about this?"

"I think Maurin's right," my guardian said stubbornly. "I don't think we should be taking stands in these labor disputes. People are only too happy to lump us in with the Communists as is, and it gets the movement involved with, well, 'Caesar's things.' That's not personalism to me. And more important"—and if you want proof he was no revolutionary, here it is; pay close attention, Panama—"my feeling is that we have to think carefully about where we want to be standing, and with whom, when this current economic crisis ends. Because it will."

I'm told Dorothy very seldom reverted to the loose talk of her Village days, making my most cherished *viva voce* quote from the saint more precious. If any reader cares to pass it on to the Vatican's canonization crew, be my guest.

"Oh, balls, Nick," she said. "Now is now."

Despite an avuncular glance my way—unsure of her best move, Pam tried to make her face simultaneously communicate that I heard people say "Balls" all the time and didn't have a clue what it meant—my guardian smiled. "And 'sufficient to the day is the evil thereof.' Is that it?"

"That's all she wrote!" Dorothy agreed. "Well, actually, I hope not. That's death."

"Pam, what is it?" my guardian asked.

"Oh! I'm sorry," I said. "I just used to know someone who said that all the time."

"Oh who?"

They must both have realized what a neglected third party I was. It was an improvised interest, as when you collar the dullard about to go neck with God-knows-whom by announcing that you *must* know where she got that dress. Pam was fifteen, didn't know the better part of valor is vagueness. Soon to do my college share of necking with God-knows-whom and then some, smoothing my undeterred hips and mumbling "Saks, Saks," I found myself lamely describing the woman you know as the Lotus Eater. Without going into the syringe bit or the Charybdean bent, of course.

"Why, I know that name," Dorothy astonished me by saying. "Isn't that odd? Nick, I was in prison with her mother."

"Which time?"

"Occoquan, during the suffrage days. I regret it now—misdirected energy." Then she grinned like a toothy iguana. "But you're always sentimental about your first time in jail."

POSTED BY: *Pam*   "Do you like her, though?" I asked my guardian on my next trip to Chicago, all tangled knees and feeling my way at the concept of admiration independent of affection.

He smiled. "Oh, Pam! Nobody *likes* her. She won't allow it: too mundane. Of course plenty of us adore her, but that's our lookout. I think she's reasonably fond of herself, but I guarantee it's completely impersonal."

By then, I'd decided I wasn't going to say anything about the illicit drawings the new draftsman at his agency made on the side. I know it sounds as if Pam did more snooping than Nancy Drew, so please remember I'm leaving out all sorts of days when I *didn't* nose around like a ferret. That Sunday back in sluggish, glazed, Chicagooey August, my guardian and I had been on our way to the zoo.

Driving past his agency's building, he remembers a portfolio he needs. Once he flicks it open on the desk in his back office, a recollected deadline dictates a phone call: "No more than ten minutes, I swear." In the outer room, its three drafting tables and two copywriters' desks deadened by weekend sunlight's optical version of a drone, Pam gets drugged on one of adolescence's most perishable moods, never felt by anyone over sixteen: mild spookiness combined with utter boredom.

Through the partly opened door, I can see the right-hand edge of an old placard, white lettering on a blue background: OU, then the much larger AN of "CLEAN," then back to smaller type for the TINE of "MUSCATINE." Brief game of eye Scrabble gets nowhere: no I, a tune. Bits of guardian's strangely artificial phone voice (when he talks on a long-distance line, I'm usually on the other end in St. Paul), half droll and half exasperated: "Well, how did he get the idea it's in the Midwest? Can *someone* explain that to me?"

Hum, hum. Flies hum, I hum. They can't carry a tune. No, I can't. On the new man's drafting table, a rough for an illustration to good old Vern Jewel's copy for the upcoming zeppelin show attracts Pam's admiring but untrained eye. What else is he working on? Heave up the pad's page, big as a skirt.

As I recall, the respective dimensions of that cock and the puny man wielding it were those of the Washington Monument and a hairless chimpanzee. At least in Pink Thing's salvage job, though, his partner is drawn in a detail lascivious enough to arouse Sean Finn's envy: not just a black button on each white cupcake, but twin worms of paler dark to promontorize the nipples. Each curl of adult femininity's parachute emblem is as caressed and embossed as the more famous hairdo up top. Overlarge in the same style as more legit Thirties cartoons, the head would've been recognizable even if the first panel hadn't provided a title: *Gabby Chatterton in 'Who're You Callin' a Dyke, You Whore?'*

Have you ever heard of Tijuana bibles, Panama? I'm sure Tim has, but can see how they might not be the stuff of father-daughter moments. Contraband more lurid than heroin, they featured famous people—either figures of real-world renown or barely disguised fictional characters like Little Morphine Annie, though I'm not sure any smut-stained wretch ever went to the extreme of fusing the two—in situations whose appeal combined crazed lust with simmering resentment. Making its way to Purcey's, one that starred Cary Grant had been squawked at by a bouquet of damn near purple rosebuds until Flora Olney of Mt. Carmel, Illinois, our most dogged reader of the actual Bible, leapt up wreathed in wrath to seize the thing and chuck it in the incinerator. So she said.

And Gabby Chatterton? Oh, she was another Thirties screwball comedienne. Her name could as easily have been Claudette Harlow or Myrna Alloy. I admit that when I met her in Hollywood a dozen years later, I felt gunshy about shaking hands.

Her own legs locked together—I might as well have had a tourniquet around both knees, from which you shouldn't infer any literal equivalent whatsoever—Pam keeps feeling like she needs to whiz but knows she doesn't. She can't figure out if what's left of her brain is screaming at her guardian to get off the phone or screaming at him to realize he needs more privacy and close his office door. Hearing his tone shift to the staccato preliminaries of goodbye, I let the pad's top page fall back down, half expecting my face to go with it in the optical effect known in old Hollywood as a vertical wipe.

Out came my guardian, who I knew had never done anything like *that*— much less *that!*—in his life. "So!" he said, scratching his head. "Off to the zoo now, yes? I'm sorry to've kept you dawdling. But I've only known one man in my life who didn't know where San Francisco was, and he's long dead."

Quoth Pam, "Could we please go to the movies instead? *Wings in the Dark* is at the Roxy."

POSTED BY: *St. Pam*   Crazed with self-important hysteria—no tune, just I and more I—and eager to erase, no, crush its cause, I spent weeks tempted to tell him his new draftsman moonlighted as a pornographer. By the time he brought me back to Purcey's after our lunch with Dorothy Day, I'd decided I wouldn't, and I didn't.

My guardian would've had to fire him. Not even for the offense so much as my exposure, tarnishing his honor as the man dead Daisy had chosen to look after her daughter. This was the mid-Thirties and the new man was everyone's junior. Plenty of people had trouble making ends meet, though I'm sure Nick paid the best wages he could.

Not that you could've convinced me then, but there are worse things in this world than illustrating Tijuana bibles, too. In that category, I'd include some people's ideas of how to illustrate the New Testament.

You see, Panama? I didn't want his unemployment on my conscience: rote concept since Chignonne's, now internalized. My silence helped keep one unspeakably filthy-minded man afloat in the Depression. It wasn't quite feeding the hungry, and definitely a far cry from clothing the naked, but I did my part.

Perhaps to my guardian's unvoiced regret (he wouldn't have voiced it to save his life), I was never tempted to convert to Catholicism. That's despite occasionally thinking I'd've made a sensational nun. Nor was I ever a pacifist, and Andy Pond among others can tell you I'm no ascetic. I honored Dorothy Day in my own way.

If the Church does canonize her, I'm glad I won't be here to see it. What, a "publicity-seeking psychotic"? (Yes, that letter was real.) It could be the most hypocritical thing the Vatican's done since they glued Joan of Arc's charred remnants back together after burning her. Unless drinking Eugene O'Neill under the table counts, it would also be nonsense to pretend they've turned up even one miracle—the minimum cover charge, I'm told, for admission to the club.

The tribute I'd like to see, and fat chance too, is a WPA-style mural in the Capitol. The Minneapolis Chippewas, Chicago Negroes, Mott Street bums, and Los Angeles Okies should be shuffling toward a storefront whose window proclaims, *Whatever ye do unto the least of these my brethren, ye do unto Me.* Front and center, her Scarecrow beside her, is that perfect pain in the hoo-ha: St. Dorothy of the Depression.

If the artist's any good, and I know who I'd hire if perchance The Unknown Draftsman's still alive, lip readers will be able to guess what she's saying: "Oh, balls. Now is now." Someone waves a union sign. In a corner, one man's contentedly flipping through a Tijuana bible.

He's their Savior, Panama, not mine. The only vital role Christianity has played in my life was its responsibility for the construction of the church of St. Sulpice in Paris. That was because I fell in love with your great-grandfather when he and his pipe were mulling other things while standing in front of it.

Even so, I'd like to know how come they treat their Good Book as if it came from Tijuana. They ransack it for the dirty parts—e.g., "The poor you shall always have with you"—that let them work off their most brutal aggressions and resentments. Why do they masturbate to the Word of God? Why is the only part of the thing they can't and won't take literally the Sermon on the Mount? How has Chad Diebold made it all Aramaic to them?

POSTED BY: *Pam*   Kuala tea: that was the pun. "Oh, no, Sir! The kuala tea of Mercy is not strained." A nonsensical joke, Panama, but you were seven. Still in the habit of threshing the uncountable, endlessly shuckable fingers of one hand with the other. Round (it was then) face crammed with the forthcoming giggle. Your Gramela's laugh at the silly capper came mostly from pleasure that, like your pretzelly ex-namesake, you were drawn to the circus tricks of words.

Yet the mouths of babes do their best work when they burst out laughing and divulge a wet secret. As I applauded with rheumatic fingers, it occurred to me that unlike intellect or even humor—if I know myself, I'd go on bawling jokes on a desert island, naked as the first day I was bored and awaiting only my gal Friday—mercy, whether strained or not, can only exist in relation to someone else.

I've tried to brew Andy some kuala tea. Opening a fresh document and setting the font size to 72-point type, I've just clacked this out in boldface: **ANDY—DON'T COME IN. CALL THE POLICE. PAM.**

My printer purred at its rare, too brief treat. Exiled to the table, Cadwaller's gun looked anxious: did it have a rival? (Flatterer! Don't worry, Pam'll be back soon.) Then I tottered out to take my best try at mercy to the foyer. If 72-point boldface type on the endtable where my mail piles up can stop Andy in time, he'll be spared the sight of my mess of pink and gray things on the rug.

There was nothing to weight it with but Kelquen's collar. Full name, Ilya Kelquen, derived from Andy's announcement—*"Il y a quelqu'un dans la maison"*—as he deposited a live bundle of tortie fur in this same foyer not long after I moved here from Georgetown in '87. The unmistakable femininity her trotting tail soon displayed was another reminder that Andy's French is a joke. A good one, though, since he treats speaking it as intrinsically humorous. ("American diplomats don't have skills, they have hobbies"—Cadwaller.)

Her collar has stayed on the marble-topped endtable since Andy brought me back here from the last trip I'll take to any vet's. Perhaps it's obvious why your mind will fix on oddities, but I remember thinking so at the time, glancing around the exam room as Kelquen got vaguely interested in a bird outside the window and Dr. Miranda explained their eyes don't close. After decades of bringing pets to animal hospitals, I'd just realized I'd have no further use for an entire profession.

That list has gotten considerably longer since dawn. No more Hardy Boys doctors, never again a *Popular Mechanics* dentist or voluptuous or frowning-lipped lab assistant hunting for a vein in my arm's tapioca and balsa. No ninepin waiters ("More wine!," or maybe more kuala tea) at La Chaumière. No more grandfatherly photographers on holiday from teaching others the craft producing exquisite images of bikini girls.

As of today, the only two helpmeets of any use or consequence to me are a White House operator and the President of the United States. And now I think of it, not without amusement, you could call mine an *assisted* suicide. Potus opposes helping folks turn up their toes-es, adding a bonus to Pam's intent to draft him as my Kervorkian.

Afterward—just so long as it isn't beforehand, Cadwaller's gun!—there'll be police. An undertaker: Gawler's, most likely, pretty much the Foreign Service's belly-up answer to Grand Central Station. Cleaning lady: I'd better make sure to leave a note to Andy and write an extra-hefty check as her bonus for wiping up the last of Pink Thing and Gray Thing. Will any of me hit the wall, I wonder? Except on television, I haven't seen anybody shot in the head since 1945.

Kelquen's collar is where it is only because depositing it in the Paris foot-locker would be too hard a farewell. In the two years since, I've occasionally caught Andy eyeing that circlet of name-tagged turquoise leather as he considers and then cancels a suggestion. That he always checks to see if it's still there is why I'm gambling my 72-point boldface shriek will stop him before he steps into the living room.

As a further tipoff, I thought of leaving my wedding ring there too. Unless he's really slipped a few cogs, to Andy that would be the difference between guessing and knowing. But trying to work it off my finger would deter the average graverobber, let alone tapioca-and-balsa me. Kelquen's collar will have to do.

Yes, Andy: like my last cat, I'll soon be nowhere and nothing. (Good *God!* Why don't those stupid, lazy bastards call? Who's running things down there today, FEMA?) Please, though, the rest of you, even if you're children: no sentimentality about the old bag's imminent reunion with Kelquen. I promise she and I would race to see which of us could cough up a bigger furball. When you call animals dumb, remember that they make themselves fewer illusions than we do about death.

POSTED BY: *P. B.*   As anyone who owns *The Mountain and the Stream* knows, my guardian, once my parents' closest friend in East Egg and later St. Dorothy of the Depression's Scarecrow, passed away in 1968 in a hospital in Davenport, Iowa. He was a few months short of turning seventy-six and had led a full if, to mimsies with as much appetite for the world as Pam's, bewilderingly renunciatory life. I still regret how a nurse's thoughtlessness flooded his own eyes with misery during his final afternoon of breathing this planet's air. Hospital-canned, but breath's breath and air's air.

His week as a terminal heart patient was the only time in twenty-one years Brother Nicholas, as he'd been known since 1947, had left the grounds of Nenuphar, the monastery between Davenport and Iowa City where he'd spent what must be one of the longest novitiates in the order's history. He'd always refused ordination; I may be the only one who knows why. I'm proud that Letter 86, the fullest of several explanations of his decision to become a monk, is addressed to "P.B.," the maximum extent to which any of us recipients are identified in print. Like the others, it makes no mention of his lone qualm about Christian doctrine, a secret he shared with me just hours before the end.

As I think I've mentioned, he'd parted ways with Dorothy over her unrevised pacifism after December 7th, 1941. Letter 45, which is the final one to "D.D." and was written soon after Hiroshima, expresses his regret at his shortsightedness: "I didn't know it would come to this, that's all. What I think you saw long ago is that it doesn't need to come to this to teach us there's no middle way." His view, not mine, but his former ward can understand his horror.

His world had turned decisively inward during the war years. In Letter 22, which was also to P.B. and came mud-scuffed to the correspondents' villa at Nettuno on the Anzio beachhead, he writes, "I'll always stick by anyone trying to alleviate suffering. But it'll never go away, and I guess not so deep down I'm one of the ones stuck trying to understand why that's our condition and not, as D____ believes, a temporary obstruction to achieving it."

The list of recommended reading he'd enclosed got whisked to shout-filled oblivion when a couple of Messerschmitts dropped out of the sky and we had to make a run for it to the dugout. It vanished along with my Anzio Bobbsey twin Bill M.'s unfinished sketch of Pam, GI-shoed and fist to chin, reading the letter from her former guardian. Since the names of the authors who'd most shaped his evolving thinking pack *The Mountain and the Stream*'s typo-riddled index (thank you, Vaughn Trapp & Co.: how did Donne turn into "Doremi"?), I doubt anything invaluable was lost. Brother, do I rue that lost sketch, though, even if Bill made up for it by doing *Nothing Like a Dame*'s jacket art three years later.

One letter his abbot returned, requesting I never make it public, was his answer to my long-brewed question—these things can be easier to bring up once there's an ocean between you—about why he'd never gotten married again. It made me laugh in a Normandy orchard, since I could practically hear his voice and see the smile creasing his face: "Pammie, what can I say? Emily Dickinson wouldn't have me."

POSTED BY: *P.A.*   In terms of his character, my guardian becoming a monk wasn't unduly hard for me to get my head around. As a social encounter, though, it was a little fidgety—for me, of course, not Brother Nicholas. The rules of his order allowed the novice no visitors at all for the first three years, then went all slack and sybaritic and let him choose one per annum. I was gratified when a letter to Mrs. Noah Gerson of Beverly Hills, California, invited me to be his first P.A.: that is, the one for 1950.

Isn't there something in the Book of Ruth about the alien corn? It was wheat and rye at Nenuphar, but the effect was similar even if they'd already harvested it. Under November's chilblained mix of cindery and violet stains, a roughly hewn bell tower reminded me of some I'd seen in Italy.

This one was whole, though: not even bullet-pocked. A man in a robe was herding a few white and auburn cattle along a rutted path. I'd been in Iowa City an hour ago, and behind my back it was sprouting nightclubs, George Groszian traffic, big-breasted hootchy-kootchy dancers now startlingly including the staid small-breasted chambermaid at my respectable downtown hotel, neon martini glasses the size of the Statue of Liberty's torch, skyscrapers, and general depravity at a dizzying clip. Then my guardian came toward me, also in a robe.

The big adjustment wasn't theological but sartorial. When a man you've known since girlhood as a reasonably snappy dresser appears before you in a roughly woven brown robe that reaches his ankles, no jury is going to convict you for feeling awkward, at least given that it's 1950. Then again, every other man in sight was dressed the same way, and *my* dull gray skirt was down to my ankles too: it had been fun to shop for that on Rodeo Drive. Kerchief over my head. You may not believe it, but the abbot's letter of instructions had included a discreet but unmistakable request to stay away if it was my time of the month.

Considering my overlapping confusions, it may be no wonder I scored a gaffe with my first salvo. The cabbie and I had kept the radio on the whole way out. "My *Gawd*, Nick!" I greeted him. "Can you believe the Chinese came in in Korea? I knew that idiot MacArthur would—"

"Pam, please," he stopped me very gently. "Didn't you get the abbot's letter? You must've, from how strangely you're dressed. We don't see newspapers here. No telephone, no radio. Or that *odd* new contraption Brother Howdy Doody had to go and spill the beans about last year," he added, his amusement indicating that some word of our diversions did slip through. "We caned him, of course."

I was still in too many places. The 38th Parallel, debauched—you wish, as Panama would say—Iowa City. Chicago, 1934; Italy. Here. "You didn't," I blurted.

"Oh, Pam! Come on, I'll show you around."

I knew I wouldn't get to see his cell. Or the rectory, for that matter. Women were allowed on the grounds if foreseen and accompanied, but not inside any of the buildings. Unornamented, as bluntly chopped in stone as if God's architect had been using his butter knife that day, they stood around me against vast backdrops of stubbled yellow. Only the grain silo behind the rectory had its familiar Iowa helmet on.

One monk walked by with a wheel of cheese, calling "Brother Nicholas" in greeting but ignoring me. Two more were sifting flour—outside, in November. Red hands. "Getting ready for Thanksgiving, I see," I said warily, to say something.

He laughed after looking confounded. "Did I really raise you? It isn't a *religious* holiday."

Why that broke the ice, I can't say—no, I can. He'd never claimed he'd raised me before.

"So what do you really do?" I asked. More cattle had just gone by.

"Oh, I've written you. Morning prayers, crack of dawn—we do tend to rattle them off a bit faster in February. Then we novices confer with our priests; I wish I could introduce you to mine. Then meditation and, in my case, correspondence. Manual labor in the afternoon."

"Doing what?"

"We make a pretty good cheese for a bunch of eremites, if I say so myself. It's sold commercially—not in California, though. Sorry. But our bread, Pam! We'll have it for lunch if you don't mind eating outdoors. I'd be baking soon if you weren't my P.A."

"And then?"

"Oh, we all go into Davenport and take in a show. No, no. In the evenings, Mass and our Office, followed by sleep and, believe me, pleasant dreams. After the first year, anyhow. The imagery changes after a while on our diet."

"Do you like it?" I asked bluntly. He was still Nick, after all.

"At my age—" he was fifty-eight that year—"it's nice to be a novice in just about any context. But let's hear about you. Who played you in the movie, anyone I'd remember? It must've come out by now."

"It did, and let's not talk about it. Rodgers and Hammerstein wouldn't let us use *Nothing Like a Dame* as the title, did I write you about that? So help me, it ended up being called *The Gal I Left Behind Me*. Whatever you do, please don't see it."

"Pammie, believe me. Whatever I do, I can't."

POSTED BY: *Pam*   The next time I was invited to be Brother Nicholas's P.A. was in 1955. I was so locked into *Glory Be* that I doubt I'd have heeded a king's summons—in fact, *especially* not a king's summons, given my democratic theme. One from Nick was different, and I realized I could move up my next trip in search of Virginia's Martha Shelton (b. 1707, d. 1745, and one of my real finds) and spend a night in Iowa City on the way.

I don't know who his annual guests were otherwise, but that was the same autumn I finally watched *The Wizard of Oz*, the black-and-white TV transmission turning the Munchkins into squeaky extras in a pygmy *The Grapes of Wrath*. Your Gramela does like to imagine the old Scarecrow creaking a Nenuphar gate open at dusk sometime in Ike's first term and saying, "Hello, Dorothy."

Anyhow, the picture that sobers the back cover of *The Mountain and the Stream*—believe me, "adorns" wouldn't be the right word—must've been taken around the year of my return visit. Flaked with motes by inept processing and badly underexposed, it shows him ladling bread into Nenuphar's oven with a long-handled baker's peel.

By then, the folds of his face had settled into their coiled life around the landlocked anchor formed by his eyes and mouth. His close-cropped gray hair was an element monkhood couldn't claim credit for, not unless it had his number long before he'd had its. He'd been wearing it that way when he'd met me at the boat.

This time the rough brown robe looked natural, of course, and Nenuphar had gone from an odd hacking of instant venerability in the Iowan landscape to a place reassuringly unchanged: a rarity in those years' hurry-up, Interstate-building America. In her latest hallucinatory incarnation as I faced the monastery, my demure Iowa City chambermaid—not even seen this trip, just recalled for her constrained manner from the previous one—had become a tight-sweatered, bosomy motorcycle moll, chewing gum as if she meant to introduce it to her newly dyed hair and clutching Marlon Brando's leather-clad back on smoky roads.

In front of me, another monk or perhaps the same one was herding different cattle, unless they were the same ones too. I had and have no idea how long cows live, and obviously none were ever slaughtered there.

"How is your, uh, Gerson?" Even if someone who went around saying Brother This and Brother That all day couldn't really complain about it, he'd always been left blank by my habit of calling my husbands by last name.

"Good," I said, which wasn't exactly true. Gerson'd long since left Metro to work for Rik-Kuk Productions, and Gene Rickey—that's Mr. Fran Kukla to you, Tim—was no boss for an intelligent man to suffer under. Since the likes of

Gene Rickey were what Nenuphar was designed to cancel, Nick had no need to hear about that.

The bakery doors were open, at least letting me glimpse the self-same kiln that's on *The Mountain and the Stream*'s back cover. A rural gal I've never been except by necessity in the ETO, but the smells of turned earth, that morning's bread, still warm unpasteurized milk, and cowflop around us were nice.

"You know, you never told me," he said. "Did you convert?"

"To Judaism? Lord, no. We were married at City Hall."

Given the how and where of Gerson's and my parting, his next question is in boldface in Pink Thing's archives. "Does he ever regret that?"

"Why, no. I don't think so. He's never said he does."

"I know I'm prejudiced—no, Pam, not that way. Around here, we don't really think of volubility as a decisive benchmark."

Remembering he didn't know Gerson—lack of talkativeness was never a problem in our marriage, neither on his side nor mine—I smiled. "Well! I guess I don't need to ask what you've been up to, though. Everything looks exactly the same."

"It isn't. And I'm not sure I like it," he answered with surprising grimness. "Let's say a couple of my recent conversations with our abbot have been tense."

"You aren't thinking of leaving?"

He was astonished. "Oh, never. Trust me, I'll die here. And with no complaints. I just want us to stay true to our principles. As the abbot does too, of course," he added quickly. "We only disagree—have, *discussions*—about how."

"What how? I mean, which? More pebbles in the sandals?"

"The long and the short of it is our cheese is getting popular. Bread too, you may have seen the brand: Flour of the Lily."

"Isn't that good, though? I do realize it's not for profit, but…"

"It does bring a lot of income for the order's other work, yes. The issue is how much of our time we've started devoting to selling the stuff. Naturally, I'm playing my part—not at liberty to refuse. You get one guess what my duty is, Pammie. Formerly a specialty."

I stared. "Oh, no," I said.

"Oh, *yes!*" he whooped, his eyes glistening with merriment. Seizing both my hands in his—a first since he'd taken his vows—he moved his elderly haunches around in a sort of caper under his brown robe. "Ad copy. Oh, Pam! For *my* sake, don't ever forget that this is a world of wonders."

POSTED BY: *Pam*   The next and last time I saw him was in the Davenport hospital. Barred from using the telephone even outside the monastery's grounds, he'd asked the staff to contact me. That took some doing.

Pam Cadwaller by then in my everyday life, I was on tour to promote *by Pamela Buchanan's* third and last appearance on a dust jacket. I'm still fond of the book even though *Lucky for the Sun* came a cropper next to *Glory Be* in reputation and sales. The spring of '68 had other plans; more than once, a local radio or TV interviewer had to interrupt Pam's chat about Parisian charms to cut away to news of the latest death or riot. I only turned out to be helpful when riots erupted in Paris itself, but by then even my agent agreed poor *Lucky* was a goner.

Flown into from habit, even Iowa City now had a Groszian undertow for real. Cars had cracked windshields and bedraggled kids sat on stoops like unemployed wig salesmen wearing the stock. Pam Cadwaller was writing checks to Gene McCarthy's campaign and I was fond of the Beatles, but neither the former nor— more remarkably—the latter seemed to have the thing under control anymore.

I didn't even need Nenuphar for contrast. While I was still *there*, my staid chambermaid mutated into a hairy-crotched gargantuess, pushing wan little daffodil junkies down onto her mound's swamp in exchange for a shot in a neighborhood I didn't know. Wondering why I hadn't just had the sense to go directly to Davenport, since in real life I'd obviously never see her again, I was relieved when Pam's rental car put open country in front of my now almost forty-eight-year-old nose on Route 80.

An audibly cubed crackle of sirens and shots was impregnating his room even before I knocked and pushed the door open. Too much to take in: he was still in a gown, but the polka dots looked silly. The TV screen was blaring flames. Bayonets in fiery silhouette: they'd called out the National Guard by then.

The remote lay on the floor. To an octogenarian with heart problems, it might as well've been in Illinois. He may not have known what it was, never having been exposed to TV. Bright with tears, the eyes he turned to me were gray yolks of disaster.

"Daisy! Bless you for coming," he gasped. "What's happened to our country? For the love of God, what's happened to our country?"

Oh, did I give the nurses hell about it. They weren't impressed: "We turn 'em *all* on mornings. Look, if I'm going to be digging impacted crap out of somebody's rear, then yeah, I'm going to watch my soaps. Sorry if I forgot to turn it off after, but he had a remote. Anyway, I ain't sure I forgot."

That was later. Now was now, and the second I'd sorted out what greeted me, I grabbed the remote and made the screen die. "My *Gawd*, why are they running that crummy movie?" I yelled. "Nobody liked it. It didn't even have a director! Did John Wayne show up yet?"

I wasn't about to let a pause make me a liar. It would've the second our eyes remet. I was just hoping that if he was woozy enough, a lot of noisy Pamela-ing might make him think it had been a dream.

"Oh, good! So you got my flowers. Well, well! Davenport. Does it have suburbs named Cushion and Afghan?"

Not my best joke, but give me a break. By the time I stopped, I saw I'd at least succeeded in making myself more real to him than what he'd seen. Only then did I pull up a chair and take his hand.

It wasn't my first deathbed, since my longtime editor at *Regent's* had passed by then. I realized as we smiled at each other that this one was different. Now no one on the planet would ever have known me all my life.

"Hello, old-timer," I said. "By now you could say the same to me."

"No, never." His voice was still feeble, but he was back on familiar Pamground. "I met you—before you could walk."

"I'm still not sure I ever learned how! But you'll be back on your feet any day."

He didn't shake his head so much as adjust its angle on the pillow. "No— let's have none of that. I wish they'd let me stay at Nenuphar to die. But my abbot. Has *such* newfangled ideas. Pammie."

Given what he'd called me as I entered, that last word was a relief. Not so the others, and I tried to remind myself that I was the unbeliever. He was a monk.

"Well, oh—I know that to you it's only a translation. Is that the right word?"

I couldn't believe I'd seen it, but that twinkle's meaning was unmistakable. "Aw, Nick," I complained. "You don't mean—"

"I—tried," he whispered, still amused. "But I just kept—asking myself. Why would God want all of us illiterate country relatives around up there— bickering, driving him crazy—for all eternity? He'd never get. Anything done. No, Pammie. Take it from—an old Chicago ad man. You've got to put something nice—in the window. But it's for here. The Gospels—are for *here*."

While I don't think any of its smattering of reviewers spotted the disconnect, no wonder his abbot's Introduction to *The Mountain and the Stream* is all about the afterlife. Something had to mask the fact that not a single letter mentions it.

"I had something I wanted to. Oh, yes. I liked the title. Of your new book," he said. "Of course, I couldn't. Keep it, but the sentiment. Sounded right. We are lucky. I promise, it'll end up in a good. Public library in Iowa. Someplace."

"Thank you. I just wanted you to see it, that's all."

"I think I'm going to sleep now," he said. "Goodbye—Daisy's little Pamela. Sorry—you came so far."

"Not that far, Mr. Carraway."

POSTED BY: *Daisy's Little Pamela*   I'd called him that deliberately, hoping he'd know why. He did:

"'No more of that—nonsense, young lady,'" he quoted himself with a reminiscent smile. "'It's Nick to you from—now on.' Just like that first day off. The boat."

"Yes."

"Was it—the *Normandie*? I don't remember."

"No, the *Paris*. Where I'd come from, not where we landed. That's one way to remember."

"Did we?" he said. "Paris." When I phoned the hospital that night he was gone.

I've never been much for tombstone visits, Panama. I've only been back to your great-grandfather's grave in Rock Creek Cemetery two or three times, always because the descendants are in town. Preferring to let the Madeleine Lee memorial watch over him there, I remember Cadwaller instead when Andy drives me past the State Department's big aircraft carrier for paper planes on C Street. But I did once go to see where my former guardian rests.

Subbing for Barbara Tuchman, since I doubt the forgotten author of *Glory Be* would've turned up on anybody's card index except from desperation, I found myself in Iowa City on what turned out to be my last public appearance as an author. Our panel was, so help me, "History and Literature: Sibling Rivals or Weird Sisters?" My first deadpan words into P. BUCHANAN's microphone were, "When shall we three meet again? Don't know where, don't know when."

Nobody got it. I'd meant to parody senescence: "We'll Meet Again" was among the most beloved songs of World War Two, bikini girl. The upturned cabbages (what's Denmark coming to?) my fellow panelists and I had agreed to call our audience couldn't grasp that old people know they're old—any more than they remembered that children, with far more fury, know they're children. So I was pretty much a bust, and before the cab was halfway to Nenuphar my chambermaid had convinced me that she was a grandmother and had voted for Reagan twice. She'd never done any of those vile, debauched things and she never would.

Accepting that their monks have passed back into being people we knew as well, Nenuphar keeps its cemetery unrestricted. Though locked at night, its gate is separate. You can even wear slacks, and times of the month were no longer an issue for me.

I told the cab driver to wait, as I had when he was alive. Of course I recognized the quotation from the final letter in *The Mountain and the Stream*, written to "Father F." just days before he went into the Davenport hospital.

BROTHER NICHOLAS

(*Nick Carraway*)

1892–1968

I wanted the world to be at a sort of moral attention forever.

There he lay, I hope at peace, under several hundred pounds of Iowa. I didn't stay long and you can't visit more than the cemetery unless you're someone's P.A., but Nenuphar still exists. It's not far from Muscatine, *dans les grands blés sanglotants.*

Part Two

1. Murphy's Law

POSTED BY: *Pam*   Brannigan Murphy crashed through the commode door at the Commodore, two Pulitzer Prizes to the wind. The diary I soon abandoned, which had already slumped from Goncourts to datebook and went white for good on our wedding day, tells me I first laid—ah, laid eyes on—my future husband on Sunday, June 22, 1941. That explains his bullnecked euphoria.

Germany's leap across Russia's border had begun history's cruelest duel of nations. The devastation it unleashed was neither here nor there in New York. For American Stalinists, the Panzers' race toward Leningrad and Moscow meant the end of the migraine clamping their brains since the Nazi-Soviet pact's signing almost two years earlier.

It's true the playwright I'd soon know as my Bran was never a Party member. Damned few were in his crowd or mine. Writing, discussing, insisting: that was left-wing Manhattan's job. A CP card smelled like an invite to hawk *The Daily Worker* outside Brooklyn shipyards or Trenton factories on cold dawns, not only a menace to our own typewriter labors but murder on a hangover. I include myself, though I was only a vague hot-to-Trotskyite. The world in flames that twenty-one-year-old Pamela Buchanan's book reviews did their best to limn blazed around a magically fireproof cocktail shaker.

Hitler's perfidy spelled professional relief for Murphy. Finished in summer '39, his anti-Nazi play *A Clock with Twisted Hands* could finally be produced without his fellow devotees of the USSR's new Jerusalem painting him as the Broadway Judas to Stalin's mustachioed, oddly hand-rubbing Messiah. Fighting words that cuckoo were everybody's meat and drink then, confusing us whenever we recollected we were all irreligious and might as well be talking about Tom and Jerry.

Anyhow, everyone in our New York knew the story of how *Clock* had been in rehearsal two Augusts earlier at the old Rosalie Gypsum Theater. Then Molotov and von Ribbentrop inked the deal to end all deals. Vast fuss in that converted burlesque house, home of the celebrated Popular Front and Center Troupe!

Leading lady Odette Clifford, angling for a Hollywood summons and needing those good notices, is all for going on. Born Karapet Parsamyan in Smyrna and darned proud of same when it suits him, director Pat Carpet—he did better on the West Coast than Odette, and here's why—wants to know what the front office thinks. The front office, in the person of John Outhouse Lavabo, professional Harvard refugee, mentions that shutting down will leave forty-eight people unemployed. His grandfather locked out eight thousand before the Pinkertons shot six, but old W.C. Lavabo was no aesthete.

The decisive voice was Murphy's own. "How could I really look Shakespeare in the eye, Pat? Or Gorky? Damn it, Lavabo. Pull the plug."

What can't be denied is that his renunciation cost him. The only new work of his to be produced since had been a pretty bleak one-acter called *Colum Firth*. Title and only breathing character, a Macy's stockroom worker trapped in a malfunctioning freight elevator after closing time with one of the mannequins from the lingerie department. As his speeches to her grew more lacerating, one slowly divined he was addressing his beloved, now dead wife. Hard today not to wince at the contrivance of naming her Cookie, letting the lunchbox-browsing widower lament "My cookie's gone" and "Gee, I wish I had my cookie back" and so on before the audience caught on with a spinal thrill the word was upper-cased.

Even if it did feature oodles of the tormented working-class argot Bran had pretty much invented from whole denim when I was a schoolgirl and there *was* a subplot about a shop steward the hero guessed was in cahoots with management, most reviewers thought Colum's monologue wasn't really Murphy in his best Murphine vein. Others saw a metaphor. The play culminated in a stymied—duh, as your Panamanic friends might say—sex act that was the most sensational thing yet seen on a New York stage; it might've gotten the production shut down if its victim hadn't been plaster.

If you find this tedious, bikini girl, I'm sorry. It depresses even *l'équipe* at daisysdaughter.com that Murphy's Wikipedia entry is a stub. Before *A Clock with Twisted Hands* finally heaved onto the Gypsum's stage, his last full-length play had been 1937's *Prometheus in Madrid*, a big enough hit to cover the alimony when his second wife divorced him in '39.

Its hero, Parnell Mulligan, was a captain in the International Brigades who learns his commanding officer is a dangerous, quite possibly insane incompetent. With the playwright's full approval, he covers up the fact to preserve Party discipline, and when John Ford's *Fort Apache* came out a decade later, set among U.S. Cavalry officers but featuring a similar plot and message, Murphy considered suing.

Or so his fifth wife told me. She got to be the widow, even taking over the dialogue balloons in *Seamus Shield, Agent of Fury*, the comic strip he'd been scripting in his final years. Anyhow, the lawsuit went nowhere once Bran's agent reminded him of Bonmarché's nineteenth-century play about a priest's heroic vow of silence under the Borgia popes, Wortsinall's seventeenth-century one defending the divine right of kings in the face of a given example's mediocrity, and so on all the way back to the good old Book of Job.

He'd married the second wife two years before he bagged his second Pulitzer, which came for 1934's *The Trampled Vintage*. (Yes, yes. You don't need to hear about Murphy's grudge against Steinbeck, do you?) That was the one whose climax cemented his and Pat Carpet's legends. After the lockout, the brewery workers starkly grouped around the body of Pinky O'Hare, the murdered labor organizer from New York, had just resigned themselves to staying non-unionized when young Russ—the illiterate apprentice Pinky took special care to inspire—started declaiming.

"No! No, listen, youse guys. Listen! I know da night is dark. But Pinky tole me—dat dead man dere tole me ["He has difficulty speaking," was Murphy's inspired direction at dat point] de moon is gonna rise. It's stormy now—and da moon will be red. *Dere!* Dere it is! See da red moon, youse guys? *See da red moon, youse guys?*"

Scrambling to his feet ["Suddenly on fire," Murphy directed, giving the stage manager a bad pause at the first table reading], the actor pointed over the audience's heads to the auditorium's back wall. As the stage went dark, a huge round scrim blazed scarlet between the EXIT signs. A couple of weeks into *Vintage*'s long run, the crowd in the Rosalie Gypsum's balcony got their own red moon to file out under, despite Pat Carpet's protests to John Lavabo that two moons killed the realism.

Bran had recouped just in time, since 1932's *The Mighty Tower* hadn't pleased anybody much. Unreconciled, he always claimed it was his homage to Ibsen, and from my one chat with an actress he'd dallied with between Wives Four and Five—they'd met while he was trying to sell a TV original under a pseudonym to DuMont's old *Roger Wilco Playhouse*—I gathered Ayn Rand was a sore subject.

His protagonist, Padraic Titan, was a thunderously successful, prizewinning…architect, just back from the Soviet Union and magnetized by a vision of a Manhattan skyscraper designed as a workers' paradise. In model form, it was prominently displayed onstage.

The sticking point for critics was titian-haired Ruby Thorp's role as Asphodel, a.k.a. Mrs. Titan. Her Act Two discovery of her husband's infidelities with Tatanyas and Sonyas who'd fallen for the rugged American visionary in one plink of a balalaika brought out her narrow-mindedness via a tearful threat to decamp. His eloquent sketches of the bliss they could share if she'd accept that genius has special needs as well as burdens fell on deaf ears, the reviewers' included.

Asphodel Titan's failure of imagination was supposed to mirror that of Padraic's backers, who felled the architect with a heart attack in Act Three by turning his plans for the Mighty Tower into a luxury building for the idle rich. Murphy didn't do himself any favors when he scoffed away real-life parallels by pointing out that, unlike his hero, he'd never been to the USSR. He wed the second Mrs. Murphy—none other than Ruby, who may've refused to start playing the second until she'd got done playing the first—a week after *The Mighty Tower* closed. Its major prop still dominated his Sutton Place digs in my day.

The first wife had been with him from the start, onstage as the corpse throughout *Things Zarathustra Left Unspoken*, his bad early play about the Leopold-Loeb case. Then she gave up acting to support her struggling playwright husband by working full time as a department-store mannequin dresser. (Gimbel's, not Macy's. Wikipedia, count your blessings.) Her monument was Murphy's first Pulitzer, in '28, for *Lo! The Ships, the Ships*—brawling Yank stokers on shore leave in Asuncion.

"Oops," you could fairly say to that, as it isn't a seaport. But otherwise, Murphy's two college summers working as a shucker on a shrimp boat out of Pascagoula had stood him in good stead. Not until his lone biographer got to work was it cleared up that the only tramp steamer he'd ever swung his duffel bag aboard was Gabby Chatterton, a three-day affair dating to his one trip to Hollywood to raise money for the Loyalist cause.

The first Mrs. Murphy, who I never met—buying a train ticket with her first alimony check, she ran a native jewelry shop in Taos before dying, much too soon, in 1940—was the predecessor twenty-one-year-old Pam felt curious about when I took over the lease. It wasn't because she'd been the same age as me when she married him; if you must know, we all were. I don't complain about any of my husbands bumping into view when they did, since I was the right Pam for all three at the time. I still can't help occasionally dottily wondering what it would've felt like to be *somebody's* first wife.

POSTED BY: *Pam*   I'd only just sat down with some people in the Commodore's bar when Murphy swarmed from the gents', belatedly pausing to check his trousers before looking back up and plowing toward us with a renewal of the heftily charismatic grin that had molarized *Time's* moralizing cover seven years earlier ("A Warning of Disaster: Playwright Brannigan Murphy"). Alisteir Malcolm, books editor at the old *Republic* and author of *Printer's Devil, Devil's Printer*, a memoir of his days running a small, Satanists-welcome press in the Twenties; Jake Cohnstein, then the theater critic for *Rampages* and years away from his public conversion to anti-Communism. Addison DeWitt, Jake's colleague from *Our Chains*, then still in the politicized early phase his delightful autobiography, *An Apple for My Eve*, calls "Red Stars in My Eyes." Besides reviewing plays for *OC*, he published tense, difficult poetry in *Orlando* magazine—at least until its Florida-based namesake, all real-estate plugs but nonetheless *primus inter pares*, threatened legal action for copyright infringement.

There were a few others I don't remember, and so much for evaluating the reportorial quality as opposed to the bias of the first remark of Murphy's to leave me poleaxed. Most likely some of them *were* Jewish, but maybe it only took one Jake Cohnstein to turn him Murphine once he and I were sharing a cab. What I'm sure of is that I was the only woman at that crowded back table, a situation Pam then reveled in.

At that age, I could count on eagerness and a gift of gab to take care of my sex appeal. Along with the Buchanan gams, on good display in a skirt suit from Saks at my carefully chosen outer seat of the booth and hopefully drawing eyes away from the ridiculous miniature hat, pinned atop my brindle mop like a powder-blue pedestal whose feather resembled the display for "Comma" in a punctuation-themed fashion revue, which 1941's daffy idea of *éclat* compelled me to wear. I was only outdone the minute someone treating prettiness as her talent was induced to sit down.

Then I was forced to behave like one more suitor if I wanted to stay part of the conversation. Not that I minded much, since my brain and my cigarette were as good at playing one of the boys as my lipstick, legs, and that stupid hat were at announcing I was one of *les biches*. But you don't want to get carried away.

The Commodore wasn't one of our usual spots, since the prices were stiffer and the drinks less so than everyone's wallets and gullets favored. Alisteir Malcolm had just gotten his Guggenheim, our crowd's equivalent of knighthood. We were seeing him off in an hour at Grand Central to spend a Vermont summer starting his admonitory novel about Benedict Arnold.

Since Arnold had a) been guilty and b) wasn't executed, the case didn't add up to a patch on your average Moscow show trial. Still, American Stalinists were ardent about sticking any Yankee Doodley wig they could on the Russian Revolution's growing pains and Alisteir's diabolically unclever essay in the old *Republic* about Lincoln's suspension of habeas corpus during the Civil War had backfired. Even in left-wing circles, the romance of the Confederacy was still in flower, and gluing Jeb Stuart's face onto Trotsky's did not have the desired effect.

Oh, Panama! The intellectual life was such a Donnybrook Farm back then. If that devil Chad Diebold thought he had me on Pam's French upbringing, her flirtation with the Communist call in the last couple of years before Pearl Harbor ought to make tomorrow's news coverage of my act of telephonic terrorism write itself.

POSTED BY: *Pam the Red Menace*　　It would be fun and not inaccurate to remind Chad I was barely out of my teens and excited by Manhattan's high-speed amoeba dance. I just refuse to trivialize things that way.

Unlike Bran, I was never a defender of the Soviet Union under Stalin. That may've been a symptom of temperament rather than belief: like all defeated factions, the Trotskyites made better jokes. Even so, my main later disagreement with Jake Cohnstein—we did some colloquium in the late Seventies, Pam subbing for a too busy Mary McCarthy—was and is my inability to see why rejecting Communism's travesty of the ideals *we'd thought* we were furthering should require Communism's apostates to scorn the ideals themselves, justice to the disenfranchised and an end to privilege and so on.

Jake said something into his microphone about once bitten, twice shy. I said something into mine about babies and bathwater. Then we baffled our audience (Bowdoin?) by succumbing to a case of the chuckles in our dilapidated way. Not having seen each other above half a dozen times since he'd turned down Gerson's offer of a job at Rik-Kuk Productions in 1954, we'd had quite the boozy, reminiscent lunch beforehand, and the polysyllables just weren't coming like they used to.

Alisteir Malcolm never got in any trouble. His slowness spared the old drayhorse from swimming against the tide when his novel *Refreshed with Blood* (the quote is Jefferson's) finally appeared in '47—and was taken as a prescient endorsement of our HUAC, not an out-of-step paean to the NKVD. To my knowledge, Alisteir never complained about the misperception, which by publication day he may have shared. Despite the officiousness he affected when assigning me book reviews—"See here, young lady" coming out at the drop of a comma, and isn't pomposity as a way of making oneself colorful pomposity at its most forlorn?—he was basically a wistful dullard, eager to participate in The Literary Life in whatever shape it took. As I recall, his final piece in the old *Republic* was a 1972 defense of black humor as the coming vogue.

Truth to tell, we'd all started glancing around fairly frantically for a waiter as soon as we sat down, knowing we'd need a lot of oiling to get through an hour when Alisteir could claim our undivided attention as his Guggenheimerized due. By the time our drinks came, the back of Addison's head was eloquently tipped to the wall at my shoulder. I could smell his hair ointment: "It's all right, I spell it POUM-ade," he'd muttered as his nape came to rest.

Murphy had pretty clearly been tanked since noon, but his liquor held him well. I will grant him virility, which in my senescence amounts to granting him Baja California as empires go. Since I was twenty-one, it was partly the virility of fame.

Fists in the pockets of a jacket impressively tailored to organize but not mitigate the Murphine bulk's aggressiveness—fond of good clothes as a mark of authority, he'd answered the letter congratulating him on *Prometheus in Madrid* from Robert Jordan Baker, the hero's real-life model, by inquiring if the International Brigades had a regimental tie—he made his feet's mild uncertainties at the nature of the communications they were receiving from the Murphine brain look like a boxer's ominous reflexes as his *Time*-cover grin led a one-man parade. When he reached us, the sweep of his muscled forearm exposed a Rolex so ostentatiously complicated it looked less like a Soviet fighter pilot's timepiece than his plane's engine.

"Sitting out the war on the home front, I see. Why aren't you defending Brest-Litovsk?" he said, immunized from his own challenge by virtue of the simple fact that he was standing up. You know, *prepared* to go, the moment the Kremlin's overlord said, "Comrades, I can do no more. Summon Brannigan Murphy."

"But I *did*. Just last month, at a party at Rose Dawson's," protested Alisteir, genuinely confused. "Oh, why—I misunderstood."

"Don't worry, Bran," said Addison without lifting his head. "We know the Red Army will knock 'em back. That's why we're doing the same." He dandled his glass.

(Oh, Christ. You'll need a glossary, won't you? Let *l'équipe* oblige. The Treaty of Brest-Litovsk ended newly Bolshevized Russia's participation in World War One; I can't imagine under what circumstances Alisteir could've felt summoned to defend it in May of 1941, especially on Rose Butaker Dawson's Cunard Heights balcony. The POUM was a Trotskyite faction whose militia ended up crushed by Spain's government to Stalin's glee if not on his orders. If you don't know what the Red Army was, screw this.)

Murphy's eyes had been prowling as if they were two lions and our table was the Colosseum. Now they found me: "Well, hello. I haven't seen you before, have I? Come on, Addison, who's the, your—"

"I do believe 'skirt' is the windmill word you're tilting at. And she ain't mine, you mug," Addison said. "Pamela Buchanan"—his flourished hand glided from under my nose to Murphy's general direction—"a party unknown."

"Didn't Mike Gold use that as a title last year?" Alisteir asked. "I might like to if he didn't. Does anyone remember?"

He knew he'd been demoted. Up against two Pulitzers, one Guggenheim was defenseless. He was pretending he could still manage the conversation even if his promised treat of getting to dominate it was history.

"Watch out for this one, Murph," Jake Cohnstein told him, meaning me: Murphy's appraising grin had been no more deflected by Alisteir's question than a locomotive by a gopher. "We haven't lured her all the way out of hiding yet, but in her cups she can sound *awfully* fond of that old man in Mexico who so mysteriously did himself in with a pickax last year."

"Oh, come on!" said Murphy, flaring up. "Christ's sake, Cohnstein. Even *we* don't say it was suicide."

As Jake's calm smirk advertised his joy in that phrasing, my future hubby grew restless. Decided Jake had only been translating for me and done an unfairly well-equipped job.

"Well, then. Little Miss You." His grin had broadened with belligerence's idea of easier game. "What *did* we see in Trotsky, back at Vassar? I can't wait to hear your expert reasons for defending a traitor to me."

Believe me, Panama, in the past eighteen months or so I'd seen that look more than once. Not on the face of anyone this famous, but some bulls you grab by the horns.

"Aw, becaw he wah so *kew*," I bawled, seizing the fat end of Addison's tie to hold it to one ear as I tilted my face and put my thumb to my lips. After frowning over it, I batted my eyes—Pam's best facial feature, remember—at Murphy like Baby Snooks.

Unlike my second and third husbands, my first was humorless. He'd learned his way around humor's shoals in the same way that in other crowds, at other bars, his gaze would sort the customers into who he could and couldn't take in a fistfight. "I think I owe you a drink," he told me.

"Another round, barkeep," Addison said. "Murph, did you mean just *this* room?"

"I've got one, thanks," I said.

He shook his head. "Not here. The hell with the Commodore. I've got some people I'm supposed to meet downtown. They'll like you."

"As she stepped into the Black Maria, Pammie heard a soft murmur of— why, could that be *Russian?*" Addison said. "And then, those coats."

"Brannigan, my train's in forty minutes. Do you mind?"

"Oh, come off it, Alisteir," said Jake Cohnstein. "If he'd asked you, we'd be sitting here coughing up your dust by now."

"And if I'd asked you?"

That was Murphy not only seizing his victory but being pretty brutal about it. Jake took the punch well, though.

"You'd have to put a pickax in my skull first. And I stand by everything I wrote about *Colum Firth.* 'See da yellow feather waving, youse guys? Does youse?'"

"Too bad. I always did wonder if I'd like it. Do you have a wrap you need to fetch?" Murphy asked me.

"Oh, look, Pammie's drink is gone," Addison said. He'd just reached over and drained it. "What will poor Pammie do now?"

POSTED BY: *Pam* Is "hooking up" what your generation calls it, bikini girl? You've got nothing on the Forties. Mine, anyway.

In fact, to hell with calendars. In Pink Thing's malleable archives, it *became* the Forties at the instant I shook my head to Murphy's coatroom question and reminded everyone the Buchanan gams weren't just decorative. Unless I'd grabbed a pair of Dottie's frillies by mistake, my underwear was fresh from our Bank Street fridge—old single-gal trick in pre-A/C days—and as usual for safety's sake on social evenings, my little pessary and tube of Nonoxynol were snug in their case in my bag.

Understand, those men were genuinely my friends. They'd never have stood for seeing Pam stumble off into the night with a writer less illustrious than they were. But those two Pulitzers were clanking like Murphy's third and fourth testicles and even Jake Cohnstein couldn't say he'd got them from Stalin.

The chance to figuratively cuckold him in advance is another reason I wish Pink Thing could serve up the full cast list of men perusing their cigarettes' glow in that combatively reflective Forties way and adjusting their specs or raking their hair around that table as they prepared to Algonquinize my hookup before they went back to giving Alisteir Malcolm his Guggen-Heimlich maneuver. No luck among those I remember, not that I've got any special regrets. Alisteir had both a wife in the East Thirties ("I wouldn't mind if Esther didn't understand *me*. I mean, why bother?" he once accurately moaned. "But she doesn't understand 'the revolution in one country,' either") and a wide-hipped, savagely cleavaged secretary at the old *Republic*'s office who, in the way of these things, had turned out to be the more demanding of the two. In one pursuit he shared with Bran, Addison was addicted to actresses; he was chasing young Terry Randall that summer. As for Jake, he'd spent all spring besotted with a pimply Paramount usher, by which I do not mean usherette.

Let me guess. You'd pegged Addison, hadn't you? Wrong, wrong. Panama, there *was* a time when men could be both witty and heterosexual—I am the woman, I was there, I laughed. Slept with a couple, too. Never Addison, but his thirty years of wedded bliss once he finally tied the knot easily outlasted my first and second marriages put together. Jake, on the other hand, bore up under the paradoxical asceticism of a man who woke up every morning juggling Trotsky-ism, dramaturgy, the Old Testament, and reveries of Tahitian lads in flyspeck loincloths. My future hubby had clearly known which of those—not the old man in Mexico, but the boy in Midtown—invited the lowest blow.

Unblessed by longevity, Jake's dingy chases after subliterates whose smiles were as rare as Loyalist victories left him pained and haggard. By way of reprieve, a couple of nights a week he'd tersely decline a third round and explain he was going out to Brooklyn to stay with his family, leaving us peculiarly touched that a man of forty as cosmopolitan as he was could still be comforted by Pop and Mama Cohnstein's Williamsburg hearth. Daisy's daughter needed some getting used to the idea that, in certain circumstances, parental obliviousness can be soothing.

As I got up, Murphy beamed in frank appreciation at the sight of Pam and gams unfolding like a whooping crane. "Buck up, Alisteir," he said to my editor, who was still befuddled by how his *bon voyage* had turned into mine. "It's not as if we're packing you off to Siberia. She'll be here in September!" Indeed the new Mrs. Murphy was.

Peculiarly, that seemed to prompt poor Alisteir to list Siberia's ingredients. "Ice, tar—"

"And so will Russia. Like it or not, gents," Murphy cut him off to advise the room at large, making up for the round of drinks he hadn't bought by offering the contents of his own skull around Odin-style. "Ready, Snooks?"

"I started out as a pacifist," Alisteir's successful Polonius groan detained us. (It was true; compensating for not having been a veteran of the Great War by establishing himself as a veteran of the peace, his dreary poems about mass dismemberment and disarmament had been collected as *A Chorister's Song in Parlous Times* in long-gone 1919.) "Can anyone tell me why does war always make everything *easier?* Damn it to hell. Last night I banged Esther for the first time in three months. I don't know—she just looked good."

"Careful, Alisteir. The walls have secretaries," Addison said. "But I never gave a hydroelectric dam for 'revolution in one country' myself. Full fathom five thy Trotsky lies, so let's just hope they win. Confess it, Bran: haven't you missed hating Hitler?"

"He doesn't know what he's let himself in for," said Murphy bluffly, already picturing how *A Clock with Twisted Hands* would let a chastened Führer know he'd just awakened Sutton Place's sleeping giant. "Come on, kid. Let's go." And we went.

The cabs on 42nd Street were sweeping along on now obscure wheels like low-flying birds in the dark. When the weather's good, what stepping into night does for Manhattan's noises and purposes is to temporarily generalize them. It creates a blissful, blued illusion of energetically flowing tranquility.

Murphy had steered me out of the Commodore and across the street by one elbow. In the cab, he offered a Murphine shoulder as a bulwark. I opted instead for Pamlatticed coquetting on my side of the banquette, my still fresh proximity to Addison's POUM-ade making me gingerly about accepting another set of male smells so soon. I didn't want to be olfactorily promiscuous.

"What were you doing with that bunch of sheenies, anyway?" my future hubby asked comfortably. "And with a good name like Buchanan, too."

"Oh! Well, of course it was Pam Slivovitz before I changed it," I drawled. "And incidentally: it was Barnard, not Vassar. I stress *was*."

POSTED BY: *Pam*   I do realize, Panama, that these last few posts have zoomed past *Pam Buchanan: The Barnard Years*. One reason I didn't graduate is that I was raring to get on, so why act differently now? I've spent enough time posing in dorms on daisysdaughter.com—modeling quaint schoolgirl fashions, exposing my strawberry pancakes and honey to bait Hormel. Overseeing the development of a body that, while never the curviest, ended up rangy and maneuverable in a number of ways I was told were pleasing.

One reason I regret pretzelhood is that those two or three inches of extra height were my social calling card in new places for decades; it takes a real lust for shyness to keep it up at five ten. One reason I won't regret making my big exit when the White House finally calls is that I just don't make entrances like I used to. With any luck, I'll be one pretzel Potus will choke on.

Far from losing my nerve, I've twice considered calling dear Bob's office to see if they can light a fire under the White House. But to someone ignorant of my plan, my impatience would be sure to sound like an old bag's pathetic eagerness for attention. Maybe I'll be dead in hours, but I'd like to go out clean, an ambition I'm sure my Senatorial benefactor will understand. He is less than three years younger than I am, and he served in World War Two.

Unlike me, however, he finished college first. Pleased as my guardian was that I'd gotten into Barnard—except in French, my grades hadn't been spectacular—its main flaw as an establishment of higher education had started to glare at me inside seventy-two hours. It had New York for competition.

To my eyes, Manhattan on subway maps resembled a lean but many-branched Christmas tree whose presents were heaped near the bottom: around Union and Washington Squares. It took me under half my first semester to winkle out where the excitement was, and the Columbia boys who were my first guides to New York radicalism should've taken vows of silence at graduation. They'd used up their share and then some of polemical oxygen.

Once I could fructify on my own hook, I didn't see much point in campus meetings about the world crisis when more consequential rallies were milling just a subway ride away: Vito Marcantonio's amplified squawk scaring the pigeons right out of Union Square, with newspaper umbrellas over everyone's heads in the rain, or the Lincoln Brigade's Robert J. Baker, no less militant in civvies, making a fist at Franco beside Garibaldi's statue after the fall of Madrid. Didn't see much point in sitting through lectures in bumble-behinded classrooms when livelier teachers held office hours in Village coffeehouses, Manhattan's buildings seeming to rear like dragons whose quarreled-over prey was sky when I'd totter back uptown after my latest attempt to find the gibbet in flibbertigibbet. Above all, I didn't see much point in wasting my Pam-prose on term papers when it looked like my best chance to join the hurlyburly.

While still notionally attending classes, I made myself the trad pest at the old *Republic* and *OC*. Did it help that the new gal ready to fetch coffee and handle correspondence was a Barnard willow among broader-beamed CCNY shrubs, spoke French, and had gams up to Sunday? I can't say it hurt. Going through Alisteir Malcolm's "Maybe" pile each week on what we called Grab Day, I'd crowd my arms with up to half a dozen books. Once I'd sorted my best bets on the IRT, I'd bash out one or even two reviews on spec as "'The Iron Gates of Life': Which Side Was Marvell On?" went unwritten for English 241. The first one Alisteir printed was a pan of a politically comatose novel by a Twenties mummy named Lady Brett Ashley, and the $25 I got paid bought the drinks at Pam's twentieth birthday party. You bet your ass I'm proud.

The proof Alisteir had a kind side was that he never told anyone I'd first come to his office toting the 1937 and 1938 Purcey's yearbooks as writing samples. But not, of course, the Fall 1934 edition of *Pink Rosebuds*, lair of the now hated "Chanson d'automne." In my days as a book reviewer, I always turned down poetry, though Alisteir stayed fond enough of his vestigial self to cover a good deal of it. Pam worried she'd wrong some real poet by seizing the chance to mete out the same treatment in print I'd met in Purcey's corridors.

I could handle damn near anything else, though, being a quick study. That got me tagged by some, not inaccurately, as glib. My ace in the hole was that I was funny, a quality then as now in even lower supply than demand in left-wing book reviewing: "Given the current world situation, in the exceedingly unlikely event of a second printing for *Farewell the Sun*, Lady Ashley's publisher might perform a public service by restoring to the 'Paris' and 'London' through which her titled characters cavort their proper names of Lutèce and Londinium, as well as retranslating their arch chitchat into the original ungrammatical Latin." Maybe you had to be there, but that squib made Addison DeWitt ask Alisteir who I was.

The review *by Pamela Buchanan* that caused the biggest flap in the old *Republic*'s offices didn't appear until the spring of 1941. Alisteir had given me the assignment in the full expectation of a demolition job, not only because that was more or less my specialty. From our point of view, shooting might be too good for the inviting fish in this gilded barrel.

In our crowd, the movies weren't taken seriously. I'd spent my Purcey's years flocking to anything Myrna Loy was in, but by '39 I'd been reeducated—by my own aspirations, always youth's cruelest and least foresighted commissars—to the point of turning up my nose at joining the crowds bleating to see *Gone with the Wind*. Hollywood was a preposterous place to us—ironically, given Mrs. Gerson's eight mostly enjoyable years there in a later Pamcarnation—and the vulgarians who ran the studios were obviously beneath contempt. So I sat down to read *The Producer's Daughter* with my pencil sharpened to a dueler's edge.

Nothing could've prepared me for the kinship I felt. In East Egg, Pammie Buchanan had used to wonder what it might be like to have a sister, and Celia Brady—or Celia Brady White, as she was by then—was the closest approximation I had or would ever come across. The last time I'd felt my own identity slithering out of my grasp this way, I'd been an eight-year-old in a Swiss sanatorium and a madwoman with chopped hair and strange hawk's eyes had been insisting I was her Scottie.

It wasn't an exact resemblance. She was Los Angeles born and bred, and our frames of experience were very different. She'd had oodles of money all her life and never thought twice about why, not true of me since the Crash.

By 1941, I scarcely identified myself to myself as *having been* a rich girl, since it didn't seem to me wealth counted until you were in a position to make decisions about it and I hadn't. As a result, my twin's politics—the prism of prisms for me then—were undeveloped at best.

Yet the tone, not only the provocations for amusement but its manner, stirred up a maddening illusion of sibling rivalry. On the page, Celia Brady sounded more like me than Pam herself had yet managed to in print—if only, I daresay, because I hadn't realized that was a priority. As a sample of how I wrote then when deeply affected by a book, here's the conclusion Alisteir printed with considerable suffering:

> *From a socialist perspective* [yes, I still cleared my throat that way; we all did], *not the least of the many delightful surprises here is the interest Miss Brady takes in Hollywood's labor situation circa 1935. While this child of privilege is blinkered, she's not blind. Nor can one dispute the poignancy given these light-hearted "memoirs" by their appearance so soon after the death of her actual father last December. Surely, if we automatically scorn the perceptions that can be gleaned from mindsets unattuned to Marxism, we only deprive ourselves of useful knowledge of the world; and the moment we deny even the most affluent a claim equal to our own on life's universal emotions, we risk abandoning one small but vital crag of a moral high ground otherwise ours for the asking.*

You'll be incredulous, but that turgid last sentence—especially on top of all the praise I'd heaped on *The Producer's Daughter* earlier—made me the Antichrist of the week at the old *Republic*. Your Gramela's shame at the style is offset by pride that I didn't falsify my reaction to give them the rap sheet they wanted, and my duffer of an editor deserves credit for printing the review in full despite formidable pressure to at least cut my counterrevolutionary ending. Even with my one concession to his woeful countenance—"risk abandoning" instead of "have abandoned"—that savagely cleavaged secretary of his refused to park her forked hams on Alisteir's lap for a week.

POSTED BY: *Pamique*   No longer a member even in poor standing of Barnard's Class of '42, by then I was sharing an apartment with another single girl on Bank Street. Still years from Nenuphar's robes, my guardian had been troubled when I wrote him in May of 1940, just as the Battle of France began, that I was a) staying in New York that summer and b) didn't plan on returning to college. I needed his agreement to keep sending me the $15 per week he'd been paying out from the tiny inheritance I was due to come into at twenty-one: the last of the Buchanan gelt, mostly generated by the sale of dead Daisy's minor Dali.

Since that basically meant he'd be staking me for a year before the whole unmagnificent sum was mine anyway, also because his scruples told him his writ didn't extend to *forbidding* the apple to fall close to the tree, Nick gave in after three paragraphs of thoughtful counter-arguments in the same sloping hand that had once announced a perfect little Paree-sienne's arrival. Since there was no other man I'd have put up with hearing *Like mother, like daughter* from, I've always been glad I didn't hear it from him.

The joke was that my new digs weren't that different from the dorm I'd left behind. The décor of twin beds, communal nightstand, and mingled stockings on the radiator was augmented only by one novelty—a small but not badly stocked bar—standing in a corner of another: a living room.

As for the other name on the lease, Murphy had hit close to home. Dottie Idell *was* Vassar: Vassar '39, not '33 as her recent *WashPost* obit claimed. By day, she was the receptionist for a West Side psychiatrist—a new breed then, at least in having chosen the career from the start rather than having helped invent it. By the Forties, Freudians were as keen on evangelizing in the face of popular benightedness as had been aviators a decade earlier.

On the ledger's plus side, he let my roommate take acting classes and go to auditions on weekdays and paid well enough to let her pillage Village vegetable stands and downtown fish markets for her great weekend passion, which was cooking. That was for pure love, since back then women didn't make a career of it except maritally and Dottie was too busy enjoying the frisky life to be on the lookout for a husband. So I ate well instead.

To be as honest as I can, daisysdaughter.com readers, I hardly remember what Dottie Idell looked like. Three inches shorter than Pam, she had hair the uncertain color of spring's first warm sun, a deviant nose that pulled up short just in time to avoid going seriously thataway, a jolly little body she was pretty jolly unabashed about in private, and a smile that turned her upper gum into a happy orchestra pit whose bright enamel music stands were waiting for players. That's really about it. She had as little interest in left-wing politics or writing as I did in acting or cooking, giving our little Bank Street nook the clemency that comes of knowing up front the twain shall never meet for long.

Unexpectedly, our truest and most playful bond was poetry. She'd declaim it with flourishes that reveled in exposing the fustian streak in Victorian sonorities—T.S. Eliot's included, and not much beat Dottie's rendition of "The Love Song of J. Alfred Prufrock" at making the shoe fit. One of her, well, dottier whims was to invent dishes based on poetic figures of speech: "I'm going to come up with a recipe for Ragged Claws if it kills me," she sunnily greeted me over a book from our living room sofa on my return from the old *Republic's* office one day, leading Pam to reflect that August was August and I liked Boucher too. Auditioning to play Louise O'Murphy in the altogether would still make more sense if there were, in fact, a play about her to audition for.

Dottie being Dottie and Pam being me, I'd've felt remiss not teaching her St. Clair Sinclair's old jingle: "To eat an oyster/You crack it foister," and so on. She was delighted, but I hardly expected to hear it burst from her lips on TV almost fifty years later. As for real poetry, even Purcey's hadn't killed Pam's private affection for the stuff so long as I wasn't asked to provide any execrable samples of my own. While I'd have died sooner than share "Chanson d'automne" with her, I got drawn into the recital game; she'd do Matthew Arnold, back I'd come with "Jabberwocky." That's how we fell into the inanity of calling our two beds Dover and Calais, as in "I left the book on Dover" or "Your laundry's on Calais."

Of course, bikini girl, you'd better believe there were nights when only one or even neither of us slept there. Bank Street didn't really suit for our dates with men. We both knew girls who'd do the you-take-the-living-room-and-I'll-take-the-bedroom bit, had signals like a shifted vase to let the roommate know she had the couch tonight and so on, but somehow it wasn't us. The aversion was to tawdriness, not candor. Three years older than I, Dottie herself had introduced me, via the name of a woman doctor, to the rubbery, unguentine world of pre-Pill birth control.

Ah, yes: the lurid sexual confessions begin. Signal event though it's supposed to be, Pink Thing's archives are vague about the circumstances under which and the perp with whom I first became trite—some more than usually aggressive Columbia boy, I do recall that. I haven't thought about it in forever.

The crushed corsage and more than usually strenuous attempt to do something about my damned hair are clues I could follow if I thought they mattered. That my mute reaction on taking cognizance of Pam's half masted, then one-ankled unmentionables was "Let's get it over with" tells me I was probably blotto.

I know I was standing up. Bump, bump. Like the hair and ear scrubbing my cheek, the chin gouging my left collarbone—bump!—stays anonymous. My back was being ground against painful, ranked protuberances—oh, my God. An elevator.

It's just as well I never told Murphy. He'd have columned firth on the spot.

POSTED BY: *Pam*   So there we are in the cab—see, youse guys? My future hubby has just unloaded a flagrantly anti-Semitic remark. Pam has done her best to riposte. If you're wondering why I didn't stop the cab instead, end this future before it began—ah, well.

I repeat: June 1941. I was four years away from seeing my radio colleague Eddie Whitling, the most cynical man I've ever known, break down in tears as we were led by the nose—you never forget that stench, never—into Dachau. I was eight years from marrying Gerson, fifteen from my first sight of Israel, and verbal anti-Semitism (we knew no other kind) was a social drawback at worst. To put it in 2006 terms, Panama, it was viler than littering but not nearly so awful as, say, smoking. Not an attractive warp, but to all but a few goys' minds, not a decisive one.

Besides, *my* decision had already been made. And in a flash too, which all bragging aside I'd hardly have you think was typical of me in those days. Dottie Idell and I had spent more nights and cloistered Bank Street weekends being just-us-gals than I probably want to admit.

"Do you really have people to meet downtown?" I asked, gauging my chin's upward tilt with finesse. High enough for the dipping Buchanan lashes to turn my eyes wry simply indicated sophistication about these white fibs. High enough to let him glimpse the flaring Buchanan nostrils would've been whorish.

The Murphy canines joined his incisors in the smile club. "Hell, yes. Couple of Spanish War vets who want to have at me over *Prom in Madrid*." He checked himself: "I really shouldn't call it that to civilians, but it ran so damned long. We got tired of saying 'Pro-mee-theus' every time."

"I'm no theater critic, but I have to tell you"—out of belated loyalty to Jake Cohnstein is my guess—"even I had a hard time swallowing that Parnell Mulligan would send his own brother to the firing squad, and honestly! Was Maria supposed to have been in love with him and not Fred all along, or just a sort of sensible gal who didn't see the point of putting off until tomorrow what you can do today? I mean, the body wasn't *cold* yet—Bran."

"Crap. You weren't there, Snooks." He hadn't been either, but the only one to point that out had been Orwell, a less than awed witness to the London production. "Anyhow, we lost the damned war. That's all the proof anyone needs I was right."

Far from bridling, Murphy was aglow with complacency at my familiarity with his masterpiece. It hadn't yet closed when I'd hit Manhattan in the fall of '38. Neither had the Spanish Republic, but the play's prospects looked better and the young Margo Channing had still been playing Maria.

Then he looked at that eye-catching Rolex of his. "You know what, though—the hell with it. I already know the line they'll peddle, and they probably got tired of waiting."

"When were you supposed to meet them?"

"Yesterday. But around this time."

"Then where are we going?"

"Why don't we have a drink at my place? If you like theater, Snooks, I can show you a piece of Broadway history. Did you ever see my play *The Mighty Tower*?" Even Bran knew that not prefacing that title with "my play" in this context risked bringing on an outburst of Snooksian laughter.

"God, no! I was twelve."

And in Paris, with a plump, depressed Daisy not Browninged yet up in Brussels. Before Purcey's, *"les grands blés sanglotants"* and that cruel little scene with poor Hormel, before—oh, who cared? I was in a cab with Brannigan Murphy, and you might not see immediately why what I'd just said was not only flattering but flirtatious.

So think about it, Panama. I was declaring that I knew exactly how old I'd been when *The Mighty Tower* was on Broadway. The delicate revelation that I'd been twelve just nine years earlier turned the Murphine masculinity from saturnine to taurine.

"If I'd had my way, Snooks, it'd have still been running when you were eighteen," he grunted, cupping my knee with one championship paw. (Two Pulitzers, eight public fistfights, "Shucker of the Month" his second Pascagoulan summer.) "The hell with the critics! *Tower* was the one. I've had better luck since, but you know that swell line of Mary Tudor's. 'When I am dead and opened, you shall find—'"

"Yes, yes! Of course I know it." I waved my hands—well, how to put this? Airily. "I'm just surprised you do."

"Hell," he said, putting the long arm of Rolexed coincidence around my shoulders. "Is that really how people think of me?"

"Why not? It's how you want them to," I managed to get out before my first Murphine kiss, as crushingly manly as a diesel truck in a barbering school.

Windows facing the river, his Sutton Place digs told the story of a bear who'd caught on too late bears don't hatch from eggshells. He'd had it done in Deco on moving in soon after the first Pulitzer, when "successful playwright" as a generic category had more sway over him, and had been trying to wrestle it back into reflecting his threatened Branhood ever since. The decorator's Bakelite and lacquer shrank from the flea-market bric-a-brac commemorating his nonexistent career in the Merchant Marine, the autographed *painting*, not photo, of Dolores Ibárurri—innocent of English if not much else, Spain's fabled La Pasionara had rendered *"No pasaran"* as "No pass around"—and the undeniably crowded and much used bookshelves. In a clench-browed way, Murphy did take himself seriously as a literary man, making it rather sad that today almost nobody does.

As promised, the central prop from his play about Padraic Titan stood before the center window in the large living room. Unfortunately, its shaft was dwarfed by the great leap into the dark of the Queensboro Bridge, no bogus architect's model and already venerable. Beyond the river's flowing coffin—odd image, but its belustered black had handles to my eyes—were Astoria, the unrevisited Long Island of Pam's childhood, the Atlantic.

We had a drink; we chatted. The unnerving haste with which he'd picked me up or I'd let myself be picked up demanded a pause to civilize us. He told me where the idea for Colum Firth's rape of the mannequin had originated: not as a symbol of political frustration—"Jake Cohnstein was full of hooey"—but after watching a religious procession in Little Italy go by. He predicted the Red Army would put Moscow to the torch before letting a single invader set foot there. "Just like in 1812," my future hubby boasted, proving his grasp of pre-Bolshevik Russian history wasn't all it might be.

Not that I saw much percentage in being pedantic then or indeed want to be pedantic now. Yet Bonaparte did view the fire's troubling beginnings from inside the Kremlin. He'd had a wonderful time there for a while. That's why "Moscowa" is among the names of his great victories inlaid in gold in the onyx base that girdles his tomb at the Invalides, even though it proved short-lived and ended in a disastrous retreat. He later said he wished he'd died the day he entered in triumph, which even Cassandre conceded was *plutôt beau* as our jonquil-hatted troop peered down at the love-cheated little clown's enormous coffin and remains the only comment of his I ever found touching. I generally dislike him. As before, *l'équipe* here at daisysdaughter.com thanks you for your attention to this utterly irrelevant matter.

Then, taking up my handbag as unobtrusively as possible—but why in hell be unobtrusive? I could've kicked furniture and yelled "I don't want to get pregnant," and that wouldn't have made it any more obvious—Pam asked to be aimed at the bathroom. I don't know if you're on the Pill or need to be, Panama, something I doubt your dad likes to dwell on even if he's in the loop. If so, lucky you for just getting to pop your birth control like a Tic Tac. Those crouching, squirted Forties preparations amid admonitory tile and porcelain were no fun at all.

On the other hand, as Dottie had more than once reminded me, they weren't optional on dates with men, unlike the answer to a question I always disliked— namely, how to make my theoretically seductive reappearance. Unless you were a hell of a lot racier than I was, it just wasn't done to skip back out in the old birth- day suit. Even Dottie, far more uninhibited than I, admitted she couldn't face that combination of road to Damascus and drama critic in male eyes.

Besides, the Buchanan bod, however friendly—thanks again, Hopsie!—didn't exactly conform to the Forties' ideal of pulchritude, with an upper endowment that didn't rival even Dottie's own petite dotties despite Pam's extra three inches of height and slightly equine hips that made it easy to tell when I'd grabbed a pair of my roommate's undies from fridge, floor, or Dover by mistake. She only ever envied me my legs—or emjambments, as we called them, amusing ourselves once again with our shared private passion for poetry.

Even though the tucked-towel look did the most for the Buchanan gams while minimizing Pam's upper inadequacies, it had just reminded me of poor Hormel. After some hesitation, I took the royal Murphine dressing gown off its hook and wrapped that around me instead, but I must've lingered in there longer than I'd realized. As I crossed the long, now empty living room from prop tower to real but inaccessible bridge, Murphy loomed up in the bedroom's darkened doorway, his torso comically Roman in a half wound sheet. "I was wondering where that was," said he, honestly disgruntled before he remembered that this was a seduction scene, not a bad day at the Lost and Found.

POSTED BY: *Pam*   Once we'd retired to the royal chamber, the old buck and wing went well enough at first. He was famous and soused, I was twenty-one and tipsy; the lamp was off, and the Mighty Tower, if thankfully not comparable to the ad, was okay. For a couple of minutes, anyhow, after which the Buchanan bod started to feel like a pummeled stairwell as stubborn furniture movers plugged away. Bump, bump, bump, not getting anywhere, Bannister. Without previous bouts of Murphine buck and wing to guide me, I couldn't tell if this was his pleasure or evidenced his lack of it.

Of course, he was as wordless as a bulldozer, and I wasn't about to ask. Even at that untutored age, querying a dieseling male face with an anxious "Is something wrong?" wasn't my idea of a great moment in intimacy. Yet while it hadn't been that warm a night, the room was growing stifling. The smacks of the burly Murphine *poitrine* on Pam's strawberry pancakes might as well have been the soundtrack to a scaremongering documentary about the Everglades.

He'd had a lot to drink, but I had no way of knowing if that was Murphy's Achilles heel or his motivation. As the minutes kept landing soggy, overheated punches, I realized my eyes were now so well adjusted to the dark that I could've written my next book review on the ceiling. Visualizing Alisteir Malcolm's face, as I helplessly did, was no great way to put paid to Pam's worry that she was on the receiving end of the two-backed version of writer's block.

Did he think he was building the goddam Moscow subway? Just too loyal to Comrade Stalin to protest the non-arrival of a train. A five-year plan, a five-year plan, a five…? Dear God, I'd be *twenty-six* when he came! My youth gone, my clothes out of fashion. Crazed with hunger to boot.

I may have actually sobbed, which didn't throw the switch either. Bran could be brutal, but a sadist he wasn't. I was honestly wondering if there was a pistol in reach when an unmistakably appreciative tail-wag in response to Pam's limp caress made me realize how the future might work.

By then, I'd've tried anything to make this gulag stint end in laggardly goo. I'd never done it before, but my hunch and hope both were that expertise wasn't a requirement. Soaking a forefinger in hard-won saliva, I did my dubious, *où est la plume de ma debutante*-ish best to stick it where red moons don't shine.

Murphy columned firth like a spout. All of ten seconds later, as I lay thinking that the always awkward transition back to one's conversational self might be a bit stickier than usual, I heard a snore.

POSTED BY: *Pam*   I was up first the next morning. Showered long, then—still heaped on the bathroom floor, my clothes looked singularly morbid—rewrapped myself in the royal dressing gown. Can't say if I wanted to provoke him, be declarative in some unformulated way, or just didn't think about it or give a fuck. Thank God, my handbag still held half a pack of smokes.

I made my own coffee, amazed by a kitchen I both could and had to walk around in. Then I sat down to figure out what I'd call myself if I weren't me. Truth to tell, this kind of instant coupling was unprecedented in Pam's not really that extravagant experience. Up to then, my occasional innings, however unromantic, had been with men I'd at least palled around with some first.

While I hadn't managed to stay friends afterward with all of them, two out of three seemed pretty civilized. I might've even managed a grand slam if

I hadn't stopped having any reason to run into my elevator deflowerer once I'd dropped out of Barnard and moved to the Village.

As for the other two, I'm still sure one if not both of their faces was bobbing among the supernumerary blobs around the Commodore bar's back table at Alisteir's sendoff. If how much of a mark either beau left on Pink Thing's archives is measured by your Gramela's inability to positively fit so much as hornrims on one or confidently light a cigarette for the other, the situation nonetheless makes it obvious we could be sociable just ten and eleven months later with no strain.

I hadn't been planning on going out at all. After we got up, Dottie Idell, still on her seafood kick, had spent the rest of Sunday afternoon dreamily inventing an oyster stew to end all oyster stews. When the phone call came from Addison, I'd practically bolted to the Commodore, to my roommate's hurt surprise.

She'd just cracked 'em foister, and all she had left to do was drop them in. I might've wavered if she hadn't gone into another of her farce poetry declamations—burbling "The sea is calm tonight" for the second time that day, my God. The first recital of "Dover Beach" had been triggered by hearing the news of Hitler's attack on Russia on the radio, but only an unfeeling ninny would *reprise* it.

If Murphy hadn't shown up, I don't know who the hell I'd have gone home with. Bless fate for at least rigging the schedule to ensure Alisteir Malcolm had a train to catch.

Anyhow, in fairness to myself, Murphy didn't really fit the bill of complete stranger. Meaning, of course, that his fame had imbued Pam's first-ever sight of him with a magnetic familiarity, creating an illusion this wasn't our first encounter. My companions' chaffing as soon as he swept his Rolex at us had no doubt helped. I got used to the double-exposure effect in my Hollywood years.

Early on, I was constantly treating people I'd only known in two dimensions as if they were people I'd known in three. They were clearly too used to it to gainsay me, even though for better or worse none of them took the advantage of that confusion that Bran unmistakably did. Since I was older and less susceptible by then, I'd have also been a hell of lot more likely to say "Hey, hang on a minute." There is a Washington version of the phenomenon, but during most Administrations the magnetic aura around a famous face seen in 3-D is more likely to be repellent than beguiling.

POSTED BY: *Pam*   Reasoning with cigaretted help that I'd *sort* of known Murphy before Sunday night was about as far as Monday-morning Pam had gotten when the man himself came bounding in, bathed and fully dressed. Apparently, a fresh shirt and slacks made the dressing-gown issue moot. It hadn't been possessiveness per se, just Bran's easily nettled sense of his own most appropriate costume.

"Hello, Snooks." Turning my head to chuck me under the chin, he grinned his *Time*-cover grin. Then he turned fatherly, not that I'd know from experience: "Listen, kid. If we're going to be an item, one thing you should know. What happened last night is never to be repeated, understand?"

"You mean you didn't want me to do it?"

"I didn't exactly say that. But it can't ever be spoken of." A Murphine finger wigwagged from his chest to mine. "Not even between you and I."

"Me," I said automatically. "But between you and me, we seem to be talking about it now."

He frowned. "I won't need help every time," he said, which turned out to be true. Even so, the single exception that proved him right isn't my fondest memory. "And I know it's got nothing to do with who Brannigan Murphy is. This headshrinker I've been seeing—"

"Wait. You go to a psychiatrist?" Call the Forties unenlightened, Panama. Picturing a man like Murphy on the couch was tantamount to learning that the Himalayas were made of construction paper and pie topping.

He looked derisive. "Of course! For research. He doesn't know I'm analyzing *him*. I'm out to paint the big picture of my times, Snooks. Like Pushkin or Gogol. I've got a play sketched that's going to knock the stuffing out of that quack, bourgeois profession, and he's one stupid bastard. I'm using an alias, and he doesn't even recognize me."

"I think you mean Balzac or Zola, Bran," I said. (Wifely of me, don't you think? I spared him repeating it in print.) "Tell me, how long have you been doing this, research?"

"Two years, give or take a month or two. I'm about ready to wrap it up. I told you, kid, he's a stupid bastard. That's just why he's perfect for me. Anyhow, he thinks my nursemaid back in Pittsburgh—"

"Wait. You had a nursemaid?" In every interview, Murphy claimed he'd gone to sea to escape the bitter poverty of his upbringing. Not until long after his death did his lone biographer check the enrollment records for Andover's Class of 1917.

"Really just a good Irish woman from the neighborhood. My parents were kidding themselves, Snooks. Poor bastards, with their delusional middle-class pretensions! Anyhow, it was before the Crash."

"Well, of *course* it was before the Crash, Bran," I said. "You were *thirty years old* when the market crashed. And living here. My God, is Mrs. Gillooley about?"

You'd be wrong to think his courtship of me that July was fueled by anxiety that Pam had the goods on him. The right word would be excitement, and for all I know that's how it worked with the other wives too. While I'm not by any means complaining, he never showed the faintest interest in getting the goods on me. After I'd turned thumbs down on Cape Cod, unmoved by my new husband's muscular memories of working on *Lo! The Ships, the Ships* there during what I thought of as the Summer of the Lotus Eater, we honeymooned instead on Maine's coast in August, Murphy often remarking that the landscape reminded him of his seagoing days.

2. A Husband with Three Heads

POSTED BY: *Pam*   Why don't they call us, Cadwaller's gun? It's not as if they're so bloody busy taking care of the planet's prospects. I was no good at science in my abbreviated schooldays, but I can read a thermometer.

If the summer that's coming is the furnace the last one was, the instructions I've just printed out for disposing of Pam could end up making me the envy of the sweltering folk left behind. Compared to the bog they'll be reeling around in, my trip into the incinerator at Gawler's could sound as refreshing as Dottie Idell's old Bank Street tradition—dear God, sixty-five years ago!—of opening the icebox door to let its frost breathe on our skins: "We've *earned* it," she'd say. "Oh, just a couple of minutes. Then August can do what it wants."

At least you've got the body for it, Panama. When the Lycra clutching your newly theatrical globes and molding your oyster become fit attire for a New York December, you'll have less reason than your portly dad to shudder at doing your Christmas shopping in the near nude. How I pity those soggy Macy's Santas.

Of course, in July's 140-degree broil, even that much clothing will have to come off, bikini girl! Let poor harried Tim go crosseyed, I want you to be comfortable. Pity you won't be visiting Provincetown anymore unless you've got scuba gear. Maybe the very tip of the Pilgrim Monument will still be above water, qualifying as landfall now only to Chekhovian seagulls.

Shan't see it, but Potus might. I picture him spending his declining years in a Texas the size and shape of Delaware. Glancing down, he spots a moldy piece of ancient string knotted around one formerly Potusian finger: "Oh, darn," he mutters sheepishly.

Unlike him, I don't think I've forgotten anything important. Checks to the cleaning lady and Gawler's; one last sentimental check each to Alley Cat Allies and the good old ACLU. Disposition of the African Adam and Eve, Ganesh, the signed La Coupole menu and the copper maquette you Cadwallers named *The African Queen*. People can take from the Paris footlocker what they like except for my mother's chaotic pages of *The Gold-Hatted Lover*, which Andy's been told to burn. I don't want dead Daisy met that way by people who never knew her.

Tucking checks and to-do list into an envelope marked "Andy" felt puzzlingly familiar until I realized how closely my chore mimicked the detailed instructions for Kelquen's care I used to leave for him when I traveled. A few years in, he gently swore he knew the drill.

One other thing I've done since my last daisysdaughter.com post struck even me as eccentric. Though I haven't autographed a book in decades, I clumped over to the trophy bookcase and took down my copies of *Nothing Like a Dame*, *Glory Be*, and *Lucky for the Sun*. Turning to the title page, not flyleaf—

author's prerogative, you know—I signed all three. Dedication: "To whom it may concern."

POSTED BY: *Pam Slivovitz*   You never can tell. Murphy, whose pearly-white choppers once dentifriced *Time*'s cover, was a forgotten man writing ballooned dialogue for *Seamus Shield, Agent of Fury* when he died in Moscow, Idaho—ah, the Murphy touch—in 1964. His *Collected Plays* (Hofstra, 1981) could probably've been printed upside down without anyone discovering the mistake. The lone biography—*Dat Dead Man Dere*, by a nice but not too talented Canadian named Garth Vader—didn't even get Garth tenure at the University of Saskatchewan.

Sadder still, as Bran's theatrical reputation winks out, *Seamus Shield* has been rediscovered by the sort of overgrown lads whose Adam's apples seem to tug their faces along behind them like skittish kites. I gather it's mostly for the artwork, but even Pam gets an occasional e-inquiry. I always write back explaining that the hero's prosthetic steel arm and curvaceous, loyal assistant, Nadya—who doesn't become Mrs. Shield until a convenient villain has torn her tongue out, arousing Seamus's pity—long postdate my trip through the marital tollbooth.

Yet for a couple of unwitting million TV viewers who dote on his vital essence, Brannigan Murphy lives. When Andy Pond calls or stops by in the evenings, he's usually horrified by which cable-news channel the mimsies are glued to, but what can I do, Panama? Am I supposed to *ignore* a television network apparently designed for no other purpose than to remind me of my first husband?

The saying that leopards can't change their spots will no doubt outlive the last four-footed example, giving the species a conversational hold on life for a couple more brow-mopping decades before the proverb fades like the Cheshire Cat's grin. Watching the spots switch leopards is one of the grimmer fascinations of my old age. Needless to say, what Pink Thing snickeringly calls the Murphy Channel has no idea it's channeling Murphy.

His politics would have been anathema to them, which just proves that attitude is the ultimate ideology. If you care to see a facsimile of my Bran's public manner, look no further than the sack of vanilla vomit manqué I've rebaptized Murph Vanity, the nominal co-host of an obnoxious hour Tim Cadwaller calls *The Thug and the Bug*. Despite an only fleeting physical resemblance, since the original Bran was burlier and didn't simper, Murph Vanity has the moxie down pat. The ability to swagger while sitting down is not a gift given most men.

The Bran I knew domestically, however, shows up an hour earlier, in the mightily towering form of Brannigan Gillooley. In this case, I'm relieved to say—I did have to bed the original—there's no physical resemblance whatsoever. But oh, the truculence, combined with an injured certainty he's more harassed than harassing, more badgered than badgering! The conviction that any hypocrisies we detect in his dust are irrelevant gnats to the deeper truths of his self-dramatization's caravan; the futile wait for him to express sympathy or concern for any creature other than himself except adversarially. The show known to Pink Thing as *The Gillooley Factor* can take me back to Sutton Place, circa 1941–42, on Clio Airways faster than dreams.

Dour, implacable, bridling at his rivals, Murphy the playwright is represented by Bran Hume, as I once inadvertently called him *aloud* to Andy Pond when we spotted him seething at a steak in Martin's. That he is the channel's official anchor, but overshadowed in practice by his colleagues, fits Pink Thing's memories of the original Bran as dramatist, social creature, and spouse to a T.

Bran Hume's compassionate side only comes out when he fawns over his favorite interviewee: that underdog Chad Diebold, in all Chad's many guises. His sense of appropriate cues for moral indignation can't help reminding me of the real Murphy's ability to lash out at the Girl Scouts as a nest of defeatists—selling us cookies on Sutton Place, one sweet little lass had innocently wished us peace, not victory, in '42—while brushing aside the USSR's collectivization famines as either Fascist lies or the fabled omelet's recipe.

Since Pam's never explained her private shock of wifely recognition, no wonder Andy's baffled I spend so many nights watching the Murphy Channel. But I'm too pretzelly for sex, my cat is dead, my latest Hardy Boys doctor has limited me to two glasses of wine a day and there hasn't been a new Kirsten Dunst movie since last October. My Bran's unwitting epigones are the closest I'll ever come to attending a séance.

Forty years dead, there my three-headed hubby is, inverted from Stalinist hack to jingo. Not that I'm implying his triple resurrection shares the original's anti-Semitism, any more than I'd care to speculate they share his craving for a womanly knuckle up the giggie. Still, I've never forgotten something Gerson said once: "Someone's always got to be the Jew."

1952? 1952. In his Packard, not my newly acquired Olds, we're driving into literal, not figurative, Hollywood. The Oscar ceremony's at the Pantages this year and we're meeting the DeWitts at the Frolic Room for a drink first. "Not to me, I hope," I say.

"No. To someone with that mentality." Gerson never much liked using Murphy's name. "I don't think it's selfish to wish it wasn't literally us so often. But once you can't think without enemies, someone always has to be."

Day in and day out, the Murphy Channel's hunt for new Jews carries on. At different times, liberals, Muslims, illegal immigrants, atheists, and child molesters, among others—spot the genuine bad apple planted to spoil the barrel there—have all fit the bill. Not that I'll be around to see it, bikini girl, but my sensational 1943 divorce from Murphy will get an odd reprise tomorrow. Once I've carried out my protest against this awful and unending war, I'm sure to spend all day as the Murphy Channel's newest Jew.

Funny, too, since I always did enjoy playing the shiksa around real ones. If I have time when the White House calls, I just may switch on the TV to turn Murphy's three-headed reincarnation into my witness. That'll be Pam's way of saying, "There! See the mess of pink and gray things on the rug, youse guys? Do you?"

POSTED BY: *Pam*   When we got cocktail-party chances to compare notes after our various escapes, it was agreed by all the later wives but Five (the widow, remember—she had something to protect) that we'd have been happier being one of the girlfriends. Didn't really know how we'd ended up as the Mrs. Murphys instead, watching the cooze scoot by. "Moral of the story is," said Four, always my favorite—touchingly, since he'd been on the skids by then, she had less worldly polish than Ruby or me, but was infinitely nicer— "there are some guys no woman with half a brain should go near *unless* he's married."

However, we were necessary, since Bran's compulsion wasn't sex as such but infidelity. The two-year gap between his breakup with Ruby and his wedding to me was the longest in his marital dossier, and everyone knew the explanation. Murphy had tried to go society, conducting an affair with an East Side dish blissfully named Elsie Dodge Plough. Closer to him in age than any of the wives, she was also rich in a way that made Bran's Broadway loot look like the sawbuck sewn into a steerage passenger's coat. That left her profoundly amused by his idea that she should divorce the Plough millions and hitch her costly wagon to his red star.

It must've bamboozled Murphy that a woman could get involved with him from priorities of her own: entertainment, mostly. When Pam met her long afterward, Fabergé-bosomed and Cartier-haired Elsie could've turned the Lotus Eater into a supplicant and poor Hormel into a puddle even at sixty. She made me laugh instead by repeating the line that had finally shut Murphy up about marriage: "Oh, Bran, why bother? Then I'd have to *do* something about you."

Would that I'd been half as brainy. As I'm obliged to keep bleating, I was twenty-one. My intelligence still served only as an emergency technique for fencing with whatever had just been chucked at me, not a way of reaching an independent understanding of what was going on. Not only a world-class chucker, my first hubby was twice my age and a colossus in the world I most wanted to move in. Even when I saw through him, it excited my youthful vanity to see through a man so important.

So far as charisma and male persuasiveness go, keep in mind that the Brannigan Murphy you're meeting on daisysdaughter.com is Pink Thing's later and wiser dismantling. The only choice Murphy gave me at the time was between being swept away and swept under the rug, and like most twenty-one-year-olds I feared dismissals from others more than mistakes of my own. Besides, that much masculinity snorting at you is a powerful convincer of one's femininity, and in those days the only definition of womanhood society trusted was a man's. Don't blame the goosey, easily rattled Pam I was if she clutched at getting her public certificate of non-Charybdean desirability from such a recognizable source.

If I'd had a better understanding of what the enjoyable part of the whole deal was, I'd have tried to sustain the romance by delaying the marriage. Even in the face of Addison DeWitt's delighted cynicism and Jake Cohnstein's amused sympathy—or was it the other way around?—it was fun to go around town as "Brannigan Murphy's new girl," the tizzied whisper that turned me into human Alka-Seltzer in public all July. I didn't grasp that wedding bells would give Bran someone to be unfaithful to, only catching on the night *A Clock with Twisted Hands* opened in December.

Addison may've been the one who tried to warn me. "Well, dear girl!" he chortled in the Oyster Bar at Grand Central the day I got back from my honeymoon. "A shock is as good as a holiday. To think even I never guessed you'd end up the *latest* Mrs. Brannigan Murphy. You know, as I wrote once, we often wondered—"

"Never mind what we wondered," said Jake. "Pam, just tell us you're happy."

"Jake! I wasn't prying. I was about to quote myself. It's a privilege not granted to many."

"You could fool me," Jake said. "And the publicists too. Remember 'Tesla Morse's ecstatic *Dots and Dashes* deserves to run forever'? Well—"

"Not this poem. I was quite young when I wrote it. Shall I clear my throat first, or just wet it down?"

"Just so long as you don't close your eyes," Jake advised. "I'll laugh you right out of your chair."

Naturally, Addison did all three. "We often wondered," he began.

We often wondered
What had been plundered
Before the wanderer
Met the panderer.
Was she a blunderer?
Asked the ponderer.
No, she was a child.
So said the wild.

"When did you write it?" I asked. "Oxford?"

"In the cab coming down here," Addison said. "But I was already drunk."

POSTED BY: *Pam*   The thunderheads that did loom over my marriage almost as soon as we got back from Maine were even triter than adultery. As I was learning domesticity wasn't my strong suit, Murphy grew more adamant that it should be my only one.

Perhaps from fear of old Mrs. Gillooley, or whoever she'd been, hobbling out of his past with a beckoning talon and a gleam in her one good eye, he'd kept no maid since his bust-up with Elsie Dodge Plough. It was a shameful thing to do to a Deco apartment no matter how goddam Marxist you were. And ah, how the lacquer grew cloudy, darlin', if you'll allow me to Gillooleyize myself. Within a week, Cinderella in reverse—the way that movie usually runs outside theaters—there I was, scrubbing and dusting. Luckily, after my one attempt at dinner had sent Dottie Idell's still moist ghost into gales of laughter, even Murphy acknowledged the pleasures of good restaurants.

He'd been incredulous that I meant to go on doing my book reviews for the old *Republic* and *OC*. Wasn't I married to a *real* writer now—and hadn't that been the goal? My bid to convert a small pantry into my workplace (it was the Sutton Place lair's only windowless room, which I'd hoped might improve the odds) got refused: "You'll put a cot in there next."

He said so as if onto my treachery. As I hadn't yet committed or contemplated any, I did feel a pang of compassion as I wondered from what recollected Gillooleyan or even pre-Gillooleyan betrayal that jeer had sprung.

Instead, once I'd cleaned up after breakfast, sent out the laundry, wiped down the lacquer, and retrieved the chrome ashtray I'd beaned the wall with last night, startling him but not altering Dolores Ibárurri's bullet-eyed self-canonization by a hair, I used to set up my typewriter at the Queensboro Bridge end of the long living room table. The Mighty Tower looked down from its place of honor as I started pecking away. Often, sensing another glower beyond it, I'd glance up to catch my hubby, in the doorway of his own monumental, in every sense, office—he had bound volumes of every press notice he'd ever gotten, annotating the negative ones with "kike-fag-Trotskyite-traitor-hooey-go-to-Madrid-and-see-for-yourself" abuse—gazing at me with genuine if baleful perplexity, a cup of cold coffee in hand.

The thunderheads receded once *A Clock with Twisted Hands* was in production at the Rosalie Gypsum. Murphy was buoyed by the imminence of his first full-length play in four years, and to Pam's relief script conferences with Pat Carpet, casting, and then rehearsals got him away from the house. Not that I ignored my chores or even moved my typewriter, but the work went more smoothly:

> *Beyond the author's dim grasp of a Europe whose politics and landscape seem to be regrettably, if understandably, cobbled together from Hollywood back lots, Rita Cavanagh's Sybil Choate is most marred by the mawkishness and triviality of the incidents she introduces to justify her heroine's belated decision to join the underground. Surely, treating schoolgirl woes and an apparently thwarted romance as motivation for her final sacrifice can only insult the brave souls now resisting the occupier in reality. Given the crisis we all face…*

Even so, my respite turned out to be shorter than expected. In November, rehearsals now underway in earnest, Murphy started pleading with me to come to the Gypsum, saying he needed my judgment: "Things aren't going well, Snooks. I can't see why for the life of me. I know this script's true Murphy." Given that he was bedding the ingenue, inviting me could've been either foolhardy or a numbskull's idea of camouflage, but I rather think he wanted me to find out. Among the wives, even cautious Five agreed our discoveries seemed key to the infidelity scenario.

As yet unaware that pea-brained but pear-boobied Viper Leigh, née Betty Schtupter one day when Brooklyn was at loose ends, had been landscaping Bran's mighty tower with her legs' pale saplings for six weeks at the nearby Peter Minuit Hotel, I went along gamely enough. That was despite being under few illusions he really wanted Pam's two cents. With Elsie Dodge Plough's eye-opening course in what a loyal New York wife could get away with still fresh in his mind, it'd been exasperating him no end that his new wife refused to see anything wrong in going out to dinner, a bar, or, sin of sins, other plays with now de-Vermonted Alisteir Malcolm, Addison, Jake Cohnstein, or whoever from the old *Republic* and *OC* when he got kept late at the theater.

"Damn it," he raged. "Don't you at least have any *hen* friends?" Oddly or not, I didn't, not then. Even Dottie Idell and I had stopped being chums once I'd quit Bank Street, something attributable mostly to a new discomfort on my end. I worried that if I saw my former roommate now, proudly showing off my still damply glued Mrs. Murphy mask, I might learn something I didn't want to.

POSTED BY: *Pam*   No, Panama: I haven't been holding back out of embarrassment. Your Gramela has just refused to believe ever since that it was at all consequential—the giggled "Dover or Calais?," the scamper, the delirium of Dottie's PJ-less warmth. I was pretty swacked the first time, and then it stopped seeming unusual. She was too light-hearted and silly, too exactly the same goofy joker in bed she was out of it, for her awkward roommate to believe our fooleries on Dover nights and Calais mornings mattered that much.

No doubt that's one reason I wasn't panicked by my usual warning images of the Charybdis temptation's price: the tension etched in the Lotus Eater's face by my mother's idlest touch or glance, poor Hormel's loneliness. Another reason was that we'd had no onlookers—myself for once included, you could say.

Yet now that I was one again, the thought of discovering I'd been wrong unnerved me. Spotting even the faintest wistful hint in Dottie's eyes that our idyll hadn't been so blithe as she'd affected would've been too horrible for words, and so that number stayed uncalled. That didn't stop me from fretting she'd track Bran's unlisted one down. Or even, in a scenario I imagined over and over, show up on our Sutton Place doorstep to confess she'd been ready to succumb to the Charybdis temptation in earnest—and with me of all people. I didn't want to know.

Unless TV counts, I never did see her again. A few months later, my nightmare was laid to rest when I heard she'd married a man named Crozdetti and moved to Louisiana, and of course it's as Dottie Crozdetti she's much better known. Thanks to some tin-eared or unduly finicky copy editor, she was "Dottie I. Crozdetti" the last time I read her name in a headline, fleetingly making me and no doubt many others hope against hope—even though the small box on Page A1 had told us otherwise—that some other Dottie Crozdetti was no longer with us. But the photo of a hefty gray-haired woman laughing in her famous kitchen was the one everyone knew, and the obit was twice as long as any Bran got when he died.

And hell, if I'd just played my cards right—no, I'm joking, dear. It's true nonetheless that, even among the few academics who still play Scrabble with

Murphy's work in hopes of spelling "Ph.D.," *A Clock with Twisted Hands* does not rate high. Titled "Time Runs Out," Garth Vader's chapter on the play in *Dat Dead Man Dere* has two epigraphs, one from Pat Carpet: "Live by the clock, die by the calendar. That was Murph." As it's a line from the play, I mildly resent the other being attributed to me: "Aaieee!"

The villain is a German industrialist, naturally in it up to his chin with Hitler, paying a weekend visit to the Connecticut home of an American newspaper magnate whose past conceals a secret. (Yes, Bran claimed Orson Welles had read an early version.) The purpose of Count von Deutrifau's trip is to silkily persuade, then browbeat, then blackmail the publisher into maintaining "America First" isolationism as his vast media empire's editorial policy. That'll help keep Uncle Sam snoozing as Adolf tears into ~~Poland France Norway Greece~~ the USSR, where "The bastard may have finally bitten off more than he can chew"—to quote the stirring qualifier looped in above the Baedeker of cancellations in Bran's two-year-old script.

Yes, the convention of the Suave Nazi was already established. But in his final rewrite, my hubby had let a few of his more teapot-sized tempests creep in. The man of the hour by first intermission, Addison pronounced himself delighted with his portrait. At the final curtain, the Count's attempted rape ("Bit of a one-trick pony, aren't you, Murph?" Addison—well, silkily—said) of the magnate's virginal, politically even more so daughter, ~~Vickie Patricia~~ Lucy, had been thwarted by her fiancé, Brendan Leary. He was ~~newly well, just last year~~ long since returned from flying for the Loyalists in Spain. Once von Deutrifau had skulked back Third Reichward, hissing imprecations, Brendan bitterly indicted America's theatergoers for their laggardliness in joining the fight against fascism.

His lies about his Spanish-American war service aboard the *Maine* exposed, the magnate was dead by his own hand. Offstage, but how I loathed hearing that gunshot. "Bit Prussian, wouldn't you say?" was Addison's unwittingly soothing comment at second intermission. "I think he should have beaten himself to death with a sled."

Well! He hadn't been watching *Clock* get wound up since November. One foot dandling toward Hollywood like a cat burglar's, Pat Carpet breaks off blocking scenes to take calls from his agent, who's angling to get him into the director's chair for the film adaptation of—this had to hurt—*A Clod Washed Away by the Sea*, an anti-Nazi play by a onetime Murphy mimic named Ernest Bellman that ran at the Gypsum for most of 1940 while Bran, hands tied by the Nazi-Soviet Pact, fumed on the sidelines. Old Floss Bicuspid, Ethel Barrymore's understudy in *A Doll's House* in 1905 and taking her first crack at political theater as Mrs. Magnate, keeps trying to ingratiate herself by fluting that she'd love to play Eleanor Roosevelt. And a certain pea-brained, pear-boobied ingenue has just grabbed a wastebasket to retch the unmistakable retches of an otherwise healthy girl in the first stage of pregnancy.

"Meta *Carpet*." That's Hans Caligar, the dignified refugee from the Berlin stage recruited to play Hitler's emissary. His accent tends to thicken when indignant: "On behalf ufa cast, I henreid [can read]. I must ask, murnau weill dalio marlene [more now while daily I more lean] brecht waltz to please you, veidt U.S.A. [why do you say], 'Avast, palatial hum'"— he smacked the script— "when *dix-sept* is salka viertel fritz lang [this set is such a virtual prison]?"

"Minute, Hans." Pat Carpet's on the phone, finger screwed to free ear like an unpopped champagne cork. "Who? Gabby Chatterton? Christ, no. Well, all right."

"You'll just have to act more impressed when you walk in, Hans," says my hubby—chipper, grandly sweatered, and betraying his agitation only with a slightly sickly *Time*-cover grin. "Acting! That's what we pay you for."

"So magnificently."

"Damn it, Hans. Viper, stop vomiting! And don't look at me like that. I told you that restaurant was no good. Where in hell is Lavabo? Listen, Herr Caligar—we're all making do, all right? We tried again just last week to get a bigger sets and props budget, but those Yid bastards who do Rose Dawson's books turned us down."

"I am a Yid bastard, Meta Morphy. My last Berlin performance was on Kristallnacht. It is *agony* for me to play this Nazi role—*crated* by an impish isle [imbecile]."

By then, you might think even Murphy would've known an anti-Semitic Irish playwright working in left-wing theater in New York might want to watch his goddam mouth. Grudgingly (Hans had had tears in his eyes), he did write a speech about Kristallnacht into Act Two. After von Deutrifau got done gloating about it, Brendan Leary—usually ready to have at the Nazi bastard for paragraphs at a time—got a surprising stage direction: "Speechless with fury, Brendan changes the subject."

Placating his own production wasn't my hubby's only worry as winter drew near. Brendan's diatribes lashed out so furiously at America's unpreparedness— "Tell those dead men lying out on the hills in Spain we're safe at home" and so on, Viper Leigh winning Murphine dudgeon when she piped her guess that, while she didn't know much about Iberian hygiene, they'd probably be buried by now—that it was a relief when the hero wound up and remembered to blast Hitler for a change.

The comrade in him at rare odds with the playwright, Murphy sulked every time another Lend-Lease shipment left for Murmansk. Pencil tapping a script whose latest caret added "buried" to Brendan's zinger, he winced whenever the papers or radio reported our Navy playing cat and mouse with U-boats. It wasn't only the actor's insufficient preparation that aggrieved him when *Clock* lumbered toward its premiere with young Hal Lime on the playbill's errata slip as the production's fourth successive Brendan Leary: one after another, the first three had gotten their induction notices.

Came opening night. It was Friday, December 5, 1941.

POSTED BY: *Pamdemonium*   I know it was nerves, but Bran and I had one of our increasingly nasty political arguments that afternoon. One of the real ones, not the midnight farces when a *very* twenty-one-year-old me used to drunkenly smack his bespoke shirt's heated front, yowling "Murderer, murderer."

I knew those were idiotic, since the rest of the time I didn't get that worked up lamenting Trotsky or the POUM. Only when I'd had a few did turning accusatory appeal to me, not to mention borrowing Jake Cohnstein's politics to get the Mighty Tower's goat. This was different: still a liquid coffin by night, the East River by day was a slow-oozing comic strip, prefiguring Bran's final career with its sun-Blondied tugboats and Dagwoody scows. Pam was sober, and my hubby's trial-baloney suggestion that Lend-Lease was a capitalist trick had exasperated me.

"Tell the drowned merchant sailors it's a capitalist trick," I mocked him. It was an awful thing to do to a playwright on his opening night, since I was parrot-parodying a line from his play. Just as bad, I was challenging his loyalty to the Merchant Marine, to which Murphy's attachment had grown stronger as his nonmembership in it receded. No wonder we were both seething in the cab.

Despite Hal Lime's scant eight days with the production as the fourth Brendan, Pat Carpet's habit of sticking the film script for *A Clod Washed Away by the Sea* inside the soiled one of the last play he'd ever direct, and a set that—bearing out Hans Caligar's objections—would've done Mrs. Gillooley proud, the debut performance of *A Clock with Twisted Hands* didn't go badly at first. Murphy did have a gift for situations that made Lillian Hellman's look like mayonnaise, and the colliding attitudes—the contempt for our weakness roiling away under von Deutrifau's praise of baseball, the magnate's undermined prowess as clay began to ooze out past his socks' gartered tops, ~~Vickie Patricia~~ Lucy's girlish dreams of a simple life in a (somewhat) less stately mansion, Brendan's clenched fists stage left and deaf Mrs. Magnate's symbolic ear trumpet stage right—all soon had the stage littered with the charred hulks of America's illusions.

Even the chuckles of recognition as it dawned that Count von Deutrifau was a Nazified Addison DeWitt were delighted, not scornful. New York opening-night audiences are too pleased by any reminder of their insider status to question its dramatic sense, and the man who normally would've—Addison—could only tackle it obliquely in his review. "The *slyboots!*" he crowed to me years later over a mai tai in the DeWitts' Topanga garden, riotously Californian and burly in one of the loud Hawaiian shirts that drove Eve up the wall and still tickled by Bran's atypical cunning.

As the Act Two curtain fell and Pam got over her annoying shudder at the offstage gunshot that ended it, my hubby was signaling his excitement at the applause with a gesture I never had the heart to describe to Garth Vader. Three fingers of one hand extended, he was smacking them against his other forearm—counting his third Pulitzer before it had hatched. It wasn't to be, but

I claim my share of the responsibility, if any, was minor. I wasn't the one who'd gotten Viper pregnant, couldn't have if I'd tried.

Act Three opened with everyone's return from the magnate's funeral, including the *coup de théâtre* of von Deutrifau's now openly displayed swastika armband. That made it even more menacing when he turned out to be bent, somewhat peculiarly—I wouldn't have *recognized* Elsie Dodge Plough's pointed cough—on marrying ~~Vickie Patricia~~ Lucy. When she resisted, the now blatantly rabid Nazi bastard hurled himself at her, tearing her blouse—and Viper Leigh screamed, as she was supposed to.

Then, grabbing her tummy as her eyes grew big as new planets, she waved Hans Caligar away and staggered offstage—which she wasn't. My first guess was panic, since over the past week or two we'd all (well, perhaps not all) been baffled by Bran's demands for a more violent rape scene.

"Come on, Hans!" he'd hectored our star at one late rehearsal from the Gypsum's sixth row. "Hell, I know it's hard for you, *Mein Herr*. It was damned hard for me to write too. Picture it this way—Viper's the Kraut, not you. That's it. You're giving it back to them for Kristallnacht!" Exuberant now, he swung his fist in an uppercut.

As Hans quite audibly asked Viper if he could borrow her wastebasket, my hubby turned to Pat Carpet. "Damn it, Pat! Do your job. Fuck Ernest Bellman." Enraged, he grabbed the hidden script for *A Clod Washed Away by the Sea* and hurled it at the cheap seats.

Our director consulted his cigar tip. "Sense memory, Hans," he called. "You're fighting your way out of the womb."

"I was quite happy there, Patkavan. Perhaps more than I knew."

"Then you're fighting your way back into it," Pat Carpet shrugged.

"That's not a memory. Do you really believe your own *Scheiss*?"

"Thanks, Hal," Pat said as his script was returned. Hal Lime wanted to see Hollywood too, and not as a Coast Guardsman on leave.

Anyhow, when Viper fled, Hans stood onstage solo in stunned silence. As murmurs told him the hall was catching on, he tried to improvise, reworking lines of von Deutrifau's caustic speech about baseball. Unfortunately, when Hal Lime took matters into his own hands and burst onto the scene, that made

Brendan's shout of rage at ~~Vickie Patricia~~ Lucy's violation—"You Hun reptile. That's strike three"—apropos in all the wrong ways. Then the curtains swept shut as the two men stared at each other.

As murmurs spawned giggles and confused applause, Murphy grabbed my arm. "Christ! Snooks, for fuck's sake get back there and find out what's happened to Viper. The captain can't be seen leaving the bridge."

Once I'd not very unobtrusively maneuvered myself down the aisle, I went up the steps to the side stage door and down a corridor to the dressing room Viper shared with Floss Bicuspid. Her own part done after Act Three's first scene, Floss was nowhere in sight; still in ~~Vickie Patricia~~ Lucy's torn blouse and beige skirt, Viper sat clutching her belly on the couch. Her face was two blue marbles above a red-rimmed, mobile Rorschach blot.

"Mascara, mascara," she moaned.

Hesitant—but she *was* an actress—I started fumbling among her cosmetics. "No, no!" Viper pled. "*Mi*scarria-, *mi*scarria—I think I'm having a misc—ow, ow, ow, ow!"

"Call an ambulance," I told Floss as her face appeared in the doorway.

"I've just told someone to. Dear God, where's the stage manager?"

"So hot," Viper whimpered. "Can't brea—"

Her temperature must've been well over a hundred. Gently prying away the slim arms clamped to her slender tummy, a tongue-biting Pam tugged buttons from buttonholes and torn collar from shoulders and then passed two slim pale arms through armholes, feeling very peculiar. It hadn't been all that long, and Viper's hot skin was moist.

Reframed things by imagining I was Murphy's first wife working at Gimbel's, and once I had the blouse off the mannequin, Viper's breathing grew easier. I had no real call to free her anxious boobies from their brassiere. I didn't yet know my hubby had unhooked, uncupped, mouthed, and squashed them dozens of times, testosteronically gorging on nipples I'd pictured as hard-centered red dollops on two shadowed and unsprung soft pears.

"The skirt too, Snooks." Captain of his own soul first, a maddened Murphy had decided the bridge could go hang. "We'll need the costume. Where in hell's Viper's understudy?"

"Why, Brannigan! San Diego," said Floss Bicuspid. "Judy ran off with that young Marine—what was his name, Walker? Ah, love on a train! Love on a train."

"Christ!" As abruptly as if a vaudeville hook from the Rosalie Gypsum's previous incarnation was to blame, Murphy's face yanked itself away. "Get Pat Carpet back here," he bawled. "And Lavabo! Lock the lobby doors if you have to. Nobody's leaving this theater until the curtain comes down for real."

Distraught, Viper looked up from her reclutched tummy. "Please, can't I? Branny, I'll stay if I have to. But—ow, ow, ow, ow."

As Murphy charged off, I hesitated. The blouse had been for Viper's sake; the skirt was for Murphy. Whose conversion into a newly founded small town named Bran, NY, I was in no shape to absorb. I'd have to get her to her feet too, feel that feverish but unhappy body knock against mine as Floss looked on.

Floss herself forestalled me: "I'll do it. We're a bit less bashful at my age," she said, misunderstanding my hesitation slightly. I didn't want to watch her taking my place. Outside the dressing room, in backstage light like Edisonized perspiration, my tuxedoed hubby, framed by a jumble of flats—one still marked "Prom in Mad II/2"—was mighty-towering over Pat Carpet.

"Snooks!" he told me. "There's nothing for it. You're going to finish Viper's part."

"What on earth are you talking about, Bran? I can't act. I'm a writer."

"Oh, hell! We can all act. If Viper can, who can't? And as for you being a— damn it, just do what I say."

"But I don't know the part," I said.

He stared the way Houdini must've after that fatal punch to the solar plexus. "After a *month?*" my hubby roared. "Christ, you've been sitting right next to me. What were you doing, knitting?"

I floundered. "Oh! I mean—of course I know all Viper's big lines, like 'Aaieee.' But—oh, Bran, it's all the blah, blah, blah in between. My God, you don't really expect anyone to remember that, do you?"

At its leisure, my brain couldn't have manufactured anything as devastating. If we'd been at home in Sutton Place, Murphy's face would've erupted for two hours without letup as the East River's prostrate Dagwoods and Blondies—

those heralds of his literary but never marital destiny—oozed mutely by behind him. But after a tense facial struggle, a stark determination to keep Bran Hume in the anchor's chair outfactored his urge to explode as Brannigan Gillooley.

"Give her a script. Let her take it on with her."

Pat Carpet looked appalled. "Bran, please. You aren't the only one here with a reputation. Jesus *Christ!* You stupid Mick prizefighter. Let's just Booth it, thank 'em all for showing up, and better luck next—"

"No. *No.* Four fucking years! Four fucking years, while you were looking up Bellman's porthole. You whoring son of a bitch. Our only other bet is Floss, and come on. At least they'll think Hans might—might!—want to rape Pam." He glared at me.

"My God, this is insane," I wailed. "Bran, my *friends* are out there"—and if I may be so bold as to quote from *Clock*, that was strike three. Even as the words escaped, I knew that now I'd have to do it unless I wanted my first and, at that point, only marriage to bite the dust instanter.

"Someone'll have to go out and tell them. And soon." Pat Carpet had just done what he did best: assert his authority in surrender. You probably don't remember his '53 HUAC testimony, though, or even what the HUAC was.

Chin rising, Murphy said, "I'll handle that"—by which he meant Murph Vanity would. "When I say it was sabotage, they'll believe it from Brannigan Murphy. God damn it, get changed, Pam. We go on in five minutes."

Smoothing his bow tie's ends, he strode off as Hal Lime rushed up. "The ambulance is here. My God, aren't we Boothing this thing?"—a vintage Broadway expression, oddly unpreserved in slang dictionaries, for sending the audience home with the play incomplete.

Pat Carpet gestured Pamward. Hal stared. Reaching rather grimly for my gown's zipper—it was low-backed, the reason I hadn't worn a bra—I stalked back into the dressing room.

~~Vickie Patricia~~ Lucy's torn blouse and beige skirt were both safely draped on a chair. As Floss tried to sponge her forehead, a still moaning Viper lay turned to the wall on the couch. She was wrapped in a blanket not all that discreetly, and the blood that darkly spidered the thighs below her barely crescented pale little buttocks made me ashamed.

"You are *joking*," said Floss as I pushed my gown's top to my waist. I was so addled I thought she meant the now revealed, less than splendid Buchanan bosom. "If we aren't Boothing, I rather thought, for the show's sake—well, I've played Desdemona, you know."

"Ow," Viper moaned. "Ow, ow."

I'd just kicked Pam's gown under the dressing table when the door swung open and two ambulance attendants bundled a stretcher through. The grab I made for the blouse just got in their way as they pushed by, spread the stretcher, and started to lift Viper onto it.

"Jesus, what's this place coming to? She'd never have cut it here in the old days," one said, and I don't think he meant Viper. Thankful its collar was already ripped, I yanked ~~Vickie Patricia~~ Lucy's top down over my head, then lunged for the skirt as they knelt to lift her.

Again thankfully, though on me it damn near invented the miniskirt, it hadn't been visibly bled on. As I smoothed the bunching over the too tight hips, Floss said, "Dear God! Your hair—I mean your hairdo." A trouper, she reached for a hairbrush; a realist, she left it lying there.

Since I'd known at first glance Viper's shoes were no go, I was crouching to retrieve my own—beaded black evening heels, all wrong for the rest of the outfit—when Viper's frightened blue eyes and "ow"-ing red-rimmed Rorschach blot went by a foot from my nose. Horrified at how fast I'd forgotten she was real and in pain, I scrambled up in my stocking feet and dashed out of the dressing room after her stretcher.

"Viper!" I called. "You shouldn't be alone. Hadn't we better notify"—well, there had to be one—"the father?"

Above the blanket's receding rim, her bobbing blue eyes stared back. She was miscarrying; she didn't really know the rules of anything. No doubt she meant to protect Mrs. Murphy's privacy. As the doors opened and she was borne into the early-December night, she jammed a hasty finger into her mouth and held it glisteningly aloft to a red moon we both knew.

"Come *on*, Pam!" Pat Carpet shoved a script folded to page 102—Viper's temperature, their hotel key's number?—into my hand. "Murph's just wrapped it up."

"My shoes," I moaned in vain. Pat swept me into the wings as Murphy shouldered his way back through the curtain to a patter of, all in all (I didn't yet know what he'd said about Viper), amazingly tactful applause.

"Good luck, Snooks," he barked, not knowing yet what I now *knew* about Viper. A *Time*-cover grin and a cheap paperback's wild eyes—once a budding pudding's twin Civil War memorials, the mimsy borogoves today, just then two orbs of everything in nowhere—passed in the night.

Pat hustled me into position opposite Hans Caligar, who clearly hadn't been notified of Viper's replacement. I'd never known he liked me until I saw his perplexity give way to a compassionate smile.

"*Mein arme Kind*," he had just time to say. "I share with you what Reinhardt said once: 'One way the theater resembles life is that it will be over sooner than we think.'"

The curtains parted. Dazzling lights blazed apocalypse. Shouting "The Führer was right! The strong only *shame* themselves when they negotiate with the weak," Hans—now Count von Deutrifau—hurled himself at me.

"*Aaieee!*" I screamed.

POSTED BY: *Pam*   Fun fact, Panama: I'd never noticed Hans Caligar had false teeth. Once he got done rather considerately mauling me between clacking hisses about the master race and Brendan Leary barged in with "You Hun reptile. That's strike three," which I'm afraid did get some laughs, ~~Vickie Patricia~~ Lucy's main job for four pages was to sit where von Deutrifau had hurled me—Wimbledon-eyed, disheveled, and in my case trying to ignore the ambulance's fading wail—as Hal Lime and Hans raged at each other. Not either actor's finest hour, but I did *try* to turn each page discreetly before I looked up aghast and conquerable again.

After Hans made his deeply relieved final exit, Addisonishly snarling, "In the theater of *war*, you will close on Saturday night—and *our* play will run forever," we got to the part I was dreading. Murphy did have some stagecraft; he knew convincing (still, just barely) virginal ~~Vickie Patricia~~ Lucy that Nazism's twisted clock ticked doomsday had to be Brendan's final task. The Murphine touch was that it took him eight pages.

As Hal Lime helped me to my feet, his face was glowing with greasepain at the shambles of his Broadway debut. Unlike Hans, however, he'd converted it into rage at his amateur costar: the difference between an old actor and a young one, I suppose.

"Oh, Brendan!" I duly gasped, turning a page. "Is it really over?" I'm afraid that drew some tittering too.

"No, ~~Vickie Patricia~~ Lucy," Hal Lime snapped, irritably deflecting my lifted script from his face. "It hasn't even begun." Godspeeded by scattered groans, we were into the climactic Murphine maelstrom.

All that saved us for a while was that his speeches were longer. Even so, I did have to jump in here and there, peddling Murphy's idea of the case for isolationism—the white-picketed garden of delights we could share if my fiancé only gave up his hobby of fighting Fascists—and not only had I never been onstage in my life, but that life had just exploded into a riot of confusions that reeled and yawed as I struggled to read ~~Vickie Patricia~~ Lucy's lines.

They kept colliding in a persistent impression that I'd been on the verge of lifting Viper to her feet to unzip the skirt I was wearing now, two brassiered pears rubbing at my suddenly pounding chest, when my Pam-hands got forestalled not by Floss's but Murphy's. With five pages to go, my diaphragm could've taught frogmen a trick or two.

"My God, you poor kid!" Hal Lime erupted. " You don't even know that you've been living in a dream world. The whole crazy madrigal's over! It's a nest of vipers out there, can't you see?"

"You're wrong, Brendan. I *did* know," I read. "But I loved it there. We were so happy. Can't we just stay in it a little longer? It's not our fight—not yet."

"No, by God. There's only one place to stop these bastards—and it isn't a fancy-pants living room in Connecticut," Hal said, glaring at the two seedy armchairs and lone floor lamp in sight. "It's the ~~Maginot Line Narvik harbor the sky over London~~ right outside the gates of Moscow. Men, real men, are dying there right now. I can't stay out. Wherever they're fighting, that's where I want to be." (Murphy and John Steinbeck could now officially reckon themselves even.)

I turned the page. "You never were going to take the TWA job, were you?" After puzzling over the problem that *Clock's* delayed production gave the play a hero who'd been living off his future in-laws for over two and a half years since the fall of Madrid, Murphy'd opted to distract the audience by introducing a Faustian temptation.

"I couldn't have. Brendan Leary wasn't born to lick anyone's boots. And honey, however much I love you, I won't kiss those fancy—Bloomingdale's—shoes—of yours, either…"

We were both staring at my stockinged feet. "These old things?" I read. "You, you, yuh, you'd never—need to, sweetheart. On our wedding night—*mmmf!*—I, I, I won't—be wearing any, silly boy! Oh, Brenda—nah, nah, nah—if you only—*aaah, ah*—promise you won't do something—*kuh, kuh, kuh*—crazy like running away to join the—*phlphphlph!!*—RAF—tomorrow, that night could staaaaaaart! *Now!* Oh, God!"

POSTED BY: *Pam*   That was when Hal Lime, at wit's end, did two things not in the script. The first was to slap me quite hard in the face. The more misjudged of his emergency surgeries was to skip two pages of script and go straight into Brendan Leary's final speech—three hundred exalted words welcoming his moneyed fiancée to the fight before berating the rest of America for not doing the same. Their only drawback was how they began: "Oh, ~~Vickie Patricia~~ Lucy! Honey, you just can't know what it means to me that you've finally seen what I've been driving at like a piledriver…"

Under the circumstances, the reviews were forgiving: even Addison's, though not Jake Cohnstein's. Everyone realized things hadn't gone as intended, and only one cloddish critic wondered why Brendan Leary had gone on to denounce isolationism right after apparently declaring that his own program was to stay parked in Connecticut, torpedoing ~~Vickie Patricia~~ Lucy's heavenly fluff every night and twice on Sundays. As for Pam, her contribution got passed over in silence except for Addison's reference—"forgiving" isn't the same as "laudatory," you know—to "an anonymous newcomer, perhaps better suited to explicitly comedic veins."

You'd better believe Bran noticed that "explicitly" when we spread the reviews out at Sardi's, the print still damp—lovely smell—on the early morning editions. I couldn't make head or tail of them myself, since as soon as we came in I'd begun downing rum like a bomb victim. Among other things, that was to make my debut conversation with Roy Charters, my future editor at *Regent's*, a bit loopy and squawky. Then Bran took me home to a dawn-grayed Sutton Place, where to my woozy bewilderment he insisted on his marital rights.

I don't know whether it was a stubborn vote of confidence in himself or his fury at my ineptitude had taken a sexualized turn. He may even have been aroused by seeing me in Viper's stage clothes, as if he'd finally demoted me to just another actress and proved I was worse than she was. Anyhow, he didn't need his usual encouragement to colum firth; if you must know, Pam's poor plum, startlingly parted and plumbed, was the object of conjugal conjugation instead. Not an experience I've ever cared to repeat—I'm not saying I *haven't*, only that I've never *cared* to—but it didn't last long.

For one obvious reason, not that I'd've wished it on her otherwise, he'd have been better off sticking to that with Viper. Chalky and tottering, she reappeared at the Rosalie Gypsum on Saturday, insisting she was well enough to perform. Since she'd been in worse pain than I was and it didn't really seem all this had been *her* fault, I toddled along to the dressing room to look in on her, but the door was closed and I didn't open it. From inside, I'd just heard Bran's voice: "Good riddance. Sorry, cupcake, but you weren't the first one to try it."

3. The Most Sensational Divorce of 1943

POSTED BY: *R.J. Pam*   Unless this desiccated tummy of mine decides it's got a craving for more pharmacology or perhaps only celery before I vamoose, it's peculiar to think I've just had my last meal. Nothing too Borgia: tuna on white, glass of milk, pill dessert. The absurdity, Panama, is that

I might not've bothered to gulp lunch at all if half my prescriptions didn't require being taken with food. Only after I'd ingested the midday triad did I recall blood pressure, etc., are irrelevant now.

The pills were from habit, the tuna's from Sutton's. How Andy Pond moaned when his last glance in my fridge told him boredom at mayonnaising a can of Starkist now comes under the heading of cooking to me, meaning I willingly pay to have it delivered to the Rochambeau from a gourmet shop he no doubt thinks has better things to do. If he saw the Martin's and La Chaumière doggie bags in the freezer, slowly frosting from nourishment to my snowblind equivalent of Nan Finn's scrapbooks, he kept that inburst of Pondian woe mute.

Fortunately, even in retirement, Andy's the type to shave *before* retrieving each morning's *WashPost* and *NYT* from his modest lawn. When they shove a briar patch of microphones at him tomorrow, he'll look reasonably spruce for a stunned old duffer. Yet I doubt he'll manage to avoid making his chum Pam sound eccentric. That didn't bother me much until I realized his briar-patched natterings might be all there was.

Are you with me, Chad Diebold? Well, *l'équipe* here is onto your nasty new game. I should've guessed hours ago there might be more to daisysdaughter. com's failure to nab even one confessed reader than its stunted graphic delights and my octogenarian confusion about how to link.

Have I guessed right, Chad? Is everyone seeing "The page cannot be found" as I input like crazy? Once your sweepers zeroed in, you only needed a mouse-click: "Please try your request later. The page cannot be found."

He can't? Well, he's probably off being rogered by some Congressman, isn't he? Split like a butterfly ballot! But I filibuster.

Chad, if I know you—and I think I do—you've already got some flunky diddling my long goodbye so I'll sound like a madwoman. I can see that doctored Pamicature from here. As the biographer in miniature of, among others, Anne Bradstreet—Chapter 8 of *Glory Be*, "A Poem"—I know as well as anyone how a bygone life can be billiard-balled to drop snugly into prearranged pockets.

Or in the event my online suicide note blindsides the White House once the media discover it and come pelting, will you and the Murphy Channel try to pretend I never existed? Pointing to the sheer impossibility of *anyone*, much less a fat-lunetted old bag with rheumatic fingers whose plumbing necessitates frequent bathroom breaks and the like, spewing words by the demented thousand, will you call my blog a forgery cooked up by some outraged committee or nostalgia fiend—Panama's dad, Nan Finn's strange son? Tim Cadwaller's name on *You Must Remember This: The Posthumous Career of World War Two* certainly fits him for the part of Pamtomimer. His hand in setting up this website most likely hasn't escaped your notice.

Short of a crash diet, he can't help the stout part. Yet I'm sure *Qwert*'s Man in the Dark will stoutly deny pseudauthorship. That's unless you've bought him off too, something that's started to strike me as no more than improbable. Don't think it's eluded me, Tim, that the Cadwaller clan is being awfully slow about its ritual group call to your lonely old Gramela. I don't give a shit if she's on vacation! At the very least my Panama must be showering by now, as you puff over your column and try harder than hell not to imagine what your daughter must look like wearing only soap.

From where I sit, Chad, Tim's your best bet to fob the thing off on. As his grandfather once said of Andy Pond when we left Andy holding the diplomatic pouch to skip out and get married at l'Église Américaine, "He's fobbable."

POSTED BY: *Pam*   Still, Chad, here's the question of questions from your Internet Pam-pal. If you are reading my blog, you devil, you've been more than forewarned of what I plan to do. Have you or haven't you canceled my White House birthday greetings?

I'm just mulling which is more like you. If it suited this slow-news Tuesday's gyre and gimble, I don't think you'd sweat a drop, much less shed a tear (he's not crying, folks; that's just ocular saliva), before you let my call go through. Yes, despite knowing how I plan to wrap up my part of the conversation. As for Potus, he's obviously free to keep talking until my nonresponsiveness annoys him or he runs out of light-bulb jokes.

You just may have decided it's more Abu Ghraib to keep Pam hunched in front of dead Daisy's typewriter—Mac, Mac. Sorry—as my fingers get rheumajulienned inputting things nobody will read in this or any other world and I wait for a surcease you've made sure won't come. In that case, Andy Pond gets to stoop unharassed for tomorrow's *WashPost* and *NYT*. Assuming, of course, he's not too upset to face the twice-a-week moped of MoDo's mood op-ed after learning tonight I won't marry him.

As I picture our dinner, in prospect again if the phone never rings—my wan birthday meal and Rochambeauvine snooze in front of *Meet Pamela* or *The Gal I Left Behind Me*—I'm mortified. That's not because of Andy's cooking, which I'm sure will be fine as food goes. Nor his eyes' readjustment to their placid Pond norm, deft as an editor fixing a typo—that's "suave," Pam, not "slave"— once they've blinked when he learns his quiet suit is being taken to the cleaners'.

What I can't stand is the reverse shot: a still alive Pam, anticlimactically present. Just an upper-Connecticut crone mulching cuisine as she paws her brain's dark for a quip she's misplaced ("Forlorn is forearmed"). Cadwaller's gun shrunk in my crotch—you senile, disgusting Cinderella!—to the familiar *vieux jeu* of my daily medicinal Rubicon cube. And the blog Clio Airways Lindberghized cyberspace with now a humiliating fantasy whose exhumation by friend, press, or stranger I'd quake at.

All because I was Pamfool enough to trust a White House promise, Hopsie! Not to mention Hollywoodized or secretly unnerved enough to make my protest depend on a call that may've been scratched from Potus's schedule after these indiscreet previews of the earful he'd get.

Can you blame me for quailing when I picture *surviving* this blog? Even if I shut down now and go read my favorite poem—"Minds crabwise interlock" and so on—from *The Pilgrim Lands at Malibu*, I've got no control over whether my readership stays hypothetical. Not after hitting "Post" scores of times since the *WashPost*'s seagull skate rugward when the windows were pale.

Bikini girl, suppose your unimaginable daughter finds my pistol-proud boasts—then learns from Wiki their tiresome author lived to a bedridden, pill-popping, marooned ninety-one? If anything, I should have died two days ago. Hoist by my own petard, I am, and here I was thinking I'd outlived my last pet. Hello, Ard! Welcome to *l'équipe*.

Ard, I don't think I can go through it again: not another "Chanson d'automne." Call or no call, I'm not sure I can face tucking Cadwaller's gun back into the Paris footlocker unfired. Even sans Potus lending an ear, my damned blog will posthumously document—won't it?—that my mess of pink and gray things was a protest against this awful and unending war.

But Ard, I'm so terrified of doing it on my own. And when, my pet? How long do we give the White House switchboard before saying "Oh, fuck this" and redecorating without a designer? It'd be one dismal irony if the phone rings ten seconds after we've made kablooie. Giving Gerson, who hated those fadeouts, *two* reasons to shudder.

Oh, Panama! I've never been so enisled and wassailed by this many decisions, not even in World War Two. The truth is, your Gramela was always no champ at making them. That's why I cast Potus as my final prompter. Ard, wouldn't Pavlov be proud?

I may seem brave, I don't know. Omaha, Dachau, whatever. If my own two cents count, not that your dad acted too interested when I was helping him with *his* book, the day of Pam's war that left me most pleased to have stood the gaff happened Stateside. But I was surrounded by women—great huge ones, with names like Viv, Tess, Babe, and Josie—and my silly pride melted once I remembered that every last one of them in our laughing, wet circle went down into the mine every day.

Feel free to look up "To the Ends of the Earth," published in *Regent's* on January 14, 1943. Yes, dear: that's your Gramela's byline. No, I didn't pose for the dumb illustration, which should've been group and by Fernando Botero.

All the same, Ard, even that journey felt like finding the trap in contraption. No more than Pam's series of contingent responses—in the crunch, saying "Deal" after Viv's "You go down with us, you'll have to stay down all day. Think you can handle that?"—to circumstances undevised by me.

Panama, Panama! This manner you dote on is my plea for a smoke as I glare at the firing squad. Whatever I made of it later, not much has ever felt like my idea from the start, my divorce from Murphy included.

POSTED BY: *Pam*   If you haven't put "December" and "1941" together, bikini girl—and why should you, born in 1990?—what turned *A Clock with Twisted Hands* into his first flop in almost a decade wasn't just its lunatic opening night. Even Bran's claim in his emergency mud-on-troubled-waters speech that Viper was in Fascist pay didn't attract too much ridicule, as it certainly should've once the hireling shakily rejoined the cast for the rest of the run. "Forgiving of him, wasn't it?" Addison reminisced in Topanga years later. "I imagine she came to him with the usual sob story about Goebbels's check bouncing and the rent being due."

The problem was that we were at war all over the world by the Sunday. Theatergoers couldn't see much merit in being scolded for our ostrich neutrality when we were losing an island in the Pacific every time another barkeep snapped on a radio. Bran tried to rewrite Brendan's least germane jeremiads to make room for Pearl Harbor, but they'd been the point and Pat Carpet, his contract for *Washed Away* (yes, they'd shortened the title) signed, was in California before Christmas. Only because *Clock* was "the new Brannigan Murphy" did it limp along for six weeks of half filled houses before closing after forty-nine performances.

It didn't win Viper Leigh fame, not even as a saboteur. From my steamed hubby's viewpoint, his improvised slander came true in court. Still, her reign on the witness stand in late May '43 only made her a star in the tabs.

Hal Lime, of course, did go to Hollywood. Pat Carpet had already slipped him a *sub rosa* promise at *Clock's* dress rehearsal of the second lead as Foyle, the hero's light-hearted pal, as soon as *Washed Away* went in front of the cameras. Most likely that explains how come he only slapped instead of knifing me.

All in all, it does seem unfair to Bran that the only person to benefit from *A Clock with Twisted Hands* was his wife. Ard knows, not because anyone ever gave me another acting job! Gerson only let Mrs. G. have a fleeting mute cameo in *The Gal I Left Behind Me*, and not only did he love me but that may've been proof. My stroke of luck was that Roy Charters was Floss Bicuspid's nephew.

Otherwise, the newly promoted editor of *Regent's* magazine—defunct since 1966, it was on a par with *Collier's* (and isn't that a big help in placing it?) in its day—wouldn't have been at Sardi's when our tense mob turned up. Instantly lost in his tweeds and office-mussed hair among our clownish tuxes and gowns, the man who'd spring me from book reviewing to go cover the home front's assembly-line Minervas and rosily riveting shipbuilders was so at home with being out of place that until he opened his mouth my first guess was he was a refugee.

When I told him so later, Roy chuckled and said he'd known right away I was: "From what was the question. You sure gave me my pick." I'm not sure he ever guessed all of them, despite being smarter than his aunt. Take it from me, Panama: if you ever worry about a man's intelligence, sleep with him. He'll never ask you another question that doesn't seem faintly stupid.

POSTED BY: *Pamderer*   Don't misunderstand. Roy and I didn't make the beast with two left feet until midway through my divorce trial. With Viper's Bran-blackening testimony still as fresh as her lipstick in my ears—must rethink that construction before I hit "Post," Ard—I knew it was all over but the pouting.

In one of his rare points in common with Murphy, Roy was twice my age. I still had fewer problems than he did recognizing that the real meaning of our blowsy, slack sex was its pointlessness. Divorce-demoralized himself, as his wife Cath—incidentally my agent after the war—had gotten a bit too overjoyed about pronouncing Manhattan "Menhattan" back in summer '42, my editor was experimenting with being un-Roylike and failing. Which brought us full circle, considering my gaga Pamquivalent when we first met.

To say the least, I haven't been around theatrical people in a while. I don't know if they still follow tradition by packing some Midtown restaurant to wait for the papers. After the kind of opening we'd had, a pack of eels spilled onto a fishing boat would've had a better chance of figuring out the right attitude. You can imagine how grateful I am Roy stayed determined to treat me as a squid netted by accident.

As I think I've mentioned, Ard, I was pretty sozzled by the time he introduced himself. That didn't make me stand out. Early on, all that had cut through the jumble of exhilarated anxiety was Floss Bicuspid trilling Ma Bell Époquishly to a nameless someone: "Wonderful! *Such* good news. Yes, of course I'll tell them. Thank you."

Turning to a dozen eager faces—did she have an in at the *Times*? Old hand that she was, could she have been speaking directly to Santa?—she indignantly drew herself up to her full weight. "Honestly, all of you! I'm quite sure everyone will be glad to hear our Viper's all right." I wonder who else Hal Lime spoke for—and how accurately he'd pegged her motives, since actors are privy to all sorts of insights they never apply to themselves—when he called out, "Thanks, Floss. We all know how noble you are."

As for me, I'd half expected to be pelted with crudités when I slumped through the door. But in the frantic limbo we all occupied, I was just another spewed bit of *Clock*'s innards, too inept to catch on that the free pass I was getting meant they'd all known about Bran and Viper. Even Hans Caligar's strenuously lively account of an avant-garde *Midsummer Night's Dream* in Zurich—"I was playing Bottom, and I was the only one who *wasn't* wearing a donkey's head"—went by without me guessing he'd told it to console me.

Two tables away (tables as obstructions, not locations; everyone was too keyed up to sit down), Bran was flashing his *Time*-cover grin and Murphying away about *Prom in Madrid*'s rough birth. Despite my breathless redisguise as the latest Mrs. Murphy, I'd done enough bloody acting for his sake tonight that I was damned if I'd go wifily Boswell-that-ends-well his monologue. A dozen conversations had turned into shrieks at masks by the time Floss said, "Here she is, Roy" and hurried to rejoin the pigeons peering out the window for news trucks: Sardi's overdressed parody of urchins peering in.

The middle-aged teddy bear who put out his hand clearly wasn't a Great White Way denizen, since his manner wasn't affected by the setting. It's not that theater folk aren't intelligent so much as that they're in a constant panic over what it's good for besides inventing demeanors, and the volatility gets fatiguing. If also, in the right wrong mood, infectious, which is why I give Roy points for patience.

"This may not be the time, but I did want to tell you how much I liked your review of Rita Cavanagh's last book," he teddy-bore down on me through the din. Now you know why I remember that one. "What was it, *Sable Coat*?"

"No, no! *Sybil Choate*," I yowled back—strident as a trident, rum punch and cigarette held in an air curtsy. "But a pose by any other name. If you ask me, she should've stuck to poetry."

"They did ask you," Roy reminded me. "Tell me, though. Do you write fiction yourself?"

"Me? Oh, hell no. Look around, Mr. Man! I just live it."

"That's reassuring," he said, ignoring the intrusion of another sham Pam who didn't concern him. "One thing I wondered about was whether you might have some competitive ax you were grinding."

"God, no! I just can't abide all these Twenties relics coming out of the woodwork to go pietistic on us. I mean, look how well their *first* idea of what life was all about worked out."

"Oh, that's right!" Roy told Sardi's ceiling. "Forgive me. I'd forgotten who your mother was. But I'm sure that's very unfair to you, so please ignore it."

"Your guess is as good as mine," I admitted to my own rum-punched surprise. Not to mention dead Daisy's, since my mother had gotten pretty damned smug about her suicide's status as the worst thing that would ever happen to me. My new candor told her an adjustment had been made.

"I doubt it'll always be," he said handsomely, a word Roy restored to its original meaning. "I'll tell you what got me curious, though: you one-upping poor Rita about Europe. Where'd all that come out of?"

Is it any wonder I reacted like a desert somebody had discovered water in? Nobody'd asked for *that* vaudeville spiel in months. Along with the rest of my pre-Murphy c.v., reprises of Ram-Pam-Pam's upbringing weren't in demand at Sutton Place. Beyond that, I'd grasped at long last that this looming head was trying to talk to *Pamela Buchanan*. Her I knew how to play.

How, yes. Why, no. Sick of the comedy I'd been miscast in since June, I was like-mother-like-daughterishly out to break the camel's back with the first straw I drew. My jalopy lingerie would've been hanging off one instep in Viper's face—Bran's too, of course—as soon as any plausible man showed interest. Ten Chignonned and *mieux Hitler que Blum* minutes later, when a newly confident Roy (I just didn't realize in which of us his confidence had grown) asked for my phone number—and a Murphy plainly alerted by John Lavabo's gurgle to the identity of *Regent's* unprepossessing top dog came toward us festooned with bluster—I murmured as I passed it to him, "My husband works at home."

"I'm sorry?" honest Roy said, honestly confused.

"Oh, nothing! Please do call."

POSTED BY: *Pam* I was surprised when he did on December 10th. I'd had other things on my mind: frying pans, fires. As my clot of a hubby moped over *Clock's* lackluster business, oblivious to the succession of sad or silly Vipers simpering or whimpering in plain and fancy sight wherever he paced, I took refuge in the wampum of a Pam-pun: *Je suis ébranlée.* I had a review overdue for *OC* of a Sebastian Knight omnibus, newly published after the surprise success of his brother's memoir—and then, from Sunday on, there was the war.

"Hello?" I said as supine Dagwoods and Blondies, strangers to conflict on the East River's gray carpet, oozed from setup to punchline past Sutton Place. Not that excitable people weren't expecting fleets of German bombers to blacken the sky with chapter after chapter of *Mein Kampf*—translated by H.G. Wells, no doubt—over Manhattan any day.

My future editor wasn't among them. "Roy Charters here. I was wondering if you'd care to stop by my office tomorrow. Around ten?"

Regent's was two spiral-staircased floors of shirtsleeved clacking and skirted swooping for copy in a stack of ten more on West 50th Street. Tucked into a corner, Roy's office was the usual editor's haven: immaculately glassy view of the never immaculate Hudson, bookcases whose upper shelves were as dense with pristine bestsellers as their lower ones were leaky with manuscripts and the competition's newsstand fodder. Its one defiance of decorum was a faded pennant from Case Western Reserve, no idle thumb at snobbery when the Ivy League was still such a password its teams actually dominated college *sports* coverage. Those were the days.

My first daylit and rumless exposure to the oval Ohio tourist brochure between Roy's overlarge ears—two lively small towns hoping their climbing visitors wouldn't dawdle too long up at Widow's Peak, a mouth whose considerable kindness was at once signaled and inhibited by its reluctance to give too much play to the bad uneven teeth in his smile's creek bed—told me how deranged I'd been in Sardi's. Not because he wasn't my type, Panama: so far as men went, I never really had one. The only one of my three husbands you'd call conventionally good-looking was Murphy.

I did like to think I had *some* sense of people's personalities, though, and Roy's was all traffic lights and posted speed limits. Then still as visibly married as the sky is blue, he was no more a candidate for a *folie à deux* than your Gramela would be for President. Tactful, too: as I took my seat in the office I'd get to know so well, the only tipoff he wasn't sure we agreed on what I was doing here was his cautious greeting.

"Thanks so much for coming, Mrs. Murphy. Now let me tell you what I'm—"

"Oh, please! It's Pam. Or Sam, I don't care."

I'd just said, *I'm a writer.* Roy nodded: "Pam then. Do you know anything about the Free French mission here in town?"

"I've met Raoul Aglion, yes. My God, hasn't everyone?"

Even with Tim for a father, I doubt you'll know the name. Let daisysdaughter.com oblige yet again. Pam's one encounter with de Gaulle's New York emissary dated to the pre-Murphine spring, when he was still making do with a spare phone and desk at—World War Two was never short on mother-of-invention wonders, Panama—the Jean Patou perfume company's Fifth Avenue headquarters. Wifeless and de-secretaried for the night, Alisteir Malcolm had brought me to a soiree at Ann Darrow Driscoll's where Aglion, polite as a just-widowed bridegroom, was going along with everyone's illusion that champagne and cake took care of his needs. Only his quick eyes were reminders of his Frankenstein brief to make his bride breathe.

His presence disconcerted my horse's ass of an escort even before the inevitable high-society "Marseillaise"—*"Allongez, enfin, dans ma poitrine,"* our smitten hostess seemed to be singing—in the foreign guest's honor. At the time, fearful of making hard-line Stalinists Djugashlivid, the old *Republic* was pretending the Free French didn't exist, a trick easier to play on phantasms an ocean away than a pleasant man in a slightly out-of-fashion dinner jacket extending his hand. So I'd shaken it instead, winning a droll look and five minutes of chat about our favorite scenes in *La Chartreuse de Parme.*

Anyhow, Roy was pleased. "You have? Even better. Here's the thing: all our readers know about them is 'plucky little band,' and that's fine up to a point. But my confidential sources tell me it's a lot more complicated behind the scenes. Here's where we exchange a look of astonishment, if you don't mind."

I beamed instead. "To be honest, I was working on puzzled. You wouldn't be trying to tell me they're still French."

"Absolutely! And it's still politics. Prewar grudges I can't follow to save my life, along with constant fighting over a very small pie and a lot of what sounds like the silliest rot if you don't have a scorecard. Well, I don't. Neither do most Americans. Can you guess why my next words might be 'Uh-oh'?"

"That could make them unpopular sooner or later." (Do I give myself credit for catching on fast? Yes, I give myself credit for catching on fast.)

"It could at that. That's one reason too many people in Washington wish they'd all go away, which we don't want and isn't likely to happen. Obviously, *Regent's* is all for them, but I'd still like to see a treatment that's more sophisticated than what we've run so far. It might help. Are you interested?"

"Of course. I'm sorry, though: what's the book?"

"You've misunderstood. I want you to go talk to them. I'm pretty sure you can handle the frame of reference, and you've got the language. They might be more willing to open up now that we're in. Do you feel like taking a crack at that for me?"

Did I? All I could think of was how different my life might be if he'd asked on June 21st. It took me a second to realize Roy was waiting for my voice to answer and not just my face.

"Damn right I do."

"Good! And, oh—goodbye, Sam. See you in, I'd say, about a week."

Like a fool, I did it in four days. And had a wonderful time, racing out of Sutton Place past Bran's darkening brow for heraldic coffee here and a timely square meal there opposite dive-bombing mustaches, hands playing bosun to invisible bosoms, and Gallic profiles too visibly down to sharing their last razor blade. They were marooned in Automats and argonauted by argot, and I hadn't rattled on so much in French in seven years. Or written it since, dismal memory, "Chanson d'automne," but now I was jotting down quotes.

Unsurprisingly, they were leery of divulging the underground's internal squabbles, those over the razor blade excluded. I made headway by patiently *pierre*-scissors-*papier*ing the Buchanan gams, saying "Oh, keep the pack" and smilingly reasoning that their common cause now would be more impressive, not less, if the U.S. public understood they hadn't all stayed blank slates politically until they leapt fully formed from de Gaulle's kepied brow. Since one of their few luxuries was that they'd never heard of Brannigan Murphy, my interviewees were surprised at how Pam excelled at nagging them on their Communists. No-shows the Occupation's first year—Kremlin spank—the PCF had since become the underground's lions of Belfort.

Then I'd come home forlorn with unconfessable envy. My brief from *Regent's* was to unravel the motives underlying the plucky little band's arrival at this point, yet the reraveled marvel was that they *were* at this point: it had clarity. Absurd as it was to see Pam's confusions as an invidious contrast—and the Lotus Eater's jellyfish leer, caught between an unidentifiable male head and a mighty wristwatch's prominent flash on a muscled forearm, had maddened me regularly since opening night with its incoherent insistence that maybe now I'd have more compassion for her—I couldn't help doing just that and indeed soon learned I shouldn't. Such incongruous goads were often to give my *Regent's* reporting more intensity.

Even so, Roy's face clouded as he turned the last page. "This is smart. But you don't have anything here from our own people in Washington. No White House, no State Department—nothing. What gives?"

"Well, of course not, Roy! They're on the fence—not ready to cut the cord yet to Vichy, you know that. Anything they say will be evasive and dull."

"Yes, Pam, it will be. And that will be revealing," Roy said, teaching me my job. "And Pam? While you're in Washington—"

"Pardon?"

"When you run down to *Washington, tomorrow,* try to talk to the Free French mission there. Lots of friction with New York, I hear. And Pam? Vichy does still have an embassy. My confidential sources tell me the number's probably in the book," Roy said, teaching me my job some more.

POSTED BY: *Sam*   Sixty-five years ago, on my first visit to my final hometown, Union Station was all herds of brown, olive drab, Atlanticized blue, and Pacific vanilla muddling through a gigantic spittoon overlooked by dull statues gagging on nicotine. Attribution forgotten and context hazy, a random fragment of poetry in Pink Thing's archives retrospectively captions the surprise poster I saw hailing our new Russian allies: *To live it hurries and to feel it hastes.*

Scrambling into a cab, I caught sight of the Capitol—not banalized the way it was to you by TV long before you eyed it for real, Panama, but a genuine L. Frank Baum surprise to someone who'd never pictured it being *part* of something. Then I was off.

Even with *Regent's* name and Roy's list of contacts, I was a nobody in a District that had been at war just over a week. Doubtless that's why Harry Hopkins never got back to me: my ur-encounter with a White House switchboard whose laziness or worse your Gramela's been cursing since dawn on her second D-Day. I had better luck over at State, where Bob Murphy, just back from overplaying our indispensable man in North Africa—no relation to Bran, he was nonetheless a bit of a showboat by Cadwaller's verdict—gave me a superbly noncommittal quarter hour. That same night, the price paid for admiring my hairdo by the nipper beside me in the Mayflower's bar was a swamping quiz once she turned out to be someone's gal Monday on the Senate Foreign Relations Committee.

I met and liked Adrien Tixier, Raoul Aglion's Washington opposite number. Met and disliked (call me impetuous, but Pam was an instant Gaullist—just add Lourdes water) Alexis Leger, later better known and no more beloved by me as St. John Perse. My stop-in at the French Embassy—i.e., Vichy—got me a three-minute denunciation of adventurers and traitors from its press attaché. It was followed by a furtive phone call to my room at the Mayflower that led to an equally furtive stroll in a bare-branched but leaf-hieroglyphed Rock Creek Park.

Not far into it, I divined what the nervous cluck beside me hoped I'd guess and forget: he was slipping info to the underground on the sly. Self-impressionable as I was, and it *was* your Gramela's first cluck-and-dagger moment, I wasn't Pamidiot enough to hint at his existence in the two thousand words I pecked out in the Sutton Place living room, rather mourning the Mayflower's bar—my *hairdo*, really? I could get to like Washington—and took to Roy on the first day of winter.

He chopped them to fourteen hundred tighter ones and ran it in *Regent's* ten days later. Obsolete Christmas trees sledded around me as I ran to the 57th Street newsstand to buy a few thousand copies. Too elated to augment the pile

with the *OC* containing the last book review ("Silent Knight, Lonely Knight")
I was to write for some years.

He hadn't flagged my piece on the cover; that wouldn't happen until the
next summer. Flipping spilling pages on a chill chalk-swept sidewalk, I panicked. Had Roy changed his mind? No. Illustrated by a graphic of the Cross of
Lorraine growing out of victimized France's swastikaed soil, there was—and
is, if only on microfilm in Luddite libraries—my story: "A Cross with Many
Roots," *by Pamela Buchanan*. And I was twenty-one years old.

Bran, you should know, was enraged by that title. I hadn't picked it or been
consulted, and Roy later swore the do-si-don't of "A Cross with Many Roots"
and *A Clock with Twisted Hands* had been too subconscious to register. Anyhow,
aside from cleaning the stain left on Dolores Ibárurri's noble nose by Murphy's
lashing of cold coffee, I couldn't have cared less what Roy called it. Mine eyes—
the future mimsies—dazzled at that byline.

I'd seen it hopping a freight atop dinky book reviews, but that *by Pamela
Buchanan* was different. Not that I had a glimmering of the *La Bayadère* procession of future Pams it was to transpose from ballet's mists to fact and now
memory. They were giving each others' tushies pats in rehearsal all the same.

The Pam loudly laughing at a bawdy gal welder's joke about idle hands
("Well, I know *that*, Rev. This one, anyhow") in Toledo. The one entranced to
be led by a WAVE along the halls of a Pentagon so new its still damp cement
made it smell like the locker room of a football team going for its first championship; we'd all learned from the great Katharine H. how over-the-shoulder
prattle simulated an off-the-shoulder gown, but I'd never mastered the gambit
and was clearly impressed. The tense one following helmet-lamp beams I kept
having to tell myself were Viv, Tess, Josie, and Babe to the ends of the earth; the
one who heard "Happy Birthday" sung to her on Omaha.

Or my sentimental favorite, however reframed in nettles by the painful outcome: the one being sketched by Bill M., my Anzio Bobbsey twin, while I read a
letter from Nick Carraway in the correspondents' villa at Nettuno. Or the one in
the scene I still grin at despite its less comic Vietnam-era sequel: the Pam being
bent back over a Capitol Hill desk in October '42 by the rangy Texan who first
put horns on Brannigan Murphy.

That *by Pamela Buchanan* gave me those Pams and more. That *by Pamela Buchanan* hoisted my flag for World War Two.

Which Murphy, you may not be surprised to hear, sat out on Sutton Place in a perfect sulk. Not only can a flop do terrible things to a playwright, but I suspect he was a bit of a coward.

POSTED BY: *Pam* As regards our soon to be vestigial home life, nobody could have been wronger than the Girl Scout who provoked him by wishing us peace rather than victory in 1942. Bran and I were at loggerheads from the moment he said, tossing *Regent's* aside, "You're really so much better at those little book reviews. Stick to your last, Snooks." Then he rose from the sofa and lumbered off to berate John Lavabo by phone for shrinking *Clock's* ads to the size of "Help Wanted" ones as the next-to-last play of his to ever see footlights slumped toward its demise.

Title and all, Murphy might—I emphasize might—have forgiven "A Cross with Many Roots" had it turned out to be a busman's holiday from those little book reviews. Roy Charters had other ideas, and Pam had just one. That was to grab any assignment he offered.

In the usual sophomore jinx, my second try, about Italian anti-Fascist groups and titled, no skin off Bran's nose this time, "Che Te Dice La Patria?," was a dud. I didn't have the language, our government's open backing made the subject much flabbier, and I never got to interview Count Sforza—which was writing up Barnum and Bailey the night the star elephant had a cold. As my editor and I postmortemed and pre-Mortimered the drab results, I despaired of getting another *Regent's* byline ever again. Then Mortimer himself—*Regent's* publisher—ambled into the office to tell us with a club man's pointless chuckle that Edith Bourne Nolan's long-nursed bill to create a Women's Army Corps had just hit another snag in the House, and Roy eyed me.

I eyed him. We both smiled. I eye-eyed him. "See you in a week," said Roy. The exile beat behind me, I had found my *boulot*.

To think Murphy had groused I didn't have any *hen* friends—and what a delightful way of putting it, too. First was Edith herself: sixty, plump, gray, unfailingly gardenia'ed, and a Congresswoman since Charles Nolan's widow had won her husband's seat after his sudden death in the Twenties. In a bonus Roy hadn't foreseen, we grew enchanted with each other as soon as she matched and, to be honest, raised Chignonne's with Madame Julien's, her own pre–World War One finishing school in Neuilly.

When that coincidence gave my hubby a pretext for the classic accusation about our affinity, I smacked his chest while sober: a first. Besides being old enough to be my mother's aunt, Edith was one of those enviable people whose faces announce that their youthful program was to sail for Olympus, unimpressed by mere swimmers' splashes in the straits of Messina. After "Skirting the Issue?" came out in mid-February, earning a wince from me for Roy's cutesy title but launching my giddy rebirth as *Regent's* rover-gal chronicler of my gender's war, I went back to her again and again, never leaving without a useful crisp quote or more guidance to Washington's wicketry of acronymic bureaucracies. She probably never realized how often my knocks at her nameplated door were for the sake of her quick crinkle of dignified pleasure at my latest news of her daughters' metamorphoses from virgins to dynamos.

At that age, every writer's ideal marriage is to his or her ideal subject—even if those too can end in a messy divorce. We get the offspring, though: articles, books. Unread in over sixty years by anyone but Tim Cadwaller, who dug up the whole slew for *You Must Remember This: The Posthumous Career of World War Two*, my progress reports on the cuke-unencumbered half of the citizenry's new prowesses in bandannas, overalls, and finally khaki have an iridescence in Pink Thing's archives I've never cared to spoil by revisiting the originals. Not until five or six assignments into my spree did Roy, watching Mortimer detain a file-burdened office filly outside a flashing elevator, see fit to mention in passing that his mom had been Dayton's first woman doctor.

That didn't stop him from blue-penciling my most ardent Pamegyrics to the all-female night shift at a parachute factory converted from turning out wedding gowns in Scranton, PA: "Brides without Grooms," April 1942. Or to the dawn-fingered Rosies filing into a shipyard to build the landing craft that figuratively and for all I know literally brought the gal who wrote "She-Worthy"—blessing, as did Roy, the dawn-fingered Rosie who'd earnestly told me, "They don't just have to be seaworthy, ma'am"—ashore at Omaha many months

later. Or to the matriculators in the Army Air Force's first nimble Women's Flying Training Detachments, hailed by a reluctantly grounded Pam (rationed on
fuel, they wouldn't let the kibitzer break the surly bonds herself) in "Finding
Mr. Wright" the next February. As that last title may tell you, Roy knew one
secret of being a good editor is to be a good smuggler.

In her own way, so was Edith Bourne Nolan. Yet my Capitol Hill fairy
godmother—and how puzzled Edith would've been to learn I thought of her
as one—had no way of guessing that the Pam who doted on feeling in league
with her was someone *neither* of us had met before. When I first interviewed
Rep. Nolan (D-Ma.), her chin-cupped reprise of her bill's setbacks as she
stroked her desk's bald spot had turned me into a previously unmet Pam who
was raring to enroll in her cosmos. Flummoxed when standing up proved we
still shared a dress size, I'd heard my mesurper downright gushily thank the
Congresswoman for her time.

In this millennium, Andy Pond can testify to Pam's love of Talleyrand's motto
as Foreign Minister: "Above all, no zeal," as useful an island of good sense in Napoleon's day as it would be in Potusville. He also knows my allergy to identification
with my species at large, let alone its cuke-unencumbered half. He'd have laughed
in astonishment at the 1942 Pam's passion as I reviewed my notes—"soldier" or
"solider"? Oh, "solder"!—in twice-drafty rail terminals, their pews snoring with
uniforms in front of the schedule board's clacking chapter and verse, or restlessly
scouted my next piece's lead sentence ("She's only a dot in the sky now") in Gulf
Coast hotel rooms too stickily dingy for the chiffonier to be hiding a phone book,
my version of Gideon in that part of the country. Until I got Roy to give me the
use of a cubby at *Regent's*, Murphy's newly dressing-gowned pacings as my typewriter tapped were those of a turnkey while I trafficked in contraband.

Trust me, bikini girl. If your private life's ever one thousand and one nights
at the opera, nothing will make you feel sane like turning fanatic. I'd've been
outraged back then by any suggestion something more brackish might be in the
shrubbery; now I'm not sure I care if there was. Those stories got written and
your Gramela's motives are dust.

As I try to reconstruct my euphoric honeymoon for one, it seems to me I
both knew and refused to know why the distaff side of the war effort had grown

out of a gardenia to set me afire. An awkwardness lurking since Purcey's days when I was in women's company was dissolved by the membership Roy's assignment file [soon labeled "BUCHANAN = ♀♀"] and Edith Bourne Nolan's blessing had granted me in the joyous conspiracy that was female solidarity in wartime.

Besides—and whether we're distaff or dat staff—we all have to discover America sooner or later. Despite my chagrin when I reflect how little my country knows what it once was when it had to be or how much it went right on being its same old hairy, wide-open self in the bargain, I've always felt lucky 1942 was my 1492: my Columbian year.

POSTED BY: *Pamericana*   Even with Dorothy Day and Nick Carraway helping me out—Murphy too? Yes, yes, I suppose, Murphy too—my pieces of the big jigsaw puzzle had stayed dainty. A girls' school in St. Paul and a few years in the Hamlet-crowded hamlet that is intellectual New York do not a brimming U.S. atlas make. Now I was flipping through notebooks to find the blank page after the ring left around my Pam-scrawl by a misbalanced coffee cup in Little Rock, a drained beer glass in Barstow, a pensive Pepsi in Pensacola, or a wet ashtray in Shreveport. Making me feel older for the first time than men who wanted to lay me, Army, Navy, and Marine recruits whose looks were still waiting for someone to shake off the developing fluid kept striking up shy or rowdy conversations in their twangs and drawls and strange urban patois as we were tugged past exhibits of rugged Appalachian carpet, girdered Great Lakes factory towns, or the Southwest's blazed ochres and evaporated lemonade.

"You wouldn't happen to be getting off here in Baltimore, would you? I've got three days. Ma'am, it'd be a privilege to show you my hometown..."

"Sorry, Corporal. Wilmington this trip for me." And I've forgotten nearly all of their faces. Not his, though: pie chin, hopeful blue eyes, smile a collection of dandy white toys his mouth had outgrown but didn't want to give up under that shock of wheat hair and slightly skewed nose. Now I knew it wouldn't cost me anything to add brightly, "Too bad, huh?"

"Too bad," he agreed, showing me grateful toys before he stood up with unexpected masculine vim to swing down the duffel bag next to my old Purcey's suitcase. Three days I could've spent kissing those eyes and just missing that nose before he went back to Louisiana or wherever he was stationed.

In mimsied retrospect, Panama, 1942's carnal throb leaves the Sixties looking like amateur hour. In ways we octogenarians have kept tenderly veiled from our generation's Brokawing hymnalists, the home-front war was our Woodstock: an orgiastic engine we gave ourselves over to, from U.S. Steel blasting smokestack lightning to Detroit's purple haze and Eleanor Roosevelt Rigby fluting away. By the time we got to D-Day, we were golden. Fulfilling a national fantasy we hadn't known was one until Yamomoto's planes turned Mamala Bay into blue acid, we were all part of the same galvanizing, mud-bathed movie.

That's why I feel riled in my dotage when Pink Thing's archives remind me that what I often recalled to Kelquen as the most libidinal year of Pam's life was the chastest in practice, a few Murphine interruptions and one other aside. Not counting trips to the devil's playground, but I often had a terrible time getting to sleep in those days. Yes, that old excuse.

At the time, I'd never have called myself frustrated, Ard. Far from it! Even as my byline matured in *Regent's*, I was in my second adolescence and first happy one, cuckoo with bliss at what I got to do. When I got propositioned on my travels, I doubt there was more than a time or two, my lickety-split mental ravishing of my peculiarly memorable Baltimore corporal from torso's dots to knees' dimples somehow out of category, when I might've felt tempted. Curious what it might be like to stoop to banality but knowing I'd be disappointed, I always fended off my Lothario Grande or Mr. Issippi, whether he was young and in khaki—the usual train and Greyhound version—or middle-aged and in a hand-painted tie (hotels).

The increasingly rare nights on my Sutton Place stopovers when Murphy sought to add some Stalingrad to our Siberia before playing the heroic Red Army casualty on top of me mostly filled Pam with wonder that familiarity could breed not contempt so much as a sense of utter anonymity. As you'll learn even if Tim wishes otherwise, bikini girl, at least strangers are individuated in bed by novelty.

Which ought to tell you that if my forbearance makes you snort, things got a good bit gamier in the good old ETO. Of course I was divorced by then, also out of my trance. If you want to get down and dirty, honey, my Columbian year teemed with more opportunities than I cared to perceive. Yet I was in such a goonily oblivious state of fulfillment, so smitten with the new excitements cramming my life in ways that reduced the poor old beast with two left feet to a pesky chihuahua, that I once left Roy stupefied by announcing the best thing about sex was the way women talked about it.

He'd just bowdlerized my favorite quote from the parachute factory's night-shift forewoman in "Brides without Grooms": "Y' know, it's just like making condoms. They darn well better work, but they only need to the once." (He lamely substituted "wedding gowns," unaware that by then busty little Cath Charters was busy pulling the ripcord on hers.) That may not sound salty to you; it was a new American music to your Gramela. So was "Why, *Henry*"— the immortal, to me, grunt of a bulky Lockheed worker when her lug wrench slipped and got romantic, not that I even tried to include that one in August '42's "Adios, Adolf. Tojo Too? Tojo Too."

So were a thousand other things I heard in my Columbian year. Except for one long-gone Scandinavian whose showpiece in a foreign tongue was "Chen-chen," I'd never known women like these. Galleon-hipped broads waved me into showers of sparks, then clinked Rheingold next to a Wurlitzer dotted with polkas and started in bellowing about the coxswain in the Azores or the sergeant in Australia. A sludge-voiced and slow-eyed freckled blonde in exile from coal country looked up from pounding Liberty ships together for Louisiana's wondrously named Delta Shipbuilding Co. to muse she'd *still* never seen the sea. Tousled farmers' daughters squinted skyward and allowed they'd figured they could fly a plane if they could drive a tractor. And they were all everywhere, roaring on city buses and reveling in cafeterias and shouldering in cuke-unencumbered droves through factory gates and past training-camp sentries.

If it was the most feminocentric year of my life, remember that my main encounters with the cuke-encumbered mob in the margin were idle flirtations on slow-chugging trains, quick Washington quizfests with pols, bureaucrats, and emerald generals, and Sutton Place Pintercourse with Brannigan Murphy. Compared to my reportorial prey, I was a more feckless sort of war worker at best. And at worst a fraud, gamely pretending I knew or cared what kept airplanes up as still wingless P-51s clanked on a conveyor belt behind a sweatily spit-curled, casually arm-grabbing, rosily riveting shout of indoctrination. But from coal mine to California—and like their more familiar office counterparts, looking up with unsinkably loose-lipped smiles to offer the leggy *Regent's* visitor coffee as I waited for Senator Bavard or torpedo-toggling, WAVE-antipathetic Admiral Canute—the broads and the slow blondes and the farmers' daughters did something so foreign to Pam's past I'd never noticed the ellipsis. It was to welcome me.

POSTED BY: *Pam*   Or welcome someone with my gams, frizzy hair, and byline who, like them, had a job to do, and like them was learning by trial and error how to be the woman who did it. Our adult self is always someone we start out impersonating, and a lot of your Gramela's later act was first put together in that Columbian year. Since my victims were unaware I was thieving, I'd swipe a roguish inflection I'd liked in Scranton to earn a grin in Ohio or a sashay from St. Louis as I went *en pointe* to peer into a fuselage in Inglewood. As I stretched my arms Samothrace-style to own the vast office sofa where I was lounging attendance on Senator Bavard, only I knew I'd seen the same pose transform farm girls into pilots in briefing rooms fifteen hundred miles south.

My need for an outer personality whose specifics I could never anticipate was so urgent that anything fatuous or tentative in my inner one got resmelted or junked on the spot. It was the psychological equivalent of a war economy, and one on which, like the country, I throve. Even when I made a total Pamidiot of myself, I'd only have gone unforgiven had I failed to spot the erratum slip. And since I'd never experienced belonging before, it was hard for me to grasp that all this was contingent—not to mention only one element in a bigger picture.

As far as I was concerned, I was reporting on a revolution, not a war. That only proves I knew nothing about either. Despite Roy's trust in my aptitude, such political sophistication as I had came from two years of Pammie-see-Pammie-do radicalism in Manhattan's kaffeeklatsches in putsch's clothing. I'd imbibed and regurgitated millenarian talk without ever considering whether I had a stake in Utopia or trying to imagine what any self-fashioned version might look like outside my Bank Street apartment. Then had come Sutton Place. You bet I was kerosene missing only a match and a wick to keep me burning.

I credit the wick for intuiting that my lack of perspective was the perspective that let me champion my home-front heroines as they deserved to be championed. After all, Roy could see *by Pamela Buchanan* as something I didn't—an ingredient in the mix. My Capitol Hill fairy godmother, by contrast, was still a Congresswoman. She could get fairly snippy about talking me down from the tree where she'd just caught me putting the feminocentric cart before the horse again.

"Pam, please," Edith would sigh over her specs. "Believe me, I do understand. Or remember. I know better than you ever will these steps are long overdue. I still think you'd do well to include a few choice reminders in your next article"—she never said "piece"—"that the point of it all is to defeat Japan and Germany."

"That's so damned corny," I'd protest. "It's what—"

"I'm sorry! Germany and Japan. Germany first is our policy," said Edith with Congressional humor. "Dear me, but I could be taken to the woodshed for getting that wrong. You were saying?"

"It's what everyone already knows is going on. It's like mentioning Sir Isaac Newton every time you eat an apple."

"Pam, here's an apple. You can't tell people something they don't know until you've convinced them you know what they do know. You can't get people to feel differently about one thing without showing them first that you feel just as they do about everything else. Columbus could only say the world was round because he wasn't claiming it was on top of an ice cream cone."

"Um, I don't think he could have. Did ice cream exist yet?"

"There you are! Neither did America. If he'd wanted to sell ice cream, he'd have called the world flat, I assure you. That's why I'm sitting here and you live in New York."

"Well, I'm thinking of moving," I said a good two decades *avant la lettre*. "So there."

"What, and see less of me? You'd be quite bored in peacetime."

"Why, are you?"

"No, dear. To be delightfully candid, people like you keep showing up. Oh, there's the floor bell. You must excuse me."

"What's the vote?"

"Goodness knows! But I'll be *such* an expert by the time I get over there. Walking slowly and nodding. Why, would you care to come with?"

"I'd like nothing better, but I've got a train to watch. I mean catch," said I as I lowered my wrist.

"Then God speed you. I met your mother once, you know. I often wondered what she'd be like if she had a cause."

"You wouldn't recognize her," I said sulkily.

"But I do," Edith said—even though, in my most ardent private substitutions of a gardenia for a wilted daisy, the shoe was on the other foot.

POSTED BY: *Pam et* It's not only because I was still learning my craft that I've long avoided rereading my Columbian-year *Regent's* effusions. By my age, one's early work is a murder mystery starring the corpse of our might-have-been selves; we know the solution but have forgotten the clues. I don't want some ripe simile or unduly athletic description to disclose a long buried Pam in the reportorial nude, peering out at the mimsies from a cuke-unencumbered version of *Le déjeuner sur l'herbe* under the impression she's fully clad.

That's the genius of Manet, of course. He shows his female viewers women who don't know they're undressed and his male ones women who don't care that they are, making the consternation general but its provocation gender-Rorschached. Which doesn't change the fact that I was—and fairly humiliatingly, Ard, so chirps my youthful vanity—*wrong*.

Goddam near everything went back to men's idea of normal a week after VJ-Day. Disillusionment left me not only alienated from those I'd adored, now docilely restored to manicures and mattress-testing, but wondering how I could have misguessed the roots of our shared exultation by so wide a mark. Yes, yes: by all means let's do note the comfort of my postwar opinion that they'd let *me* down when I'd spent my Columbian year struggling not to do the reverse.

Didn't I opt for Vichy myself when I turned my ETO tales into *Nothing Like a Dame*, whose inscribed copy to Edith incidentally got no response?

Not that I know for individual fact what became of my home-front pinup gallery. Since my original '42–'43 notebooks are long lost—I didn't make much of a habit of saving such stuff until the Paris footlocker said it liked midnight snacks—I've also got no way of learning, and the reason's as mournable as it is metaphorically apt. Founded in the 1890s, *Regent's* had its house idiosyncrasies. The one you'll chortle at was its prim and, by 1942, notorious principle that people who weren't public figures had a right to privacy.

Thanks to that rule, which didn't get junked until the end of the war, Edith Bourne Nolan was one of the few to appear in my stories under her real name. Even in my stories from the ETO, anyone under the rank of major rated an alias. Since every war correspondent from Ernie Pyle down knew nothing tickled the home folks like Lieutenant Nephew's or Pfc. Soninlaw's mention in print, Eddie Whitling used to scoff at my scrambles to think up false monickers. But Roy liked the tradition—because it was eccentric and archaic, because it was our version of Eustace Tilley's butterfly-examining monocle in *The New Yorker*—and warned me only against excessive whimsy. No Oglesby in a brassiere factory, no dentist from Tuscaloosa.

Along with the magazine's other arthritic stricture—the first photograph printed in *Regent's* showed the mushroom cloud over Hiroshima—that shibboleth helped "To the Ends of the Earth," which got me a sweetened paycheck from Roy for hazardous duty and a breakfast call from the Office of Production Management's harried press flack. "For God's sake, Pam!" spouted a certain future historian for whose work my Gerson, gaga for Grant and Lee's baseball teams, turned out to be a hopeless sucker.

"Why, hello, Mr. Catton. Thank you, I'm well." (Yes, daisysdaughter.com readers—'twas he. He was doing his bit like everyone else, and half the fun of belonging to my generation is that we all first bumped into each other at a Hitler-staged *bal masqué*. That was often to make our civilian careers seem like the costume, not the restored identity.)

"Pam, for God's sake, don't you know it's *illegal* for those women to be working the mines? Yes, we know about them. Yes, we know they're only doing it to free up their men to go get shot at in Tunisia for the duration. And yes, that's why we're doing our best to turn a blind eye. It's not going to give me an easy week now that you've gone poking around with a flashlight."

"Poor man. Try drinking! Say, I've got an idea much neater than whiskey. Why not make it legal?"

I believe the current term is *venting*. Legalizing mine work for women wasn't something I'd been rash enough to advocate in print. I'd learned a bit from Edith by then about what the traffic would bear. A measure of which was his answering groan: "Are you joking or crazy?"

Since the women coal miners of Riceville, Tennessee—the wildcats, as they called themselves—are the most lost to history, they're the ones whose *noms de guerre* in *Regent's* I regret most. As I do the nonpreservation on film, other than soon to be extinguished Pamavision, of their imposing waddles and big-gloved hands unexpectedly bared for quick tasks by a tug of too few teeth and then regloved the same way. Shins that Hogarth had drawn with babies curled around them now braced to absorb a pneumatic drill's recoil. Or the lack of any audio record, unlike Pam's faint D-Day "Thank you" at the National Archives, of their voices' gnarled grain and lewd laughter.

Someone not lost at all, on the other hand—like Edith Bourne Nolan's, his Congressional title let me use his true name in *Regent's*: I quoted him on shipyard absenteeism in "Liberty Belles," October 21, 1942—is Murphy's first cuckolder. He was also the last unless you count Roy. Then and later, my main reaction—unless you count dentitioned chuckles—was bewilderment. Didn't he know there was a war on?

My hunch is his answer would've been "Yes, indeedy." That form of wisdom was beyond the why-Henry'd, ungamahuched Pam who realigned her newly delingamed gams with my purse as a guide and rode home on the bus sans underwear, wondering if his pleasant receptionist collected or labeled the ripped panties she found in his office wastebasket. I suppose *l'équipe* here at daisysdaughter.com owes him anyway for the chance to parade some proof I wasn't a complete wallflower at the orgy. Otherwise, Murphine Stalingrads aside, I'd be telling the depressingly sexless story of a ninny who spent her Columbian year in drydock.

Enough, though! Ard, enough. The phone may still ring and I've got to make up my mind, my pet, about keeping my date with Cadwaller's gun if it turns out not to. The thought that all too many of you may never read anything else about the women who helped win World War Two has just curled this close-cropped hair of mine.

What does it matter if the Fifties re-encased them in Eisenhowerite Lucite? They did what they did and I saw it. Not to drive your dad nuts or awaken Manet's competitive ghost, Panama, but I doubt even you in the Christmas-ornamented altogether would be a vision as thrilling as the first pilot I saw jogging in a baggy flying outfit to hoist herself into a cockpit and trundle down a muggy runway as tough grass grayed and bent at Avenger Field, Sweetwater, Texas—the place names are real—one morning in February 1943.

At least in *Regent's*, her name was Jessica Auster of Coos Bay, Ore., and she was the dot in the sky in the opening sentence of my Houston-datelined rhap-sody—with a detour to Delaware, where Nancy Harkness Love was training her own batch of flyers—to the Guinea Pigs, as the women in Jackie Cochran's 319th WFTD were known. Google *Nancy Love* and *Jackie Cochran* for pictures that ought to hang in every college girl's dorm; each noncombat mission their outfits flew freed up a male pilot for a combat one. They flew thousands.

I'd be embarrassed to tell you how often these fat-lunetted mimsies of mine have gone over every image available of Avenger Field with a magnifying glass held to my Mac's screen. As I look in vain for Jessie's tight locket face and maybe even a caption that would restore her true identity and unmollusked hometown, I think I might know her even in dorsal view; she had a way of slumping her weight to one hip and bracing the other with her far elbow out. No luck so far, none. But if she's alive and reads this blog, perhaps she'll recognize herself and comment in time.

"Edith!" I complained when I stopped back in Washington to fill out the picture with my usual dose of brass-hat imbecilisms and cuke-encumbered leg-islative rhubarb. "Do you know they don't even get military benefits? They're going to be flying bombers to England, for God's sake. Does that sound like 'Civil Service' to you?"

"No, dear. It sounds like 'flying bombers to England' to me. Do you know how many the Eighth Air Force lost over St. Nazaire last week?"

"Not that many. Seven."

"You *do* live high on the hog."

"Well, I've seen the factories."

"They're certainly doing good work. You might try the graveyards. Or let's hope POW camps. What on earth do you think we need night shifts making parachutes for?"

"The airborne."

"With luck, yes. Maybe by summer, but I didn't say that. As for the benefits, do you think I haven't had Jackie and Nancy both on the phone? May I say I called *them* with pro forma apologies. They know we have to think about what—"

"The traffic will bear. Yes, I've heard."

"Pam, I haven't been interrupted since my second term."

"Sorry," I gulped. "Not pro forma, either."

Edith beamed. "Nonsense. There's no other kind of apology at your age. Feel free to pretend differently if you can make it amusing. And brief. I'm afraid I've got a committee meeting."

Taking advantage of an acolyte's permission to burn incense by getting incensed, I'd gotten into the habit of bickering with my Capitol Hill fairy godmother on our first long train trip. It was to Iowa—*les grand blés* still, no longer *sanglotants*—to see the first WACs graduate from officers' training school at Fort Des Moines: "Gold Bars for a Redhead," *Regent's*, September 9, 1942. Four hundred sixty-six women marched past the podium in broiling heat, their heads swiveling at "Eyes right" to snap Congresswoman Nolan and Colonel Oveta Culp Hobby a mass salute under their trim overseas caps. But when Edith prodded me, I couldn't, *couldn't* tell her why I'd snorted before my eyes resparkled with newly moist awe.

That distinguished woman had spent a lot less time than I did riding in talkative wartime rail coaches instead of gardenia-friendly compartments. She'd almost certainly never heard the universal service nickname for the khaki envelopes perched atop those determined coifs: *cunt caps*, if you must know. Decades later, as we watched the usual surprise horde of out-of-town laddybucks with strange marsupial accoutrements spill past our red light on Constitution Avenue, chanting "We're here, we're queer" and so forth, on what we District ancients always forget is Gay Pride Day—perhaps luckily, Bruce Catton was years in his grave—Nan Finn voiced her fuddlement: "Can someone please explain to me why they want *that* word back? Pam, do you have a clue?"

In spite of having a good deal more than one, I decided on reflection against telling the glorious girl my Fort Des Moines story. Dear Nan can garble a meaning the way Mozart could dash off a concerto, and often to as charming but chancy effect.

Once I got my own cunt cap in the ETO, I refused to ever call it anything else, embarrassing even Eddie Whitling sometimes. It had looked awfully stylish on the redhead of my story's title: Lieutenant Connie Ostrica of New Haven, Conn., at least after Roy asked, "Where's New Heaven?" She'd been as articulate as her distant lips' switch from frictioned dismay to electric amusement had promised when, sizing up my best bet, I'd accosted her in the barracks with my usual explanation that I needed a viewpoint character. Or tailor's dummy, in intra-office *Regent's* parlance.

While I don't think that figure of speech influenced my choice, there's always a chance it did. If she wasn't among the one in every thousand WACs who became casualties, Connie could've had her choice of lives. Mrs. Gerson used to half expect to run into her in Hollywood, in some scenarios after marquee proof she'd taken the name I'd invented for her in *Regent's*. The probability is she just got Eisenhowerized into a baby factory for some executive.

Those unshrinking-violet eyes of hers made me sure he'd have money. He'd travel a lot too, keeping him serenely ignorant of her half waking languors as *by Pamela Buchanan* got tucked discreetly below the pulsatingly pulpy title (*Connie's Secret*) of one of those lurid Fifties paperbacks on whose covers I'd occasionally spot her lookalikes gazing back at me in airport book racks before I grimly returned to reading Cotton Mather's sermons or Washington's report from Fort Necessity for *Glory Be*. Anyhow, Connie should know—if she's just Googled "Ostrica" for old times' sake, if she's come across daisysdaughter.com's SOS from Potusville, if she's tempted to give me a reason to re-footlocker Cadwaller's gun—that it was for her sake I took up the cudgels with my Capitol Hill fairy godmother on our ride back from Iowa.

"Edith, for God's sake!" I demanded. "Why aren't they getting the same pay as men holding the same rank?"

"Why, are you?"

"I'm not in uniform."

"Those come in all kinds, my girl. I've been wearing this one since 1925. Find your shop and stick with it. I must say this morning made me miss my old nursing rig."

"From where?"

"Italy! Back in the first war. Had the most dreadful roommate too. Lord, she threaded the boys like popcorn. Pam, I hope I don't need to remind you my bill sat in committee for nearly a year. I'll do something about pay grades when the time is ripe."

"What about command authority? Honestly, what good is it even calling them officers when they can't give anyone orders outside the Women's Army Corps? Even Oveta Hobby can't, and she's in *charge*. Any dumb fuh—fool of a sergeant can tell her to go fly a kite. How could you let them get away with it?"

"They didn't get away with anything. *I* did, and it took some doing, and I absolutely forbid you to bring up command authority in your article. Do you have any idea what a red flag that would be? They'd be asking me next if I wanted girls at West Point."

"Don't you?"

"Pam, Pam. The laughter would be ribald and the issue would be lost. I do think you ought to profile Oveta, though. Interesting woman, and the sooner this isn't always about *me*, the better."

"You know it's ridiculous she's only a colonel, don't you?"

"Of course I do. I sometimes think it's preposterous I'm not President, but that's what the traffic will bear. Are you riding all the way back to Washington with me, dear? We'd have such oodles of time to discuss my imaginary Presidency after I've napped."

"No, I change in Chicago. I'm on my way to Detroit."

I spent three days there for "The Mighty Flowers." ("Oh, no, not again. I'll apologize to Bran," my editor said, and I said, "The hell you will, Roy. I've *had* that fight.") In my own regulation bandanna and less than form-fitting sack suit,

I watched new Sherman tanks get trundled chassis by ring-scarred chassis along one assembly line until their gun-needlenosed turrets were lowered onto them from another. That tempted me into an analogy about bees descending on daisies and gardenias which I gather, see title, must've survived Roy's edit. Not until the ETO would I learn our mighty flowers weren't up to snuff design-wise, outgunned by most Panzers and blazing like matchbooks at one well-placed shell. But we built fifty thousand of them, Panama—and we won.

Gloria Kamenica is almost certainly dead, though. Cadging each other's cigarettes in a typhoon-foamed tavern, she and her three henchwomen—galleon-hipped Anna, Myra, Billie: my private toast to my Columbian year—were a long way from maidenhood even then. Retrospectively breaking my heart, they were shy about showing re-muftied, once again "classy" me their homes, sending me back at closing time to my suddenly effete room at the Tuller despite Pam's Rheingoldilocksy epiphany that I'd only capture Gloria if I could describe her cuke-unencumbered (Guadalcanal) tenement apartment.

The communal bathroom down the flavorful hall to which her sturdy legs carried her now dekerchiefed hair and robed peekabosom at the end of each long day. The fire escape she sometimes sat on for a final smoke and beer, listening to the trucks, the radio playing "Who Wouldn't Love You" across the way and the 4-F down in 3-G banging his better half. Too tuckered and suddenly disconsolate to even find a nightgown, she crept into bed—and when I got back to Washington next, I was beside myself.

"*Edith!* Do you know the trick they're pulling in Detroit these days?"

"That depends on which and whose. I'll stick with a qualified yes unless the sun now comes up in the West there."

"Even when they're doing the identical work, management gives the women different job titles. Guess whose salary is smaller! And their union won't do anything."

"Dear me. You'll be telling me next there isn't one female shop steward in the whole plant."

"Of course not, and the joke on me is that I spent years twitting away at cocktail parties about the wonderful, progressive labor movement. But all those idiots can think about is what'll happen after the war."

"What a coincidence! So am I. Oddly enough, so is the NAACP. It wasn't easy getting the defense industry to open up all those skilled jobs to black folk, but manpower's manpower. It's going to be interesting to see what Los Angeles looks like by 1960, since I very much doubt they're all champing at the bit to move back to the plantation once we've won this thing and so does my colleague from Watts. Have you been to California yet?"

But *Regent's* had an actual Negro on the racial beat: light-skinned and bow-tied Jim Bond, a decorous ex-Communist whose scholarshipped voice retained only the faintest burr of his Mississippi upbringing. Jim and not Pam wrote "Collard Greens and Palm Trees," along with "If We Holler, Let Us Go" and "The Black Hawks' War." When he came back from Tuskegee, I'd just got done writing up Jackie Cochran's Guinea Pigs, and he and I did exchange one awfully wry grin in the halls. The only time we were at odds was when I heard he'd complained about my turning Joy Sterling, as I'd called her, into the viewpoint character for "The Fuse."

"Jim, let's have this out," I said when I saw him after *by Pamela Buchanan's* account of life at Huntsville Arsenal had come out. "I don't think you've used a woman as your tailor's dummy even once. What does it matter what color she is?"

"In Alabama? Did you try asking her that?"

"I didn't need to, it was the thing's given. I quoted her manager on all that instead."

"Her white manager."

"Yes! And he was my pincushion"—*Regent's*-ese for a villain. "Did you even read it before you went storming off to Roy?"

"Twice. I was looking for one hint your little Joy was angry."

"But she really wasn't—" I floundered at Jim's smile. "Oh, hell. You think she was putting on an act for me."

"No, Pam. I *know* she was putting on an act for you."

"Wouldn't she have for you, though? For different reasons?"

"Sure. But we'd have both known it, which is fun."

"I wasn't down there for fun."

"Are you sure? Pickaninny docility and all, you did make her sound like somebody I might not mind too much to meet." Now drolly natty, he adjusted his bow tie. "I think it was 'face of a Gauguin' that did it."

POSTED BY: *Pam*   And yes, Panama, speaking of art, the mimsies have seen them here and there. Those T-shirts that revive a famous image of a woman in a polka-dot kerchief rolling up her sleeve and flexing an arm, with a different face and "She Can Do It" replacing my way-back-when's obsolete "We." Andy Pond and I have agreed more than once that sometimes it's just goddam strange to have lived so long.

Lord, I do wish I liked H*ll*ry better. Sent her some money last year, guessing I'd croak before she fucked it up. Quit once she cosponsored a flagburning amendment. How can anyone not grasp Old Glory does, has, and must stand for the right to torch it if you're so inclined? Something I never have been, even now. I couldn't.

I suppose you'll vote for her too, bikini girl. By 2008 you'll be old enough to lose your polling-booth cherry and she'll inevitably run if Potusville hasn't declared martial law by then. I wish I hadn't spotted the Evita hidden in "inevitable," but that's what your Gramela gets for too many readings of *I Was Dolly Haze's Monster* back in Beverly Hills in the Fifties.

Ostensibly scribbled by the perp, that true-crime confession was quite the nonfiction shocker in Ike's day. Slavered over by the silly for its illicit licentiousness, it was reluctantly savored by the literary for its elusively elucidating prose. Hadn't glanced at a page in decades until I fumbled forth my sunbleached copy from between *The Producer's Daughter* and Brother Nicholas's *The Mountain and the Stream* after your and your dad's last visit to Washington. Kelquen's tail drew a mustache on me as I painfully crouched.

Yes, well! Now it's just you and me, Ard, my pet. Do you suppose a woman president would be worth sticking around for?

Naturally if she were *me*, the question would answer itself. Pamus, I'd be called. Talkily stalking the West Wing with my mobile bower. Would you like to be one of them, Panama? Special Assistant for Chen-Chen and Patois?

The pills from lunch do seem to be having their standard effect. It's a pretty woozy hour as a rule here at the Rochambeau. I shouldn't be posting at all, since Ard knows what I've spilled. But on the assumption this is the last day of my life, I don't honestly care. Or shouldn't, considering my nonbelief in any hereafter.

Speaking of which, my silly pre–Pearl Harbor roommate on Bank Street could really be extraordinarily silly. Do you know what that divine goose said once, resting her newly showered chin on poor Pam's collarbone? This, with a nod at my typewriter as I clacked away at some pointless book review: "Do you suppose they'll ever invent one of those that can contact the afterlife?"

"They have," I said curtly, pulling the page. "And for God's sake, go away, Dottie! Or at least put something on. I'm on deadline."

POSTED BY: *Pam*   A sludge-voiced slow-eyed freckled blonde exile from coal country who'd never seen the sea put me on the trail that led me to exasperate Bruce Catton. Mellie Branch was her *Regent's* name, and she was the tailor's dummy in Pam's New Orleans–datelined "Liberty Belles." A random question over coffee—"Won't let you work in the mine back home, huh?"— won a cascadingly freckled reply something like, "Oh, no! I'm too young and elfin, you see. But some do."

It took me three months to make time to find out if Mellie was fibbing about the women she knew who'd put on miners' helmets to free up their husbands and boyfriends to wear Army ones, since Roy hated blind alleys. Once I got there, it wasn't easy to ingratiate myself. Riceville doesn't welcome many strangers, and I was a five foot ten gal from up north whose cheapest overcoat, carefully chosen, and scarf still Hollywoodized me.

At least I knew better than to go around bellowing what I was after. I just loitered wherever I could, waiting as unobtrusively as possible to spot a woman who'd look to my uneducated eyes as if she might work in a coal mine. After a weekend of diner meals I ate in slow motion, practically memorizing the *Knoxville News-Sentinel*, Viv fit the bill: cinder-crisped hair yanked around without ceremony by a shrewd possum face, hefty in a mackinaw as she ordered coffee. You can scrub and scrub, and later I'd watch her try. After a few months, that dust isn't on your skin—it's in it.

She was plenty guarded, too. Yet if I was a long way from nattering about undergrounds with Raoul Aglion's plucky little band, I'd also come a long one in my Columbian year. Rheingolding with Gloria, letting GIs down easy on slow-chugging trains: Pam's third and hardest-won language was American.

I'd never speak it aboriginally, more like ab-derivatively. But I could fake it like a burglar playing plumber, and it was all preparation for getting Viv of Riceville, Tenn., to recommend blueberry over lemon meringue. And next to concede she wouldn't mind a piece herself.

My main advantage was that being female meant I couldn't by any stretch of the imagination—not only hers but oddly, salutes bounced off cunt caps or no salutes bounced off cunt caps, mine—be official. Another was the nametag on the striped peppermint blouse behind the counter. If it'd read "Joe" instead of "Jo," I'd've been out a quarter in exchange for a grudging admission that it was a windy day.

Instead, after reglancing at Jo—still the nearest thing in sight to a cop—and visibly wrestling her opinion of me until she'd pinned it for a count of three, Viv finally said, "Well, I guess I could—maybe, maybe—get a couple of us together to gab at you if you want. Can you wait 'til next Sunday?"

I shook my head. "No—that's not what you *do*. See what I mean? I need to go down with you, into the mine. Can you fix it?"

"Brother! That ain't allowed." And her pie plate was as empty as a Hoover campaign promise. My best guess was I had five seconds tops.

I rolled my eyes and leaned back. "Just look who's talking, sister. Since when did that stop you?"

Made it. Viv's eyes went crafty as we smirked at each other. But then her glance fell on my nails. Unlike the Elizabeth Ardennes tapping away at my Mac, which are as chipped as a summer camp's Christmas lights, back then they were as saucily redcapped as ten little drummer boys.

"You go down with us, you'd have to stay down all day," she warned. "Think you can handle that?"

My worst imaginings had had Pam back above ground and catching a Greyhound to the Knoxville train depot before noon. "Deal," I said instantly. Anything else would've made that manicure Viv's decisive, derisive, and final impression as she thanked me for the pie and rose.

"We don't bring nobody back up unless his back's broke," she said, pleased. "Eat down there, too."

It took her another day to talk the other wildcats into it and agree on how to sneak me in. The morning after that, stepping out of Riceville's lone hotel into a dawn chill that bit like a cobalt T. Rex—and decked in a borrowed mackinaw and overalls whose hindering creaks made me imagine I knew how sculptures must feel when they're still under wraps before the public's big "Ah"—Pam became the covert center of a cuke-unencumbered huddle that shuffled me into the pit's elevator cage past a shift boss distracted by Viv's razzing about his sorry hat and sorrier cob.

If any of the men crowded in with us noticed I was Pamtraband, they kept it to themselves. But they were mostly watching their shoes. Then a bell rang and the cage started its descent so loudly I was petrified.

What in hell had I been thinking? The motor's ratcheted gloating was at least mostly steady, unlike the runners' interrupting shrieks of wheels on ungreased metal and the stranger thuds from farther down the abyss each time we unpleasantly paused. Under the cage's canary-yellow light bulb, the faces packed around me looked like carvings, whittled by a knife that got blunter with distance until I realized my eyes were straining for some way to escape. When the gate opened and my fellow passengers startled me by turning alive again, we were eight hundred feet down.

In spite of knowing there'd been dozens more miners waiting behind us at the pit, I'd stubbornly kept imagining a single tunnel, no longer than Riceville's lone hotel's lone hall, with a couple of wheelbarrows' worth of prop charcoal tipped over at the far end to mark what must, must be my room's door. Before me stretched the chambers and railed passageways of Appalachia's answer to the Louvre, and nobody'd seen fit to tell me earlier that down here blackness wasn't a color but an element.

Not only was electricity's sole purpose—suddenly grasped at last and for good—to illustrate, not even illuminate, bituminous blackness. What my frost-seared lungs were gulping was the taste of blackness. What I instantly dreaded was the sound of blackness cracking.

I've never spent a day in such terror, Panama. I'd do Omaha or even Huertgen over first. They happened outdoors, up where people belong.

"Stick with me awhile, Miz Buchanan," Viv said. "Then we'll sort of pass you around."

To get up to the face on Gallery Eight, which was where my wildcats were working, we had to climb first into shuttle cars that clanked for a century on rails whose gleam got reprolonged at each curve. Then we were shunted onto a siding where wheeled coal gondolas the size of the Cardiff Giant's coffin were waiting to be loaded and sent back down the track. Past that was another dim labyrinth of darkness headlamps could pierce and darkness they couldn't, hacked like squares left solid in the mountain's big crossword puzzle.

"Room an' pillar," Viv explained. "See, all that's coal too. It's what's really holding the rest of this up."

Not only was my voice a squeak, it was the dumbest question in the history of the industry. "Is it safe?"

"Haw. Hey, Tess! Miz Buchanan wants to know. 'Is it safe?'"

"Why, sure," Tess said with equanimity as she slumberlumbered along. "Right up to the ver' second the whole danged works comes crashin' down on our heads to kill us all without warnin' or a prayer of rescue, mine work is safer'n golf."

"There now. You see?" Viv asked. "You one of them lady golfers, Miz Buchanan?"

"No, I don't think so."

"I just only wish people didn't keep laughin' an' makin' merry so darn loud all the time down here," said Tess. "Y'know that jimmies my concentration something fierce."

"Now that's a point of view. The singin' is what gets to me. Naw, Miz Buchanan—we're just teasin' you a little. You go right ahead and sing if you want."

POSTED BY: *Pam*   By midmorning I was almost used to how faces could be extinguished as they swiveled. Or no less unexpectedly bloom whole and real, snowwoman-eyed in a lamp's beam and apparently bodiless: held up only by will and grime. Since I was working too even if it didn't look like it to the men who'd learned by now I was an interloper, I'd started prodding my brain to find words to convey the quality of cold this deep underground: cold that wasn't weather, had never known breeze or seasons, hadn't even been air or experienced noise and motion until it was forced to exist as something other than earth. "Cold unaware it has a rival for humanity's affections," the printed version read, more archly than I'd like.

What kept getting harder to remember was that the coal I watched broken up into chunks once it had been extracted, then shoveled into barrows to crash into gondolas for the long sluice down the rails that ended with its unimaginable rise to unimaginable daylight, was the *point*. It seemed insane that nothing more than a few billion idiots' need for fuel up on the surface explained this vast underground effort. The how and the what of it kept killing the why. A year ere I saw Anzio, it was Pam's introduction to the nature of combat.

Of course the cuke-encumbered miners just hated having the wildcats down there, not only from superstition—"We're supposed to be bad luck," Josie said. "Cain't say what that makes you, Miz B."—but for the implied reproach. In a vital industry, they were exempt from the draft. Their fool friends Dave and Steve had enlisted anyway, leaving them to share these bowels with Dave or Steve's uncoupled ball and chain.

Willing to wink patriotically otherwise at the law, management drew the line only at women handling explosives. Viv told me that would've provoked a mass walkout, war or no war. I so desperately wanted the image for "To the Ends of the Earth" that I described unidentified "hands" planting a charge, not outright misleading my readers but letting them picture Babe packing dynamite in the plug Josie'd just bored before Viv twisted the detonator. I wouldn't do it today, but I wouldn't need to.

As promised, Pam got passed on from crew to crew, gritting my teeth at every wave of a gloved hand or wobble of a headlamp that sent me between two pillars past light-scarred curved rails, barrows' oncoming trundles, or an acetylene torch's gassy blue flute solo. Even the rattle of pneumatic drills and hungry gondolas on their way back from the shaft's base didn't drown out the dim and, to me, unpredictable blasts when a charge got set off in some other gallery.

Since they couldn't leave their own jobs to lead me to my next underground heroine, my heart was always in my throat until I spotted an identifiably female strand of cinder-crisped hair straying from a hard hat, an upper loll of overalled but recognizably female bosom above a billowing belly and under a pivoting two-by-four in the gang detailed to roof and timber a passageway between two galleries, a bulge of unmistakably female hip bent over a jackhammer at the face, or an irrevocably female crook-toothed grin at the controls above a rolling caravan of coal-crammed bins. Nothing else proved to me that I too could exist down here.

Then ego stole back in. Even as I crouched, clutched stanchions, or measured my vocal volume for "Babe, can you talk during this?" or "Tell me about yourself, Tess," the fear I'd now managed to squelch thanks only to their nearness was thrilling me at how I could function. Trust me, there's nothing like your first day down a coal mine to trigger narcissism's inner shrieks. It helps one hell of a lot when you know going in it'll be your only one.

Came noon at last. Since the cars shuttled us back to the big, higher-ceilinged chamber at the shaft's base for lunch break, Pam's flooding sense of reprieve (the elevator cage wasn't moving, but it was *there*; it could be scrambled onto and its button smacked in a jiffy as everyone else died horrible deaths) was doubtless one culprit in turning me Pamidiot. Another was my small picnic hamper from Riceville's lone hotel, as out of place among their scuffed and scoured lunchpails as were its contents—biscuits, cold fried chicken, thermos, frayed but clean cloth napkin—among slablike ham sandwiches on bread less white than gray. Just as bad, while I should've been and was grateful the wildcats ate as a group, once we were sharing two benches I couldn't shake a feeling I'd convoked them.

Food makes women talk about sex just as women's presence makes men think of food. But my God, those Tennessee Gargantuas! Time's blurred some of their vocabulary but not its lubricity. With a coal-dusted hand, Josie wiped crumbs and a worm of errant fat from her lips: "Now, my Andy was always a Saturday nighter. Two beers at Prew's an' it's hello Mommie with his pants 'round his ankles. An' now he's sandily committin' the sin of O-nan in O-ran."

"Armored, ain't he? They ain't in O-ran anymore."

"Engineers. But he just better not be dippin' it in some belly dancer's snuff-box. He don't know where that's been since the Bible."

"Sunday was always Stevie's and my day for the old hunchy-punch," Tess reported. "Man, I felt like a bowling alley. I do hate goin' to church with nothin' to look forward to."

"Nothin'? *I* can think of somethin'." Those fingers waggled, and Josie must've weighed two hundred pounds! You didn't want to picture her trips to the devil's playground. For weeks I couldn't help it even on mine: those Andean slopes, that overhung El Dorado.

"That ain't an *occasion*, Josie. That's like brushin' your teeth and callin' it dinner."

"Well, I sure ain't sure how much longer I'm supposed to keep it parked," said Babe. "On our first date ever, Dave told me I look like Mary *As*-tor. Live by the sword, die by the sword, what I say."

"Ain't Dave stationed at Benning? Shit, that ain't so far. Meet 'im in Chattanooga and he could Astorize the living whimsy out of you."

"Naw, they're gone. Shippin' out for hairy old England, I think. Anyways, Viv, we know you got nothin' to complain about. Even with Dolph splashin' around for pure laughs wherever in the South Pacific."

"I still got plenty to complain about," Viv said tensely as I reheard her dawn jeers at the shift boss with new insight. "Dolph done it to me first, you know that. And in peacetime. How 'bout you, Miz Buchanan? We all seen that ring."

"And we were lookin' too," said Tess. "Where's your man serving?"

"Oh, he's back in New York." I was startled. Could I lie Bran out of his dressing gown? Decided I couldn't. "He's not part of this, though," I said clumsily.

"Just sitting it out? Where, Park Avenue?"

I knew it was a movie address and not a real location. "Something like that."

"Well, now. Lucky you."

"Could've fooled me!" I chirped—and pay close attention, Panama. I'm about to commit the first of two Pamidiocies that only seeing "To the Ends of the Earth" in print cured me of cringing at. "I envy you."

Two of them snorted and three knocked wood. "Havin' a good time with us, Miz Buchanan?" Viv asked.

"Sure, who wouldn't?" I said, misunderstanding. "I can't help thinking of that old cartoon."

"I'm sorry. Which old one?"

"You know. With the two miners, and one of them saying, 'For gosh sakes—here comes Mrs. Roosevelt!'"

Do I bless myself for not saying "In *The New Yorker*?" Every day. To the last wildcat, eating or not, they looked—and what a surprise this is too—stupefied.

"Why, I'm not sure as I see why that's funny," said Viv. "It's true she ain't been down here yet. But even Mrs. Roosevelt can't be ever'where at once."

"Not even Mrs. Roosevelt," Babe nodded.

"Anyway you know she would if she could," said Josie. "She's just doin' what her husband cain't like we are."

"You know something?" said Tess. "I sometimes sort of tell myself she *is* here. It helps on them hard days."

"You too?" said Josie. "And Babe, you?"

"Oh, yeah."

"I'm sorry again," said Viv to me. "I've learned in this war that it takes all kinds. But what is your quarrel with Mrs. Roosevelt?"

"Why, not a thing," stammered I.

"Then please don't speak against her in this mine."

POSTED BY: *Pameleanor*   One price I paid was a considering look from Viv as everyone got ready to go back to the face. Discarded helmets seized, gloves replucked and retugged. "You could just wait here if you want, Miz Buchanan," she offered. "We'll only be doin' a lot more of the same, and we know a lady like you ain't used to the dust. All mornin' I'd hear you comin' when I heard you coughin'."

I wasn't sure whether the possum's good opinion of Pam *qua* Pam was salvageable. The Pamela Buchanan who only materialized when led by a *By* was the version of me that had to be saved.

"Oh, sure," I said. "Hell, Viv, why don't you take the afternoon off too? So far's I can tell, they don't need you around here at all."

Not that it matters, since "To the Ends of the Earth" would have been written regardless. Still, who knows? Maybe she was a bit fond of me in my exotic way herself. Her face split in a proud smile.

"Now that's a point of view. Drink tea," she suggested. "Maybe go get our hair done."

"No. Why don't we go to the movies? See what Myrna Loy's up to."

"All right. If that's what you like to do. Haw!"

"What's funny, Viv?" Tess turned to ask as the shuttle cars jolted.

"Why, me and Miz Buchanan are goin' to the picture show. Don't it look like it, though?" Viv shouted back as we started rattling down the tunnel in earnest.

You could say none of the rest of them ever came back, not in movies or anywhere else. Between them Viv and Josie agreed on at least a half dozen other pits employing wildcats for the duration, something only a summoning telegram from Roy stopped me from confirming. But I've never found a history book, Mr. Catton—or Google hit, bikini girl—that mentions the lewd and massive female Tennessee coal miners of World War Two. They've stayed underground.

If Eleanor Roosevelt Rigby had only visited them, Tim Cadwaller would've had all the documentation he needed. Instead, never reprinted since 1943, *by Pamela Buchanan's "To the Ends of the Earth"* is the only record Viv, Tess, Babe, Josie, and their sisters ever existed—unlike Jackie Cochran, Nancy Love, Oveta Culp Hobby, Edith, or for that matter Raoul Aglion, Adrien Tixier, Alexis Leger, and Count Sforza. Reliable news source though *Regent's* was at the time, since the revelation that finally sank Roy's by then moribund magazine two decades later only pertained to the cold war, at least one letter to the editor accused me of making the whole thing up. All Pam can say is that, five years before H*ll*ry Cl*nt*n's birth—if only as a visitor, if only for a day—I was down in that mine with them.

POSTED BY: *Pam*   If not for Roy's Western Unioned NO PLACE LIKE HOME AND NO TIME LIKE NOW, handed to me in unexpected exchange for the picnic hamper at Riceville's lone hotel, your Gramela might've come back from Tennessee with a more earthshaking tale to tell, not that *Regent's* or any other publication would have printed it. In fact, I'd have been lucky Gitmo didn't exist back then.

I'd nearly forgotten the vague tip I'd passed on by the time Roy and I went out for a bite after putting "To the Ends of the Earth" to bed. His choice of eatery was a *Regent's* joke, since nothing made him seem more Ohioan than rejoicing in the Carnegie Deli after spending half his life in Manhattan. Long after the war, when I suggested popping in for some cheesecake to his ex and my agent, Cath Charters goggled as if I'd asked Queen Elizabeth whether she'd like her picture snapped at the Tower of London. Then she hailed a cab to introduce me to a chic *pâtisserie* four avenues over that came and went in a year, nicely summing up the difference (taxi too? Taxi too, since we could've walked it in less time) in how those two Midwestern transplants took to New York.

Anyhow, Roy's gaze ignited with back-burner concern after his last pleased burp of pastrami. "Something I can't forget to tell you. That girl whose family got kicked off their land? It never happened and you didn't hear it. My confidential sources went mesugar."

"Meshuggah," our ancient waiter growled as he slapped down the bill. "Jesus."

Only two weeks later, I needed a blink or two. Babe! Who did indeed look like Mary Astor if you'd knocked out one of Mary Astor's front teeth, given her a voice like syrup, and steamrollered her face on a very wide piece of bubble gum. When I'd crouched down next to her in midafternoon, she'd been laying ventilation pipe.

"Can you talk during this?"

"Oh, sure."

"Tell me about yourself. Where's your family?" In that bygone America, believe it or not, knowing where people came from was still widely believed to establish something useful about them.

Well, that was a story. Marriage had brought her to Riceville, but her kin had owned land nearby for a century. Now they were in a Knoxville boardinghouse and unhappy about it, notwithstanding that Uncle Paul had already found work in a sawmill. The government had ejected them and dozens of other families in Roane and Anderson Counties just weeks earlier.

"And we don't know why and we ain't supposed to talk about it, even to complain," said Babe in three-quarter profile, her irritated eyes the two "a"'s in Mary Astor's name as she huffed. "I bet Mrs. Roosevelt don't know. There'd be hell to pay if she did! We're Americans."

Oh, Panama! The Manhattan Project. Babe was talking about Oak Ridge. Our government had taken over those tracts of land in eastern Tennessee to build the plants that were going to produce the enriched uranium for Fat Man and Little Boy out of anyone's sight. Ten miles from where we knelt in darkness, the appalling future that crowned our victory was hauling its engines into place.

That bomb never went off in your Gramela's work, then nor ever. "They even wanted Babe's real name," Roy warned. "Luckily, I could tell them in all honesty I didn't know it. But *Regent's* is now officially sworn to secrecy, you at the top of the list. I vouched for your ability to put any and all disquieting intimations in your war reporting out of your head, but don't be too surprised if someone looks you up to make sure. Shall we go?"

Once we'd parted—hatless Roy headed at a fast clip (the pastrami must've protested) back to the office, Pam on her bundled way to the Plaza for a newly apprehensive drink with Oliver Watson, my newly acquired divorce lawyer—I found myself waiting on a light at 57th and 7th next to a familiar profile, furred for a concert and coiffed for a beheading.

I suspect we'd both have preferred pretending the other was a museum display. But you can only sneak so many peeks before you mistime one. "Hello, Mrs. H.," I said a tad grimly.

"Oh! Hello, little Pamela," said the Lotus Eater. "Dreadful slush, isn't it? At least your shoes won't be much of a sacrifice. Are you going to the Ellington concert? No, you can't be in that."

I was in my perfectly respectable daytime pumps, Rosalind Russellish skirt suit and camel coat, and deep enough into my career to feel bewildered by the reminder that some women still had a use for evening gowns, jewels, and satin heels. She was forty and extravagantly moneyed, thanks to the surprisingly kindly looking gent who'd pulled off a glove to beamingly prepare for an introduction his wife didn't want to make. Now he was doing his best to mistake it for a white kitten with five playful feet. Unlike the L.E., he looked as if he might be looking forward to Duke Ellington's music, not merely adding his starched and studded shirtfront to the *de rigueur* event the herd across 57th was pawing each other's bracelets to congratulate itself for attending.

"I've been," I said, which was true. Bikini girl, I'm sorry I dismayed your dad by confessing I don't much remember it. We were all simply living our lives, for God's sake! Not deliberately trotting from one of Tim's future stations of the 20th-century cross to the next. Joy Sterling long since forgiven, Jimmy Bond had taken me to the debut concert two nights earlier. Then he'd written the *Regent's* appraisal—"Taking the Genteel Train," a knock at the Carnegie crowd's belief that its plaudits were in any sense a promotion for Ellington—that drew a few protesting letters from the East Side when it came out in the same issue as "To the Ends of the Earth."

"Why, then! Then good for you to show the flag in spite of your domestic troubles," said the Lotus Eater. "Of course I haven't seen Bran Murphy since— oh, sometime in the Twenties. But I have to admit I'm surprised my old beau took so long to realize you've got more hair on your chest than he does."

"Excuse me?"

"Good Lord, it's a compliment. I know I couldn't have done all that scrambling around for *Regent's* at your age. Too frightened every last minute. That's death! Wouldn't your mother be proud of you, though?"

"Oh, you're Pamela *Buchanan!*" her husband eagerly broke in as the light changed. "Such a pleasure, I'm afraid I'm an avid—"

The L.E. and I were glaring at each other, ignoring the mink and velvet swarm toward condescension. "Why don't you go ask her, you witch?" I said. "You know where to find her."

It shook the Lotus Eater more than I'd have believed the Lotus Eater could be shaken. "You were so little. You misunderstood everything—saw it all exactly backwards," she blurted wretchedly, her face newly Camilled in its chinchilla collar. Then she and her husband plashed through the slush as Pam stood there baffled by whether I'd just heard an honest delusion or the L.E.'s last trick.

While I probably caught sight of her in Manhattan a half dozen times afterward between then and the Sixties, I don't recall us ever exchanging another word but for arctic greetings when the igloo was too confining for mutual obliviousness. But by Roy's and my final meal at the Carnegie Deli, which was in late '66 or early '67—my God, twenty-four years after "To the Ends of the Earth"—I was in a sable coat myself. Cadwaller's gift on our eighth anniversary.

I'd just come from Cath Charters' office after signing my contract for luckless but lovable *Lucky for the Sun*, something I knew better than to mention. The informal contest between them over expat Ohioism and pastless New Yorkery had been settled on Cath's terms. Its sine qua non had been that they both were successes and Roy was one no longer. Most likely he'd have retired by then any-way, but he hadn't expected to do so in disgrace as his magazine foundered.

Poor old *Regent's*. Already dinosaured by TV, it hadn't been able to survive exposure as one of the too numerous magazines, foundations, and other institu-tions that spent the Fifties living the life of Sidney Reilly on the Central Intelligence Agency's largesse. Adding insult to injury, the money'd stopped flowing several years before the story came out—soon after Jack Kennedy's incredulous, "Jesus Christ, why? Are we going to send Castro an exploding subscription?"

Eager to get back in JFK's graces after the whole Bay of Pigs flop, Lang-ley turned off the spigot in mid-'61. Yet Roy had not only known about the payments, which had been Mortimer's call. He'd agreed to let traveling spooks use assignments as cover and shaped foreign coverage to reflect Agency views. Though I didn't have the heart to ask him if he'd played middleman in my case, that may well have included Pam's smattering of Ike-era *Regent's* pieces date-lined Paris.

Was I indignant? Not really. I was a diplomat's wife by then, familiar with worse things done in worse causes. Besides, I knew Roy too well. "A Cross with Many Roots" had been my first grazing contact with his inclination to see *Regent's* as a helpful policy instrument in league with Washington's shrewdest minds. Those jokes about his confidential sources were both revealing as jokes and telltale as preludes.

Besides, in the days of the war, it had made sense to see us as all being on the same team. Roy was too trusting to realize mores had changed. Of all the institutions he'd put his faith in, only the Carnegie Deli never let him down.

I hadn't been up to New York in a while. Still knew I no longer needed to fret about running into the Lotus Eater, as I'd read her obit by then. Of course Carnegie Hall looked unchanged, but the Beatles had played there three years before. Their newly piratical, flowing-locked progeny swirled around Pam in a seizure of chic as I got out of the cab two blocks south. Still at his old table—as I've said, only the Carnegie Deli didn't let him down—a Roy now as wrinkled and whitened as a sea cow's proboscis looked up from a caravel of pastrami.

"My doctor would kill me if he knew," he said once he'd stood up for an eight-eyed peck and, readjusting our respective specs, we'd sat down. "He's trying to anyway, so what the hell. I'm not sure which of us gives the other more zooris."

"Tsuris," our waiter snapped as he slapped down my menu. "Ah, tourists. Welcome to New York City."

My old editor beamed. "I'm sorry, young man. I meant grief."

"How are you holding up, Roy? Thanks, I won't need it. Just cheesecake for me."

"Ah, Pam." Roy glanced at the wall where his sketched portrait still hung. "All that really hurts is reading that I was a bad editor, because you know that's not true. I was a good one. I was just a very bad Richelieu."

POSTED BY: *Pam*   As you may've gathered, daisysdaughter.com readers, another reason "To the Ends of the Earth" has stayed memorable is that it was the story I came back from reporting to learn Bran was suing me for divorce. The grounds were desertion, which I couldn't especially argue with. And adultery, which as it happened, Pam's why-Henrying on Capitol Hill to the contrary, I could.

It might have been different if his lawyers hadn't named Jake Cohnstein as co-respondent. But if you've damned near forgotten I was still Mrs. Murphy, I leave it to you whether to grouse at my inept storytelling or salute my blog's positively Jamesian way with lacunae.

Oddly or not, it had never occurred to me to leave him in my Columbian year, since at one level I never quite grasped I *could*. At another, I'm afraid I'd come to rely on my marriage as an all-purpose preclusion. Imagining a Pam at liberty to get off in Baltimore for a *folie à* Corporal, invite any Detroiter I fancied to my room at the Tuller Hotel, or turn a stack of new parachutes back into wedding gowns before they got packed for the Airborne would probably have alarmed me right out of my skin.

All the same, his wife's wartime blossoming from a little book reviewer into a gallivantingly slangy American broad most available at our local newsstand can't have put many songs in Bran's heart. Since everything I was doing felt gloriously natural, its improvised artifices not only included but exulted in, even I didn't recognize the extent of Pam's metamorphosis until I saw it in not my hubby's face but Mr. Carraway's. On the way back from Fort Des Moines, a switchyard snafu in Chicago left me at loose ends I knotted by going out to Oak Park to visit Dorothy Day's former Scarecrow.

During what proved to be our last pre-Nenuphar reunion, we were as glad as ever to see each other. Nick tactfully avoided bringing up Murphy: in a Manhattan restaurant soon after my marriage, my ex-guardian's and new hubby's only meeting had left the future Brother Nicholas appalled even before Bran's jovial, "Never got your hooks into old Daisy yourself, did you? Believe it or not, Nicky, I've got a couple of stories about the ones that got away from Murph. Say we wait until Snooks here goes to powder her nose." Under Nick's cherished out-of-place magnolia, as I stubbed out smoke after smoke, recrossed now adult gams, and waxed all Walt Whitwomanish about Sherman tanks, WACs, parachute factories, my favorite editor, and my favorite Congresswoman, I saw in midsentence I now bewildered him.

A moment later, his affectionate murmur of "Just give me a sec to empty that ashtray, will you?" told me he'd counted on Pam to bewilder him one day. Because he was Nick, bewilderment wasn't worry's synonym unless I was unhappy. At fifty, his age then, you've either harnessed the world or accepted that it gallops on. Now that he found me incomprehensibly whole and wholly incomprehensible—not only to himself but, so I dared hope, to her—his duty to Daisy was finally done.

Having known me since my toddlerhood and the U.S. of A. since his Penrodic own, Nick had always expected both Pam and times to change. Not so Bran, since fame was a game of musical chairs he'd won and the famous never think the music will start up again. It didn't help that his own writing wasn't going well; his final play, *The Two-Faced War*, wouldn't reach footlights until after our divorce, and then in a miserable little theatrical club out in Brooklyn.

Unsurprisingly, I was the villainess. But I was in the ETO by then, so unmoored from my strange interlude as Mrs. Murphy that Addison's delighted V-mail report seemed to not only describe but be addressed to a caricature.

I'd honestly thought I was doing my marriage a favor when I shifted my typewriter to *Regent's* offices. That just left him alone to brood afternoons under Dolores Ibárurri's coffee-stained portrait, glaring at volumes of press clippings now ominously labeled "1928," "1929," and so on. When I was putting up in

Manhattan—I'd quite unconsciously stopped saying "home" by mid-'42—our arguments could have rocked the gulls pocking Dagwood and Blondie over the East River into peeling off for Brazil, then still noncombatant.

I should admit I welcomed those duels. They were my reprieve from the importunings of the Pam who'd start up her old golem writhings whenever, another trip under my belt, my train wound back into Grand Central. The Pam who gave as good as she got in our fights was soon another of my emergency wartime selves: I could've fashioned her lines from a coma ward. If I was brutal, remember I was quite young and battling for a new life I loved against a two-time if also two-timing Pulitzer winner. I knew nothing of middle age.

"Jesus *Christ*, Snooks!" Bran protested one day, bourgeois at last. "At least keep your voice down. You're shrieking like a goddam fishwife."

"Oh? Den say, den—why don't youse write a play about me, Moiphy?" My next jab hit even lower, and thanks to uniforms on slow-chugging trains it wasn't uninformed. "As if anybody ever goddam talked that way!"

Injuring him no less, my peripatetic e.e. comings and goings worsened Pam's neglect of her domestic duties. The housewifely ones, I mean, though as I've said the undressed ones eventually devolved into looking to Flaubert's productivity for inspiration as to frequency and to the Eastern Front for pointers on intimacy. As murky windows and unwiped Deco lacquer deepened Bran's gloom, I grew exasperated. What a woman he could be sometimes.

"For God's sake, then! Hire somebody to clean the place. Never mind your fucking principles, think of *her*. She's out there half naked, starving, nibbling a crust of bread from a garbage can, and wondering why noble Mr. Murphy believes in the proletariat too much to toss her a bone. Now I know why Stalin's wife shot herself," I said. It may tell you something about my assimilation of my marriage as pure theater that I could toss in a woman's suicide by gun without an admonitory tingle from dead Daisy's file in the archives.

My hubby winced for other reasons. "Not sure I could afford it, Snooks. No, damn it. I don't mean we're facing eviction. But I was really counting on *Clock* to run and run."

Given what charwomen charged in those days, that was patently Bran experimenting with himself as the beleaguered hero of Sutton Place. He still had a great deal more money than I was earning from *Regent's*. Then again, having it isn't the same as making any, and the sad truth is that he did have to give up his East River view by '45 or so. Thus began the downhill slalom that ended when Wife Five, who'd only come in looking for the butcher's phone number, found him slumped like a deflated circus tent over the latest balloon filler—"Kill me then, you mad beast. There are thousands more like me"—for *Seamus Shield, Agent of Fury*.

Nonetheless, even a marriage both parties suspect is obsolete goes on making demands as a situation, and for whatever it's worth I was more active in trying to solve them. Until my divorce summons, a good slice of my income went into paying the wages of Trinka Solynka, lately of Danzig, who came in twice a week to spend a few dreamy hours losing at tic-tac-toe to our furniture.

Trinka had piano legs but a bosom any concertinist would love. Raven-haired when the agency first sent her over, she startled us both when she went permed and platinum for New Year's, proudly trotting out "hairtresser" as her first trisyllabic American word. Even though I couldn't have presented Bran with someone more unlike myself if I'd spent a year hunting, I wasn't remotely conscious of hiring a substitute for anything but menial chores.

He and I had never really had it out about Viper Leigh. Something in me balked at playing the betrayed young bride; I may've intuited our twenty-year age difference would let Bran intolerably act the adult as soon as I started mewling. Once I'd got over being *ébranlée*, I'd simply started treating his infidelity as a known fact between us, leaving Murphy guessing about any private little grave mound under Pam's frost but handing him the role of overgrown boy instead.

That suited my hubby, since it gave him permission to go on acting like one. The more so as, reluctant to summon Viper too vividly by name, I'd pluralized her as "your chippies." Once she recovered from miscarrying, he picked up with her where he'd left off: the dates on the bill for the room at the Peter Minuit dawdled on into mid-January, when *Clock's* dismal run ended. Soon after that, I was away so often that Murphy didn't require a love nest for their or any other dalliances.

As for that little grave mound, of course it was there. It had never happened to me before, except in the childhood petri dish of nonsensical loyalties where a budding pudding kept insisting that the Lotus Eater's treachery with her beefy beach rutter—but for his Rolex, now more faceless than ever—should count. Yet it was always the metallic fact of having been cheated on that grabbed the headline in Pam's mental tabloid. The gent responsible seemed fatuous, silly, a bit trivial: when I tried to picture it, no more than a pair of vague hands palping pale, now peeled, bare little pears.

That had felt like the wrong image to try lighting wifely anger's torch with, and I'd soon learned to shut it off faster than the L.E. could say "That's death." Once I was launched on my Columbian year, I grew increasingly confident that squalid little Hormel's belated dressing-room revenge had been a fluke. One thing I'd known since childhood about the Charybdis temptation was that it made people unhappy, and well! I wasn't anymore.

POSTED BY: *Jake Damstein*   As ludicrous as it was for my hubby's divorce suit to name Jake Cohnstein, something Bran knew as well as any man Jake hadn't actually gone to bed with, it had a vital geographic plausibility. Since April '42 or so, still mourning the Mayflower's bar but not the pinch on my cash flow—taking refuge in the trad magazine ploy of making no identifiable individual responsible for them, *Regent's* was laggardly about reimbursing expenses—I'd been putting up on my Washington jaunts at Jake's cramped new digs in Kalorama. Leaving even Addison at a rare loss for words, he'd gotten himself commissioned at forty-two, joining the Army's Office of Public Affairs.

"You ought to meet the fellow I share a desk with," he told me with amusement during my first stay with him, over a Wisconsin Avenue lunch I now recognize as an occasion comparable to Roy Charters's discovery of the Carnegie Deli. Over Nan Finn's or Laurel Warren's shoulder, I sometimes still see two talkative ghosts in the truncated booth that's tucked just behind Martin's Tavern's unchanged front door.

"Anytime, Jake. Say, these crab cakes are good."

"They always will be even after I'm long dead, but listen. Heck is a good old boy from Somewheresville, South Carolina, and his favorite advice to me on any subject is 'You ain't in New York no more, Coan-Steen.' But Pammie, I'm a

hopeless civilian. I just can't make myself say, 'That's *Captain* Hebe to you, Lieutenant Redneck.' Strange times, don't you think?"

"All around, though."

"Exactly!" He was pleased I'd understood so quickly. "All around. Pam, I
could swear I'm happy here."

Having lived in Washington far longer than he did—and *pace* my old
Capitol Hill fairy godmother, never having been bored once in peacetime—
I wonder if Jake understood the difference between place and occasion. New
York can trust its glamor to hold sway even when nothing special's happening.
To everybody but us lifers, the District's allure is at the mercy of events. When
it's in default mode, outsiders are usually prepared to believe our so tellingly
manufactured capital has consequence, yes. Excitement, no.

The exceptions are rare: the Kennedy years, the Watergate summers. In the
mimsies' experience, the war was the greatest exception of all. For forty-four
months, Pam's future city—overcrowded, inconvenient, the Mall visitors think
of as so eternal clogged for the duration with temporary office buildings whose
windows looked like a centipede's legs—had the charisma of Babylon.

For Jake, its attractions were multiple. Instead of sniffing they weren't all
idealistic, today I'd rather say there are ideals and ideals. In recent years, whenever Andy Pond has driven a grumpily fat-lunetted Pam down Pennsylvania
Avenue, I've never caught sight of the genuinely touching statue of the Lone
Sailor at the Navy Memorial without seditiously picturing a tin casting of my
old friend Jake Cohnstein standing nearby—hands in tin pockets, tin smile
mildly askew, and nerving himself to offer to make the Lone Sailor less lone by
buying him a tin drink. Which the Lone Sailor's flesh-and-blood forebears quite
often accepted, and not always naively.

He did try to be discreet during my stays, but war is hell and hotels were
mobbed. I still remember how nonplussed Pam was the first time she awoke on
Jake's living room couch to see a young soldier emerging from the bathroom,
reclad in yesterday's uniform but with freshly showered hair. Either no fool or a
huge one, he kept ostentatiously patting it before he left.

Fond as Jake and I were of each other, our breakfast—Sergeant Kowalski
did not participate—was strained. In fact, I felt furiously resentful, with the

extra ragged edge that comes of red clouds hiding unlooked-at bluebirds. I do
remember the word I kept wanting to toss at him was *selfish*. It wasn't only that
he seemed to me to be taking advantage of the war in ways I'd felt maritally
and professionally immunized from. Back in pre–Pearl Harbor days, I'd happily
commiserated about his ushers and such without ever meeting one face to face.

In this case, not only was commiseration plainly uncalled for, but it was
so clear no emotional attachment was in play—no tenderness, no smiles, no
friendship or soft lingering poetry—that I felt enraged on my gender's behalf.
"My God, it's true!" I snapped. "Men *are* all alike."

"Hope springs eternal," Jake yawned over toast.

"It's always so easy for all of you, isn't it? Just find 'em and fool 'em and so on
and so forth until the bloody cows come home. Whether it's wham, bam, thank
you ma'am or wham, bam, thank you Stan."

"I didn't have to fool him, believe me. But maybe the grass is always greener
on the other side of the hill."

"Which means what?"

"Just that one cliche deserves another. Sorry, but Addison I'm not. How
did it go? 'We often wondered what had been squandered…'"

"Plundered."

"I always did say he's more sentimental than I am. Whatever became of
that friend of yours on Bank Street, anyhow? I liked her that one time we met."

"Oh, she's married, I suppose."

"You suppose. By the way, which of you got married first?"

"I couldn't care less. Does it matter?"

"You tell me."

"She did," I fibbed. "I just didn't like her husband."

POSTED BY: *Pam*   As for the cuckolding of Brannigan Murphy, which
I'd better make haste to describe in all its why-Henry'd, cuke-encumbered
detail, the only thing Bran's lawyers got right was the city it happened in. It
could also scarcely be called Pam's doing, since I just wanted a quick quote
on shipyard absenteeism to stick into "Liberty Belles." When I put my head
in Edith's door to ask her receptionist which Democrat on the Naval Affairs

Committee would do, she gave me an appraising look after recommending a young Texas go-getter, still in his mid-thirties but already in his third full term. "Just make sure your ear is the only thing he talks off," she said wryly.

Of course my hair was the usual electrified oatmeal. But in a tight outfit of Pan Am blue, the closest Saks could come to approximating Connie Ostrica's WAC uniform, the Buchanan gams were on exceptional display. You can only be so modest at five-ten, especially when fashion is doing its part for our troops in more ways than one by not wasting fabric on anything except the shoulder pads.

That's why the energetic tick-tocking of female hips in snug skirts is as much part of my wartime way-back-when as greasy GIs in fatigues, and did we ever *need* those shoulder pads, too. No man's eyes would have reached our faces otherwise. Anyhow, I was reasonably sure I could induce the Congressman to give me five minutes.

He gave me twenty, the cuckolding of Murphy included. Once I'd been gladhanded into his inner office (slatted blinds; pictures of his wife, FDR, himself with FDR, but not of himself with his wife; law books, and the peculiar Scotch-tape redolence of warmed wood, upholstery, and paint in a Congressional office in an Indian-summer October back before air conditioning made life in Washington more comfortable and less sensual), I think Pam got to ask one question. A quarter hour later, virtually the next sound from her mouth was a moan.

The accent had gotten less baffling early on, devoutly though I hoped the Congressman never had to say "I'll be leaving Abilene" when the matter was urgent, clarity vital, and his audience Northern. But in all my many days, I've never known another transition from blather to screwing that was such a continuum. It was as if copulation was only volubility by newly physical means, just as his monologue had been physicality barely restrained by its obligation to stay verbal.

I'd also never been literally bent back over a desk. I couldn't tell you just when the large hand gripping my right elbow for emphasis got tag-teamed by another pulling my shoulder-padded left shoulder close for greater confidentiality. Or when the plough nose boring in beneath his hooded eyes bumped mine as the Congressman's most sensitive feature, that rangily dewlapped but oddly dainty mouth, went on berating and beseeching me to understand the war, America, and then himself in ascending order of difficulty. His huge ears hung palely in the background like an elephant hunter's trophies.

Shipyard absenteeism? Good God, when he thought of the sacrifices our boys were making in New Guinea's muddy jungles, the mere mention of shipyard absenteeism made his blood boil. I hadn't been to the battlefronts—but he had. (Indeed so: on a VIP junket whose vague agenda had roused Douglas MacArthur's ire. With full Rooseveltian backing, its true goal was to let the Congressman claim status as a veteran in every *political* campaign from then on.)

As for himself, he was proud to have worn his country's uniform during this great struggle. (He probably hadn't had to have it drycleaned more than once, since it got mothballed the instant FDR ordered all members of Congress holding military commissions to go on inactive duty. His stint as a Lieutenant Commander in the Naval Reserve had served its purpose, and the 1942 elections were coming up.) Excuse his French, but the Congressman was, yes, *God-damned* proud to have shared those boys' dangers, however briefly. (His one flight as a kibitzer on a bombing mission had lasted two hours, but the Silver Star they pinned on him for it looked good.)

Whenever he thought of the pitiful lad whose belongings he'd packed up with these very hands to send 'em on home to his Momma—well, not *his* Momma, of course, bless that fine lady; the lad's Momma. Bless her too—shipyard absenteeism incited the Congressman so much he wanted to smite people. Why, if *he'd* been that kind of slacker, the good folks back in the Hill Country who'd chosen him as their representative still wouldn't have rural electricity.

Did I know he'd done that in his first *year* in office? Not even thirty yet, by God, not even elected to his first full term; sent here by a special election they'd all said he didn't have a prayer of winning. And *that*, young miss, was the sort of gumption these United States needed if we were going to prevail. Could I please tell him how we were going to honor those poor boys and their Mommas' sacrifices and make rural electricity worth enjoying and get this damned thing over with when it still took us two *months* to get a Liberty ship from first rivet to christening?

"Forty-five days," I gasped into his nostrils, and the Congressman's craning nose inhaled my words. His vast ears only heard a reason to expand on what he was expounding.

It wasn't just Liberty ships! It was destroyers, and battlewagons, and transports and landing craft and big goddam aircraft carriers. We needed all those by dates certain, in tonnages and numbers the Committee would be glad to provide—and as a longtime friend of the working man, by *no means* was he going to let anyone put all the blame on shipyard absenteeism. Owners had to do their part too. Did I have any idea what pathetic—yes, *pathetic*—percentage of capacity America's industrial plant was running at, *nine full months* after Pearl Harbor?

"Sixty-eight percent," I gasped. "But the September figures aren't out yet."

Well, now. Well, now! Maybe I *was* in some position [I'll say: his belt buckle was gouging my bellybutton] to feel the Congressman's engorged wrath at the idea of business as usual during this hour of national peril. Did I know I was a fine example of a fine, fine young American woman? *Regent's*, was it? Old Mortimer was hiring them younger and prettier these days. Smart, too! He hadn't had much of an education himself—just a degree from Southwest State Teachers' College of San Marcos. He reckoned that made him as good a man as any. Where had I gone to school?

"Barn—"

That's just what he'd thought! Did I see, did I *feel* the holy power and the wonder of Barnard and Southwest State Teachers' College of San Marcos marching toward victory together? Could I grasp his American metaphor? Did I know that in New Guinea's jungles he'd seen other fine women just like me— nurses, tending our brave boys in muddy tents by a single lantern's light as the ground shook from Nip bombs. Nobody was asking anybody where they'd gone to school out there. He'd been lonely, far from home; never mustered up the courage. Yet just from pure gratitude, he'd always wanted to—just one kiss—wanted to—

In this changed culture, Panama, the sound of tearing underwear would signal violation to any movie audience worth the salt in its popcorn tubs. Yet while desire, as a conscious choice, didn't enter into things on my end—no time—neither did protest. If you must know, the hand that pushed down those nettlesome undies after a moment of too-many-nooks snags was my own.

They ripped when his hand took charge at mid-thigh, and unlike a White House intern of a later day, I wasn't much on souvenirs. Stuck under yesterday's handy *Evening Star* for propriety's sake, those just-bought panties from Hecht's ended up in his office wastebasket. All in all, your Gramela can think of quotes from *by Pamela Buchanan*'s oeuvre that did my wardrobe less damage and made my knee-locked bus ride back to Jake's less tense than "'Shipyard absenteeism is our Achilles' heel. "Work or Fight" must be our motto,' said Rep. Lyndon B. Johnson (D-Tex.), an up-and-comer to watch on the Navel Affairs Committee."

Thankfully, Roy fixed the typo without comment—and for Lady Bird's sake, I've thought of pseudonymizing LBJ. But if I make it to 1968 on daisysdaughter.com, calling him Congressman Austin Driskill here will only add confusion to our encounter in the White House a quarter century later. Sexually, the reprise was a fiasco. We both had other things on our minds: Ho Chi Minh in Lyndon's case, Cadwaller's tense presence in the dining room at the opposite end of the East Wing in mine.

By some lights, I know I'm an also-ran. Even today, the District's awash in old prunes happy to wheeze away at the drop of a martini olive about their hump with Jack Kennedy. I'm still not sure I didn't get the better bargain. While neither was renowned for his consideration *after*, you did feel you had Lyndon's full attention *during*—not cool Jack's forte, so we're told and I can easily believe. That knee-trembler in Congressman Johnson's office in my twenty-third year also left me in no doubt why he was by far the greater legislator of the two.

I mean, one saw the fraudulence. It was transparent. Yet it was fraudulence transfigured and exalted. It was fraudulence whose very transparency communicated his conviction that it was only a method and the end it served, whether selflessly national or throbbingly personal, was all the more ennobled by the contrast.

Even as my panties ripped, I'd felt overwhelmed by my enlistment in a great cause. My Pan Am–blue skirt hadn't been shoved up to my ribcage for more than ten seconds before I *knew* we'd defeat the Axis. I quivered as throngs of shipyard workers practically punched each other for the honor of being first through the gate.

Briefly. Then a disheveled and, in pre-Pill days, anxious Pam was babbling "Bathroom?"

He'd already stepped behind a screen. "Hallway," he called over a tap's gurgle soon augmented by a cuke-encumbered one.

My gratitude when the thirty-sixth President's biographers confirmed his habit of peeing in his office sink was considerable, since I did wonder at the time if I was dreaming. I did my best to pull myself together before returning to his outer office, but one look from his receptionist told me my odds of fooling anybody would improve on nonexistent only after I'd left Lyndonville.

"One piece of hard-won advice, hon. The next time you make an appointment, you ask me first if he just happens to have a little ol' meeting at the White House comin' up. You ought've seen the last gal to come out that door when he knew he'd be seein' FDR in an hour. Jeepers, *she* looked like a plucked chicken. Here, lemme hold that compact steady for you."

At least in New York circles, my divorce from Murphy got judged 1943's most sensational as it was. If Bran had known his cuckolder's identity and named him in the suit instead of Jake, my hubby might've accomplished what he always so forlornly hoped to: alter history. Of course the problem with altering it that early is that nobody will ever know the history that's been altered.

POSTED BY: *Pam*   As soon as I took a breath and rescanned the papers handed me by a bailiff making his fourth trip (hence Roy's telegram) to *Regent's*, I understood why Murphy'd been so upbeat at breakfast. Saw what his lawyers were counting on in naming Jake Cohnstein: in exchange for keeping Jake's actual preferences out of the courtroom, I'd be forced not to contest the divorce. Winning one on the charge of adultery guaranteed my hubby wouldn't have to part with a dime.

They were taking no chances that, while I might love Bran less, I might love Sutton Place more. Even though I didn't care about the money, something Murphy revealingly never believed, the gambit of casting Pam as the cheat made me so furious I decided I didn't give a parachute how much dirt got tracked as I stomped out of that corner.

Since Roy and Cath Charters had split up by then, I was halfway to my editor's office to get the name of his attorney when spotting Jimmy Bond made me realize I'd better put in a call to Jake first. When I hung up half an hour later, I was giggling.

"Why, Pam. None of you ever asked," he'd said, tickled himself at my astonishment once he'd broken the news that was to leave even Addison dumbstruck when it came out in court four months later. "It's one reason I wangled this commission. After David enlisted, I wanted to do my part too."

I felt much better once I knew my only regret would be Viper. Roy's attorney was in uniform and on Wild Bill Donovan's staff by then, so I had to find one of my own: Oliver Watson, Esq., whose funereal shingle between a florist's and a jeweler's on Amsterdam Avenue had a touch of *Et in Arcadia ego* I liked. A week after I'd been served, Pam countersued, naming Viper Leigh as co-respondent. With a late-May court date, it was on.

It'll sound medieval to you, bikini girl. Back before prenups and no-fault ruined things for the spectators, a contested divorce could be a real prize-fight. Despite having written a couple of forgotten bestsellers, I'm not sure I've ever given masses of strangers more reading pleasure than I did during the eleven days Murphy and I made the beast with two left hooks in a Manhattan courtroom. Aside from letting Congressman Lyndon Johnson lope to 1600 Pennsylvania Avenue with a clear head, calm loins, and renewed faith in his star, it was probably my major contribution to the war effort.

Since as a celebrity Bran wasn't movie-star caliber and it was only a trial for divorce, not statutory rape, my hubby and I—not to mention Viper Leigh and Trinka Solynka—may not have done as much for morale as Errol Flynn did when "In Like Flynn" became a battle cry from New Guinea to Casablanca. But if there was a Bronze Star for salaciousness, as opposed to Flynn's chimerical Medal of Honor, all four of us could have put in for one.

POSTED BY: *Pam*   You're welcome to hunt up the full transcript. Since I don't have all day and may have less if the phone rings, I'll just give the highlights as I remember them. Having uttered one of the more startling sentences heard in any divorce trial up to then, I don't see how you can blame me if I make it the last word.

Murphy's case was in trouble as soon as Jake Cohnstein took the stand in his U.S. Army captain's uniform. Even Oliver Watson was in the dark about what we had in reserve. Jake and I had both hoped it wouldn't come out during discovery, and it hadn't. We knew they'd had a detective prowling Washington for some conquest of his who'd tell all about their frolics—or, more likely, could be blackmailed into placing me not only in Jake's apartment but his bed, naked as foolscap and playing Cohnstein-scissors-paper for all I was worth.

What would that have been like, I wondered? Odd thought, since I never knew if he preferred to take the girl's part himself and invariably had to stop picturing a nude Pam sharing the dark with newly feminized and knowledgeable Jacquina. Anyhow, we weren't sure they'd located any such creature, but we hoped to forestall them.

Did, too. After taking Jake through the roundelay (yes, those dates sounded right; no, we'd never so much as kissed), Bran's lawyer was still incredulous at our indifference to the mud they could dredge up with the simple words "We believe it speaks to the witness's credibility and character, Your Honor." The warning shot he decided to try was exactly what we wanted.

"Well, of course you're a lifelong bachelor, Mr. [affecting a touch of neuralgia, Jake rubbed one shoulder] Captain Cohnstein. In fact, the common expression is 'confirmed' bachelor, isn't it?"

"I don't know where you get your information, but I'm nothing of the kind. And as a happily married husband and father, I resent what I believe you're insinuating."

POSTED BY: *Pam*   After the recess—and you'd better believe Bran's baffled lawyers asked for one—Oliver Watson, briefed by then, took over. "I believe you were saying you're a happily married man, Captain Cohnstein. Is that correct?"

"Yes. I married the former Sharon Halevy on August 12, 1921. We're the proud parents of David Cohnstein, born in May of the following year."

"Is your wife present, Captain Cohnstein?"

"It's thoughtful of you to ask, Mr. Watson. That's her in the second row."

"Would you rise, Mrs. Cohnstein?"

And she did, beaming: Sharon Halevy Cohnstein, who'd stood under the chuppah with a still troubled Jake when pleasing Pop and Mama Cohnstein was the one act whose value he trusted. She'd lived blissfully ever since—raising their boy, pleased by her husband's success in Manhattan, and content to cook and play checkers with no further carnal demands on her rotund physique. Sharon and David were the "family" he'd let us all misguess was his parents when he spent nights in Williamsburg, deeply satisfied by the respite from his and the world's complexities.

"Is your son in the courtroom, by any chance?" Oliver Watson asked.

'I'm afraid not. He's a waist gunner on a B-17—'somewhere in England,' as they say. I'm sure you know that's all they're allowed to tell us when they write home. I'm glad to say that David does often."

After that, Murphy's lawyers could've shipped half the District's rough trade up to Manhattan to tell tales. They wouldn't have dared call one epicene specimen. It was bad enough they hadn't realized the effect of *Captain* Cohnstein showing up instead of the civilian Bran remembered. To besmirch a B-17 crewman's only dad as his wife and the crewman's mother looked on would have made them Hitler's pinch-hitlers and Hirohito's pinch-hitos. Over celebratory drinks that evening, only Addison stayed irrepressible: "You're just lucky the boy isn't a tail gunner, Jake. Brother, would that have brought down the house."

When I think of my friends, I think I must've had something. Still, we were hardly out of the woods. Even if Jake's testimony had made hash of the adultery charge, we hadn't been able to crack Viper Leigh. With much Murphine encouragement, she was under the impression she could be the next Mrs. Bran if she played her hole card just right.

POSTED BY: *Pam*   Having swapped Sutton Place for my editor's donated sofa in the study of his Upper West Side apartment—where I slept alone, at least then—I'd spent a restless spring. The trial's preliminaries kept me cooped in Manhattan and unable to go on the road as often as I was addicted to.

I did get to Texas and Delaware in February for "Finding Mr. Wright," whose title's true secret wink was Roy wishing me well in my own new sky. Then I spent a week in New Mexico in April for "The View from Ward Three." That report on the Army's Albuquerque nursing school was both my final home-front piece for *Regent's* and my first experiment in making Pam herself a story's tailor's dummy, since "the patient" volunteering for mock bandaging, splinting, sponging, and comforting was none other than your Gramela.

A few short takes from Washington on quickie trips aside—and yes, I'd avoided reinterviewing LBJ—those two pieces were my only reprieves from the drudgery involved in becoming the latest ex-Mrs. Murphy. After my Columbian year, I had days when it drove me half batty to wake up feeling engulfed again by an environment and characters my journeying had largely left behind.

That meant not only Murphy himself, now an infuriating clown as he flashed *Time*-cover grins and told whoppers for a stenographer's benefit. It meant tepidly circumlocutious, porcelain-pale, easily flushed John Lavabo and the cast of *A Clock with Twisted Hands*. All of them but Hal Lime—bruited for a supporting Oscar by now after playing Gunnar Dyson, the wisecracking Swede who ended up staying behind to cover his squad's escape, in *Corrigedor Story*—got shaken down for their two cents and wooden nickels regarding Bran and Viper.

I did like seeing Hans Caligar again, especially after his denturized elevator mutter of "Remember, the smart only shame themselves by negotiating with the shtupid." Yet I'd found myself blush-worthily eager when Viper's own turn came to be deposed, swiftly setting it down to a yen for revenge.

That yen was disappointed. In a polka-dot dress all wrong for March and warning us what to expect in May, she'd played the tearful innocent much better than she had ~~Vickie Patricia~~ Lucy, not that Pam had great grounds to scoff there. No, she'd never had anything "like *that*"—nice moue of disgust—to do with Mr. Murphy. She didn't go with married men, and had liked and admired me much too much [insert two-way stare here] to even think about it. Yes, she'd been up to his room at the Peter Minuit those five times. (We knew it was more like fifty, but five was all the hotel's former night clerk could confirm.) But only to help him with his revisions by reading ~~Vickie Patricia~~ Lucy's new lines, and she'd never removed so much as a hairpin.

Yes, she'd been admitted to Bellevue—no, not the psychiatric wing!—on December 5, 1941. Only for unspecified "abdominal bleeding," though, not a miscarriage. The verdict was an early period and bad cramps. The hospital records bore her out, but in those days it wouldn't have taken much pleading from someone as lissome as Viper for Bellevue's Kildare-was-here not to have written everything down.

And she was sorry, but would we—would we mind? Her high-school fiancé, really the only boy she'd really loved, had been killed at Kasserine just last month. It was awful to answer these questions when she was still grieving for him.

Unsurprisingly, when our gumshoe checked, said boy's genuinely grieving parents were stumped that Betty, as they knew her, had flashed out of Flatbush in June 1940 without a toodle-oo to now mantlepieced Phil. Even so, Kasserine Pass was Kasserine Pass: our worst defeat at German hands before the Battle of the Bulge's opening days, and we didn't know about the Battle of the Bulge yet. Grieving parents are grieving parents, and Viper was so good Oliver Watson had made up his mind he wouldn't challenge her testimony directly.

We knew we had to call her if they didn't. I'd named her, after all, but Oliver was dreading what it would do to our case. That changed once Trinka Solynka took the stand.

POSTED BY: *Pam*   Remember, they were still trying to nail me on desertion. Trinka's job was to describe Bran's life after Mrs. Murphy started wanderlusting all over the country—just for the romps and nectar, I gathered. A pitiful picture she gave too, applying that artless accent like dill on a turbot: sad Mr. Murphy shutting himself away for hours before emerging to test the pillars' lack of give, Samson-style, a stricken expression on his sadly beardless face (she mimicked him slowly, regretfully checking). Gulled Mr. Murphy gazing at gulls under the portrait of Dolores Ibárruri—the *other* Mrs. Gillooley, and why hadn't I seen that until now?—in the vain hope I'd swoop in on my broomstick and start sweeping the kitchen.

It was just how Bran behaved when I was on hand, and it wasn't Pam he was mourning. It was inspiration's failure to pipe up now that Dolores no longer leaned down. But I don't think Trinka ever understood what he did for a living, or indeed that he wasn't just a millionaire—her exaggerated estimate of his place in the cosmos—by dispensation of strange American gods. Certainly in her day no evidence of his labors had made it out of his office except when she emptied the trash.

As indifferent as I was to the money angle, it did annoy me that Trinka was Murphy's witness when my signature was the one on her checks. My whispered question whether that could be brought out earned a look of woe from Oliver Watson, since it would indicate financial independence and he *did* care about the alimony. It was not only what I was paying him for but, if all went well, with.

More infuriatingly, Bran's lawyers made bold to ask Trinka about the Murphys' conjugal relations—and she quite naturally reported they were non-existent. Of course they were, when she was there cooking or cleaning! She wasn't a live-in maid, and Miss Hormel (not called) to the possible contrary, I wasn't an exhibitionist. Yet Trinka had been an awed if dictionaryless witness to some of our rawer fights, and her recaps of those gave spectators their first real prickle of juridical porn. Spoken in lisped and zaftig Danzigzags, "An' then Mist' Murphy say I never knew how good Colum Firth had it—an' she say well I sure rather look at Vacheton Moment than *that* God damn thing" had a tawdry allure so fleshy Trinka might as well have been kneading her own mammarial concertina at the time.

I hadn't seen myself impersonated since Purcey's callous halls. In this case, any fool could see and hear that Trinka's regal tut-tuts, airy chinlifts, and dismissive those-little-piggies flutterings of fingers were the fruit of spellbound attendance at Brooklyn movie palaces.

Still, as I watched her burlesque a Pam I knew had never existed, one thought kept insisting it was fertile. Dear God, was Bran determined to turn us *all* into actresses? And bad ones at that? Bolstered by Addison's lunch-break mutter of "You know, I do wonder if Murph's been smiting the sledded Polack on the ice," that intuition convinced me to lobby Oliver Watson for a fresh line of questioning when Trinka returned to the stand.

My attorney hated the idea. With all our attention focused on Viper, we'd never raised the issue during discovery. Like most trial lawyers, Oliver had a horror of asking questions whose answer he didn't know, and he was still nettled at Jake and me for keeping Sharon Halevy Cohnstein's existence hidden. But with Viper herself due to testify next and still unbudgingly backing Murphy's story, he reluctantly agreed.

Before he got to it, he had to take Trinka back through her whole morning's testimony—chivvying her as to whether Mrs. Pam hadn't *really* said Thus-and-so instead of Such-and-such, etc. With her Danzig-in-distress English up against his curlicued kind, it was so tiresome it bored even me, and I'd been the one God damning the Mighty Tower to begin with. It was late in the day before Oliver, fresh out of pickable bones and splittable hairs, gave me a helpless glance to see if I still wanted to go ahead. I nodded.

"Ah, before we let you go. One last question, Miss Solynka. By any chance, in the past eight months, have you yourself ever had—ah, sexual congress? With your employer?" Even Oliver couldn't keep it straight that Bran didn't pay her wages.

"What? No!" Trinka cried just before giving Lyndon Johnson's afternoon delight my worst scare of the trial. "*She* go Congress! Not me."

"No, no. That's not what I'm asking. Miss Solynka, have you—yourself— ever had illicit relations with Mr. Murphy?"

Trinka thinking hard was like a steam shovel waiting for its operator to show up. "My aunty she come say hi one time. Was bad?"

"No, no. Have you—your honor, may I have a word with my client?"

Since he was sitting behind me, I didn't actually see it. Languidly coughing to draw Trinka's attention, Addison raised both hands for a gesture involving a circled thumb and finger, a forefinger and movement.

As her first moment of total understanding during an ordeal that puzzled and frightened her dawned, her face bloomed happiness that she could be helpful at last. No wonder Bran enjoyed banging her.

"Oh, *boinky-boink!* Yes, yes, yes, yes. Tuesday, Thursday, Tuesday, Thursday. But never when Mrs. Pam home"—and her face went from virtuous to sly. "When she go Congress."

POSTED BY: *Pam*   That was how Viper Leigh went from being the final witness scheduled on Bran's side to the first called on ours. To say she was seething is to remark Versailles cost money, and that polka-dot dress was history too. When she marched her upthrust pear boobies and tight-skirted rear past Bran's table, her icepick heels were stabbing the floor like Trotsky's comeback in the role of Banquo's ghost.

Unlike Trinka, whose testimony is what gets *Murphy v. Murphy* cited in dictionaries of American slang ("boink, v.: sexual congress; wide 1943–45 service, Broadway use; from 'boinky-boink,' n.; earliest known citation…"), Viper didn't say much for the books. She sure made a splash in the papers, though: RED PLAYWRIGHT PROMISED MARRIAGE, STAGE CUTIE AVERS ["Bombers Pound Hamburg"—see p. 4]. VIPER'S HEARTBREAK AT LOST CHILD: 'MY POOR MUFFIN,' SHE SOBS ["Algiers Conference Wraps Up: Churchill Pleased"—see p. 9]. TWO-TIME PULITZER CHAMP CAN'T EVEN SPELL: 'PETER MINUET TONITE?' MURPH'S MASH NOTE READ ["Attu Battle Ends with Mass Nip Suicide, Says Army"—see p. 15].

I wasn't prepared for how much her confession hurt. You get used to seeing these things as circuses, Panama. Then you remember how once there you were in the forest. I hadn't known Murphy first took up with Viper in October '41, before she'd been cast in *Clock* and just two months after our return from Maine. I could have lived without learning their nickname for me was Helen Keller. Nor had I known he'd had her on the same Sutton Place sofa where he and I—early on, early on!—had done our best to widen Dolores Ibárurri's eyes once or twice.

Remember, not only was Bran my first husband. For what now seemed longer than he'd deserved, I'd gone on thinking he'd be the only one.

By the time Oliver finished leading Viper through her Peter Minuit minuet, my hubby's lawyers were peering under their chairs for a briefcase to piss in. Out to discredit her, they fell back on trying to bully her into admitting she'd set out to entrap Bran by getting preggers. Was that a mistake, and not only because Viper'd succeeded in provoking compassion for that tiny Murphine seahorse flushed into the sewer system. When they pushed one time too many, her eyes glistened.

"I'm sorry, would—would you mind? I'm sorry. I'm doing my best, but— *oh, Phil!*—my fiancé was killed at Kasserine Pass. And he never even—we never. And it's so awful, so awful, you see—to be answering these dirty sex questions, when—*oh, Phil, Phil, Phil!* Oh, I'm so sorry, Your Honor." [MURPHY TRIAL BOMBSHELL: BRAN CALLED VIPER'S USO WORK IN PHIL'S HONOR 'WASTE OF TIME,' SAYS WEEPING FLATBUSH GIRL. See p. 45 for Yankees win and all sports coverage.]

Once Viper swept her boobies back off the witness stand, I probably shouldn't have been taken aback at how anatomically—I mean automatically— she joined our circle outside the courtroom. Doing their best to form a coral reef of friendship inside a surf of reporters, Roy Charters, Addison, Jake, and (this was heroic; I loved her for it) Sharon Halevy Cohnstein weren't expecting it either. I'd just yowled that I needed a drink when there Viper was, reaching out: "Pam! I'm so glad it's over [*sic*]. I just hope I helped."

Actresses, honestly! The latest role is the only one. It doesn't matter to them how vivid your memories are of their late-1941 performance in *I'm Fucking Your Husband* or their polka-dotted turn in Spring 1943's discovery hit *And I'm Going to Lie My Cute Can Off About It, Too*. Not to mention a part that Viper, then delirious, had been unaware of playing: her feverish skin and pears' contribution to *Miss Hormel's Revenge*, a chamber piece I didn't want revived. As she grabbed my arm and I inhaled her perfume, thrust upsettingly back to the last time we'd been in physical contact, all I could do was stare into her breathily bright-lipsticked face.

"I hope *you* write a play one of these days," she told me. "Wouldn't that show him? And I'd like to be in it if I could."

At which I must've stared twice over. Even in his Topanga garden, Addison was delighted by the memory. "Isn't the power of the unconscious splendid?" he mused. "She can't have realized what she was implying."

"Oh, not a chance of it." Then I hesitated. But I was older and a long way from that dressing room, and Gerson was nowhere in sight. "Even so, I swear I got worried the first words I typed when I got back to Roy's were going to be 'Act One.'"

He didn't bat an eye. "She *was* pretty. Dumb as cornstarch, but pretty," he said fondly, and never brought her up again.

POSTED BY: *Pam*   Up until Viper's testimony, my four months on the sofa in Roy Charters's study had been as unstained by carnality as the New York edition of Henry James that loomed over me. But that night, not without a certain grim inner mutter of *plus ça change* on Pam's part, my editor and I had our first fumbling go at the old buck and wing. Volcanic it wasn't, and when I finally met the woman whose bra cups Roy may have been hoping I'd fill— bustling Cath Charters was no more than a name to me then—I saw how the Buchanan bod might've started out looking like a bit of a stretch and ended up seeming like a bit of a letdown.

On my end, once I'd quit counting the Marquands between (Sinclair) Lewis and (Walter van Tilburg) Clark, I spent most of the ten minutes it took feeling mystified that anyone as brainy as Roy could think sex as a *deed* was a cure for loneliness. As opposed to tender confirmation it had been defeated, my own lost ideal. That notion must be more afoot in the land than I'd gathered, and so on.

Once Viper's stint on the stand was done, so I learned from Garth Vader's *Dat Dead Man Dere*, Bran's lawyers begged him to let them barter for the best alimony deal they could. Yet my hubby was the same Murphy who'd taken *A Clock with Twisted Hands* on his back and staggered a few more blind steps up the mountain before letting the opening-night audience leave, and by that time he didn't care about the money either. He wanted self-justification. To get it, he was depending on the oldest unofficial rule of American jurisprudence: you can't wrong someone hateful.

In the good old tennis court of public opinion, I can't say he failed. Not going by the jolly men in later years who'd react to being introduced to Pam by playing the asinine trick of snatching their bee-stung hand away and chuckling as their upheld palm implored my mercy. Making a joke of it, yes, and swinging back in for the grip. Still putting me on notice they knew I had a shiv in my purse.

In a suit brown as autumn, Bran had testified much earlier. Consulting his own interlocked Pulitzer-winning hands, he'd won a few stunned looks from his soon-to-be ex as he described how he'd encouraged my writing. Did he mean "You're really so much better at those little book reviews"? Had he known it was going to be my excuse to abandon him, he wouldn't have lied about thinking Pam had talent: "I wasn't under oath then, Your Honor" (*Time*-cover grin). A loyal husband will do these things to protect his home's harmony.

I'd been furious, but Oliver hadn't been able to damage Murphy much. Neither Trinka's boinky-boinks nor Viper's Peter Minuit minuet had come out at that point, and my fussbudget lawyer was no match for Bran at charm or stagecraft. By my own turn, my hubby's case was in much worse shape, and Oliver was concentrating on refuting the desertion charge. His purpose in walking me through my *Regent's* assignments wasn't only to remind everyone that I hadn't been rowdying around the country for fun, something Roy Charters's testimony had already confirmed.

What Oliver hoped would sink in was an ultimately patriotic contrast: Pam singing democracy's arsenal while Bran sat on his. Pam watching Sherman tanks roll out as *Colum Firth's* author played mannequin games with Viper Leigh; Pam freezing her pants off in a Tennessee coal mine as on Sutton Place Trinka gave demonstrations of how to play the accordion lying down. Was my lawyer glad Viv and the others had taken me down the shaft on a Tuesday.

"And as you watched them plant the dynamite that afternoon, Mrs. Murphy, did you have any inkling that at the same moment, in New York..."

"No, of course not," I said, thinking all this might sound very different if Bran and Trinka's boinky-boink hour had come at the end of the day. Except for one anodyne sentence, however, my happiest and then most disconcerting Riceville memory had stayed unmentioned in print.

I hadn't expected Bran's lawyers to take me through the same itinerary. Soon I understood what they were listening for: a fractional hesitation, a small but fatal shift in tone. "Mrs. Murphy, did you ever commit adultery in Tennessee?"

"No."

"Did you ever commit adultery in Michigan?"

"No."

"Did you ever commit adultery in Texas?"

"No"—and suddenly I was terrified they'd ask about Washington, D.C. But Jake had immunized me there; it never crossed their minds.

There was one other state I had to brace myself for. Its tourist brochure was looking at me and we'd made the beast with two left feet that morning. I only kept my poise by remembering that adultery *with* Ohio wasn't adultery *in* Ohio, something I thought Roy would laugh at that night but he oddly didn't.

"Mrs. Murphy, according to your husband, you—ah—increasingly lost interest in the physical side of marriage even when you did put in an appearance at your home. Is that your recollection too?"

"My God, I don't know what Bran's talking about. No matter how tired I was, all he had to do was ask. Well, grunt."

"Order in the court."

"But in fact, your—ah—conjugal intimacies did occur considerably less often as time went on, didn't they?"

"The way I saw it, that was really up to him."

"Should we take that as meaning you had no interest on your own?"

"Well, I never turned him down. If you mean was I raring to go, though, then probably not."

"Why was that, Mrs. Murphy?"

I looked at Bran. Bran looked at me. Oliver Watson looked alarmed. Dolores Ibárurri looked askance.

Viper stared from a stretcher. Trinka danked me for hiring her. Edith Bourne Nolan rubbed her desk's bald spot. Connie Ostrica snapped a salute off her cunt cap. Viv's possum face hawed.

Gloria Kamenica clinked a Rheingold. Mellie Branch had never seen the sea. Jessie Auster squinted skyward, and docile Joy Sterling had been angry, so angry— so incredibly angry behind that Gauguin mask as she snapped off the fuse.

Oh, fuck what the traffic would bear. "Hell, I don't know," I drawled. "But to tell you the truth, I just got tired of having to stick my finger up his ass every time."

POSTED BY: *Pam*   In the rowdier tabs, the standard paraphrase was "I got tired of goosing him": meaning identical, connotation desexualized enough to get by. The genteel equivalent was "I got tired of priming the pump," which actually struck me as cruder—the way a too vivid imprecision will.

It didn't matter. The authentic quote was all over New York by the cocktail hour. It landed with the first wave in Sicily that July. Until *Nothing Like a Dame*, it was the single thing strangers were most likely to know about me—the main upside being that Pam was dead Daisy's daughter no more.

Since you were all of eight years old during the Presidential sexual imbroglio I call Billingsgate and you appear to've survived its linguistic acrobatics unscathed, you may be marveling that "I just got tired" and so on could make me notorious or Murphy publicly ridiculous. But over sixty years ago, women weren't supposed to say such things. Not in courtrooms, anyhow, as opposed to coal mines or Detroit saloons or Toledo cafeterias or Albuquerque nursing schools.

As for Bran, he'd spent fifteen years as the cock of theatrical New York's walk in an age when cuke-encumbered writers were proud of behaving as if they typed with their fists and read books with their teeth. To infantilize him in that Gillooleyan way struck at his *literary* virility. Had I been old enough to understand what bags of jellied nerves and impostures so many men are, I probably wouldn't have done it—no matter how fed up I was with the stupidity of our marriage, and hearing our suddenly sad, puzzled sex life called "conjugal intimacies," and Roy's prim red-eared face three rows back.

Whether I *regret* it, I can't say. The mystery is I'm not sure Murphy did. Except for the alimony, which I'd told Oliver Watson not to get too "Tallyho!" about—and it was the part he'd looked forward to, too—it was all over on June 4. When I saw Bran nearby on Lafayette as I peered for a taxi once we'd each been released from our knot of reporters, I half expected him to do something he'd never done while we were married, namely hit me. As he recognized his tall one-arming wife among the sailors, instead he looked abashed, relieved, and damned near grateful.

"Waiting for a cab?" I called, since we couldn't go on eyeing each other uncertainly until they'd won the war.

Grinning, he shook his head. "On my way to the subway, Snooks. I might as well get used to it."

"Oh, balls, Bran. You know I'm not going to take you the way Ruby took you. I've never cared."

"Too bad. I thought it was my ace."

Hands in his pockets, he was being buffeted by uniformed foot traffic out to learn for sure whether the Bronx was up and the Battery down. We'd both just caught on that this was goodbye, and he was Brannigan Murphy; he had to dominate it. After some facial fidgeting, he made up his mind: "Oh, well. 'We'se did have good times onct. Didn't we'se, Baby?'"

Spoken as the hero clutched a dismembered Macy's limb, that wheezer was *Colum Firth's* curtain line. What would have devastated Murphy if he'd known was that my speechless reaction came partly from uncertainty about what he was quoting.

"Oh, come on!" he ragged me. "Can't you at least say, 'Bran, I never knew. *You* were the Mighty Tower'?"

Asphodel Titan had been crouched over her husband's corpse when Ruby Thorp spoke that line in 1932. At Murphy's insistence, she'd begun unbuttoning her blouse as the lights dimmed. That baffled even young Addison's quick thumb through Freud—and dear God, I thought. Does every literary marriage end this archly?

"Christ, Bran." I was honestly angry all of a sudden. "All right, if it'll make you happy. 'Listen, it's our fight too. And if need be, we'll go to the ends of the earth.'"

"That's not mine." Then he looked hesitant, mentally flipping back through the scrapbooks to 1928: "Is it?"

"No, mine. Well, a woman I called Viv. I guess you never read it."

"Was that Tennessee?"

"Yes," I said bitterly.

Bran scowled. "Well, just so you'll know, Snooks—I didn't fuck Trinka that day. Or Viper either. It just wasn't worth it getting back up on the stand to say so."

"Oh, really? No boinky-boink for poor Mist-Murphy? Were you trying to *write?*"

"I was too worried."

If it was a lie, he'd convinced himself of it. When two people realize they've never understood each other worth a damn, the least they can do is agree they've misunderstood each other more intimately than most: any breakup's consolation prize.

"Oh, Bran," I said. "Go to hell. Do you even remember my birthday's on Sunday?"

Fishing out a handkerchief for me from his jacket's breast pocket—his manliest act of the war had been to accept the restrictions on new tailoring in stoic silence—my now imminently former hubby took his best guess. "Twenty-two?"

"Twenty-three." And I meant to be affectionate; it just didn't come out that way. "Too old for you anyhow!"

His face darkened, then grew confused. "Bye, Snooks," he said and blunderbussed my cheek. "Good luck."

I wished his back the same. The *M* was for Murphy, the snotrag's in the Paris footlocker. Whether or not the White House calls, whoever finds me here will find it there.

POSTED BY: *Pamela Beach*   Sixty-two years ago today, as late as noon—as *late* as *noon*, Mr. Spielberg—they were still arguing over whether to evacuate Omaha. Write off the landing, bring away as many of those miserable upholstery tacks as they could and redirect the supporting troops to one of the beaches where the thing had gone better. On the command ships, they couldn't see and weren't in radio contact with the handfuls of soaked survivors who'd finally gotten to their feet and uttered their own equivalents of "Oh, fuck what the traffic will bear" before starting up the bluffs under fire.

Still far out to sea ourselves, Eddie Whitling and I couldn't see them either. By noon, we'd gotten ourselves off the *Maloy* to hitch a ride in on an LCT packed with artillery that was scheduled to land in early afternoon. It wouldn't; everywhere around us were slewing and bobbing landing craft of every type. They'd either tried to make the beach and been driven off by the obstacles that were supposed to have been blown by then or were being held back by new, contradictory, or out-of-date orders from either the command ships or the Coast Guard cutters slicing through the seaborne traffic jam to keep us megaphonically herded.

Nobody knew for sure what was happening anywhere. Everything between us and the smoke-shrouded beach itself looked like the most abominable mess. But everything behind us just looked stupidly safe.

On top of that, they'd told me as far back as Portsmouth I wouldn't be allowed to disembark. Only Eddie had official license to, being cuke-encumbered and killable. Our LCT's skipper had been told through a megaphone to only let Miss Buchanan of *Regent's* observe from the bridge before I got sent back aboard the *Maloy*.

Aside from *You Must Remember This: The Posthumous Career of World War Two*, most books only mention one American woman correspondent who successfully waded through Omaha's surf late on D-Day. My better-known rival Martha Gellhorn of *Collier's* wasn't supposed to get ashore either. Unbeknownst to each other, we used the same subterfuge, which put a smile on Tim Cadwaller's face when he told me so.

Tim didn't know where she got her corpsman's Red Cross–marked helmet and brassarded jacket. I know where I got mine, though: Eddie. Our LCT had finally been cleared to start the run in when he beckoned me to one of the few spots aboard that wasn't a bramble of legs, gear, and sea wash and puke. He had the stuff bundled inside a GI rain poncho he'd stuffed under the last jeep in line to be offloaded.

"Make up your mind, Pamita." He had to shout in my ear above the engines and Coast Guard megaphones. "You've been bitching since England about what men can do. Are you game?"

"Why in hell didn't you ask me before now?"

"Jesus Christ! And let you *think* about it? I'm not that kind of monster. Other kinds, sure, you bet. But you don't mind those."

Whoosh! A rocket barge had just loosed forty fuming spikes beachward over our heads. We'd both just discovered how nervous we were by stupidly ducking. "Where did you get it?" I bawled.

"What the fuck does that matter?"

"I can think of one way it could!"

"If you mean is he alive, of course he's alive. Look around! We haven't taken one casualty yet."

"And what am I supposed to do if I've still got that crap on when we do? Say 'There, there, soldier'—but I've got no morphine? Huh?"

"Don't put it on now, you dumb twat. Wait 'til we beach and move fast. Then ditch the helmet, that's what they look for." (It was thoughtful of Eddie not to specify whether he meant our boys in need of a medic or snipers in search of a target.) "Are you coming?"

"Damn close."

"That's not what I meant. Are you coming ashore with me? I did this for you. It's the only damn thing I, Eddie Whitling, will ever do for you. Yes or no!"

And yes I said yes I will yes, as they say, and here I am with a gun in my lap and my mind now made up. I suppose *l'équipe* has known all along there can be only one end to Pam's second D-Day.

For once, Ard, the pleasure's all mine. No Eddie to shove a Red-Crossed GI helmet at me, no Roy to charter me, no Edith Bourne Nolan to set me on fire. No longer a difference between squandered and plundered. And as of now—*as of now*; wasn't that how I began?—no phone call from Potus to give this old bag her cue to settle this hash.

I'll give *him* until sundown. Once the color of evening most closely approximates the indigo hue of the tracer-flicked sky over Omaha when I heard "Happy Birthday" sung to me at the Vierville sea wall by a dozen dazed relics of dawn, I'll leave a mess of pink and gray things whether he's listening or not.

There, now. It's settled, or will be once I hit "Post." Then I'll be back in an LCT sloshing toward Omaha as the sea starts to grow cascading gray fir trees from the German artillery and we see that Martian alphabet of destructive contraptions that still haven't been blown. As one boat to starboard becomes a black bathtub with a half dozen swimmers, the next one starts noodling to portside—and a Coast Guard megaphone barks through the explosions, *"LCA Five-Two-Twelve, you are not a rescue boat. Stay on course for Dog Green."*

Ard, I'm nobody's rescue boat, not even my own. All I can do is stay on course for Dog Green. Here we go.

POSTED BY: *Pameleanor Rigby*   Only because Murphy's *Collected Plays* lives up to its title is *The Two-Faced War* even in my library. I've never read it and now never will. Yet Garth Vader's *Dat Dead Man Dere* seconds Addison's report from the aisle that lizard-blooded "Catherine Steptoe," gadabout whoresspondent for *Majesty* magazine, was transparently Bran's old Snooks turned Medusal.

My impotent yet homosexual lover, Solomon Roth, is some sort of spatula in FDR's kitchen cabinet. We're in cahoots to bleed the Red Army white by delaying the onset of the Second Front. That I was played by Viper Leigh, apparently willing to let courtroom snakes lie in exchange for lead billing, certainly rang my old *plus ça change* gong.

Enter a ghost from Catherine's past: Fingal O'Flaherty, a one-legged, eyepatched—dear *God*, Bran—alum of Madrid. He very nearly derails our scheme. As the curtain falls, we're congratulating each other on having made my shooting of Fingal (Addison claimed he woke up and clapped) look like suicide.

Even though Viper pointblank refused to be discovered in bed with Catherine's mother—poor Floss Bicuspid! At least she dodged that bullet—Garth Vader does his Saskachewanful best to argue that Bran was exploring new themes. But his old bogeys took precedence, and his anti-Semitism had progressed from social bluster to typewriter. According to Addison, devious Sol Roth made Shylock look Methodist. Despite Garth's pro-Murphyism, *Dat Dead Man Dere* adds the further damning detail that the psychiatrist Bran had started seeing in 1939 was also named Roth.

Anyway, you might think he'd learned his lesson about writing plays that could be overtaken by events. *The Two-Faced War* opened a week after Normandy. Dachau made headlines ten months later. If there was a single valid *aperçu* in Bran's Murphine stew, even the most perceptive theatergoer couldn't see it.

Once his back vanished and I was left with his stancher, I soon gave up finding a cab. It was a pleasant June evening, and the sailors' on-the-town whites had started glowing like ice cream among the wheat of khaki and the chaff of fedoraed civvies. Besides, a taxi ride felt too personal in a way. You can turn queenly and tumbriled in a Checker's back seat. I'd spent ten days in the tabloids: I walked.

I strolled up Lafayette a while before I started tacking randomly westward, as one can when WALK and DON'T WALK are calling the shots and sunset's fingers choose you like a recruiting poster. Unless I wanted to tramp until it was pitch dark, sooner or later I'd have to either cab it or play IRT ladybug to get back to Roy's, the only bed in New York I had a key to. He'd left court early, giving me a glum feeling I'd walk in on his idea of a victory feast—some *echt*-Roy combination of champagne and potato salad.

It was just as well my editor was allergic to shellfish. Otherwise, he might've cracked the desperate game of code I'd played with my austers and ostricas and kamenicas and joysterlings and lamellibranchia, never quite admitting it to myself until one sunset finger showed me the Hudson and Pamique had to face that she wasn't just ambling at random. I wondered who'd lapped up the dish I'd passed up when I bolted to the Commodore to meet Jake and Addison nearly two years ago.

I also didn't know if Roy would be robed in pajamas, for months just his attire when he came to the study door to wish Pam goodnight but in recent days a quiet invitation. Yet my hunch was he too knew the jig was up on our sad-sack bid to behave like generic New Yorkers. Tonight would no doubt be understood by us both in advance as our valedictory try, the kind of sex—and there are many worse—that amounts to a friendly handshake without clothes. You get snagged on wondering why the other times weren't like that and then the question answers itself. As frightened as I was of the new freedom plaguing my brain with Pams insisting they need no longer stay phantoms, I wasn't such a fool as to think keeping things going with Roy was any solution.

Hell, at least Sharon Halevy Cohnstein could cook. Not that I'd find out in person until my birthday on Sunday, when she and Jake said they wouldn't take no for an answer. Luckily, she kept kosher, forestalling any chance of a too painful parallel to Pam's uneaten meal. If I'd been Jake, I'd have stayed snuggled up next to her in Williamsburg forever.

Back last December, it must've been at about this time of day—though dark and freezing—that I'd finally come up out of the mine. Fresh air, live air, air that moved without dynamite! Even though Viv, Tess, Josie, and Babe didn't act as if they were in any hurry, the sudden leaps of their jokes hither and yon as we emerged told me a strain you get used to isn't the same as a strain that's gone away. Unless I was fooled by the novelty of hearing their voices in unconfined space.

Pam's ultimate experience of belonging while being treated as exceptional was stolen from me all too soon by its converse. The only sentence in "To the Ends of the Earth" that alludes to it is mundane, thanks partly to my editor's alert blue pencil: "The women have convinced management to build them a communal shower, its hastily nailed broads ["Pam, you did mean 'boards,' yes?"

asked Roy] already water-warped and the unchinked gap between palisade and roof open to the biting winter cold."

That doesn't begin to convey my consternation when we ambled into the same rough structure, marked by a hand-painted *Wymen Only*, where I'd put on my loaned overalls ten hours earlier. That had been bad enough, but I hadn't been outright naked and neither had they. Now hissing water through a door I hadn't noticed this morning stilled Pam's garrulity at being back from the ends of the earth.

A long way from Purcey's, where even in the basketball team's locker room nudity had been far more a matter of glimmers than striding—can you see better now why tormenting Hormel with *ma plume* was so unforgivable?—and even farther from Long Island, where a budding pudding in search of information as yet unsorted into categories had peeped at a fifty-year-old Scandinavian housekeeper in the buff, I wasn't prepared for the matter-of-fact unpeeling that began as soon as the outer slat door was shut and hook-and-eyed. I was still twenty-two, and the wildcats were so—well, *ungainly*, the damning word (please note ambiguity as to damnation's recipient) that popped into my mind. Josie's Andean slopes, Babe's Bazooka-pink breadth. Tess's ropy back and wattled glutes. Since I'd known her the longest—three days—Viv's cinder-crisped Van Dyke alarmed me most.

Even if I'd brought a towel, to wrap myself in it would've been a mortal insult. Theirs were all over one shoulder or trawled. All gingerly meekness, I joined their shuffle into the shower stall, where at least we were a bit more spread out.

As they laughed and tossed their only bottle of shampoo (it was as harsh as lye) back and forth, anonymity wasn't in the cards even so. Not only was the gal from *Regent's* as anomalously gangly as a Manhattanized Schiele among Tennessee Boteros, but of course they had to tease me about my mere smudges of coal compared to its deep ingraining on them.

"Ain't *you* a waste of good Ivory!" called Tess, herself the color of a Paris church from wrists to elbows and forehead to clavicles. "We ought to report you to the Production Board." They all hawed with delight, and understanding that I was the object of that delight—not malice, delight—humbled me. They were tickled and pleased I'd stuck it out in the mine, but not because I could do what they did. They went back down to the ends of the earth every day. I hadn't particularly earned their respect. So far as recognition went, I doubt any of them cared what I wrote in *Regent's*.

I'd simply been somebody who wasn't there normally and could have stayed away if I'd chosen to, and the wildcats didn't expect much of a nod from the world up top. Mrs. Roosevelt I wasn't, God knows. But as folks say in Tennessee, I'd do, and I was just catching on that I was surrounded by the most magnificent female beauty I'd ever see when Viv called, "Hey, New York! Think fast."

While you might guess looking up at Eddie Whitling's shout to see the tricolor break out atop the Eiffel Tower was pretty hard to beat, catching that shampoo bottle was your Gramela's happiest moment of World War Two. I laughed and called back, "Not wasted on me?"

"Hell, it's wasted on us," Viv barked. "Ain't you got eyes?"

"Ain't on me yet," Babe drawled. "Mary *As*-tor, read me 'n weep."

To dry off I borrowed a towel still damp with Andean moisture. When I looked up from my bench for my stored clothes, the other women—still nude—were gathered under the outer stall's lone light bulb. "Miz Buchanan," Viv called, newly flinty, "would you please come join hands with us? It won't take but a minute."

As I stepped between Josie and Tess, I'm sure I was beaming. Couldn't wait to find out what new treat of this companionship was in store! The tumble of imaginings had barely gotten to urine-drinking when I realized all the wildcats' chins were lowered and their eyes closed.

"Babe, I think it's your turn," Viv murmured.

"Okay." Babe bit her lip. "Um, Lord—we thank you for this day. We're sure grateful nobody got killed or even hurt. We hope you don't mind all our rough talk and foolin'. And, uh, we'll be back tomorrow! You know we'll stick at this. If it helps, we ain't even gonna say a word about Oak Ridge."

She didn't call it that, since it hadn't been named yet. That's what she meant, though.

"And the swap is we pray you'll send as many of our boys back in one piece as you can see your way clear to. But if you can't, we'll stick at it anyway. You know us. Amen."

"Amen," they all said.

"That was good, Babe," Josie said quietly. Tears were streaking her cheeks.

"Wait. Don't break the circle." Troubled, authoritative, Viv's eyes were on mine. "Miz Buchanan—*please*."

"Oh! Amen," I said for the first and last time in my adult life. But their looks stayed disturbed though they went on being polite. I wasn't sorry to be handed Roy's telegram.

Otherwise, I'm not sure I could have faced that night of killing loneliness. I had practice, but it's different when however unreasonably—and I knew it was—you can vividly recall a moment of feeling its opposite.

POSTED BY: *Pamhattan Hellodrama*   Somehow I found myself down at the dockside. Nipped or should I say Japaned into a bar, Italian or Irish—Costello's, McGinty's?—and asked for a gimlet. Looking down a counter thick with hands resting steins next to shot glasses, the bartender said, "Ma'am, you bring out the artist in me."

Despite my foolish choice of drink, though, Pam did know a bit about New York. I expected to nurse my gimlet undisturbed and did.

An hour or two later I'd've faced mauling. By midnight I could have risked being chained in the cellar. Yet it's all about sunset. And stopping at one drink, since two would've announced I'd brought my chain with me and was hoping for some gents' assistance. But I could stay here in safety for as long as I nursed one or it me. It was the color of cactus in Albuquerque.

Nurse Harmony, Nurse Cass, Nurse Sandy, and Nurse Sigourney. Had I really called them that in "The View from Ward Three"? I had and now it was too late to take back from print. Just my millionth or so reason since "Chanson d'automne" to never attend a Purcey's reunion. Oh, bikini girl: as in Harmony Preston, Cass Lake, big Sandy Hingham, and Sigourney Keota. I'd kept imagining they were the new Clara Bartons bandaging, splinting, sponging, and comforting the gal posing as a casualty.

Their St. Paul equivalents would have fried me in oil and called it a transfusion. Especially now that they knew. Forgive me, Panama: that gimlet was muddling.

On my way back from New Mexico, I'd stopped off as usual in Washington for a chinwag with Jake. We were still planning Sharon's materialization in court, and his wife was terrified. Then a visit, my last, to Edith Bourne Nolan. As she and a smiling plump fortyish bespectacled woman looked up, Edith beamed: "Pam! I've wanted you two to meet for so long. This is my daughter Ariel."

"Big date?" the bartender asked as I stood. Oh, I knew New York, where lies are appreciated for their artistic effect. Truth's poor reputation is that it's got none. "The biggest," I said, and he said, "Good luck." Nice man, McGinty.

I'd missed the cellar by inches, the measure of the fringe of newly embattled light cuffing the Jersey side of the river. Heavy ships slogged toward the Narrows, then still bridgeless, and Manhattan's massed buildings were suddenly women saying goodbye. I cut back in to Greenwich and then went up Hudson; south of Abington Square and near the corner of Bleecker, I gazed at a remembered window. Who knew who was living there now or why or anything much, really, and I had no idea if the Pam I'd hatched over a gimlet to put on new armor in my awful and unending war was a betrayal of or way of staying loyal to its two former occupants. But I made my small adieu.

POSTED BY: *Pam*   As I think I've said before on daisysdaughter.com, every supposedly brave act I've performed has been your Gramela's plea for a smoke as I glare at the firing squad. Far from being any exception, my journey to the Second Front exactly a decade after thirteen-year-old *Pamelle* saw New York's skyline materialize from the *Paris's* prow stands as the proof. To stay in the United States would've meant deciding with nobody's help whether to take the Declaration of Independence at its word, and Joy Sterling could've told me that's long been an invite to madness.

"Roy, I could stand to get out of town for a while." It was Monday, June 7, 1943: 364 days before D-Day. I was in his corner office at *Regent's*, perched Rosalind Russellishly on my editor's desk with gams crossed at the ankles and my back to the Hudson. The nails on my cigarette-forking hand were as ragged as red surf.

"I thought you might." Did I dare guess my editor's owlish expression was hiding relief? As things turned out, our handshake without clothes had lasted all weekend. We'd teetered right on the verge of transition from the kind of confusion that staves off a decision to the kind that demands one.

"I've been wondering whether maybe it's time we did something on Hollywood's contribution to the war effort," Roy mused. "It's not your standard topic, but would you be interested? I know he's washed up, but Ronnie Rea—"

"No, no! I've had it with the home front," I said and felt a twinge as I noticed Murphy was getting his wish. "Wherever they're fighting, that's where I want to be."

Part Three

1. The Voluptuous Allure of Hollywood

POSTED BY: *Daisy Clover's Daughter*   Pam's a map in the mirror now, especially when I risk beaming at myself. The griffins have come home to Proust, Hopsie! My dentition's foxhole of gold-cusped good humor turns my hoisted mug into a misinformed jack-o-lantern primping for Christmas. Yet to the mimsy borogoves, a gaze at my grinning reflection feels more like looking at the former Yugoslavia. We kept it hung together while we could.

Not that any raving beauty has been lost. The only photograph of me in *Vogue* was a black-and-white one of Mrs. Gerson in her Beverly Hills garden when *Glory Be* came out, and the flowers had to do most of the work. Still, I doubt I ever looked better than I did when twenty-seven-year-old Pamela Buchanan, bestselling author of *Nothing Like a Dame* ("A delight!"—Celia Brady, *Phoenix Sun*), came down the ramp from a silvery, still propeller-shimmery C-47 Dakota and let her gladdened skin get tipsy on the lavish blue champagne of a Los Angeles nonwinter one day in early 1948.

Catch the mistake, Tim? I still kept making it two and a half years after VJ-Day. DC-3 Constellation, not Dakota. The planes weren't in olive drab anymore, neither was I, and nobody would ever call me Pamita again if I saw them coming. Wrong continent, his own book had omitted me outright, and what a prick Eddie Whitling had been, really. Everywhere but Dachau.

The studio car was waiting on the tarmac, a more minor perk in the way-back-when in case Potus bridles at my *lèse-majesté*. Wouldn't you know those eyebrows of his anywhere, even Larousse? The proof was that three other cars stood there too, admitting men in cayenne, cardamom, and ginger sport-coasts—sorry, sports coats—who only looked at me with interest once I helped myself to my own Lincoln's back seat.

Sorry, gents! You could've been currying favor with me since the Rockies. And right you are, Bacall I'm not. I'm told she could end up playing me, though. Ta.

She didn't: Lauren Bacall, I mean. Neither did Maureen O'Hara, Dorothy Malone, Donna Reed, Barbara bel Geddes, Jane Russell (you wish!!, as Panama would say), or Daisy Clover, all of whose names got bruited at some point. Past forty by then and matronized by her Penelope to Fredric March's three-striper Ulysses in *The Best Years of Our Lives*, Myrna Loy was on nobody's list except Pam's schoolgirl one, unconfessed even—or especially?—to Gerson.

I did meet her once, though, and I hope you'll agree a tongue-tied Pam has novelty. I practically demonstrated the sailors' manual through my lipstick as the Nora Charles of my reverie-prone Purcey's youth graciously waited for me to either give her her hand back or at least name a price. There was bougainvillea behind her, and a ridiculously pleased-looking tea set laid in front of her. People favoring Truman's reelection lounged and lunged around, and one measure of the laughingly bovine wedge of inanity I became is that I remember feeling impressed by the *pensée* that Anzio was a long way off. (Well, yes, Pam: some 6,370 miles as the cow leaps. Montaigne slept undisturbed.)

I'd love to say every last word she spoke is engraved on my heart, but the coroner will need a working knowledge of cuneiform. I did reassure her Harry had my vote, of course—my unpremeditated goodbye to leftist capriciousness, represented by Henry Wallace on the 1948 ballot. In memory yet green, Myrna Loy's eyes were the mint that made a good Democrat out of me.

POSTED BY: *Pam*   Early on in what I had no idea would be my eight years in Hollywood, the random materializations of its familiar b&w gods in carelessly Californian color did make one feel like Alice among the playing cards. Miss Loy's blossoming on the old Pygmalion's veranda was one of only a few such encounters—my crimsoned introduction to unwittingly Tijuana-biblical Gabby Chatterton being another, the majestic third coming soon to a website near you—to turn me gawky in near Hormelic earnest.

After all, I'd interviewed generals, slinking my byline through SHAEF rub-a-dubs where Metro's old boast "More stars than there are in heaven" meant something more soldierly, not to say shoulderly: my Pam-pun to sloshed Eddie and a couple of periwinkling stenographers from Ike's press gang in a pub two weeks before Normandy. A hint to our intake and jitters was that they found it hilarious.

In fact, during the spitball stages of *Nothing Like a Dame*'s Metro-morphosis into *The Gal I Left Behind Me*, Gerson had the notion of getting Omar Bradley to appear as himself. His cameo would've reprised the pate-massaging press conference during the Bulge when Pam Buchanan of *Regent's*, not yet renamed "Peg Kimball" and still uncast to boot (Barbara bel Geddes did *Caught* instead), had asked whether he could confirm that a whole regiment of the 106th was gone—just gone!, and Tim Cadwaller's future favorite author, Kurt Vonnegut, gone with it into a German POW camp—and there was interest. The Pentagon, as we were learning to call it, saw such quasi-commercials as useful in cementing everyone's dazed understanding that its wartime encroachments were now a fixture of our national life.

The new Army Chief of Staff's schedule proved too crowded, and too bad. When I think of the reliable uncles, worried lawyers, and thoughtful apothecaries Brad might've gone on to play for Metro—and had played, only opposite the Wehrmacht and under Eisenhower—I know I'm just wishing more of you had gotten to appreciate the helpless respect the flamboyant owe those able to assert authority without theatrics.

No surprise Mark Clark, the long-nosed dolt of Anzio, offered his services in Brad's place. One red-leatherette afternoon at Chasen's, Bill M. nearly choked with laughter as I described the eager telegrams from Clark's PRO, and Bill had always liked him better than I had. Protecting the two disrespectful combat men in Bill's *Stars and Stripes* cartoons from the brass hats who wanted them to reform, or at least to shave and wear less raggedy uniforms, was the best thing Clark did in the war. Anyhow, Fifth Army's former commander didn't end up in *The Gal* either.

If only that were true of Bill, since our friendship didn't survive Metro's fictionalization of him as smirky, doodling "Chet Dooley." Everybody knew a cartoonist for "The GI News," how inspired, could only be one person, and as late as the Bicentennial I'd sometimes get muttonholed by an Insomnia Channel watcher eager to know whether our romance was what had busted up Bill's first marriage. When I explained it had been fabricated, they looked knowing as only ignoramuses can.

Knowing darned well he'd never laid a glove on me, Bill was genuinely upset. "That first night at the villa, I showed you a snapshot of my wife and kid," the last letter I ever had from him went. "Mind telling me how that got turned into Chet Casanova and his etchings?" I'd be flattering the Buchanan bod if I thought what truly got his goat was that the plot had Chet—that damned Hal Lime!—lose me to Walt Wanks as Eddie "Harting," Eddie Whitling's *nom de Metro* in the final scenario.

The Gal I Left Behind Me's release into unimpressed reviewers' captivity lay far ahead when we had our Chasen's tête-à-tête. Or tête-à-tit, as very nearly happened when Bill stood up to find a phone as Deanna Durbin squirmed and brimmed by. I'm not even sure why he was in California, since Hollywood's massacre of his own book was only a gleam in *Variety*'s eye at the time. It could be he'd just come to Chasen's to see if the chili was everything Louella said it was and then stayed on with me for the sauce. Or our waitress, taloned to be the next Linda Darnell and resentfully aware, those purloined loins receding like an unanswerable—not by my eyes, anyhow!—knock-knock joke, that we'd be no help.

I'd seen him in civvies before, since we shared a publisher and he'd done *Nothing*'s dust-jacket drawing of his pal Pam a year earlier. Yet that afternoon in Chasen's was the closest we came to recovering our old *esprit de* beachhead, as the sense of a mighty, unreasoning engine clanking away all around us was uncannily similar. Darting like his brain's inky infantry, Bill's eyes hadn't quite lost the impishness that had welcomed mine as new playmates in the correspondents' villa at Nettuno.

When I first blinked at his baby face, I'd been still itchily jeweled by sea salt under my newly issued correspondent's togs. He'd been perched Aladdin-style in a knit GI cap atop an ammunition crate in some prewar Fascist's vacation home that now boasted *two* splendid views of the Tyrrhenian Sea. Through the more recent of them, our Navy's maneuvers were already halfway to Hollywood: Busby Berkeley with an ocean to play with, chorus-line landing craft enchanting a somnolent tender as durable as Esther Williams. And all that was already four years ago, a fact that, like our plush postwar America in general, seemed preposterous but encouraging.

"Who was it named us the Bobbsey twins?" he asked out of the blue— red leatherette, brown Scotch, and violently violet Linda Darnelly nail polish, rather—once I'd got done spiting Mark Clark's face. "Capa?"

"Bob? No, never. Floyd Young. He only came up from Naples for the day."

"I wonder why he took a dislike to us?"

"He only came up from *Na*-poli for the day," arch Pam repeated. "I heard he had to borrow a change of pants when Anzio Annie hit paydirt, too."

"Yep, that must've been it."

"Of course it was! He was jealous."

Even so, I'm proud to say Bill thought too well of our friendship to let us sink into nostalgia's bog head-on. As we'd both learned, that was what you ended up doing with people when the war was *all* you had in common. Or ever expected to, and my shoulders still recoiled at Eddie Whitling's already resoftened mitts squeezing them at *Nothing*'s publication party last spring.

Because I loved him, please note Bill's thoughtful way of steering me back to now. "So who's going to play him in your movie, huh? Way I remember, William Demarest would be about right."

"Who, Eddie? Oh, Floyd! That fraud? He probably won't even be in the script. Not that anything is for sure yet. Even me, so help me! Honestly, Bill, you wouldn't believe this place."

Prescient words, though I didn't know *The Gal* would end up skipping not only Floyd Young but Anzio. No correspondents' villa, no alternately wary (something might happen) and riotous (something had and here we still were) trips up to the First SSF's dugouts along the Mussolini Canal. And definitely no "The Angel of Anzio," the title of my March 1944 *Regent's* attempt to resurrect the laughter and efficiency of one of the three American nurses killed by a direct hit on their hospital tent in early February.

We'd all hoped the front-line troops wouldn't hear, but there were no secrets on that beachhead. One look at a map would tell you why. Unlike the front-line troops, correspondents could get back to Naples for a break whenever it got to be too much or our deadlines piled up.

"Shit. I like it because I don't need to," Bill said now, meaning Hollywood.

"Oh, me neither. All this is fun, but I can't wait to get back to real life."

"That's funny," he said with a slightly Darnellized grin. Roguishness, which I first took his mood for, made him look even younger—and in fact, cub though I'd been in the ETO, Bill spotted me a whole year. What had evened us up into temporary twinhood was that he was my elder in combat.

"Why, pray?"

"Aw, hell, Pam. When you used to tell me bedtime stories about the ritzy life in Manhattan, you know what it sounded like? One hint: not a play. Bragginham Murphy or no Bragginham Murphy."

"A movie," I guessed.

"On the nose. Now I've met those people—Jesus, have I—and I keep wanting them to be your old movie. You know? Indulge me, you stupid bastards, what's it to you? Here's a nickel, I got plenty."

"Well, you earned them. I—"

"No, no. Sorry, that's a whole different rant. The deal is, they're all listening to me ramble on, and to them the *war's* the goddam movie. Is that just how the whole works works from here on in?"

"How which works works?"

"Everything. One man's newsreel is another man's musical, and never the twain shall meet. Where's Linda Darnell, anyway? I'm empty."

"Well, of course I left out the boring parts back then. I'm a writer."

"I mean the whole house of cards," he said stubbornly. "In Italy, at least I could—no, fuck that."

"Fuck what, pray?"

"The minute I start thinking the war was the one true part, you know what I'll be? I'll be *obscene*. I'll be more disgusting than Georgie Patton. At least he thought it was wonderful while it was going on. Uh-uh, Pammie. Let's talk about something else."

"I'm trying, but I've only been here a month." With some interest, Bill's eyes waited for me to clarify whether I was being sharp with him. So I said, "Shit, I haven't even slept with Lassie yet."

"Uh-uh. *I* get Lassie. You get Rin Tin Tin. We're the goddam Bobbsey twins, and I ain't gonna be the one to shock our public."

"Don't worry," I said, suddenly hilarious on all eight cylinders. "Your kids'll look like—"

"What?"

But I'd changed my mind about that joke ("dogfaces") and pointlessly said, "Ronald Reagan." Bill only thought it was funny because he'd made up his mind it was going to be.

It's hard to explain these delicate shoals, Panama. Whatever *The Gal* made of us, Bill and I really had stayed chaste as siblings during the war. Now peacetime was turning us into ex-adulterers, anxious not to spoil our reunion by reawakening the ghosts of rutting. Just as well we were interrupted—and by an expert on these matters, too.

"Vy, *Beel!*" a tall voice said. "Sergeant, I haven't seen you since Alsace. And such a nasty cartoon that was, with only the officers at the stage door! There were millions of you poor boys, millions. I did what I could."

Our four eyes crept up the ETO's best-known human Christmas tree. Old enough to be our mother too, and Miss Dietrich was acting it even if she didn't look it. "*Vot* are you doing in this awful place?" she scolded.

"Uh, just having a bite. Then we stayed on. Hic and all that. Say, aren't you here too?" Bill rather timidly asked.

"Not Chasen's! This *room*—this *booth*. You are in *Poughkeepsie*. Didn't you tell Dave who you are?"

"Marlene, I don't know who he is either. It just seemed sort of sensible to keep it mutual."

"So vy didn't *you* do something, then?" As the female, I'd been promoted to accountability. "But ach, my manners! I'm so magnificently sorry. Who are you?"

"This is Pammie Buchanan," said Bill. "She covered the ETO for *Regent's*. We spent a while dodging shells at Anzio together. Shit, we probably should've still been collecting them. The she-sell, seashell kind, I mean."

Once Miss Dietrich heard I'd been to the war, like her, she softened. Then brightened, Rockefeller-Center-of-attention-style: "Oh, yes! Yours was *Nothing Like a Dame*. I remember. *Excellent* title, that's why I bought it."

"My God, if I'd known you were—"

"No, no! It was such a pleasure—such a luxury, Miss Buchman—to read one book about the damn war that wasn't personally autographed. Finally, my real opinions could leap out, pawing here and goring there. You'll forgive me, won't you?" As if producing a diamond-bearing rabbit from a top hat, she held out a deal-sealing hand. "I didn't know you were so young."

Mesmerized, I watched my own ringless fingers vanish. "Until now, neither did I," I said. "I sure admire what you did, though. I know they hate your guts for it in Deutschland."

Did they ever, and they haven't stopped. However long she'd been away, those newsreels of *their* Marlene entertaining our GIs must've made them feel even Father Christmas had changed sides.

"Hoo! Ask a German what he loves and you're inquiring about his pastimes. Ask him what he resents, and…but *didn't* we meet once back then, Miss Buchman? Maybe London, maybe Luxembourg. I think you look familiar."

"Oh, it's—possible, I suppose," I chirped, winning a snort of delight from Bill. "I'm prac'ically positive I've seen you somewhere before too. No, we honestly never did. But thank you."

Thank you? My, oh, my. "Ah! Too bad," said Miss Dietrich. "There weren't so many of us over there. I loved the boys, I loved the boys! Still, sometimes one does want to pull down the shades on the candy store and drink one's cocoa in peace. You must've known Janet Flanner, though."

Kind of her to offer a substitute, don't you think? But Bill and I were still so stupefied we hadn't even asked her to sit down.

"No, I never met her either. A nice editor did tell me once my writing sounded a bit like hers, but of course it did! It's called imitation—knowing who your betters are."

"Then we are different. In my case, I wouldn't have the faintest curiosity. Or belief. But *Beel!*" she cried as if she'd just arranged for him to reappear from somewhere now that I'd been scooted back to kindergarten. "Tell me, how much longer do we have you in town?" Ah, the Hollywood "we."

"I'm getting on a train to Taos Thursday morning."

"Oh, family?"

That was me asking, since Miss Dietrich probably didn't know Bill hailed—
had hailed?—from New Mexico. He'd told me a lot about it in conversations
longer than any I bet he'd had with her in Alsace.

He shook his head. "Book club."

"Such a pity," Marlene groaned. "I have a sneak preview. Usually I stay
home and do the ironing, but this one I made with Wilder. We are both *alte Ber-
liners*, so we know the little lies stuck on at the end don't matter."

"They did in Berlin," Bill pointed out. "And they were kind of big, and—
stuck on at the beginning, and—where was I?"

"No, no! It's a comedy. We shot there too, it's nothing but rubble and big
masonry eyes. Anyhow you might have liked it."

"I still could," Bill said. "Hell, I still *can*, can't I? Even if I pay for my ticket?"

"Now you'll be making me weep. Bill, you must absolutely flee this place.
Miss Buchman, will you please see he gets on his train? We don't deserve him.
Only the poor dogfaces did."

No doubt it's only in my imagination that she receded inside a giant soap
bubble, beaming *"Adios"* to us both. Since otherwise the silence might've lasted
until Dewey defeated Truman, I said, "Why, that's odd! Marlene didn't seem a
bit worried about *me* being corrupted by Hollywood. Do you think she knows
something we don't?"

"Sure of it," Bill mumbled. "Pammie, be honest. Doesn't all this ever seem
bizarre to you?"

"I think I've got the advantage of you there. Never had a normal." I thought
I was joking until his helpless nod made me wonder whether, by raising me so
wrong, dead Daisy had equipped me right. Since I didn't want to give her credit,
the vaudeville routine went on: "They split my atom in the cradle. I remember
Einstein saying, 'Goo-goo.' He looked so funny in his polo outfit! I'm sorry, Bill.
Something's really bothering you."

"Oh, Christ, I don't know. Bothered? Sure, bother me with Marlene Dietrich, and lobster and hotel keys. Try that line out on the guys in the foxholes. I'm
luckier than an Irishman with a dentist."

"It wasn't luck! It was talent. My God, was it talent. And they aren't in foxholes anymore, so there."

"Nope. They're in graves and I made a bundle. *Time* put those two jokers of mine on the cover while I was still drawing sergeant's pay. What was every other GI hoping to come home to if he didn't get his ass shot off? God willing, a wife; God willing, a job. And we got the bestseller list. Pammie, help me out! I'm sorry, but there aren't that many people who would know. Don't you ever feel shitty?"

"When I compare your book to mine, you'd better believe I do."

Some author Bill was, since he just looked annoyed. "That's not what I meant."

"I know, but leave it be. Leave it be," I repeated, a locution Pam had never used before. "They had their job, we had ours. And you could have gotten your ass shot off lots of times. So could I have once or twice."

Beyond him, Chasen's was up to its favorite conjuring trick. The opening door's brief reminder of prosaically (!) sunlit Beverly Boulevard revealed that what we'd been lulled into taking for a homey setting was a den of specially lit vaults, its human swag briefly caught in the act of getting up to visit other money. By now, however, even the draftsman in Bill wasn't interested.

"You weren't in the Army, remember? I was. If you'd gotten killed, it would've been an accident. Just an awful, horrible, awful fucking not supposed to happen, like the nurses. We'd have felt lousy for, I don't know, maybe a week. A *week*, Pam! You know what that means."

"Sure I do, Bill. All this flattery is making me dizzy."

I wished he hadn't mentioned the nurses, and not only because—along with lots of other things that didn't fit the tone—they'd been left out of *Nothing Like a Dame.* Nor was I sure Bill had ever read "The Gates of Hell," *by Pamela Buchanan*'s report from Dachau, whose most opportunistic stratagem he'd have seen right through and probably been offended by. Leave it be, leave it be: I was a writer.

"Just listen, will you?" he said. "For me it's the other way around. The Army thought it was getting another rifleman, more meat for the grinder. But even my Purple Heart was for a scratch—and here I am. Guess who I owe it to? Maybe I even met the guy. Then I tooled back down the road in my little jeep and he got it instead."

"This is the stupidest horseshit I've ever heard in my life," I told him, an exaggeration that would've had Murphy beaming at his unwarranted reprieve. "*Instead?* Everyone could've been anyone, you know it. Guilt is a form of vanity."

"Sure is," he agreed with an aplomb that told me the charge's only surprise was that it was conversational, not internal. "Because there's always that other little voice. You know it."

"I've got lots of voices, Bill."

"It's the one that keeps saying, 'That was the best of it. You're done. At twenty-six, kiddo, you're done. Drink up.'"

"Well, you aren't. And even if you were, so's Goya."

"That's funnier than you think. I didn't know what my book was turning into back home—I mean here—until some egghead attacked me in an art magazine. Now, *he* kept bringing up Goya: 'Los Desastres,' you know. Point was I'd given folks a sort of Uncle Remus war, because Goya had headless torsos in trees and I never drew one corpse."

"Why, that's absurd," I said, not least since I'd never realized he *hadn't*. And I knew—and I know—Bill's cartoons by heart.

"Well, I'm a pretty simple boy. Being *unfavorably* compared to Goya still felt like a heady brew. But I did think about it, account of Whacksmith sounded so sure, and right or wrong I told myself, 'Same subject, buddy. Different jobs.' Goya had to show people what war really looked like, didn't he? The guys I was drawing for already knew. They didn't need that—from me."

"Uh-huh. And if you're curious, you just told me what's eating you."

"Besides Linda Darnell not coming back, you mean? I was really just trying to kill some time."

"Oh, I know that. Heaven forbid we should pretend you matter, Bill—to you, to—me or to anyone. But it isn't about coming back in one piece, all right? Or even making a bundle."

"Can't make you feel sorry for me, huh?"

"Wrong again, because I do. Bill, Bill! I'm so smart it's scary. Marlene was right too, only I got distracted."

"That's what she's for. That's the formula."

"Listen!" I commanded, exhilarated by my prowess at being maternal or perhaps only sisterly. Though not a twin, for that had been a battlefield promotion revoked by Bill's talent. "What's gone wrong is you can't love them anymore."

"Can't love who?"

"Whom. You can't love the guys in the foxholes the way you did when they were in foxholes now that they aren't in foxholes, and it's driving you crazy. You can be as good as anything, you can draw until your fingers bleed, and you aren't ever going to have an *audience* you care about that way. Not that I mean to pick a fight with the Catholic Church," I lied, "but sainthood isn't about the saint. The best saint in the world is only as good as his flock."

"Honey, were we really in *Italy* together?"

"Oh, fuck you. Fuck you in Napoli while the chambermaid watches us," I said and gathered I'd better move on. "I was writing for fat-assed civilians in Darien and places. Of *course* I want those idiots to think *I'm* wonderful! You were drawing for the guys and you miss thinking *they're* wonderful. How can you now that they're all back to buying Studebakers, cheating on their taxes and voting Republican?"

I'd love to tell you Bill shouted "Eureka!" and strode forth from Chasen's a new man. I still think I was right, but that's not how life works. "Maybe so," was all he said. Then, "Did I ever tell you what I was going to do with my two jokers?"

"No."

"I was going to kill them. I ain't sure when I knew, but one day I knew that had to be the last cartoon. They were going to be the last two guys to get it in the ETO the day the war ended. It had to be them."

"Why, pray?"

"So it wouldn't be anybody else! It was every GI's nightmare. It was mine."

"What happened?"

"Oh, *Stars and Stripes* nixed it."

Fresh out of other ideas that excluded disrobing, our waitress finally brought our next round. Still wearing a shriven look—maybe Cary Grant had starred in *I Was a Male War Bride*, but Carole Lombard's plane crash had retired the lead in *I Was a Male War Widow*—Clark Gable came through the door, his broad shoulders maneuvering from the ever problematic street into a realm where he wasn't unusual. I raised my glass: "To Oz."

Ruefully, Bill smiled. "To Oz."

POSTED BY: *Pamzie*   Or to one damn Oz after another, as Tim Cadwaller—another latecomer who thinks it's all about Bert Lahr and 1939 Technicolor, not Bill's and my cherished L. Frank Baum—puts it in *You Must Remember This: The Posthumous Career of World War Two.* Each turned into Kansas as we left it, and still you fucking children wonder why my generation boozed. We didn't have that many constants.

I still rue how Bill didn't stay one of Pam's. That's not only because his two jokers are swapping tales on Parnassus with Paul Bunyan and these mimsy borogoves you know as your Gramela's glaucomedic eyes watched an imp in a knit cap scrounge for paper to draw them on. However little Bill's cartoons resemble that odd duck Sean Finn's perverse comic books about the superpower diaspora, Nan's strange son reveres him and would plainly have given anything, anything!, for intimate converse with my Anzio Bobbsey twin face to face. I might have had a decent chat myself with Sean for a change when we compared adult heights at the glorious girl's Christmas party a dozen Yules or so back if he hadn't looked crestfallen—and accusing, which was a bit self-promotional if you ask me—at hearing that his hero and I were no longer in touch.

Bill's later adventures on Clio were stranger than mine, and that's why I like to picture us bumping into each other on layovers now and again. We'd have caught up as propeller and then jet engines reorchestrated our century's tornado: me watching a succession of hemlines go up, then down, then up, then down on the Buchanan gams, Bill testing how much history could crowd that cherub face without turning its grins Luddite or worse. The reverie gets iced each time Pink Thing's archives reconfirm that Chasen's was and now always will be the last time we met.

Since he had his pride and Chet Dooley had offended it, even Pam's services as a Los Angeles sherpa were declined with a non-answer to my welcoming telegram—or did it just go undelivered? Only Western Union knows—when Bill came back in '51 to watch Universal shoot his two jokers and then stayed on awhile. Unlike me, unless Pam's mute parody of an extra in *The Gal I Left Behind Me* counts, he ended up on the screen himself, acting or pretending to alongside Audie Murphy in an adaptation of *The Red Badge of Courage*—a project that made my second husband suffer. Passionate to see history resurrected on film, Gerson had been trying to get a Civil War picture on track forever, but Metro's pashas let Dore Schary do that one.

Once or twice during *Red Badge*'s looping, Mrs. Gerson, as I was by then, saw or thought she saw Bill chowing down at one of the commissary's long tables. Unsure if he'd forgiven me for *The Gal*, I knew that was no place to find out, especially since Huston was there. He was contentedly stroking the jaw-bone of an ass as usual with those prehensile fingers, and I'll never figure out what made a smartypants like Lillian Ross fall for *that* sawdust-leaking act.

I also had and have no idea if Bill took the part as a lark or was trying out a way of being "Bill M." whose propinquity vis-à-vis Bill M. would make sense to him. He only appeared in one other movie before giving up the whim, cel-luloid's help in objectifying intimations of spuriousness clearly not having done for him what it did for Audie—who held them at bay for fifteen years by play-ing in Westerns whose only tension was the abiding mystery of his imploringly boyish face, not Dorian Gray's so much as our own Dorian Khaki's. While an actor he wasn't, that Medal of Honor we remembered was a sort of inoculatory super-Oscar.

According to *You Must Remember This*, which I don't doubt is trustworthy research-wise even if I never did read it all the way through, Bill next decamped pen, pad, and helmet to Korea, that reject pile of bits of World War Two that hadn't been fought at the time; it wasn't his war. More touching for Pam was learning that he'd gotten his pilot's license sometime in the Fifties and was soon flying his own plane, since the motivation for that grab at autonomy was crystal clear to his fellow passenger on Clio. I hadn't forgotten watching Jessie Auster turn into a dot in the sky.

Trying to be good for something while denying he was good *at* something, as Tim puts it in one of his better guesses about the man, Bill made a quixotic run for Congress and lost to some Republican windmill. He didn't go back to full-time cartooning until Eisenhower's second term. Then he stuck to his last for thirty years, and as I recall he only brought back his two *Stars and Stripes* jokers for Omar Bradley's funeral. But not ex-President Ike's, and my hunch is Bill couldn't bring himself to draw that pair saluting *any* politician.

When the newspapers said he was ailing with Alzheimer's, of course I wrote him. Going by the photographs, my knit-capped Aladdin had certainly blown up into a Jeremiac bullfrog, but by 2003 Bill's onetime Anzio Bobbsey twin was no very succulent morsel either. Got no answer, didn't expect any. Something like ten thousand other people had been moved to write to him too, and they were on more intimate terms with him. They were mostly perfect strangers, and at best I'd have been an imperfect one.

POSTED BY: *Pam*   When you're as ancient as we were and only I still am, the most persistent revisers of your own muddled first-draft sense of what the whole shebang was about are other people's obituaries—from Bill's three years ago to, a good deal more recently, Dottie Idell's. Not so the twenty-odd inches the *Post* gave in November 1986 (the *NYT* was stingier, and Tim, Chris, and I all said "Fuck 'em") to ex–Lieutenant Commander, then Ambassador "Hopsie" Cadwaller. In that case I already knew my own emotions blindfolded.

It was a few weeks after we'd buried your great-grandfather that catching sight of *Nothing Like a Dame*'s brittle spine in our living room's newly insensitive bookcases gave me my first real pang of mortification at its light-heartedness since Bill's and my boozy afternoon in Chasen's. My one and only World War Two, and I'd vamped it up into 253 pages of taffy.

Even though *You Must Remember This* does its best to exonerate me, I'm afraid Marlene Dietrich was right. I'd always been able to hedge my remorse by deflecting it into contempt for *The Gal I Left Behind Me*'s worse inanities, but the bungled screen version had long since stopped airing even on the Insomnia Channel and the silly, flirty book was still there. *My* book, *by Pamela Buchanan*, with Bill's fond cover art its major value to collectors even then. Coquettishness wasn't his specialty, but he'd given me a saucy come-hitler look and added a fun comma of Garbodacious cleavage when I lankily modeled fists to hips and chin atilt in surplus fatigues.

Wined and dined by a waxy Andy and now rewined in the Georgetown house I sold inside a year to take up my falcon roost at the Rochambeau, a Pam then only in her mid-sixties pulled *Nothing* out to ponder Bill's already unrecognizable caricature. Wondered what had become of the original, then got hugely annoyed at how my Greta-garbling thoughts had tricked me into a maudlin, movieishly mawkish, blundering double meaning. Tossed the book, grew gradually aware my wineglass wasn't a pet—i.e., summonable by flopping my hand in its general direction—and refilled it. Soon was quoting and requoting my favorite made-up line for Judy Garland: "Toto, I'm blotto."

I refuse to blame Cath Charters. For *Nothing's* vapidity, not my 1986 hangover. Roy's ex was not only doing her job as my agent but did it damned well. When I crossed my legs and put up my hands in her office, I didn't have a clue what sort of book I wanted to get published, and note phrasing. Everyone I knew was getting contracts for them and one rather felt one was traipsing around in last summer's organdy without a Random House advance. I was frantic to catch her interest, also to divert it. Never did learn for sure if amiably meowing Cath knew about my Pleistocene sessions of the old buck and wing with Roy during my divorce from Murphy.

So I made haste with the bright, evasive anecdotes: "From Co-Respondent to Correspondent," "Never Ask for Towels on a Troopship," "Mark Clark's Nose Is Out of Joint," "Undone in London," "Omaha Ha-Ha's," "Eddie's Norman Conquest," "Hurtin' in the Huertgen," and the dismal rest of *Nothing's* eventual table of contents. Pam's thought was that once I'd got done thawing the icy crap out of her, we'd get down to what I'd really seen, and while all I may have meant by that was anecdotes with a grimmer, more crimson-laced, whey-faced palette, now I'll never know. What Cath knew was the sales figures for *See Here, Private Hargrove*, to which—forgive me, Bill—*Nothing* got *favorably* compared.

"Well, there's your book," said my agent, though I'd only dried up because I was nerving myself to talk about Dachau. Not the easiest topic to carom off a bright laugh in a Midtown aerie, with Cath's green nails adding busy ticks of New York ornamentation to the silver baptismal cup—bought for a GI Bill song by one of her young authors in Rheims—she used for mint juleps come sunset. "How fast can you write it?"

Answer: pretty fugging fast. Five months: April to September '46, in the furnished apartment I'd rented in a Brooklyn rooming house. Not a New York I'd ever known, but Sutton Place, the West Village, and the Upper West Side were looking like three on a match to me. Lifting dead Daisy's typewriter out of the Paris footlocker, I ignored the Lotus Eater's malicious invitation—chauffeur-capped for some forgotten bit of Twenties zaniness, she was peeking out of a snapshot in the backwash of curios underneath—to hoist the window's sash and scatter my mother's chaotic pages of *The Gold-Hatted Lover* to the winds. Then I Smith-Coronated a kitchen table where Pam would never slice a single onion, much less spend an idle May morn dotting muffin dough with cherry bits in nothing but my borrowed shoes, and started clattering away like Perle Mesta's bracelets. I mostly ate cigarettes.

After going to the then considerable trouble of getting my ETO *Regent's* articles photocopied, I doubt I looked at them even once. The scrupulous Pam who'd written those had been able to welcome midnight as I hunted for an appropriately valorous evocation of "smelly" before one a.m. gave me my lead: "Rank means very little at this crossroads south of St. Vith, where rankness is the key to your fellow Americans' respect. Climbing out of our jeep to be briefed on the situation, which looked tricky but promising, by Captain Maxwell H. Folger [how had Roy let that one by?], 24, of Coffeyville, Md., we felt disgracefully scrubbed and pink..."

And so on for the rest of "Tiger! Tiger!," *by Pamela Buchanan's* 2,000 pungent words about life in a tank-destroyer battalion ten days after the relief of Bastogne. Yes, we were ornate in those days, Panama: had to be, to prove to Hitler and our readers that no obscenity we saw could blunt our sensibility. Now I had no one to do justice to but me and I knew I was trivial. *Gloriously* trivial, like the bright yellow cabs going by in no fear of artillery spotters or the ball game blaring from the sidewalk.

When one doubleheader stopped my fingers in midair, I was nearly done with a bit of foolery about Eddie quizzing a perspiring Vichy mayor on the local Calvados and fromages. To keep the mood light, I was skipping the coda that his former nonstituents were preparing to hang him. The astonishing urgency in the announcer's voice had me wondering what counterattack or map coordinate "Cookie Lavagetto! Cookie *Lavagetto!*" was code for, but Red Barber was speaking in clear and I heard thimbled roars. Then I went back to batting out *Nothing Like a Dame* as if I were lustily joshing at a party.

Which I often also did for real, since those same unabashed cabs pumpkined me into Manhattan more nights than not from my Brooklyn digs. Once the postwar edition of Midtown enfolded me, the heaped lights looked like avalanches in reverse, breviaries in an aviary: I'd last seen them dimmed to keep U-boat captains from figuring out whether the Bronx was up and the Battery down. Any wingding whose backdrop was Rose Butaker Dawson's Cunard Heights balcony or Ann Darrow Driscoll's Central Park zoo would've had the rest of their riffraff combing the hospitals if I was a no-show.

I'd been to both houses in my last Pamcarnation. But when I got back from our European war, both those salty pillars of society—Rose, the Picasso collector at the pinnacle of art's meeting with commerce; Ann, the blonde ingenue famed as the first bride to scream "I do" from the top of the Empire State Building—took me into their fold as if we now shared something too obvious to speak of. I lost touch with Ann when she left New York after a notoriously botched mid-Seventies facelift, but the bowl old Rose had finished glazing just before her death in 1997 got sent on to me by her granddaughter. UPS delivered it in Etruscan shards, but I was flattered all the same.

POSTED BY: *Pam*   As I was, bikini girl, truly, when your dad dedicated his damned book to me. His passages Egyptologizing my now mummified *Nothing Like a Dame* (Henry Holt, 1947) and its 1949 screen mutation could still have benefited from Roy Charters's blue pencil. "The hilarity of these faded reminiscences [mine is part of a lineup, given away by Pam's wilted corsage] can make us wonder if their authors were idiots," writes Tim, taking the bull by the horns as he never does conversationally. "But they weren't. They were crazed with relief because it was over. If you ever come across *Nothing Like a Dame* at a library sale, treat it kindly. You're holding the postures and japes of a sensitive woman who'd seen atrocious things. Now she's trying to convince us as merrily as she can that neither she nor her generation were scarred for life when they sailed on the *Titanic*'s return trip to face down King Kong."

Bizarrely mixed analogies aside—we didn't smash into a hairy black iceberg, did we?!?—I do wish Tim had asked me before he volunteered to play Pam's shrink in print. Trauma, please! Ask the boys under snow in the Ardennes about traumas, even though you'd have to sew that one's fucking mouth back on to get an answer out of the dumb fuck. Jesus Christ, Eddie! What had that dumb fuck been thinking to go back for his fucking *gas mask*, something even the dumbest GI tossed on his first route march? Jesus!

Consider the odds that I sounded like a glib, shallow ninny because I bloody well *was* a glib, shallow ninny, like most people that age—not really that much more advanced than yours, bikini girl. Since turnabout is fair play, my diagnosis is that your dad's the one playing shell games with bonnets and bees: overcompensating, as the Floydians say, for the fact that he'll never know what it was really like.

And soon nobody will. No one at all on this groaning, valiantly sashaying planet; not even dear Bob, whose clout with this administration is clearly more minimal than he suspects. Leaving out Vonnegut, whom I regret I've never met, he's almost the last of them left whose name people will recognize in the obituary. Besides Norman, obviously, whose own clacking cubby in Brooklyn I learned many years later wasn't too far from mine. Sure can't say the same for the respective results of our labors.

Of those gone on ahead up the bluffs, I suppose Bill's obit affected me most. "Come on, Pammie! Cut yourself some slack. The nurses aren't in mine either," I reheard him say as the Jan. 23, 2003, *WashPost* slid out of lunette range and became an annoyed Kelquen's hat. I rescued it as she shook it off, more slowly than she might've when younger. "What's that line from Whitman everyone loves now? 'The real war will never get in the books'?"

"Oh, Bill! At least you tried."

POSTED BY: *Pamita*   Once my manuscript was moored like a cockleshell among Holt's dreadnoughts, I did have misgivings. They just aren't those Tim attributes to me. Four different editors tried to talk me out of reprinting "The Gates of Hell," my May 17, 1945, *Regent's* report from Dachau, as *Nothing*'s very peculiar appendix. One of them suggested I at least give readers fair warning by prefacing it with the Webster's definition of "incongruous," and I took Doc Selzer up on it too: "Not corresponding with what is right, proper, or reasonable; unsuitable; inappropriate." The whole garish misstep was dropped from the paperback, even from the hardcover's last dozen printings.

A few otherwise *Dame*-smitten reviewers chided my "immaturity" (*Boston Carbuncle*) or "surprising tastelessness" (*Savannah Klaxon*) in subjecting readers to that final, I swear, "cold shower" (*Sacramento Malaprop*). One or two oddballs admired the discordance; I learned from Gilbert Seldes, no less, *Krazy Kat's* champion back in the Twenties, that the best writing in the book was the page Holt left blank between the main text and "The Gates of Hell." Pro or con, those were the exceptions. The vast majority of *Dame's* glowing notices ignored my odd appendix, like diners too stuffed with turkey to mention the hostess had soiled herself, the universal stain browning her wiggly white satin, as coffee was served.

Their deafening silence was why I agreed to an appendectomy when we went back to press. But Tim got his mitts on a first printing, and did *You Must Remember This* ever go to town on Dachau's there-and-not-there. I could so easily have set your dad straight, bikini girl! I knew my motives for reprinting a sample of my war reporting, and the agenbite of inwit played no part. They weren't conscience-stricken; they were vain.

Only my never met champion Celia Brady pegged it in her review: "Now that she's finished clowning, the lovely Miss B. would like us to know she can so play Hamlet." Bingo. I didn't want readers of what might be my only book to think giggles were all I had on when I hopped out of the cake, and I was proud of "The Gates of Hell." It was the hardest piece I'd ever had to write, and its opening line—"This pile died in a boxcar"—had won the admiration of none other than Cyril Connolly.

Anyhow, were I fifty years younger, I'd be tiddling my nose at Tim now in cyberspace. With one obvious exception, who left us long ago—brain aneurysm, 1965, Saigon—nobody, Panama's dad included, ever divined the identity of the tailor's dummy I'd anonymized in *Regent's* as "the soldier": "Quite possibly for good, the soldier's face changed" and so on.

He was the very same fellow who'd rollicked through the rest of my book barking bon mots like traffic commands: "'Oh, hell,' Eddie groaned. 'It's the seventh Calvados to the rescue'...'I don't know about you, Pam, but I think Field Marshal Montgomery just told us to turn left at the snow job,' Eddie said... 'Shut up, Eddie, for Christ's sake,' I told him. 'I've had it with your masculine wiles.' 'I've had it with yours too,' he grunted. 'I've hated you since Normandy.'" If those tastes of our wit strike you as caviar, by all means start haunting library sales. Not counting selling my own, which I won't ("Glad I could help you out, kiddo—whoever you were, are or will be. All my love, Bill"), there's no such thing as a copy of *Nothing* I can make money from, so I'm not being mercenary.

Since I never called Eddie anything but Eddie in the print version of our romps, only our fellow ETO correspondents knew that the Dame's breezy side-kick was famously sepulture-voiced Edmond Whitling, then known as "the conscience of radio." Not unmasking him was what he came to my party to thank me for, so he said, waiting for his gratitude's full range of meanings from abject to insulting to sink in. By my lights, his own war book, a stentorian thing called *The Rough Draft of History*, had exactly one joke in it, the dedication: "To my dear wife, who not only kept the home fires burning but let me feed my rough drafts to them when I got back." Don't blame Pamita if she never got to his ruminations on Dachau.

"The Gates of Hell" had paralyzed me until I hit on misrepresenting him as a nameless GI. Then every other element fell into place. We all took short-cuts in those days, and I suppose using Eddie gave me the clutchable point of familiarity I needed to get on with it. In my defense, as I'd reminded Bill in Chasen's, everyone could have been anyone. Eddie hadn't been quite Eddie— or even Edmond Whitling, his other masquerade—since we came upon the death train.

No guards, no locomotive, no explanation. Just a stench as big as the Prado under a low pewter sky that kept it sealed in over thirty or forty boxcars and flatcars packed with former people, none alive. Preserving my sanity for your benefit, Pam wasn't Pam either, and when she resurfaced in midafternoon—in a squabble you'd better believe I left out of "The Gates," and it's Maggie Higgins who should've thanked me for that one—I was aghast. As Tim Cadwaller charitably says, having only *appropriate* reactions to Dachau would be proof of psychosis.

Even so, it was not-Eddie—not not-Pam—who broke down when he saw the impractical souvenir of life as a human being one claw was guarding: a toothbrush. That was probably the origin of his transformation into "the soldier" in "The Gates of Hell." Angrily rubbing his jaw and smacking his face, he detached himself from the "we" of the lead, the plural vanishing as mysteriously as the collective narrator who introduces Charles Bovary.

No, daisysdaughter.com readers. I'm not even going to try to describe all we saw. Doing it once in dulcet magazine prose nearly killed me, and I was lots younger and spryer then. Just more game all around, you might say. But as a sample of what doesn't get in the books and didn't in *Regent's*, I'll tell you about Eddie's and my first test—which we passed—in the etiquette of genocide.

Not that the latter term was current back then, just as the former one isn't today. It was a practical dilemma, because we'd yelled at our driver to stop and scrambled out as soon as we came upon the train some minutes after the Thunderbirds' leading patrols. ("Thunderbirds" meaning the U.S. 45th Division, oddly enough Bill M.'s old outfit until he'd been detached to *Stars and Stripes*. They'd been at this since Sicily, too.) Three or four cars down, we saw that it stretched on and on.

Eleven months after D-Day, Eddie and I knew each other best when wordless. Here was the question we asked with our skins: now that we knew, when did this get redundant? The two thousand or so *other* dead Jews could be not unreasonably assumed to be more of the same. Oh, we might spot one whose specs still encircled his I-was-a-tailor stare at the sky, proof he'd stayed a person until nearly the end. Maybe one ex-little girl would be clutching a doll: human interest at last!

Faced with that much formerly human immobility in closeup, we two felt frantic to reconvert ourselves into mobile, aggressive, not-dead Americans by jogging back to our jeep to barrel by on four wheels. The now aging stink of the former people's final excretions was still being caught up with by the younger and friskier smell of their corpses, as if they'd expired while trying to write their names on each other in feeble dribbles of pee and crap: nothing else left to communicate, nothing else left to write it on or with. Prim Roy was fretful about letting me say "excretions," much less the word that in 1945 would've shocked

printers and made our readers ask what this world was coming to. "LET ME SAY
SHIT I WAS THERE IT WAS SHIT IT WAS SHIT IT WAS SHIT PAM," I Telexed from
Munich in a pointless fury.

More etiquette of genocide: so long as we were on foot, we understood
smoking was verboten. By contrast, a jeep's zip-a-dee-doo-dah air of having
somewhere more important to go excuses all kinds of callousness vis-à-vis the
scenery. Our nostrils were pining for the fragrance of our future cancer to dull
each new intake of feces and carrion.

Etiquette of journalism: the camp lay ahead and it was our story. If we
stupidly tramped the whole length of the death train like two amateurs, other
reporters might beat us to Dachau. Too well and too wretchedly to say so out
loud, we knew how we'd feel if some brisker rival, say the *Herald Trib*'s Marguerite Higgins—Pam's ETO doppelganger, younger than me by all of three
months—went bucketing by as we trudged alongside the follow-up Thunderbirds who'd unslung their rifles, perhaps for some illusion of potential to affect
the situation, back at the first flatcar. Ever since the Russians had come upon
Auschwitz and with local urgency once the Brits to our north had found Belsen
two weeks ago, being first in on a concentration camp's liberation had been
every war reporter's new grail.

No fair, I thought: Maggie'd already gotten Buchenwald. Eddie could be on
the radio tonight. With *Regent's* longer lead time, I'd have to work twice as hard
for *by Pamela Buchanan*'s piece not to sound dead on arrival. And above all, we
knew that the farther we walked, the farther we'd have to walk back, plodding
past faces we'd now recognize or particularly memorable tesselations of bodies—unless our GI driver, no master of the initiative even when what lay ahead
didn't start him gibbering "Jesus," trundled up the road on his own. Doubtful,
and we'd gone too far to wave.

Well, we paid our respects. Couldn't see how to avoid it, since neither of us
wanted to be the one to bleat "Enough" and bolt jeepward. Of course we were
each hoping the other would crack. We'd seen bodies before, but killed soldiers
did and no doubt do tend to be reasonably healthy and well-fed and young
and clothed. And shod, though I'm not sure why bare feet make such a difference. They do, like bare diarrhea-dribbling gray rumps and shrunken penises

and one ex-child's small nipples, which somehow unlike her eyes struck me as closed.

"And here I was counting on you to be the weaker sex," a re-Eddified or rather rebenighted Eddie was to say at *Nothing's* party. "Why do you think I took you along?"

"I'm sorry: took me along?" I said and his grin lost wattage. We'd both attended enough Royal Navy briefings in England to know that, in that particular ice-cube voice, "I'm sorry" meant "Release the hounds." When a man's sense of irony deserts him enough that putting you in your place is his idea of finding common ground, he's done.

Anyhow, we followed the tracks on into the camp, and if you've never visited what's left of Dachau—never have myself, so don't know how much has been prettily, *tactfully* preserved—you should know "camp" is a misnomer. Like the industrial complex it was, Dachau was built to last. Dozens of buildings spilled out over many walled areas as migraine-inducingly as typography in an alien language.

Henry Ford would have felt right at home there, I daresay in more than one sense. Do you know that son of a bitch is the reason we still know a book called *The Protocols of the Elders of Zion*? Talk all you want about Mercedes or Siemens. I've never bought one of Ford's fucking cars in my life.

POSTED BY: *Pam* Neither I nor any elderly Thunderbird could tell you what Dachau looked like, though. We never saw it as a going concern. We saw it in bankruptcy, with all the mess you'd expect when a business goes under: its inventory scattered and suddenly puzzling, its former foremen unemployed. Its product no longer in urgent demand.

In Metro's 1949 flop *The Gal I Left Behind Me*, Eddie's and my trek got telescoped into screen shorthand of wondrous puerility. Once this pause for a world-historical postcard in The Gal's itinerary had been identified by a sign reading "DACHAU" over the entrance to what appeared to be a converted cattle ranch—and was, left over from some recent oater; the camp's real outer wall was brick, its name unproclaimed by any similar logo—a brief but thoughtful reaction shot showed our dismay.

Yes, we *frowned at the bad,* to quote the children's book whose pastels kept leaking into daisysdaughter.com's legitimate recollections of Chignonne's. DIS-SOLVE TO a Glenn Millerized VE-Day in Hitler's old Munich apartment, true as to setting but not a lot else. That's when Eddie "Harting" in his lovably testy way finally explodes: "Will you shut your trap, Peg? I've loved you since Normandy." Me or rather "Peg Kimball," spunky to the last: "Not London?" THE END. Inserted closeup of Adolf's portrait rolling its eyes no doubt just Pam's later hallucination.

In the nonhallucination, the tracks didn't let up once we were inside the grounds, the grounds?, the grounds. With nothing else to guide us, we followed them. The GIs we saw flitting here and there before they melted into or vanished behind one warehouse or workshop or another—if you can't picture how exhausted men flit, it's the same fast-slow-fast as a firefly's dusk squiggle, only more unshaven and cantilevered by equipment—might be under orders that would veer us off course.

The earth was vile mud streaked with random silver. Cadaver, face down in puddle: a journalistic detail, should maybe make a note of it before I forget. (I did neither). Brains stove in and showing. Dogs somewhere barked urgently. Clammy rain mugged the air without falling. The fresh batch of cattle cars we saw as we came up to the railhead were empty, but the unscrubbed shit-stains—take that, Roy—and reek told us they hadn't always been.

Beyond them, past a stubby bridge over an undredged, just as well, canal, a squat guardhouse with a gun tower broke an unending tall shiver of wire fence. Three or four jeeps were already wedged in the badly paved gap between the bridge's far end and the guardhouse's archway. In helmeted mottlings of drab coats and grime, a few dozen of our boys clustered around them.

"We guessed right," someone nearby said exultantly. Unscrambling my mind from not-Pam paralysis, I realized Eddie's voice had surprised me because I hadn't heard it or even not-Eddie's voice since we'd come upon the death train.

And yes, Panama, this was it: the famous encounter between our fabled Wrigley-chewing naivete and the Nazis' ultimate *Gesamtkunstwerk.* I doubt I'll get much credit for admitting on daisysdaughter.com that the pajamaed stew of not-quite-former people on the far side of the guardhouse archway's gate—yes, *that* gate, with the inset motto, smaller than its iron twin over the aperture of Auschwitz, reading *Arbeit Macht Frei*—reminded me briefly of Purcey's during our one night fire drill.

Since I was there, however, I also grow caustic when that moment is depicted as if it *resolved* much of anything. Let alone rescued any of them or ennobled any of us at the touch of Uncle Sam's wand. It didn't, and it wasn't a moment either. As the rain we never saw falling made us all miserable anyway, the meeting of Wrigley's and *Gesamkunstwerk* went on for several chilly, clumsy, crowded and— I'll say it—tedious hours, because nobody really knew what to do.

In fact, it went on for days, not that I witnessed all of them. By early May, under a sky the plump blue china of an uncomprehending Bavarian barmaid's eyes, I was in Munich with writer's block, not Dachau's begetter's problem if you've ever tried *Mein Kampf*. Fingering Hitler's own copy—well, one of many, I suppose—I briefly considered feeling envious, then thought better of it.

The regimental CO had orders to keep the not-quite-former people penned until medicos and documentation crews reached the scene. The only reason things kept happening just the same was that something had to. If you must know, leaving aside the corpses and the clatter of machine-gun fire from behind us on the other side of the canal, the climax of the liberation of Dachau was a lot like being stuck on a mucky outdoor subway platform at rush hour.

Machine-gun fire? Oh, yes. As I may have mentioned, before the officers stopped it, we machine-gunned a few dozen of the camp's guards out of hand. I didn't watch it happen, but I later saw their crumpled bodies in an unmistakable, deeply satisfying ("PAM HAVE YOU GONE CRAZY ROY") domino arrangement in front of a wall. True, those who got machine-gunned were unarmed by then. Ethically speaking, we didn't have any business machine-gunning them. They probably shouldn't have been machine-gunned until they had no hearts left to speak of.

Most of us had gotten here by walking past the death train. We killed all the dogs too. In my earshot, a light colonel from one outfit got into a shouting match with a brigadier from another over who had responsibility for the camp, ended up pulling a .45 on him; it didn't seem unreasonable. Nobody got court-martialed over anything at all that happened the day we liberated Dachau.

In the one photograph I've seen that I believe shows Pamela Buchanan of *Regent's* on the spot on April 29, 1945, just weeks before the birthday that marked my first quarter century as a speck of life on this bloodstained beach-ball, my head has started to turn away from the *Arbeit Macht Frei* gate as my blurred paw reaches up to my breast pocket. But if it's the moment I remember, in fact my would-be grip's retreating. At a loss, the GIs nearby had started to push cigarettes and candy into too many hands through the bars until some shavetail lieutenant shouted at us to quit.

Unless we had thirty thousand packs of Wrigley's and Lucky Strikes coming out of our pink assholes, we were fueling a melee. "Lt waving arms—POWs [*sic*] yelling," my mud-smudged notebook scrawl reads. Then, amid the cries of resharpened despair from up front—and of indifferent and baying, otherworldly celebration from somewhere farther back in the scrum of not-quite-former people—I heard a croaked summons unmistakably addressed to me.

"Mar-ga-ret Mitchell," some not-quite-former person was calling. "Margaret Mitchell."

POSTED BY: *Melanie*   I was tentative as I approached. Squeamish? Yes, squeamish. The mob of hands that gripped the gate had knuckles as prominent as buboes. If you weren't there, you'll never truly know how the distinctiveness of eyes is that they're the only part of a human body that doesn't and can't get dirty. They all stank like latrines. "I'm sorry, I don't understand," I said.

"Margaret MIT-chell," he repeated and I naturally thought Dachau had driven him mad. I couldn't have gotten it more backwards. Behind me, two more jeeps had wedged their snouts into what was fast becoming Dachau gridlock. I heard some sort of fracas break out: "My orders are to *secure this fucking camp*. These men aren't under your command. So help me, sir, if you don't—"

"What the fuck are you, Colonel? Some kind of guardhouse lawyer?"

"Margaret *Mitchell!*" my inmate—my, how the proprietary instinct runs deep—raged at seeing my attention divide.

"Yes, yes. Margaret Mitchell," I tried to reassure him. "*Gone with the Wind.* Yes, yes, yes. Americans! Statue of Liberty."

As you may have gathered, my second guess was that he was babbling the only American name he could remember. Again, I couldn't have been more wrong.

"*Hilfe!*" came a wail from deep inside the compound. Automatically, I jerked my eyes to the sound. Dully, I watched what happened next happen. Armed or not, officer or enlisted man, that's all anybody on our side of the *Arbeit Macht Frei* gate did. Just before it vanished among scrabbling fists and fingernails, the guard's face had looked like a turnip that screamed.

"*Please!* I am Nachum Unger. Nachum Unger, Nachum Unger! We are colleagues. Was it in Technicolor, and did Paulette, Paulette—Paulette *Goddard!*—play Scarlett? I'm Nachum Unger—Nachum Unger, the poet! My work was as the cinema critic for the *Yiddisher Togsblat* in Dresden. For the love of God, colleague, tell me! Did Selznick succeed?"

"Does it matter?" I marveled inanely. But it did. His face was fierce with triumph.

"Margaret Mitchell!" Nachum Unger boasted. "David O. Selznick. 'Scarlett O'Hara she was not beautiful, but men seldom realized it when caught by her charm as the Tarl-ton twins were.' Eight years I have been in this place. I swore my reason to live would be unique—so unique they'd never guess. *Here I am.* Please tell me, colleague!"

I gaped. Honestly, Panama, should I have told him—Nachum Unger, Nachum *Unger*, weighing eighty pounds and reeking like a latrine—that I didn't know? That *GWTW*, six incredible years ago, had been infra dig in Pam's suddenly silly, newly obtuse Manhattan set? My role representing the United States in social situations as your great-grandfather's wife lay well in the future. But this was its stinking, surreal ("SORRY TOO INCONGRUOUS ROY," my editor Telexed back, deleting our whole dialogue) prototype.

"It is a cinematic masterpiece, Mr. Unger," I said formally. "Feel free to tell your surviving readers so."

Nachum Unger's chin lifted. "Thank you, colleague." His unfoulable eyes gleamed.

"No, no." I reached out a grotesquely healthy and corpuscle-crammed Pam-palm to cover his knuckles' gray stones. (Should never have washed it.

Something faint but real about the 20th century could've outlived me, could be yours to pass on in fainter and fainter turn.) "Thank *you*," I told him, for I did understand I'd just heard a tribute to something about America I'd never held in proper awe.

Brother, was I about to be upstaged. The new female voice that crashed in beside me was so disorienting I thought it must've come from inside my own skull: "Put a sock in it, Melly. I don't know why *you're* here, but I've got a job to do. Did they really kill that guard with their bare hands?"

"Yes," I said. "Jesus, what are you doing, Maggie?"

Bewildered, I was staring at compact-mirror range into the determined face of one the greatest war reporters of the atrocious century we shared, ravishing even in the overcoat and oddly earflapped cap she'd scrounged in an apparent bid—hadn't even crossed my mind, and evidently didn't need to—to disguise her femininity. Dear, it was sweet of you to say your Gramela should be as celebrated. But if you want to please my lesser ghost, honor Marguerite Higgins's giant one. Face the ocean when you do.

Friends we weren't, though, then or ever. "What do you think I'm doing, 'Pamita'? I'm going in. My God, you don't even know who's supposed to be in the VIP hut in there. Von Schussnigg, Léon Blum, Niemoller! I'm sorry for these poor bastards too. But amateur hour is *o-vah*."

And she'd already gotten Buchenwald. In my defense, remember that even colonels and generals lost their heads the day we liberated Dachau. Remember that Maggie and I were both twenty-four, and Dachau wasn't yet, well, *Dachau*. Given her looks (sexier than mine, no matter her garb) and reputation (ditto), the accusation implied in calling me "Pamita" was an outrage I couldn't abide.

"Hey, *fuck you!*" I screamed. "Fuck you. I got here first, Maggie! I got here first."

"So did the Vikings. Now get out of my way."

In "The Gates of Hell," the *Arbeit Macht Frei* gate opens somewhat mysteriously: "As if the demand for liberty of those within could no longer be contained." It's bullshit. I was standing right there when, after a quick check on whether the arguing officers were paying any attention, which they weren't— that was when the light colonel jerked his .45 from its holster—Maggie started to prise up the restraining bar I hadn't noticed, incidentally proving which of us was the real deal.

The thing she hadn't counted on was that the once and future people all straining against it had no stake whatsoever in letting anyone *in*. They only saw someone about to let them *out*, and I doubt they even registered Maggie was female. That can't have been a too significant distinction in there since around 1936. The second the restraining bar was loose, she went from bulky-coated human champagne bottle to cork in a latrine-smelling flash flood.

If the gate's outward swing hadn't pinned me behind it, I'd've been as buffeted as she was. I'd lost sight of Nachum Unger too, had no idea if—inspired to reclaim anonymity for the same reason he'd clung to his name—he was part of that frail and foul exodus. Nor did I see him once the crowd was recooped, or when I went back the next day in a foredoomed attempt to refind him.

Your Gramela's only exportable Dachau memento: when the inmates sluiced out and the gate's bars slammed into me or I banged into them, the *r* or the *i* in *Arbeit Macht Frei* cut my forehead, three-fourths of an inch above my left eyebrow. Half a century later, when my medicine-cabinet mug shot showed me the tiny scar was lost for good in crinkly Clio Airways routes, I confess to having mixed feelings.

At some officer's shout, a few Tommy guns rat-tatted. Our boys had fired in the air, but the shots stopped the flood anyway. Some of them trying to apologize as they did so—and the single word "Pal," spoken in a Tulsa twang in Dachau's miasmal air, was never to sound so moving or so inadequate to me again—the 45th's GIs moved the protesting, all too used to being herdable not-quite-former people back into their compound, desperately trying to avoid actually pushing them or aiming weapons: "Ya gotta wait, pal. Doctors are coming. Food's on the way. For your sake I hope it ain't Spam, buddy! You know Spam? Spam?"

Not a soul understood him, but his face must've been comic: I swear someone laughed. The sound could have made a bird gasp.

Just as the last of them were being squeezed back behind the gate, another GI grabbed my elbow to propel me inside. "Mac, what the fuck are you doing?" I shrieked. "Do I look Jewish to you, for Christ's sake?"

"You were bleeding," he blurted by way of atonement, mixed with a hint that I'd pulled a fast one: something any snail could do. Probably a replacement, he looked as if his unlined face's inadequacy to everything it was being asked to react to would make his eyes resentful rather than generous in old age.

Quoth droll Eddie in Munich: "Easy mistake, Pamita. You *are* on the skinny side. Plus, that beak—"

I pitched a pillow at him. "I didn't say I was complaining, did I?" he called. Stomping out of the room, I stomped back to my typewriter. Three words aside—"by Pamela Buchanan"—the scrounged page rolled into it was still blank but for the swastika watermark.

POSTED BY: *Pam*   If you've figured it out, you're faster than I was. It wasn't until my third straight day of being blocked on "The Gates of Hell" that I smacked my still Band-Aided forehead at my stupidity. Good God, why hadn't I kept my mouth shut and bled? A little more thinking fast and I'd have succeeded where Maggie had failed. What a scoop: the only correspondent to experience Dachau while caged. Hell, the bonus I'd gotten for "To the Ends of the Earth" would've ended up looking like bus fare.

Thanks partly to that, none of Maggie's biographers mentions the *other* woman reporter on the scene that day. Her mischief with the gate does show up in the more scrupulous accounts of Dachau's liberation and is this old bag's test of their reliability. Miss Higgins's own published report, incidentally, had Eddie and me guffawing, since she and a photographer had apparently ended the Holocaust, which we didn't yet call it, single-handed. In fairness to her, I repeat: twenty-four.

She's my road not taken, Panama, not that I flatter myself I'd have gone along it as far as she did. Partly because it had no sequels—unlike Maggie, I'd never go through anything like that in front of a typewriter again—I did feel miffed when "The Gates of Hell" didn't make the cut for the Library of America's two volumes of classic World War Two reporting, unlike not only some of Maggie's stuff but Eddie's radio report from Dachau: "Better tell Junior to go out and play, folks. I come before this microphone with eyewitness testimony to a crime against mankind that must never be repeated…" But Marguerite Higgins is buried in Arlington and she deserves to be; for not only that war but Korea and Vietnam.

When I respotted her near the jeeps, she was plainly the worse for wear. I think she'd actually gotten knocked down in the panic when the Tommy guns blatted skyward—and if ever a sky deserved killing, it was that one. Tossing a breath up at those tightscrolled curls under her strangely earflapped soldier's cap, she looked back at the gate with pride. Not complacent, hard-won. In memory, for we never met again, I salute her. If the books only put one gal at Dachau, I say give it to the braver of us two.

Then she got out a notebook coolly enough to turn Pam's impulse to mimic her into intolerable monkey-do. As I started past her to make my way back over the stubby canal bridge instead, secretly begging only to be somewhere not raw with the imprint of livid events—in Dachau? Good luck there, Miss Buchman—I heard her say, "Colonel, Maggie Higgins, the *Trib*. Do we have an estimate yet on the numbers?"

"In there? My God, none."

If I was looking for Eddie Whitling, which I'd like some points for thinking I wasn't, I was lurching the wrong way. He was still on the compound side of the canal, trailing behind a squad of Thunderbirds along the fence to see if he could talk to anyone through it without risking his or their electrocution. (The juice was still live.) What hindsight tells me I was after is bound to strike you as grotesque. Not unlike Eddie, I was looking for a little bit of Dachau I could call my own.

I wished "Tiger! Tiger!" hadn't stressed stench. Now I'd sound like a real broken record, all nose and no brain! Dogs would do better. The six I'd just lurched past, what made them journalistically interesting? Got it: even in death, thanks to their pelts, they looked warmer than the fifteen or twenty near naked or naked former human beings I could see sprawled in plain sight between mud and silver. If only it would rain in earnest. No, Roy had teased me for my devotion to weather.

American trucks were starting to groan this way from the camp's main entrance, so slowly they clearly didn't understand anything. Near the second cattle train—or was it now the first? The shit-stained and shit-stinking but empty one, near the railhead—a lone MP with a snagged brassard was already posted to direct them here and there with stupid traffic flags. He had a GI handkerchief knotted over his nose and mouth against the smell.

"Howdy, cowpoke!" I brayed. "Robbing the train? Stick 'em up! That gold'll never reach Tucson, Tom Mix. Bang, bang, bang!"

Fumbling with his stupid sticks—too slow, too slow!—he jerked the kerchief down. "Ma'am?"

A few seconds later, he said, "Ma'am, I can't move from here. How can I help?"

Pam was pretty sure he couldn't, but I did have a list. If I'd had my druthers, Pam definitely wouldn't be on her hands and knees in this icy foul muck. Lord knew when we'd get to change to dry clothes! I wished Pam hadn't just vomited, partly because that reminded me of all the food she could eat anytime she or I liked.

I wished that hadn't reminded Pam of Dottie Idell in our kitchen before Pearl Harbor, especially since thinking *that* had just taken the horrifically inept hop, skip, and jump of thinking Sharon Halevy Cohnstein—instantly scooting in front of a substitute stove out in Williamsburg—shouldn't be allowed to exist in a world like this one. Above all, I wished Pam hadn't started blubbering because her forehead's new ruby still smarted and she was fresh out of dulcetly literate *Regent's* descriptions of bodies and stink and the awful factory clatter of machine guns and euphemized human shit everywhere. What I'd have given for Pam's one lucid thought since noon to have been something other than a venomous reflection as she stared at Maggie that life's always greased for you when your hair is pretty.

I wished the stupid MP and his fucking dumb little furled flags would wave the trucks to run over me when they finally got here. Oh, Panama! Never mind that Maggie Higgins wasn't scared of trying to get into the compound, however irresponsible that sounds. She wasn't scared of *writing* it. On my hands and knees in randomly silvered mud, I was feeling sorry for myself with starved bodies reaching for the sky around me.

The hands that helped up not-Pam turned out to be Eddie's. "It's all right, Pamita," he said, atavistically batting away the reek of my pukey breath before a grimace signaled he'd remembered what replaced it: Dachau's. "It got to me too."

And notice, as I only did a week later, his admission's implication that I hadn't *seen* it get to him back at the death train. Men always try to treat our hearing and our sight as two sovereign powers, brokering alliances with one or the other as it suits their notion of *Realpolitik*. They can't even be selfless without hoping we're eyeless.

POSTED BY: *Pam*   "The Gates of Hell" takes dramatic license in compressing all its perceptions—and omissions, says a wry vegetable-chopping voice or two—into one afternoon. In unforgiving fact, it wasn't until we forced ourselves to go back the next day and split up to poke around as much of Dachau's vast layout as possible that Eddie completed his metamorphosis into "the soldier" by discovering its abandoned Brigadoon. Spotting a portal in a discreetly walled brick compound north of the inmates' stinking barracks, he stepped into a haven of *Gemütlichkeit* homes and tended lawns: housing for *Hauptsturmführers*, *Sturmbannführers*, *Obersturmbannführers*, and *Standartenführers*.

The one he entered was cozy, with the one and only unprefixed Führer approvingly sizing up chintz from his gilt frame above the mantel and the familiar boiled-potato smell of humid German kitchens, whose gestalt always does make cooking seem like another ablution. People had sat down to meals here. Upstairs, one room held a boy's playthings: rocking horse, toy train set. Children had been raised here.

Think of that, Panama. Because it's associated with your earliest memories, you love beach air's freighted tang. Today, are those onetime tykes' nostrils doomed to quake with nostalgia when they walk past cesspools? Funerals bother them: of their five senses, one that should be stimulated isn't. In food shops they're suckers for especially stinky cheeses, like the ones they misremember Mutti used to buy. For no reason they can name, coffins strike them as a waste of money.

And no: it wasn't their idea to be born there. It's never anyone's idea to be born anywhere, and we get no say as to when. Unlike our exit if we're in the mood, and this pretzel should know.

In the master bedroom, which like the whole building was infuriatingly undamaged—our boys had looted the liquor, left the rest—the soldier saw a feather bed. From pure campaign habit, he threw himself on it, stretching out from crusty boots to crewcut; booze was the only other thing nobody in the ETO passed up. We claimed beds even when we hadn't felt tired until then, knowing our illusion of wakefulness was just exhaustion held in check by nerves.

Just as the pillow's wings nunnified the soldier's now helmetless head, obliterating the ticks of the watch on the forearm hooked under it, he turned his eyes to the wall. Like all those in this house that faced the inmates' barracks, it had no windows.

Thanks to a grippable bedpost, he was back on his feet right away. When Eddie agreed to let Pam borrow not-him for "The Gates of Hell," he claimed his hands were swabbing at his clothes without a say-so from his brain. He even felt bad about grabbing the bedpost, and his scalp was telling him he wouldn't rest easy until he'd found some shampoo. Just not theirs.

However pooped a man may be, some beds just aren't worth sharing with their former owners. Of course "I'd just pictured that pillow under Frau Major's fat ass" was too crude an epiphany for the soldier to think it, but I did try to hint at the sexual dimension of Eddie's revulsion by scattering some women's unmentionables on the carpet. They'd probably been there, Frau Major having presumably packed in a hell of a hurry. Men just don't notice.

From his next remark, Eddie must've regretted giving me that glimpse of an Eddie whose body was jerked by morality's strings. We were in the gloomy domed basement of Munich's Hofbrauhaus, site of Adolf's proclamation of the Nazi Party's program in 1920 and now, a few unmoving migrations later, one of the 45th's regimental CPs. The Germans took it back eventually; the night Cadwaller and I revisited in 1959, glum tourists playing glum hooky from a glum NATO conference, a group sing broke out, swaying tankards and all. "Let's get the hell out of here," my third husband grunted.

Four days after Dachau's liberation, what was Eddie's next remark? This, with a forced and hence authentic grin: "Natch, if you'd been there with me, Pamita, the story might've had a different ending. Huh?" He even got his eyes to twinkle, which was like watching television be invented in a crypt.

"Oh, *Eddie*," I said, disgusted. And for the first time, sorry for him, the reaction that fatally lingered. Pink Thing's archives keep maintaining *Nothing*'s pub party was when chipper, compulsively self-estranging Eddie Whitling crossed from irrepressible to helpless. That's wrong, though: it was in Munich. So often, what we remember as our perceptions are just belated confirmation of something we've known latently forever.

"I wonder if they made beer there?" he said restlessly, which was chivalry of a sort. He was groping for an acceptable halfway house between his manner and my mood. "You didn't see a brewery, did you?"

POSTED BY: *Pam*   I hadn't, which doesn't mean there wasn't one somewhere in Dachau's maze of workshops. And though I hesitated briefly over dead Daisy's typewriter—good detail, too patly yeasty an irony?—the American woman who wandered through "The Gates of Hell" didn't see a brewery either. Fudging was one thing, outright invention another.

For instance, it was a meek Hershey bar, not my idiot Lucky Strikes, that the nurse was on the verge of pulling from her breast pocket to push through the *Arbeit Macht Frei* gate when the shavetail lieutenant shouted at us to quit. That kind of thing was all right. So was resorting to an anodyne "Later" to get her inside the prisoners' compound, something I only did under escort the next day. Not without a teeth-clenched inner "Fuck you," I admit, since my rival—her deadlines were tighter, like her skirts and her curls and her coiled pissy cunt—had shedaddled by the time they let us correspondents in.

I'd reluctantly introduced the nurse after realizing the soldier couldn't see everything, not only because his perspective was limited but because no such entity was within human grasp. As I wrote in "The Gates," there was no *everything* to Dachau. Something would always be left out, had to be—the story of a single shoe in that place could've filled an encyclopedia.

So like the soldier, the nurse just wandered. Unlike me, she didn't throw up, much less turn a lone MP into Hopalong Cassidy; she was a professional. As she went through the barracks, she was assessing which emaciated not-quite-former people had a chance. (In fact, I was looking for Nachum Unger. As I've said, in vain.) Around the time the soldier came upon the officers' quarters, the nurse found the camp's infirmary.

Naturally it was for the guards. Unable to grasp that not only were they prisoners but their former victims weren't, its tenants—poor halitosal Hansel, down with a corn—had been monstrously indignant, so I was told, at being ejected (poor greentoothed skeevy Erich, did you shiver with the flu?) to make room for a handful of inmates.

All the same, it's true that, like the soldier and the nurse in "The Gates," Eddie's and my paths recrossed outside Dachau's modest crematorium. Modest, you ask? Oh, yes. Unlike Auschwitz, Dachau wasn't an extermination camp. The thousands who died there died unsystematically: shot, worked to death, succumbing to starvation or disease.

Mauled by trained dogs for entertainment.

In the usual tangle, the couple of hundred as yet unburned bodies our soldiers had found heaped almost to the rafters in the storehouse next to the crematorium were still there. Roy rightly made me cut an overelaborate simile about indecipherable chalk at the top of an oversized blackboard, but I was trying to get across the strangeness of looking *up* at mortality. Ever since, I've believed we stick it in the ground to make that state inferior to our own.

Anyhow, that's when I turned and saw Eddie. While I wouldn't understand for years that the final sentence of "The Gates of Hell" was also my goodbye to my quip-happy ETO Virgil, I was proudest of it for a note of doubt I don't think my editor ("BEAUTIFUL ROY") ever caught. Tapped out in Munich on dead Daisy's typewriter in a two a.m. litter of balled-up pages, overflowing ashtrays, half filled bottles, maimed copies of *Mein Kampf*, and Eddie's new snores, this was it: "Four living creatures despite it all, their eyes met."

POSTED BY: *Pam* Hand it to our road-not-taken minds for their ability to miscast us worse than Hollywood at its most Zanuckleheaded. Not only was my mother no caregiver and hence incapable of raising one, but Pam's only real-world try at "There, there"—comforting a miscarrying actress who'd slept with my husband in a delirious dressing room—had been a mangle of hamfisted Murphine commands and Pamcentric confusions. When I first tried out being my own tailor's dummy in "The View from Ward Three," I'd played not soother but casualty: a mock patient mock–ministered to in New Mexico by the trainees I'd named for my old schoolmates.

I'd even felt uncomfortable writing "The Angel of Anzio." That was partly because I'd never made a heroine out of someone dead before and partly because I hadn't really known the jolly warm girl I called Dolly Rydell in print. (Even on a beachhead, you can move in different social sets.) When I waded onto Omaha three months later, terrified our wounded would call to me when my only hypo was a pencil, I'd ditched the Red Cross–mooned helmet that made me look like a corpsman faster than you could say Florence Nightingale. Yet I ended up feminizing the same disguise in *by Pamela Buchanan*'s final report from the ETO, possibly earning Bill M.'s disgust if he read "The Gates" and spotted the imposture. If he did—and he had an inscribed first printing of *Nothing*, after all—he never mentioned it. My only excuse was that a real nurse would've been as helpless.

Of course, one advantage of writing for a fat-assed civilian readership in Darien and places is that nobody from Roy on down asked what one would be doing up with front-line combat troops. That's why Gerson, who'd never been in the military, surprised me by taking my dissimulation for granted. "When I first read that—in *Regent's*, not to brag—I was touched that you wanted to imagine yourself as a healer," said the perplexingly (my head was still stuffed with the unbroken crockery of New York cliches) thoughtful man who wanted to put *Nothing* on the screen.

It was the day after my arrival in Los Angeles, and he was showing me around Metro. Delectably spread for the sky's giant blue appetite, this part of the lot was all whitewashed buildings, soothing lawns. A Swiss Alp got heaved up and relowered beyond them by unseen but cursing workmen. Brisk staffers on errands hurried past somebody dressed as Napoleon.

"I didn't have much choice," I stammered. "I mean I couldn't have been *me!* I wouldn't have known how. But I couldn't bring myself to be no one—omniscient—not there. A God's-eye view made no sense. And then just by process of elimination, you know, why else would a woman be in Dachau?"

Not at all rudely, Gerson gave a *very* dry chuckle. "You're right. There are limits. But ach!" (That was deliberate.) "We'll settle."

"Yes, there *are* limits! Do you have any idea how—my God, how presumptuous that would've been?" If that left him thinking I'd considered dressing myself in a not-quite-former woman's filthy togs at the typewriter before I virtuously rejected imagination's promotion and wasn't just trying to worm out of a gaffe, so be it.

"As a matter of fact, I do. That's why it'd be a relief to quit trying. Hopeless, but I feel obliged. Shall we go off the lot for lunch?"

"I'm not sure I'd know the difference, so it's completely up to you."

Nodding, he took Pam's elbow with rare calm for someone shorter than me. How many actresses he must've steered to water. The real Gerson touch was that he didn't tell me which we were doing, paradoxical reassurance I was in good hands.

"I'll tell you something that'll help," he offered, correctly interpreting my stare at all the roofless cars. "Hoping, Miss Buchanan, that you do stay on a while. No, L.A. isn't a real city—that part's true. It is a real place, though. The problem for most East Coasters is that they can't see the forest for the palm trees."

"Problem for or problem with?"

My future second husband laughed. "Oh! That's when we get into personalities. But if you're shrewd enough to ask, my guess is that you'll love it here. I do."

"It's Pam," I said a bit late. "By the bye."

POSTED BY: *Pam-Luc Godard*   We'd been married several years by the time Gerson, in a rage—not at me—confessed he'd masturbated to *Dame*'s jacket drawing shortly before he placed a movie-rights call to Cath Charters. I'm not trying to shock you or make you think ill of him; the point was his zest for thinking ill of himself, a subject immune to my input. We always agreed on so much except the standards the ideal Gerson should be held to.

If he'd been puckish about it instead of self-lacerating, he wouldn't have been the Gerson I wed in '49 at L.A.'s City Hall; the Gerson who never knew that made two of us, although my understanding was he'd had the actual book propped in his briefly locked office and I'd just gotten the drawing's lines entwined in a Tijuana-biblical, Myrna-loyal reverie the night before I flew to California. Lax shiksa that I was, I hadn't felt too incriminated. But Gerson's penis just blamed him for everything, and its owner put too much stock in individuality's sacredness to care that most men did it the other way around.

How many marriages founder in confusion over which one's job it is to heal the other? If you think ours foundered over a silly mental picture of Gerson killing the snake to my book's cover art, oh please. We were happy before and after that confession. If in temporarily separate ways, we were even happy during, since we both knew his determination to insist some remote core of him was unhealable wouldn't outlast Pam's astonishment that he could mistake such flimsy stuff for his core.

Besides, every marriage has its defining time of day, and ours was breakfast, not midnight: Gerson plucking at his orange juice and making jokes at *Variety* as if it were a child that needed a giggle. Me going through decorators' brochures and sorting invites to the Wilders', the Kellys', and the Governor's Ball until *Glory Be*'s stirrings dungeoned me most nights in my study.

My second book included, all this was unimaginable to me as I began learning my part in what became the incredibly dithering, protracted—and given the results, wasted—chore of turning my first one into a movie. Cath had wangled me a screenplay deal, citing my gift in *Dame* for quick he-she byplay; I later learned she even reminded the studio I'd been married to Bran, a sort of credential by osmosis. Nonetheless, I had to be partnered and immediately was. After our lunch (off the lot, French, delightful), Gerson led me to the writers' building to meet a sofa with the power of speech named Wylie White.

Reputedly handsomer before booze began playing Rodin, he'd been married for a while to none other than Celia Brady, whose memoir *The Producer's Daughter* I'd tormented Alisteir Malcolm by reviewing so rhapsodically for the old *Republic* in another life. But I never got to meet Wylie's ex, not even to thank or spank her for her answering praise of *Nothing Like a Dame*. As I learned from my first eager inquiries while scanning the room at Hollywood parties, she'd moved to Arizona on doctors' orders shortly before I reached the West Coast. So my flickering hunch we'd get along like long-lost sisters never got tested outside print: two slim books whose dust jackets (hers annoyingly pictureless) I had a tendency to catch for years peering up side by side each time I unpacked my library.

If not Celia, then I'd hoped to be teamed with Bettina Hecuba, whose credits went back to Griffith and who'd won one of literary Manhattan's rare dispensations from charges of whoring in the California sun. Smart as a tick, she kept in New York's good graces by impersonating an unrepentant golddigger; I knew I had it made when *Dame's* first reviewer compared it to Bettina's expertly addlepated *Now and Then, There's a Girl Such as I.* Horrified by the thought of *two* women, neither one shackled to Hollywood (Bettina at least kept five pert toes wiggling East), witching it up on their payroll, Metro's preference was for a male's wise hand. Or wise back, my usual view of Wylie as he slept off the three double martinis that had washed down an elephant's idea of too few peanuts at lunch.

We got along like gangbusters when he was sleeping, not too badly when he pawed himself awake. Overseeing three other movies' progress at the time, Gerson had given us marching orders whose fundamental irrelation to reality I was too new to Hollywood to appreciate. Once I did, I understood how men of his caliber might put up with peddling treacly illusions to the public for the sake of the interludes when they got to enjoy the more gallant illusions they'd cooked up for themselves.

Gerson was no hack, far from it. He was a man deeply fired by earnest beliefs, including that movies could and should be better. He'd admired my war reporting, and far from bemoaning "The Gates of Hell"'s inclusion in *Dame's* first printing, he told me I should've done that all the way through—interlarding each chapter of comedy with "The Angel of Anzio," "Bacchanapoli," "The Day the Tide Ran Red," "Tiger! Tiger!," and my other ETO pieces for *Regent's.*

"They're *both* true!" he told Wylie and me firmly. "And if we can make an audience see they're both true, they're both always true—the slapstick, the horror, yes? Yes?—then I think we end up showing them that this was a very *American* kind of war. Unless, Pam, you're really from Winnipeg."

"The truth is she's really from Winnipam," said Wylie. "Peg is her name. I love how he says 'American,'" he went on once Gerson had left. "It's like hearing a virgin say 'Cunt.' Say it often enough and open sesame, the Great Bush will appear."

"Oh, I like it," I said.

"Cunt? So do I. No wonder you wish I was Bettina. That's the reason I drink, you know. I'd never touched a drop until you—"

"No, you jackass. The way it matters to him."

"It does," said Wylie shortly. "But I've been around longer than he has, Peg, and one thing I know about Hollywood is that it takes a very smart man to be a real idiot. I'm only a mildly smart man. I'm perfect."

"You must've cared about something once. Just for me, can't you pretend? I promise I won't be in Los Angeles long."

"I am American. I don't need to."

I decided to ignore his implication Passaic wasn't in the U.S.A., and we settled down to reconciling the Pam Buchanan of *Regent's* with *Nothing's* Dame, little knowing—all right, Wylie probably did—she'd turn into The Gal. By my next birthday, in spite of my collaborator's damn near sestinal siestas and morning yawns of "Tell me again about the lighter side of Dachau," we had a script I liked. Then a schoolboy, Jean-Luc Godard might've liked it too—especially the Godard of *Les Carabiniers*, one of Tim Cadwaller's favorites. Even with a Balkan blank like Metro's Tod Paspartu directing instead, it could've made a reasonably good movie, that is if it'd had a snowball's chance in Trader Vic's of ever being made.

Since I didn't have a clue, I was beginning to enjoy myself. On Metro's tab, I had a suite—though not bungalow—at That Hotel. Could look down from my window on its pool's frescoes of paunchy gents toasting at rest, their sunglasses as declarative as a firing squad's blindfold, among magnificent girls in Newton-defying bathing suits as waiters circulated and bellhops trotted out with plug-inable phones. While you won't believe it, Panama, in those days a telephone's status was indicated by its heft and Bakelite sheen, not its resemblance to a metal hangnail.

Appearing poolside myself, the Hollywood equivalent of a debut at the court of St. James, struck me as both unnerving and a bigger commitment than Pam's signature on my Metro contract. I'd learned at Anzio, no less, that too much sun turned me freckled and peeling instead of gorgeously tanned, and the Buchanan gams were my only feature that gave me any hope of passing for suitable human scenery. Still, it was either that or binoculars, and after a week, having bought a demure but not wholly unchic tartan two-piece and my own shiny firing-squad blindfold, I wrapped myself in a hotel robe and went down.

No doubt it's just Pink Thing's archives having fun that I recall those with *The Naked and the Dead* on their laps looking up to trade competitive glares with those starting Irwin Shaw's *The Young Lions.* Having just about finished John Horne Burns's *The Gallery,* I was rather bleakly thinking Napoli had kept a few secrets from the Bobbsey twins when a bellhop startled me by plugging in a phone next to my chaise. It was Gerson asking me to be his dinner date at the Gene Kellys: "I was supposed to be holding Lily Hellman's hand. Not really her cup of hemlock, but Betsy Blair [then Mrs. Kelly] is doing *Another Part of the Forest* over at Universal and if you're Lillian you tend the greensward. But she's flying back East to nurse Hammett. Thank God," he added decisively, careful to erase any insult I might feel at being asked so late.

Odd sightings around the pool or on the Metro lot aside, that soirée was my introduction to Hollywood's real trick photography: the kind taken by your blinking eyes as familiar screen faces turn 3-D. Yet in a variety of Beverly Hills and Bel Air homes that spring, sometimes as Gerson's date and sometimes (I *had* written a bestseller) on my own, I noticed most of them were sheepish about these lesser selves, for lesser they indubitably were. Manhattan magnifies, Los Angeles shrinks; the difference is the sky. One reason actors like living there is that it lets them pretend they're in proportion.

Male stars, especially, had overeager manners tinged by worry that a ringer like Pam might know truths fame had denied them about the complex mummery of behaving normally. As they waxed lyrical about tennis or havered after substance by subscribing to *Newsweek,* retreating indoors to read it to demonstrate the indifference of an *homme sérieux* to May's mesmeric soar, they seemed more victimized than even Murphy by masculine faith that a noble thing called "real life" existed out beyond this palisade of artifice, not a dichotomy to confuse most women in either Monte Carlo or Weehawken. It came out in questing, jousting grins and a positive mania for conversational premature ejaculation, as if guessing what you were about to say did more to prove their bona fides than putting up with listening to it. Not to smash any altars, but the one I've got most in mind is Bogart; I've never had so many perfectly passable remarks get brutal-ized before they were halfway out of my mouth by clackingly chopper-proud pseudo-savvy. ("Uh-huh! Those burp guns could cut a man in half." Well, no: they were .30 caliber, not .50.)

Yet even the women were likely to worry you'd catch them out somehow, pointing in vindictive triumph (they could fathom no other kind) at the give-away mistake—the tinsel!—in their otherwise convincing bean dip. At fame, all of them were experts. In ordinary situations, they were as touchingly unsure of whether to act snooty or abashed as centaurs at the Preakness.

Would you like to know the party game those silly, enchanting people were all sure defined them as regular folk, breaking the ice for newcomers? Charades! Trust me, oh, that's just the thing to make you feel you're on an even footing with Gene Kelly, in whose facially mobbed living room I once had to act out Milton's "Come and trip it as you go/On the light fantastic toe." But these were Hollywood's great middlebrow years, when the vogue was to impersonate the Versailles edition of suburbia.

As always in movieland, one motive was fear. Though McCarthyism was years away from being coined as a term—by Herblock, incidentally, the *WashPost*'s op-ed Daumier; in Sean Finn's pantheon, only Bill M. shares that plinth—and its eponym was still an obscure freshman Senator from Wisconsin, the House Un-American Activities Committee had reached L.A. a year before I did and the Hollywood Ten's contempt convictions were still on appeal. Since Hollywood's politics ranged from a balletic pink (the Kellys) to Kremlin red (Pat Carpet, by now as indigenous a transplant as most of Southern California's flora), it made sense to take cover in aggressive normality.

His own teenage membership in Passaic's small chapter ("More the size of a limerick, not that the Irish kids stopped throwing rocks") of the Sparta-cist League now a wry memory—"It was mostly a way to meet girls," he told me, which I knew wasn't true but knew he wished had been—Gerson was well placed to be kind about it all. "When backing Wallace for President is a show of intransigence, you wonder what Norman Thomas must think," he murmured one night, backing me in his Packard down a long driveway after we'd heard some drunken hyphenate lecture his shrunken caliphate about Henry's good sense: the approximate equivalent of praising Nixon's idealism. "Still, who am I to talk. Pam, can it be you've seduced me into voting for Truman?"

I got you another, Miss Loy. My big advantage was Harry's decision, ignoring the State Department's qualms—even Cadwaller, then unknown to me, had thought it was rash—to recognize the new state of Israel. Then we pulled up at That Hotel, where as usual Gerson's goodnight was confined to the warmest of smiles.

He took me to parties; sometimes I even asked him. Unless driving time counts, however, we hadn't gone out *à deux* since our French lunch. If I thought about it at all, I was operating on the assumption that our social life was purely professional, just as so much of Hollywood's professional life struck me as purely social.

When I got to the office next morning, Wylie was recumbent but wakeful on the couch. "What do you know, Peg? They tossed it," he said, nodding at our script. "Now can we get to work, please?"

POSTED BY: *Celia Brady's Sister*   I hadn't understood anything, since my impression was that once we gave Gerson what he'd asked for, that was the movie Seattle and Bangor would see. Yet even though he had some authority to acquire properties on his own, he wasn't an *independent* producer: in lot parlance, a Metro gnome, not a Metro pasha. The pashas had read Wylie's and my script and vied to mime "By the licking of my thumb, something wicked this way comes" at charades. In a sign he thought his authority could use shoring up—more often, he strolled in on us in the writers' building unannounced, a gentler way of asserting it—our next confab with Gerson was in his office, not ours.

"Well! We had a good four months at least, you two. I'm proud of our work, but of course all good things must come to an end." That was my first hint, confirmed by variants on the same template I saw from a wife's vantage point on his later productions, that Gerson hadn't been able to help urging Wylie and me to write the script we had to give himself the bliss of believing such a movie could exist. In fairness to him, you never knew: something might always slip in under the radar.

"Anyhow! We're tag-teaming this. That's the word from on high," he told us. "Pam Buchanan, I'd like you to meet your new alter egos. Wylie, you must know them by now."

Because some people's faces hurl their legends at you even if their preferred publicity photo dates to 1922, I'd known as soon as we walked in that the plump dwarfess in platinum ringlets and kohl-rimmed kewpie-doll eyes on Gerson's rich couch could only be Bettina Hecuba. Indeed my heart had kicked, since I had no idea what a big disappointment she'd be. (Short version: despite my best efforts, I never got Bettina to consider the possibility that I might be, well, Pam! Potential kindred spirit, fellow voyager. More Hollywoodized than her bubbly books let on, she had no interest in meeting anyone *like* her.) The man doing his best to make his share of the couch look like a pleasure boat's flying bridge was another curdled old hand turned monkey's paw, Claude Estee.

"Bettina, you're the wizard." Gerson's lips crimped with what he later admitted—to me, not the room at large—was a renewed awareness she revolted him. "How do you see the problem?"

"This thing you've got here is a hemorrhoid that wants to be a trapezoid," she said. "It's all here, there, Anzio, whatnot, Paris, craziness, dead people we never met when they were vertical and cannot give a fig about. What I see is the old triangle. Bill and this Eddie, sure we change the names. Which one's she going to end up with?"

"And we lose Italy," Claude Estee said. "We get all three of 'em to Merrie Olde, then bang, on to France. Frolics ensue."

"But that never happened," I protested. "I only ever *saw* Bill in Italy. And Lord knows, we never—"

"Lesson One," said Bettina, acknowledging me at last but only as an intruder. "Nothing. Ever. Really. Happened. If you ever say that to me again, you'd better learn to say it in Chinese. It'll do as much good and you'll have a new party trick when you head back East."

"So who *does* she end up with?" Gerson asked. Though I was staring madly in all directions, I think I caught his eyes flicking away from me as he did. I was too squirmy about hearing her answer to pay much mind.

"We argued, but I like this Eddie. Reason? She and this Willie or Joe or whatever are the same age. Babes in the woods—wah, wah. Enough with the diapers. He can't teach her much and what audiences like is a broad being taught. Eddie's older, got more seasoning. I see Gable."

"We aren't quite at that stage yet," said Gerson. "Anything else?"

"Yes. All these exteriors," Claude Estee said. "I don't know if you've even had this script budgeted, Noah—"

"No, we haven't."

From the "I knew it" glances Claude exchanged with Bettina, I gathered this was an interesting admission. "You know it's impossible," Claude went on. "Primo, this ain't *Birth of a Nation*. *Deux*, Bettina and me don't do the great outdoors."

"The goddam *war* was outdoors," I protested. "What about the fucking *war*?"

"Kung pao, foo yong, chow mein," crooned Bettina. "Chiang Kai-shek," she added with relish.

"Lesson Two," Claude informed me. "They know how that ended."

"Damn right," my neighbor guffawed. Wylie'd never pretended he had any loyalty to the script or to much but his paycheck.

"All right. There's a lot more to do. But I think we've come to a meeting of the minds, as my dear wife would say."

Once I knew Gerson better, I knew how he'd been suffering. With his passion for seeing history resurrected on film, you could say he was *fluent* in kung pao. He'd been forcing himself not to speak it to protect his position, and remember: the imaginary movie he'd gotten Wylie and me to write had meant more to him than to me. I'd already lived it, written some of it in *Regent's*, mocked some more of it in *Nothing*, and profited all three times. Gerson was the purist, not me.

"This'll work out, Pam," he told me bravely. Also wrongly, but still. "I know it's a lot for you to digest. But these three know what they're doing."

"Yeah, we do," Bettina snorted in the polished corridor—to Wylie, I noticed, not Claude. "If he did, we'd all be in gravy."

POSTED BY: *Pam*   "Who's Gerson's dear wife?" I interrupted Wylie as he started to brief me on our new subordinate roles the next Monday.

"You don't know? Oh, of course you wouldn't. Stella Gerson, née Negroponte. Older than him, I think—she was a publicist here for years. She was in Carole Lombard's plane crash," he said and looked impressed. "That crack of his was darker than I thought, and I'm good."

"I thought Carole Lombard was in Carole Lombard's plane crash."

"So were twenty-odd other people, Peg," Wylie reminded me. "That must make it hard on Gerson. I know it did on Stella's friends. All over town, it was 'Carole Lombard, my God! Oh God, we've lost Carole *Lombard*.' Not that Carole Lombard, Carole Lombard, Carole Lombard didn't deserve it. You know she was the best of us by miles. I know for a fact Stella G. thought so too."

"Were you one?" I meant one of Gerson's wife's friends.

"Stella? I'd have sold her out in a handclap. But I did like her, yes. Sorry to see her go that way, her demotion to 'among others' in the papers the next day included."

Having just spied a heel's Achilles heel, I wondered if he'd say the same of me if I flew into a mountain with someone better known. Too bad Wylie White (d. 1980) has long predeceased me, his credits petering into sitcoms and silence in the mid-Sixties and his long Hollywood novel unpublished.

Be that as it may, when Pam eventually laid eyes on a photo of the first Mrs. Gerson, I felt obscurely relieved we looked nothing alike. No mystery he'd cherished her, but my husband knew when people are gone. Her picture was right out in the open in our den. I saw no reason to move it.

I hadn't come upon a locked room that held fifty more lit by tapers. I wasn't urged to do my hair like her—and good luck *there*, Antoine of Beverly Hills—or consider work as a publicist. I hope you share my relief, bikini girl, since it'd be a shame if I had to gum up what *l'équipe* hopes is a reasonably entertaining daisysdaughter.com post with that sort of drivel. It's the bane of all Hollywood fiction, for all I know including *Lost Weekends Under the Volcano*. Wylie never showed me a sentence.

As for our own sow's purse from a cow's ear, nearly all *Nothing Like a Dame's* new script shared with its predecessor was its title. That eventually went too. Gerson did his best to look regretful when he told our quartet at one story conference that Rodgers and Hammerstein had pulled their considerable Hollywood clout to scotch the title despite Pam's earlier copyright.

"Hey, fuck you, Richard. I got there first," I muttered. "Are you really that possessive about your shirts?"

"I'm sorry, Pam?"

"Nothing. Nothing, like a dame." Privately, however—yes, we were an item by then—Gerson and I agreed it was just as well. At least *The Gal I Left Behind Me* had no association with me.

The way tag-teaming worked was that Bettina and Claude, old monkeys' paws at construction and Wylie's and my bosses in all but name, would rough out a sequence and messenger it down the hall for us to tart it up into dialogue. Then they'd rework our version by plugging in road-tested jokes from their earlier movies, which plagued Wylie mostly because he didn't have the stature to crib old jokes from his. Then they'd decide the whole outline was wrong, reshuffling scenes as carelessly as Imelda Marcos sorting shoes before they put us to work on new ones to fill the gaps they'd just created. Even granting *The Gal* was one of the worst movies of 1949, the wonder is that it wasn't one of the worst of 1965.

I found Pam had a knack for claptrap, which possibly should've worried me but didn't. (Youth is resilient, old age couldn't care less. Middle age is doubt's swamp.) The process had so little connection to anything I'd learned to call writing, let alone my own life, that I responded to it as a light-hearted transformational game. Soon I'd even learned to sling the one unanswerable argument in story conferences: "The audience will go for it." Since nobody in Hollywood is an audience and no member of a real one believes himself or herself to be an interchangeable cog, what gave any of us a claim to insight beats me, but it was never challenged.

That said, I could still get three pairs of eyes to roll heavenward by betraying my ignorance of basic rules. And with no regrets, not in the case I'm thinking of. At one caffeine-fiendish meeting at which Gerson was present, Bettina, Claude, and Wylie were wrangling over the latest plot hole ripped open by tag-team genius, namely how to dramatize Chet Dooley's discovery that Eddie Harting was The One writ purple in Peg Kimball's heart. If nothing else, I was grateful my Anzio Bobbsey twin's new cognomen was in place, as I had honestly cringed at hearing them all call him Bill. Even Gerson, whose voice I otherwise enjoyed.

Nor was I sorry Pam was now Peg, as Wylie had presciently christened me. Of the three of us—and by now I could hardly remember the kung pao that in the real ETO, Bill, Eddie, and I had never been a "we"—only Eddie had kept his first name, simply because everyone except me liked it. Anyhow, they were tossing around stupid ideas: for instance, a letter home to my "parents" Chet might guiltily read before posting it. I wondered briefly if it was worth turning Chinese to bring up the kung pao of a polo accident on Long Island and a Browning in Brussels.

"Oh, shut up, all of you," I said instead from the couch. I'd taken over Wylie's recumbent posture, since around Bettina and Claude he sat up. "Why can't he just spot me coming out of Eddie's room the night the Bulge starts?"

Not to pat myself on the back, but silencing Bettina Hecuba was no job for an amateur. Or maybe one *only* for amateurs. "For God's sake, Pam!" said Gerson. "We can't even hint you were fucking."

Unlike me, he wasn't foul-mouthed. Indeed I rarely heard him use the word in the all-purpose and flavorful adjectival incarnation that all of us this side of Omar Bradley had learned to deploy in the war. He was just respecting convention. Except possibly in private, "fucking" was all anyone in Hollywood called sex.

I sat up. "Jesus Christ, that's all we ever *did* do. Kung pao, foo yong, chow mein," I added, whirling on Bettina. "Chiang Kai-shek! Chen-chen," which didn't quite come out of nowhere: those kewpie-doll eyes had just reminded me of the Lotus Eater's. Then I saw my future husband's face.

So, I'm afraid, did everyone else. And—"I'm sorry, Gerson," I said witlessly. "I thought you knew."

Was it his inadvertent declaration or mine that settled things? We often tenderly bickered about it. In any case, that night Gerson asked me to dine *à deux* for the first time since our French lunch: at Musso & Frank's, later our marital favorite, which incidentally proved he had no intention of keeping us under wraps. His goodnight gesture was a dry but lengthy kiss.

A couple of days later, in my suite at That Hotel, kisses were succeeded by mutually shy—we mostly kept it under wraps—but satisfactory fucking. Yet the gesture this old bag still holds in her heart is that Gerson didn't propose until after *Variety* announced the next spring that *The Gal* was a box-office bomb.

POSTED BY: *Pam*   After thinking Seattle and Bangor had a rare treat in store, I'd almost forgotten the goal of all this nonsense was to ship something to theaters. Hence my surprise when one day that fall—the temperature doesn't drop, but everyone can feel summer's bored air lift and go bother Ecuador, taking its shed snakeskin along and leaving a tenderer shimmer behind—our tag-team quartet's latest wad, chartreuse by now in Metro color-coding, came back with the pashas' magic endorsement: conditionally approved for production.

"It's just another movie now," said Gerson with a hint of reprieve. Cigaretted and bare-chested, his body paler than Pam's was by then, he was still hopelessly, sniffably, uniquely, and hence adorably Gerson. "I'm sorry, Pammie. You're well out of it."

"I'm through? Pink-slipped? Time to start packing my bags?" Meet my first unmistakably Hollywoodized thought: unless I wanted to start footing the bill for this suite myself, we'd have to find someplace else for our fucking.

"Oh, you and all this are still on the budget. So's Wylie. That is, I convinced the pashas to renew his contract."

"You know he's a wreck, don't you?"

"Everyone does and him better than most. But I owe him for when Stella died. He identified—well, whatever was left. If I had, I'd still be gibbering."

A passenger on a plume of cigarette smoke, a rare ghost of mangled Stella Gerson, née Negroponte, curled upward to rejoin Carole Lombard. Then it dissipated. "Chen-chen," Gerson said.

Plucked from Pam's memories in story-conference extremis, the cry to the dealer to start the next game was already one of our codes. "Chen-chen," I murmured back.

True to its Chinese nativity, its meaning altered with inflection too. "Oh, Pammie! Do I have time?"

"You'd better make some," snuggling Pam told his ear. So tucked and folded, corpuscle-crammed, peculiarly and proudly vulnerable. So oddly like the anus

in reverse of our brains' publicly displayed, disgustingly exposed digestive sys-
tems. To spare you any more detail regarding the images that used to pop into
Pam's mind unprompted, see Tim Cadwaller, "The Holocaust as Pornography,"
in *You Must Remember This*. His not unastute guesswork makes a natural sequel
to the chapter that precedes it, "The Holocaust as Sacrament."

Not least because I kept such Hieronymian bosh from Gerson, a few pink
slipups over the years aside, the fucking was satisfactory. "Oh! You should
know," he said with a proud chuckle as he dressed. "This is mildly interesting. I
think we've cast you."

They had, but I didn't meet the young New York stage actress recruited to
play Peg Kimball until her wardrobe tests. It was the moment when the phoni-
ness turned real and kung pao fled for good.

We were supposed to pose together for a studio photographer. Turning
a corner, I ran head-on into a sparkling gal in the identical correspondents'
uniform I'd worn in the ETO, from cunt cap and shoulder flash to constantly
tugged skirt and low-heeled, slightly clunky pumps.

I think they'd cheated on the stockings; ours were never that sheer. More
saliently, I'd never had a nose that daringly darling, lips as ripe, or eyes anything
so radiant. My blue-gray ones were attractive, but they were weather, not live
gems, and Antoine would go to his grave unable to convert my brindle mop into
her shiny bob. She was also a good few inches shorter than me, making her, I
suppose, Peg Kimball's exact height.

"Oh, I know it's confusing!" she said with a silvery giggle, perhaps aware
the claim flattered me. "Let's get ourselves sorted out here and now. We're both
Peg, but you're Pam. And I'm Eve."

As I hope my readers if any appreciate, I try to avoid cliches. Still, they
really do say this in Hollywood: "We're ready for you now, Miss Harrington,"
someone called.

Yes.

POSTED BY: *Eve Harrington's Pal*   Yes, though my dearest Hollywood
friend's biographers generally hurry past her flop screen debut—often casually indicting Gerson, to both Pam's and Eve's fury, as the hack that gentle

man wasn't. *The Gal I Left Behind Me* was the movie she outraged Broadway by coming West to make mere days after she'd collected The Theatuh's prize trophy for starring in *Footsteps on the Ceiling*. Given *The Gal*'s reception, it's astounding she didn't bolt back to the stage by the next train.

As movie fans know, she didn't. From her saucy success in Red Riding-wood's film of *Footsteps* and then Charles Eitel's *Saints and Lovers* to her haunting job as abandoned Queen Disa in John Wilson's much Oscared adaptation of Shade's marvelous *A Distant Northern Land*, her career after *The Gal* was all mistletoe and laurels. Contradicting the fables told against her in New York, she never once except teasingly reproached Gerson or me for making her screen debut such a dud.

Out of touch with Addison DeWitt since I'd come West, I hadn't even known he was married to her, an eyebrow-raising break with form for him. But I was delighted when he came out to the Coast himself and they set up housekeeping in the hills above Malibu. Unabashed at living off his wife's earn-ings—"Good Lord! So did God," he crowed, flourishing a hand at our dazzling surroundings—and amusing himself by sporting atrocious Hawaiian shirts in their sun-medallioned garden as he chatted with servants in the most debonair pidgin Spanish I've ever heard, he tucked cigarette holder in mouth and went back to writing the taut, spiky poetry he'd begun with, producing three slender books critics called almost Shadean as well as my second-favorite memoir after *The Producer's Daughter*, the jaunty *An Apple for My Eve*. By the time he died in '72, prompting his wife's retirement from pictures, I doubt most people even knew he'd once been Manhattan's silkiest, nastièst drama critic.

He was still back in New York, bracing his bride via bouquets and tele-grams, when *The Gal* finally sneak-previewed in Glendale on April 14, 1949. As I've said already, it's a miracle my friendship with Eve survived. Unlike, as I've also said already, mine with Bill M., not that Bill was on hand. I'm not sure when or where he saw it, but his letter about Chet Casanova's etchings only reached me in July.

I'd never seen *The Gal* myself until Glendale, and so help me I had no idea Chet Dooley would come off as such a pusillanimous fink. An initially charming one, true, with an engaging line of boyish patter, but only because Peg Kimball was a ninny. Even after tag-team genius had started prepping Chet to come off second best in The Gal's maturing affections by concocting an unreliable streak, I'd gone on picturing, well, *Bill,* who had no more duplicity than an M-1 and couldn't even be shrewd without his eyes reaching out to pull you into the fun. Then you could enjoy his shrewdness as boyishly as he did.

Besides, on my one visit to the set when Hal Lime and Eve had a scene together—a dozen feet of mocked-up Normandy farmhouse behind them, live chicken whose trainer was clucking and flapping his elbows just outside camera range—Hal had looked about right and been personable. His slap of Pam's face the night of *A Clock with Twisted Hands'* premiere had briefly retraced itself in our gazes. Then we mutely agreed the actor who'd belted me was a Hal he'd left behind him.

The problem was that I had gotten so used to the Hollywood trick photography of seeing actors in three dimensions that I'd neglected how different their effect could be in two. Hal was well on his way to specializing in seductive weaklings with a gift of gab. Unfairly, since he'd only been doing his job, I never could cotton to him much after seeing how expertly he'd worked out Chet Dooley's libels of Bill.

During the first reel or two, I hadn't paid much attention to the fact that I was watching a dull botch. However far it strays from kung pao, it's fun to see your life impersonated, and I snorted at not only a tired character actor's pretense that he was Roy Charters but at a bookless office Roy wouldn't have given *Regent's* janitor. When Eve minced onscreen, I couldn't help but be bewitched by the fantasy that those were *my* self-frisking hips, my life-welcoming lips, my cuddly new bosom, my hair and my voice. Regarding the actual Buchanan bod in Glendale's fuckless aftermath, I realized Pam's enchantment had had its painful side.

Like the monkeys' paws at construction they were, Claude and Bettina had made Eddie Harting a veteran writer at the same mag who treated The Gal with derision in the opening scene. Announced with a brazen final quip, his departure for the looming Second Front was what provoked her to barge into the faux Roy's office in an "Ooh, I'll show *him*" snit and lobby for her own ticket to the ETO ball. A far cry from my own jump out of a Charybdean frying pan after my divorce from Murphy, but no facsimile of my bullnecked first hubby—much less Dottie Idell!—marred the screen. As far as the audience knew, Peg Kimball went to war a virgin. Kept her bloody cherry for a good ten seconds after the fadeout too.

In the third reel, Chet Dooley turned up, introducing himself in a London blackout—Peg's, from brandy—with "Yep, I just got back from Anzio": Claude and Bettina's one concession to kung pao. When Hal Lime smirked as he said it and I heard titters at the wolfish undertone, I whispered aloud, "No, no." Every scene from then on with him in it had me writhing and sick.

Only upchucking in Technicolor all over Bettina's toupee (she was the toadstool sitting in front of me) would've done justice to my feelings about Chet's farewell to The Gal and *The Gal*. As rear-projected Sherman tanks rolled by silently (!) in the background—all out of proportion, but that was kung pao—he passed Peg Kimball a snapshot of his wife and baby. Just what Bill had done the first night at Nettuno, a bit of business I knew had been nowhere in any script from cream to chartreuse. Couldn't begin to guess—oh, yes I could: Wylie was the one who got summoned to set to troubleshoot in emergencies— how it had ended up onscreen.

No longer an up-front announcement of his marital status to ease the long-legged newcomer's anxieties, it was now a confession. It was Chet's guilty way of indicating he was taken and had led The Gal on. Then Hal Lime wandered away to be soundlessly flattened, so I hoped, by rear-projected Shermans, free-ing Eddie and me to frown briefly at Dachau or rather "DACHAU" before our VE-Day confession of love.

Nobody in the lobby could've been stupid enough to interpret the tears ruining my face as praise. Gerson was uneasily chatting with two Metro pashas; he reached for my arm, but protocol stopped him from following. His back to them but nonetheless self-destructively, Wylie was raising a flask to his mouth like a bugle. Meanwhile, the civilians—as even I had gotten into the thoughtless habit of calling them—were reaching for the comment cards like Italian women about to hack up a still living horse.

Oleaginously, Hal Lime was trying to edge in between the two Metro pashas poking Gerson. Eve was nowhere to be seen and told me weeks later she'd fled before Normandy. "You know what we say, Pam," called out Walt Wanks, the bullfrog in a turtleneck who'd played Eddie Harting without much interest in the job. "There's always the next one."

"Not for me, Dub. Tell Gerson I'm leaving, willya?"

POSTED BY: *Pam*   When Gerson, normally not one to pound, pounded on the door of my suite in That Hotel, his face mixed relief with outdated panic. He'd thought from Dub's message I was leaving Los Angeles, had had to endure many more minutes of lobby autopsy before he dashed after me. We had a long hug while he mumbled healing-sounding things to me and I did the same back.

"Chen-chen?" he asked, still mildly worried. We both knew fucking wasn't in the cards, and yet we'd never slept in the same bed without it. Nor was either of us in any shape to acknowledge that doing so would set the seal on our domesticity, though you'll soon read proof I'd intuited it.

"Chen-chen, Gerson, but—what? You know, how?" What would happen once *The Gal I Left Behind Me* had been pushed out to sea in flames had never been discussed.

"We'll work on that later. But I told the desk to put the room bill on my personal account from now on."

After some surprisingly awkward undressing (baring the Buchanan bod from habit, I turned to see a constrained Gerson in T-shirt and boxers; except after sex, he didn't sleep nude, and in his own home favored striped pajamas of a vaguely European type), he was off to slumberland by express train. Remember, he'd had a more exhausting night than I. His hour with the Metro pashas in Glendale had forced him to fake a confidence not only untrue to his feelings but insidiously confirming their opinion of *The Gal*. Only outright belligerence— impossible!—might've worried them into wondering whether he was right and they wrong.

Oddly moved to realize I'd never watched Gerson fall asleep before, I sat beside him. Even reached out to experiment with stroking his hair, then pulled my hand back as if burned when I recognized which bond I was parodying. As for Pam, despite the fact that I'd hardly been in the mood either, going fuckless

left me sleepless. After a prowl or two around the suite—discovered there was
nothing interesting to see on its prototype TV set, a.k.a. the bathroom mirror—
I parted the curtains and looked down at the pool. At this late hour, of course
it was deserted.

The pool itself was still brightly lit, presumably on the off chance Carole
Lombard's plane's pilot might spot it in time. Yet from the chaises and tables
to the famously pink but now murky imitations of the Palais Royal's walls that
framed it, its surroundings were dark. Mine, all mine!

After wrapping the Buchanan bod, still in the pointless altogether, in a That
Hotel robe, I grabbed my cigarettes. Having made sure Gerson's breathing was
even, I slipped out. So bored he'd clearly hoped his ornate uniform would do
the job without his waking help, an age-speckled doorman stirred downstairs:
"Pool's closed, Miss."

"I'm naked under this," I said impulsively. "Want to see?"

Blearily looking me up and down, he considered the idea. Then he said
"No" so wryly we both laughed. "What the hell. Just tell them you found the
door unlocked, okay?"

"Sure thing. But won't that get you in trouble—Admiral, sir?"

He smiled. "I'm not the guy who locks it."

Once he'd ushered me through, I found a prime chaise. Someone's abandoned copy of *The Naked and the Dead*—or was it *The Young Lions?*—lay
broken-backed below my feet. Every hunter of tranquility knows that in a state
like mine you're better off waiting for thoughts to come instead of chasing after
them. Especially if the lure of water's nearby, you need only put out the bait:
yourself.

Feathery and Lombard-light, they settled as I tried not to disturb them.
Between Glendale and Beverly Hills, each time the studio car I'd shanghaied
had proved privilege's uselessness by stopping at a red light, Pam had grown irritably aware that her fine fettle of outrage at everything under the moon except
me wasn't the whole story. Now, drawn by the pool and the noncomma of non-
cleavage in the terrycloth V of my plush robe, the rest could peep into view.

My indignation at *The Gal I Left Behind Me*'s travesty of Bill had hidden
abject, cowardly relief that now no one would ever guess my most bathetic war-

time secret. What's unnerving about Hollywood distortions is that they can hit on camouflaged kung pao as easily as not. At that June story conference, only a monkey's-paw coin toss whose upshot I'd awaited in panic—"We argued, but I like this Eddie"—had stopped *The Gal* from spilling the beans.

Oh, crap; oh, Christ. Of course, you fucking fools. Of course I'd been in love with Bill! I was *crazy* in love with my Anzio Bobbsey twin, as in love as I've ever been with any man up to Cadwaller. I'd let Eddie Whitling pound Pam's socket from London to Bavaria to see if I could learn to ignore it.

It stayed not only chaste but unmentioned. If I once or twice told myself I'd seen a certain something in Bill's cheerful eyes, it was probably delusional—or just a friendly, accepting, possibly agreeing but unverbalized reaction to seeing the same something in mine. I do realize daisysdaughter.com hasn't been long on evidence I'm dainty, but did that snapshot of his wife and baby do me in. Besides, so much had already been spoiled and wrecked and shot up around us that I knew I could never do anything to spoil our beachhead twinhood. If Bill did do any fooling around in the ETO—and remember, he was young, adorable, far from home, and even by 1944, famous: famous at twenty-three, sweet Jesus—he kept it out of his memoirs. Aside from helping me out of the odd dugout, he never touched me once.

In a token, I suppose, of my helpless respect, he doesn't in my favorite recurring daydream of us either. As I recline on a looted, luxuriant couch at Nettuno, wearing only dog tags, I'm letting—letting!—him sketch me in the nude. One arm hooked behind my head, I'm smiling as his eyes flick back and forth from his pad to the newly lush Buchanan bod.

Unlike *Nothing Like a Dame*'s cover art and my old friend Rose Butaker Dawson's broken bowl, that drawing exists only in my mind. If it ever existed in his, by now it might as well be at the bottom of the Atlantic. Or the Tyrrhenian Sea.

POSTED BY: *Pam*   Never shared even with Gerson, since by our rules I'd have only had to if he was going to be introduced to Bill in my company, that little secret was to add another irony to a cranium bulging with them when these astonished, then amused mimsies scanned Tim Cadwaller's defense of

The Gal I Left Behind Me. "Of course it's untrue to 1944–45," he blusters. "So what? It's preciously true to 1948–49, which we remember less. The only generalization I've ever allowed myself about movies is that they're always really about how life looked to people at the time they were made."

Pompous, no? "Allowed myself" is beneath you, Tim. No reader does or should give a fig about our inner tussles. So you wished you could sleep with luscious Eve Harrington? That makes you stand out from the crowd.

I'm not saying it's charmless. Nobody else cares and I can't help being tickled when people like Tim vouch for the kung pao of eras that predate their birth. As you know, Panama, I'm fond of your dad. On my generation's rotting behalf, I'm flattered our whole moldy shebang means so much to him.

How it must drive him berserk that he'll never *know* Hollywood's voluptuous allure in 1948–49. Much less what the ETO was like in 1944–45.

What was it like? I'm not sure I can say after sixty-plus years. Pam's gone from gal to pretzel. Traducing *Dame's* cover sketch, my medicine-cabinet mug shot burlesques the breakup of the former Yugoslavia. And I just don't think about the war that often.

Sorry, Tim. I know it was your dream of dreams when you set up this website: your Gramela's reminiscences of 1944–45. Normandy, Anzio, the liberation of Paris! All of which I lived through, saw, smelled, ducking at times and waving at others. But I'm going to be a mess of pink and gray things come sundown and I don't want to waste my last hours. Let Dachau stand for the rest.

Trucks droned by and sweaty men jerkily plodded. What do you want, Mr. Cadwaller? I was awfully young and lived superficially, and to tell it all properly would need a book as fat as—though I hope far more readable than—Edmond Whitling's forgotten *The Rough Draft of History*. It was only a war long ago and I can't believe the world is still interested. Much better just to fast-forward to me in 1949, still lying poolside in a darkened hotel.

There, as I recall, I did make an attempt to cull and preserve some bits of kung pao now that I'd seen what Hollywood could do. Since I was near bright floating bought water [fix later, Ard], I thought of how I'd watched more than one LST (Landing Ship, Tank) come off the stays in Memphis and New Orleans shipyards. Seeing one at the surfline—reversibly, thanks to those huge things' shallow draft—as enough wheeled and tracked vehicles rumbled out to make you think it hadn't been their transport but their factory, wheels and tracks thrashing Mediterranean water and then gouging Italian sand, had made me gape even though I'd just disembarked myself and briefly looked back.

Boxes and cases and bidons and crates of supplies were stacked up everywhere, not looking as high as they actually were. They were half interred, camouflaged, tented. We got shelled every day and nothing we held was out of German artillery range. Too tizzied by my own survival to understand the meaning of the corpsmen pushing past us to where Anzio Annie had sent up gouts of sand and some darker soft rocks and green and red sticks, Pam's giggly talking jag after her baptism of fire (I was here! It was there! Here I am! How amazing) ran its hysterical course without Bill interrupting. Then he brought me ever so gently back down to earth: "Come on, Pam. Those guys in the Hermann Goering Division may be fanatical Nazis, but they're only human. You know they'd never hurt *you*."

That was all of a week before one German pilot in a hurry dumped his bombload wherever and I heard someone call "Nurses too." Then someone else in the villa called out "How many?" as we dumped our coffee and grabbed for our helmets and pencils and someone called "Three." Someone stopped and said, "Jesus. Not Ellie Farnsdale," because she was the one we all worried about. But someone called, "No, she's all right. She took charge."

Even though his old division held a sector farther west, Bill's favorite outfit when scouting material was the First Special Service Force, a joint Canadian-American commando brigade. They did things Bill knew he'd be accused of fancifulness for using in his cartoons, like electing one of their favorite lieutenants mayor of a pocked sun-blasted village out in no man's land they'd moved into for the fun of it and renamed Gusville.

Most units didn't have favorite lieutenants, but the Force wasn't most units. I got treated to dinner out in Gusville once; my waiter was a German prisoner picked up on patrol. So I was led to believe until he took off his coalscuttle helmet, quit glaring, and laughed, "Ma'am, I'm from Toronto. We just felt a mite bored and like goofing around. No disrespect." The next time we went back we were told he'd been killed.

That was Anzio. But not *Anzio*, a Cro-Magnon opus starring Robert Mitchum as a war correspondent more likely to try eating a typewriter than use one, which I walked out on twenty minutes in. It had no kung pao at all. That was five less than I lasted at *The Devil's Brigade*, leaving a blessedly empty Washington theater to go surprise Cadwaller at the Department once I got fed up with red-faced William Holden insisting he was Robert T. Frederick, the First SSF's CO.

Not much against Holden, Panama. But by '68 he'd seen better days and in '44 Bob Frederick hadn't. He was my definition of a leader of men and out of combat you'd have taken him for the only prof at a small Midwestern college who could order kung pao beef without fear and saw that as the limit of courage, though never civility.

If Bill ever noticed I always decided to hitch a ride with the Navy back down to Naples when he did and back up to the beachhead when he did, he was too kind or just worried—not shy? As Jake Cohnstein said, hope springs eternal—to mention it. If you had dispensation, it was easier than hailing a cab in Manhattan. Our side's water taxis plied back and forth constantly, ferrying wounded men one way and materiel the other.

Far enough out to sea to be sure any shore guns in the mood for a potshot would only liquidate water, we'd watch the coast's toothy towns and lumpy spearmint-sprigged squeezes of batter slide by. Casualties in flapping or newly sliced uniforms shared the rail on the down trip and equipment was lashed at our backs on the up. As if the sight reminded us that Italy would've been overseas even had it been peacetime, it was most often then we'd find ourselves chatting about our lives in the States.

Taken in fall '43 by the troops climbing the boot from the heel up, the word for Napoli by the time I first saw it was *requisitioned*. Requisitioned hotels, requisitioned apartments, requisitioned bottles glug-a-glug with requisitioned wine. Requisitioned women, girls, and boys with toothpick legs in wide short pants easily shed, getting by however they could in the khaki, jeep-revving, saluting and placarded, occasionally kilted (Highlanders), kepied (French officers), or even turbaned (the Moroccan goums) carnival of the Allied rear echelon. In Naples, distinctions between "liberated" and "conquered," like those between "requisitioned" and "pillaged," had never been more than semantic.

Skirts up for food! Kneeling, gobbling, and swallowing for a promise of medicine. Bent over a jeep, oil drum, or desk for a vague guarantee of a job scrubbing pans. Brisk trade in C rations, cigarettes, jump boots, chewing gum, jerricans, typewriters, watches, gasoline, blankets, daughters, and penicillin. Dogs mostly were spared, at least boys don't get pregnant and I didn't know half of it. The Army censors and Roy only let me print a tenth: "Bacchanapoli," *Regent's*, April 12, 1944.

On my five or six jaunts there, Pam the good girl (well, I was, Panama! An Anzio Bobbsey twin, as deficient in Italian as I'd been when I was trying to interview Count Sforza, I never sold so much as a pair of black-market stockings. Never walked even once down a rot-smeary, rat-scrabbled, rut-perfumed street fondling a virginal pack of Lucky Strikes, flushed with disquieting awareness that the one with big eyes or the one with small children would do anything at all if I could only explain it. Hell, no. Your Gramela had 'em, she smoked 'em) mostly knew the classy end of the Napoli bacchanal. Those were the parties thrown by Naples's scuttling mobs of Army and Navy PRO's for visiting firemen from brass hats and editors to Congressional junketeers and USO stars. They had real Stateside brand liquor and something hotter and fresher than "O Sole Mio" on a working gramophone.

Got away mostly unscathed, twisted and no doubt unsatisfyingly unhillocked nipples aside, and never went until I was sure work, tap, tap, tap, was done for the day. While I never saw Bill at those, his absence proves nothing. I couldn't be everywhere and there were usually several of them going on.

But the Second Front was my story, had been Roy's goal for Pam all along. Once I'd finished "Bacchanapoli," I knew I'd better get a move on if I wanted a prayer of seeing D-Day from a landing craft's prow. Hadn't once thought of scheming to get ashore, that was Eddie Whitling's improvised gift. What I did know was Bill wouldn't be going, since Italy's guys were his guys.

He only got to France when they did in the second landing in August. Once I knew we shared a country again, I passed up opportunities to bump into him. By then I had a cynical, talkative, quip-prone, and humiliating reason to avoid him.

His sendoff at Anzio had been fond but unsatisfactory. "I'll see you, Pammie. Who knows, maybe even in New York. I'll find out who's in Grant's Tomb if it kills me." We didn't even hug. You'll have a hard time believing this, bikini girl, but back then people only embraced in public if they were Italian, related—which we had been, but weren't now—or lovers.

In Naples, I sued a general who'd twisted my nipples to let me fly as cargo on a C-47 hop to Gibraltar. Saw the Rock for the first and last time. Adios, Bill.

England was barrage balloons over Parliament, "Ma'am" in pubs and every other street's still smashed eyeglasses from the Blitz staring in a daze at my long gams and cunt cap. It was Ike pacing the Southwick House lawn in our reportorial circle, chain smoking, realizing I was the one correspondent he didn't know. "*Regent's*, huh? Where you from, Miss Buchanan?"

"That's a hell of a long story, sir. But I digress. So, the Free French…" He cracked up damn near gratefully. Knowing what his burdens were, I've boasted since that I once made him laugh.

England was also almost instantly Eddie, who bragged he'd do better when he wasn't knackered by liquor and did. I was in that overwrought condition where it seems like a miracle that anyone at all wants to sleep with you. Yet there had been those nipple-twisting Napoli generals, not to mention Floyd Young, and I knew my real willingness—how well life prepared me for life as a Foreign Service wife, all in all—was geographic. I needed a new country to be fuckable again.

We sailed for the invasion aboard the *Maloy*. A DE or destroyer escort, not much interesting about it except it was the 29th's floating headquarters and one of its bridge signalmen was eighteen-year-old Ned Finn, years later the cigaretted, alcoholic DCM to my Cadwaller in Nagon. (Deputy Chief of Mission, Panama. Honestly, bikini girl! Respect your great-grandfather and whatever you do, don't end up hungry in Naples in wartime. I don't and I can't want to see you that way.) Shaking hands on Plon-Plon-Ville's long jetty before he brushed dear Nan and then their children forward, we knew better than to pretend we'd had the remotest cognizance of each other on invasion day. Like Cadwaller, Ned and I both knew how huge, clankingly scary, and monstrously impersonal it had been.

Twisted this way and that by the waves, bumped by the planet's indifference against that Martian alphabet of German obstacles, a few dozen of morning's waterlogged dead were still being prepped for eternity's surgery when I—I, Daisy Buchanan's daughter, I, Ram-Pam-Pam; I, Pomme—waded past them on that one and only day. Not wanting to make every step a slogging flounce, but you know how it is with surf. Your choice is Columbus or an anonymous corpse. Then I ditched my misleadingly Red-Crossed helmet before anyone could feebly or urgently call, and Eddie and I each got to work chasing up somebody who still had the power of speech to tell us about it.

One thing about an invasion beach is that for the life of you you can't tell where all the *junk* came from. Look at one of the most often reproduced photographs of our men going ashore, snapped from the landing craft they've just left, and your eye is caught by a mystifying tangle of white on the ramp. Toilet paper, bandage roll? No, Panama: kung pao. By the time I reached Omaha there was junk everywhere. Gear that had burst its stuffings, bloodied French phrase books, even a typewriter from some clerical unit clearly sent in too soon. Armed Forces edition of a pulp paperback called *The Dark Deadline*. It was as if we'd hurled our attics at the Germans, not our army.

The clutch of first-wave survivors Eddie induced to sing "Happy Birthday" to me was on the shale near a trackless bulldozer. Some were still wearing their waist-cinching life preservers, those odd cummerbunds of D-Day that, more than any other single detail, bring back Pam's twenty-fourth birthday when I spot them in photographs. But they were all so bewildered that, incredibly, not one wanted to smoke.

The few who reached the sea wall had stayed huddled there in a trance of fear, taking more casualties but uncommanded, scattered, mostly weaponless, and at a loss for any behavior except waiting dully for themselves or someone else to get hit, like children in a brutal orphanage, as one hour piled onto the next and wreckage piled onto wreckage. Eventually, once the Navy's destroyers started chancing destruction themselves by steaming dangerously inshore to pelt the bluffs with five-inch shells (Cadwaller's corvette's popgun played its part), Norman Cota, the 29th's assistant commander, had pried some Rangers, engineers, and gamer infantrymen to their feet to take and clear the beach exit. These boys hadn't been among them, though. Since six-thirty a.m., they hadn't been among anyone.

Mr. Spielberg? That was Omaha. Not your hardy Ranger outfit, with its forty-two-year-old (!) Captain Tom, that somehow recovers from being annihilated at the waterline to get up the bluffs and start wiping out Jerries in twenty-five intrepid minutes. At low tide the real Omaha, unlike yours, forced them to cross at least a hundred yards before they got to dry sand, much less shelter.

Anyhow, companies that have just been annihilated don't slaughter anybody. They aren't in the mood and the 29th, unlike the Big Red One, had never seen action. I will never understand why that massively planned invasion's planners pitched an unblooded unit at Omaha, unless they knew that whoever landed first was going to get massacred and the choice of the virgin 29th was sacrificial.

And oh, Mr. Spielberg! Indulge me, I'm elderly and I shan't be around too much longer. Where did those paratroopers come from? Paratroopers— behind *Omaha?* They landed on the Cotentin side and any patrol sent out to rescue your private would've started from Utah. With Carentan still in dispute, Eddie and I couldn't even get over there until June 13 or so. But Utah Beach wasn't gory enough for you, was it?, so you cheated. You cheated for the exciting sake of your bloodbath.

Don't misunderstand, daisysdaughter.com readers. My fight is with thrills disguised as kung pao, not D-Day's enshrinement alongside Bunker Hill and Gettysburg. No doubt you'd believe your Gramela if I said I'd witnessed all three.

It took us dull weeks and weeks to nudge the Germans out of Normandy's hedgerows. The Battle of the Bocage was Brad under apple trees beside his command trailer, bareheaded unless Bernard Law Montgomery was due to visit. With its Aussie and tanker badges, Monty's beret required a helmeted Brad so that *our* wispy-haired general wouldn't look like an *American Gothic* farmer in newsreels. It was a luckless, fuckless Eddie and a luckless, fuckless Pam scouring narrow, tree-Gothicked, hotly jammed roads as we looked for a story that wouldn't just be the same one with altered coordinates and a different unit and more dead cows.

We said the hell with it one day in July, flagged down a truck headed beachward to flag down a supply ship returning to England. Spent two nights making naked kung pao in a Plymouth hotel before Pam, safety-pinning her otiose bra's broken strap, retreated to London to tap out "The Stalemate." It never saw print: when we got back to France, Operation COBRA had started. The bocage gave way at Falaise.

Paris was a mezzotint kermess, possibly the only one those urbanites have ever yielded to without restraint. Paris was a mass: de Gaulle's. Paris was flowers, Mme Chignonne's and the Paris footlocker's poisoned, therefore preauthenticated kung pao, from dead Daisy's typewriter on top of *The Gold-Hatted Lover's* amok drafts to two velvet cases holding one engraved gold syringe—beyond a glint of doubt, my mother's, its minuscule *Give me your answer do* identifying it unimpeachably as the Lotus Eater's Charybdean gift—and one unengraved silver one. Q.E.D., the L.E.'s own, despite Pam's fallibly colored memory of the one time a budding pudding had seen its roseate gleam in the L.E.'s soft paw.

Put both syringes back and snapped both cases shut, haven't looked at them since. But I know they're still down there, trapped like women miners in snapshots and rubbish. All I ever rescued was dead Daisy's typewriter, determined to make "Like mother, like daughter" come true only in the arena where I had a track record—*by Pamela Buchanan*—and knew she had failed.

What you won't see on the footlocker's lid, much less in the kung pao–challenged (Glenn Ford! Kirk Douglas!) *Is Paris Burning?*, are two palmprints: Pam's own. Months late, Eddie'd just read "Bacchanapoli," and I'd rather not consider that he might've been imagining my long gams as toothpicks and my bloomers as shorts. Yet Paris addled me too, and we spent a week in a swim of notional identities and light-hearted transformational games ("Pretend you're nice today, Eddie. All day," I commanded. He said "Okay": did a crackerjack job) before we woke up one afternoon and remembered somebody'd told us Patton was on the Meuse. By the time we got to it ourselves, his columns had stopped: no more gas.

I had even less use for Patton than Bill did, from his high-pitched squeaky voice to his humps with the Red Cross girl we all knew was his niece: two bits of kung pao *Patton* left out. Of course the whole thing is just a big musical, with the hard-working (on film) Spanish army as both the Sharks and the Jets in its lavish production numbers. The niece killed herself, by the way.

Worsening weather, rain in our bones where the marrow had been, forests so dark and grim breadcrumbs would've been useless: that was the Huertgen. Navigation skills boxed and outfoxed by too many trees, we kept getting lost, which was scary. We'd orient ourselves by which way the beat-up stretcher bearers were jogging, shamed—at least I was—that spotting them was a relief.

Division after division got put in and chewed up there, to this day no one knows why. For the first time I felt disgusted around combat generals, not just rear-echelon ones. So we said the hell with it again, headed back to now dripping and pigeon-gray Paris to fuck-booze-munch-ablute some more. But played no light-hearted transformational games, our tribute I suppose to knowing the war had gone bad.

You know what falling snow means in this story, don't you, bikini girl? If you don't, your dad's been remiss. The Ardennes was where outfits bled white in the Huertgen and the grass-green new 106th got sent for either a reprieve from or a mild smattering foretaste of combat. Ten Panzer divisions hit the thinly held line.

On the mend after Holland, one debacle Pam neither witnessed nor wrote, the 101st Airborne got pulled out of its rest camps, shuttled up to hold onto Bastogne. In swirls of icy confetti not far from Neufchateau, I watched the trucks rolling by and heard a shout I still cherish.

"Hey, *Regent's*—hey, red! Miss Buchanan! Remember me? Carentan! Hey, what the hell is new since?"

"Beats me, soldier! Everything!" I was walking in icy confetti and mud alongside. "Where you headed?"

"Some shithole!"

"Well, I know that, sonny! Some help..."

His tailgated face had vroomed on before "...you are!" Identical but for his shout, other trucks came bumbling and lumbering through icy confetti. They didn't even have winter overcoats, Panama. Like most of our army in Europe, they didn't have a lot of practice *defending* much either, but they turned out to be good at it. More determined, in fact—and you might as well know what Ike, Brad, and Patton all knew—than our reluctant GIs ever were when attacking. That's why the Germans only broke when the weather did and our fighter-bombers could hit them.

That was the Bulge. But not *The Battle of the Bulge*, a largely snowless—and mudless, witless, characterless, pointless, indeed everything but deathless—affair that may have the least kung pao of any movie I've seen. I can only imagine management's mixed feelings at District movie houses when they saw Mrs. Cadwaller march up in the Sixties and Seventies for the latest World War Two epic. They knew I'd yell rude things and hoot before walking out early, but without me they'd have been screening the matinees for mice and cockroaches, from *Rome Dead Ahead*—with that callow idiot Chuck Troy impersonating the GI I was sure he'd never been in real life—to *The Bridge at Remagen*. Seen on Tim Cadwaller's recommendation when I'd about given up (of course all these movies litter the index of *You Must Remember This*), only *The Big Red One* had what makes kung pao irrelevant: the right poetry.

As the war's way-back-when grew more distant, what frustrated me most was even the costliest epic's inadequacy at conveying even a pitiful facsimile of the *size* of the thing. It didn't take place in bespoke bits of landscape churned up in all too visibly limited ways that wouldn't annoy the banks, TV aerials, and Volkswageny flows of vacation traffic just off camera. It was our everything and Europe's everywhere.

The few vestigial bits of what you're pleased to call ordinary life—whose return inside a decade to West Berlin, even, no one who'd seen it as rubble and big masonry eyes would ever stop finding preposterous—were what seemed pointlessly contrived and stupid. Even in exhilaration, we Americans were mundane to ourselves, of course, but amazing to everyone else. In the real town of Remagen, when I saw a woman the age I am now clucking endearments as she fed her cat an unbelievably precious sardine, I almost jumped out of our jeep to go smack the demented old hag. Yet I'd have done the same for Kelquen.

Never saw *Schindler's List*, Mr. Spielberg, and sorry. A man who can't get Tinkerbell right isn't my idea of a good guide to Auschwitz and by then I was seventy-three. But my Dachau you know: "I'm Nachum Unger—Nachum Unger, the poet. We are colleagues. *Here I am.*" And you know its kung pao, which I've never recorded until a soon-to-be-gone-with-the-wind Pam did: "Hey, fuck you, Maggie! I got here first." If he heard me, Nachum might've had a thing or two to say about that.

As for Pam's own failure, well. Withered as they are by now, the Glendale memories in Pink Thing's archives say I'd find Peg Kimball's kung pao–less antics with Chet Dooley and Eddie Harting in *The Gal I Left Behind Me* excruciating. That one started with me and so I bear the blame. Hearing Andy Pond tell me he'd rented the damn thing for my birthday would've been reason enough to seize Cadwaller's gun even if I'd been feeling merry up to then.

Yet over the years, I've also told myself that for Peg Kimball's 1948–49 to do justice to Pam's 1944–45, *The Gal* would've had to last sixteen hours, be unwatchable, cost half the country's GNP, and require its audience not to bathe for a week as part of the price of admission. Breaking new ground in kung pao, Eddie Whitling's Flynn would appear as itself—and if I knew it and its owner, demand top billing too.

I didn't write *The Naked and the Dead* or even *The Young Lions*, let alone *The Gallery*. I wrote *Nothing Like a Dame* instead. Pam may just lack a novelist's urge to transmute haywire events into concentrated truths, alchemizing how-it-was into a raftered here-I-am. Much less, with wretched "Chanson d'automne" at once the exception and the proof, a poet's: "Minds crabwise interlock, with luck, and scuttle/Then it's done."

That's from Addison's "To My Wife on Some Anniversary," if you're wondering. It's in *The Pilgrim Lands at Malibu* and too few anthologies. When I was actually at work on *Dame*, yanking each day's final page from the roller so I could shimmy into Manhattan via pumpkining taxicab, I never felt I was recording. I felt I was living, suiting my priorities.

As for the rest, isn't it enough it all happened? And has stayed imprinted, untransmuted but there, on my elderly mimsies, nostrils, cerebellum, and skin. Like everyone else's from Bill M.'s to Cadwaller's, Pam's Second World War will all only unhappen at the instant I die.

Sorry, Tim. I can't do it, though as you see I've just tried. It's futile. Just waves slapping bodies, engine noise always, food out of cans. Too many cigarettes, hairy black icebergs, mud and shouts, fucking. Sometimes I wake to a thunderstorm and think they have our range.

POSTED BY: *Pam*   At my age, however, one's memories dwell as much or more on what *didn't* happen, which can mean things that might've but didn't or things you aren't wholly sure did. The day in 1951 when thirty-one-year-old Pammie Gerson, a blissfully childless producer's wife who hadn't yet conceived *Glory Be*, realized her life in Los Angeles had crossed over irrevocably from a light-hearted transformational game into confining if pleasant kung pao had elements of both.

Gerson and I had been married two years. As I've said and his warm letters after our divorce confirm, we were happy. When Pink Thing plays safecracker, though, I'm forced to accuse myself—for his sake, not mine—of treating my second marriage as a respite. A lulling sanatorium stopover, prefigured by Metro's whitewashed buildings and green lawns on my first Gersonized tour of the lot.

That morning in our now twice redecorated Beverly Hills home—Stella Negroponte's picture, what did I care?, still watching from the den—my husband had let out a swiftly muted cry. The script he'd found in his briefcase was supposed to have been messengered the previous day to some actor or actress whose name I don't recall. He was addled enough to reach for an already emptied juice glass.

"Pammie, I hate having to ask. Could you please, please run this up to Malibu? We're in horrible rewrites on *That's All She Wrote*"—one of Gerson's sorrows, originally based on Abigail Adams's correspondence. "You know I'd do it, but I don't have time."

Was I resentful? It's possible. A request that mars your day's plans is as nothing irritation-wise to one that interferes with none. A week had gone by since my welcoming telegram and it was obvious Bill M. wasn't going to take Pam up on her offer to play the knowledgeable Los Angelena while he was back in town.

If he had, of course I'd've had to tell Gerson the truth *The Gal* had so nearly hit on. It would've been worth it to see Bill again. And possibly, now it was all in the past tense, confess to him too, with the amused valedictory laugh at my youthful foibles I was getting so good at. Sometimes one quick candled look in a restaurant gives you all you didn't have in an instant, sparing both parties the trouble of having lived through it but nonetheless curing regret.

In a modest rebellion once Gerson's Packard scooted offscreen (our front window was Beverly Hills Panavision), I phoned up the DeWitts for a lunch date. Since I'd be going out their way anyhow, I'd drop off the script after a good meal and some enjoyably surf-pearled Manhattanish banter. I was ignoring a stricken face's plea of the sooner the better.

Luscious Eve was off shooting: Manley Halliday's *The Night's High Noon*, I think. Addison said he'd be tickled mauve just the same. As usual, he proposed their Filipino cook's warthog sandwiches—his delighted description, not mine. But I'd spent lots of time in their yard's pilgrim lands and the day's warm but wild breeze had me craving the Pacific in closeup. In a rare feat, I convinced him to putter down from their hill and meet me in Eve's and my favorite restaurant, glassed-in and exclusive but hunkered out at the far end of a weathered fishing pier near Porto Marina Way.

The juxtapositions of leather wine list and fried seafood, fine china and sandals, wind and protection from it defined the California I'd come to adore. God, how Tim and I both loathe Joan Didion, who flatters East Coasters by treating such stuff as a vulgarization without ever explaining what it's a vulgarization of or how you go about vulgarizing something unprecedented.

In a Hawaiian shirt that was dreadful even by his standards—"Jekyll and hydrangeas," he bragged—Addison dropped into the facing chair. I was instantly overdressed by comparison in a bronze silk blouse, copper scarf, beige toreadors, low-heeled fawn shoes, and modest peach handbag. When friendship's unflustered edition of silence came over us after updates and gossip, we gazed at the beach's dotted idyll: tiny lovelies with their interchangeable Chucks, gulls soaring like punctuation hunting the sky's nonexistent sentence. He looked so tranquilly pleased I decided to tease him with beatitude's opposite: "Do you envy them, Addison?"

Judging from how his eyes had to drop as well as turn to meet mine, he'd misunderstood me slightly. "Oh, Pam! We're all creatures and the rest is verbiage. That's really all my verbiage is about."

Our food came. Recalling now dead and obscure (not in that order) Sinclair St. Clair's Provincetown jingle from Pammie's childhood, I recited. Tickled purple, Addison wanted to memorize it: "'To eat an oyster/You crack it foister/ This part is moister!...' Wait, what's the last line again?"

As we crunched back over gravel to our metallurgic cars, the beach's squeals and caws becoming audible as their source grew invisible, I remembered Gerson's script with distaste. "Addison!" I called, eyeing it in the back seat. "Do you know where Blank Blank lives?"

"My dear girl, I'm a poet. I study how people live"—grand sweep of his car keys—"not where. To find my way home, I just keep going up."

In an un-Gersonishly hasty scribble, the address was on the envelope. I still needed help. Damn few of the surf-facing houses on the coastal highway's beach side sported visible numbers then or maybe now. Too prey to fans, not yet called stalkers but anathema all the same. Mailmen must've loved Malibu in 1951.

As for why I've long forgotten the name and even gender of the star Gerson was pursuing, your guess is as good as mine. Mine is that the erasure is Pink Thing's archival way of mimicking the fact that Glen or Glenda never starred in that film, title also gone to oblivion and evidently unproduced. I'd know it if it were among my second husband's credits on imdb.com, a website whose name I sometimes read as "I'm D.B.": Daisy Buchanan.

Near Topanga Canyon Boulevard, Gerson had said. More irked at that sweet man than I could ever remember being, I parked when I got to it and set out, the script swinging like a second handbag to metronome my real one. Found one boite with a fearlessly displayed address under twenty digits lower than mine, so at least he hadn't been lying. But its neighbors' expensive roofs and protectively recessed, unnumbered doorways wandered away from Pam's sight as if queuing for an invasion of Canada.

Nothing for it: I'd have to find someone to ask. The odds of spotting any Malibu resident in reach of my halloo on the *highway* side were about as good, though for the opposite reason, as seeing convicts wander at will outside a maximum-security prison. They kept to themselves, those exiles from availability: on the beach side, with architecture to match. When you drive past, you're really looking at their houses' anuses, not facades.

Spotting a thumb of white with its nail painted blue in an unfenced gap between two boites, grimly aware the breeze had played hob with a hairdo that had been hobbled even at Antoine's, I plunged into the sand, my miscast shoes sinking like miscast actors' hearts. Out back, since the beach was the whole bloody point, I knew I'd see somebody hallooable. Maybe even, by good fortune, run right into Blank Blank him/herself.

To my shock—but why? It wasn't that unlikely—someone hallooed me instead. "Why, Pam! Pam Buchanan. That *is* you at last, isn't it?"

Turning, I found myself face to face with a woman's apparently decapitated head. We weren't precisely eye to eye, since her pleased blue ones, pellet nose, and rich red pulpit mouth were perpendicular to mine inside a dark crater of tangled bangs and between two slats of the house's raised beach-side deck. The rest of the railing was mostly screened by bright Navajo rugs, explaining the Mary-Queen-of-Scots effect.

"Well, hello!" I said, purse and script dangling at my beige toreadors' flanks. I couldn't remember who the fuck she was.

"This is so nice! Come around that way," said she with a lift of her chin, meaning the stairs on the deck's far side.

As I did as told, I was racking what was left of my brains after lunch's two bottles of Riesling. I knew her face wasn't famous, but then what was she? Director's wife, actor's mistress, child star's mother? My guess is I'd met some two thousand of movieland's crème de la foam, and she really could have been anybody. In Hollywood, you never knew when a forgotten handshake would turn out two years later to be the shakee's conception of sisterly intimacy. Unless her chat dropped a hint or she tactfully recognized the problem—had she looked tactful? Hard to say, since California faces can be as friendly without implying tact as Manhattan ones can be tactful without implying friendliness—and told me her name, I was stuck.

While I wouldn't call it a hint, it was certainly intimate. As I reached the top step and all of her sat up, naked as the day we were born, her small breasts stopped pouting and grinned.

She hadn't sat up before then, you ask? You don't know California. Hands to her sides like a swimmer at rest, upper baubles two dark stoppers on those little brown jugs and thatch going from crackle to cruciform as I came up the stairs, she was taking the sun and had even reclosed her eyes. Ten more seconds was ten more seconds.

"Isn't it wonderful? After all this time too. I didn't even know you lived out this far," she said eagerly, drawing up her knees. Only for balance as the deck braced her palms, though, not from self-consciousness.

"Me? Oh, God, no. I'm just, ah—" My purse and Gerson's script fidgeted as if I was unsure which was the right token.

"Oh, of course. I should've known from that handbag you didn't, shouldn't I? Rodeo Drive's satchel is Malibu's porte-monnaie." Proving that, whoever or whatever she was, she did have an eye for the telling detail.

Her grin counted on me to appreciate it, too. Her question asked Pam's approval, but before I could answer—how I would've beats me—she'd deduced that my fidgets, along with my pause on the weathered top step, might have a meaning that surprised her.

"I'm sorry! I'm stupid from sun. It never crossed my mind you were shy. 'Nothing like a dame!' But I can—"

As she tilted one haunch, her eyes still on me politely, the arm that reached for her towel was at once ceremonial and a genuine concession, what with every inch of that compact body plainly craving more radiance, heat, breeze, and salt air. Craving everything except the gull droppings, so far as I could tell.

"Oh, no. It's perfectly all right," I told her, showing a cool I didn't feel by stepping onto the deck proper. Of course anyone who adds "perfectly" to "all right" doesn't know what he or she's talking about and is hoping to fool people. "I'm just—"

"Silly, isn't it? He likes me dark all over," she cackled. "Marry in haste and repaint at leisure, I guess. I'll be black by the wedding. Of course you can't come."

See what I mean about friendliness without tact? "Oh, I'll live," I said.

"Let's just hope I do! Say, is that your new book? Please tell me it is." She meant Gerson's envelope. "Of course you remember how I loved your first one."

Did that help? Not much. Of Pam's two thousand or so dabs of movieland's crème de la foam, maybe six hundred had said they loved *Nothing*. Some two hundred of those had gone on to strenuously demonstrate they were familiar with *Nothing*'s contents. The other four hundred plainly felt just knowing *Nothing*'s name was enough. "Take that, Joan," I can almost hear Tim say.

Speaking of tact, you may wonder why Pam—a well-bred product of Mme Chignonne's, Purcey's Academy, and briefly Barnard—hadn't opted for civilized honesty: "I'm so terribly sorry, how do we know each other?" and so forth. With much winning facial and gestural embroidery to convey only a fellow member of our overcrammed crowd would understand my plight.

Well, it was a bit goddam late for that, bucko. Couldn't tell someone naked who was acting this fond of me I didn't have a clue who she was. As soon as I'd considered the *noblesse oblige* route, I'd imagined breezeblown dark bangs and cruciform crackle catching fire in the sun to cinderize her to parchment. In other words, I'd pictured this whole mirage vanishing, putting paid to a trance I wanted to end but not that way.

"This? Oh, no. Just somebody else's script. I'm just—"

"We've seen enough of those!" the Great Unknown laughed. "I'm making sun tea. Would you like some?"

"I'm sorry?"

"You don't boil it. Desert trick. Put it out in the sun and it steeps." She nodded to a screwtop jar of auburn liquid on the railing that I hadn't noticed before. I doubt I'd have noticed if she'd had an ack-ack gun hooked there.

"Wait a sec. I'll get ice and glasses." One tanned arm scything out at me, the Great Unknown made as if to stand up. "Sugar or lemon for you?"

"Oh, neither! I'm just—"

Seeing *more* of that trim practical body wasn't my idea of a health program. Nor hers, since trying to rise started her coughing.

"Oh, brother! What an awful racket. Let's make it worse, see." Squatting on her heels Indian-style—in profile, but my *saints*—she reached for cigarettes. "Want one?"

"No, thank you. You see, I'm just—"

Whoever was puissant enough to like the Great Unknown darker all over and get his way, he wasn't a movie star, big-league director, or paunchy gent toasting beside That Hotel's pool. All three kinds of panjandrum said "Next" when a bathing beauty turned twenty-five and this one was closer to my age, Hollywood death to us both if we hadn't had brains or other connections. The smile and her limberness had made me hesitate, but her cackle had been the first giveaway. My own raucous whoop, Pam's party trumpet by the New Frontier, had budded in 1950.

"Maybe I should just let you finish your sentence," she laughed, squatting and smoking. "I haven't let you get a word in edgewise. And you're Pam Buchanan, for Christ's sake! Who I've waited so long to meet."

"I'm sorry," I said. "I'd love to stay awhile, truly! But I can't! I'm on duty, you see. I can't find Blank Blank's house and I've got this stupid purse, script, to deliver."

"Oh, is *that* all?" The Great Unknown scrambled up, stood near Pam. Pam guessed the Navajo rugs were only decorative after all. "It's the one with the blue awning, just down there." She aimed with her cigarette hand.

"It looks like a mausoleum for tropical fish," I said.

"God, that's just like you! It used to belong to Monroe"—and she hesitated—"Monroe Stahr. But he died without ever living there."

Now that we were side by side, the most obvious difference—I mean aside from her being so richly naked, Pam so impoverishedly clothed in Rodeo Drive's copper, bronze, and beige best—was that I was taller. I don't mean we were twins, just in the same general league looks-wise. Yet she was a pure emanation of Los Angeles, I a collection of scattered lives from East Egg to war that had wired itself into a semblance of nativity. I'd thought it genuine because I'd unconsciously thought it temporary.

I could live out my life here and still only be bivouacking. I'd never offer my skin to the sun with such assurance my reward would be the Pacific's answer to Chanel, from faint tingle of cinnamon to heat of proud driftwood.

It only lasted a beat, as actors call seconds. Then I said, "Thanks ever so much! See you later."

"I hope so."

I was back down the steps when she called me. "Oh, Pam!"

I looked up, which I'd never done before at her. Since it was a clear day, they must've seen that smile and those dark stoppers winking all the way from Redondo.

"Yes?"

"Come back when you've dropped it, why don't you? I'll give you sun tea. Or if you like, wine! One bottle between us and I bet you'll join me."

"Who knows? Maybe I will," I called over my shoulder as I floundered in costly beach flour. My purse and the script were now Malibu skipoles: inadequate ones, neither reaching the ground.

At the one with the blue awning, I got told Blank Blank wasn't home. A woman servant accepted *The Script Not Taken* on her hermaphrodite employer's behalf. Once I'd agreed with Manuela I had a car waiting, not precisely a lie, she showed me out at the street door. As I trudged up on the highway side past a Greyhound bus I'd neither catch nor ride to the convertible I duly got into, drove away in, and soon traded in for an Olds, I realized I'd never know for sure behind which of these hideouts the Great Unknown lay waiting with sun tea.

Why did it matter? Wasn't that a relief? Oh—scythe, my foot. You're so fucking easy, you know? You're so scared of cigarettes, too much sun, and name-lessness. The Great Unknown wasn't death or the devil's dark bride.

Did you really think daisysdaughter.com had gone supernatural? No, no. As I'd told Bill at Chasen's three years earlier, I had lots of voices in my head. But they all belonged to real people, including the Lotus Eater. Her little cry of "That's death!" had sent me from a gimlet to the ETO. Then this and that happened and here I was now, too beigely burdened and frightened to answer that cry's contradiction in Malibu.

"I am California," the Great Unknown's bare skin had whispered as we stood side by side. "I'm sun, money, plenitude, joy. I was the victory in the war that you saw and the proof is I know nothing of it. I'm the reason you came here and the champagne that kissed you when you came down the ramp, and you should have listened to both poets you know. We are all creatures and the rest is verbiage. Here I am. What we might have done if you'd accepted my sun tea wouldn't have bound you to any future at all, don't you see? We'd both have been back in our lives before midnight. But you might have had a few naked hours as the Pam you most dream of—*still, still*—before it was too late, since youth is the one god I, California, have been cursed by my makers from Cortez to Metro to kneel to. You can't have everything, can you?"

My one gesture indicating I'd like to broker a compromise was fairly pathetic. Once I'd tipped the sand from my shoes, I didn't put them back on, walked back up to my car with them hung from the hand Gerson's script had been in and hot asphalt and mica bits searing my soles. How my eyes scoured those hooded pink houses as I walked past them on the burning road, number-less, cuneiform, cruciform—oh, drat.

I loyst her.

2. *Glory Be*

POSTED BY: *Pambidextrous*   I know, daisysdaughter.com readers if any: this is certainly adding up to quite the Guinness-bound amount of verbiage for an online suicide note. The more so as Pam's second D-Day is still in Leopoldinely robust bloom outside my window.

People who only own digital clocks don't know what a glad little company of mimes they're missing. Watching two p.m. perform its sailorlike semaphore just now, I thought what I often do: Ned Finn's hour. Bridge signalman on the *Maloy* off Omaha, remember? Spared only by a premature death from witnessing his and dear Nan's strange son's career as a disturbingly licentious creator of comic books derived from his upbringing in what he calls the superpower diaspora.

To think that when I knew him as a child in Nagon, all that brat cared about was *The Longest Day*. Ned and Nan's paperback copy looked like a card deck afflicted with leprosy (the climate's doing, not Sean's, just so I won't be misunderstood) by the time Ambassador Cadwaller's wife replaced it with her own. I suppose we can count ourselves lucky he's moved on, puberty no doubt a big help on that front.

Tim Cadwaller thinks highly of Sean's stapled output, from *Lovely Sybil, Meter Maid* to *Cynthia's Icicles* and *The Brothers Vane*. To my imperfectly concealed dismay, they've even discussed collaborating on some sort of fairy-tale saga stuffed with souvenirs and fantasies of what used to be called the American Century, disguised as some implausible relic's bleats and croons from the good old *Titanic's* engine room. Can't say as I'll regret not being around for that one should it materialize, thanks to Cadwaller's gun putting paid to my memories of the real thing at long last.

As for Pam's birthday fecundity, what I can I say? After a lifetime as a writer of, *Dame* aside, more or less careful prose, I do feel a mad glee at yoicksing on without a second look. It's probably obvious to anyone who knows writing that I'm not in it for the style, much less the sneaky bracketing of surface randomness into a gunsight's hatchmarks that always lets my betters claim the reader pulled the trigger. That doesn't mean these fat-lunetted mimsies and rheumatic fingers of mine would so terribly mind a *bit* of encouragement from you mysteries out there. Still no comments when I homepage, and would it really kill you to chime in with a kind or unkind word?

But even if you're Panama, please don't try to dissuade me from using her great-grandfather's gun. With or without the White House's telephonic Potus *ex machina*, I can't think of a single argument or unlikely promise of transcendence this bloodstained beachball could offer that would tempt me to wake up in one piece on June 7—or D Plus One, as it was in 1944. The blog sent forth can never be recalled, Chekhov was right about pistols, and daisysdaughter.com will have wasted your time if you don't see a mess of pink and gray things on the rug at the end. Finito, *dans le tapis sanglotant.*

In the meantime, disbelieve *l'équipe*'s wordflow if you like. If I were sailing under literature's skull and crossbones, I could point to those tales Conrad's Marlow ostensibly starts telling after dinner and continues as the coffee grows first cold, then moldy, then unchucked only because the Malayan houseboy has died of old age. As I'm inputting in real time, my preferred example is nonfiction: *I Was Dolly Haze's Monster*, initially titled *The Confessions of a White Widowed Male* and meant for an exclusively diagnostic audience before its editor, one Dr. John Ray, saw reason in the form of paperback greenbacks. Gerson and I once shared a table with that dull man at the Gene Kellys'.

On the drive home, we agreed it was extraordinary that someone could have sat across a table from the now notorious "H.H." and be so unperfumed by either magic or cyanide. In town to visit his brother Nick, all Dr. Ray wanted to talk about was the book's screen chances. Don't blame Gerson for being evasive. Typically, my warmhearted husband was more curious about whether the poor little girl really had died in childbirth—which was when, interestingly, Dr. Ray grew evasive.

Though I was kind enough to murmur a hard-won warning ("Charades") once coffee and dessert showed up, I'm a writer. I was most fascinated by the introduction's claim that the perp had dashed off the whole incredible Taj Mahal in fifty-six presumably harried days. Nicholas Ray's boring brother assured me it was true, and I know I'm not in the same league as a stylist or nostalgist.

Nonetheless, if Dr. Ray's patient could do his thing in that timespan, you'd better believe Daisy Buchanan's daughter can do my lesser mine in this.

POSTED BY: *Pam*   Nothing emblazons the Fifties notoriety of *I Was Dolly Haze's Monster* like Gerson's familiarity with it. My husband read very little but history in his non-Metro hours. In Stella Negroponte's room, as I thought of the den, a whole wall was grimmed up by what Civil War buffs know simply as the *O.R.: the Official Records of the War of the Rebellion.* Its 128 volumes contained every scrap about every scrap from Grant's after-action report on Fort Donelson to Lee's lost message at Sharpsburg.

To either flank, more bookcases massed reinforcements. Presidential biographies, books on the Revolution and the Founding Fathers, the opening of the West and the mind of the South. During too much of my second marriage, Pam's mute nickname for Parkman, Catton, and Beard was Winken, Blinken, and Nod.

As you may've recognized, Gerson's bent was American. Wylie White had pegged him as an unrequited wooer, and I'm afraid the future mimsy borogoves had a mite or mote of condescension in them as well. However jostled Pam's unbringing, I was a near Mayfloral member of the old circus troupe. Jamestown on the Fay side, dimly related on the paternal to none other than James Buchanan—our fifteenth President, Panama, and quite the worst until recently. The DAR's wastebasketed importunings made our mailman sweat even before *Glory Be* came out.

Indifferent to that heritage at thirty, I was bemused by Gerson's attachment to squabbles, warbles, and battles that had been legislated, warbled, and turned into sculpture's equine equanimity well before his own Ellis-aliased clan's arrival during Teddy—not Franklin—Roosevelt's Presidency. But could I really have assumed his motives were *social*, proof I didn't know my man worth beans? Still horridly alert to distinctions between Mayflora and Mayfauna, which Dachau had horridly honed instead of obliterating, I did know that caring in earnest about which Adams came first was no way to blend in.

"Honestly, Gerson," I told him when he corrected me. "It just doesn't matter all that much to us."

"Oh, Pammie!" he said fondly but shrewdly. "Have the grace to say 'me.'"

"If you care, then why don't you care about Europe? Since you don't." I introduced bookshelves.

"We did! And look where that got us."

"We didn't and look where that got *us*," I raged obscurely.

"Let's make a new rule," said Gerson. "No plurals."

"That's a good one," I agreed with affection. All his best insights were terse. "Much better than the silly one about no studio gossip after sunset."

He smiled. "It's all right, Pam. That one was conditional. To be honest, I meant the boulevard."

POSTED BY: *Pam*   Not that we knew it, but Gerson's ulcer-sparing Boulevard Rule—its new name, cited whenever I came from Beverly Hills to collect him—would be obsolete in under two years. Unlike most Hollywoodites, Gerson refused to treat television as Goneril to the big screen's Lear. The more stymied he grew at Metro, the more the new medium brought out his idealism.

At dinners and even breakfast, he'd lecture Judas-eyeing stars and execs—and then Pam, more indulgent but no more convinced—about TV's educational wonders, magical accessibility ("Look, Pammie. Fran's on. Why don't we get in the car, fight traffic for an hour, and *drive* to the living room? You see?"), and best-of-both-worlds blend of privacy and community. Democracy, too: "Let people turn up their noses. Thomas Jefferson wouldn't have. I trust Jefferson more." Once he dragged Jefferson in, I should've known then and there he was going to quit Metro for Rik-Kuk Productions, the Burbank-based company owned by grimace queen Fran Kukla and her husband, Gene Rickey.

Even after the reality had failed his hopes—and I can't imagine I'm spoiling anyone's idea of suspense on *that* score—he stayed scornful of the old screen's gibbering hostility to the new. We were good chums after our divorce, swapped many letters with international postmarks. I recall one of his from '58 that spent half a page of its friendly three excoriating Hollywood's gaudy depiction of the tube-fueled rise of a folksy demagogue.

To Gerson's now uninvolved but still perceptive eyes, *A Face in the Crowd*'s pose as a political warning was hogwash. Its hysteria's real fuel was movieland's hatred of television, "and the real joke is that the *jealousy's* political," he wrote.

"They know Lear buckled to McCarthyism—and Goneril was the dragon slayer. Goneril, not Cordelia. Cordelia was just literature."

Buckle they had, and ingloriously too. Hollywood's one overt protest against the witch hunt predated Pam's time: the planeload of movieland luminaries, Bogart among them, who boldly flew to Washington to stick up for our First Amendment rights. Exercised them again by recanting, Humphrey Dumpty included, as soon as they got back to the Coast. By my second wedding day, covert protests were the rule.

Those included Gerson's own. He hired a lot of blacklisted writers under pseudonyms, not only at Metro—everyone knew "Kent Clark's" super screenplay for *Lean Over the Bridge* was really Wayne Bruce's cowled attack on serving more than one master—but to cook up TV scripts once he'd moved behind his more spacious desk at Rik-Kuk. Thanks to Gene Rickey, that was also when the Boulevard Rule became the Cahuenga Rule, though Pam's new Olds nosed its way to the Valley to pick him up less often than her old convertible had in Culver City days. Since most of our dinner invites were still in Los Angeles, it made more sense for him to come down to me.

Of course, the actors who got named by Pat Carpet and others were out of luck. Unlike Greek tragedians or typewriter-chained trick or treaters, they couldn't don masks. Even though Potusville is spiky with comparisons, it's hard to explain what the blacklist felt like. My advice to Tim Cadwaller, which I'm still fairly pleased with, was that any Hollywood histories of the period that focus on the plague are accurate as to our mood. Those that ignore it are equally so.

Doublethink, Orwell called it. I imagine the years of the blacklist were a lot like the worst AIDS years if you were heterosexual yourself but had friends at risk. With practice, you could switch without forethought from gloom to frivolity a half dozen times while crossing a room at the Kellys'.

Gerson often ended up trailing behind me, since he knew dozens and dozens of people affected; I only a few from my past. One of *Dat Dead Man Dere's* saddest chapters describes Bran's bellicose arrival in Washington, vowing to tell the HUAC to go fly a kite before a clerk explains he's been dropped from the witness list. ("The Chairman wasn't sure who I am, hey? Well, I know who *he* is, God damn it," blustered Murphy, there being reporters about.) When the subpoena came, Hans Caligar decamped back to Germany and joined Brecht's Berliner Ensemble.

Even Jake Cohnstein's brush with the witch hunt was minor. Hoping to stay on in Washington after the war, he got turned down for a job with the new CIA and could guess the reason or reasons. Hence Jake Cohnstein, Professor of Drama at Whitaker College in Chambersburg and author (1954) of *It Was All Theater: From Brannigan Murphy to the Moscow Show Trials.*

Good book, incidentally. Much as I lamented Jake's turn to the right in public and private, it was legitimate, and he Jakishly alienated Red-hunting yahoos by wrapping up *Theater* with a "review" of McCarthy's Senate subcommittee that judged its hearings purely as neo-Muscovite drama: prefiguring my recognition of the Murphy Channel as Bran's right-wing triple doppelganger, "Comrade Joe" was his title. I not only enjoyed our one campus debate but wish we'd had more, since getting fizzy and fuzzy with him before and after was so entertaining.

He and Gerson got along, too. On our New York trips in the Fifties—Bloomie's for me back when it was unique, Fourth Avenue's used bookshops for him back when they were plentiful—Jake was our usual dinner companion unless we had to attend some Metro or later Rik-Kuk and network frouhaha. Too proud to recruit a prop female and too guarded to introduce pals with real beards, he made us a trio, never a quartet. Partly just to reassure myself she'd survived Dachau, I'd have liked to see Sharon Halevy Cohnstein again, but that warm woman had grown more reluctant than ever to leave her Williamsburg nest.

Their son David, the B-17 waist gunner whose invisible presence in a Manhattan courtroom had made Jake's testimony unimpeachable, had been shot down in the first big raid on Schweinfurt just two months after *Murphy v. Murphy* wrapped up. If Sharon had asked, I'd've had no choice but to tell her what I knew about the end product when a parachute—I hoped not made in Scranton—failed to open. She wasn't the type, but I'd met a few.

Their wryness together surprised me at first: Jake and Gerson's, I mean. Now matter how dwindled from militance to mild mindset, Gerson's sympathies were firm enough to normally leave him constrained around harsh anti-Communists. Maybe New York gave him license, as if the witch hunt was only happening—though of course it wasn't—out on the Coast. Besides, though my husband was ten years Jake's junior, they'd grown up in similar milieux before Gerson moved to L.A. in the Thirties. When Jake asked why, my husband told him more than he ever did me: "I just felt too many people had already had the life I would've had if I stayed. You know the feeling." Jake agreed he did.

They shared the same Thirties cosmology: Scottsboro boys, Kirov's murder. Jake enjoyed demonstrating he hadn't *forgotten* his Trotskyite days, just as Gerson liked showing off he hadn't forgotten his East Coast ones. Why be evasive, though? The spark of their shared amusement was as plain as the shiksa between them from our very first dinner at some Italian place in the Village.

Not the usual Hollywood visitor's idea of fine dining, but Gerson loathed "21." "When I'm eating a meal, I like to be on firm ground as a diner," he told me. "I don't like to moonlight as the maitre d." There any pasha from Metro's New York office or, later on, network bigwig could interrupt our meal on a whim, stopping my patient husband's fork or coffee cup with box-office this and ratings that. And Pam had no objections, since "21" was predictably the Lotus Eater's favorite lair under Eisenhower.

As two Gersons goodnighted one Whitaker prof, Jake laughed. "Take good care of our Pam, Noah, please," he said. "I'm invested, you know! I was her *first* Jew." Waved, strolled toward the subway—Williamsburg-, not Chambersburg-bound.

"It just seems unfair!" I told Gerson once we were strolling ourselves. Balmy night for December; we'd only hail a cab when we tired. "I'm your bloody wife and if I so much as mention the word, you look for the pogrom in your martini. But *you* two—oh, no. You can joke all you like, but heaven forbid I join in."

"Minority privilege, Pammie." Gerson was in a good mood. "It's the one kind you'll never enjoy."

"Even if I converted?"

"You'd be a fire engine on a golf course." Then Gerson looked anxious. "Pammie! Jake didn't mean, did he..."

If Jake had, my husband would have been perfectly pleasant, but only if warned. Thanks to the way he'd learned about Eddie Whitling, one rule on

New York trips was that I'd never introduce him *unadvised* to anyone I'd slept with, giving me a fairly sheepish five minutes when I hung up after Roy Charters asked us to cocktails. Unsure of the rule's rules, I had no idea what I'd do if we ever faced lunching with Dottie Idell, but no Crozdettis were listed in any edition of the Manhattan or even Queens, Brooklyn, Bronx, New Jersey, or Connecticut phone books between 1950 and 1956.

My turn to laugh, though. "Oh, God, Gerson! No. My name would've had to be Paul."

That amused him for blocks. He kept calling me Paula for the rest of our stroll and in the cab we flagged down near the Flatiron Building. Kept it up as we spun through our hotel's door. With new decorum, he stopped when we got in the elevator—just before, needless to say, it might've got interesting.

POSTED BY: *Paula*   Though it was no longer fucking in either temper or name, that side of our lives had stayed satisfactory. We had our signals, our favorite spots around the house and on each other, our understood preludes and aftermaths. No matter how tempted Gerson might be to get dressed or read, he knew I needed five minutes' Pompeiian stillness before we uncoupled. Especially with Eddie Whitling behind me—well, I had certainly better rephrase *that*, Ard—Gerson horizontal charmed Mrs. Gerson with the same virtues he had when vertical and clothed: thoughtfulness, humor, paradoxically self-assured diffidence.

Demanding he wasn't, and since he was Gerson, I took it for granted this was his preference and had no complaints of my own. What a relief for us both that he was so civilized! And he was, so stalwartly and helplessly it drove him to despair.

At least to Pam, though, he only voiced that despair once. What he told Stella Negroponte's photo is none of my concern, but I'm sure he'd stayed courteous, good-humored, paradoxically self-assured, and the rest of the bland bit when Stella was around in the flesh. Otherwise, her picture wouldn't have been on open display in the den: not if Gerson was Gerson, as he couldn't help being.

The once followed a celebratory Musso & Frank's dinner. Gerson had given the pashas notice he was switching to their Antichrist—television—as the new head of production at Rik-Kuk. One natural way to cap off the night would have been to triumphantly turn on our set, tiny regatta flags that spelled out "SCREW METRO" fluttering on its antennae. At a time when prissier households—especially movieland's—preferred keeping theirs hidden behind cabinet doors (it fooled nobody, Panama, wasn't meant to; simply acknowledged the sight was a rude one), our big fifteen-inch RCA Gleason was on bombastic display in the living room.

In those days, however, TV stations went off the air at the witching hour. My mind boggles at the mobs of Fifties-born children conceived to either "The Star-Spangled Banner" (newlyweds) or a test pattern's monotone foghorn (younger sibling, perhaps calmer, perhaps not). In our marriage, spawning any such diapered thingummy wasn't on the table: Pam's one stipulation before I'd said yes, agreed to by Gerson with not only alacrity but something like gratitude. But from our usual preliminaries—him jangling the car keys, me instantly shoeless with an "Ah!" in the foyer—neither Mr. nor Mrs. was in any doubt we were going to screw Metro by screwing.

Once the bus cleared the hill, though, he felt distracted. (I mean literally *felt*: to me, from collarbones to knees. My feet were less sure, rubbed the sheet like a hunchback for luck.) At least by his considerate standards, the post-coital Pompeii was brief. Then he turned on the lamp.

"Gerson, what is it? Aren't you"—as always when light fringed his fine hair that way, I was reluctant to say "sleepy"—"tired?"

He was glaring so fixedly at the opposite wall that I thought he was going to suggest putting a TV set in the bedroom, one thing we'd agreed we'd never do. I'll spare daisysdaughter.com readers the multiple rounds of "Well, whats?" and "Oh, nothings"—married life's version of "Row, Row, Row Your Boat"—it took to get something out of him.

He still wouldn't look at me, though. "Nothing, I guess. I just thought it would maybe be different."

"Different? We ran out of different on our first anniversary. Good riddance too! I just looked damn silly in that Frederick's stuff. You must know what you're in for by now."

"That's just it. No, it's not! But it's part of it."

Gently down the stream. Merrily, merrily and so forth.

"Well, don't we know what we're like? That's what makes it nice," I said. "I know what you're like. You know what I'm like."

"Do I?"

"What kind of question is that?"

Life is but a dream! Row, row, row.

"Pammie!" he finally said. "What's the one thing *everyone* knows about you?"

"Nothing, so far as I know."

God, it was awful for him. "The whole *world*. Knows you put your *finger*. Up Murphy's *ass!*"

"Thank you, dear, for reminding me. So?"

"*So!* Don't you ever once *consider*. Putting your *finger!* Up—" he'd run short on breath; it came out as a squeak—"*mine?*"

I was baffled, since I'd done that and worse to him. He'd done much, much worse to me as I lay there and quailed, though I have to admit those bits usually ended up striking me as funny, not vile. But only, of course, in my Pamagination. I kept its unwelcome glimpses of ransacked disgust as sequestered from him in bed as I did my Dachau flashbacks out of it. Never really sank in that Gerson horizontal and Gerson vertical might both be gripped by dread he'd missed the important part.

"Why, I never thought you'd want me to. That's all," I said, knowing it wasn't.

"I don't even know if I do! Fun it doesn't sound like. That's not the point."

"What is?"

"I don't know! But it's here somewhere." He smacked the bed. "Here."

If you ever find yourself in a like situation, Panama, listen to me. Do it, don't do it, try something else next time and if it's a bust, laugh! And skip off in the nude like a wood sprite, bikini girl. But don't offer.

"Why, Gerson," Pam offered, both hands waving helplessly. "I mean, I suppose I could or whatever, if you—"

"No!" he literally shouted. "I can't explain, but never. Not once I had to ask. Don't you see—" and here my Gerson spoke the dignified words that inadvertently restored our marriage to its old easy terms, at the cost of a distant ship scooting away—"now it would only be painful."

I couldn't have quashed that chuckle if our lives had depended on it. In a way, Gerson's did: a life where, without needing to ask, he could be someone other than Gerson, Gerson, *Gerson* every cursed minute. Because he was Gerson, he gaped at Pam's chuckle and then understood it. And because he was Gerson, he sheepishly smiled and then laughed.

I've never sent a man to prison before or since. In my defense, he went willingly, and they say jailbirds get rattled easily when they're on the outside. I can't imagine and wouldn't want a marriage or even friendship without laughter, but beware when it's the only language of endearment you share.

Once we'd gotten done laughing, he looked at me tenderly. "Ah, Pammie. Not me! Not us, I know. Let's both try to get some sleep, what do you say? I've got my first day of school with Gene Rickey tomorrow."

"Oh, that's right!" I said. We managed a few rounds of married life's happy version of "Row, Row, Row Your Boat" before he switched the lamp off again.

Whether Gerson's omission of *Not you* from the litany was deliberate, I can't say. Yet I sometimes marvel he didn't stick a TV set in the bedroom, which I've still never done in my life. Kelquen used to sleep atop the one I've just glanced at in such puzzlement, since it can't be ringing.

My God! That's the t

POSTED BY: *Gramela*   Elephone, yes. It was the elephone. But all clear, daisydaughter.com readers! Pink Thing and Gray Thing are in their proper casings. Cadwaller's gun is relapped and unused. I still know Potus's voice only from TV.

It was Panama, daisysdaughter.com readers. (Meet the legend at last.) Panama, her dad, granddad, mom, dog, and kid brother, all clustered on speakerphone. "Hallooo, Grammie! Happy birthday. Oh, Scarf, just stop it. Scarf, now!"

I fumblingly lowered my pistol. Great-grandfather's gun, meet great-granddaughter's squeal. I could've fired midway through and she'd never have known.

"Oh this is so sweet of all of you perfect dears," I squawked back. At my advanced age, you can pull that crap out of your hat without blinking. Do you think we don't know how we sound? "It's so nice to be remembered."

"We don't need to remember you, Gramela! We know you! We all love you! Scarf too. Scarf, say happy birthday in dog!"

"Pan, don't be silly." That was her dad. "Oh, Christ, what am I saying? Go right ahead."

"Is Scarf new?" I asked to ask something.

Tim groaned. "To Scarf first and foremost. Three months, says the pound."

"You've got to meet him, Gramela!" Panama squealed. "He is adorable."

"If I don't shoot him first," said her mom. "Pam, you remember my favorite couch?"

"Dozed on it often as CNN played."

"No more. *Siempre los desastres.* But how are you really? The truth."

"Still right here with you! Knock wood."

"Ouch! Hey, Pan, quit."

Chris cut in. "Pan! I'm not saying it's wrong for you to hit your little brother. He'll never learn otherwise about girls. But that's the oldest dumb joke on the planet."

"Shit, Grandpa Chris. That was just my excuse, not my reason."

"Oh, all right then. Hi, Pam."

"Hi, Chris," I grinned. (Grinned? Oh, yes. I've had this gun in my lap since 6:20 a.m. Right then it too just felt like part of the family.)

"I guess you know my dad would be thinking of you," he said without false pomp or unctuousness. "We're not him, but we do what we can."

"Well, I'm certainly thinking of Cadwaller. But I don't need a birthday for that."

"Neither do I," Chris bragged affectionately. "I wish he could've met Pan, though. She's turning into such a cutie, one of these days this old man may ask her to pose in the nude."

"*Grandpa!*"

"I only wanted to prove I can scandalize *you*, my young miss…"

"Oh, BFD. Guess what, Gramela? At my school? At my school, we call scandals flipflops! They're all just what we have on our feet."

"Oh." Love of language comes first and then you grow discriminating. "Is your father still there, dear? How's the next book coming, Tim?"

"Oh fi—"

"*Liar!* Black liar. He hasn't been working on it at all. Dad just got back from France, Grammie! I'm sooooooooooooooooo jealous. He *worships* Marie Antoinette."

"News to me, Tim. And I damn near wrote a book about her once," I said, chortling but flipflopped. "What would your grandfather say?"

"No, no. *Marie Antoinette*, ital, a movie," Tim laughed. "It's not coming out here 'til October, but I saw it at Cannes. It's pro-Marie, too. The Europeans were booing, but I swear I think it's wonderful."

"October? Yes, that sounds interesting," said I pleasantly, toying with Cadwaller's gun. "Yes, hello, Scarf! *Hello.* But my God, Tim: who plays her? Who could possibly get me to sympathize with that—"

POSTED BY: *Kirsten Dunst's Oldest Admirer*   Son, as they say, of a bitch. Son of a bitch, son of a bitch, son of a bitch! Son of a bitch, son of a bitch, son of a bitch! Son of a bitch, bitch, bitch!

It was Ned Finn who realized that was the lyric to Beethoven's Fifth. You'd hear him singing it under his breath in our tiny embassy in Nagon when a file went missing or the Department asked for something absurd. Nan told me the Finns used to bellow it on car trips, only their youngest barred from joining in by infancy and then delicacy. Ned died before she got permission, and then of course Stacy Finn ended up with the best reasons of all to sing "Son of a bitch" to the Fifth Symphony.

Until mine. Damn this country! When all's said and done, damn this country. It can push and gnaw away at you until there's no bloody give left. It can drive a dotty old bag who's read too many obits and too many news reports of a senseless killing to hike up the Paris footlocker's lid, ignore her mother's chaotic pages of *The Gold-Hatted Lover*, and wait for a White House phone call or an Omaha-indigo sundown to do herself in. And then this country, this country!, springs its favorite trap. Flipping through "Coming Attractions" as if it's no matter at all, this country, this country!, casually asks, "Don't you know Kirsten Dunst is Marie Antoinette?"

October. Could I phone the White House myself and gently explain dear Bob got my birthday's date wrong? Then sit here for four addled months with

Cadwaller's gun, ordering buckets of tuna salad from Sutton's as *Siempre los desastres* splatters cable and each morning's *WashPost* makes my woozy head orbit with obits just so I can close mimsy borogoves that have seen Kirsten, my Kirsten, as a queen—as a queen! And Tim, curse him too, had to tell me it's wonderful. Why couldn't it at least be one of her lesser efforts, not that there are many of those?

For personal reasons I've often wished she'd star in a gals' romp set in New York in the early Forties: *The Refrigerated Lovers*, say. But Versailles will do in a pinch. Oh, Ard, oh, Ard! The world goes all to mud in your head and then silver sparkles at a theater near you.

Gerson's shade groaned at the way tag-team genius would've Metroized my new dilemma: batty Peg in a trance as she sets down the elephone ("A bit more unsteady, Miss Harrington") and her liquefied thoughts about the gal she'll leave behind rivulet down her face's cracked map. Stuff and nonsense. I had all those Cadwallers and a very annoyingly voluble dog on the line. Barely had time to coo "Oh, I do like her" when Panama rebolted from the blue.

"Grammie! For once in your whole stupid life, will you say yes to Provincetown? We're all getting fed up, it's disgusting. Stop being such an old bag, you old bag."

"*Pan!*" That was her mother.

"That's all right. Panama, good for you," I told them: them, since she already knew. "I can't, dear. I really can't travel and I'd be the most awful fuss if I did."

"Not this year!" Chris boomed. "Sorry, Pam, but we're putting a gun to your head. We've hired someone to help out just for your sake. She deals with geezers like us [he wasn't a diplomat's son for nothing] all the time."

"What's her name?"

"Moesha, oh—Moesha. Hang on, it's right here. Moesha Kendricks. Wow! That's a very odd question to ask off the bat."

True, but I couldn't have asked them to send me a picture and its caption was my only substitute. "What of it? I'm elderly," I said. "One foot in the grave and one in my mouth. I'm fucked if I know which is which anymore."

"But you do know we all wish you didn't say things like that."

"Why on earth not? Tick-tick-tick. No fountain of youth I can see in the neighborhood. Can you?"

"The reason we don't like it is it's your excuse for everything and you aren't dead yet," Tim put in. "Grammie, Dad's hired her. That's settled. Come on, will you think about coming?"

"Pleeeeeeeeaase, Gramela?"

"All together," Chris commanded. Muddled elephonic roar of group Cadwaller "Please," frantic barking.

"All right! I'll think about it. Just to shut Scarf up," I said.

"Yay!"

Duty done, the Cadwaller carnival was shifting its focus: I was audibly one item in a big family's day. I say so with no resentment, since if calling a pretzel like me was the *highlight*, I'd flee such bores by speedboat. Then Panama burbled again:

"Gramela, I nearly forgot! Did you listen to the iTune? Did you like it?"

"Dear, I'm sorry. The I-Tune?"

"The song?"

"Oh, yes! Yes, I did like it. Believe it or not, I was humming it first thing this morning. Well, trying to. Can't say I got very—"

"Oh, good! I'm so glad. Okay, chen-chen!"

"Chen-chen!" I called.

"She's gone, Pam. You know her. Faster than a speeding bullet."

POSTED BY: *Pink's Newest One*   Panama's faith that my frail life is enriched by exposure to the Panamanic beeps her generation decoys its hips with is one of those pumpings of teenage enthusiasm even a faux relative as gamy as me knows better than to trample on. I can recall Pam's failures to get Daisy interested in anything at all that interested me. Guessing my methods were inept, I never grasped that for my mother the source was what invalidated it.

I'm also not blameless, since at Panama's age you can't tell the difference between an occasion and a newly announced hobby. Unconvinced by Andy Pond's and Nan Finn's praise, I'd never been to the FDR Memorial until Tim brought her along to see it for *You Must Remember This*. Hadn't quite understood how it tumbled on, with varied rushes of water that grew magnificently still at the final pool marking death.

That was two warm springs ago. Past cherry-blossom time, but before District air's summer mimicry of car exhaust. Though I was still grumpy about my new wheelchair, I was relieved we'd brought it.

I got re-grumpy when I saw a shrunken (he was lifesize) Roosevelt seated in my chair's less gadgety prototype at the entrance. Not part of the original design, as I tri-grumpily knew from the *WashPost*. The tapdancing-challenged, or whatever the handicapped bloody call themselves these days, had lobbied for a representation of their fellow cripple sans illusions.

Nicophobes had lobbied equally successfully against any depiction of him with cigarette holder. If you asked *my* generation, which clearly no one had, that was denying Toscanini his baton. Bunny lovers had wrangled over letting Eleanor Roosevelt Rigby's statue show her in her fur stole. Ridiculous, just ridiculous.

"Oh, he wouldn't have liked that at all," my dentition and I grumped at the spring air, meaning the chairbound FDR. "He really did keep it hidden from us."

"Yes, Gram. I think I've read that once or twice," said Tim fondly. "I haven't been making up this damned thing off the top of my head, you know."

As Tim rolled me on, however, I grew touched. The sculpted and, to my eyes, inevitably Dorothy Day-ified breadline was the turning point. Strange to think it was now *my* generation—Pam's "us"—for it hadn't been at the time. To a Purcey's girl, all this had been primarily an adult business, and like all adolescents we'd concluded they'd fashioned the world as it was then by choice.

Skirling nearby, alarmingly naveled and hipboned—that was the day Tim looked at her and said, "Help me, Pam. What am I going to do?"—Panama was earplugged as she softly crooned. So often to my eyes, all these gadgets' purpose seems to be to redefine formerly demented public behavior as sane. Still, I did understand she meant no disrespect. It just wasn't fathomable to her that one kind of self-definition could preclude another, a pliability I hope stands her in good stead.

Then one of her croonings took me aback, seeming as it did to indicate she was hearing messages from another world after all. Tunelessly—the tune's fault, I soon learned, not hers—she chanted, "In the *Nine*-teen ... *Twen*-ties."

"Panama!" I demanded. "What on hell's green earth are you listening to?"

She couldn't hear me. When I re-asked in sign language, grimly bracing the while for some concert-challenged group to bustle up and arrest me, one earphone popped out of her Goya-dark curls. After providing some zoolike name I can't place, she said, "They're really one of Dad's bands. So don't tell my friends! But I like them when I'm alone."

"No, dear," I said as curls got ready to reseize their plastic prey. "The song. What is that song?"

"Oh, I like it a lot." Teenage logic. "It's like, it's like sort of like when you tell us about the way-back-when. It's called 'Being Boring.'"

"Well, I like *that!*" I said, tossing my head back with a dentitioned laugh. Not sure if she'd just proved she was young or growing up. And away from me.

"No, no! It's about how all of you were *never* boring. Listen." Before I could protest, her unabashed fingers had reprogrammed the gadget and fitted the plugs into my kidnapped ears.

My generation isn't comfortable in earphones unless we're over Schweinfurt. *My* generation feels at a loss for appropriate facial expressions to assume when we're listening to metallic chipmunks mate under the keen observation of two cinnamon-sprinkled dark eyes and a smile lost in curls in breath-kissing closeup as if we, not the chipmunks, are unwilling specimens in an open-air lab. Not that I'd have told Panama, but hearing slithers of electronic dots and dashes in tense situations isn't completely unfamiliar these days to *my* generation: EKGs, MRIs.

Yet this young doctor's murmur did have its soothing side, even if it did go on and Panama's face was a goddam billboard Panamanically selling toothpaste, breath mints, skin moisturizers, false eyelashes—no, those were real—and impossible bliss. Tim was hovering somewhere as Potusville temporarily rearrayed itself, old-family-retainer style, into my Washington.

Quite the backhanded compliment, I thought quadri-grumpily, eyeing FDR's gigantic I HATE WAR hewn in stone. Not boring. Most centuries don't get even that much credit in Panama's ledger, I suppose.

"Did you like it, Gramela? Did you like it?"

"Oh, yes. I did. Confusing, mind! But nice." Not sure I meant the song.

So it began, although my great reprieve has been that I no longer need to contend with Panama's face in closeup as I listen. Far from thoughtless, her e-mails give me full instructions every time on how to mouse-click the downloads into sonic existence on my Mac. Far from oblivious to my age in other ways as well, she only sends me songs she guesses or hopes will speak to Pam in some way.

They may well, but most of the time I'd be the last to know. They're in a language that's indecipherable not because it's a lost one but because mine soon will be. I can't tell if I find them excruciating because they're chockablock with chipmunks and EKGs or from pain at my own ignorance. Only occasionally does a bit of pidgin make sense to me, the case with Panama's most recent offering.

But I don't know whether her tastes are esoteric or trite. Tell me, daisysdaughter.com readers, has anyone but Panama even heard of a cater-whauler who calls herself Pink? Charming name, bound to warm me as I downloaded. I had the opposite reaction to the song's title, since I could remember a winsome number yclept "Dear Mr. Gable" and sung by the very young Judy Garland in *Broadway Melody of 1938*. If this unknown Pink's unknown ditty confessed a similar infatuation with Potus, I couldn't imagine what Panama could be thinking.

Once I'd dutifully listened, I went back to her e-mail. Understood better its quip about Pink's career suicide. The photo or twelve my curiosity got me to hunt up online had me nearly choking. And I'd thought *Panama's* dress code left too much too decipherable?

Mouth like a jaguar's, too. Eyes like twin six-guns enjoying the suspense at a birthday party. Will flags shoot out, or something else?

Other than that, I know just two things about her. One's that her voice is a syrupy bray I'll never learn to call musical. The other is that she's got more guts than the entire Democratic Party—oh, than all of you, all of you! All of you should be shamed.

I wasn't lying on the elephone just now, bikini girl. I can be evasive but I don't lie. As I fetched Cadwaller's gun, I did find myself humming "Dear Mr. President" in my aardvarky croak. Your Gramela was damned if she'd let that half naked child with the jaguar mouth and laughing six-guns for eyes be any braver than me.

POSTED BY: *Pam*   Googling tells me her CD didn't do very well, though. Stendhal's fabled pistol shot at a concert is anathema to Americans. But just as hearing Pink's pained warble a few days ago first prefigured and then bolstered my birthday resolution, so now glad tidings from France have prompted an unlooked-for crisis.

Isn't that always the crossroads, Tim? "Dear Mr. President" or *Marie Antoinette*? Go down fighting like Pink in June, hold on for succor from Kirsten in October? I wonder if they know each other, that would be grand.

Oh, damn! Oh, damn. Like so many people my age, I can't help missing simpler, less ambivalent times. In my case, this morning. Now I may not know until Potus rasps in my ear or the light fades to indigo on upper Connecticut which of my imaginary great-granddaughters I'll honor in the observance or the breach.

Half a century ago, when Gerson chose, accepting froth was the suicide option, not the vote for life. And no, I don't mean leaving Metro and movies for Rik-Kuk and TV; I mean the decision that broke Pam's heart. You could call it the worst review *Glory Be* got and, to the extent any writer writes for anyone other than him- or herself, I'd written it for him. Yet he wouldn't have been Gerson if he'd stayed mine. Civilized, soothing, thoughtful, and diffident: he was all of those things and more. Timid, no. The lone coward among my three husbands was Brannigan Murphy, not Noah.

His choice and Pam's heartbreak—our final his-and-hers hotel towels, you could say—were still hanging unseen in the future's darkroom when my second book made its first blurry appearance in a mental snapshot I'd thought was of something else. (Sorry, Chris: you're the photographer, not me. It was good to hear your voice, though.) If not for that, I guarantee I'd have burned it instead of sharing it on daisysdaughter.com.

In a rare treat, since we usually went to him, Jake Cohnstein was in L.A. New at Rik-Kuk, still optimistic, Gerson'd had the very Gersonish idea of one-upping the live dramas still common then by using the medium to recreate legendary theatrical performances of the past: *Hamlet* as Sarah Bernhardt had done it, say, albeit obviously with another actress impersonating her impersonating him. In that case, only a very primitive and soundless screen version survived.

On our last New York trip, listening to Jake rue all the fabled productions he could only describe to his Whitaker students at one or more removes had been what first got my husband thinking. That was his reason for inviting Professor Cohnstein out to the Coast to discuss a possible change of career. If Gene Rickey approved and Jake agreed, he'd be producing the series, which Gerson had provisionally named *Proscenium* and Pam, unconverted by her husband's home-screen neo-Platonism, kept calling *You Scrim, I Scrim, We All Scrim for Ike's Grin.*

On Jake's last night, we'd arranged a mini-reunion featuring Addison, whom Jake of course knew from pre–Pearl Harbor days, and Eve, whom he'd never met. Once he and Gerson drove off to Burbank, I'd spent a pleasant day alternating between overseeing the cooking and cleaning—likely to show up in slacks, Eve was still Eve Harrington—and reading the papers. News story datelined Dien Bien Phu, anonymous whispers of trouble on the set of *A Star Is Born.* Brief and maddeningly photoless society-page item on Celia Brady's new life as the wife of a real maharajah, not Hollywood pasha, in faraway Jaipur. He'd shown up on a stallion and she rode a tame tigress at their wedding; I'd definitely never get to meet her now.

The meal went off without a hitch, if to Gerson's regret without a Hitch. Despite Rik-Kuk's eager pursuit, *Alfred Hitchcock Presents* premiered a year later under a different aegis. While I felt bad for Gerson's sake and wouldn't have minded meeting *Rear Window*'s director in other circumstances, I wasn't sad he'd declined our dinner invite. We'd have had the Hollywood-party problem of two contending spheres of interest—figurative in Eve's case, damned near literal in his—and also wouldn't have quite been among friends anymore. Gerson assured me his manners were exquisite, but obviously Hitchcock couldn't have helped introducing an element of uncertainty.

Stella Negroponte welcomed us for coffee. A ritual best understood in the *Nine*-teen *Fif*-ties, even in our relatively booze-unfueled house, bikini girl, as setting out a half dozen cups of interesting liquid for guests to observe as they went on drinking. Everyone was cheerful, a monochrome-shirted (for once!) Addison included. Drunk or sober, the den was his favorite room.

"Do you know this story, Noah?" he drawled. "As Pushkin lay dying, he was asked whether he cared to say goodbye to his friends."

"No, I don't. Did he?"

"Yes and no. Looking up at his bookshelves, that great poet called feebly, 'Farewell, friends.' But whenever I walk in here and look up at your proud towers, I feel I should say 'Hello, children!' instead."

"Feel free to borrow whatever you like. I'll be pleased," Gerson said. "I'm done with them."

"No, no! Just admiring. Damned good improvement on the real brats we've got to meet. Oh, Jake—so sorry."

"Not at all," said Jake. "It's been ten years. Has it really? Yes. The tree I planted for David in Jerusalem must already be taller than I am. It was around Sharon's size then, probably what made me pick it. Something familiar." He smiled.

"Oh, that's nice! Maybe I should disguise myself as a rosebush," Eve said. Legs tucked and a propping thumb and forefinger inviting us to guess where the picture frame's other half was, she'd turned a couch into her boudoir as usual. "*Then* Addison might write a poem about me. Damn you! I'm nature, too."

"Of course you are, my love. But with a welcome hint of the supernatural that rocks my agnostic bent to its shoes. Talent knows its limits. Well, actually it doesn't if it's talent, but it knows its strengths. Five years ago next month, isn't it?"

"Yes, sweet man. Do you think enough time's gone by that we could show our faces on the Great White Way again?"

Addison frowned in mock calculation. "Not quite, but I'm fairly sure enough magazine covers have. Why, d'you want to go?"

But Gerson wanted a flashback, which socially was very un-Gersonish of him. He spent enough time dragging conversations back to his menu at work; as a host, he was a devoted audience. "My God, Jake. Jerusalem. When were you there?"

"Early '49, not too long after the armistice. The CIA had just blackballed me, so the passport was a bit of a problem. It may have been the only time being Jewish made my life easier."

Gerson winced. "How so?"

"It's a topsy-turvy world we live in, Noah. I only got one by swearing under the table I wouldn't need it long. In other words, I wasn't visiting—I was plan-

ning to emigrate. Once the most junior Israeli consular officer hears the magic
word *Aliyah,* the State Department turns on the spot into the walls of Jericho."

Eve laughed. "Why didn't Arthur Miller think of that?" she wondered prettily.

"Ah!" Addison said. "He only wanted to go to London. Bit hard to frame
a desire to see your own play staged by my former countrymen as a religious
imperative unless you're mad as a hatter. Not that they shouldn't have given him
the damn thing, of course."

"Hell, why didn't he just lie?" a well-brandied Pam bandied on her way to
the decanter. "The SOB does call himself a playwright, after all."

"I did. And I only call myself a professor," Jake said as my husband looked
perturbed. I hadn't had a chance to ask him how their final meeting with Gene
Rickey had gone. "Of course it was a leedle embarrassing at the other end when
I had to put down me shovel, dust off me American hands, and tell them Jake
Cohnstein had changed his mind. Which I never had, but they didn't know
that."

"You weren't tempted at all?" Gerson asked.

"No, not for a minute, Noah! Israel was David's dream, not mine. Fulfilling our fathers' dreams is a dove disguised as an eagle, but fulfilling a son's is a
vulture disguised as a phoenix. Of course he never knew they'd call it Israel. To
him it was Palestine."

"We were going to have a child," Gerson said unexpectedly. "My first wife
and I, I mean. But they died." I decided to dawdle a bit over replugging the
decanter.

"What did the Israelis do anyhow—" that was Eve calling, oblivious and
grinningly ginned—"toss a coin?"

"I imagine it was a mite more fraught than that. Naming a child is responsibility enough," said Addison steadily. "Naming a book is my limit. I wouldn't
want the burden of naming a country if it were only bloody Monaco. And it
wasn't."

"No, it wasn't," Jake agreed. "I will say going there did give me something
I'd always wanted to see. Certainly not in my Bolshie days, even though we pretended. Noah here probably won't want to admit it was pretending even now,
but it was."

"Oh, no! Oh, no," I said, swooping back in between them. "You two aren't going to have *that* conversation again."

"No, Pam. We aren't." By Gerson's Smirnoff-again-on-again standards, that was downright brusque.

"What was it you'd wanted to see, Jake?" Addison asked.

"A beginning." If any of us had ever wondered what he'd looked like at twelve, that grin was our clue. Then it matured into his familiar one: "Then again, that was why I took it into my head to hope the CIA had room for the likes of Jake Cohnstein too, so clearly I'm not choosy. You always want—just once!—to be present at the creation."

"Oh, the *tree!*" said Eve. "Ad, are you sure you don't want to have children?"

"Not the tree." That was Gerson. "The country."

"Yes. Imagine watching *Oedipus Rex* without knowing she's his mother, Addison! That's one trick this show of yours for Gene Rickey can't manage, Noah. Well, I saw it. There were still burnt-out supply trucks on the road to Jerusalem."

"I envy you!" Gerson said with a stare at the walls. "Look at this crap and pity me. No matter how often I read the British band played 'The World Turned Upside Down' at Yorktown, I'll never *hear* it. I've got it on an LP, of course. But I'll never be there. I can only imagine that one drummer boy on the left in tears."

"Noah! You surprise me, I must say."

"I'm not picturing him naked, you son of a bitch," said Gerson in the closest he'd ever come to acknowledging Jake's sexuality to his face. "Just in tears, in tears."

"I'm picturing him both." That was Eve. "Yummy. Naught but a drum."

"Why, you bloody bitch! We *aren't* having children. Even pets." That was Addison. "I won't risk it. God help the servants."

"All right with me! I'm a plant. I'm random. Six of one, half a dozen of the other. Screw you."

"Jake, I do envy you," Gerson said with new formality. "I know that's why I keep trying to go back in the time machine. I used to read all this"—he nodded at Winken, Blinken, and Nod—"and tell myself, 'Well, it's belief disguised as escapism!' Now I worry it's just escapism disguised as belief."

"You'll prosper in TV, m'boy," Addison muttered, crotchety with Scotch.

"Ad, I simply can't accept that," Gerson said promptly. "Not yet."

I'm no great fan of *Never*, Panama. Not even with your great-grandfather's gun in my lap. Drunk as I was and we all were by then, Gerson taught me two of the noblest words in our language: *Not yet.*

"Well, it's not really such a privileged experience as all that," said Jake. "Why don't you just go yourself?"

"To Israel? Don't tease me, Jake. Even if I didn't have—obligations, I'm much too old to start over that way."

"I meant on your next vacation, Noah," Jake explained after a moment. "Come back and tell me how tall David's tree is."

"Oh a visit! Oh of course. No reason not to at all," Gerson fumbled. "I just got confused. Forgive me, Pammie."

"So are we all, I think," Addison said after another moment. "I'm quite comfortable with that myself, but someone's got to drive. Eve?"

"I'm pretty trinked too."

"Yes, dear. But there isn't a police officer in this city who'd write you a ticket. I have an accent, an unknown face, and a helplessly supercilious manner even I loathe. I'd be in the hoosegow before you'd finished redoing your lipstick for the nice patrolman."

After they'd all gone home—even Gerson, if home meant upstairs; even Jake, if home meant our guest wing—I lingered on in Stella Negroponte's room, pretending I cared about the scummed glasses, miniature Boot Hills of full ashtrays, and mostly virginal, incipiently spinsterish coffee cups. Luz's job in the morning, but I thought I'd at least make a start after my nightcap. And spot the mistake there, since some minutes later I was blurrily realizing that now at some point I'd have to get up and collect those scattered clothes too: that quadruple-cupped bra, that zigzag-buttoned blouse, that repeatedly pleated skirt, and those four-legged undies. All four of Stella's eyes were watching but neither of the bitch's mouths moved.

Stupid, but I'd never before heard my husband express erotic longing for any other entity but me. He was as incapable of infidelity even with the dead as any man on hell's green earth. Any marriage made of more than toothpicks can survive an adultery, and in hindsight I knew I'd committed more figurative ones in the last year of mine to Murphy than Bran had the literal-minded kind. Not for lack of trying, but even he couldn't take on four hundred sixty-six marching women at once.

Glimpses of each other's unlived lives are the real abyss: the ones that imagine you a stranger or dead as Stella Negroponte or someone who never existed. We've all got them and yet spotting our spouse's is intolerable. I'd just found out about Gerson's Great Unknown, which unlike mine had a name and location. At least I'd had the goddam decency to keep Pam's to myself instead of blurting it out in my cups.

"Look, Gerson," I giggle-gurgled on the rug. "Here's my cunt. You never call it that. Cunt, cunt, cunt! Stella's watching and she's naked too."

But since he was asleep upstairs in European striped pajamas, he didn't answer. At one level I'd have given a lot to see the look on his face if he were awake.

"Gerson, did you ever find out your first wife's anus is just a *leedle* hairy? Not that I'm complaining. Do you want to know what Dachau smelled like? Do you want to know what Dachau tastes like? Sharon, stick your tits in her! Punish her. Fuck her. Cram your mompricks up her."

"Oh, God! Oh, Pam. I thought you'd never ask. God, I'm naked too! I'm so shy and old now. Here's my kitchenized fat deadboy twat. Shove a burning B-17 up it please, why don't you? It's all I ever think about anymore."

"The hell with that! Let me suck dead Stella's smell off your nipples. What do I care, I'm drunk and I have nightmares and I haven't written a word in five years."

POSTED BY: *A Pamographer*   Not quite true, by the way. Even if you don't count letters—to Cath Charters, to Brother Nicholas, to Jake himself—I'd done two or three pieces for *Regent's* on the voluptuous allure of Hollywood. Roy had liked them well enough to wonder if I'd be interested in turning movie reviewer, but even if I'd felt qualified (I didn't), it was obviously impractical with Gerson at Metro. By the time he moved to Rik-Kuk, someone else's byline was handling the faint praise and beheadings.

Anyhow, if you're still with me, bikini girl, you may as well know your Gramela's first venture into cyberporn is a drastic abridgment of what really poured out. So it may surprise you that I came downstairs the next morning able to return Stella Negroponte's gaze without flinching. Then I glanced around Gerson's library.

"Oh, all right then!" I said. "*À nous deux*. I'm going to prove him wrong if it kills me."

Shades of Peg Kimball in *The Gal I Left Behind Me*. But you see, if we aren't Jewish, we don't have an Israel. We're stuck here in the crap we've got around us. By now even the Israelis know the feeling.

"Sorry, Pam?" It was Jake, preposterously showered. I'd clean forgotten our guest wing was right off the den, but his face didn't hint he'd witnessed or overheard anything out of the ordinary. I remembered from Sergeant Kowalski days that he was a deep sleeper.

I got us both coffee, a ritual best understood—in the *Nine*-teen *Fif*-ties, Panama—as a necessary binge of quick slurps and mild "Ows!" while avoiding contemplation of last night's harlequinade of glassware. "Hungry?" I asked.

"Starving." Lips stung by the cup's rim, he smiled. Then asked in turn, "Hung?"

"Oh, maybe a leedle." I could've strangled myself, but he didn't react. Pam had the unnervingly alluring thought that being caught would've been more permissible if I'd been the guest and not the miscast host.

"Yes, me too. Hope I can get some sleep on the plane." Not bothering to put hand to mouth, he showed me his fillings. "Tenure interview tomorrow."

He wanted me to catch that, so I did. "You're turning Rik-Kuk down, aren't you?"

"Uh-huh. I didn't much like myself last night, Pammie. Or anyone on hand, to be honest. I know they say Hollywood does strange things to people, but I didn't think Jake Cohnstein would succumb in under, what's it been? A week. For one thing, I'm not used to hearing Jake Cohnstein assertively call Jake Cohnstein Jake Cohnstein in conversation. Are you?"

"No, but—" I decided not to explain that I'd thought I knew the reason. "But you have to remember we aren't like that when we're working."

An irrational "we," I agree, for Pam to include herself in. Yet the Hollywood "we" isn't functional: it's tribal.

"It's not just that. Ah!" His coffee had cooled enough for a nonstinging mouthful, the reward for all those burnt sips. You're frightened it'll stay that hot unless you demonstrate you're willing to suffer for its sake. "I think Noah's a dreamer. Pam, you've met Gene Rickey."

"Sure. But Fran's the horror."

"Lord help you if she's worse. I'm not used to people who call Shakespeare Willy. Or to hearing myself called, variously, Jack, Jerry, and Joe."

Out before I thought, it broke one of our rules. "What, Gerson didn't tell you?"

"Tell me what?"

"Odds are you'd have to give up being Jake Cohnstein, at least in the credits. Gene was trying things out. Jack Clamstone, Jerry Cumberland."

"Why couldn't I have been? Gerson's Gerson. I couldn't watch much of *That's My Fran*, but I did get that far."

"Oh, well. Noah Gerson is only going to sound Jewish if you live here. In Minnesota it goes right by. But Jake Cohnstein just sounds"—I felt helpless, but it was awfully early—"Jewisher."

"Hear that, Noah?" Jake said. "Nah, nah. The game is done—I've won, I've won. I'm Jewisher."

My bathrobed husband reached for his mug. "Are we still talking about Jerusalem? Good. I wanted to hear more."

"No, Hollywood. But I don't think we've met." Jake put out his hand. "I'm Jack Cornhole."

"No, that would never—" Gerson's face sagged. "That's a no, I take it."

"Afraid so. I was planning to tell you on the way to the airport."

"We couldn't—"

"Really, no. But I do thank you for the offer, Noah, and the trip. God knows I saw a lot."

POSTED BY: *Pam*   Assuming you've read it, something Amazon says isn't likely, you may be baffled by my insistence that rapturous *Glory Be*—forgotten now, scorned in the groves of academe, but in the *Nine*-teen *Fif*-ties, Panama, *by Pamela Buchanan*'s second and last bestseller—came out of solo squalor under Stella's gaze, self-sick and she-sick and seasick from those towering waves of suddenly inadequate Winken, Blinken, and Nod. Don't be. Up until Cath Charters placed it at Random House, the full title was *Glory Be: A Beginning.*

My original plan was to end with a verbal closeup of a British drummer boy—sorry, Eve, fully clothed—beating "The World Turned Upside Down" at Yorktown. It didn't work out that way because I realized I wanted to end with a beginning, leaving the outcome in now notional but once real suspense. I brought the curtain down instead with the Shot Heard 'Round the World. The book didn't call it that because they didn't yet.

Since I soon learned that nobody then or now knew whether a redcoat or a militiaman fired the war's literal first shot at Lexington, I left my nameless final protagonist's allegiance ambiguous while tempting the reader to guess he was an American rebel: shades of the unidentified "hands" I'd described a decade earlier packing dynamite in "To the Ends of the Earth." Also a classic example of why academia's tenured ninepins revile my kind of history. My final image was a verbal closeup of a finger tightening on a trigger: by a coincidence I was conscious of long before sharing it with you, just how my life and daisysdaughter.com will end 231 years later if Pink wins her battle with Kirsten. Closing line? "They say he pulled it soon after eight in the morning on April 19, 1775."

Not the best sentence I've ever written, no. Just the best *last* sentence I have, as of now anyway.

Some planned opening chapters were discarded as well. The Vikings got lopped and so did Columbus. As I've mentioned, I began with "A Landing," and Panama? Sorry: I'm a writer. If I couldn't bring myself to revisit Provincetown for a *book's* sake, there's no chance a ring of jolly Cadwallers on the elephone, barked at and barged at by a lively little dog, will persuade me.

Gerson-led, Gerson-loving, I set myself rules. Pure narrative: no anticipation, flashbacks, or reflections outside each bit's time frame. Each chapter hung on an incident, a moment—even just "a sort of anecdote," as Mencken had described the Scandal. I honed the writing, ditching not only *Nothing's* careless prattle but my old *Regent's* molasses. Like my other two books, *Glory Be* had jokes in it; I did want to make Gerson smile. But no *mugging.*

From "A Landing" on, chapter titles were abrupt. My rule was never to use "The," which was falsely defining. It was always "A Cargo" (first slave ship docking at Jamestown), "A Misfit" (Roger Williams: last words, "Rhode Island"), "A Sermon" (Cotton Mather), "A Storm" (Franklin's kite), "A Fort" (the untried George Washington in the French and Indian War). And so on, from the well-meant, off-rhyming with "cargo," but now archaic "A Negro"—Crispus Attucks, of course—all the way to "A Morning." Off-rhyming with "landing," you see.

Ah, Cadwaller's gun! How it depresses your owner's widow that April 19, 1775—and all that goes with it, from Minutemen to "If this be treason, make the most of it" and so on—has been appropriated in our day by the crackpots who wrathfully style themselves militias. Generations of high-school history teachers got driven to despair by my compatriots' fabled hostility in every poll to their topic, and now this.

And curse liberals too, for ceding the whole beautiful thing's imagery to their opponents just because its unsophisticated musketry embarrassed them. Unless April 19, 1775, belongs to all of us, it can't belong to any of us: the lesson a pigheadedly Mayfloral Pam learned from her Gerson's stubborn library-shelved conviction that he had a claim on events predating his family's arrival at Ellis Island by a century or more. I wrote *Glory Be* to hold him when he began to despair of believing that it was a claim on much.

No, I had no formal training. One proof's that it took me two years. Each moment laboriously researched, sites (all but one) visited, each chapter written and rewritten until I could've staged my own ticker-tape parade with typewriter ribbons. And no, the reviews weren't all glowing. My old friend Dwight Macdonald had company. But I spluttered whenever "cinematic" popped up as a term of abuse, often with a slighting reference to my then current roots— an Americanism if I've ever coined one, by the way. Though my Los Angeles address wasn't fudged, Cath and Random House agreed I'd better leave Pam's marriage to a Hollywood producer unannounced on the dust jacket. But *Vogue* and everyone else profiling me printed it.

So what and of course! Perhaps you'll see what they couldn't. I meant to give Gerson one movie Metro's pashas would get no chance to dicker and euchre into eunuchhood; two dozen fabled historical prefilm occasions Rik-Kuk Pro-

ductions couldn't turn thumbs down on. Take it from me, daisysdaughter.com
readers: if you want to make the movie or TV show of your dreams, write a book.

Near Pulitzer miss or not, *Glory Be* isn't in much repute nowadays. Tenured
ninepins sniffed from the start, since *Lux et Veritas* is Latin for "No amateurs
need apply." By the mid-Seventies or so, none did—and my God, *narrative* was
a term of abuse! So was "entertaining," so was "brisk." When one ninepin calls
another's book "highly readable," both parties understand the next step is cudgels at dawn.

Glory Be's author is a minor member of a forgotten breed. The most recent
online citation of my once much loved book is a mention in some ninepin's
withering dismissal of yesteryear's "popular historians." Scorned for being more
interested in the reader's pleasure and my own prose than substance, I'm a min-
now alongside bigger fish in the barrel. They include not only Gene Smith and
Cornelius Ryan, whose letter apologizing for Pam's deletion from *The Longest
Day* ("I left out Marty Gellhorn too") is in the Paris footlocker, but—here's
where this old bag's jaw dropped—Barbara Tuchman.

Barbara Tuchman? No, really? I'll take that with bells on, you unwitting
flatterer. Good Christ, how that woman could structure and write!

POSTED BY: *Pam*   It wasn't all Gerson, too much Beverly Hills, or disgust
at having shown Stella Negroponte Pam's Coos Bay. The blacklist was on my
mind too, despite my regretfully scrapped Salem chapter "A Trial." Arthur
Miller had dibs. The play whose London production he'd been denied a passport to see was *The Crucible*.

By the time *Glory Be* reached stores, the witch hunt was waning. Brave as
ninety-five mice confronting a rat, the Senate had finally censured McCarthy.
That didn't spare me from being attacked in left-wing circles, some of whose
circlers had known me in my old *Republic* days. I was guilty of knuckling under
to the Age of Conformity with a craven *American Heritage* hymnal—a charge
repeated as late as 1965 in his lugubrious *How the Red Faded Out of Old Glory*
by a creaky weathervane you've met before. You old fraud, Alisteir Malcolm.

Not a bit of it. Pam was as fed up as any of them with the flatulent com-
placencies of the *Nine*-teen *Fif*-ties, from its scrims for Ike's grin to his true

grandson Howdy Doody capering on General Motors' strings. Now a dyed-in-the-Loy liberal Democrat, I hadn't forgotten our Thirties hopes. Gerson and I did our best to stay chipper; blowing our brains out was at best Plan D, only rarely discussed and only while driving, ever Los Angeles's Ferris wheel for conversational caprice. Yet even before Jake's visit, in moping moods my husband would worry as we drove that spending one day in Fran Kukla's U.S.A. would convince Lafayette it had all been for nothing.

Privately readier to agree with him than he yet was with himself, more likely in later years to think the Marquis's IQ was all in his wig anyhow, I wrote my book to not only hold Gerson but buck both of us up. I meant my look back to prompt him and any other readers it might attract to look forward. To restore, if saying so's not self-aggrandizing—oh, what the hell if it is? I'm just babbling unheard out in cyberspace anyway—a sense of possibility, accident, circumstance, hope.

In two words, of beginning. It wasn't called *Glory Was*. My people weren't preserved in aspic. With a few grim exceptions (spend a month with Cotton Mather and a taxidermist won't have you), they were urging us to go forth and do likewise in our own metamorphoses.

The catch any author will recognize is that what I was doing to hold Gerson took me away from him. Not only on my research trips, since there wasn't a lot I could do about the fact that California's part in stirring up the American Revolution, however prominent in my own case in 1954–56, had been fairly limited in 1620–1775. Even at home in Beverly Hills, pacing and typing in my heretofore barely used study above Stella Negroponte's room, I was a Mercury astronaut before they existed, my only hairdresser a pencil for weeks at a time. I believe Antoine scraped by.

Luckily, my husband had never had to count on his Mrs. for cooking or cleaning. Nor did the servants need Pam's compass to navigate our house, since both Luz (the housework) and Ava (the kitchen) dated from Gerson's first marriage. That was how redecorating, which I'd never given a tinker's dam about, had become my early declaration of Pamhood, though I swear I never once waited, let alone hoped, to hear Luz crash into a sofa where a clear path had been.

Yet now there was many a Saturday and Sunday when my husband, home from Rik-Kuk and increasingly weary of Winken, Blinken, and Nod, could go well past sunset more likely to hear a peep out of Stella than me. Being Gerson, he wouldn't have put it that way on a dare, but he did mutter sometimes.

"Why, Gerson!" I tried to reason with him. "I used to spend all day here waiting for you to get done working. Never once complained."

"Not on weekends. And I wasn't right on the other side of the ceiling the whole time," he said, nodding upward. "I can still hear you sometimes, but I can't see or touch you. It's an *adjustment*, Pammie, that's all."

If you'd like proof Gerson loved me, he didn't bring up the most obvious difference. His job at Rik-Kuk was supporting me, trips to Jamestown and Boston and the site of Fort Necessity now making that dog-tongued receipt drawer bulge more. Though *Dame's* royalties had kept me in Antoine and toreadors (the pants, Eve, not the bullfighters) for the first year or two of our marriage, even then all the big bills were his.

If every marriage has one boast kept untarnished, ours was a good one: we never once fought about money. He did that with Gene Rickey, not me. We weren't to be reprieved from all marital cliches, however. I was two-thirds of the way through my manuscript when he wretchedly asked—at a ten p.m. dinner, gone cold: Ava did chicken salad for lunch a lot in those days—if I was having an affair with someone back East.

"Someone" was the Hollywood note, since the faint implication he'd know them was leverage grasping at straws. I'd put him through a lot if he was thinking like a producer, but that's not the only reason I gaped. Living people weren't especially real to me in those days. Airplanes, trains, hotels, taxis, whole cities—Boston, ugh—were simply obstructions I had to put up with for the sake of one building, one church spire at daybreak, one hill young Washington had cantered along, one fringe of trees, or one library. The full Pam materializing only when I'd made contact, I slid through the rest like a ghost.

"No, Gerson, no! My God," I said. "If I were having an affair with anyone, I'd be having it with you."

Didn't quite hit the right note, did it? He didn't think so either. "Say the word, Pammie. Name the day."

I didn't mean to be glib. I meant to be poetic: "April 19, 1775."

He looked down at his plate. "I'll be in Europe," he said.

POSTED BY: *Haroun Dam-Raschid*   Oh, buck. I'd bucking well bucked us up good and proper, hadn't I? But I was in the literary opium den, greedily puffing on a pipe shaped like a Colonial fife. Turbaned and scimitared, I was mentally sauntering among the perfumed lemons and melons of history's seraglio, murmuring "That one" to Qwertyuiop: my Smith-Coronal, many-eyed vizier. The eunuch had no say! By that stage in *Glory Be*'s composition, I could no more have braked or redirected myself had I been a bullet.

The truth is, Gerson's obtuseness mostly just maddened me. Couldn't he grasp the rose in the nettle? Not only was my book my gift to him; it was his to me. If not for my husband's quaint and then frighteningly unreliable passion for Winken, Blinken, and Nod, I'd have never understood, never cared, never experienced this world's true fourth dimension: yesterday. Never have discovered a past I now saw had precipitated me.

Knowing both sets of my forebears had been on the scene, I searched as if drunk for Buchanans and Fays. Dead Daisy's daughter wanted one chapter to serve as a not too conspicuous marker indicating her stake in the emerging pattern. Never found a good one, but in my own mind I settled on a metaphoric substitute. Too little known planter heiress Martha Shelton (b. 1707, d. 1745) became the heroine of Chap. 15, "A Romance."

In an episode I saw as crystallizing the new fluidity of social relations in the still apple-carted, British-aping, yet inchoately freedom-seeking colonies, she'd alarmed the proud Virginia Sheltons by falling in love with one Alfred Wiggins (b. ?, d. 1767), the family tutor: mathematics for her brothers, pianoforte for her. Alarm turned to outrage when she married Wiggins once his seven years' indentured servitude were up. All was posthumously forgiven when Shelton Wiggins (b. 1745, d. 1806) became a captain of the Continental volunteers, cited for unusual valor at the Battle of Brandywine—you had to turn to *Glory Be*'s appendix, "The Aftermaths," to learn this—and a friend to both Patrick Henry and Jefferson. No mean trick, incidentally.

"Saltsbury" still stood outside Culpeper, where Cadwaller and I were to buy a *pied-à-terre* we liked many Indian-summery years later. Already visited once, it was Martha Shelton's home I was off to, with a stopover at Nenuphar to see Brother Nicholas, when I confronted Gerson's true anguish. I doubt my husband had ever seriously worried I was parking the Buchanan bod gams ahoy to welcome the penetrating historical insights of Philadelphians and Richmonders. That was just the comic-book sexualization of his deepest dread.

He always drove me to the airport when he could, with a goodbye kiss as pleasantly dry as those we'd exchanged before we ever slept together. But this was a night flight, and I suspect that's why he couldn't take it. He was gripping the steering wheel like a fatal X-ray.

"Gerson, are you ill? I thought the chicken salad was a little off myself. But you know how Ava gets when she thinks you've repoached—sorry, reproached—her."

Knowing it would have trouble speaking, his mouth meticulously squared itself. "I swear," he said, "I swear I never think about it when it's me who's flying. And if we're flying together, Pammie? Then I can always tell myself, 'Well, at least...'"

He didn't need to finish that one. "Yes," I said. "Me too."

"Do you, can you, have any idea how I hate to leave—how I hate *dropping people off*, at airports? I've never told you, but I wait every time. I sit in this car and I watch the takeoff. Day or night, I follow the plane with my eyes until it's not there anymore. Then I just hope it's still somewhere."

"Gerson, Carole Lombard's plane—"

"Please don't call it that. No, never mind; that's not the issue. I know everyone always will. But now you do it all the time, all the time!" he cried, meaning flying rather than misnaming Stella Negroponte's plane. "All the time."

"Well, I've got no choice now! You know that."

He let that one pass. "I don't want to have to ask Wylie White for another favor, Pammie. I don't want it to happen again! I couldn't stand it. And even when you're *home*, but up there, you know—working—I start imagining it's already happened."

"Oh, love! Gerson, I promise. I vow. History isn't going to repeat itself."

"How can you say? How can you know? It's random."

"I'm not. And I'll never be."

He looked at Pam for confirmation. What did he see? The yes in my eyes, the no of my nose. The mixed-up thou of my mouth. Through my clothes, which he always could read like a book, the dotted I-I of Pam's nipples. The nave of my navel, the us of my—ah, screw it. I knew I'd get in trouble sooner or later. I still rate that moment the most intimate Gerson and I ever shared.

Notice what I didn't say: *And I'm not pregnant.* We'd never spoken of his gar-bled admission to Jake that Stella had been, which he didn't realize I'd heard and I gathered nobody knew. Wylie White would have told me if Gerson and the first Mrs. Gerson had shared the happy news before she boarded. Nonetheless, in my own writerly mind, saying I wasn't pregnant wouldn't have been true— and in Gerson's mind, since he loved me, it wouldn't have been true either.

I kissed his cheek. "I've got to go."

Go I did. Come back in one piece every time—no real suspense *there*, is there?—I did too. Except in the Clio Airways sense, where crash victims I was fond of litter daisysdaughter.com's landscape, I hadn't then and miraculously still haven't ever known anyone who died in a plane wreck. Even David Cohn-stein, a B-17 waist gunner who planned on surviving the war to go to what he called Palestine, was only a name and the same curly-haired snapshot in Sharon's purse and Jake's wallet.

Despite dully guessing that Wylie had had to suck in his breath and then nod before they opened his future nightmares' Pandora's box, I'd always been most conscious of the *fact* of Stella Negroponte's death, not its manner. It had never sunk in how haunted Gerson must be by its manner. He'd never tried to turn me into Stella. Not without reason, he probably thought he'd married her opposite. Yet I'd terrified him by threatening to undo that all by myself.

Perhaps because that parting had been so intimate, the reunion was shy. As if our Boulevard Rule from Metro days now fit Pam, not him, and its geography had been reversed, we were past Sunset before he asked, "Go well?"

"Yes! Oh, Gerson, I'm so close now. I've already done Lexington. The only big job I've got is to get Martha to pop out Shelton Wiggins and then bury that bitch for good, tie up a few loose ends, and—I'll be done."

Even to myself, I'd never said it before. Selflessly, Gerson wreathed me in smiles. By the next light, he'd grown a wee bit less selfless: I heard a tick of Gersonish mirth from the driver's seat. Nudged him.

"What, little man?"

"I thought I was the only one who called her 'that bitch,'" he said with amusement. "Never to her face, of course."

"I swear I'll make it up to you. Really, not that much longer!" I tried to remember how non-authors computed. "Two months at the outside. Can you wait? Oh, please wait."

Wait, Gerson did. Wreath me in even more laureled smiles when *Glory Be* came out and became a bestseller, he did. The West Coast pub party was at Romanoff's, and I don't believe he was harboring any Bolshevik schemes. Knowing him as he did, I'm sure the decision that ended our marriage wasn't taken until an hour at most before he told me, and that was only because he'd woken up earlier. That was on the vacation that, flush with new royalties and Random's promise of more, I insisted on treating him to make up for it all.

Just the same, I watched *Glory Be* miss out on the Pulitzer alone. Had my twenty minutes of banter with Jack Kennedy, the winner, alone. Well, no, not *alone*: it was a banquet at the Waldorf in spring '57. In those days, they didn't officially announce the also-rans, so in theory Pam Buchanan was just a fellow guest and author rather than a thwarted rival. If you were in the know, though, you knew; I knew. He knew, and he was there alone too. Off at some horse show, Jackie was a no-show.

What a different book this might be—Ard, I'll fix later—if I'd had a bit more bosom, was three inches shorter, and Antoine hadn't messed up the perm. But I digress.

The name "Gerson" appears nowhere in *Glory Be*. While in his family's case the connection would've been literally nominal, since it was an Ellis Island alias, I'd hunted for suitable Gersons as well as Fays and Buchanans, thinking the gesture might please or tickle him. Had no luck on that score in Philadelphia or Culpeper, the Great Meadows a.k.a. Fort Necessity, Nantucket, or Boston. Yet my second husband isn't missing from my second book, even though it probably went right by in Minnesota.

While I worked on the thing, he'd had only two distant competitors. One was Jake Cohnstein, which would certainly have added more apoplexy to Alisteir Malcolm's *How the Red Faded Out of Old Glory*. The other was Stella Negroponte, but that would have just upset Gerson—whom Pam, in that annoying habit I picked up from dames in hard-boiled movies and fell into with all three of my husbands, had never called anything but Gerson in conversation or letters. Not this time, though, and the last two words I wrote were the first two I'd imagined on a hungover morning two years gone. On a page headed "Front Matter" and destined for Random House, I typed, "For Noah."

3. *Gerson's Hope*

POSTED BY: *Pam*   Unless you're on the lucky side of forty, you'll know which two passing remarks in my last batch of Pam-pages are sure to bring a hail of cyber-opprobrium down on *l'équipe* here at plucky little daisysdaughter.com. But *That's My Fran* fans can lump it.

Once Rheuma One, new nickname for my gnarled forefinger, clicks "Post," we don't look back. No matter how much abuse you hurl, I'm not going to delete "grimace queen" or recant my 1954 line of dialogue, in casual—all right, not very—conversation with Jake Cohnstein, tagging Fran Kukla as "the horror." Observe me instead as I lift my ancient hand from the mouse and revolve it to jab Rheuma Two upward in solitary grandeur.

If I've got any misgivings, Panama, they're about your Gramela's venture into cyberporn. That I do wish I'd left out; it's the sort of thing Sean Finn would dream up. Let's just hope Tim restrains him from too much of that in their collaboration.

For Tim's marriage's sake, he'd better stay more alert to his surroundings while he's at it than I was during *Glory Be*'s composition. If making the beast with two hard covers hadn't been Haroun Pam-Raschid's command to

Qwertyuiop for most of '54, all of 1955, and some of 1956, my wily Smith-
Coronal vizier and I might have been less stunned by Gerson's announcement
of his plans in December of '56. I'd have been as heartbroken in the immediate
scheme of things and as happy for his sake once I'd knocked some perspective
into myself, just less stunned.

Thanks to our ten p.m. dinners and now hurried breakfasts, I knew in cut-
lery-clinking detail what Fran and Gene Rickey were putting him through.
Itching as I was to get back to my upstairs seraglio, I still thought I could
indefinitely postpone compassion more active than conversational bandages.
Measuring my authorial megalomania for a marital straitjacket more than I
knew, I also thought *Glory Be* would be enough to balm all Gerson's wounds:
not only those I'd carelessly inflicted with my jolly multiple reprises of Stella's
final flight and distracted impersonations of her footsteps pacing the ceiling,
but the ones that bathed his brain in blood daily in Burbank.

Fat chance. I could've been Winken, Blinken, and Nod rolled together; I
could've been Barbara Tuchman herself. My book's case for the defense still
couldn't have matched Fran's, Gene's, and Rik-Kuk's case for the persecution.

POSTED BY: *Pam*   *That's My Fran* was the nest egg, and I'd hate to have
been the vet who examined the golden goose after that one came out. Costar-
ring Hippolyte Lecteur—Americanized as "Hy Lector" in the credits, he was
an ex-bandleader who'd had a minor hit dueting with Piaf on a novelty song,
as if French popular music is ever anything but, called "Coûte Que Coûte,
Cocotte"—the series's back story was that Fran had met her French husband
as a wacky WAC in Marseille. Now he played the accordion and sang in the
swank San Francisco nightclub where she kept trying, etc., etc.

Squawking, *That's My Fran* ruled the roost at One Eye, as the era's foremost
broadcast network was known in the industry and as a pretty dubious-sound-
ing after-hours joint in the meat-packing district was known to a few of Jake's
acquaintances in Manhattan. Yet the proof the Age of Conformity wasn't mis-
named was that Fran Kukla ruled at both.

Not all men in gray flannel suits were immune to an urge to slip into something more comfortable. After the only time Jake, never too happy camping,

got hauled off to visit the cabaret One Eye, we got a dazed report in his next letter. Our Fran was the orange-wigged specialty of all three female impersonators he'd seen before finishing his lukewarm paper cup of Eureka Gin, giving a whole new *echt*-Fifties meaning to *mon semblable, mon frère.*

Giving it another, the legitimate One Eye was home to the now visually squared radio voice of Eddie Whitling, its evening newscast's most ponderous marble jaw. Knowing he'd be forced to defer with penguin-suited chuckles to my ETO ex didn't do wonders for Gerson's mood when, corporately summoned to New York, he had to put on a tux and dithyrambulate around the room at network powwows. As he used to say, their only purpose he could see was to settle who had the best dentist.

Though I probably did a worse job than I thought of hiding my frustration at being yanked from *Glory Be*'s better world, I used to go with him when I was on the East Coast. My presence made face time with One Eye's star embalmer of current events at once easier and harder on Gerson. Our glass-clinking small talk would have sounded as civilized as quoits if you'd heard it on tape. Only Eddie's grin kept my husband advised that, by the obnoxious rules of his sexual poker game, prior bedding topped a wedding. His crayoning eyebrows intimated that in the sack his Pamita was someone Gerson wouldn't have recognized, infuriating me more because he had a point.

Naturally, I voiced neither fury nor cause in our taxicab autopsies (if four-wheeled L.A. after dark is a Ferris wheel, four-wheeled New York after dark is a penguin morgue). Nor did I ever feel the faintest commemorative flutter in Eddie's presence. Among other things, his always boiled eyes were now slightly thyroidic, as if inside his muscularly groomed face a circus clown was struggling to get out.

Luckily, if only in the limited sense of the word implied by the French military attaché who once reminded me with some annoyance that it doesn't *snow* on Devil's Island, Gerson was spared the day-to-day running of *That's My Fran*. His name danced on unseen strings in its credits only as it did in those of all Rik-Kuk shows: "Noah Gerson, Executive in Charge of Production." Gene Rickey oversaw the nest egg while Fran clucked and mimed flying, repaid every week in her ego's ransom of fuzzy canned laughter.

Brought aboard, he was told, to give Rik-Kuk pedigree, Gerson asked for and got a free hand. The other was usually wrenched up between his shoulder-blades by Gene Rickey's armlock before noon, a figurative ordeal so painful that inside a year my husband, no sybarite, had hired a literal masseuse. Busy upstairs with Pocahontas, I never felt jealous of Ursula. Both Luz and Ava damn near put on mourning, though.

Even when his pet projects limped onto the air, they'd come down by then with Rickeyfied worms. One that caused Gerson special grief was *Shocks of Recognition*, which up to its first pilot had featured a panel of eminent modern-day historians interviewing actors made up as Adams vs. Jefferson, Burr vs. Hamilton (neither armed, fortunately), Lee vs. Grant, Custer vs. Sitting Bull, Mark Twain vs. James Fenimore Cooper, Babe Ruth vs. Ty Cobb, Stephen Foster vs. (the real) Louis Armstrong. By the time Rik-Kuk sold it, to Arthur Schlesinger Jr.'s chagrin—it was the reason he'd started wearing those natty bow ties—it had mutated into a quiz show called *Wasn't That Us?* which lasted thirty-odd incredible years. So I learned when, numb after a hospital visit during Cadwaller's long dying, I turned on our (soon my) set and stared briefly at its Eighties iteration, now hosted by an amiable dunce named Mack "Paddy" McMartin. No mean hand at hat tricks himself, the one-term Congressman we'd hardly known had turned District dross into Hollywood gold.

It wasn't all like that. If it had been, Gene Rickey's armlock would've soon been partnered by his other arm choking Gerson's windpipe while leaving him a free hand, and my husband had an inner realist whose job was to keep Noah fed. I don't much recall any of them, but Tim Cadwaller tells me *Molder and Maunder* is a good courtroom series, *Curt Rasp, FBI* has its gangbusting moments, and *Here, Biscuit* (child star and dog rehashing the myth of Sisyphus in suburbia) is funny as you-scrims for Ike's grin go. Rik-Kuk's four Westerns—*Giddyup, The Chesterfield Clan, Ten Steps Back,* and *Lasso*—were often a cut above the other twenty or thirty then on the air.

Still, the fate of *Proscenium* tells the story. With his passion for seeing history resurrected on film, my husband hadn't abandoned his fantasy of Lazarusing unpreserved great moments in theater after Jake turned him down. Far from it, since he now had the goad of proving Jake wrong. They could be competitive, those two, and a line in Jake's letter describing the male after-hours Frans—"But I'll go back if Pam wants to, since she might enjoy it"—had left Gerson peculiarly irked.

He reworked and polished his brainstorm; he got Orson Welles's phone number. He set his mouth firmly and went back to his desk with Welles's rumbling laughter still in his ears. I'm afraid even his wife, descending from Haroun Pam-Raschid's study with her brain still orgiastic and modulating with difficulty to an environment where other people breathed and spoke, had begun to find Gerson's hope comical. Even if the silly thing ever got broadcast, it could hardly make up for all the slop and crud, Rik and Kuk, I-scrims and you-scrims surrounding it.

Yet when *Proscenium* did reach the air, it was no ratings disaster. Done in only by the wane of live TV, it ran three years and is ranked among the highlights of what Tim swears is called the medium's Golden Age. The only one disgraced was Gerson. What's worse is that he was under few illusions from the moment One Eye gave its blessing and Gene thanked him for not giving up.

Six p.m. was early for me to relinquish *Glory Be*, but I wanted to watch the Democratic convention. As I came downstairs, Gerson was bidding his masseuse adieu: "I'm sorry, Mrs. Clydesdale. I'll try to do better next time."

"Bad day in Bearbank, darling?" I asked as Ursula clopped down the sidewalk. By then, whether he'd gotten pummeled at work or at home, Gerson's smile and his wince were inseparable.

"Most people would say not. *Proscenium*'s a go."

"Oh, my God! Which play do they start with?"

"Sarah Bernhardt in *Hamlet*. Just as I planned."

"Then what's wrong?" Light dawned. "Oh, crap! Who's the actress?"

He was ashen. "Fran wants an Emmy for drama. She's crazed."

POSTED BY: *Pam*   Even those who agree she was a horror—and Tim Cadwaller seconds me, perhaps more reliably as he never knew her in person—also acknowledge that Fran was a trouper. Well, of course! That's like saying Napoleon was always a soldier. They had what draftees don't: motivation.

She got her Emmy, too. Not for drama, though: comedy. Not many thigh-slapping, roaring-with-laughter Americans ever knew *Proscenium*'s original intent had been to elevate them, but the industry grapevine bottled wine off Gerson's comeuppance for years.

Too anxious to more than pick at Ava's guacamole, he turned on the set an hour early, fussing with its rabbit ears. Watching TV felt more active then: a challenge to our ingenuity. To make him laugh, I brightly asked, "Why is tonight different from all other nights?," but he didn't think it was funny. Vaporous with postpartum authorial confusion about what magazines and other people's books were for, I busied myself elsewhere, barely heeding the brawls and shots in the living room: "Give me ten minutes to get out of town, Pard? I'll give you Ten…Steps…Back." Then Gerson called, "Pammie, it's starting."

"*Pro*-SEE-knee-yum!" the announcer boomed as Greek masks of comedy and tragedy played musical chairs before settling in place. Doing his research, Gerson'd had the Pantages Theater mocked up as one from the Belle Époque, but Gene Rickey had scotched his plea to dress the whole audience in turn-of-the-century evening wear. Only the first two rows got outfitted, and they were the ones shown filing in.

As Cornelius Ryan might put it, the text was abridged too far. That was partly thanks to One Eye's ninety-minute time slot and partly because Fran wanted a grand entrance. "This is a hell of a lot of rhubarb and rhubard and ketchup and crotch rot before I show up," she'd muttered, and Gerson had agreed to open with Hamlet's first soliloquy.

The Pantages curtains parted to reveal a rampart at Elsinore, empty for five full tense seconds. Then Fran swept in, magnificent in a black wig and doublet. She actually looked more like Sarah Bernhardt in the photographs of Bernhardt costumed as Hamlet than I would've guessed she could. For a sixth and seventh full tense second, I wondered whether Gerson's hope might possibly come true.

Fran extended an arm. "*Ohhh*, that this too too solid flesh would melt!" she groaned thrillingly.

A wave of delighted laughter crashed into a surf of applause, making the looks of studious Belle Époque-y concentration from the period extras in the two front rows look even daffier in the reaction shot. And understand: during three weeks of rehearsal, Fran had worked terribly hard. She'd not only memorized the surviving chunks of her part, but listened to Gerson explaining Sarah Bernhardt's grand manner and the period's theatrical conventions. He'd told me that there'd been moments in the final run-through when the mutation of Fran into Sarah and then Sarah into Hamlet had even him forgetting she was Fran, an obvious thrill for more than one reason.

Yet not only had a junkie just heard the sound of auditory heroin. A trouper had grasped the jig was up, and old Fran hands in the know swear you can't see her blink. Of course Gerson and I were too unnerved by the laughter to realize that *Proscenium*'s star, unlike the prince she was playing, was making her greatest decision in a heartbeat. On live TV, with Rik-Kuk's future at One Eye riding on the outcome and eighty-nine minutes to go.

She rolled her eyes. "Brother! What I'd give for a cheese Danish," she told the camera. "If this diet don't kill me, my stepfather will."

As it's available on DVD, I don't suppose I need to rehash all of *Proscenium*'s legendary 1956 slapstick *Hamlet* here on harried little daisysdaughter.com. I've met stubborn folk who refuse to believe it was all improvised, but they didn't know Fran Kukla. Nor could Fran have guessed that her whole career—the burlesque days, the TKO bit parts, the radio stint, and the four seasons of *That's My Fran*— had been preparation for this astonishing cavalry charge into the jaws of death.

Everyone I've talked to has a favorite gag. Fran accompanying "When we have shuffled off this mortal coil, must give us pause" by holding up her hands squirrel-style and glancing at them, then us, in toothy consternation; I've had that one reprised to my face many times. Fran popping up midway through Polonius's burblings to gasp, "Kind of like listening to John Foster Dulles, isn't it?" Or the famous moment when the actor playing Horatio, who like the rest of the cast had been struggling to stick to the text up to then, answers the speech that ends "the triumph of our pledge" by asking, "Sweet prince, is Pledge among our sponsors?" She whirls on him with a glare of affronted hauteur, all the funnier since it was genuine.

And Gerson? In our Beverly Hills living room, Gerson looked as if his dentist had decided to try eye surgery after strapping him to the chair. We watched with clenched jaws and tensed paws, and soon we didn't dare glance at each other. After Gerson's murmured "No, no," neither of us spoke a word. Then Fran picked up Yorick's skull, rubbed her own wigged one, and bawled, "Forty-nine cents for *cabbage?* Cripes! What's Denmark *coming* to?"

Oh, Panama! I damn near keeled over laughing. So did my pained yet undeluded husband, recognizing that the game was done—and Fran Kukla had won, had won. We roared, we snorted. My Gerson slapped his thigh. We laughed 'til we cried.

POSTED BY: *Pamlet*   You know the rest, Tim. All three Borsht Brothers coming out of retirement to send up Junius, Edwin, and John Wilkes Booth's 1864 version of *Julius Caesar.* Fran's own return doing Eleonora Duse as Camille. Once they realized having a historic production for reference wasn't pertinent anymore, it got easier: Jimmy Durante's Cyrano. Perhaps in worse taste, George Shearing's jazz *Oedipus Rex.* None was as inspired as the spontaneous original, but Pam did learn in a letter from Eve—dehusbanded and sans TV, I was living in Paris by then—that the Hal Lime demolition of *Doctor Faustus,* with Fran's dowdy *That's My Fran* costar Mamie Dwight cameo-ing as Helen of Troy, was a scream.

And no, Tim: I'm not offended by your opinion that *Proscenium's* forgotten and solemn original concept had an *echt*-Fifties middlebrow pathos. I agree that the show everyone roared at was more original and just plain better. But even granting that Gerson had an ultimately triumphant longing to see the past revived in modern configurations rather than starting fresh, I'll never buy your contention that the mistake made by earnest fellows like him was to see TV as too literally a medium—a novel way of transmitting the traditional—rather than a new art form in its own right.

It's simple, young Mr. Cadwaller: nobody my age will ever keep a straight face when we hear television called an art form. "What's Denmark *coming* to?" we're more likely to bawl.

Not counting DVD Kirstenings or my first husband's three-headed resurrection on the Murphy Channel, I don't watch much anymore. I certainly couldn't take more than a cringing minute or two of the hideous sitcoms an aging Fran Kukla did when her ego was driving her time and again to recapture people's love of *That's My Fran*. By then, she didn't give the Frank Uklas who impersonated her after hours (there were four Frans at the Stonewall rebellion) much room for exaggeration.

When I wonder what made her so strident, it's probably no surprise I circle back to the one aspect of Fran with which I felt an affinity. Do you know, I think it was all about her hair? When she did Bernhardt and Duse on *Proscenium*, she wore a wig both times, but on any series she starred in, a wig wasn't an option. That orange frizz of madness was her television trademark, staying unchanged even when her blurry eyes and turgid jaw had no more flexibility in reacting to events than the cameras whose glassy stare she seemed by then to be emulating for mimetic protection.

When I was revolved if not resolved to face my own follicular sorrows in salon mirrors, did Pam ever consider a wig herself? Oh, hell no. By the early-Sixties heyday of Baez and Bardotlatry, I was too used to being out of competition, and anyhow my straits were less dire. Fran's orange frizz put my brindle mop in perspective, and *my* hairdressers were encouraged to do their very best, not their worst. Above all, I wasn't parading my coif in front of millions of viewers who adored me for making women look stupid.

I can think of a few silly shows I've enjoyed over the years. I was quite fond of Goldie Hawn on *Laugh-In*. Still, I'm afraid I never so much as sampled the series you and Panama used to rave about, Tim, even at the FDR Memorial— *Roseanne the Umpire Slayer* or whatever it was called—and I'll never know what people mean when they say they're addicted. The only exception in my case had several motivations besides quality.

I'd never paid any mind to daytime TV, but a husband wincing at IVs at Bethesda Naval Hospital makes habit go by the wayside. Until I switched channels after my brief exposure to Mack "Paddy" McMartin in his game-show host guise, I hadn't known *The Good Life with Dottie Crozdetti* existed, much less that it had been running opposite *Wasn't That Us?* for years and years. Then there Dottie was in her kitchen, brandishing a plucked chicken by the neck and puffing her cheeks to go "Buck, buck, buck."

Pamique almost didn't recognize her pre–Pearl Harbor Bank Street roommate, now grown much stouter and grayer as well as forty-five years older. The wayward nose, blonde hair, rosy complexion, wide prominent cheekbones, dimples, and unpredictably tossed chin—all gone. Only her blue eyes and mischievous small teeth were the same.

All through Cadwaller's long dying and up to Dottie's retirement too soon afterward, I never missed an episode. Yet unlike Fran Kukla's *Hamlet*, *The Good Life with...* has never been on DVD. When I read Dottie's obituary, one of my odder thoughts—I don't think it would've displeased her—was that now maybe everything would come out at last, the many seasons I'd missed included. Now I'll never know.

Kirsten, you'll have to watch them instead. I'm sorry, darling: Pamlet's made her decision. You lost.

Yes, Ard: I'm back on course for Dog Green. I've got Pink in the landing craft with me and we're holding hands. She's wearing the very Googlable low-cut black thingamabob she barely had on at the 2003 Grammys, with the vent up to here that shows off her thigh tattoo and her strap boots. I generally prefer her blonde and rather hope she won't sing before we hit the beach, but her jaguar grin is fierce and she looks adorable.

POSTED BY: *Pam*   Come to think of it, the invisibly tanned Gerson who stayed in touch after our divorce could've probably given me some tips about handling this endearingly light little gun in my lap. Just lucky he didn't have access to weaponry after *Proscenium*'s broadcast, and not only because back then he didn't know a safety catch from a light switch.

Yes, he'd laughed. He confessed he'd been crimping his lips not to since Fran's John Kukla Dulles ad lib. I'd been crimping mine since the actress playing Ophelia sashayed onstage belting out "Love for Sale" after "To be or not to be," answering each of Hamlet's rebukes with another jitterbugging chorus. Sadly, she never worked for Rik-Kuk again: Fran was still Fran, and the routine had crowded her.

Gerson wouldn't have been my Gerson if he'd managed to sit through Fran Kukla's *Hamlet* stony-faced. That didn't mean he took any pleasure in his dream project's success on these terms once we'd darked our TV set and the first congratulatory calls started jangling. When he went up to bed, he looked shattered. When he came down to breakfast, he looked glued.

Whatever he'd used, he'd done a practical job with the pottery, without much regard for aesthetics or more than approximating his former appearance. "You know what, Pammie," he said. "Maybe I'm not cut out for TV."

"You're not cut out for Fran, we know that. But she's the paper doll, not you."

"She also understands this country better than we ever will. Not even saying that's good, bad, indifferent, just true."

"No plurals," I blurted maladroitly, making him stare. Weren't *we* a we? Hadn't I just called us one, for heaven's sake? But I was speaking as Haroun Pam-Raschid. *Glory Be* was due out in October.

Even so, the return of my authorial dementia was stoked by fresh compassion. I do and must think the feeling was genuine, no matter how gaga. Now that *Proscenium* had turned into what it had turned into—and if Gene Rickey's nighttime call had been gushing, his morning one was an eager bark for more classic plays to lampoon—I was more convinced than ever that my book was Gerson's only hope.

Making me believe I was not only right but that he agreed with me, he threw himself like a lemming into planning *Glory Be*'s Romanoff's party. He didn't have much else to do, since he'd taken himself off *Proscenium* as soon as Guapo Borsht was mentioned as a likely John Wilkes Booth. The bathrobed, striped-pajamaed man I knew in those days—"I've let Ursula go. This is Frau Schildkraut"—told a pleased but puzzled Gene that he was shut away working on an idea for a sitcom about a zany American war correspondent who'd met a Buchenwald inmate she felt sorry for.

Though less depressed than Gerson by *Proscenium*'s mutation, more than once forcing myself to look sympathetically down in the dumps when all I could think of was *Glory Be*'s imminence, I did feel oddly agitated by what it all meant. In my youth—first time you'd called it *that*, Pammie!—even the least reflective of us had been sure we were duking it out with mighty times. In the Thirties and Forties, believe me, inconsequentiality wasn't our worry. Now the game was done—we'd won, we'd won—and our reward was Fran Kukla's *Hamlet*.

In odd hours, which more and more of them were—no one's ends are looser than an author's in the final countdown to publication, and besides my marriage had gone funny—I chivvied those fleas around the track. I wanted my mind to arrive at some sort of declaration on the topic of whether heroism was a demand forced on people by necessity or a thrilling ambition irrespective of circumstances; whether it was the poem or what you did when the world said you had to so that you could go back to whatever you defined as poetry—silliness, merriment, pratfalls, and comfort. I look pensive in my photo in *Vogue*.

When it finally came out, *Glory Be* didn't do as well as I'd hoped. It's possible my yardstick was to blame, since I wanted and at times expected it to wreak havoc on the 1956 election, somehow giving us President Kefauver; to destroy Gene Rickey as Carthage had been destroyed, tossing Fran on the pyre like an orange-frizzed pine cone; to improve my hair, *gonfle* my tatas, and restore my Gerson to what he'd been when I'd met him. By more middling standards, the thing was a smash. It spent months on the bestseller lists, neck and neck with *Profiles in Courage*—a book conceived, let's say to be polite, out of a muddled impulse not too dissimilar from mine by one of the most cautious politicians in America.

I suppose I shouldn't have sold the TV rights to Rik-Kuk, but Cath Charters said they'd made the best offer. Though the series never materialized, that the book was even bought should tell you what kind of success *Glory Be* was. Anyhow, by then Gerson didn't work for Gene Rickey anymore. The sale was a betrayal only of a Gerson he'd left behind him, and his answer to my letter confessing it was amused.

That was after I'd gritted my teeth and forced myself to keep a promise I'd made when Martha Shelton was alive. To be honest, I hated the prospect of tearing myself away; I loved the interviews, the book signings, the meetings with strangers I didn't need to worry about impressing. I already *had*, you see, and it was heaven to know going in I'd have to club kittens in public before anyone expressed a doubt about how wonderful I was. But I'd told Gerson I'd make it up to him and God knows he was owed.

"Gerson, I want to take you away from all this," I told him in early December. "My treat, don't even think about the cost. Right now, Random House would probably send a virgin to my doorstep if I crooked a finger! Well, whatever. Just name a place and you're there—with me, of course. No one else."

"Anywhere?"

"Anywhere at all. Tahiti! I'll get the globe from Steh—from the den and you play eenie-meenie-minie-moe."

He smiled his new pottery smile. "Never mind the globe."

POSTED BY: *Pam*   Israel had just fought and won its second war when we saw the same burnt-out supply trucks Jake Cohnstein had on the road to Jerusalem, the Israelis having left them as memorials to the convoys. Mere Angelenos, how we two gasped at that brawny sun when we came off the plane holding hands (skittish landing). Pam hadn't been the hat type since the ETO, but a white one the size of a truck wheel was the first thing I bought.

In what I've learned isn't an uncommon reaction, our new surroundings felt inexplicably familiar. In my case, though, the big peekaboo and wink of the sun's eye around every corner wasn't religious. Fans of daisysdaughter.com must've gathered by now that spirituality isn't my pool hall. For all nine days we spent there, Palestine never stopped reminding Pam of a more militant California.

Tel Aviv was what Los Angeles would be if it were fighting for its life. Imagine seeing burnt-out supply trucks on the road to Pasadena! Imagine tanned surfers become darker paratroopers, battered old freighters in San Diego's (Haifa's) sparkling marina, a girl with eyes dark as tamarind and hips expert as miniature race cars serving falafel, hummus, and olives in Malibu—well, Tirat Karmel.

Our home base for much of the trip, Jerusalem was a sadder but wiser San Francisco. One afternoon, the Negev was the Mojave, but with a lone tank's hulk parked, cannon aimed at unseen Salt Lake City: the Dead Sea. I'm afraid Nazareth reminded me a bit of Bakersfield. And so on, leaving me disarmed, often exhilarated, and sometimes mysteriously or not so mysteriously upset.

With a harsher sun browbeating stonier ridges and more determined plants, the hills that cradled the kibbutz we were driven to above the Plain of Esdraelon were the rugged Middle Eastern cousins of those I'd wound my old convertible and then my new Olds through so many times to Topanga. The local Addison— there was one, the mayor—offered us mint tea, not daiquiris, had defended San Bernardino in the '48 war (game leg introduced as memento), and spoke of

Herzl and the Dead Sea Scrolls, not botany and Keats. The local Eve wore a blue kerchief, had three children and a rifle: "Oh, drat!" her Los Angeles counterpart exclaimed some weeks later when I shared with her what I hadn't with Gerson. "And me left helpless with these silly brass knuckles"—her jewelry.

Of course there were differences. The livelier street life in the cities, the dustier, shabbier cars. Gritting its feeble surf as if here came the important part, the thin sea hugged in close, didn't stretch like the Pacific to beyond of beyond. The music stayed stubbornly foreign. Aside from a few bleary ones in cafés, the only TV set I saw was in our room at the King David Hotel—unused, as may go without saying.

Yet my double vision didn't only turn the DeWitts into kibbutzniks. It reframed most Israelis I met. More vigorous, brisker, and far less prone than Californians to talk about real estate—well, then, anyway—they still weren't total strangers to me. That wasn't because they were Jewish and mostly spoke English. It was because—oh, at last, Pamidiot, think of Addison!—they were *transplants.*

Volunteers. Not a place you were born, one you heard of and struck out for. Then looked to your mettle, new companions, and wardrobe to make "This is who I am now" stick. That's no longer true, wasn't by my first trip back with Cadwaller in the Sixties. Even by 1956, it may have been waning if you'd seen Israel earlier. But it was only eleven years since Auschwitz. Eight since nationhood, independence, the Jerusalem convoys battling to get through to the city.

And Gerson? He was Gerson re-Gersonized. More Gerson than ever, yet a Gerson I'd never known. I wasn't sure anyone had, Stella Negroponte's photo not being partial to divulging confidences. In Wife Two's mental lists of our husband's attributes, "nimble" had never loomed large. Now he scrambled over rocks, stood on walls, leapt at stairways. He chortled at victories, exulted in landmarks, shut up for a change at Masada. He was camera-crazed the first day or two; I appear goofily white-hatted in much of the evidence. Then he stopped taking pictures, and I doubt he noticed. Let alone had guessed why.

"I'm so glad you met a me," said Eve in Topanga the following February. "You watch! One day all the Eves will take over. Who was the you, and where was she? Beersheba? Eyeless in Gaza?"

"That's just it. Not a Pam to be found—and I looked."

I waggled a ringless finger that's now long since become Rheuma Three and keeps Pam Cadwaller's wedding band captive between two grim knuckles. At my age, you can catch yourself stupidly inspecting your own mitts in wonder: "And you were there, and you." It seems unbelievable all ten of them did the whole trip. Eyes are one thing, but *fingers?* It doesn't stay interesting long.

Still, it had been two months, and I laughed. "But there wasn't a Gene Rickey, either. For Noah's sake—and Israel's!—I hope there never is."

POSTED BY: *Pam*   Midway through dinner on what I thought was our final night in Jerusalem, we were joined by a ghost. I had to take his word for it, though. Spiritualism isn't my pool hall either, and the man who pulled up a chair at my dazed invitation was visibly as corporeal as the next corporal (he'd been one). The ghost I kept squinting and failing to see was someone he had been, not was.

To prepare us for what I thought was our looming return to Los Angeles, once Gerson's and my food came Pam broke a vow I'd stuck to all trip. For the first time in nine days, I brought up *Glory Be*. Cath Charters had been keeping me posted by telegram, and for the first time had mentioned the chance of a TV sale. Yet if I thought asking Gerson's advice on my book's I-scrim-for-Ike's-grin prospects would either attract the expert in him or make the topic seem less Pamcentric, I was wrong.

He glanced around the King David's restaurant. Doing the same, since our flight was tomorrow—I assumed he'd understood my impulse and wanted a farewell panorama—the vestigial war correspondent in Pam once again liked how the Israeli Defense Forces had apparently never seen much point in dress uniforms. To an IDF officer, more declaratively if they were senior, short-sleeved and open-necked khaki was a fit rig for meeting anyone from movie queen to foreign minister. The only nod to formality was that most I could see had been pressed.

I liked how even the smartest cocktail dress announced itself as merely occasional, as functional here as pants and boots might be the next day. I liked how even a room this Britishly elegant declared that the purpose of buildings was shelter from wind and night when they came.

All this was California grown purposeful, California with urgency. Yet Gerson atypically seemed to be eyeing what other diners had on their plates.

"What do I think?" he said at long last. "Pammie, if Cath sells it, let her. Put the check in the bank and don't get involved."

"But Gerson, it's my book, for God's sake. I can't just walk away and let them ruin it."

"They won't," he said, chewing tranquilly now.

"They won't?"

"Nope! They'll just make a bad series. But the book is a book is a book. That's all she wrote, you could say."

Why didn't I just give up, try again on the plane? A touch of Haroun-Pam-Raschid, I presume. "Well, I'd at least want a say in the casting," I protested. "I can't let some Gidget play Martha Shelton."

Gerson smiled. "If she's pretty, why not? A paycheck's a paycheck and Gidget must live. Pammie, no one on earth knows what most of your people looked like, acted like, sounded like. Not many would care."

"I would and I do. I know exactly what Martha looked and sounded like. If Shelton Wiggins walked in here, I'd recognize him in a New York mi—"

"Oh my God. That's ben Canaan," Gerson furiously whispered.

Was that the ghost? No, it wasn't. Not mine, at least. Still, even *Glory Be*'s author couldn't bridle at that interruption; it had been ben Canaan's tanks that had reached the Suez Canal only a month ago. Yul Brynner crossed with Paul Newman, his new eyepatch firmly in place, he joined a large table of archeologists and filmmakers after raking the room with a cerulean gaze I thought turned most chilly when it passed over me.

"I never realized I looked *that* American." I meant to make Gerson chuckle and did. Three different people at three different stops had told us of the latest military celebrity's bitter estrangement from his blonde U.S. wife, unlike Pam a real nurse but no paragon. She'd scuttled back to the States like a shiksa iguana once she caught on after the '48 war her Ari meant them to live at Gan Dafna, not here in ritzy Jerusalem. The most memorable verdict came from San Bernardino's game-legged defender: "Like an actress, she knew she'd been miscast. But here we can't play first one part, then another. He's mistrusted Washington since."

"Gerson, don't stare," I reminded him.

"Ah, why not? I don't know if you've noticed, but someone's staring at *you.*"

I hadn't. When I scooted my gaze over my salad fork, guided by Gerson's "Nine o'clock" to his wineglass (he'd learned tactics somewhere: from Stella?), he was still staring steadily and didn't look away either. Once our eyes met, he smiled, dabbed his lips with a napkin, stood up, and walked over.

"I didn't mean to be rude, only sure," he explained, all smoothly muscular middle-aged vigor and rubicund skin. "You are Pamela Buchanan?"

"Oh, yes! Of course. I—"

I'd reached for a pen and come up with a spoon. I'd looked at both his strong hands for a copy of *Glory Be* that stayed invisible. I'd looked back up for help at his well-tended face and wide smile.

"Colleague, why didn't you tell me Paulette Goddard had ended up out of the running? I really think I could have handled it, you know."

Did I stare? I stared. Did I gasp? I gasped. Did I leap to my feet as silverware clattered, Gerson vanished, Ari ben Canaan winked, and a wineglass smashed somewhere? I did. All Jerusalem became a mute wedding orchestra.

"*Nachum?* Nachum Unger, the poet?"

We held out our hands and they waltzed.

POSTED BY: *Pam*   Eventually—I think our coffee'd come by then—Gerson grew back first one eye, then the other. A mouth I'd seen somewhere before requested some sort of modest assignment. For a while all he'd been was a shoe.

My Gerson and I had been married eight years. On April 29, 1945, I'd talked for eight minutes at most to a reeking, eighty-pound Dachau inmate with unfoulable eyes. But I'd said "I do" to What's-His-Name at L.A.'s City Hall as kids peddled their papers and routine Cadillacs shuttled. I think we went to Musso's afterward, can't be sure.

Nachum and I were wedded by history—the ultimate shotgun marriage, I know. I don't think it's unkind to invite you to guess which day was more memorable to not only two but all three of us.

The best fuck of my life was my only experience of group sex. It took place in the restaurant of the famous King David Hotel in Jerusalem. No carnal desire was involved. There are things I've done in reality—bent this way agreeably, bent that one less so, crocked on brandy or wine—that I wouldn't blush to admit half as much. I'd never been unfaithful to Gerson, but that night I committed public, conversational adultery.

Our voices and eyes did the deed right in front of him. We tore off the clothes of the years as he sat there. Do I dare to think we liked having a watcher? As waiters roved, khaki and cocktails went this way and that, palm fronds past the windows mimicked a chuppah and muttered rustling applause—and all stayed perfectly civilized—I played Nachum's strumpet as I never had with or for Gerson, much less with another man as he looked on and sipped coffee. My own inmate took me as a ship takes the sea.

The ugly word I detect I'm avoiding is *ownership*. If it applied, it was mutual. The whole heat of our sex—and I remind you once again: waiters, Gerson, Nachum didn't take off so much as his wristwatch—was that we owned each other without either being the slave.

And Gerson? Gerson might've grown up in Nebraska. He'd never seen history's ocean before. He'd studied it, read everything he could get his hands on about it. He'd gone crazy trying to imagine it. But the waves' crack and the wild air, Panama! The joy of two glistening, mermish bodies as we gasped, splashed, got smacked around, rose, and rioted in the surf of our little acre of history's ocean: he'd never had that in his life. My poor Gerson had gone from eunuch to cuckold. Had no one to accuse except Martha Shelton and Hitler.

Occasionally treating us as a plural for politeness's sake, Nachum told me his story. The displaced-persons camp north of Munich where he'd spent ten months after being sprung from Dachau had separated Jewish survivors from German POWs by only a tripwire: "We got the impression you Americans thought we'd *all* made a mistake. But as you can see and we all learned, you do make damned good ice cream."

A return to now blasted Dresden struck him as a handsome invitation to swim down and reclaim his stateroom in a sunken ship. His decision to turn illegal had been made with his feet, which walked all the way to Trieste.

"How did you live?"

"I'd broken into one of your warehouses, took five cartons of American cigarettes. Back then—you remember, colleague—eight would've gotten me to Madagascar. When I reached Palestine, I had one pack left. Here it is."

Reaching into his pocket, he held it up, now wrapped in Karloffian tape and cellophane. But you could still make out the camel.

"Will you ever smoke them?" a faint Gerson asked faintly.

"Oh, I don't smoke. Would you like one?"

Fainter still: "No, no."

Some years later, Nachum told me he always offered. By then he'd married the woman who said yes. She lit one every anniversary until the pack was gone.

Trieste still had enough of a Jewish community for him to make contact. He was passed down the line: four months, that part took. Finally he splashed ashore through black surf one night near Caesaria among scrawny kids, impatient Haganah guides, and a woman who started wailing she'd left her overcoat behind; they'd made it to the trucks before the Royal Navy patrol boat's searchlight came on. Three weeks later, equipped with an old bolt-action rifle and eight rounds of ammunition, he was on the front lines in Jerusalem.

Now he was a columnist for *Haaretz*. "Movies?" I asked, and he shook his head: "No, colleague. Politics."

"And the poetry?"

Nachum grinned. "Oh, well. By the time I'd learned it well enough to think of trying, I must say writing poetry in Hebrew struck me as redundant. Colleague, what about you? Tell me about the book you wrote."

Did that ever turn out to be an awkward bit of post-coital pillow talk! Of course I thought he meant *Glory Be*, but Nachum didn't know it existed. He looked unabashedly baffled when I started going on about the Pilgrims' landfall and the French and Indian War. Meaning to pay me a professional compliment by treating it as a given, my colleague meant that I must've written a book about *our* war—our own bit of history's ocean, swirling until it knocked us together on April 29, 1945.

And I had. I just didn't especially enjoy explaining that mine was an uproarious American romp through Europe that featured the Holocaust as a clumsily appended afterthought, scrapped outright in the later printings. Can't say for sure if squeaking *Nothing*'s title when Nachum wouldn't take "Oh" for an answer counted as a third awkward moment or just the second one's continuation by other means.

"And your role?" he asked Gerson pleasantly. I don't know if he meant the war, my book, or our shared century, but my husband was too honest to choose any but the least boastful option. God knows it pained him, though.

"Me? Oh, I turned it into a movie."

Slipping the Karloffian camel back into his breast pocket, Nachum beamed at us both with real fondness. "*Damned* good ice cream," he said.

POSTED BY: *Pam*   Nonetheless, that let Gerson back in as more than a land-locked peeping Tom. He was allowed to have hands now. Once he saw he'd been granted permission to perch on the messy bed we'd made of our bit of history's ocean, he was even allowed, a bit gingerly, to broach topics. Since Nachum had already told us about the 1948 war, my husband wanted to hear all about the one that had ended a month ago with ben Canaan's tanks on the Suez Canal.

But Nachum was a real Israeli, impatient above all with simplicity. He knew what Gerson wanted to hear: the IDF on the offensive, armored spearheads in the Sinai. Ben Canaan and Landau conferring over a map, goggles around their necks in the lead chariot's blue-starred, Hebrew-lettered shadow as sun-baked dust swirled and they seized the initiative. Paying my husband a backhanded compliment (they were to stay great friends for years), Nachum refused to give Gerson that movie.

"Remember: we colluded," he told us. "I've got no love lost for Nasser, I'd shoot him without batting an eye if that raving pan-nationalist bastard showed up at my door. But we *schemed*. Not exactly a first for us, since we made deals with anyone and everyone to get as many Jews out of Europe as we could."

Note the "we," Panama. As I've said, "This is who I am now." Also note its upcoming contradiction, though.

"Well, it was justified," said Gerson primly.

"Of course. You'll get no argument from me. I just wish they'd made a few more! But this was different. Suez wasn't survival, it was power politics:

our little Israel on Broadway at last. Suez was us in league with the British and French, our former imperial masters—no great love lost there either, but we've obviously learned you don't always marry for love—plotting in secret to smash Nasser and Egypt, who deserved it, to hell and gone. It must just *confound* our so recent allies that in London and Paris, Suez is the foreign-policy disaster of all time. But in Tel Aviv, Haifa, and this very room, Suez is a triumph and the latest glory of our already much laureled IDF. Same plan, same war! Different publics."

"Have you *written* this?" My husband looked incredulous.

"Oh, Noah!" Nachum laughed flat-out tenderly. "I've not only written it, I've said it on radio. To a mixed reaction, yes. Did you think we'd stop arguing just because we're a country? It would be like the British learning to cook. Or Americans forgetting how to make movies."

It wasn't until we were exchanging addresses that Nachum confirmed Pam's stymied ghost-seeking stare by admitting he wasn't Nachum Unger at all. No, not an impostor, Panama: a successor, one Nachum ben Zion. "Not the most inspired choice, colleague, I agree. But as I think I told you both, trying to write poetry in Hebrew struck me as redundant."

"Oh, hell! I'll never get it right," I laughed, remembering Jake introducing himself as Jack Cornhole and also playing the shiksa for the first time in hours. "Didn't all of you always tell me changing your name was giving in?"

"Well, colleague. A lot depends on what you change it to."

"And where." Gerson's voice was muffled, but whether by his mouth or my ears is anyone's guess.

Nachum went on out into his city; we went up to our room and made love. Whether I felt I had something to make up for or was just compensating for one act of infidelity or fidelity by performing another is anyone's guess too. If I'd known it was our last time, I'd—oh, hell, bikini girl, I probably wouldn't have done anything much different. We were us, knew each other too well for surprises to register as anything but impersonations. In bed, anyhow.

When I woke up, Gerson was out on our balcony. From my pillowed point of view, Jerusalem was just a blue sky and murmurs of traffic. I stood up and it metamorphosed into the vista my husband had been looking at for an hour.

I doubt he'd taken much of it in. Now that he knew there'd be world enough and time for that, looking at it while still trapped in the guise of a tourist must've been distracting and annoying. When he turned to me, he'd visibly spent most of that hour harrying his face and voice to brace for whatever followed what he'd audibly and visibly determined had to be the first words he spoke when he turned to me if they were going to get said at all.

"Pammie, I'm staying."

POSTED BY: *Pam Kukla as Sarah Bernhardt in the King David Hotel* Not only because a lot of it's just too atrocious but I don't have all day, there's no way I'm going to attempt a full reconstruction of the two hours that followed. What I'll be leaving out, like what I've got no choice but to put in, definitely wasn't married life's version of "Row, Row, Row Your Boat."

It was just more, abominably more, of Gerson's and my perversely bright-morninged, surreally—well, to one of us—Palestinial version of the witching-hour colloquy no marriage can survive more than one of. The other stranger's facial expressions and vocal rhythms blind you with rage at their idiot resemblance to the spouse you loved. Noticing nose hairs feels like apt cause for butchery. Yet maybe the timing wasn't altogether inappropriate, since as I think I've mentioned, some marriages are most themselves at midnight. Ours had always been most itself in the morning.

Here are a few—how to put this?—highlights. "Say it, say it! Just say it once, that's all I ask. Did we *disappoint* you, Gerson? *Huh?*"

"No plurals," he said reflexively.

"All right! Did *I-aye-I-eye-I* disappoint you?"

A fire engine could've gone by under our window just then and been drowned out. That "I" went on for a good eight or nine seconds, and Maria Callas, eat your lungs out. Of course, I didn't have to worry about staying on pitch.

His lips crimped. "Yes, you did. But I'm sure I also disappointed you. Many, many times."

With no anticipation from my eyes, I felt my cheeks go Niagara. "No, never, not once, never! Never once, Gerson. Never," I blubbered, then corrected myself. "Well, *now!* I mean, obviously: now. Did I mention now? Yes, definitely now. It only takes one. Hell, just ask my muh-mother. Oh, laugh, please please laugh! Your Pammie muh-made a joke. *LAaauUUuGH!*"

"I'll listen to anything you need to get said, but will you stop screeching? My God, Pam, you sound like—no, that's too cruel."

I didn't stop screeching. It's a wonder the King David didn't throw us both out—or the city authorities, what with all those wonderful old buildings burnt to ashes. (Because the fire engines couldn't get through, Panama. Because no one could hear the *sirens*, Panama. God! I get sick of holding your hand, bikini girl. I do.)

"…It's *because* I'm American, you bitch!" he finally screamed back. I'd never heard him scream before. "My God, this is what I was *promised*. My God, don't you understand that here, here, *here* is the country I always wanted, imagined, *prayed for* the United States to be? Because I knew it *had been*, once before I was born? It's like a man whose mother is fat, dull, old, and stupid—she smells bad, Pammie! She doesn't read anymore, can't even write her own name. She sits in her own caca and rocks back and forth and laughs at Fran Kukla. She's shoving, shoving more cookies in her mouth, more baloney, more hot dogs, more! I don't know how she even finds room for it all when she's got Gene Rickey's cock in her mouth, but she does. Then one day he finds a photograph of her as a young girl."

"And can't wait to screw the bejesus out of her," I said coolly. "My! This is getting interesting. I can't wait to write to my mother-in-law in Passaic. But oh! That's right. She can't read anymore."

Later. Was I packing, unpacking? Was I trying to smash the lid of Gerson's suitcase down on that sweet man's hands? He'd let slip that he'd already phoned Nachum ben Zion for help with a place to stay: *my* Nachum, *my* fellow swimmer in history's ocean. Didn't a fire engine loaded with ice cream outrank a new supplicant? Guess not. I know that at some point I wadded up his silly European-style striped pajamas and hurled them in his face.

"*ANSWER ME!* I need to know. If I were Stella! If I were Stella, Stella, that bitch Stella! Would you still? Well?"

He looked perplexed. Then, although it's just as well I didn't recognize it until shortly before its imprint on my memory began to fade some months later—if I had, I'd have gone for him with jaws for hands and teeth for nails; wouldn't have rested or stopped until satisfied that not only I but nobody would ever see that look again, now that his face no longer had the tools required to produce it—he looked compassionate.

"You never knew her. She'd have just gone wherever I went."

"Well, I'm Pam Buchanan! Pam Buchanan, not that stupid fucking, fucking cow, and you never even *asked!! ME!!! Shithead!!!!*" I screamed.

We looked at each other dumbfounded. Not only had it blatantly never crossed his mind to ask me to remain in the Promised Land with him; it hadn't crossed mine until provoked that he hadn't. We knew each other better than we wanted to right then, and we'd never wanted to less.

That well-meaning idiot honest-to-God scratched his head. "Oh, Pammie. Come on. I mean—I suppose I could have, yes. Maybe. But really. It would've really just put more of the burden on you. Wouldn't it? Having to say no and feel rotten. That wouldn't have been fair—and now, I think, it's too late. Isn't it?"

"*Yeaaaahh*, it's too late. You know why? You want to know why? *Now*, Gerson, *now* it would only be *painful!* Oh, where have I ever heard *that* before? You want this up, up, up! you *now*, Gerson? *Huh?*"

And you might think that by the rules, namely none, of a marital witching-hour colloquy—even one held perversely, well!, let's just say idiosyncratically, in the morning, with Jerusalem's astonishing and yet never astonished skyline playing the backdrop to him, then me, then him, but never us—there can be no such thing as going too far. You'd be wrong, and now we both knew it.

It wasn't a question of wrecking my marriage. That had gone out the window an hour ago and something in me was already wondering what it would be like to be free. It was a question of whether we'd be able to exchange a civil word if we ran into each other thirty years from now. He'd thought I knew and understood him better than that and now he'd never be sure.

He looked at me, made up his mind what he was going to say next. Didn't look good—my bet and instant fear was Charybdis—but then he unmade it. Said instead, "Well, Pam, the game is done. You've won, you've won."

Knowing I'd lost, I wept. Saved our future by insisting that random moment of cruelty didn't define me. Brokenly agreeing that there was no Gerson, let alone plural, still up to me to define, leaving a Pam he might not despise as my only salvage job, I sat on the bed, half drowning my apologies in tears and half coaxing more tears with new apologies. He sat down there next to me soon enough.

What can I say? It worked. I've got forty fond letters postmarked Israel to prove it. Unless she threw them out after his death, his widow has at least that many, with a variety of postmarks, to him from me.

Saying "It worked" doesn't mean one sob or apology was a whit less than genuine, Panama. It just means that salvaging a Pam he might not despise was the agenda. I couldn't have cared less what sort of person I actually *was*, you know? I cared about what sort of person Noah was: someone I desperately wanted not to despise me. Believe me, if I'd had to fake being a Pam he might not despise, I would have. I just don't think I did.

The third hour, for my single worthwhile accomplishment of the morning was that there was a third hour, was much calmer and quieter. One proof was that we heard a fire engine, though distant and plainly racing toward somewhere nowhere nearby.

In fact, the third hour was gratifyingly gentle. In a muted way, the third hour was one of the best we'd ever had. There's nothing for marital harmony like the transition to speaking of your marriage and the selves that you were or affected to be in the past tense.

One fragment: "No, I'm not saying it was ever a temptation for you. That's not who you were. But because of what you were—not Jewish—it couldn't help being an option. That's all: an option. It's your option to move to Cincinnati. That doesn't mean I think you'll do it."

"Not *that* miserable," I mumbled.

"Good. And I asked myself, do I really want to go back to living surrounded by people for whom anti-Semitism is even an option? Even if I don't believe the ones I know and trust will ever take advantage of it?"

I stirred, punched a friendly wet pillow. "Was that when we were at Yad Vashem?"

"Ah, Pam! You know me better than that. Masada."

During the third hour's last half, I was no longer sitting but lying on the bed. And yes, there was a moment or two when a friendly two-way suspicion dawned that the last time we'd ever made love might be demoted to the next-to-last time we'd make love. But we knew we couldn't risk it; the second hour was too recent. The third hour, though a promising child, was still a long way from first grade.

"Noah, you're brave," I blurted up at him at the end of the hour.

"That may be the only thing I've ever wanted to hear someone say about me." He bent to give my forehead a dry kiss. "And since you did—and since I'm glad, I'm honored!, it was you—let me have that as the thing I carry away from here. I'm going."

I can't say I'd have *minded* if, just for pleasantry's sake, he'd seen fit to tell me Pam too was brave. But you can't have everything, as I'd once been reminded by a whisper of skin on a beach deck in Malibu. That I'd won the third hour and the promise of knowing him for the rest of his life was plenty enough to keep.

He looked at his watch. "You've missed our flight, of course," he said. "Bad timing."

As I too got to my feet, since not seeing him to the door would only have told him I'd mistaken a hotel for a hospital, one final two-way recognition decided to stay mute. We'd both just realized I'd be boarding a plane soon, for Noah a special anxiety back when he'd been Gerson.

Even if my flight out of Israel did turn out to be Carole Lombard's plane, though, he was safe now. However anguishing, the death of an ex-wife wouldn't be history repeating itself, and I'd been one for at least an hour. The papers Pam's lawyer mailed for his signature three months later were a civilized formality, at least so far as we two were concerned. Purely mental though it was in his case, poor old Oliver Watson was visibly strained by *his* first trip to Palestine. Noah sent them back with a joking note about the Galilee I'd left behind me.

"On my way out, I can ask at the desk and have them phone you," he offered. "For your sake, I hope you won't have to stay on an extra day on my account."

It was silly, but maybe not getting my "You are, too" in the bravery sweepstakes had rankled a bit. It wouldn't have had to mean any more than another driver's thank-you wave after passing into the turn lane.

"Oh, I don't know," I said. "Now that I'm a free woman, maybe I'll stay on a couple. I'd kind of like to go back to Tirat Karmel."

"Tirat Karmel, really? What do you know? I wouldn't call that one of the highlights. But, well, vive la dee-ferance. I did like that funny little restaurant."

"Me too. Noah, will you do me a favor?"

"Of course."

"When you get to Nachum's, can you ask him how you say 'The Great Unknown' in Hebrew?"

POSTED BY: *Pam* I didn't go, no. (Duh! As you children say.) I shunned Tirat Karmel on later trips in the Sixties and Seventies, even though I alone in the bus or limo knew of a little restaurant that served the most divine, divine, divine!, hummus, falafel, and olives, brought to your outdoor table if you were in luck by a girl with eyes dark as tamarind and hips expert as miniature race cars. I'd inhaled her skin: "I am Israel. I'm sun, valor, hardship—and joy. I'm the most daring thing you'll ever do if you've got the nerve. Are you Jewish, by chance?"

"Would it really matter?" my skin babbled back. But she was fetching the next table's water by then.

I still hope Israel's Great Unknown wasn't killed in any of the wars. She'd have been getting on by my last trip: 1979. For her sake, not mine, by then I obviously had to hope she wasn't still waitressing.

Instead, when obliged as expected to stay over an extra day, I ate a meek last supper alone in the King David's restaurant. Was disgustingly, disgracefully relieved when ben Canaan's surviving eye didn't show up to rake me over the coals as a whore combined with a hypocrite and coward, two things your true whore— I'd seen Napoli, remember?—never is or could be. An American, in short.

Flew back the next morning to the land of Fran Kukla's *Hamlet*. Yet of brave Martha Shelton and so much else. Still unsure whether one citizen's idea of a promise betrayed is another's idea of its fulfillment.

Perhaps the real prayer is that neither's decision will ever be final. When I think of Israel, that's certainly the hope of a philo-Semite like me.

Philo-Semite, you ask? What of your cleverness in spotting all those signs to the contrary? Oh, I swear. You're children. As I should've started telling you much earlier on daisysdaughter.com, you're all too fucking easy.

Yes, I belong to my generation. With the mother I had, not to mention the father, I could not help but be conscious of Jews as Jews. Smart ones can spot it eight decades later at Nan Finn's Christmas parties, and unless they've got no humor—not bloody likely, not least given the goyish occasion—they dig it.

Me too, though I've got to be awfully bombed on Nan's hopeless Chardonnay before I talk about Noah's death. I yawp on instead about Pam's first trip to Israel. If only thanks to the fact that I saw it before most of my auditors were alive, that keeps them interested until I'm outdone by the next round of canapés.

I swear, if Andy Pond were Jewish or could even fake it—had the odd bit of *crackle*, you know, along with his brain's fine imitations of the weak lovely music Mozart would have composed if he'd lived into his eighties—I'd have probably married him ages ago. I'm still the shiksa and I know the drill. In the first decade or so of my final widowhood, it was my favorite way of being socially sexy.

I've been called a kike hag. Before you rise up in outrage, demanding the coiner's name, I assure you he's beyond your reach. His name was Nachum ben Zion—born Nachum Unger, the poet. Nachum only bothered to mince words when he was dealing with people who might misinterpret them.

He said it ("Oh, colleague! You're such a...") at a round table on the patio of the King David Hotel in Jerusalem one night in the spring of 1965. I'd just learned of Eddie Whitling's death in Saigon. Nachum's wife—a sabra, by the way—was the only one who even rolled her eyes. Noah did blink before he chortled, but then Ruth rattled something off to him in rapid Hebrew and he started to laugh helplessly. Never did find out what she'd accused him of. Ehud Tabor, whom Hopsie and I knew from when he'd been Hopsie's Israeli counterpart in Nagon, grinned at me and said, "They do come in handy. How's Nan Finn these days?"

As for Cadwaller, he knew damned well he'd better be the quietest laugher. But he beamed over his pipe: "I'd never put it that way myself. But you'll have to admit the shoe fits, dear."

I'm sure Noah would've been disappointed but refused to judge had he known Nachum emigrated to the United States after Israel's invasion of Lebanon: "Next year I'll be seventy, colleague. At my age, you can't help wanting to live in a country where 'rockets' red glare' is a figure of speech." Hired by some think tank, he used to show up on TV a lot when the Middle East was the topic. He died in 1995 in Passaic, oddly enough all of six blocks—not six million—from Noah Gerson's childhood home.

POSTED BY: *Pamorana*   As for me, I might've stayed on in Los Angeles for decades, happily ogling girls in Newton-defying bathing suits and looking for the Great Unknown at parties, if Luz and Ava hadn't decorated our home for the Gersons' return. Coming into the den to see that forlornly tinseled, eternally Pam-sized Christmas tree next to Stella's picture just about did me in. I moved on.

Though Noah didn't even need to ask for me to send him his first wife's photograph, I was touched when he wrote back requesting one of his second. He had a particular image in mind, a pensive shot of Mrs. Gerson in our old Beverly Hills garden. Being Noah, he hoped it wouldn't be too much trouble for me to get him his own print of the picture of *Glory Be*'s author in *Vogue*.

Even though it cost me a marriage—and would it be a happy ending if I'd kept him unhappy? Sorry, I'm not that big a narcissist—I wouldn't have missed seeing Israel in 1956 for the world. I wouldn't presume to articulate what its existence back then meant to most Jews, much less "the" Jews. Nor am I the one to fathom what its existence must've meant and still does to most Egyptians, Palestinians, Syrians, and so on. I do know what it meant to some of us goyim, especially if we hailed from Los Angeles.

How could we not catch our breaths? Never mind Hollywood. Israel was the greatest movie any bunch of impatient Jews ever created, a cinematic masterwork. And it was real.

I know for fact that attitude used to drive a lot of Israelis nuts. Yet my second husband was not only, as he'd said, American, but a filmmaker. Even with Nachum ben Zion as his caustic best friend, eleven years of living there never knocked the awed Panavision out of him. Who are you to say it should have? *Aliyah.*

Noah Gerson died in June '67. He was shot through the head by a sniper just hours after the documentary unit under his command had photographed something not seen in two thousand years: Jews praying at the Wailing Wall.

They were young Israeli paratroopers with slung Uzis, but they were there and so was Noah. The world gasped at those images of history resurrected on film.

The ben Zions sent me the picture printed in *Haaretz* and taken sometime earlier that day. Halfway out of a jeep, Noah's wearing something he never did in Hollywood: sunglasses. His right hand, slightly blurred, is reaching for what may be a candy bar. His smile could part the Dead Sea.

You won't understand, but I knew him. I can't regret it happened when it did: I mean, before. Before too many displaced Arabs, too few Americans, and a good many Israelis, Nachum ben Zion sardonically in the forefront, started wrestling with the fact that history resurrected wasn't history redeemed. Before the fulfillment of all his hopes my Noah filmed at what I know was the happiest moment of his life turned so sour.

Before the Panavision epic he loved and loved living in got degraded into an endless, relentless TV series, its production values unimproved by the abandonment of the early seasons' rousing black and white for muddy, perplexing color and its travesty of *Hamlet* with any number of real corpses unresolved by the emergence in Israeli politics of any number of Gene Rickeys. (To Bibi or not to Bibi, that is the question.) Before Nachum ben Zion said the hell with it and ended up dying in New Jersey. Before even Noah would've had to face knowing his Israel had started down the gray road to becoming, as the United States has or must and even California may, just another country.

Part Four

1. Lucky for the Sun

POSTED BY: *Pamtonia Fraser*   I'd been living in Paris a few weeks when a book *by Pamela Buchanan* about Marie Antoinette thrummed in my head one wet morning, flapping little dust-jackety wings. That should tell you two things, the more obvious being that Paris is one unignorable city. Try to demote it to a mere environment and it'll just crawl in your ear as you snooze *à l'Américaine*. The other is that, nine months later and counting, getting over my second marriage had its up days and down days.

Unless you count a private title whose silliness should've warned me I was belling too many cats for comfort—*La Brioche, C'est Moi*—not a word of it got written. Until festive Cadwallers' voices crowded a speakerphone and Tim's news knocked me off my game, I hadn't thought of that phantom book in decades. Having put mimsies and Rheumas to work checking imdb.com, I see the movie's derived from some other broad's bio instead. Oh her.

A title, a marriage to last year's Nobelist. A dozen fat tomes ruing their old lives as trees. No doubt a mansion or two stuffed up some pastoral cleft in Dickinham or Stropshire. Some women still can't stop grasping at trophies.

Was she invited to the set at Versailles? Would you like to meet our star, your Ladyhood? Pretend to flip through the script, meanwhile licking your lips as she kicks a leg, buries mirth in her prayers, tips laughing wheat and rye sideways in a honeyed tumble? Then jumps up and offers you strawberry pancakes—Ard, I'll fix later—while pretending she'll ever care who you are? No, she's not *oblivious* to those cobras in your Ladyhooded eyes. Not only do you overrate your own subtlety by a mile, but your prey is much brighter than anyone thinks. She's just indifferent, your Ladyhood—indifferent.

Kirsten, at least I was American! Pardon me as I scoot back my wheelchair, set aside Cadwaller's gun, and frog-march this old bag's indignant kidneys on a tour of the rug. If the White House calls before I simmer down, I'll give Potus elephonic pink and gray things blasting like a bucket of soggy confetti made of vomit and worms. Hell, I may not tell him it's a protest or even greet the man first, just leave him puzzled and deaf in one ear.

Yes, Ard: that's just one more reason to stick with my new pal Pink in the landing craft. Too depressing to creep like anybody into a District theater to see *Marie Antoinette* in October, knowing that if I'd played my cards right I could've been at Cannes in May. Champagne with Kirsten before I paraded amid bigger, more golden bubbles of music up the red carpet on her perfumed arm—only, of course, because I'm so doddery and she's as sweet as she is talented. Honestly, what else could it be?

POSTED BY: *Pam*   Beyond Paris and self-pity—and on the second count, I might as well have called the thing *Vainglory Be*—I can spot several reasons for Pam's impulse to pop Marie Antoinette between hard covers. One: I'd turned thirty-seven, Antoinette's age when she died. That had been on an October day probably not too unlike those I saw previewed in each wind's flips of wet leaves on my walks in the Luxembourg Gardens, not far from the flat Pam had rented in the rue St. Sulpice.

Two: I was twice-divorced damaged goods, had good cause to think my female charms were themselves now *ancien régime*. Remember, I'd just spent eight years in Hollywood. At thirty-five, actresses who fell short of beautiful started mud-wrestling for the chance to play Thelma, the heroine's cranky old well-weathered maid.

Three. The most obvious cue shouted from every train schedule that included Brussels. At the age of thirty-seven, which I knew dead Daisy would be much happier to hear styled "the same age as Marie Antoinette" while leaving her daughter out of it, my mother'd put a gun in her mouth to play lollipow.

Never written, my Antoinette would have been my third book. Had I done it right, however, it would've been the first by Daisy's daughter. By now I felt I'd done enough living of my own to absorb that role without feeling swiftly exiled to tininess, oafish feet clumping on stairs and a gluey maternal disappointment cowling my every wail.

For one thing, I was old enough to understand Daisy's chagrin was provoked not by what kind of daughter she had but the fact that she had one; *still* had one. A less thoughtless, more loving, less selfish child would've vanished along with the polo-dispatched proto-Potus who left her a widow and still smirks in scalloped photographs in the Paris footlocker.

After closing up what was left of my life in Los Angeles (discharging Luz and Ava was no fun: I might as well have had to tell them Gerson had died), then spending some meaningless months in New York—Pameata's for-old-times'-sake fling with beflabbed Eddie Whitling still makes me shudder—I'd come to France with a very different program. When Cath Charters pressed me on *Glory Be*'s sequel, I'd looked at the cup from Rheims on her desk and started talking about Americans in Paris during the Revolution: Adams, Jefferson, Franklin, our envoys. Plus John Paul Jones, a favorite of mine long before I met his fellow sailor Cadwaller. As eager as my agent not to repeat the long drought between *Nothing* and *Glory*, I thought I was improvising.

As usual, I wasn't. Having lost a husband to Israel, Pam was probably looking for her own other country. Besides, I had a notion of doing a whole cluster of histories that would depend on the Revolution for interest and point without ever confronting July 4 directly. I'd pay a circuitous tribute to Herman Melville's profundity in a letter to Evert Duyckinck—"The Declaration of Independence makes a difference"—by never dealing head-on with the white whale staring every last one of my readers in the face.

What vanity I had then, bikini girl! I'm glad I gave up that scheme. To be honest, as a writer I think I've had a few innings. Still, your Gramela could never have sustained an approach that refractive for tale after tale, alluding obsessively to a heart of the matter I refused to call by name even once. I was probably seduced into thinking I could do anything by Cath's green nails tapping the baptismal cup she still used for mint juleps.

Despite missing out on a Guggenheim as I'd missed out on the Pulitzer, I had enough *Glory Be* royalties to convince even a Frenchman I could sign a year's lease. *La gloire américaine* was in bookstores by then, not that it did well in translation. No great surprise and, by my lights, a bit of a compliment.

Definition of *mon quartier*'s welcome to the former Ram-Pam-Pam: for the first month or so, I used to strip with the shades up just for company. In nothing but heels and biology's clover, the Americaness dared the Tour Eiffel's tip to come get me: "Red rover, red rover, send Juliette right over." Anytime I came home from seeing that odd goddess sing in a nightclub, I'd've had her stripped in a handclap to let me lavish one lonesome fan's gratitude. You kidding?

I wasn't completely marooned. A few Yank reporters Eddie and I had palled around with when Europe was the ETO were now based in Paris as foreign correspondents, bemusedly following the spectacle of a drunken Marianne playing *Hamlet* that was the French Fourth Republic in slow-motion free fall. To keep my hand in as I mulled the elusiveness of my newly fugitive book—Antoinette or John Paul?—I knocked out a piece for Roy on the parliamentary debates during that fall's five-week governmental vacuum, including the session where I finally saw Janet Flanner plain. Just not too plain, since the doyenne's harsh visage kept her as unapproachable in person as Pam's somewhat rusty reportage in *Regent's* was to hers in *The New Yorker*.

I can't remember who invited me to the party in honor of Lady Diana. (No, Pan—not your much mourned Diana. This one was a different kettle of tiaras.) It certainly wasn't the hostess in person, since I was as negligible to her social set as I was dwarfed by Janet Flanner in print. Primarily known as a TV producer's ex-wife who'd written a bestseller—which there were a lot of in those days—I wasn't out of the club, just no trophy.

If *l'équipe* weren't feeling pressed for time, I'd e-mail Tim to see if he has a clue whose arm I swept in on, since Tim and not Pam is the keeper of Cadwaller's datebooks. Hopsie wasn't much on the old Proustian tapestry, but a jotted "Met Pam B., brought by [???]" might appear.

When I say *costume party*, Panama, you shouldn't picture later generations' sloppy Halloweens, where the ambitious guest is dressed as a giant beer can and someone in more of a rush scribbles a hasty mustache under his or her nose as if that's all you need to be Proust. They were galas, much mulled by all hands before one's final choice of Josephine or Athenaïs de Montespan knocked one's checkbook off balance like a staggered boxer. Our hostess had rented her *arrondissement*'s foremost relic of *ancien régime* vainglory, now a Boucher-and-Fragonardy art museum whose hall of mirrors, mimicking Versailles's less palatially, was for hire in the evenings. That semi-public venue would account for Pam's inclusion in the guest list, since I certainly never saw the inside of our hostess's home. In my whorily Hollywoodized way, I might've rifled her correspondence, stolen some incredibly precious gem she'd left lying around in plain sight.

My best chance of identifying my mystery escort would be to recall his disguise, but Pink Thing's archives have gone fluky there too. False mustache, director's megaphone, priest's soutane, or *sans-culotte*'s cap? Anyhow, I'm positive Pam's date wasn't the mock Talleyrand I saw early on, ostentatiously hobbling and caned to draw attention to the lame foot the real Bishop of Autun had the poise to trivialize.

Watching the counterfeit clump by on parquet that gleamed like Parkay, I remembered my favorite quotation from his model. Oddly, it's Tim Cadwaller's and Sean Finn's too, even though Tim's no more a reactionary than I am and Sean's deepest beliefs may be a puzzlement even to him. It's the only admission of nostalgia that shrewd voyager through multiple regimes ever allowed himself: "Only those who lived before the Revolution know how sweet life can be."

Pam's own choice of costume was dramatic to no one but me. How many people here would even know I didn't doll up like this every day? It had still gone through several demolitions. I'd thought of the obvious choice first, then eyed my mirror in earnest and accepted that five foot ten of flat-chested me couldn't do Marie Antoinette. Maybe in print, but not in person.

To try John Paul Jones would've been mischievous, especially with a male escort. But he'd have had to be an old friend for the stunt not to rock him with social unease, and I had none of those on this continent. Finally, in an ambivalent nod to now shuttered Chignonne's—Cassandre had tried to keep it going, but educationally, grief is no selling point—I went as the Madwoman of Chaillot. Paste diamonds from Madame De's, a wild wig from La Ronde, a wild gown I was assured by some fool at the Marché aux Puces had been worn by Lola Montez. If it had and it could have been verified, I couldn't've afforded it.

Max! That was his name. An émigré I'd met in Hollywood. Introduced, Pink Thing now tells me, by Barbara bel Geddes on the set of *Caught*. What was he doing in Paris? What was his last name, who had he come as? Tim, can't you help?

I found Buchwald dressed as a Pilgrim, a self-amused self-advertisement. Already a classic, his column's Frenchification of the first Thanksgiving—oh, Panama, haven't you ever read it? Your dad did at ten and nearly choked laughing—was due for its by now traditional *Herald Trib* reprint. Along with the hornrims that always reminded me of two TV sets who'd decided to get married and give birth to his nose, his unrepentant cigar under his Kilometres Deboutish headgear first marred, then produced the effect.

We scarcely knew each other, but he was in a genial mood even for him. "*Pam!* Is that you under those stormy chickens?" he bawled in his Bronx ice-cream mixer of a voice. "You know, one of these days you're going to have to tell the rest of us poor Americans what you're really up to! Every one of us is trapped here like a fly in amber, but not you. We all know the Qua-tree-ème Hooray-Pooh-bleak isn't long for this world, but you don't look like the death-bed type. What gives?"

"Why, I—if you really want to know, I'm putting together a book about American diplomats and sailors in Paris," I said, still my standard answer when pressed. Even Cath hadn't heard about my project's bosomy but shadowy alternative. You somehow don't want to confess you're thinking of gluing Marie Antoinette's head back on for a smooch through a hole in the calendar until you've got a reasonable-sounding, unrevealing explanation for why.

He chortled. "Don't you think you'd better meet a few first? You'll change your mind in a heckuva hurry. Like I keep telling you, we're the ones trapped here. Trapped here! Lafayette, Indiana, we are trapped here. Send help, for God's sake."

"Not from now," I said. "Then."

Switching to the Matchmaker Channel, he blinked happily. "Then I've got just the man for you. Follow me! Gangway! *Bande-chemin.* Let's see some horn-pipe there, De Grasse. *Merci. Merci-donnant.*"

Even if you don't happen to be the author of a book whose opening chapter describes a landfall at Provincetown, you don't disobey a stogie-smoking

Pilgrim with TV sets for eyes. In my mad gown, stormy chickens slipping down over my vision at one step before they bucked at my next, I followed him. Imagine my feelings when Miles Standish parted kings and queens and led me to John Paul Jones.

Who, unlike Pam's impish facilitator, had taken enough care with his costume to be smoking a clay pipe, not one of his usual briars. Who, as Pam needed under ten minutes to conclude, must rank up with the dullest, most pedantic, irritatingly self-satisfied (about what, good Lord? The chance to cover his follicularly challenged dome with a tricorn? The subsequent opportunity to point out to me, the author of *Glory Be*, that Jones was unlikely to have gone wigged at sea?) pompous asses I'd ever met.

Whose surprise request for my phone number—God, hadn't he hated me as much as I hated him?—had me privately strangling stormy chickens at the thought he might use it. Panama, meet your great-grandfather.

POSTED BY: *Pam*   Briar-piped and so bereft above the ears of anything to interest a barber that I scanned the sky for pigeons anytime his fedora was doffed, Cadwaller looked more himself in a dark suit by daylight. So did most Paris Americans.

When I'd last seen the city, my compatriots and I had been most identifiable by our helmets and cunt caps, our khaki and olive drab, our jangle of leggings and jeeps and bazookas. A dozen years later, sober business attire was the giveaway, distinguishable from its European equivalents by its refusal to be considered, evaluated, rebuked, or in any way interpreted as fashion. I didn't notice how carefully Cadwaller's version of the American funeral accommodated European views by retaining two features they could grant had style—first by clarifying itself as a choice, second by being expertly made—until I fell in love with him.

By my final trip there—in the *Nine*-teen *Nine*-ties, Panama, not long before your dad started going each spring—too many of the Americans I saw were shouting our well-known uncle's name by looking and above all sounding as if they'd given up on the fat farm a month before breaking out of the funny one. At times I regretted my old schoolgirl uniform's local mufti, but by then I was past the age of nationality. Nobody gives a rap what country women in their seventies are from, since we all look pretty much alike and everyone knows which country we're heading to.

It'd taken him four phone calls to get me to agree to lunch. First I'd pleaded work. "Perhaps for the best. I'm fairly busy too," he said, and the next day I read the latest on our sale of arms to newly independent Tunisia with an annoyed sense of having had insiderdom thrust on me.

Next I'd pleaded flu. "The French winter is nothing to sneeze at," he said, leaving me dumbfounded by whether I'd just heard the worst joke of all time or was talking to a man too obtuse to realize he'd made one. Then I'd pleaded work again.

"Bad luck for me. But I obviously don't want to intrude on your book," Cadwaller said. When I wanted to know what made him think I was writing one, he politely inquired, "Don't book-writers write books?"

That was cloddish even by his standards, I thought as I hung up and eyed my Smith-Corona's twenty-six tadpoles. No longer Haroun Pam-Raschid's wily vizier, it would soon resume its original guise as dead Daisy's typewriter if I didn't give it something to do with my hands soon.

As bad or worse, every phone call from Cadwaller was a reminder of my unpleasant discovery that Art B. thought ill enough of Pam to make fun of her. He was renowned as the least cruel of humorists. I couldn't think of anything especially stupid or gross I'd done to bring out his unsuspected malicious streak.

So what if he'd spotted a prettier woman or more interesting man over the Madwoman's wildly gowned shoulder? He could have just mimed his cigar was in need of an ashtray and I'd have been none the wiser. No need for the prank of pretending a dullard like Cadwaller was the closest I'd get to meeting a reincarnation of the persistent eighteenth-century men who'd voyaged back from the New World to ask for alliances, backing and fighting ships to command.

The only reason I'd decided beforehand to accept Cadwaller's invite to lunch by the fourth time he called was that I badly needed some sense of myself as a working stiff. If I was stuck playing the poor man's Janet Flanner for *Regent's*, I could do worse than to cultivate the envoy in practical charge—of course there was some Ikean figurehead over him—of looking out for our interests on the diplomatic end of NATO. Even if it spoke a whole Britannica about diplomacy Dulles-style that someone like him had the job.

"Anytime I watch Paris fishermen, I'm distracted," he said as we broke bread on a bistro's glassed-in sidewalk on the Quai Voltaire. "Winter or summer, which is the means and which the end boggles me."

"Speaking of ends and means, I'd sure love to know what de Gaulle is thinking right now. Do your Embassy people have an inkling?" I said. (Top that for a reportorial segue, Janet F. All right, so she could've in her cradle.)

Cadwaller's eyes bid farewell to the fishermen. "Oh! Believe me, we'd like to. Still, even we know that's the wrong question in a way. What de Gaulle is thinking and planning will be what historians poke at. What de Gaulle is *feeling* makes the rest Q.E.D. except for one mystery: his timetable. *Entre nous,* can you imagine what sort of mind it must take to harness emotions like his?"

God! He was even drearier than I remembered. Reconsidered the appeal of Flannerizing myself on the spot. *"Entre nous,"* for Christ's sake! His accent hadn't been too bad, but still.

"I'm learning what sort of mind it takes to be interested," I said brightly, since rudeness might at least enliven things.

"I'm sorry. I hadn't grasped it was my topic. You're kind to point it out, but excuse me. You won't want to hear this, Pamela. Please muffle your ears."

Using and then tossing his napkin, he stood. I hadn't even noticed the drunken American serviceman belaboring a waitress back near the zinc bar, but nothing was background to Cadwaller. Not if it involved his compatriots.

"Marine! Brace. You're a God-damned sorry excuse for a God-damned disgrace, do you know that? Brace! Leave this poor God-damned woman alone. Is this your idea of how to behave when you're wearing our country's uniform on foreign soil? Brace, I said. Now put down a good tip and get out of everybody's God-damned sight until you're sober. You got that, Marine? Yeah, you got that."

He came back to the table, abashed. "Sorry, Pamela. Forgive me, but I can still speak Navy when I have to. Even if it weren't the job, I'm afraid that sort of behavior would just drive me up the wall."

He looked up at our waiter. *"Désolé de vous avoir fait attendre, monsieur. Pour madame, le poulet Chaillot sans orages*—yes, Pam, you're sure? Not the *huîtres* claire St. Claire you were looking at earlier? All right. *Pour moi, le homard ensor-celé par les asperges blanches. Et une bouteille de—un moment, je vous prie."* He'd switched to the wine list. *"Ah, voilà. Un château d'aube irait bien, qu'en pensez-vous? Ca ira? Merci bien."*

Handing over menu and wine list, he reached for his pipe and tobacco pouch. "Anyhow, Pam, I didn't mean to bore you about de Gaulle. Professional weakness plus private fascination: what a deadly combination that can be at times. I'm sure I do go on. Now, what would you rather talk about? Have you read Dutourd's wonderful new book *Les taxis de la Marne*? Of course I'm not literary. You'll know better than me"—puff—"that's why I'm curious."

Oh, Panama! That was your great-grandfather. I married him.

I wouldn't want to know the woman who didn't.

POSTED BY: *Pam*   I also don't mean to embarrass you, since we're now describing a man whose blood started running thirty-two years later in your own untroubled, happy-to-be-here veins. So let me just get this out of the way. The first time Cadwaller and I hit the sack wasn't looking too special until he demonstrated that solicitude wasn't something he saved for restaurants. Understanding Pam as no other man had (I don't mean they hadn't done it, just that even thoughtful Noah Gerson hadn't recognized any special under-standing was in play; the gurgle far down in my throat stayed Sanskrit to him), your great-grandfather, the distinguished American diplomat, gave head to Daisy's daughter as if it not only was going but had gone out of style, leaving him as the lone expert. At least until his long dying left him incapable, nudg-ing him to go down on me was like asking Bach to hum something pretty.

So that said, daisysdaughter.com readers, can we move on? Trust me, and I believe you may on this score by now, people only natter about their sex lives when there's a problem. If they're *bragging*—definite problem. We never bragged, didn't need to. Our never tamped contentment was as plain as the pipe on my Cadwaller's face.

In my garrulous widowhood, inattentive to everything except prompting more talk, only decorum has stopped me from asking Andy Pond how it looked from the outside. Not decorum in the Emily Post-It Note sense: concern that some eddy of woe washing up from Andy's mouth to his eyes might betray an old unhappiness at either his exclusion from our glow or having no comparable one of his own. Believe me, bikini girl, any concept of good manners that isn't backed by real reluctance to cause pain is horseshit. The rest might as well be the rules of parcheesi.

Even so, Cadwaller and I didn't hit the sack until a month later, proof he shared my concept of manners. He knew bloody well he could've had me kicking the ceiling from the moment I started gasping *l'Américaine*'s opinion that *Les taxis de la Marne* was a marvelous, fiercely controlled but passionate, oh!, *splendid* book, and Jean Dutourd her living French writer of choice ever since *Une tête de chien*. (Was and is: my age and still with us, he's become an awful right-wing curmudgeon, atrocious as only an octogenarian French curmudgeon can be. But those sentences still run clear as brooks and forge ahead as muscular as bouncers.) In later years, my third husband looked amused when I'd hound him to confess whether he'd considered scooting me around the corner and up to the Hôtel de Lille's fifth floor for a quickie before dessert.

Even if he did—and why *wouldn't* you tell me, Hopsie?—he'd briefed himself enough on Pam Buchanan to worry about putting me at risk with too much casualness or impetuosity. Knew I was newly divorced, could deduce it hadn't been my idea from the circumstances. (Yes, Mrs. Gerson's solo return from Jerusalem had made the next-to-last gossip item in some columns, more curious then than now about book-writers' doings.) Knew I'd been married at twenty-one to Brannigan Murphy.

Whatever else he'd learned or decided not to about my past, the whole scroll was clearly no testimonial to knowing what I wanted from life. Carrying tact to a fault, he didn't demote his predecessor from "your husband" to "your ex" until after our own marriage, and by then he'd met Gerson and watched us together when Noah came to Paris to scout funding for his country's infant film industry.

The one bit of homework Cadwaller saw fit to share didn't come out until he was walking me back to the rue St. Sulpice. "I've read both your books," he advised apropos of silence. Even twenty years later, that habit of treating his side of conversations as information for others to make of what they would, unmodified by any attempt to steer your reaction or even concede it should produce any, could still drive me crazy.

"Thank you. But the question is your timetable," said Pam with my second-best mischievous smile. (Wrong profile, but he *would* insist on the gentleman's place on the street side of the sidewalk.) And he wasn't even looking at me, the dummkopf. Who cared about the traffic? Not me.

"The second three weeks and the first one ten days ago. It was the bonus of you turning me down so often, but I don't see why I should be thanked. Haven't told you what I thought of them yet."

"That's not what I was thanking you for," I cooed.

Damn you, Cadwaller! Never mind the new swirls of snow or the frog-marching bicycles. My eyes are blue-gray weather that were once Civil War memorials in a budding pudding's face. Now my mouth is so lipsticked (1958!) it looks like two crimson bananas visiting Arlington Cemetery. My smart winter Chanel suit—smart? It was brainy on my part, brilliant on Coco's, and whoever invented January was a genius—conceals a paucity of bust I'm hoping won't disappoint you in the sack.

Or in the summers.

Coming to a halt, he looked up instead at St. Sulpice, never the most highly regarded of Paris's many heaps of ecclesiastical stone. That's not only because it's on the Left Bank, away from the smug medieval in-crowd on the Île and far from Sacré-Coeur's white *bombe glacée*. The real reason is that it's impressive without being especially graceful or inviting, just a couple of determined towers that don't leap into the sky so much as announce that this is as far as they got and there's no reason the sky should care.

"I did get it from your books that you aren't pious, Pam, so I doubt this'll offend you. Might bore you, but I'll take my chances and it won't be the first time. I sometimes ask myself why religion is the only human impulse that rates monuments this moving. Aren't there other things we all know? Of course they tried during the Revolution, secularizing them into temples of nature or whatever, but it didn't take. One thing I'll say for churches is they're damned good at not letting anyone mistake them for anything but what they are. This one got in just under the wire—eighteenth century."

I'd wanted a flat in this neighborhood because I remembered what the Place St. Sulpice looked like full of roistering GIs and kissable Parisiennes. Now it had come down to one forty-seven-year-old man in a fedora and raincoat, looking up at St. Sulpice's towers with his hands clasped to his back as snowflakes bothered his eyes without especially disturbing them. Below the raincoat, black suit pants and black shoes kept his black silk socks hidden.

But when he'd sat down to lunch, I'd idly noticed something I now realized he only expected to be detectable to someone interested—that is, European or female. What, Pamimbecile? Oh, of course! That meticulous pattern of miniature diamonds woven from ankle to cuffed shin.

"Cadwaller, I won't rest until you tell me! Who's your tailor?"

Looking over Pam's way at last, he beamed at me curiously. "What a peculiar question! I don't have one in Paris, just a haberdasher," he said, and we knew.

POSTED BY: *Goldilocks* If you wonder about the heading, daisysdaughter.com readers, that's what Chris Cadwaller called me during the first completely cheerful conversation we brought off after his father's death. I assume anyone who's stuck with my blog through thick and thin gets his teasing gist. But if she hadn't had it already, Callie Sherman would've earned Pam's undying enmity for a remark she made one night in late 1967 or early 1968.

Not only alive, Cadwaller was in the room, albeit out of earshot. At the far end of our living room's shoebox (Georgetown houses are narrow), he was chatting with an also still alive, thankfully not yet ostentatiously blotto Ned Finn.

Can't recall the occasion. Were we welcoming the Finns back from Berlin, packing Andy Pond off to Lisbon, repaying the Shermans for putting us up in Hong Kong so soon after Cy had taken over there from still mourned (bum ticker) Stu Wiesenthal? It could've been any of those or a half dozen other twinings of the State Department magic carpet. Not too far from Pamela Harriman's glossier pile, our place on O Street was the rug depot between Cadwaller's two Ambassadorships, and Callie's serene command of blueblood crassness always could give even Potus's fabled mother a contest.

"*Que voulez-vous*, Pam? We all go back to our own kind sooner or later," she said, lifting her hands to mime scales of injustice. So far as any of us could tell, some ancestor of Callie's had ordered those scales of injustice from La Scala. Family heirloom now. Say what you will about Italians otherwise, fine crafts-men. Etc.

"The homing instinct," Callie went on, now resignedly bearing an invisible orb and scepter. "Don't we?"

That was after she'd worked both Murphy and Gerson into the conversation. No, no kids with either of them either, Callie. Thanks. Thought you knew that. Oh, just making sure? I see. Since you didn't want to commit a faux pas. Lovely. Yes, Chris—*whom you've just met, again,* Callie, in his jeans jacket plus tie and his scruffy Sixties beard—is Cadwaller's son from his first marriage. No, he isn't an FSO or even Peace Corps, didn't emulate his dad after all; he's a photographer. For a living, not a hobby. The dark-haired little boy peeping up at us, stunned by most things but comforted by a firm paternal trouser leg on one side and a pro-tective maternal skirt on the other, is Cadwaller's young grandson Timmy.

"Oh, Callie! I don't think I even have a kind," I said warmly—warmly to the point of boiling, in fact. "Of course I weep alone sometimes to know I'll never belong to yours. But hell, you can't have everything."

The one time I met Clare Boothe Luce was frosty and unmemorable, but all women my age are in her debt. "*Quel accent de cirque,* too!" I said, knowing I was safe on that count. The remnants of Callie's Critchloft Academy French were catch-phrase jewelry, worn for effect. The language was a stranger to the interior of her brain.

Between us, Nan Finn's face went out of synch—mouth swearing spon-taneous fealty to Pam, which delighted me, even as her eyes brightened and hardened in her none too adept faux Callie. One reason the glorious girl never mastered either of our styles is that she'd have had to start by accepting they were two different ones. That would make one of us *wrong,* a model Nan Finn *shouldn't* emulate. When we were together and she was captivated by both the Dame and the Duchess—cf. the White Rabbit: "The Duchess, the Duchess! Oh, won't she be savage if I've kept her waiting!"—she was never more adorably herself than when she tried to mimic both of us at once.

Do I even need to mention that Callie and I were also great friends? Espe-cially given how prominent in our small world both Cy Sherman and Hopsie were, the intra-American *comme il faut* of the old Foreign Service gang didn't leave us much option. Luckily, we were also at the age when it's possible to enjoy someone hugely without liking him or her at all.

"We all have one, I think, and I don't see any point pretending it's not a comfort. If I thought you honestly meant that, I'd have to feel sorry for you. The loneliness of the unique thing! So awful if genuine, so trite as a pose. 'Oh, no, no one like me in the whole, whole world,'" Callie moaned witheringly. "You wouldn't condemn Nan here to that, would you?"

"My God, I'd never condemn Nan to anything," I yelped at flagship volume, abetted by the fact that on one side my warmth was now genuine. "But in fact I don't think there's anyone like her in the whole, whole world. Do you?"

By now, Nan's eyes and mouth *really* didn't know which side to take. Or rather, which of us was taking hers. Since she wasn't a ninny (this isn't about perceptiveness, bikini girl; it's about susceptibility), you could see her mind make an intrigued little nest around the fact that Callie Sherman was the one advocating tribalism. Pretty rich from the most genuinely—that is, pointlessly—exotic woman I know: "The only White Russian princess born in Bucks County, Pennsylvania," Cadwaller once called her in private.

Nan's nose was charmed to find its owner under discussion. It tossed up and her laugh followed, faithfully as Christmas after Thanksgiving.

"Oh, of course I'd be thrilled to think I was unique! Right up to the first time it scared me. Maybe it's all about *mood*," she blurted triumphantly to coast out of the giggle, and now you know why I was fond of her.

However, Nan had refined one social skill to a subtlety that neither I nor, to my knowledge, Callie ever needed to acquire. That was an ability to carry on— merry, eager, and charming—while monitoring her husband's liquor intake. Despite having known both Finns for years and seen Ned in the bag too often, I'd only noticed those flicked checkups and adjustments for the first time earlier tonight.

For a change, I'd restrained myself from joining any group Nan was in right away. Brightly anecdotalizing Berlin to Andy Pond and some other people, she seemed as oblivious as a hummingbird to the third cocktail Ned was hoisting across the room. Then came the outflung arm—oh, it was gorgeous; Nan Finn at that moment would've been Balanchine's envy—that let her pivot on Cy Sherman's shoulder, almost weeping with laughter at her ineptitude in letting the Vopos take her passport the first time she went through Checkpoint Charlie, to block someone's view of Ned's too ruddy face.

Whose view? Not just anyone's view. The view of her husband's new overlord at the Department. That self-important ignoramus was holding forth about LBJ's South American policy (*sic*, I must say) in yet a third conversational cluster *over Nan's shoulder*. And to think Cadwaller and I had once discussed whether I should find a way to ask her if she realized Ned didn't hold his liquor well at parties.

Note the phrasing, Panama! God knows my generation drank like Cossacks raiding an Indian reservation. Plenty of us drank like Cossacks raiding an Indian reservation in Dublin on New Year's Eve. In those days, the issue and only litmus test was conduct, not intake. I'm still not so sure we were wrong.

I doubt Callie Sherman ever appreciated Nan Finn's furtive artistry. Still, she and Cy obviously knew about Ned, since they'd had the Finns in Frankfurt when Cy was Consul General and Ned was a junior officer on his shakedown consular tour. We'd only gotten them when he came as Cadwaller's No. 2 to West Africa, a chronological disadvantage that nonetheless made me gratifyingly sure Nan was ultimately more mine than Callie's. We'd never have been evenly matched rivals for the glorious girl's allegiance if warmer feelings for Mrs. Cadwaller hadn't offset the *droit de duchesse* of Callie's first dibs.

Incidentally, I assure you I'm describing social life exclusively. Nan was guileless, Callie had no interest in people as human beings, and I was—well, I'll take refuge in saying you've met me. But I was about to glimpse the pathos of Nan Finn's furtive artistry, which was that too often it was art for art's sake. No matter how good she was at deflecting attention from either Ned's condition or her own anxious tabs on it, sooner or later he had a way of announcing it himself.

Late 1967, early '68? Then he'd had three foreign postings: Frankfurt, West Africa with us, West Berlin. One stint in Washington before this one. Two-thirds of the people in that room knew the signs! Could instantly read the newly silly grin, loud voice, and reddened face, the newly boastful and either unwittingly or indifferently private humor. "Jesus Christ," he'd just bawled too happily at Cadwaller. "Jesus Christ."

Please, I thought: for Nan's sake, not the later blubbering. The rubbish about his adolescence in the Navy. Then I recounted the room and saw that worry was misplaced. With the tactical sense—not quite intelligence, is it?—of drunks, Ned Finn only wept at more intimate gatherings.

"Jesus Christ," he guffawed, now blatantly crimson. "Of course we pretend to put up with it. But so long as we're the ones keeping them safe, hell, Ambassador! We all know we don't need to give a *shit* what the West Germans think of Vietnam. So do they, nosy bastards. Jesus Christ."

Then came the fatally lopsided rictus of inward amusement. It followed the first obscenity as faithfully as Waterloo followed Elba.

Above Cadwaller's imperturbable smile, I saw his eyes give Ned the mute Georgetown-shoebox version of "Brace." Though Hopsie'd wrestled his conscience, his fondness for Ned had kept him from mentioning the drinking in his DCM's fitness evaluation even in our last year in Nagon. He knew after that he'd no longer be able to protect him directly.

Like most of us, I was fond of Ned too. He was a good, wry man when sober, and a merry one after one drink. Just never learned how to pace himself, but Callie's eyes savored her victory anyway. That Ned had been Cy's made her opportunism—or was it real, deep contempt?—even crueler.

Not our kind, *Pam. Why don't you just admit it?* Cadwaller meanwhile was exerting authority by answering Ned at dull length in a voice hard as brick, brooking no interruption so as to keep him braced. Yet he'd have had to go on for an hour to stop Ned's grin from sloping and slopping around like his face's pet puppy. It was getting impatient for the next chance to say "Shit" too loudly in a Georgetown shoebox whose human eyelets included a new boss Ned clearly dreaded and loathed, and Hopsie couldn't have kept it up for an hour: he was the host. As for the hostess, I'd just seen Nan's face ready itself for its lonely pilgrimage.

Unless the shoebox's contents got rejumbled fast, she had no choice at all. Cross that room on her own, pretend there was something silly and fetchingly Nanlike she'd realized she wanted Cadwaller's thoughts on. Ambassador, should I take up a pipe? So tempted by meerschaum. Be still, Ned. Be still.

We'd all know anyway, though. Callie Sherman would know most of all. My Nan!

"CADWALLER!" I roared like a lioness, making small Timmy Cadwaller stare. Young Sean Finn, too. "CHARADES! That was the plan, Hopsie, wasn't it? I'm tired of waiting! Isn't everyone else?"

"Frankly, no," murmured the Duchess. "Cy and I must be going, in fact." But the Dame had just won the look on the glorious girl's face, and you never won that look, Callie. Not once.

She was fifteen and drooping with gratitude now that she'd gotten help with the prom float. If it wasn't such a hardy snowball in hell, even your heart would've melted. Then Nan's eyes Morsed a worry; I gestured a quicksilver reply. Yes, we'd manage things so Ned would only guess, not perform. Sit close and do what you can to keep him from rising or shouting. Coffee for all, not just him.

I saw Nan most recently in April, I think. So hard to believe she's about to turn eighty! Seemed and was younger than her age back then, seems and is younger today. What was once a necessity is now a gift, as Andy Pond said of her ingenious ingenuousness. Yet it's as unaware as ever of its hard-won uniqueness.

Every once in a while, through her own face's latter-day skein of vintage Clio Airways routes, that nose lifts. Christmas still follows Thanksgiving.

"Oh, Pam!" she said as we sat at La Chaumière without Laurel Warren for once. "When I think of Ned, I swear I just don't know. He might have gone the same way as a history professor. That was the first dream, some college in Oregon. Then he took the Foreign Service exam for the hell of it. Sometimes I think it was too confusing for both of us. When we were posted abroad, we had everything rich people do except money. When we got back home, we had everything middle-class people do but experience."

POSTED BY: *Pam*   Quite, quite late that night—*Mmmmmmmmmmmm!*— when I told Cadwaller what Callie had said, he chuckled in pity. "I don't envy foreigners who have to learn English," he mused and, being Cadwaller, seemed quite prepared to leave it at that.

"Hopsie, come back! Setting the bloody alarm clock can wait. Why?"

"Take 'kind,'" he explained, setting it anyway. "A very simple word whose meaning when it's an adjective is nearly the opposite of its effect as a noun. Callie's the noun and you're often the adjective, but they can't print your pictures in dictionaries."

"Mmmm. Not looking like this, that's for sure."

"I'd buy it," he pleasantly said. "My English could use brushing up."

I doubt even Callie would've made her remark in front of him. He had a great trick of affecting just enough ignorance of female chat's flashing cutlery to obliviously drop a plate on the floor and stand waiting.

My third husband gave advice to four Presidents in spite of knowing three wouldn't take it and the fourth (Gerald Ford) wouldn't understand it. One Cadwaller ancestor had played a minor role at the Constitutional Convention in Philadelphia, but smallpox did in that vote against the three-fifths of a man clause. Nothing would have disgusted my Hopsie like a suggestion that some family portrait of a fellow whose nose looked like a persimmon gave him any special say in the matter.

That said, the Dame can't pretend the Duchess was completely off base. We all do have our limits at experimenting with universality and that's all there is to it. I've sometimes wondered if it says something vile about me that Pam could never picture falling in love with someone who wasn't American.

Of the three men I married, Noah Gerson's grave in Jerusalem is the proof of all proofs that he was as American as could be. Never either Noah's or my favorite writer, Melville did have that one moment of clarity. The Declaration of Independence *does* make a difference and there are no restrictions on how.

As for Brannigan Murphy, not only was he as made-in-U.S.A. as Custer, Velveeta, or Wrong-Way Corrigan, but I suspect that as much as fame was what drew me. He'd been on the cover of *Time*, but I doubt I'd have cared had it been *Paris Match*. He undid the last of Chignonne's bun, for which I thank him.

As for your great-grandfather, Panama, I've made one rotten job of it here on still loving, still mourning daisysdaughter.com if you don't see that the Cadwaller who clapped a pipe in his mouth and took on the job of steering a fighting ship named the *Bonne Femme Pamela* from midlife to old age didn't need an ancestor's portrait to broadcast his place of origin. Character did the job by being sure enough of its own inner resources to put me on notice from Day One that the only way I'd ever disappoint him was by dying.

To say he let Pam "be herself at last," as you children might be nitwit enough to not only say but find deep, is preposterous. I always had been, you always will be, and once you've seen India it's hard to call that an accomplishment. There's just a big difference between doing it helplessly and doing it without qualms, sure of the marital steadiness bracing you as you meet the waves. If the sight of Nan Finn disrobing to change into the glorious girl's swimsuit in the improvised shelters of Nagon's fairly casual idea of beach privacy, soundtracked by a orchestra of surf, did more than once give me paws—see Fran Kukla's *Hamlet*, Act III, Scene 1—I'd still refuse to label it thwarted longing. It felt more like nostalgia.

When my romantic patriotism worried me—and it *is* a form of bigotry, no question—I discovered the farthest my imagination could strain was to sketch a Pam who'd married a Frenchman. If a gal wants to feel truly American from breakfast to armpits, in my observation that's the shortcut of shortcuts. Even Celia Brady's marriage to a maharajah wouldn't touch it, since those generous Indians delight in surprises. Unlike the French, they know surprises change nothing.

So imagining Mme Pamela had its Yankee Doodley attractions. Even so, the moment I had us mentally installed in the Faubourg St. Germain—him Tour de Francing *Le Monde*, why was he a stockbroker?, me scrambling my eggs and translating all of Dutourd into English for some American publisher—his face would warp into that of Hy Lector, born Hippolyte Lecteur. An accordion wheezed, my hair was now a crazed orange. I dove overboard (why were we in a lifeboat?) and never looked back.

When Chris Cadwaller phoned one day in early 1961 to tell us he'd just gotten married to a nice girl from Rouen, even a man as urbane as his dad was briefly nonplussed. Not that he'd have allowed himself to show it had anyone other than his wife been watching. We felt taken aback for another reason besides Hopsie's son having married so young—nineteen!—or his springing the news as a fact on the ground. A French daughter-in-law felt like an intrusion of Cadwaller's job into our personal life, as if Chris would soon show up hauling not a plump, bright student wife but a briefcase bristling with Quai d'Orsay memoranda. After doing it all day at work, at home Hopsie didn't want to *negotiate*.

As you know, Chris, I adored your bride on sight and do still. As for your dad, he wasn't the adoring type. The single exception flattered me beyond measure and was on public display only as a beaming given, never once a performance. He'd still grown very fond of Renée by midway through dinner. Two virtues you fast learn to prize in a Frenchwoman are practicality, apparently doled out at birth to all XX-chromosomed customers—and placidity, no more common in Paris than statues lionizing Napoleon III. To find them united was like meeting Rapunzel.

Even at twenty, from round eyes to round hips, a then brunette Renée announced herself physically as a pleasing arrangement of circles and spheres, a yé-yé-banged and chubby female Olympics logo whose gold, silver, and bronze Chris had won all at once. At nineteen, he was still tense and wiry. I knew already in which direction I'd bet on that Jack Sprat contrast to resolve itself.

Chris, I did make sure first your head was turned at an angle that made it unlikely you'd spot my smile and guess—and you would've—what prompted it. Did you think of it too and hide your grin from me? I couldn't help but be bemused that just three years had gone by since the new Mrs. Cadwaller, still all wet as a stepmother, had come in search of aspirin into our never too lockable bathroom. That was how I'd embarrassed an even wirier, just then *much* tenser Chris in the grip of solo Brigitte Bardotlatry, which at least on some grounds had turned out to be prescient.

POSTED BY: *Pam*   That happened much too soon after I'd first met Hopsie's son in the summer of '58, when Cadwaller's ex relented and sent Chris to Europe to visit his dad before Exeter reclaimed him. Cadwaller hadn't asked her until we were married, his way of protecting me.

He wasn't going to let sixteen-year-old Chris indulge any illusions his verdict on Pam was of practical consequence. Nor would he permit the first Mrs. Cadwaller to canter her yes or no around our upcoming nuptials. By then she was back in the marital saddle herself as Eileen Downslow, arbiter of the horsy set in Middleburg, Va., and whoever coined the happy phrase "Sugar wouldn't melt in her pocket" has my fondest salute.

Of course, the night we met Renée three years later, it didn't take Cadwaller long to figure out Chris's refusal to alert us beforehand. *"Payback!"* he boomed, for him downright lustily, and leaned back in his chair. "I am getting slow. You didn't meet Pam until she was Mrs. Cadwaller either."

"Yes!" a Chris who'd also surprised us with his first scraggly beard crowed from the floor, enjoying his reward. "I had to for form's sake—you understand, Dad. Now we're even." He might've done well in his father's profession, but he was already fondling a Leica.

"Chris, *assez!*" said Renée. *"Tu as déjà un tas de photos de moi."* Panama, if your grandmother thought he'd taken lots of her then, she must rue her youthful innocence now.

As for my own wedding to Hopsie, it had been a fairly bundled-in affair in the crunch. The Qua-tree-ème Hooray-Pooh-bleak's deathwatch had gone into overdrive that spring, keeping Cadwaller burning midnight oil and Andy Pond yawning at the Assemblée Nationale; I think one day in late May was the only time I saw Andy unshaven. I was stuck with a wrapup on the political situation for Roy I kept having to update, then scrap.

By then just about everyone this side of Sartre had accepted that de Gaulle had to come back and take over. Now that he'd waited them out, he was making conditions. Allies he'd bully without anyone's by-your-leave. Only the French had to ask first.

It did drag on, though. As June loomed, we realized we could be living in sin until de Gaulle, France, or even we just keeled over. "Something degrading about needing the General's permission," Cadwaller muttered and pulled strings to book us a nooner at l'Église Américaine. It was handy to not only our Embassy but the Palais-Bourbon, where it was all happening.

We came out to find Andy Pond tapdancing next to an Embassy Chrysler.

"It's over, boss! De Gaulle is Premier with emergency powers. He does know them, doesn't he? He won."

"Oh, *Hopsie!*" I yowled. "We got it all wrong! We weren't waiting on him. He was waiting on us."

Very few people who worked with my husband would have called him romantic, but they didn't know him or understand us. He looked mildly amused, and I defy Hollywood at its swooniest to match the one word he said quietly: "Timetable." Cleared his throat, spoke more loudly: "Andy, how long? The emergency powers."

"Six months."

Cadwaller nodded, impressed. "He is good. Any shorter, why bother? Any longer—well, well! And maybe my, my down the road. Well, Pam, I've obviously got to get on this. Mr. Pond, you're not quite off duty. Can you give Mrs. Cadwaller some sort of honeymoon? Not that one."

At least outside a bedroom or with others present, that was the closest to lewd I think he ever came. But it *was* his wedding day. And it was to me.

Did the new bride pout and complain, kick at the church or the car tires? Did my new husband pat my hand, have to tell me *in public* how much he loved me? What bilge. Risking it though we weren't alone, as Hopsie got in the car we exchanged one grand look of naked pride—and you can have your fat photo albums, your West Point swords, and your Mendelssohn. I wouldn't swap my third wedding for anyone's.

Romantic is as romantic does. All three of us and then quite soon (honk!) two of us knew Cadwaller was adding to his burdens by delegating Andy to look after me. His logical place was at Hopsie's side, something neither Andy nor I would have dreamed of acknowledging either before or after the car pulled away.

To do so would point out that Cadwaller *had* just told me in public how much he loved me. That faintly Micawberish "Mr. Pond" had been a shout of it if you knew him well. We both knew him well.

You didn't look very different then, Andy. Forty-eight years ago, you had the same smile. It's never stopped saying—well, mildly mentioning, to make it more active would misrepresent you—that a man who's never known what he's waiting for had better learn to take pleasure in breezes, interesting random events like the fall of the French Fourth Republic, bright ads on passing buses. Its private amusement makes me wonder at times how Ned Finn would have made out if he'd learned to accept all of himself without splitting it into Ned drunk and sober. For all I know, it makes Nan wonder too.

"Well! At least we know what's off the table," you said. "Would you like me to take you to—?"

"My God, Andy! No. I've got a piece due for *Regent's* I can finally finish. I know you've got to get back to the office, but can you just give me the lowdown in the taxi home? It's not far."

POSTED BY: *Pammie, Ram-Pam-Pam, Pamelle, and Pamita* All the same, I'd been married under six weeks when Cadwaller told me his son was arriving in Paris next Monday. I couldn't remember the last time I'd had to deal with anyone's child for longer than an inept nod and coo.

On the first night, I'd only swapped a few words with a very tired kid before Cadwaller showed him his room. All we were to each other was images. If I say mine of him was an unfocused Polaroid and his of me was an Edvard Munch painting, believe me I'm not being vain. He was sixteen and I wasn't.

I hadn't caught on at all to what I was in for until the next morning. "Oh, no, Hopsie, no!" I begged, pleading as I never would've for him to keep me company on our wedding day. "Not the deep end of the pool."

"Pam, if he does dislike you, my presence will only force him to hide it. Creating a whole other source of resentment, since confusion doesn't have many outlets at that age. Anyhow, I've seen you swim." We were alone. "You swim beautifully."

A whole day with a teenage boy. Eve's idea of heaven, to Addison's laughter. Not mine. True, if Cadwaller's child had been a sixteen-year-old daughter, I could be crooning all this on tape from a straitjacket.

"After six short weeks of marriage, not to mention seventeen long, wretched years of containing my deepest urges, I now had poor Christine Cadwaller in my vampiric power. Hungrily, I led her to the Hôtel de Lille—*non, non, je ne peux pas vous le dire, Maigret! C'est trop affreux. Au secours!*"

What of it? As Addison said, we're all creatures. Before the spell breaks when bikini girl—Panama!—scampers away, I've seen looks not enough unlike mine on her father's face. Does that mean Tim's a monster? Am I? As I've said already, in my generation it was all about conduct.

I had no idea what behavior of mine might be suited to Chris. Serious lad: jacket and tie at breakfast. Exeter drill, sign of respect to his father, notice to Pam that this wasn't his home if I claimed it was mine? I was clueless. I must say his look at the croissants was choice.

Because worry needs something to focus on, I'd focused on weather. It had rained for three days, now it was only overcast. Oh, damn. Now it was *all* up to me.

We started down toward the Seine from the Opera Quarter. As unconventional as Cadwaller could be in private, to live on the *Left* Bank just wasn't done. Unless you were too junior to matter, the French simply wouldn't take you seriously.

I was wondering if I was supposed to hold the boy's hand. "Chris, how is your mother?" That was desperate.

What a rare and wondrous lad you were, you roly-poly grandfather. Walking down the rue Gambon, which like all Paris you'd never seen, you formally drew yourself up: "Miss Bucha—Mrs. Cad—oh, well, Pamela. I hope you'll understand, but I obviously can't discuss my mother with you. It's not on."

I was too touched to laugh. Glimpse of Cadwaller's youth, replete with some Exeter teacher's phraseology. I hadn't been fishing, since I knew all I needed to about Hopsie's first wife. He'd never once voiced an *opinion*, but when pressed would give me her Bartlett's best-of. From bedroom to courthouse, the quotes hadn't been pretty, and going by photographs, neither was Eileen Downslow. Nice enough horsewoman's body, but that face I knew from Purcey's. It hadn't improved in adulthood.

"All right and I'm sorry," I said. "I wasn't trying to pry. Just make conversation."

"If that's all you want, tell me about yours."

I didn't stare long, since even then I knew Hopsie. He'd never have burdened or furnished his son with the fact that my mother's final choice of perfume had been cordite: Browning No. 5.

If Eileen Downslow had seen fit to mention it before Chris boarded a trans-Atlantic plane, I'd have bitten her nipples off, but I doubted it. My society-page gleanings told me she was quite happy with her new husband's millions, the more so as he didn't get to Middleburg often. All Hopsie's first wife ever really cost me was a White House invite in the Kennedy years—Jackie preferred her fellow equestrienne.

"Oh, Chris! Mine died a long time ago." Since at his age all adults were Methuselah, he'd be unlikely to grasp that could mean I'd been younger then than he was now. "That's really all there is to say."

Not completely fair to a sixteen-year-old boy, but I think wholly reasonable. He was still right on the cusp when fair and reasonable are two different things.

"Here's the Seine! What shall we do now?"

Wrong question. I was the adult: that didn't make him child but jailbird. He just looked at me quizzically.

"I know! Let's take a *bateau-mouche*."

Believe it or not—and my guess is that only people who've lived in Paris for years will have no trouble doing so—I never had. Seen them plying the Seine every day, obviously: tourism's latter-day landing craft, their serrated cargoes of open-air theatergoers attending to a microphoned Marianne. Still, the odds were starting to look good that Chris would appreciate Paris more the less it was Pammed all to hell for him. The more microphonic the better, any substitute mother would do. Barge's flat hull and threshing engine a substitute Cadwaller.

Bought our tickets, took our seats. Chris glanced around, neatly combed. Young or old, nobody else here was in a jacket and tie, gray pants, and polished penny loafers. Even the schoolchildren who'd just flashed by to gobble three rows were in shorts and sticky thin shirts. The pleasantly bicameral American couple behind us looked more than capable of leading my wordless ward back to our Embassy if I threw myself overboard. The engine's threshing would finish the job.

It was so long ago that American tourists were a huge improvement on American businessmen. Panama, you'll never understand your great-grandfather's world—or Ned and Nan Finn's, or Andy's, or mine—until you grasp how baffled we were when some otherwise reasonable compatriot of ours would turn out to be here to make money.

Came Chris's first confidence: "I like boats." It was followed by the first twitch of a smile quickly withdrawn, accompanied by the first Cadwallerish nauticalism. "Of course you can hardly call this thing one."

Did I put my foot in it? Oh, hell, what else was Pam here for? Hopsie, you might have given me a *bit* more to work with. Hobbies, whatever.

"More than horses?" I said.

He looked at me with a schoolmaster's pain. Had I not understood what wasn't on the curriculum, barred from the syllabus? "It's really a false dichotomy, don't you think?"

"They teach big words at Exeter."

Oh, *good* volley! It's a wonder you aren't at Wimbledon, Pam. Also a cause of profound regret to the both of us right now.

"Words aren't big or small," Chris said impatiently. "They're either the right size or the wrong size. Dad said you were a writer."

Believe me, that was no invitation to start chatting about my near Pulitzer miss for *Glory Be*. Not when I could hear him saying, "I like books. Of course you could hardly call that thing one."

We lumbered out into midstream. Started chugging upriver past the Île de la Cité with godawful slowness. Our microphoned Marianne started her lecture.

"À votre droite, mesdames et messieurs, voici la Conciergerie. C'est ici qu'enfermée dans un cachot, la reine Marie Antoinette a passé les derniers mois de sa brève vie. Elle n'avait que trente-sept ans quand elle est montée à l'échafaud."

Tap-tap-tap. "Heuh! La'ies and gentlemen, on your right is the Conciergerie. Here Queen Marie Antoinette was imprisoned in the final months of her life. Her age was just thirty-seven when she walked up to the guillotine."

Of course I knew it all blindfolded, had since Ram-Pam-Pam's childhood. That was why Eddie Whitling had barked in my ear: "Never mind the tourist spiel, Pamita. She's dead, okay? End of story. Screw your schooldays. Get us back to the Préfecture, for Christ's sake! De Gaulle's probably there by now."

My GI shoe was propped on our jeep's dashboard. I was Lucky Struck under a cunt cap. Waving the match out, I started laughing: "In this mess? Eddie, if you knew French drivers, you'd know French *tank* drivers are not to be fucked with. Nooo! No more champagne for *you*, Jacquot! My God, Eddie, look at them! Just look at them. Christ, are we going to have to go all the way down to the Île Saint-Louis to get there?"

"Et maintenant, à notre droite, l'Hôtel de ville. Brûlé à l'époque de la Commune en 1871, reconstruit peu après. C'est ici que le 24 août 1944, au soir, sont arrivés les premier chars libérateurs de la Deuxième D.B. du Général Leclerc."

Tap-tap. "Heuh! On our right, the Hôtel de Ville, the mayoralty of Paris. It was burned in Eigh'een Seven One during the Commune, but soon afterward rebuilt. Late in the evening of August Twen'-Four, Nine'een Fort-Four, here arrived the very first tanks of General Leclerc to liberate Paris."

Even at midday on August Twen'-Five, Nine'een Fort-Four, Captain Dronne still looked exhausted. Bearded, diesel-soiled, the usual oddly soft pallor around red-rimmed eyes where his goggles had been. In the summer of 1944, I was always distracted by the French Second Armored Division's abbreviation to "*2ième D.B.*" Couldn't help reading it as "the second Daisy Buchanan," which unlike the first had gotten to Paris.

As they say, Paris is worth a mess. "Pamita! Ask Dronne how many tanks in the recon unit."

"*Mon capitaine, combien de chars aviez-vous?...* Just those three over there, Eddie. And half a dozen halftracks."

Montmirail, Romilly, Champeaubert. Beating Callie and Cy by a number of years, those were the names of the first three Shermans in Paris. Speaking of Callie, I liked the slogan painted on Dronne's jeep: *Mort aux cons.* The tanks and their crews were stinking with diesel, cordite, and Normandy too, not that the Parisians flocking around them cared.

"Three? This city was still crawling with Krauts last night. What in hell was he, a canary in a coal mine?"

"*Mon capitaine, s'il vous plaît...* Eddie, he says his orders were to get here. He doesn't recall any discussions of his prospects or fate once he did... *Pardon, mon capitaine?* Eddie, he'd like us to join him in a glass of wine."

"You sure he didn't say a barrel? Whoof! Don't translate that part."

Our *bateau-mouche* was turning the corner at the tip of the Île Saint-Louis. Backing, engines threshing, clumsily maneuvering.

"*Et maintenant, droit devant nous, vous pouvez voir la Tour d'Argent qui est un des restaurants les plus célèbres de Paris depuis la Belle époque. Le monde entier de la gastronomie connaît le fameux caneton.*"

Tap-tap-tap. "And here in front of us as we turn we can see the Tour d'Argent, the most famous restaurant in Paris. The whole world of digestion knows the pressed duck from the, uh—*oh, merde, quoi! Oh, pardon*—the Beautiful Time."

It was the hardest one yet. And just when I thought I was getting used to this time-machine Shinola, too.

"Oh, Georges—it's our last day," said my mother. Eleven months from switching her cosmetic allegiance from Jean Patou to Browning No. 5, she was a puffy oversized pastry on a pink hotel bed. "I think we should take Pammie somewhere special for lunch. What about the, uh—the Tour Doesn't?"

"*Ah, non, Day-zee. C'est beaucoup trop cher.*" Georges Flagon, who incidentally could have afforded it easily, waved a budget-minding finger. "*Et puis tu sais bien que ton mari n'aime pas beaucoup devoir monter un tas de marches. Pas vrai, Pamelle?*"

Here it came. Oh, Panama! This was me at twelve:

"Yes. And *even* if it weren't *expensive*, Mother—and *even* if you'd remembered Georges has trouble getting up *stairs*, Mother!—it would still be just too *corny*, Mother. *La Tour d'Argent! Mon Dieu, comme je m'amuse! Tu te rends ridicule, mère! Et tu ne vois même pas que je te le dis à ta gueule, mère*"—fingersnap—"*parce que tu ne comprends pas le français quand on parle vite. Mère.*"

[If you must know, and I suppose you must: "The Tower of Silver! My God, how I'm laughing! How ridiculous you are, Mother, and you don't even know I'm saying so right to your pie-hole, Mother"—*claquement des doigts*—"because you don't understand French when it's spoken fast. Mother." Oh, Panama. Panama, Panama, Panama.]

I expect the fingersnap was what did it for Georges. "*Ah, non, Pamelle! Ne parle pas comme ça, hein? D'accord.*"

The fluttering eyelids in the fat and sickening destroyed beauty of her face. "I'm sorry, I didn't understand. Have you and Georges agreed on another place we could go? Honestly, it doesn't matter to me! I was just trying to please you, Pammie—and I'm awfully hungry."

"*Et à notre droite, mesdames et messieurs, vous avez Notre-Dame.*" Tap-tap. "La'ies and gentlemen, we are of course now looking up at Notre Dame."

"We made it! Hey, you guys. I think we're here. Ain't that the Perfecktour across the way? I know I'm sayin' it all wrong, Miss Buchanan."

"Hell, no, you aren't, Luke. The perfect tour sounds right to me. Just scoot us in as close as you can, willya?"

Six days they'd held that building across the *parvis* from Notre Dame as the insurrection flickered and flared and the Allied commands wrangled before sending the Second Daisy Buchanan and our own Fourth Infantry in. Its walls were bullet-starred and smoke-scorched. Why the Germans hadn't just blown the Préfecture de Police to hell Warsaw-style when they still had tanks and artillery and ours hadn't reached the city is something I'll never know.

"Jesus," our driver gibbered in a very different tone from the way he was to say it eight months later when we came upon the death train. A heavyset redhead in a bursting sweater had just mushroomed in his lap and kissed him, and she didn't look as if she had plans to move on.

"Come on, Eddie. Let's let him make time with her! We'll never get through this on four wheels anyhow. God, I bet the Parisians don't know whether to shit or go blind. They've hated the *flics* for centuries. Now the cops are the heroes of the insurrection."

"Don't lose me, Pamita, I'll drown in frogs. Say, what kind of country puts its goddam police headquarters opposite its cathedral?"

"All of them, Eddie, don't you know that? Just in different ways and sometimes you can't even tell which is which."

Burnt-out *camions* in the courtyard with FFI markings. The building's defenders were eager for cigarettes. The soldiers who'd liberated it were eager for wine, but it had all been poured out six days earlier to free up the bottles for Molotov cocktails. Some crazed Wehrmacht captives were looking around as if trying to guess who would protect them from whom.

Came Pam's first Paris *collaboratrice*, her head shaved and stripped to a lumpily unsexy slip already moist with her fellow Frenchmen's saliva. A swastika crudely daubed backwards—four years of this, and they *still* didn't know the alignment?—over her firmly closed eyes, her hips still metronomically brisk from pure Parisienne habit as she was shoved through the courtyard. Don't know if they'd decided she'd had about enough or wanted someplace more private to get started in earnest.

Does it sound like a movie to you? Just too corny, to coin a phrase? But I saw it, I saw it: the white stars on our Shermans, the bright summer haze stamping everything with instant eternity. The oceanic crowds, the flags and the flowers as more halftracks and jeeps became islands of GIs crushed under Parisiennes and someone called out that von Choltitz had signed the surrender. On a balcony, a small girl was baffled by why she'd been jammed into last year's Communion dress to watch a circus hit town. Hoping for a smile, I sailed my

cunt cap around like a lasso, but she was looking for someone to make sense of
it all and I wasn't much help. I saw it, I saw it, I saw it.

"Eddie! This one *mec* wants to know if *we* know when de Gaulle's getting here."

"Ain't that grand? Four years of waiting for us, then it's *merci* and boom and
back to waiting for *him*. What are we, chopped liver? Ah, fuck you."

"*Mon copain vient de vous dire qu'il pense que le Général de Gaulle arrivera bientôt.*"

"I, uh, speak some English. Please tell your friend that refusing his invitation to copulate does not mean we think a brief cry of '*Vive l'Amérique*' would
be inappropriate."

"*Et voici le Louvre.* La'ies and gentlemen"—tap-tap—"*le Louvre.*"

Massive stairwells, tiny but endlessly multiplied clatter of shoes. In my blue
coat and bobbing jonquil hat, I was ten years old, nine years old, eight: "*Ram-
Pam-Pam! Eh, Pamelle. Eh, euh—l'Américaine! Bouscule pas, garde ton cul. Eh,
Madeleine! Vas dire à Chignonne et Cassandre que nous autres, on n'en a rien à
foutre de la Joconde. Mon sourire à moi est vachement mieux. Tiens, prends ça!*"

"*Et là—toujours le Louvre.*" Scripted joke. "It does go on for a bit."

That was when this part of the Louvre began to look different from not
only the previous part of the Louvre but the rest of Paris. We only understood
why when first the previous part of the Louvre and then the rest of Paris began
to look more like it instead. Our microphoned Marianne squinted skyward.

"*Ah! Enfin un peu de soleil. On a eu bien de la chance qu'il ne pleuve pas!*" As
weather reports weren't part of her script, she mentally groped before saying,
"We are lucky for the sun. *Et maintenant, à votre gauche, l'église américaine de
Paris, la première église américaine construite à l'étranger.* La'ies and gentlemen,
on our left, the American Church of Paris. This was the first church constructed
by Americans in a country not their own. *Oh, mais madame! Madame. Merde!
Pardon, le micro. Qu'avez-vous, madame? Qu'y a-t-il, enfin?*"

"Miss Bucha, Mrs. Cad—Pamela. Are you okay?"

"Sorry, Chris, sorry. Yes, it's all right. *Ce n'est rien, mademoiselle. Mille par-
dons. Ça va.*"

Engines backing, engines threshing: as we docked, all this somehow made
it more vivid than the trip had that we'd been on a river the whole time. Back on
land, I decided directness might be what Cadwaller would advise.

And I'd outlived her.

"Chris, how old do you think I am?" I asked as we walked.

Not only did that catch him off guard, he was still young enough to feel obliged to stop and study me physically before framing his answer. "I don't know. Old enough for Dad, I guess. Say, was that the church where you—"

"I'm thirty-eight. Yes, it was. And I wish you liked me better."

Astonishing me—even your grandpa admitted he wouldn't have done it if he'd been a year older—he took my hand. "Oh, but I do now," Chris said very seriously. "I didn't know grownups cried."

POSTED BY: *Pam*　　Chris's stepmom got the worst reviews of her not wholly unspittled life when my third book came out in 1968. Yet my look at three ages of Paris, three ages of Americans in Paris and three ages of myself in Paris is still my own favorite among the blinking, huh-durn-near-forgot-our-manners trio you'll meet if you search for books *by Pamela Buchanan* online. It also has my favorite among my titles, and God love the faulty English of Paris's *bateau-mouche* Mariannes. Even as I sat bawling my brains out next to a concerned young Chris Cadwaller, Pam's authorial instinct was laying burglar's hands on *Lucky for the Sun*.

After the me-me-me of *Nothing Like a Dame* and then the ruthlessly I-omitting *Glory Be* (Pam's self-equation with Martha Shelton was a secret I took to her grave), I found a new bridge between the two. One reason I like the book is that I like myself in it. On most of its pages, I sound like a fairly lively, likable—sane!—human being.

I don't think it was all imposture, though of course some of it was; I'm a writer. Despite everything else going on in 1966 and '67, writing *Lucky* made me happy as neither *Nothing* nor *Glory* had. I even got in touch with La Tour d'Argent to ask if I could include their recipe for *caneton* as an appendix. I thought the gesture might give special pleasure to at least two readers—one all but guaranteed, as Chris was sent the first copy, the other conjectural but fondly imagined a full quarter century after Pearl Harbor.

Blame the slow grind of the publishing mill for the drubbing I got. One welcome exception was a belated rave from my never met champion Celia

Brady (White, Singh) in Jaipur's *Pink Courier,* a name that prompted a blink or two. I didn't yet know the Pink City is Jaipur's nickname. Still, I doubt praise from a maharajah's wife would've cut much ice with my Stateside critics.

Even I could see that whatever the ideal season might be for a book like *Lucky for the Sun,* the spring of 1968 wasn't that season. It reached stores midway between the Martin Luther King and Bobby Kennedy assassinations, and you'd better believe most copies just sat there until remaindering put them out of my if not Simon and Schuster's misery. Aside from *Lucky's* brioche not being in huge demand, it was obvious its author had led a fairly privileged life—once again, duh! as you children say—and by the late Sixties people like that were being measured for rhetorical tumbrils.

Even though Hopsie had only needed to hear the first minute of Chris's talk about the *caneton* to understand that he was really praising his new stepmother and it was all right, the big lunch with my sixteen-year-old stepson I used as my penultimate set-piece came in for special abuse. Maybe that was unavoidable. Other than a passing remark that it was the first time either of us had eaten at La Tour d'Argent, sharing my private motivation for taking him would've upset the book's tone.

Owing to a similar reticence, my dedication—"To the memory of Marie Antoinette and la première D.B."—got smacked around everywhere from the Salt Lake City *Pillar* to the Chickamauga *Post.* Above all, my epigraph from Talleyrand got cited as proof of my political insensibility and obliviousness to the crisis we all faced. On *Lucky's* pathetic book tour, whose only silver lining was getting to see Nick Carraway in the Davenport hospital one last time before he died, I never quite figured out how to explain to hostile under-thirty interviewers that one could know how sweet life had been and still be *for* the Revolution.

To whatever extent a middle-aged white woman writing checks from her Georgetown home to Gene McCarthy's Presidential campaign could be considered the equivalent of one of the Commune's *pétroleuses,* I was. Not one bloody critic noticed that Pam ended her description of visiting the Mur des Fédérés at Père Lachaise with a superficially valedictory, sneakily prescriptive *"Vive la Commune."*

It was my recognition that the world was changing in a way I applauded but whose cost to things I cherished I knew I'd regret that had gotten me started on *Lucky* to begin with. Not wholly unlike, so I speculated, Talleyrand himself, I thought one could mourn the soap bubbles tossed up by a bygone era's values without either advocating those values or failing to support the need for new ones to replace them. I still wish I could remember the full name of the émigré who brought me to the costume party for Lady Diana.

I call an ability to do both at once the true mark of civilization. The minds capable of doing only one or the other on either side of the Sixties divide struck me as equally pigheaded, equally smug. That's why I used to turn even Cadwaller's pipe upside down when I'd rant about campus protesters desecrating libraries and so forth, then stomp upstairs to write another fat check to the McCarthy campaign. Tim, isn't there some aphorism that would explain what I mean about believing in and acting on two contradictory ideas at once?

As my book came out in the States, Paris was being taken over by barricades and street battles for the first time since its liberation from the Nazis. Back in their customary role of truncheoned proof that there's no thug like a uniformed one, the once again hated *flics* were firing tear gas and advancing on student demonstrators who, while providing one inverse example after another of the forgotten wonders of shampoo, threw prised-up paving stones back and retired to the next barricade. The Tour d'Argent was wreathed in green and gray police smog.

It went on for weeks, looking worse even on TV than the aftermath of the Stavisky riot Ram-Pam-Pam had glimpsed thirty-four years earlier on my way to the Gare du Nord after my mother's death. When it ended, something's back had been broken, and I'm not sure anything ever grew to replace it. What neither side knew was that they were brawling over who won bragging rights in France's last command performance on the world stage.

Cadwaller's feelings were mixed at the time. He knew de Gaulle had to go, had set aside private fascination for professional antagonism ever since *Le Général* had pulled France out of NATO. Incidentally forcing its headquarters' relocation from Paris to—where else, mother mine?—Brussels. Yet Hopsie loathed chaos, passionately believed in dispassionate discussion. He'd already made his only exception to that rule, and she was the one arguing with him.

He was also personally alarmed, as was I, when we realized Chris and Renée must be in the thick of it. We didn't hear from them for weeks, but their stories were as inevitable as the way Nan Finn's giggle follows her nose's upward toss. Depositing Tim with a friend, Renée had calmly plodded off to volunteer in the improvised infirmary set up by the students inside the Sorbonne once they realized the *flics* were checking all the hospitals after every street battle. As for Chris, trained by his father to recognize that a U.S. passport was a responsibility as well as a privilege, he knew he couldn't join the demonstrators. Instead he took the best photographs of his life. They were later published by Kaylie & Gallagher as *May or Mayn't*, the book that interested Amherst in hiring him.

When Cadwaller got done leafing through it the next year, he set aside his pipe and looked at his son thoughtfully. Behind us on the self-same rug I'm planning to splatter with a mess of pink and gray things come Potus or sundown, Renée was leafing through *The Golden Book of the American Revolution* for seven-year-old Timmy's benefit, clucking here and humming there to teach him how a woman would interpret it.

"Well, Chris," Hopsie said. "You'll never convince me all this was any sensible way of getting what they wanted done, done. I abominate it! I don't despise it, but I do abominate it. But you did convince me it had one thing she's taught me to revere. No matter the setting, the season, the reason, the anything."

"What, Dad?"

"Beauty." Soon after Cadwaller's long dying ended, Chris told me that was the compliment from his father he'd prized most. Since he was knocking away tears and the morality of all confessions, large or small, is their timing, I waited a few years to tell him it had also been mine.

Sometime in the long afternoon of crowded gabble that followed Hopsie's burial, placid and nonliterary Renée surprised me by volunteering to try translating *Lucky for the Sun* into French. Touched as I was, my favorite of *by Pamela Buchanan's* books was an eighteen-year-old flop by then and I seriously doubted—what with the raw feelings stirred by everything from Reagan's visit to Bitburg and the placement of Pershing missiles in Europe to our then current peccadilloes in Central America—that too many Frenchmen were baying for an elderly *Américaine's* elderly book about our share of their capital.

I also knew it was a gesture to her father-in-law, not me. Before I could find the right way of showing how touched I was while letting her off the hook, she saw she had to attend to Tim. He was twenty-four when she spotted him tearing up over his grandfather in our Georgetown kitchen, and imagining the lifelong effect of all those Olympic hula hoops and spheres rubbing and saying *"Ah, chéri"* left me awed for neither the first nor last time at Panama's dad's sexual sanity. But I digress.

Back in 1968, everyone who didn't scoff at *Lucky for the Sun*'s epigraph slammed me instead for its closing sentence, and a few greedy reviewers did both. It was taken as more narcissism, but I meant it as a reproach, a regret, a commemoration: a memory, in short. When I think of how much more painful a reproach, regret, and commemoration it's become in Potusville's day, I could bawl more loudly than I did on the *bateau-mouche* almost half a century ago.

After the set-piece of my big Tour d'Argent lunch with Chris, my final chapter paid homage to Dutourd's *Les horreurs de l'amour* by imagining a long walk through the city, starting at our Embassy and going on to the replica of the Statue of Liberty near the Pont de Grenelle, Edith Wharton's first Paris apartment at 58, rue de Varenne, and the plaque in the rue de Lille marking the building where Adams, Franklin, and John Jay had signed the treaty ending our Revolutionary War. Its last stop was the Place St. Sulpice, which I described as I remembered it on August Twen'-Five, Nine'een Fort-Four: mobbed with islanded GIs in jeeps and halftracks and happy Parisians celebrating under two determined towers announcing to the sky that this was as far as they got. There was no reason why the sky should care, but they did.

Then I wrote the most bitter, most grateful, most puzzled, most complicated line of my career. This was it: "And of course, we were loved."

2. The Art of Nagon

POSTED BY: *Pam*   In my favorite snapshot of Hopsie from our time in West Africa, he's wearing a top hat and looks debonair. His eyes are two crows' nests that have just sprouted crows' feet. One hand tips a glass in salute, though neither it nor his smile is greeting the camera.

For a reason that would've struck me then as too obvious to articulate, I know the little girl watching fishermen haul long nets from the sea can only be Nell Finn, the older of Ned and Nan's two kids. I'm almost positive the boisterous American back and raised hand Cadwaller is facing belong to Nell's father. Ned could be very funny at that time of day.

Naturally, I know that's Rich Warren in preoccupied jaw-rubbing profile behind them. Seated nearby, our USIS man's wife Laurel is the only one glancing up into the lens. She looks feline, something Laurel could never keep up for long. The canary in her mouth is about to be set free with a grin.

Even more than the fishermen behind them or the gray palm-frond roof of the gazebo they're in, one detail proves that they're all in Nagon. Hopsie's top hat aside, the men—him included—are all in swim trunks. Laurel Warren has a swimsuit on too. So does Nell Finn in the background.

Cadwaller had worn his Ambassadorial topper in all seriousness earlier, but I assure you clapping it back on now wasn't his way of lampooning whatever ceremony he'd been to in Ouibomey. An hour away down Nagon's coastal, sunlit and palm-slashed, only fully paved road, it was the official capital, thanks to its preserved royal courtyard from the old tribal days, its Portuguese fort from entrepreneurial seventeenth-century ones, and its convent-cum-nursing school-cum-leper colony left over from France's *mission civilisatrice*—euphemism for colonialism. Plon-Plon-Ville, where we all lived, was the administrative or, as Ned Finn called it with binary irony, the working capital.

When I asked her, Nan couldn't recall either which Nagonese occasion required our Ambassador to gussy up in the same rig that our London envoy would have less dehydratingly worn to Edward VII's coronation back in 1901.

Hopsie would have been indignant had anyone mocked maintaining the custom in equatorial Africa. He valued punctilio for being to public diplomacy what a signature on a treaty is to negotiation. Not only the thin skins of Africa's new republics but our and even their former masters' determination to wish them well by symbolically vouching they were our sovereign equal in the great hall of nations demanded top hat and white gloves.

Knowing the rest of us would be at the beach, he'd come straight there and changed to swim trunks whose pattern, thanks to the snapshot, I now remember better in black and white than in color. Were those pale whorls blue or green? Now that we were behind our invisible intra-American palisade again, since the fishermen certainly didn't care, he was wearing the top hat to waggishly parody his role as the chief of our much smaller Yankee Doodley colony.

If my daisysdaughter.com readers are wondering, at the time young Nell Finn was the only American girl her age in the country. Now in her fifties, she still acts and sounds thrilled to no longer be singular when I see her at Nan's Christmas parties. But like the rest of us, Nell says she wouldn't have missed Nagon for the world. Spin the globe all you like, you won't find it today.

POSTED BY: *Pam*   Hopsie always did have acuity. Moments after that snapshot was taken, he ended the joke by handing the topper to me before racing Rich Warren—onetime UCLA lineman, '46 season only: once Laurel entered the picture, he got tired of having to fake humorless animosity before every snap—down to the surf for a swim. Any longer, and the juxtaposition of rank and good fellowship might've turned buffoonish or self-satisfied.

As for me, I'd been Pam Cadwaller long enough not to model his Ambassadorial chapeau. Didn't matter how tempted I might've felt when Nan Finn's giggle summoned me. Bringing up the Kodak that in Nagon followed Nan's laugh as inevitably as Valentine's Day follows Christmas, she called, "Marlene! *Marlene!*"

Panama, I'm not optimistic high-school teachers of English even know this themselves, much less explain it to frizzily tress-stressed, only fizzily attentive bikini girls. But parody has all sorts of dimensions. It needn't be intentional to be not only ironic but, variously, acrid, bemusing, or even rhapsodic. Indeed parody is often most poignant when unanticipated and accidental. It has its own gift for beauty and pain. In 1962, it was the art of Nagon.

What were we parodying? Camelot, most strikingly, in our hairdos, costumes, and Kodak-immobilized gestures. Our version was contemporary with Washington's famous one. But we were six thousand miles away at what most people would call the ends of the earth—even though, to those of us on the spot, it looked and felt more like earth's beginning. Visibly, that didn't stop us from turning the beach a mile or so west of the bony long concrete Rheuma of Plon-Plon-Ville's jetty into our sham Hyannisport.

As one of the kids on the post idly snapped off the tail of a small wall-scaling lizard—impressed every time by no blood or evident consequence, though perhaps it's as well lizards can't talk—we were no less visibly mimicking intimate East Wing soirées in our now petrified hand dances and profiled palaver on those dreary government-issue sofas of ours. They were backed against the grainy cement-block walls of the tin-roofed blockhouses most of Plon-Plon-Ville's diplomatic community called home, and the equestrienne's influence had to've been seismic for Pam to risk that little black A-line cocktail dress. Not my best look, even if I daresay the splendidly crossed Buchanan gams were still in business at the old stand.

Did even Carol Sawyer, whose wide face was as Dutch as a tulip crossbred with a windmill, try those *Breakfast at Tiffany's* bangs that year? No TV set in sight in any photograph: none in the country. But the Scandinavian hi-fi unit ceding its place of honor only to the Finns' liquor cabinet is a hoot.

Very enjoyably, we were also parodying ourselves, one of the treats of reaching the prime of life and recognizing that the ship is more or less built. Except for my Hopsie, we were all in our mid-thirties to early forties, the age when the furnishings of one's impressionable youth—cf. Nan's "Marlene! *Marlene!*"—become pleasurable as shared tokens. Anyhow, in the Foreign Service one soon learns that one's personality on arrival at any new post is bound to be parodic. It's not only enhanced for quicker ease of recognition by the new pack of strangers but adjusted for climate, local customs, housing, and the social origami of everyone else's anecdotes of their previous one.

Parody that *Glory Be*'s author might've been more struck by than most: until our first contingent made landfall, there'd never been an American Embassy in Nagon. No one had preceded Hopsie and me, Virgil Scoleri the Admin guy, and a de-Laureled Rich Warren, along to scout buildings for the USIS library. We docked at the tip of Plon-Plon-Ville's bony Rheuma, staring at the fishermen's pirogues drawn up on the beach.

The Embassy compound was still being built. Until we did it the first time, no flag whatsoever had been hoisted up its new flagpole. No American flag had ever flown with Nagon's sun-boiled sky as its backdrop.

The reason we'd come by ship from the Ivory Coast wasn't only that even Air Afrique only landed every third day. We had supplies in the hold: file cabinets, typewriters, desk chairs, our new President's portrait for the Embassy wall. For the rest of our time in Nagon, we waited for ships the way you wait for phone calls. Thanks to the Sears, Roebuck catalogue, each few months brought us another delivery of goods from the home country unavailable here: bright red coolers, Scandinavian hi-fi sets and records, sneakers and blue jeans, toy guns.

Beyond our coastal camp lay the rest of Nagon, unmanned by any personnel of ours other than Buzz Sawyer's native assistant at the USAID irrigation projects upcountry and a couple of Peace Corps kids nobody liked. (Snobbery about non–State Department representatives of America is a Foreign Service perk.) Beyond that lay a whole strange continent, as yet uninvestigated by any of us but known to tumble on grandly and frighteningly for thousands of miles.

On display in every American blockhouse, its pages tenderly reprised by the kids on the post long after they'd grown mossy and chipped, the Sears, Roebuck catalogue emblazoned the values, still exotic on this continent, to which we hoped to win all of its allegiance someday. Referring you once again to *Glory Be*'s opening chapter, "A Landing," do I really need to say one more word?

Hopsie did. Nautical as ever, he bought a small motorboat for the Embassy out of the contingency fund six months in. We traded one of our wry private looks once Pam saw the name he'd had painted on it: *Pélérin*.

I christened it one day after filling one of our sacramental few Coke bottles with seawater, wearing a kerchief and sunglasses that strike my eye now as a Jackie move blended with a tribute to Priscilla Alden. Then we, Ned and

Nan Finn, Buzz and Carol Sawyer, and their kids all clambered in—Hopsie at the wheel, happy to be skippering again—to skim across the Plon-Plon-Ville lagoon for a picnic with Rich and Laurel Warren and their two boys. Showing their usual streak of affable but stubborn eccentricity, the Warrens had chosen to live in the lone American blockhouse on the far side—Rhode Island, as I sometimes called it.

POSTED BY: *Pam*   Parody of a *nouveau riche* faux pas: the Finns' four Nagonese servants, outdoing Buzz and Carol Sawyer's three and the Warrens' austere two. Of course the Residence had six, but Cadwaller's rank clarified that as an official outlay and not a personal preference.

Realizing that she'd embarrassed herself by adding a kitchen boy to cook, houseboy, and laundryman had the glorious girl clutching her head as soon as Carol congratulated her. Since she obviously couldn't fire Kindassou, there all four of them are in their white-buttoned white uniforms with nine-year-old Nell and her younger brother. Louis's extra prestige as the cook is advertised by his toque and prosperous bulk.

"Pam, what was I thinking? I just didn't know how I was supposed to say no," Nan wailed once she and I were safely out of the country, meaning we'd borrowed one of the Embassy cars and drivers to zip over the border for a quick shopping run to Nigeria. We had no PX, so the Brits' Harrod's-parodic NAAFI store in cosmopolitan Lagos was our backup between Sears consignments.

"No to who, Nan? Not Ned."

"No, Louis. He's been doing this for a *lot* longer than I have. I've only ever hired babysitters, and I didn't know Kindassou was his cousin."

"So are the other two, I expect. But you know it doesn't really matter," I told her. "So you and Ned are shelling out eighty dollars a month instead of sixty, big deal! That's probably raising the per capita income by something like fifty cents. Anyhow, your cook's better."

Remember, I was the Ambassador's wife: that was rash. I didn't need to add *than Carol Sawyer's* for Nan's eyes to quicken with covenized glee. We'd been in Nagon long enough that I knew I could trust her not to rely on my favoritism for leverage when Carol was around.

Then she clutched her head again, contemplating an unfortunately mental NAAFI shopping list. "Oh, God! Those pretend M&Ms the kids like. In the tubes. Help me. Smilies? Sillies?"

"Smarties," I said and we both laughed. " 'Pretend'?" I added, and Nan grew even younger.

Parody of the cold war: innocently and now *there's* a first, the Soviets had located their Embassy compound in Ouibomey. Nobody in Moscow had grasped that it was only the ceremonial capital and the rest of the diplomatic community and all the Nagonese government's ministries were in Plon-Plon-Ville. But their home-office bean counters wouldn't let them scrap the little Kremlin they'd built next door to the leper colony, so they showed up at big receptions looking fairly wilted. They'd had to tool like mad up the coastal road for an hour in their unairconditioned (more scrimping) black Zils.

They couldn't very well not attend. Just as Dobrynin was later in Washington, their Ambassador was the dean of the diplomatic corps. Beating us by a week, the leisurely Brits by two, and the resentful, foot-dragging French by a month, Shishkov had been the first to present his credentials to M'Lawa at the unfinished Palais du Président. Stuck waiting in Abidjan for Virgil Scoleri the Admin guy, we'd been pinning our hopes on the West Germans, but Rommel would have turned in his grave at the way that fool Klaus Schlitten lingered in Cairo.

Relations between Cadwaller and his Soviet counterpart were impeccably frosty, the more so as they rather liked each other. That didn't stop Hopsie from leaping forward, pipe-wreathed and happy in his white linen suit, to shake glum but optionless Vasily Vladimirovich's hand with crackerjack pleasure at our first diplomatic shindig after the Cuban missile showdown.

Speaking of frosty, the Soviets' Buzz Sawyer wasn't noticeably more competent than ours. I'll never forget how that obese Odessan, who'd rented a *band*—M'Lawa's own, for hire between Presidential events: it was the only one in the country—blanched in his obsidian suit when a Soviet trawler triumphantly offloaded the USSR's latest gift to Nagon. To us Americans, those six spiffy new snowplows were marvelous to watch as the enormous things, blades blazing, swung overhead one after another on derricks against Nagon's sun-boiled sky.

One ended up on a concrete plinth in front of the Palais du Président as a sort of trophy of Soviet interest. It *was* machinery, after all, and the trawler had also delivered a hefty shipment of cement. At least the Snowplow Affair let Buzz off the hook for the eight thousand screwdrivers USAID had shipped to a country that probably had fewer than eight thousand screws to use them on.

Parody of Pam's marital past: just a couple of blocks nearer the beach than ours on the Boulevard St. Michel, the name unchanged from *mission civilisatrice* days, the tiny Israeli Embassy's blue and white flag flew. Plenty of countries didn't even bother to have diplomats in Nagon, since there just wouldn't have been much for an Ambassador from Costa Rica, say, to *do*. But the Israelis put in an envoy wherever they had recognition. Ehud Tabor was their man, handsome as a rock pool and black-haired as a jaguar. I can't help noticing that I look unusually uninteresting and marginal when he's nearby.

Poised as he was, Ehud's most ambitious event turned out to be Israel's biggest disaster until the opening days of the Yom Kippur War. New movies usually reached Nagon a year or more after their release, and we never knew what we'd get. I still remember the oddity of seeing my old friend Eve Harrington dubbed into French in *The Magpie Did It* in the dank dark of the Bijou Castafiore, Plon-Plon-Ville's largest movie house. So Ehud had to go to considerable trouble to get a print of Hollywood's bouquet to his nation's birth: the lavish Panavisioning of Ari ben Canaan's headstrong early years, shrewdly stopping short of the post-1948 marital tribulations that might've turned the concluding reels into *Cat on a Hot Tin Kibbutz.*

Or maybe those were just missing, since the reels that did turn up in Plon-Plon-Ville weren't numbered and the projectionist had to sequence them by guesswork. Our own Yankee Doodley colony included, the whole diplomatic corps and Nagonese cabinet—fortunately, President M'Lawa was in Paris—were sitting on folded chairs in the Israeli Embassy's only large room, from which they'd had to cart out the buffet tables as we waited outside for a couple of Ehud's locals to turn it into a screening room. Ehud had no choice but to go ahead and hope for the best.

Oh, God! Haifa, Jerusalem, shipboard, Gan Dafna, Jerusalem again, all seemingly cued by Nell Finn playing hopscotch. The movie opened with a prison break, but it didn't work out: soon everyone we'd seen escape was back in stir. They declared independence, then bombed the King David Hotel in an apparent ruse to lure the British back. The opening credits burst upon us an hour or so in, triggering a doomed hope we might get our bearings. Then they declared independence again, briefly—"Seen it!" someone called—and two or three people came back from the dead. After some inconclusive fighting, everyone ended up behind barbed wire in a detention camp on Cyprus.

"C'est tout ce qu'il y a. Il n'y en a pas plus," the projectionist said resignedly. We all staggered out into the night like zombies.

"Ehud!" an instantly cigaretted Ned Finn called, fumbling with matches. "Old man, I just want to tell you how personally sorry I am the whole Zionism thing didn't work out." Marlboro lit, he glanced around whimsically: "I wonder what they'll use this building for now?"

"Well! A cinema would be my guess, Ned. It seems to have a future there," said Ehud, too experienced not to be droll but swiftly taking refuge in a cigarette of his own. Then he raised the hand forking it: "Herr Ambassador, thank you for coming."

A stricken face stared back. "Please, under the circumstances understand I can voice no opinion. None," Klaus Schlitten said and departed.

"What the hell, Ehud. It wasn't that bad. Just like life!" I told him. "Anyhow it was fun to see Jerusalem again."

"Oh, yes! I'd still like to visit," said Nan Finn eagerly. "Ned too, of course. Wouldn't you, honey…?"

POSTED BY: *Pam*   The wonder and pity of the art of Nagon, Panama, is that we were surrounded each and every day by geography and people movingly determined not to be a parody of a country. On the map, Nagon was just one of the Nigeria-dwarfed crinkles near the notch of the African elephant's ear. Yet a flag is a flag and a national anthem is an anthem.

Yes, they might've had to turn to a French vexillologist—one guess why he'd prospered between 1958 and 1962—for help designing the flag. Its patterning of Africa's eternal green, red, and yellow still flew proudly over Plon-Plon-Ville and Ouibomey, as well as from a maze of white poles outside the

Palais du Président on the coastal road between them. And yes, they might've been ridiculed in the Paris press when the anthem's author wrote asking Cocteau's blessing as an Academician on the lyrics, but it was bellowed nonetheless at every public event. Well into adulthood, the former kids on the post could still sing it, even though Nagon no longer existed:

> *Le peu-ple nagonais s'élève!*
> *Le peu-ple nagonais s'élève—euh!*
> *Des siècles de souffrances sans trêve—euh!*
> *Sont brûlées par Le soleil d'aujourd'hui.*

If you're curious: "The Nagonese people arise!/The Nagonese people arise!/Centuries of suffering without respite/Are burned by the Sun of Today." Yet the Nagonese people had arisen, if only in Plon-Plon-Ville's sports palace to wildly cheer France's formal cession of its colony, mere weeks before the Palais du Président started to do the same. I doubt a single American didn't mutter "Uh-oh" at his or her first sight of that thing bulking up along the coastal road. Its resemblance to a massive box of sugar cubes was so striking that Ned Finn used to wonder if one good monsoon would turn it into a puddle.

It cost three million dollars, which may not sound so pricey until I inform you Nagon's budget that year was eight. The rectangular vats of water lining the coastal road opposite it were supposed to complement and reflect the maze of flags facing them, but they had no drainage and were soon covered in thick green scum. The detail that earned Hopsie's "Well, well" as we mounted the steps to our first reception there was that the main entrance featured a revolving door with a ten-foot wingspan.

That was Jean-Baptiste M'Lawa's own idea, copied from his favorite hotel in Nice. He'd been the only real choice for President, the plebiscite a mere formality. The chunky Polytechnique-trained economist had led the delegation that negotiated Nagon's freedom. Written largely in Switzerland during his Geneva period, his tome *Les problèmes de l'Afrique moderne* had influenced the Constitutions of three other former French colonies by the time his own country's turn came.

He could even have argued, not unreasonably, that his massive box of gleaming sugar cubes was just what *le peuple nagonais* needed for daily proof they were a true nation, on a par with not only Liberia or Laos but even *notre bonne mère la France*—the anthem's lyric in colonial times, rhyming touchingly if none too convincingly with *confiance*. Yet not many of them saw it, and you can guess what subtracting three million from eight gets you in a country that has only one paved road running longer than five kilometers. At the time, Nagon's per-capita income was $87 a year.

We didn't need to drive too far north on the inland trunk road, whose asphalt gave way to ochre mud just past the sports palace and Army barracks, to find villages whose children had bellies like canted Rand McNally globes and legs like compasses. Their mothers' breasts had stretched into tattooed tube socks stuffed with two desiccated tangerines. Round mud huts with thatched roofs clustered near baobab trees on bare plain. Hump-necked cattle so bony that they didn't look likely to supply much but the future skins for tom-toms hobbled and swayed here and there. The kids on the post got very excited when we spotted a lioness looking up at us from the guts of an eviscerated antelope.

Our reason for making that trip was a doctor who'd written Buzz Sawyer asking if *les États-Unis d'Amérique* were feeling flush enough to splurge on buying him a bicycle. We brought him a Vespa instead, which turned out to be dumb. Where would he find gas, how would he pay for it? Even though the older Sawyer boy glowered like a candle in shorts when Buzz unracked Tommie's bike as a substitute, he'd been slotted to get a new one for his next birthday and that Sears consignment was due in six weeks.

Well after the sugar cubes got stacked up on the coastal road, construction languished on the Assemblée Nationale. At the time of M'Lawa's overthrow, the delegates were still meeting at the Hôtel de la Plage, venerated by the kids on the post because it had real ice cream. The École d'Administration did open, but M'Lawa didn't even wait until its first class of white-shirted, pen-proud students had graduated before he ordered the cadres of French administrators who'd stayed on after the handover to go home. He did it because *Le Monde* hadn't mentioned the new nation of Nagon even once in its generally sober columns since the business about writing to Cocteau for approval of "Le soleil d'aujourd'hui"'s lyrics.

God, how the kids on the post loved that anthem. But my most dramatic memory of it is instrumental. Along with Ned and Nan Finn, Cadwaller and I were in the reviewing stand when Nagon marked the first anniversary of independence. Fretful of protocol, the glorious girl had asked me to ask him if it'd be all right for her to bring her Kodak. Since the Finns' seats were two rows below ours and hence even farther away from M'Lawa's canopied chair in the top one, Hopsie thought it would. He still knew Nan well enough to warn me to warn her to take pictures of the parade only: no pivoting to gaily snap us, Vasily and Krupskaya Shishkov, the Schlittens, or Ehud Tabor, and above all not the President himself. He had bodyguards.

Then I took my seat next to Etiènne Maurice N'Koda. Decorated by both Vichy and the Free French and still wearing those medals, he was the grizzle-bearded former French Army sergeant who now headed the nation's armed forces. After the bright-kerchiefed and singing upcountry village women with their baskets of manioc, the students at the new École d'Administration in their pen-proud short-sleeved white shirts and stiff new black shoes, the wimpled latest graduates from the Ouibomey nursing school, and the clerical staff at the Plon-Plon-Ville Monoprix store had all filed by, the demonstration of Nagon's military prowess was the parade's climax.

As the Nagonese Army appeared, the Presidential band crashed into "Le soleil d'aujourd'hui" and N'Koda leapt to his feet. A bit uncertainly, everyone else in our row did too. I didn't dare look behind us to see whether M'Lawa had and would've had no way of knowing if he'd done so first or second.

Arms swinging, eight hundred men marched smartly past us in four companies. The first three were shouldering bolt-action rifles and the last one was equipped with rubber truncheons and riot shields.

Then came four jeeps. Then came five rumbling snowplows, their blades thankfully raised. As the last of them passed us, N'Koda abruptly sat down. With some hesitation, so did the rest of our row, though the anthem hadn't ended.

Once Nagon no longer existed, I don't know what became of its anthem. Yet "Le soleil d'aujourd'hui" lives on tenderly in the middle-aged memories of the former kids on the post. They sing it now at Nan Finn's Christmas parties:

Frères et soeurs nagonais, sourions!
Vainqueurs dans la lutte contre le temps!
Commençons le travail ensemble—euh!
Dorés par the soleil d'aujourd'hui.

Once again, if you're curious: "Nagonese brothers and sisters, let's smile!/ Victors in the battle with time/Let's all get to work together/Gilded by the Sun of Today."

You'll have to forgive me, bikini girl. The mimsies have just informed me I'd best excuse myself for a bit.

POSTED BY: *Pam*   Proof parody knew the difference between itself and burlesque, at least where Pam's marital past was concerned: no Irish flag joined the Israeli one in the Plon-Plon-Ville sky. But I remember Rich Warren's washboard forehead the day he came by the Residence to ask whether I'd mind if he included *The Trampled Vintage* in the USIS library's collection of significant American plays.

"I know it's dated and not even his best. But it did win the '34 Pulitzer for drama." Trust Rich to use added specifics the way others do "well" and "you know."

"What, those idiots?" I drawled in the lavish voice I'd discovered at forty had been lurking here and there in Pam's throat all along. His forehead almost went from washboard to page of a phone book before he caught on that *Glory Be's* author was joking—well, mostly.

"Rich, of course I don't mind! So long as you don't ask me to act in it, I couldn't care less. But it was thoughtful of you to even wonder if I'd be bothered"—that wonderful little compromise between "annoyed" and "upset."

"I've learned late in life that thoughtful's my best trick," he said, going from frown of concern to smile. "Awful football player! Just awful. Ask Laurel."

I'd gotten the hang of him enough by then to know self-deprecation was his way of being friendly, not neurotic. So I was just letting him know I liked him: "Awful for UCLA, you mean."

"Oh, sure."

"Rich, you've just stumped me. What *is* his best?" I asked, since I knew no such category.

"For my money? *Lo! The Ships, the Ships*, but don't trust me. Laurel played Conchita when the Mask and Grease Club revived it in college. You all think she's so pleasant, but with castanets she's a spitfire."

"Then why not get that one? It won a Pulitzer too."

"Out of print."

"Poor Murphy," I mused. "You know I hadn't thought of him in forever? Then someone"—Jake Cohnstein, but Rich didn't know him—"wrote me last month he's doing the word balloons for a comic strip. From Broadway to the funnies, all in one lifetime."

Rich grinned. "Don't ask me to feel sorry for him. I've spent my whole life in the funnies."

"I thought that was Buzz," I said and we laughed. However inevitable, at least in those days, our USAID man's comic-strip nickname fit him like a dropped anvil except in one abject sense. His lonely hobby was woodworking, which failed utterly to interest even his own sons until he carved Tommie a wooden Tommy gun after the toy one they'd ordered turned up missing in that Sears consignment.

Neither Rich nor I knew our Yankee Doodley crew would soon be coping with a complication that put any hint Buzz was a figure of fun out of bounds. Ridiculous he still was, but too painfully. Parody of John Updike, disliked by me for its literary derivation nearly as much as its boorishness: Ned Finn's affair with Carol Sawyer. It ground along for four months as the rest of us writhed.

And yes, in case you haven't noticed: the Finns and the Sawyers. I think the coincidence irritated both families, especially since the tin-roofed American blockhouses of our DCM and our USAID man faced each other with only a low wall between them on a straggling dull street five minutes' walk from the Embassy compound. For one thing, they didn't remember the Twain books well enough to be sure what sort of jokes they should make. No great lacuna to Buzz, that was a torment to Ned. If seeing Carol's wide face aslop in voluntary sweat for a change was his idea of great-great-great-grandfather Huckleberry's revenge, all I can say is I hope his ancestor would've been ashamed at how the family had gone downhill.

Dismal enough if we'd all been back in the States, illicit rutting was inexcusable in our little colony, which at its peak could muster under a dozen American adults in all. To spare you confusion, *l'équipe* has skipped over a few of our

Embassy's lesser factoti here on sneakily efficient little daisysdaughter.com: we had an econ attaché too, not to mention two secretaries that the spirit of Camelotian parody, along with a blank spot in Pink Thing's archives, forces me to rechristen Fiddle and Faddle. Still, what a tiny group we were. In our special circumstances, the real crudity was that he and Carol both knew no one had the luxury of throwing their bad behavior back in their faces—Ned's often silly and flushed even without booze's help, hers oinkier than ever.

You couldn't just toss them aside like an Updike paperback before reaching instead for the glowing, rock-steady best of Cheever (the Warrens). Not only would that mean chucking Nan out with the bathwater, but we were all stuck here until our tours' various ends. You learn fast overseas that the fabric of intra-American life can't be allowed to unravel. With its talk of sports and old movie stars and its familiar idioms, it's all you've got to keep the unrelieved exoticism from turning excruciating.

The only one who could've braced Ned was Cadwaller, who loathed confronting subordinates about their personal lives. Our DCM might be inanely plying his dowsing rod with his back turned to Lake Superior, but his work hadn't slipped and, except intramurally, he wasn't disgracing his country. Either of those sins would've had Hopsie giving ex-Signalman Finn pungent proof this Ambassador *still* knew how to speak Navy.

Partly at my prodding, since I couldn't stand it for Nan's sake any longer, he was getting ready to read Ned the riot act anyway. Then the whole piggish thing unmistakably lapsed the night Carol, wearing a sleeveless flowered dress and a tight-cheeked smile, is sweeping away invisible warders with those stocky Dutch arms and a Marlboro has been left to burn itself out in an accidental-looking ashtray in the foreground.

But while it went on, we all knew. Amiable Rich Warren forced himself to stop laughing at Ned's jokes—even "Born Toulouse, I've lived my life Lautrec," sung *a l'improvvisatore* apropos of nothing but surf one night on the merry ledge between first and second drink at the Hôtel de la Plage. Laurel looks on more than one occasion as if she wants to *spit* out that canary.

If Buzz didn't know sooner than most, he should've had himself shipped in one of his USAID packing crates to some World Museum of Boneheadedness with the standard stencil on the box: "**A GIFT FROM THE PEOPLE OF THE UNITED STATES.**" Maybe even the kids on the post knew. And poor Nan: of course the glorious girl knew. How could she not, given that proprietary glow in the background of all three of Ned's eyes—nature's plus cigarette's—as Carol, caught turning in closeup, stares with a nearly crazed facial push-pull of panic and sexual smugness?

At least among the minor players in our old Nagon crowd I've bumped into since, the only one who didn't know was Virgil Scoleri, the Admin guy. For pure bullnecked obtuseness, Panama, not much beats your lifelong bachelor who *isn't* a homosexual.

"Ned and *Carol?*" he bellowed as all five of his eyes (specs plus half finished drink) bulged. He couldn't grasp that not only were we at Nan's Christmas party but Carol was coming out of the kitchen.

Nan still invites her, and that old fool Buzz comes too. We never see the truck that brought Carol or the vacuum cleaner that annually goes into reverse to cough out her husband. Yet while I could've sworn Nan herself was out of earshot—at the room's opposite end, she was trilling like three sitcoms as she bid goodnight to the Warrens and greeted the dear, translucent Bergs from her and Ned's West Berlin days—I've never spotted Virgil Scoleri, the Admin guy, at any of her parties since.

Or anywhere else, but that doesn't prove anything. It's just pleasant.

POSTED BY: *Pam*   If any daisysdaughter.com readers are let down by my apparently declining interest in sharing Pam's inner tribulations and torments, which I certainly do hope you've enjoyed in *l'équipe*'s earlier posts—the anguish, the drama, those fun muddled longings—I invite you to put two and two together. In Nagon, there weren't any. Never underestimate a happy marriage's benison.

Instead, when I'd consider my lot in my early forties, the Pamela Buchanan Experiment felt as if it'd been reasonably well achieved. And a damned close-run thing too, as the Duke of Wellington would put it. I well knew how easily my middle age could've been a series of shipwrecks: stripping with the shades up? "Red rover, red rover"?

Now, for the first time in my life, I was most prone to boredom when alone in a room. I just didn't have any special country I was itching to wander in between my own ears. Our frequent book shortages between Sears consignments, Lagos trips, or someone's home leave put paid to my only other reason to crave solitude when I had no literary project of my own underway. I did write a great many letters and was told they were wonderful by Gerson, Jake, Eve and Addison, Nachum ben Zion, and even (I only wrote him the once) Wylie White.

Other than that, when Hopsie was at the Embassy and I didn't have him to talk to, something I'd still be doing ecstatically if we'd been granted a century on a desert island, I liked spending time with my fellow wives and those of Nagon's grandees. While it's true an hour with Celeste M'Lawa would explain rather better than any number of books why her husband turned dictator, she hadn't had anyone killed and could make any limo ride go by in a flash.

Yes, Ard: I avoided saying "nonetheless." As for Carol Sawyer, preferring her company to being alone could've been a sign of either raving despair or deep contentment: in my case, the second. I had six servants to oversee, things to plan, obligations. The short version is I was an Ambassador's wife and found that it suited me.

Besides, if you don't know me by now, then God help you. Nagon, on the other hand, no longer exists, and in the time that remains me I'd like to resurrect a few bits of its memory. As Marlene Dietrich once said in another context— but to my face—there weren't that many of us over there.

Parody of Twain, much more to my liking: Nell Finn's brother Sean and the two Sawyer boys in their rolled-up jeans and white T-shirts, poling a raft improvised from the lids of a couple of Buzz's USAID packing crates around the Finns' backyard. Like all of Plon-Plon-Ville just then, it was under two feet of water. Monsoon season quickly explained why all of our tin-roofed blockhouses were built three feet above ground, since Hopsie had to roll up his pants past his shins and carry his shoes and socks to wade across the compound from Residence to Embassy for a month. He usually lit a fresh pipe beforehand, nautical being as nautical does.

Parody of suburbia: both Sawyer boys and the Warrens' two lads racing around with toy six-guns beneath the frown of Ouibomey's seventeenth-century Portuguese fort. That was the day we all caravaned at the invitation of Nagon's Minister of Education, Culture, and Tourism to tour the country's most viable cottage industry, at least in this century: tchotchkes for export to Afrophiles.

Carol Sawyer spent the most time in the stalls where women were sewing floral and faunal appliqués and bunting on bright panels of cloth for wall hangings. Laurel and Rich—and more unexpectedly, Hopsie—lingered in those where craftsmen tapped tiny hammers to assemble copper maquettes of miniature figurines: king under umbrella in palanquined processional, man-woman-child family unit akimbo, the whole thing smaller than a tea tray. Cloddishness being as cloddishness does, Buzz Sawyer offered advice to the woodworkers hollowing out tribal masks and gluing on straw hair dyed purple. As for me, the wooden sculptures I liked best were the statuettes, nude, gaunt, half life size and including the pair who stand guard in my living room today: the African Adam and Eve.

Other than Nell, the kids on the post couldn't have cared less about copper figurines that weren't toy soldiers. But the boys didn't know enough about imitating gunslingers to even yell "Bang." Instead, they were shouting *"Pan, Pan"*—the French equivalent of "Bang, bang" or "Pow, pow." The school they went to in Plon-Plon-Ville was a holdover from *mission civilisatrice* days, all instruction in the language of *notre bonne mère la France.*

Nor did they have access to American comic books, and thoughtful Rich Warren looked troubled. "When we get Stateside, they're all going to have a hell of time with baseball," he said. His voice's dawdle when he got to "all" was for Ned Finn's benefit. We all knew his unathletic son was a worry, and where was Sean? Probably up on the fort's ramparts, patting a Portuguese cannon in his private sacrament. He didn't like cowboys and Indians, just war.

Ned himself didn't grasp the nicety. "Hell, Rich, how come?" he burbled. Not from interest, only because he hadn't thought of a joke that would attract attention back to him.

"Because nobody's taught them," Rich explained patiently. "I've tried with ours, but they'd rather '*Pan, pan*' with the other kids."

Ned guffawed. "Christ. Were you taught? Was I?"

Now that his affair with Carol Sawyer was done, he tried to win the laugh he'd clearly noticed he'd been cheated of at the Hôtel de la Plage. "Born Tou-*louuuse*, I've lived my life Lautrec…"

POSTED BY: *Pam*   Not parody but proof no one who wasn't there will ever have a clue what Nagon in 1962 was like: one or two years ago, his old Gramela mentioned to *Qwert's* Man in the Dark how puzzled I was that movies and for that matter fiction so seldom explored the kinds of lives the likes of us had led abroad. Off the top of my head, I could think of only one movie whose hero was a U.S. Ambassador: *The Ugly American,* starring Marlon Brando as what a few Foreign Service vets speculated at the time might be an impersonation of Cadwaller. If so, and it strikes me as unlikely he'd have been informed enough to know Hopsie existed, he certainly made a briar-sucking hash of it.

I'd seen the grown-up Nell Finn at Nan's not long earlier. With her oddly delighted, enthusiastic wistfulness—beats wistful enthusiasm, I agree—she'd mentioned how isolated that omission sometimes made her feel when the Finns came back Stateside. Everyone else her age had scores of period TV shows—and later, dozens and dozens of drivelingly nostalgic movies—that approximated their childhood experience. She had no choice but to cherish a brief glimpse of two frightened State Department children in *The Ugly American* as Hollywood's only acknowledgment that families like hers had ever existed.

"She's wrong," Tim said promptly. "Tell her to try *She Wore a Yellow Ribbon.* I bet that brings it all back."

I marvel sometimes that he makes a living doing what he does. Never having seen it myself back in the Fifties and only dimly recalling the title, I asked Andy Pond to Netflix or Nextflick it. Sat there bored mindless until Pink Thing blessedly reached for sleep's mallet.

What on earth were you thinking, Tim? A pack of shaggy-dog stories set in the Old West—at a *cavalry* outpost, for Lord's sake? Mating rituals, drunken sideshows, and people riding away as everyone lauds life in The Cavalry as if it's some sort of secret society? You hardly even see any Indians, or I hadn't before sleep's mallet came down.

When I called him back to complain, Hopsie's grandson only snickered. "Oh, well. There's always *Walkabout*. I know Sean Finn likes that one."

"Dear God, and what's *it* about? No, don't even tell me. I'll give it a try if you say so."

Tim laughed. "No, Grammie, don't bother. It's about the kids on the post, not the grownups."

"Oh, really! Where are they?"

"Nowhere. There aren't any."

POSTED BY: *Pam*   Parody of cosmopolitanism, overheard by the Ambassador's wife as, stepping over a disquietingly cluttered but not bad drawing of shellbursts and multiply waving Stars and Stripes, she passed a clutch of Searslessly idle children at our Thanksgiving party in the Residence: "Are you Pan Am?" chirped some young Sawyer, Warren, or Finn to another. "*We're* TWA. They give you wings, you know."

Parody of World War Two, bemusing to not only onetime ETO correspondent Pamela Buchanan but onetime Signalman Second Class Ned Finn, onetime Marine medic Rich Warren, and onetime Lieutenant Commander "Hopsie" Cadwaller: all the kids on the post but one were nuts for it. Bored silly with voicing Kraut rat-a-tats and welcoming Frenchmen, Nell Finn volunteered to be a nurse once in a while, but the boys weren't big on being wounded, much less tended. They all wanted to be killed.

On the beach in toy helmets, splashing off the *Pélérin's* placid bow. "Aaagh!"

"Come on, men. Only two kinds of people are staying on this beach. The dead and those that are going to die!"

"*Pan, pan, pan!*"

Nine-year-old Nell didn't even look up from her Enid Blyton book, brought back along with the Smarties in the most recent NAAFI haul from Lagos. "*Merci, Amerloques! Vive l'Amérique. Tac-tac-tac. Hilfe,*" she called and went back to her reading.

Her brother was the real obsessor, enraged when the other kids on the post faltered. Since Tim Cadwaller knows Sean Finn, he knows something about Ned and Nan's only son that most daisysdaughter.com readers presumably won't. (I have no idea how popular or not his odd semi-obscene comics about the superpower diaspora are or ever will be, the forthcoming—so his mother says—and bafflingly titled *Yuiop* included.) That's the peculiarity that his first name's pronounced as spelled: that is, "Seen" and not "Shaun."

Nan's still fairly sheepish about that one. The proof's that I only heard her tell the story once in Nagon and never since. If you've known her forty-five years, as I have, you know that's a statistic without peer in Nan Finn's anecdotal repertoire, and she's normally not abashed about telling stories where she's the fool. Sean's name had been her worst gaffe back in Frankfurt.

The glorious girl had been stuffing that pillow of future little boy under her dress—I couldn't imagine her pregnant!—for going on eight months when Cy and Callie Sherman, the mighty Consul General and his wife, came to dinner for the only time at the very junior Finns' hopeless little apartment. Having settled herself at dead center of their one comfortable sofa, predictably not noticing that left Nan a choice of hard chair or standing, Callie asked the inevitable question.

Or not so inevitable, since Nan's inward clutch of her head told her she and Ned hadn't talked names in months. For either boy or girl, the primary mystery back then: we'd have found knowing a baby's gender in advance pure sci-fi. Still do, really, but obviously not our headache or lookout.

Anyhow, *Callie Sherman* was asking. That meant people with a proper sense of how the thing was done always had a name ready. At a loss and having used up all the quick-wittedness at her command by instantly rejecting "Adlai"—it was October 1956—Nan's just-clutched mind leapt at a recent crumb from the *Herald Trib*. By then a lush if not the world's fattest heroin addict, Errol Flynn was shooting a movie in Biarritz.

He might be a wreck, but how she'd loved him as Robin Hood. His son was named Sean—in like Finn!—which sounded offbeat but elegant. But the name was much less common then. So much so that Nan Finn had never heard it spoken aloud.

When she blurted "Seen," Cy cleared his throat. Callie's chin lifted—oh, Callie, how could you! Yes, even you. That poor girl, so frightened of what you'd make of dinner she'd damned near forgotten she was pregnant at all.

That was when Ned Finn had his great moment in archery. Fitting his Marlboro's arrow to the bow of his lips, he blew cheerful smoke. "We always thought it sounded better that way. Didn't we, hon?"

The problem was afterward. With all the pugnacity and bitterness Ned did his best to transmute to good cheer before letting it surface, he wouldn't back down: Sean-pronounced-*Seen* it would be if they had a boy. That's how his gallantry coarsened into another opportunity to demonstrate unrepentant Ned Finn-ness, and of course he never considered—nor did Nan, I think—that their son was in for a lifetime of correcting telemarketers and people to whom he was applying for jobs.

That was the boy who patted Ouibomey's cannon, begged Nell to cry "*Tac-tac-tac*" as he jumped monotonously off the *Pélérin*'s bow and read my old acquaintance Cornelius Ryan's *The Longest Day* until he'd made a tropically dropsical card deck out of the sixty-cent Fawcett Crest paperback Ned had bought at Idlewild. Once in a while I'd consider telling Sean-pronounced-Seen that both Ambassador and Mrs. Cadwaller had been on hand, but was stopped every time by what I'd be in for. Besides, his own dad had too, and surely pilfering that Davy Jones locker of anecdotes would be enough to sate even insatiable Sean.

I still wasn't prepared for the sight that greeted me at the beach on my forty-second birthday. That would be Nell's brother gripping a toy rifle, wearing a toy helmet and cartridge belt: nothing unusual there. Unlike the burnt cork smeared all over his face.

I sat up. "Nan *Finn*, for Christ's sake! We're in Africa. How can you let Sean run around playing Amos and Andy? Not that the fishermen care, we aren't quite human to them anyhow. But my God."

"Pam, don't you think I know? He doesn't think he's in blackface. He thinks he's playing One-Oh-First Airborne. That's what they did when they jumped into Normandy, that's what Sean does. You of all people should know it's June 6."

"I'm sorry. He has *got* to scrub that off before Cadwaller gets here."

"I'll try!" Then she drew up her Nan-knees and hugged them. Looked out to sea, crimped her lipstick.

"What is it, honey?" That too was rash, and not because I was the Ambassador's wife. She didn't notice, though.

"Oh, Pam. He screams. He screams, he screams, he screams. I hope the Sawyers don't hear it, but I know they do."

I couldn't help thinking how glad I was the Residence was five minutes away from the Finns and the Sawyers. I'm afraid that wasn't because I could've gotten there quickly in a pinch.

"He wanted me to sew him a parachute," said Nan. "I'm all thumbs. What's going to become of him?"

"*Geronimo!*" Sean yelped, hopping off the sandfloured trunk of a fallen palm. I hunted how to console his mother without egregiously changing the subject.

"Hell, Nan. Back when we were kids, he's the one who'd've had a career all lined up and waiting. Remember Al Jolson? 'How I love ya, how I love ya—my dear old Swanee…'"

Turning, she tossed her nose up and giggled softly. "Don't worry, Mrs. Ambassador! I may be pretty hopeless. But I'll never take that picture."

POSTED BY: *Pam* One thing you should know about the snapshot of Hopsie at the beach is that I'd never seen it until Nan, too tactful to present it in person, mailed it to me in a manila envelope a few weeks after Cadwaller's funeral. Used as I was to her little camera coming out on every and any occasion, I'd never thought twice about the forty-odd photo albums that march along the bottom shelf in her den as if she's trying to recreate the now vanished Berlin Wall. When I asked to see the Nagon scrapbooks the next time we had lunch, she looked shyly pleased.

An hour later, I looked up in wonder. "And we used to make fun of you!"

Unlike Chris, the professional in the family—well, now *there's* an interesting slip, Ard—she was only a shutterbug-crazed Foreign Service wife. Yet as I paged through her hundreds of photographs, nearly all black and white with mounting smatterings of color, I had moments of thinking they were the civilian equivalent of the famous ones my ETO acquaintance Bob Capa had taken of Omaha Beach under fire.

Imagine everyone teasing Ned Finn's giddy better half as she got out her Kodak yet again to click off shot after shot, not all of them unattractive by any means and none deliberately so, of Carol Sawyer during the four months her husband was screwing his want of courage to that sticking place. These were occasions and so must be preserved. The photographer's feelings were unimportant when the moment was irrecoverable.

Chris never got to Africa, to his regret. A young dad scraping by as an Agence France-Presse stringer in those pre-Amherst years, Cadwaller's son couldn't afford the trip and Hopsie knew better than to offer to foot the bill. We saw them on trips to Paris instead. Pivoting in her swimsuit or little A-line cocktail dress under fire, framing our Yankee Doodley colony's oddly Hopperized Norman Rockwells and Rockwellized Edward Hoppers in front of the Rothko-komo of Ouibomey's Portuguese fort or random Jackson Pollockries of palm fronds, Nan Finn was the chronicler of the art of Nagon.

"My God, Nan." I'd already decided against teasing her about Ehud Tabor's centrality whenever he appeared, since I had no idea what'd happened and strongly suspected nothing had. Movie fandom by other means, that was all. "What's going to become of all these?"

"Oh, the kids are still bickering. But Sean says they're the only thing he's ever asked for, so... So."

"Well, well," I drawled, clapping the album shut. "Parachute sewn at long last."

By the time Hopsie got back from his swim—along with Rich Warren, he'd been detained in the surf once a couple of the kids on the post begged to clamber onto their shoulders to play Dinosaurs, brawling and shoving as the waves smashed in—the top hat was safely stowed with the rest of his formal wear in the Ambassadorial limo's trunk. And I've got to describe that car, which looks as impressively odd as a scarab butler when it appears in Nan Finn's photo albums. Unless other small posts took advantage of Andy Pond's inspiration, there may have been no other Ambassadorial limo like it in the world.

Our bean counters at the Department hadn't budgeted for a limo, thought our new Embassy's half dozen Chryslers would be adequate to any Nagonese occasion. Cadwaller dug in his heels, and if you think personal vanity was involved, bikini girl, you'll never understand your great-grandfather. He was damned if he'd let the United States look as if it did things on the cheap or took

Africa's newest nation less than seriously, and we didn't yet know what Hopsie's Soviet counterpart would be rolling around in.

The bean counters just went on farting back at him until Andy, back from Paris by then and reassigned to the Secretariat, had his brainstorm. Even though the Checker Motor Corporation of Kalamazoo, Michigan, was baffled by our request, you could sway a U.S. business in those days by explaining American prestige was involved. Yes, incredible as I know that sounds.

When our Checker rolled off the assembly line, it may've been the first in the company's history to be painted black. It was probably the first to be fitted with twin flagpoles on its hood. It was definitely the first to swing on a derrick in Nagon's sun-boiled sky before it was lowered and rolled down the Plon-Plon-Ville jetty as the kids on the post cheered. Even Hopsie couldn't resist when I said we had to repaint its meter's little tin pop-up flag in Betsy Ross's honor.

After all, it was originally red—and that wouldn't do. Once Sean Finn got to work with a six-year-old's debut squint and his watercolors and we showed Pierre how the meter worked, our chauffeur got a great kick out of making our limo's tiny Old Glory go "ding" as we pulled up in state outside the Palais du Président, the Hôtel de la Plage, the other Embassies, or the fort at Ouibomey. One thing Cadwaller knew was the distinction between silliness and style. That little tin flag was our announcement that the world's mightiest nation was also its merriest, as indeed we often were in Kennedy's time.

God, how the kids on the post loved that car. Even Nell, so often exiled by the boys' passions: we used to find Barbie dolls propped on the dashboard. As for her younger brother, maybe because for once he'd been treated as skilled, our Checker limo may have been war's only rival in Sean-pronounced-Seen's affections. When given permission, he could spend an hour making the jump seats go up and down and toying with the meter whose tin flag he'd painted, and that was how his mother convinced him to scrub off the burnt cork before Cadwaller joined our beach picnic.

"I told him I wouldn't let him go in the car if he didn't. And I couldn't've, really, could I?" At the thought that practicality gave her less credit for ingenuity, her face touchingly clouded.

Then Hopsie stepped out in his cutaway, a wrapped package in his hands, and greeted me with a rare but appropriate public kiss. An additional reason for me to cherish Nan's snapshot of him in his top hat and swim trunks is that it was taken on Pam's most memorable birthday in Nagon: my forty-second, June 6, 1962.

On the beach? On the beach, which wasn't just any beach. Brackish tall palms in gray fright wigs and bearded coconut jewelry lined the seaward side of the coastal road like a defeated army long forgotten by nature's generalissimos and still awaiting its Dunkirk fleet. Beyond them was an impossibly floury strip of iridescent white sand, deserted except for the fishermen hauling in their long nets as waves boomed in all the way from Brazil. I don't know currents, but that's how unstoppable they looked, their mile-long blue chess sets swelling from distant pawns to white-tipped rooks before they heaved up and crashed at last, spreading carpets of ermine a hundred feet wide for the sun to parade on.

The sky was as blue as Easter-egg dye and so enormous your eyes begged your chest's help to measure it. Occasionally decorated by a tiny freighter or trawler docked at its fingertip, the long bony Rheuma of the Plon-Plon-Ville jetty pointed toward St. Helena for the benefit of any clouds ambitious to visit where Napoleon had died. Nearer us was the abandoned tugboat, stubby mast aslant and deck awash even at low tide, that the kids on the post treated as a sort of waterlogged haunted house.

Then came the rock breakwater near the frond-roofed gazebo where we most often made our American camp. Tommie Sawyer and Sean-pronounced-Seen used to squabble over who got to Iwo-Jima the flag both boys insisted should be taken on every expedition, which can be seen slapping Star-and-Stripily away between a palm trunk and someone's bare shoulder in quite a few of Nan's snapshots.

To the Nagonese, it was all just *la plage*. We called this stretch Finn-Sawyer Beach, since they lived nearest. Warren Beach—or Laurel's Beach, as uxorious Rich tried to get us to call it—was several kilometers east, beyond the jetty and near their lone American blockhouse on the far side of the Plon-Plon-Ville lagoon.

Aside from the fishermen and an occasional religious procession—white smocks and chicken feathers, half Catholicized voodoo and half voodooized Catholicism—we and our red Sears coolers had it all to ourselves. If M'Lawa

or his successors had ever found investors to put up some resort hotels and figured out how to lure tourists, by now Finn-Sawyer Beach would make Cancun
look as seedy as Monterey. When your Gramela imagines it Cancunized, any
thoughts of a lost Eden are doused by a single remembered statistic: a per capita
income of $87 per year.

Somehow, I don't think the fishermen or even the religious processions
would mind telling our unspoiled African paradise to go fly a kite.

POSTED BY: *Pam*   My birthday fell on a Wednesday that year, but nobody
was going back to the office after our picnic unless you count Virgil Scoleri,
who'd never left it. Issuing visas to the smattering of well-off Nagonese who
wanted to visit the States and the larger but more penurious number eager to
emigrate, helping the occasional U.S. citizen who'd not only found his or her
way to Plon-Plon-Ville but needed a passport replaced or had run afoul of the
police or the Hôtel de la Plage's concierge, plus staying abreast of political and
economic developments in mighty Nagon, so electrifyingly vital to our interests—well, they called it a hardship post, but not because of the workload.
There were plenty of days when everyone but the duty officer knocked off by
midafternoon.

Luckily for the rest of us, Virgil Scoleri loved to be duty officer. Like all
Admin guys, he secretly thought it was *his* Embassy and could swagger about
at will, receiving the mute homage of file cabinets and typewriters temporarily
reprieved from serving false masters. Normally the color of cooked pork, he'd
gone the color of raw sirloin the day Cadwaller found him, in a stupor of fas-
tidiousness, erasing Ned and Buzz's penciled jottings from previous months on
their shared office's wall calendar.

Since I was the Ambassador's wife and it was my birthday, that day the
gathering didn't only include our core group, as I'd come to think of it. The
Embassy's lesser factoti were there too: Duncan McCork the econ attaché with
his grabby short curly-haired wife, the two secretaries I've dubbed Fiddle and
Faddle. No doubt attractive to their own age group, to Pam's eyes they were as
sexless as government-issue pens in the two-piece bathing suits that advertised
their topic-free youth.

Which may tell you middle age and/or my third marriage had changed me, but I digress. Sunglassy and wrists clasped in a few of Nan's snapshots, the real outsider in our birthday beach gang—and one visibly undaunted by that status, as his own sense of insiderdom was portable and indifferent to ours—was the Agency's junior man in Lagos. First name Carl and last name redacted, if only by Pink Thing's apathetic archives, he was in Nagon on one of his periodic wild goose chases. To Cadwaller's gratification, our Embassy had no spook of its own; he generally had the regard for CIA that a cabinet-maker would have for an arsonist.

We couldn't not have invited Carl [Last Name Redacted], since he was putting up at the Residence while chasing his latest wild goose. A few bits of conversational confetti over the last few months, badly glued together in the Agency's Nigerian toyshop, had convinced him Vasily Shishkov was thinking of defecting.

Oh, it was such silly stuff, Panama! Even if Vasily had been, which I doubt, he was smart enough to know that proclaiming himself Benedict Arnoldov in a post as minor as Nagon would be lucky to get him three paragraphs on page A22 of the *WashPost*. Then a glum apartment in Bethesda instead of a house in Silver Spring and the same old unairconditioned Zil of a Krupskaya instead of a sensationally hubcapped new T-Bird of a mistress, with nary a book deal in sight. Still, they all had to keep themselves amused somehow.

"Any kids of your own, Carl?" I brightly asked Langley's man from Lagos early on, before Hopsie'd shown up in our Checker limo and while Sean Finn, miniature paratrooper, was still skulking around and yelping "Geronimo!" in blackface. Screwing a glass of white wine turned zephyr-pale by sunlight into sand, he'd just hefted a coconut and mimed lobbing a forward pass at a couple of puzzled Warren or Sawyer boys, apparently without considering it would've thwacked their small torsos like a cannonball.

Because Agency hands all got their dialogue from the same TV hack advised to stick to the corsair note, he bared jaunty teeth and said "Probably." I gave a wry snort out of habit, meantime surprised by my aversion. It took me years to recognize that what made the core group the core group was that we were the ones who were parents, Hopsie included thanks to invisible Chris and me by the osmosis of stepmomhood. If not, more osmotically yet, by *Glory*

Be, which Rich Warren had thoughtfully included in the USIS library *without* asking me first. Even dim Dunc McCork and grabby short curly-haired Beth might've made the grade if they'd had children.

Astonishing me, Carl [Last Name Redacted] next had the gall to lift one wrist-clasped hand to put the brakes on Rich as he approached with a wine bottle to refill Pam's beckoning glass. Such things just weren't done on Finn-Sawyer Beach.

"Something I've been meaning to ask you, Mrs. Cadwaller," he said easily. "Can I trust the boys at the Residence?"

Oh, crap. Did they never tire of this folderol? The things I did for you, Hopsie! We'd caught on fairly fast that the Agency visitor's professional vanity was insulted by the task of blending into our little community even on an idle afternoon at the beach. He was itching for his proper element and due: solo conversation. Only the Ambassador's wife could oblige him without giving him the jackass satisfaction of establishing a pecking order where we just saw Ned, Buzz, Rich, and so on.

"Trust them with what?" I said and stifled a laugh. Having circled around behind Carl [Last Name Redacted], Rich Warren was brandishing a now recorked wine bottle, a CIA-braining leer of mock savagery distorting his genial face. "You can trust Pierre with a car. Implicitly and explicitly, you can trust Kojo with a chicken. Those are their jobs."

"Take a note to Ouibomey. I can't go myself. Too conspicuous."

"I'm sorry. You want one of our boys"—and yes, bikini girl, we did call them that; I won't lie—"to pedal a bike sixty kilometers and back for your sake? And my God, don't you know Ouibomey is the one place in Nagon where a white tourist won't surprise anybody? Borrow Nan Finn's camera, for Christ's sake. Visit the snake house, see the fort. Honestly!"

His sunglasses regarded me pityingly. "My mistake. I thought you were in charge of them. Maybe I'd better speak to Cadwaller."

"Feel free to go right ahead, but not today." I was watching Fiddle and Faddle rise and fall with each wave, frog-kicking with their temporarily unanchored legs but conversationally gesturing with their hands and rapidly tossing hairdos. They weren't that bad, just young and silly.

"Well. I'm not sure when I do is completely up to you, Pam."

"Of course not, but it is up to Hopsie. And that's the second good piece of advice I've given you in my patriotic way. Can't you give it a break? Carl, does this beach really look like the goddam Bay of Pigs to you?"

Carl [Last Name Redacted] grinned again, his teeth as impeccably white as his sunglasses' two scoops of Pam-twinning black ice cream were dark. "Damned if I'd know. But that's a rotten thing to say about your husband's secretaries."

It was my turn to look at him pityingly, not that my glance made a dent or I expected it to. One thing about the Carls of this world that may explain quite a lot of CIA's history is that they don't care if their guesswork is accurate. What's important is that it sounds shrewd.

He'd still spent three whole weeks under the Residence's roof, making me marvel that his take on the Cadwaller marriage could be so blitheringly wrong. Of course it never crossed his mind that I might've been watching Fiddle and Faddle because I was fed up with spotting twin Pams being targeted in his sunglasses. The truth is that when Faddle got killed by a shark a year later, even Hopsie had to concede it did wonders for her memorability.

Carl [Last Name Redacted] clearly thought he'd zinged uppity—and jealousy-crazed, aging—Mrs. Cadwaller but good, though. "Maybe I could ask *them* to go to Ouibomey," he offered in case I'd missed it the first time.

"Better not for their sake. The snake house unnerves the fuck out of them."

"What's in the snake house?"

"You don't know that either? Well, one helluva big, dusty old python, Carl. What rattles Fiddle and Faddle is that he gets let *out* of the snake house once a day to slither fairly unpredictably around Ouibomey by his priest."

"His say what?"

"Priest. It was one of the voodoo cults M'Lawa was going to ban, at least along the coast. Not the image our Président wants for *le Nagon d'aujourd'hui*. Of course he doesn't give a damn about the rites upcountry. But it brings in a bit of tourist money, so the python stays."

"You've seen him? On his…constitutional?"

"My God, yes. Cadwaller fed him a couple of very unhappy palm rats we'd taken along just in case. Very much an honor, since the Russians are right there in their appalling compound and they've never been asked. That did more for us in Ouibomey than fifty bags of rice."

"Great moments in diplomacy," Carl [Last Name Redacted] said.

"Mmm-hm. You boys might want to try it sometime."

POSTED BY: *Pam*   I've got no idea whether or how he ever got his silly note to Ouibomey. Either way, the upshot was plainly zilch, since Vasily Shishkov went on his pudgy Krupskaya-chained way to his next post in Buenos Aires some months later, his phantasmal memento a slow wink at Cadwaller. I was certainly glad to be shut of our man from Lagos when he unscrewed his wine-glass and ambled down to the waterline to hail Fiddle and Faddle. They were emerging from the surf like two moderately toasted marshmallows in search of more burning.

The Buchanan bod and I were on good terms that year, sharing a hiya-Old Paint-howdy Buffalo Bill brand of mutual amusement. Provoking male interest wasn't a priority; I had Hopsie's, which was private and more guaranteed than sunrise. So I had no qualms about letting the good old gams prop up my favorite white swimsuit in public. Africa did play hell with my skin, birthing orangeade ant farms of new freckles on my shoulders and arms. I knew I wouldn't learn their actual hue and staying power until the tan that spawned them stopped being a year-round one. Back in the States, they mostly faded, but the damage was done.

Whatever science says to the contrary, I'm also sure three years of African sun also hastened my hair's premature graying. I found I didn't mind at all. Even before I started having the first of Antoine's several District successors cut it skullcap-short in my mid-sixties, the old brindle mop looked rather better in b&w, by which I don't just mean in Nan's photographs. Yet only after we'd returned from Africa was I especially conscious of it as a transformation. Like the freckles, up to then my newly slate-and-seagullish peruke had simply seemed to be Pam's Nagon incarnation, subject to reversal once my circumstances changed.

That was how I looked when Nan waggled her Kodak and called, "Marlene! *Marlene!*" It's safe to say the resemblance was minimal, making the glorious girl's delight a susceptibility based on affection. When I recall how that merry face was crisped an hour later by tears she'd sooner have died than let drip in front of us, I might still have a hard time forgiving her husband if Ned weren't decades gone.

Even so, the one I shouldn't forgive and doubt any of us did is Carl [Last Name Redacted]. My guess is he'd approached Cadwaller and gotten Hopsie's brushoff by then. Anyhow, he was the one who, between last white and first pink gnaw on a drumstick, looked around and said brusquely, "Where's Finn?"

First off, any of us would've called Ned by first name. But secondly, whether or not Nan was sitting right there—and she was, forwarding a roll of blank film through her camera until she saw that tiny "1" appear in its odometer—something we all knew better than to ask in public in June of 1962 was "Where's Ned?" Even Rich Warren's eyes couldn't resist the roundup establishing that Carol Sawyer was also missing. The day of my forty-second birthday, their affair was still in the present tense.

Luckily, Buzz was down at the waterline. We could hear him instructing a couple of annoyed kids—his own—on how to flip the *Pélérin*'s outboard motor out of the water before beaching it. That may've left Nan more bereft, though I never saw them stoop to the tag-teaming social protectiveness of spouses whose spouses are straying. She was still the glorious girl, and anyhow Buzz would've muffed it.

She knew that silence would tempt one of us to leap in with a fib, decoying Carl [Last Name Redacted] at the intolerable price of confirmation that our whole gang was aware of Nan's marital Calvary. It's all the more garish when it's sympathetic.

"Oh, Ned!" she instantly piped up, her thumb mashing the Kodak. "I think he ran back to the office awhile. He finally got that meeting with N'Koda, and"—her free hand mimed Ned typing, or possibly playing "Roll Out the Barrel" in a whorehouse—"while it's still fresh in his mind, you know!"

"Huh. Well, at least someone's…"

Even Carl [Last Name Redacted] knew better than to say "on the ball here" as a swimsuited Cadwaller sat by with a look of placid interest. "Bound to read that one," he finished instead, which was at least a generic insult to the Department rather than our post in particular.

"I'm sure he's coming back, though, Pam," said Nan, deflecting attention back to my birthday at some cost to keeping Ned's *other* can of worms sealed. "You know he wouldn't miss the champagne!"

"Carl, how soon do you head back to Lagos?" I wondered with deep pleasure.

"Yes. We've all been asking ourselves when we'll lose you," Rich Warren said so affably that even Carl [Last Name Redacted] had no choice but to take it as dismay. But Laurel looked as if the canary in her mouth had just struggled energetically.

"Oh, Pam! How thoughtless," Rich said then, refilling my wineglass.

"I'll take some of that too, Rich," Carl [Last Name Redacted] said a tad sulkily. "Well, I don't know yet when I—"

"I do," said Hopsie serenely, his straight-stemmed favorite briar sticking out like a pleased tollgate. "Your boss cabled as I was leaving for Ouibomey. General effect, he can't do without you, so Code Quick Brown Fox and so on."

"I'm supposed to decode those myself, sir," Carl [Last Name Redacted] said.

"It wasn't coded. I'm afraid I was just being whimsical. Dear God, Pam, how does the rest go: 'over the lazy hedgehog'? Senility at last! How I've waited."

"What about—?" The Agency man's face thickened. He couldn't discuss the real reason for his three weeks in Nagon, even though we all knew it. The Finns' new black dog probably did, being an alert sort of mutt.

"Oh, Lagos thinks we can monitor things on our own for now. Any new wrinkles, of course we'll let the toyshop know."

And no, Panama: I wasn't too surprised when your great-grandfather later admitted he'd very nearly slipped up and said "Lagos agrees." The cable from the station chief there had been a reply to no less than three from Plon-Plon-Ville recommending that Carl [Last Name Redacted] pack his bags instanter.

"I'm pretty sure friend Vasily was just playing out the string for the hell of it," Hopsie told me that night in our bedroom, where we'd made love any number of times to the arrhythmic scuffle of a monsoon-fleeing palm rat's claws on the tile floor. "But even if he'd been halfway serious, an approach that clumsy was making us laughingstocks. What did it for me was Klaus Schlitten asking if

Americans always did their Christmas shopping so early. When Klaus sounds bright, you know we're stupid."

That was later. On Finn-Sawyer Beach, as we all fought to contain our relief at Carl [Last Name Redacted]'s imminent exit, Laurel Warren started to talk with much brio about her last shopping trip to Nigeria, puzzling us slightly. Incapable of being dull, she still usually spun her conversational gold from something less NAAFI-chafflike.

Then we realized her quick eyes had spotted Ned Finn coming down to us from the Embassy Chryslers parked behind our Checker limo. Presenting an altogether unnecessary new case of wine as the alibi under his Marlboro's pilot fish, he was clad by then in the Sears-consignment jump suit he affected that year in his off-duty hours: odd vanity seventeen years after the war's end, combined with safari effect he no doubt hoped we'd see as droll. For Nan's sake, Laurel knew, something animated had to be going on when he reached us, giving him time enough to redaub some familiar, jolly Ned Finn-ness on the stark face of a contented adulterer.

"Well! Of course they're just hopeless for music, so I finally asked—oh, hello, Ned—finally asked if they've even *heard* of any other composers besides Elgar. And with great pride, they brought out a dusty Nigerian pressing of *My Fair Lady*. I nearly died! We're down to our last Coltrane, and Rich always says Brubeck gives him arachnophobia. But you like show music, don't you, Ned?"

"Oh, God!" said Nan, gallantly turning into half of a happy couple on a dime. "Six straight months of *The Music Man*. By the end, even Kindassou could halfway sing along to 'Seventy-Six Trombones,' and not only doesn't he speak a word of English but he doesn't know what trombones are and he's never seen seventy-six of *anything*."

"I was hoping to get Louis on 'I Got the Horse Right Here' while he was serving the meat the night we had Shishkov over. But *Guys and Dolls* showed up broken," Ned grinned, smuggling himself back into husbandhood. "Blame Sears all you want. I'll never forgive that son of a bitch Roebuck."

"We can loan you *The Sound of Music*," I said. "I've about had it with that one. Even Hopsie's started singing 'Edelweiss' with a Cockney accent in the shower—'May you bloomin' grow.'"

"Only when there's no hot water," Cadwaller reproached me mildly. He understood distraction was vital, but he *was* the Ambassador.

"I think we've still got *Oklahoma!*," Laurel offered. "Do you have that one, Nan? It skips on 'Oh! What a Beautiful Morning,' but—"

We instantly knew it had been a mistake. In one of Laurel's rare miscalculations, addressing Nan Finn instead of her husband had made it too obvious we were plying the glorious girl with compensatory gifts. For a fraught second, Nan's face tried to keep gaily going. Was that Rodgers and Hammerstein or Rodgers and Hart? But it was Rogered and Hammerheart, and two rocking-horse slivers of private Atlantic shimmered in her lower lashes. As the surf boomed in fatal encouragement, she jumped up like a soldier hearing gunfire, dashing sand from her bare thighs as if she'd just felt it start to crawl upward.

"Well! I think I'll go for a walk," she announced. "Do you feel like one… Laurel?"

"Can't get fat, can we?" said Laurel, which was ridiculous. Physically, she was a watchmaker's dream of well-organized economy, a swimsuit virtually her version of her husband's football rig in college. Still, even someone as graceful as our USIS man's wife needed some ingenuity to make getting up to join Nan look indolent instead of hasty.

"Hell, what's the problem?" Carl [Last Name Redacted] grunted peevishly, showing teeth amazingly unchipped by his spectacular tumble down the ladder from intruder to complete boor.

"No problem, old man. She gets homesick," Ned Finn said, crumpling an empty pack of Marlboros and patting his jump suit for another. "We've all been in Africa awhile. Is Nigeria your first foreign posting, Carl?"

Which was the closest Cadwaller's adulterous DCM ever came to justifying his behavior in front of Hopsie and me. And yes, Ned at least had the grace to look troubled as his wife, awkwardly reaching out to vague blue air for nonexistent banisters, descended toward where the *Pélerin* was beached.

If you knew Ned Finn, though, the flicker of self-disgust that followed did him no credit. Rather than provoke him to change his ways, it was far more likely to end up massaging his conviction that he was the tragic protagonist here, his sessions with broad-beamed Carol Sawyer a Byronic protest against life's confinements. I didn't want to watch the facial mutations I was sure were coming: stoic compassion for his own much misunderstood Ned Finn-ness, self-indulgence retooled as sodden valor by his jaw's new set as he lit his next cigarette. That otherwise intelligent man's oft-foiled narcissism fouled his brain with rubbish sometimes even when he was sober.

As Carl [Last Name Redacted] began explaining that he couldn't really talk about his other postings, Finn, I stood up. "Sorry to leave you, gents. This old broad needs some exercise too."

"Going for a hike of your own, dear?" Hopsie asked.

"Have we even met? No, a siesta. I'll be worn out by the time I wake up."

POSTED BY: *Pam*   My towel, straw hat, and tropically swollen Dell paperback of *The Guns of August* in tow, I picked a spot where Ned and Carl [Last Name Redacted] would be inaudible unless an invasion fleet suddenly materialized offshore and got them shouting. After I'd spread the towel out on that millenia-milled sand's warm cake batter under a couple of palms whose coconuts I made sure had fallen—no point inviting Fran Kukla-ish punctuation, was there?—I barely pretended to commune with Pam's better as a historian before trading propped elbow for chin-pillowing forearms.

Though out of earshot, I still had a view of the whole of our now scattered American crew. Soon enough it included Carol Sawyer plodding her red-suited way up to our picnic site. No dummy, she'd taken care to be seen ebulliently mothering her own two boys and one dragooned Warren down near the surf beforehand. When it came to deflecting opprobrium, Ned favored alibis, Carol credentials.

The next time I looked over, she was as happy as a teapot, enjoying a rare stint as our Yankee Doodley colony's sole incarnation of the female principle. Normally, Nan, Laurel, and I would've been tossing that job around like a beanbag: the Ambassador's wife because of her status, Laurel thanks to her wit, Nan with any reminder that she was the glorious girl. Yet we were all three absent for once, and even short grabby curly-haired Beth McCork was an asterisk near the stove-in tugboat, midway through one of her tense little squabbles with Dunc about where she'd hidden his balls and when our econ attaché might next get a glimpse of them.

The backsliding tide giving them gilded new yards of wet sand to do it with, Fiddle and Faddle were crouched with mute giggles, remolding a sand castle the kids on the post had left unfinished to the shape of a man. At the moment, red suit perched on red cooler, Carol Sawyer—who knew enough to know she played the part better with her mouth shut—was queen of Nagon's America.

Even by Ned and Carol's low standards, this broad-daylight stunt was atrocious. She'd brought the broad and he'd brought the daylight, and if I knew Ned, resentment at our man from Lagos's superiority had found a characteristically convoluted outlet. Not only a bachelor, at least on Nagon jaunts—no one was sure if he'd diddled Fiddle, but we could all tell he'd addled Faddle—Carl [Last Name Redacted] was a traveling salesman whose suitcase's contents by some lights had more zest than ours. CIA's unfailing belief it could claim greater glamor invited ridicule but was also impervious to it, leaving Ned torn between the jokes he could make and the envy he felt at protection from being one.

Whatever he and Carol had done and wherever they'd done it—if only for Sean's sake, he'd damned well better have known our Checker limo was sacrosanct—the urge to shove something in somebody's face was unmistakable. He didn't care that the face ended up belonging to his wife.

To my further annoyance, the Ambassador's wife had been their Get Out of Jail Free card. Nobody would have violated Pam Cadwaller's birthday with a public scene no matter how many oinks we overheard from the wings. For Cadwaller to make an issue of it, a bare-heinied Ned would've practically had to bellyfish Carol in front of me, her bared paps no coins from Ali Baba's cave— odd image, Ard, have I used it before?—but two much-chewed and slobbery pacifiers. And yes, if you're wondering: I knew I was distracting myself. It miffed me that I had no real justification for feeling hurt by Nan's choice.

Given the available cast, who could she have asked except Laurel Warren? Despite being Pam or even Marlene, I was still Mrs. Hopsie when the chips were down. She couldn't have picked me as her confidante without violating protocol and, for all she knew, putting her husband's future at risk. She had no idea in what terms Cadwaller and I might discuss things and people when we were alone. Nobody did and even you, daisysdaughter.com readers if any, never really will.

When I looked down the beach, Nan and Laurel were already nearly to the abandoned tugboat. I knew they'd turn back before reaching it, since Beth and Dunc McCork were still putting the dumb back in dumbshow and would guess something was wrong even if Nan'd managed to compose herself by then.

Unknown to the glorious girl and her consoler alike, little Nell Finn was wandering behind them, either pining for her mom to remember she too could play nurse or just hoping for a respite from being the only American girl in the world by appearing in a painting finally captioned *Three American Women on The Beach, Nagon, 1962*. As the fishermen hauled in bushels of still living silver in their long nets, the Finns' new black dog thought it was all a grand game.

Sioux-Sioux? No, that's got to be wrong. The mutt's jokey handle was some other Ned Finnism, since he named all their pets: revenge on four legs, I grasped, for Nan pronouncing Sean "Seen." Then faraway Laurel reached out—stumbling, consoling?—to grab tiny Nan's arm.

"Lech," I contentedly told the sand under my chin, so fine-ground just exhaling could faintly but decisively repattern it. Pam not only knew she was quoting but, to her mild surprise, caught on she'd just accepted who'd said it to whom thirty-five years ago. Under the skies of an Africa that neither dead Daisy nor the Lotus Eater had ever seen, I could afford to make jokes now that I'd avoided those shoals.

However, Finn-Sawyer Beach wasn't done demonstrating the art of Nagon. After my quiet Pampiphany, I must've dozed a good while. Indeed for over an hour, since Hopsie's squeeze of my shoulder woke me to a visibly different edition of the ocean's peacock courtship of the sun. Our whole Yankee Doodley crew was grouped around me: Ned and Nan, Rich and Laurel, Buzz and Carol, even the misfit McCorks and Fiddle and Faddle. Nell and Sean Finn and the Warren and Sawyer boys.

Only Carl [Last Name Redacted] was blissfully missing. Since he had to pretend Lagos needed him badly, he'd impatiently borrowed one of the Chryslers to drive back to the Embassy compound.

Hopsie had clearly waited to wake me until just a few minutes before things would've devolved into blatantly detaining everyone for sleeping Pam's sake. Common enough at some posts I've seen where the top man and his spouse, particularly if he's a political appointee and not a career FSO, treat the whole staff as servants blended with movie extras, exercising that kind of Ambassadorial prerogative never sat well with Cadwaller. As for me, I was muddled, since I'd spent all afternoon slipping in and out of recalling that this was my birthday. I was about to get a stranger reminder of it than anyone except my husband could've possibly known.

"Back among us, Pam? No bad dreams to speak of?" he murmured tenderly, too low for anyone else to hear, as he passed me a champagne flute. Then stood: "Do we all have champagne? All right, Kids on the Post. You can sing now."

Happy to be singled out as performers, since they weren't champagne drinkers—your great-grandfather knew how to give even children their moments, Panama—they took a clustered big breath. *"Happy birthday to you— happy birthday to you…"*

Can't you guess what startled me? Sean-pronounced-Seen, face now scrubbed of burnt cork but still wearing tin helmet and clutching toy rifle. The older Sawyer boy's wooden Tommy gun, sawn and glued together from a USAID packing crate by ineffectual but not thoughtless Buzz. The younger Warren lad's plastic-foliaged toy helmet and pistol, the older one's prized child-size Army fatigue pants. Sean only the most persistent of them, keeping it up well after the others had tired, they'd all been playing D-Day.

It had been eighteen years since Pam Buchanan had waded ashore at the Vierville exit. Since the beachmaster shouted at Eddie Whitling and me to get out of the way of the first trucks to reach Omaha as a lone Spandau still hammered. Since Eddie had gotten a few stunned first-wave survivors in life-jacket cummerbunds to sing this same song to the goony broad passing out Lucky Strikes they were too dazed to smoke. *"Happy birthday to you—happy birthday to you…"*

The children now singing would never believe and might even be surly at learning that this, not their cries of *"Tac-tac-tac"* and repeated debarkings from the stubbornly innocuous *Pélerin*, was the closest they'd gotten all day to recapturing the real D-Day. It may've been as they sang that Pam's blue-gray eyes, once a budding pudding's twin Civil War memorials, acquired the secret name daisysdaughter.com readers know them by today: the mimsy borogoves.

As always happens when children sing "Happy Birthday" to grownups, their voices tangled over what to call me. Sean and both Warrens' bland "Mrs.

Cadwaller" bumped the Sawyer boys' truculent "Mrs. Ambassador." (Thanks, Carol, and no: no love lost on my end either.) Both were outdone by Nell's audacious peal of "…dear *Pamela!*," for which I cherish her. For a shining brief moment, winding up in West Africa in a skirtleted swimsuit and now grayed brindle mop as champagne grazed my lips and Barbara Tuchman sat near me seemed like the only conceivable outcome to all my yesterdays.

Hopsie later apologized for not having anticipated the echo. While he naturally knew about my Dog Green serenade, he hadn't considered the kids on the post's outfits, which after all were their standard togs at play. With his usual skill, he decided to ensure my forty-second birthday would coin a fresh memory and not just a cartoon overlay of an existing one.

"It's nice to hear you all sing together," he told them. "Can we have one more? Something from here—from Nagon."

Emboldened by the smile I'd flashed her when she sang out *"Pamela!,"* Nell Finn appointed herself concertmaster. Happily, she started chirping with an indifference to the other kids as eerie as if she'd been blind: *"Il était un petit navire, il était un petit navire—qui n'avait ja!, ja!, jamais navigué…"*

Before the boys could join in—or worse, didn't, unwilling to let the lone girl lead them—Hopsie stopped her with a pleasant chuckle. "I think that one might be a bit long. Bit grim, too! I'll never understand how the French came up with a children's song that's a charming tribute to cannibalism."

"Believe me, I do," I drawled, then added *"Et toi aussi, non?"* to Nell to console her. She giggled, luckier than I'd been at Chignonne's. However deranged a companion Sean Finn might be as they grew up, she'd never feel like the only American *child* in the world.

The other kids had made up their minds now. Jostled only by Sean's squelched "Oh, say can you see," Sawyer and Warren boys—and soon Sean and Nell, too—gave me my relic, now theirs as well:

"Le peu-ple nagonais s'élève!

Le peuple nagonais s'élève…"

"Perfect." Excusing himself with a smile, Hopsie returned as they finished the anthem, carrying the package he'd been holding when he stepped out of our Checker limo in his cutaway. "Happy birthday, dear."

I unwrapped a maquette of copper figurines from Ouibomey: a queen on a palanquin held up by eight bearers. Then I looked closer and gasped.

"*Hopsie!* How did you…"

It was us. As you know, Panama, from fondling what three generations of Cadwallers call "The African Queen," the woman on the palanquin is a depiction of me as I was in Nagon. The bearers are Nan and Ned Finn, Carol and Buzz Sawyer, Laurel and Rich Warren—and Fiddle and Faddle, making Dunc McCork's rank-conscious brow wrinkle when his and Beth's turn came to examine it. But they'd only been in-country six months and our Embassy secretaries predated them.

"Nan gets all the credit," said Cadwaller. "I borrowed a few of her snapshots."

Of course they aren't detailed resemblances. Yet the Ned has a mimed cigarette's copper stub in his mouth, the Buzz's long neck and pot belly are mimetic, and the Rich has UCLA scratched on his chest. Aside from Nan's miniature camera, the women are recognizable mainly thanks to their varying heights and some try at reproducing their hairdos, though I doubt it gave Carol vast joy that she's most individuated by being the stockiest. As for me, my identity's signaled by the crossed Buchanan gams as I lean forward with upflung arms, something I could've sworn I'd never done in life until I came upon myself making the identical gesture from an identically seated position for Nan's Kodak during our first New Year's Eve party at the Residence.

Hopsie himself isn't depicted. But all things considered, I think you'll agree he needn't be.

Nan was tickled by her contribution, Ned visibly thirsting for more than champagne. Fiddle and Faddle were transfixed by themselves. Laurel was wry—"Are my arms really that skinny?"—and Carol was a beaming Medusa of seething resentments. Buzz was mostly just gloomy at the prospect of having to do the whole goddam thing over in woodwork before his wife's first birthday at the next place they were stationed in.

The most delighted of us is missing from the maquette, as are all the other kids on the post. I'm sorry, Panama: I don't mean to deprive you. In my note for Andy Pond, "The African Queen" has been earmarked to Nell Finn—or Professor of Comparative Literature Helen F. Eichler, as she is today. She was still tilting it this way and that like a tiny ship on her palms' sea when the rest of us started packing the Chryslers with towels and Sears coolers, picnic baskets and wine and champagne bottles, the flag and the boys' weaponry.

No great huge hugging farewells, obviously. We'd probably see every last one of each other tomorrow and back here at Finn-Sawyer Beach in a week. Or Warren Beach, since Rich and Laurel had gotten Cadwaller's agreement to take their boys home on the *Pélérin*. It looked like a fun ride, skipping off to go far out around the Plon-Plon-Ville jetty's long Rheuma toward the lagoon whose breadth kept the Warrens' privacy intact.

"Hopsie," I murmured, "would Pierre mind another half hour? Once they're all gone, let's go for a swim."

He squinted down the beach cheerfully. "You know, the fishermen are *awfully* far away. There isn't a religious procession in sight."

"Oh really?" I said as I waved at the departing cars.

So we propped my birthday present where we'd be able to keep an eye on it from the water. It looked nice on top of our swimsuits. As my fifty-two-year-old husband and I ran down to the surf, we smacked past the sand castle Fiddle and Faddle had turned into a golem, its sand feet now lapped by the returning tide. Since they'd left as well, we never did learn which captain or king he was their beach-party tribute to.

POSTED BY: *Pam*   If you go by Department records, Cadwaller's Ambassadorship—the first to Nagon in U.S. history, one reason he prized it above India in some ways—ran from mid-1961 to mid-'64. In Pink Thing's archives, which I'll go on considering truer than calendars until Potus or sundown puts paid to me, the bean counters' mistake is their failure to grasp that 1962 lasted twenty-three months in Nagon. Finding itself unusually happy there, it decided to stick around awhile.

Our 1962 was when M'Lawa still occupied the Palais du Président and also when our core group was all present and accounted for. The first departure— the Warrens, for Athens—came in what bean counters would call August 1963. That was all of a month before Faddle's shark pulled her down off Finn-Sawyer

Beach when she went out too far one day, taking that living emblem of 1962's fluff prematurely as well.

And yes, since I'm not wholly immune to middlebrow yardsticks: 1962 was the year Bobby Kennedy came to Nagon. Mind you, we got him for just seven hours, since Nigeria beckoned. He slept in Lagos that night, and did Carl [Last Name Redacted] ever dine out for years on *that* Agency briefing.

Carl's luckless station chief was in Philadelphia on home leave. It's only fair to add he shot himself for wholly unrelated reasons, and Ned Finn was just skylarking when he used to claim otherwise. By the way, I'm sure among themselves they talked every bit as uncharitably about diplomats as we did about spooks.

Since we knew we had just seven hours, never had "Le soleil d'aujourd'hui" sounded so endless as it did once the first jet ever to land at Plon-Plon-Ville's airport had rolled to a halt. (Yes, they'd built a new runway for the occasion. Now they had two.) As Cadwaller and I stood beside Président and Mme M'Lawa, I blessed Nagon's skimpy military budget. Ruffling that forelock as we'd all seen him do, just never in color, Bobby had no idea he was stalking past the entire Nagonese Army, stiff forearms perpendicular to their bayoneted bolt-action rifles in the old French style.

Our DCM had had his work cut out for him talking N'Koda into excluding the snowplows of the *1er Régiment Blindé*. Not only would explaining their presence to a baffled Robert Kennedy have used up a good hour of our seven, but the Soviets might well have claimed it as a belated feather in their cap. Whatever else I've had to say about Ned Finn on daisysdaughter.com, he was good at his job. If the price of keeping those snowplows off the tarmac was the creation of the Nagonese Navy, I'm sure the Pentagon never missed those two mothballed minesweepers.

Since the kids on the post wanted to be reviewed too, Cadwaller himself had taken charge of another negotiation to ensure the helmets, the toy rifles, and the wooden Tommy gun stayed out of sight. On top of that, Hopsie'd had to mollify a Buzz Sawyer disconsolate at being denied an upcountry caravan to tour USAID's best irrigation project by granting forty-five precious minutes of our seven hours for a slide-show simulacrum that had the rest of us wanting in anticipation to chew our eyes out with our own teeth.

Here they came, and I was taller than he was. My big hat—protocol, not preference, Panama—probably didn't help. Those blue eyes didn't like to look up unless he was the only man sitting down in a room where everyone else was standing.

"Welcome to Nagon, Mr. Attorney General."

"Thank you, I know where I am, Mrs. Cadwaller," he snapped back.

It's conceivable it was meant as a joke. Yet even if he'd had the instinct for drollery—and no way I'd know—he didn't, unlike his brother, have the right face for it. Some men don't.

Or the voice, since to be humorous and peremptory at once only works among courtiers. We were, and I damned well do include myself, professionals. If Nixon had won in '60, we'd all have performed the identical chore.

Similarly, some broads have great gams and some don't, my guess as to one reason Ethel Kennedy's greeting was no huge improvement. I'd seen her eyes narrow as she and Bobby came off the ramp, but what was I supposed to do? Though my hemline was more than respectable, we were in equatorial Africa, where sheath cuts were hell before nightfall. The Department's advisory had said nothing about affecting Amish dress to put our VIP's Mrs. at ease.

As we shook hands, she squinted. "I've broken my sunglasses," Ethel Kennedy said. "Do you have a pair I could borrow?"

We both knew I did: the pair in my other hand, which I'd naturally removed as soon as the jet's door hatch swung open. I passed 'em over, she poked 'em onto her nose. "Thank you," Ethel Kennedy said. And I had to take her to Oui-bomey.

That wouldn't be until after our formal session with M'Lawa at the Palais du Président, and to be fair her little laugh when she was escorted to our Checker limo wasn't at all unpleasant. Still: it was *our* Checker limo. Not only beloved of Sean-pronounced-Seen Finn but envy, not that she'd have believed it, of the Soviets.

Perhaps it's in her husband's favor that he seemed to pay no attention at all to what kind of car he was in. Then again, unlike Ethel and me, he wasn't on one of the jump seats. Realizing I'd forgotten something and hoping neither of our guests had enough French to follow, I spoke over my shoulder.

"*Pierre! Faut pas faire le truc avec le petit drapeau aujourd'hui, compris?*"

"*Oui, madame.*" Hopsie gave me a nod, but Pierre's day and opinion of Kennedys were both spoiled. He enjoyed making Old Glory pop up on the meter.

"I don't understand why he can't just ride with us," said Bobby, meaning M'Lawa. Of course we were doing the whole motorcade bit, the vast convertible whose rear seat contained the Président's broad back and Celeste M'Lawa's scarf rolling ahead of us in a mobile cat's cradle of motorcyclists. "It'd save a lot of time."

"Sorry, sir, it wouldn't," Cadwaller said. "At best you'd just have the same conversation twice. M'Lawa's very proud of the Palais du Président."

"Christ. As if I care whether I meet Kosygin at the White House or, or—Dixie Liquor." Opened at the Georgetown end of Key Bridge the year Prohibition was repealed, that stubby little place—booze shop to New Dealers, Fair Dealers, Ike's-grins, Camelot, Great Society, and now Potusville—has a charm only District lifers can fully appreciate: nongovernmental longevity.

"Sir, I'm sorry. It's different," I explained, leaning forward as we hit a bump in the coastal road. "Your brother didn't build it himself."

"Oh, yes he did," Ethel said, a Kennedyism if I ever heard one.

"Dixie Liquor?" I said. Whenever Hopsie tried to reproach me, he ended up weeping with laughter all over again.

POSTED BY: *Pam*   Luckily, Bobby was too distracted to notice the sixth snowplow on its concrete plinth in front of the Palais as we drove through the gates, though I think Ethel gave it an odd look from her jump seat. But the prelunch session with M'Lawa didn't go well. Overflowing one of the only five Louis XVI chairs in Nagon—most likely the reason Celeste was indisposed—he said, "Please tell Mr. Kennedy I'm sorry his President has only one brother."

That was Hopsie's translation, and Bobby's face tightened. "He's got two. He had three. Christ! I've been briefed on this man. Do you mean to tell me he *hasn't* been briefed on the President of the United States?"

He'd misunderstood M'Lawa's point. "*Moi, j'ai des millions.*" I have millions. "Every man in Nagon is my brother. Every woman in Nagon is my sister."

"Well! There must be a mother in there somewhere," said Bobby. "I hope."

Cadwaller's brows arched at his impatient glance. "You won't want me to translate that, sir."

"When I don't want you to do your job, Ambassador, I'll tell you."

Even he may've realized that was a mite rude. Over lunch with the Nagonese Cabinet, which found Mme M'Lawa miraculously re-un-indisposed, he made amends of a sort. Eyeing the local version of *choucroute garnie*—the meat was wild boar—he turned to Cadwaller. "Peasant specialty?" he murmured, giving the grin I'd started to think he saved only for newsreels.

"Technically, yes, sir," Hopsie murmured back. "But the only real one they've got is no food whatsoever."

Wearing my sunglasses (of course I never got them back), Ethel wasn't at all bad in Ouibomey. She was good at the nursing school, very good at the leper colony. I think she was bored at the Portuguese fort, where our guide laid it on thick about the legend that the walls of its dungeon still ran wet with blood one night a year: *des siècles de souffrances sans trêve*, as "Le soleil d'aujourd'hui" had it. I'm pretty sure she never grasped what the priest at the snake house was trying to tell her about the python. She'd seen eight countries in nine days.

She did her best at the artisanal shops, concentrating hard before she picked out two pretty good maquettes of copper figurines: "Not really my area," she'd mumbled to explain her frown. "Jackie can be pretty merciless, you know." The woodcarvers' African Adams and Eves, male dowsing rods and female genital pineapples in full frontal view, never had a chance of boarding her jet. She was still Catholic, and the 1962 version of the white woman's burden—cosmopolitanism—had its limits. It's just as well she never saw the Nagonese version of Christ on the cross in Plon-Plon-Ville's oldest church.

Then we got back in the one of the Embassy Chryslers whose air conditioning Virgil Scoleri had determined still worked best, Hopsie having retained our Checker limo and Pierre to trundle Bobby back to the Embassy compound after our lunch at the Palais du Président. As we started back down the coastal road, ahead of us were two motorcyclists on loan from M'Lawa's cat's cradle, impressively clearing no traffic at all. Behind us were another Chrysler for the security boys, a third for the traveling press, the Portuguese Ambassador's green Mercedes, an old Citroën holding Nagon's Minister of Education, Culture, and Tourism, and an even older Renault that sardined Plon-Plon-Ville's one newspaper editor, Nagon's one radio-station manager, the lyricist of "Le soleil d'aujourd'hui" and West Africa's one female pop celebrity, whose Francophone version of "Blowin' in the Wind" was a regional hit. "Dominique" was the flip side.

"What on earth do you do for real shopping?" Ethel Kennedy asked me. "Clothes."

"Oh, for everyday things, we've got Lagos. Or the Sears, Roebuck catalogue! But for anything special, we usually wait until we're back in the States on home leave."

"How can you stand it? I'd go nuts. Just bonkers. Loony, insane, certifiable."

She gnawed at a cuticle. "Say! That's pretty. Is that the Atlantic or the Mediterranean?" Ethel Kennedy said. "Can you ask the chauffeur?"

POSTED BY: *Pam*   Taking Ethel to Ouibomey got me out of attending Buzz Sawyer's AID slide show, which I heard from a canary-popping Laurel Warren had been marred by too many views of Buzz's older son hands to hips in front of grateful Nagonese. Then came one mention too many of what a bright, concerned lad Tommie was.

"Do you want me to adopt him? I've got plenty of children," Bobby icily barked. Not our seven hours' highlight for either Buzz or Carol, since of course that was the muddled, irrational dream.

I also missed the visit to the USIS library, where Bobby instantly checked whether *Profiles in Courage* was on display and one of Rich's prize English speakers got halfway through reciting "Hiawatha" from memory before Bobby said, "Please tell him we have another event." However, I was on hand for the failure of Ned Finn's joke, which all of us felt bad about for his sake.

He'd been searching for the right one for weeks. If the Sawyers had fallen prey to a fantasy of having Tommie appreciated as a quasi-Kennedy in African exile—*recognized*, might be the *Prince and the Pauper*-ish word—Ned's dream was Ned Finn-ish. He wanted to uncork one quip so amusing that Bobby might repeat it to his brother back at the White House. Like so many men his age in or out of the government, Ned had never had a President he identified with until now.

Aware it couldn't be too impertinent, he wanted his joke to convey a nearly ineffable mix of wry aplomb, fealty, and metaphorical connection. When he tried his favorite on one of the only two people on the post who'd met JFK (the other was Cadwaller), I told him I thought Jack would be tickled. What we'd overlooked was that it'd never reach Jack except through Bobby, whom neither Hopsie nor I had ever met.

Worse, while Ned had worried he might have to force the setup himself, our visitor gave him the perfect opening. That made our Yankee Doodley crew's humor warrior look as chuffed as if he'd just been seated on a charger.

"And in emergencies?" Bobby asked once he'd gotten over his incredulity that we had no telephones, just the teletype machine for cables. When we needed to make a phone call, we drove over to Plon-Plon-Ville's main exchange and paid our money like the rest of the queue. "Revolution, natural disasters, Amcits who need evacuating. What do you do then?"

This was it: Ned Finn's apotheosis. I'd never seen him so happy without either a Marlboro or a drink. "Well, sir," he said, "if all else fails we'll probably just carve a message on a coconut."

(We geezers get so tired of *explaining* things, Panama! Jack Kennedy had done that to signal his crew's survival after his PT boat was sunk in the war. The coconut sat on his desk in the Oval Office. Everyone knew it. Back then, familiarity with all things Kennedy was as axiomatic as *Roseanne the Umpire Slayer* is to you.)

Kodak ready, Nan giggled. Since Ned wasn't in Coventry anymore for boffing Carol Sawyer, Rich Warren readily chuckled. Robert Kennedy's eyes, on the other hand, could've turned the Caribbean into a skating rink.

"Are you making fun of my brother's war record, Mr.—uh, Finn?" he asked in the deadly tone that treating a question as a pure request for information can have. "Do you even have one yourself?"

Ned was staggered. "Oh, no, not at all," he muttered, meaning only to disavow any mocking intent but inadvertently killing the sailor who'd Morse-lamped *Reported chaos on beach* from the bridge of the USS *Maloy* on the morning of Pam's twenty-fourth birthday. "Oh, why, uh, sir"—he'd just stopped himself from saying "hell"—"it was really just a joke about Africa."

"This continent has terrible problems," Bobby upbraided him, which certainly helped clear things up for everyone in the room. Oh, we'd had our suspicions—but we just couldn't *know*. "I don't think whimsy's an attitude many Africans would appreciate, do you?"

"I realize that." Ned was still poleaxed. "But, well—as you can see, there aren't any present."

"And the one I just saw right outside that window?" Bobby asked keenly.

"The night watchman is deaf, sir," Cadwaller said.

POSTED BY: *Pam*   What a prick. Spin it any way you want, but *l'équipe* stands fast: what a prick. I know Bobby's biographers say he grew more compassionate after his brother's death. Daisysdaughter.com has no reason to disbelieve the conversion's pain or sincerity. May I point out that a good few of us manage that pole-vault to adulthood based on less of a loss.

Afterward, we tried as best we could to bathe our seven hours in dazzle. The Nan Finn of today recalls it as marvelous, but her husband dragged himself around like a sick cat for three days. I caught Carol Sawyer screaming at Tommie, normally the apple of her eye. Cadwaller's carefully worded report to the Department—while he had no C Street enemies he knew of, this one would be scrutinized on Pennsylvania Avenue too—was able to judge the Nagon stop as at best a middling success. He was pleased when I told him Ethel was good at the nursing school and better at the leper colony, since that allowed him to praise her role unreservedly. Hopsie left out my request for my sunglasses.

Though I found Jack more enjoyable on our brief acquaintance, I'm not sure but what America is better off *imagining* Kennedys. The beauty was ours and they only instigated it. Our mimicry was the real magic, since we were acting out our ideal of them without constraint by truth's cold shower. It must be wrenching for the current members to realize they're doomed to emulate a clan that never existed.

"M'Lawa's no good," Bobby told Cadwaller as our Checker limo ferried them back to the airport. Cat's cradle of motorcyclists, etc. "Anyone else in line for the job?"

Ethel gaped in her Jules Verne agony. "The night watchman? Bob, even for you, that's—"

"No, dear. The President we met this morning. What's his opposition?" Bobby asked Cadwaller.

Hopsie started explaining the animosity between Nagon's upcountry tribes and the coastal one most endowed by France's *mission civilisatrice* to which M'Lawa and nearly all of the Cabinet belonged. Bobby cut him off: "No, no. A man. All this means nothing unless there's a man. Is there one?"

"N'Koda's a northerner. But he's ex-colonial too, and so far the Army's stayed loyal."

"Why didn't I meet with him?"

"You shook hands at lunch. But M'Lawa would no more permit a private meeting between you than—if you'll permit—you'd give Jimmy Hoffa the keys to your home."

"You did ask, though."

"As best we could without myself being declared persona non grata and N'Koda put under house arrest. It's not much to my liking, but you should know that by now our reputation precedes us."

Bobby let that one go. "Who keeps tabs on N'Koda?" he asked.

"Ned Finn."

"The coconut man? Oh, I want someone else on that file."

"That's really not possible. I don't have a chief of political section here," Cadwaller explained. "It's Finn or no one."

Probably the first time since '61 I'd heard him call Ned by last name only. But we were in a car with Robert Kennedy, and Hopsie had been in the Navy.

"Can't you do it yourself?" Bobby asked.

"Not without shredding my relations with M'Lawa. Of course I'd do it if instructed that was our policy."

"Then assign someone else," Bobby said. "I don't give a damn about your bureaucratic State Department chart."

"No reason why you should, sir. But N'Koda might, since he does know who's senior after me at this post," said Hopsie blandly. "I'm afraid your only option would be to have Ned sent home and replaced. I'd call that drastic."

Bobby gave him a surprisingly friendly smile. "That's not a word that comes up too often around me. But if all it takes is a phone call to Rusk, then—"

"Obviously my resignation would be on the Secretary's desk the next morning," Hopsie explained. "That's unless our teletype machine here broke down. I do enjoy making my own personnel decisions, but I've never thought I'm indispensable."

Bobby looked at him. "Family money, Ambassador?" he guessed after a moment. Now, *that* was class.

"Oh, I'm sure Pam could keep me. Any book on the horizon, dear?"

"You're a writer, Mrs. Cadwaller?"

He looked worried. New information, late in the day. People like Robert Kennedy are likely to treat whatever hasn't come up as something you've been withholding. Never mind that you withheld it because you know you're minor in the big panorama.

"Oh, hell, yes. When I feel like it," I brayed. "I just haven't felt like it since your brother beat me out for the Pulitzer."

"Excuse me?" Words not too many people ever got to hear from Bobby Kennedy's lips, I'll wager. Starting with the family maids.

"Mr. Kennedy," I said. "When you see the President next, would you mind terribly giving him Pamela Buchanan's affectionate regards?"

"Pamela Buchanan? Who the hell's she?" Ethel asked.

"Me. As I was then, Mrs. Kennedy. As I was then."

POSTED BY: *Pam*   Since the downside of dealing with a restless mind is often its upside within hours, most likely the Attorney General had forgotten about getting Ned axed by the time they hit Lagos. Cadwaller never heard a peep from Washington about it. And despite Bobby's antagonism to M'Lawa, I know for fact that the coup that took place toward the end of our twenty-three-month-long 1962 (it was July '63 by the calendar) bore no White House fingerprints. Our house blusterer Virgil Scoleri was sure he smelled Russians, but his evidence was so stupid even Dunc McCork told him to put a shoe in it.

God, how the kids on the post loved that coup. It was the first one any of us had witnessed, and we had front-row seats at its outbreak. That wasn't by accident, since it was timed for our Embassy's annual Fourth of July reception and cookout. Besides the usefulness of knowing where M'Lawa and the entire Nagonese Cabinet would be, along with most of the diplomatic corps, N'Koda had an idea the date would make it harder for the U.S. to complain about a revolution. Let alone withdraw foreign aid or refuse to recognize his new government, which he confessed to Hopsie and me over drinks at the Palais some weeks later had been his chief worry.

"And the Soviets, *Monsieur le Président*?" Hopsie asked.

"Mr. Cadwaller, you know *parfaitement bien* they'll recognize anybody. Only Americans play hard to get."

The Fourth was sacred anyway to the kids on the post, since to them America was a distant planet they'd been expelled from and this was its orbit's perihelion. I looked forward to it too, but getting ready for the damn thing was no bowl of cherry bombs. In Nagon, coming up with a day's worth of uniquely American-type activities that didn't involve toy helmets and wooden Tommy guns, along with a menu of uniquely American-type food, wasn't the easiest chore, and I never missed our nonexistent PX more. Useful the rest of the year, the Brits' NAAFI store in Lagos was no help on Independence Day.

Among other things, we could get hot dogs, hot-dog buns, and ground beef for burgers. Hamburger buns were the missing Grail. The Finns' cook thought he'd solved that one year by rolling beef patties in the shape of hot dogs, but even the kids on the post couldn't eat them. They looked too much like turds.

That was when I decided nothing was *really* more American than Southern-style fried chicken. Not only could we get the birds, which weren't plump but were edible. For a reason neither we nor the Nagonese ever, ever alluded to—not even in front of the seventeenth-century Portuguese fort at Ouibomey, and definitely not on the Fourth of July—our cooks took to the spicings as if they'd, um, invented them.

Dear God, you children can be slow. What do you think those enterprising Portuguese had been exporting, anyhow? Whose blood do you think legend claimed still ran wet one night a year on the walls of the Ouibomey fort's dungeon? Did you even wonder what that line in "Le soleil d'aujourd'hui" about "centuries of suffering without respite" alluded to? At the time, U.S. visa and immigration policy gave considerable preference to applicants with blood relatives who were American citizens. Every Nagonese who applied had thousands of them. They just had no way of knowing, much less proving, who any of them were.

The kids on the post moped at being deprived of guns outright, so I compromised by confining them to the Revolutionary War. Hadn't I seen a Sears-consignment toy musket in Sean-pronounced-Seen's arsenal? He looked exasperated: "It's a *Civil* War musket, not a Continental smoothbore. And they take so darn long to reload!"

Some tyke, that Sean. No wonder Nan and Ned looked woebegone every time they remembered him. He only decided the musket and the now moldy tricorn hat Hopsie'd worn as John Paul Jones would do once Laurel and Carol aroused his jealousy by outfitting the Warren lads and the younger Sawyer boy as the Spirit of '76.

Carol sewed a blue panel with a colonial circlet of thirteen stars over the fifty-state version on one of the Embassy flags. The Presidential band wouldn't part with its snare drum, so Laurel improvised with a tribal tom-tom from Ouibomey and two wooden kitchen spoons. The flute was from Ouibomey too, but a flute is a flute is a flute.

Nell Finn was glumly contemplating life as Betsy Ross again. Unlike Carol, she couldn't sew any more than Nan could, which had made the whole act a bit Marcel Marceau at our last Fourth of July. She brightened up when I suggested Pocahontas and lent her a copy of *Glory Be* bookmarked at "A Princess." Instantly, Tommie Sawyer decided he'd be an Injun brave, but don't misread puppy love there. By some peculiar boyish measure, he now outranked them all—Pocahontas had no tomahawk.

Bunting on the Residence, bunting on the Embassy. Paper red-white-and-blue bouquets topping each corner of our compound's walls. On the Residence's tin roof, portraits of JFK and wife and M'Lawa and wife flanked the banner bearing Pam's favorite motto and her cheerful translation: "THE DECLARATION OF INDEPENDENCE MAKES A DIFFERENCE/*LA DÉCLARATION D'INDÉPENDANCE, SANS BLAGUE* (Herman Melville, *romancier Américain*, 1819–1891)."

Sousa, *Victory at Sea*, and "Seventy-Six Trombones" playing on speakers. Aromas of hot dogs and sizzling fried chicken, so strong in the heat they almost knocked out Plon-Plon-Ville's two olfactory constants: motorbike fumes and cowflop. In Bermuda shorts, Faddle was stocking our biggest cooler with Coca-Cola, a rare treat even the kids on the post understood must be saved for the sacred day. They usually made do with the local French product. In the Embassy's garage, we'd set up our movie screen and 16mm projector to show the creaky Hollywoodisms we could rent without busting our budget: Gary Cooper as Lou Gehrig in *Pride of the Yankees*, Ronald Reagan as George Gipp in *Knute Rockne, All American*. I'd decided a sports theme was both Yankee Doodley and benign.

When I stopped by to get the name of his projectionist, Ehud Tabor laughed helplessly. I didn't really expect anyone to play close attention to the movies, though. They were just there to forestall people thinking there was nothing to do, the eternal crisis of the Plon-Plon-Ville diplomatic corps.

The drill was that our American gang was on hand by midmorning. Then the diplomatic corps showed up, followed by the Nagonese Cabinet. The vital thing was that M'Lawa—and in our final year, N'Koda, who continued the tradition—had to arrive with the full crowd on hand, and heaven help the luckless Nagonese official who dawdled in after him. As for us, our main worry was that Ned Finn might be not only well oiled but leaking lubricant by the time the Président arrived. Luckily, he too remembered the nearly disastrous timing of his Nagonized version of *West Side Story* last year—"M'Lawa! Say it soft and it's almost like freedom/Say it loud and you'll weep as you read 'em"—and was sticking to beer.

He wasn't bad with the new Soviet Ambassador, either. Vasily Shishkov having left us for Buenos Aires, his replacement was a fellow named Goliadkin we all thought was a charlatan. The Central Casting types often have that effect, precisely because you meet them so rarely.

"I'm glad to see at least a few of your indigenes survived," Goliadkin said heartily as Nell trotted by in her Pocahontas feather, rolling a Sears-consignment hula hoop. Nobody'd told her what they were for. "What tribe is the little girl from?"

"She's a Kulak," said Ned offhandedly. "Unless you'd like something harder, Mr. Ambassador, would you care for a Coke?"

"I've counted coup!" Tommie Sawyer bopped Nell with his tomahawk. "Now I've got to scalp you. That's the rule. *C'est la règle, Nell, tu le sais.*"

"Tommie, ouch!" Nell said firmly as he tried to wrestle her to the ground. "*Et de quoi parles-tu, hein?* We don't scalp girls in our tribe."

"Oh, *ta gueule.* C'mon, please? I'll let you be the first to give *la lèpre* money outside Monoprix next time. Nobody else has hair long enough to get scalped."

"Oh, go scalp your mom. *Fous-moi la paix,* Tommie! I'm Pocahontas. Now give me back my hoop."

"I can't scalp my own mother," said Tommie disgustedly. Sometimes, I think Buzz and Carol's bid to get him recognized as a quasi-Kennedy wasn't so far-fetched.

"*Monsieur le ministre!*" I called. "So good of you to come. How goes *l'Éducation, la Culture et le Tourisme?*"

Of course he wanted to reminisce about Ethel's visit to Ouibomey, our increasingly tattered social habit ever since. "Naturally, we dream of *her,*" he said with a reverent nod up at Jackie's photograph on the roof. "*Elle parle Français, vous savez?*"

"*Bien sûr.*"

Then that beetle-browed shy academic—he'd written his dissertation on Alfred Jarry's African influences—surprised me. His eyes grew furtive, his voice intense. I was no longer engaged in social diplomacy, but the political kind.

"Mrs. Cadwaller, please pass this on to Washington. If I could host Jacqueline Kennedy here for even one day"—a no longer academic finger went up—"a coup of that magnitude might make me the most popular man in the country. I share the New Frontier's ideals. I—"

Philippe Paul-Christophe P'kapa was interrupted by the opening notes of "Le soleil d'aujourd'hui." In Nagon, it only played on one car's horn, as if the blatting of a cat's cradle of motorcyclists wasn't enough of a giveaway.

"*Monsieur le ministre,* please excuse me. I must greet *le Président.*"

"As must we all. Sooner or later," the Minister of Education, Culture, and Tourism said resignedly as M'Lawa, massive in a boxy electric-blue suit, exited his Presidential convertible. Its buttery Catskills honeymoon bathtub of rich leather upholstery made it the only car grander than our Checker limo in all of Nagon.

Whatever that Polytechnique-trained economist turned dictator was, stupid he wasn't. As he entered our compound beside tribally shawled Madame M'Lawa—Celeste favored Pierre Cardin on most days, but this was her official regalia—his eyes needed only one sweep of the scene once they'd rested on his own portrait atop the Residence roof to spot the dominant fact at our Fourth of July reception and cookout.

"*Où est le général N'Koda?*" Where is General N'Koda?

"I'm the luckiest man on the face of the earth," Gary Cooper's voice maundered from the garage. Then we heard gunfire.

POSTED BY: *Pam*   Cadwaller stepped forward. "*Monsieur le Président*, I have no way of knowing what's going on. *None*," he emphasized as M'Lawa stared, because our reputation did precede us. "Until we learn more, I must strongly advise you to return to the Palais du Président immediately. We have no local communications here."

M'Lawa hesitated. Too many thoughts were gnashing gears behind that hefty forehead, and he had no way of telling which were significant. The mind of a dictator has to make room to not only brew his own schemes, but monitor the hypothetical ones of a dozen or a hundred other men—including, just now, Hopsie's own.

"I strongly advise it," Cadwaller repeated. "You have only your bodyguards with you. Think, *Monsieur le Président*. The Presidential Guard is at the Palais, not here. They're your best hope to retrieve this situation, whatever it is."

From far off in that muggy still air came a grenade's sharp but humidity-muffled crack. Later we realized it must've been the attack on the radio station going in. Audibly nearer us and coming closer every second, we heard grinding engines and shouts, along with more rifle shots—more likely exuberant than hostile, as they had no opposition up that way—from the north end of Boul' Mich. In case my daisysdaughter.com readers have forgotten, that was where the Army's barracks were, across from the sports palace.

"*Monsieur le Président*, you don't have much time," said Ned Finn briskly, flicking away a Marlboro as he returned from a quick inspection of the street. "I don't think they've blocked the road to the Palais just yet. But their advantage right now is that they know exactly where you are."

That clinched it. Though his eyes said he hadn't worked everything out— one gear was still sticking—M'Lawa nodded. *"Voiture!"* he commanded his nearest bodyguard. *"Celeste!"* he called to his wife, who at the first shots had started for the Residence porch as if guided by her own portrait glowing on its hot tin roof. *"On y va."*

Without waiting to see if she was obeying—he could always get another wife, but had only one Palais du Président—he turned and let his bodyguards muscle him out of the Embassy compound. They were only muscling humid air, but habit is habit, and Celeste M'Lawa said *"Oh, et puis zut"* and scooted to join them. As more gunfire erupted, she found time to grab my elbow with a startlingly mischievous smile.

"Mon Dieu, how I've longed for this day," she confided. "This damned kerchief! You will visit us on the Riviera, won't you? *Le soleil d'hier m'est beaucoup plus agréable."* After a quick one-two *Parisienne* cheek peck, then she was gone too.

"Christ, Ned!" said Hopsie with uncommon relief once we'd closed the gates behind them. "That was close."

"Damn close," Ned agreed. "You see Celeste head for the Residence? She knew."

"What was going on?" That was Bermuda-shorted Faddle, clutching a half eaten hot dog.

"Hon, he was on U.S. territory," Ned explained with a grin of reprieve. "If he'd thought fast enough to ask us for asylum, Jesus! By the time we got an answer from Washington—"

"He'd have been singing 'Edelweiss' in my shower," said Cadwaller. "And then what if they'd tried to take him by force? N'Koda's too smart for that, but a mob is a mob."

Were we ever in for a shock. *"Let them come!"* mad little Sean Finn shrieked, gripping his toy musket. *"'If they mean to have a war'—"*

"'Let it begin here!'" whooped Tommie Sawyer in his fierce Iroquois war paint.

"Oh good God," Hopsie said as the full lunacy of the kids on the post sank in. "Pam, round up *all* the kids and get them the hell inside the Embassy. No, the Residence. I don't think there'll be much shooting, but they don't know it's real."

Sean burst into tears. "Yes, we do. Yes, we do."

"Nan, Laurel, Carol!" I called. "I'm going to need help."

Cadwaller meanwhile had bounded up to the porch, where the microphone set up for the official exchange of Independence Day greetings stood under Melville's banner. "I must ask the Nagonese Cabinet to leave," he announced. "We cannot offer you any protection. Buzz! Handle that. Members of the diplomatic corps are naturally free to stay here or return to their own Embassies as they wish."

"Are you joking, Ambassador?" Ehud Tabor called out merrily. "These are the best seats in the house."

"Yes, and there's a great deal of beer," Klaus Schlitten chimed in.

"Goliadkin," said Hopsie, away from the microphone and back down the porch steps. "Your call, of course, but I think it might be best if you *did* stick around. We don't know what's happening in Ouibomey—unless, of course, you know what's happening here," he added, now wry.

"It wasn't us either," said the Soviet Ambassador. "Cadwaller, it really wasn't you?"

"Nope," Hopsie said. "And my word on that too. Tell your government. Goliadkin, you don't think the Chinese—?"

Goliadkin laughed. "How would we know? How would anyone?"

The grinding engines, exuberant shots, and chants from the far end of Boul' Mich were getting steadily more thunderous. As Buzz Sawyer shepherded the soon-to-be-former Nagonese Cabinet toward our compound's rear exit, Rich Warren mounted a ladder to take down M'Lawa's and Madame M'Lawa's portraits. He took down JFK's and Jackie's too, puzzling me until I saw his inspired idea of hooking them to the compound's front gate.

As for me, I was rounding up children. Two Warrens, two Sawyers, Sean-pronounced-Seen—oh, my God.

"Tommie!" I shouted. "Have you seen Nell Finn?"

His lip curled. "The squaw?"

Finally—and I must admit satisfyingly—I lost my temper with the Sawyers' little princeling. "Listen, you brat! Do you want to have a fight with *me*? *C'est ça que tu veux?*"

May I remind you that he was in second grade and I was five foot ten? Is this the right time to mention that after the kids on the post saw a French-dubbed version of *One Hundred and One Dalmatians* at the Bijou Castafiore, I'd caught more than one of them looking at me as if eccentric, literally lofty Mrs. Cadwaller was a certain someone's Plon-Plon-Ville avatar?

"Pam!" Carol Sawyer exploded. "I'm sorry, but you can't yell at my son. If there's yelling to do, I'll do it, all right? Nan's got her hands full with Sean and no wonder. Can you please find Nell on your own?"

I stared around. Rich had killed John Philip Sousa, but our houseboys were still surreally bringing our remaining guests drinks. The oncoming engines and glad cries and rifle shots were vying with exhilarated diplomats' laughter and banter. Then with new woe I recalled what I'd seen rolling out our compound's front gate just after M'Lawa and Celeste bustled through it.

Unsure how close the rebels were by now, I knew I didn't want to unbar and reopen the gate. Blessing myself for choosing a pantsuit and sandals that morning, I forked left gam and then right over the compound's low wall and saw Nell immediately. Under her Pocahontas feather and clutching her hula hoop, she was staring transfixed up Boul' Mich.

What she was staring at was pretty transfixing even if you'd seen Paris liberated. Like the four clanking behind it, the lead snowplow was packed with perspiration-oiled soldiers hanging off every stanchion, rifles raised and mixing cheers with lusty renderings of "Le soleil d'aujourd'hui." Crowning them in the thick shimmer of heat were big portraits of N'Koda and Nagonese flags. No red ones, I noted swiftly, alleviating Cadwaller's most urgent concern.

Trotting alongside and behind were the reserve N'Koda had smuggled in from upcountry: a few hundred of his tribal kinfolk from the north. Gaunt-armed and bony-shouldered in the sleeveless ribbed cotton undershirts that were pretty much the *mission civilisatrice*'s only notable contribution to non-coastal Nagon, they were armed with upcountry's traditional hunting weapons:

machetes and iron bows with cloth grips and slung quivers of grim iron arrows. Quite a few of them were wearing one of Buzz Sawyer's eight thousand screwdrivers as a festive pendant on a lanyard around their necks: "Smart man, N'Koda," Cadwaller said later. "Even-steven."

"Nell, what on earth," I stammered at the top of my lungs. Realized I'd better walk and not dash to her: someone running might look like a target. Her pinched grave face looked up.

"If this be my fate, I must submit," she said calmly—a line adapted from, so help me, the Pocahontas chapter of *Glory Be*. Some distant part of me felt flattered.

Frenzy came first. "For God's sake!" I screeched. "What is *with* you damn children?"

"Oh, that's simple!" she said, clearly pleased and surprised to be asked. "We don't know what's expected of us. Richie Warren thinks that if we guess right we'll all get to go home to the States, but he makes a lot of stuff up. We all do." Then she turned to face the rumbling snowplows.

Right, right! The snowplows. I'd grown moderately used to jiggling the infant Tim Cadwaller on our Paris visits to Chris and Renée. I'm pretty sure I'd never tried to hoist a nine-year-old.

"My hoop!" she implored as I staggered while lifting her, that stupid feather going right up my left nostril. So I had to bend back down to grab that too. Then I ran and dumped Nell on the far side of the compound wall before scrambling over myself. Lost a sandal and my pantsuit tore on a snag.

Once I'd got her inside the Residence, I had a glum chore to perform. "Carol," I said. "I'm terribly sorry. You were completely right. I had no call to blow up that way."

Looking up from a sofa between Tommie and the younger Sawyer boy, who was still dolefully toying with his Spirit of '76 flute—not unintelligently, she'd made him take off the head bandage—Carol relished her new Get Out of Jail Free card. My tantrum had cost me any right to go on obliquely exiling her for oinking it up with Ned the summer before. Not that I'd ever been rude: Hopsie would've caned me. In a group of women this small, you could still do a lot just by whose conversational gambits you seized on.

"We all know it isn't an average day. It's just—Pam, if you were a mother, you'd know how sensitive they are at that age."

I would love to report Tommie was pulling the wings off flies just then. But if so, he was only pulling them off with his eyes.

"Tommie! *Je vous demande pardon. J'avais tort,*" I said.

"Say thank you, Tommie," Carol prodded. "Be gracious for once in your life."

"Why?" he said sullenly. "Just because Cruella's married to Dad's stupid boss?"

I looked at Carol, she looked at me. Then we shared our friendliest laugh since the Sawyers got to Nagon. "Yes," she said.

"Darn tooting," I said. "But never mind. It's all right."

"What's happening, Pam?" Nan Finn asked. "Outside."

I beamed. "Well! Since I'm not a mother, I'm going right back out to find out."

POSTED BY: *Pam*   I'd barely stepped onto the Residence's now diplomatically jammed porch when Nan followed me. "Oh, I mean the hell with it," the glorious girl laughingly said, holding up her Kodak. "When'll I get a chance to see this again?"

"What about Sean?"

"Cruella, thank God *you* own a copy of *The Longest Day.*"

"Signed, too." Something clicked. "When's Sean's birthday?"

"November. Did I tell you what I'm trying to get him?"

"Uh-uh."

"A cannon from Ouibomey. The Portuguese consul still has some sort of squatter's rights at the fort, and—oh, my God. That's them."

Indeed it was. Festooned with shouting and singing soldiers, one after another of the snowplows of the *1er Régiment Blindé* clanked and squealed over crumbling, patchy hundred-degree asphalt past our Fourth of July frieze of diplomats greasy with fried chicken, Bermuda-shorted secretaries munching hot dogs, and white-coated Residence houseboys passing Coca-Cola and popcorn. As each of them reached the gates mounted with our portraits of JFK and Jackie, there were cries of *"Vive l'Amérique!"* and *"Vive le Président Kennedy!"*

"Propaganda," Goliadkin said. "N'Koda coached them. They don't know what they're—"

"*Nous t'aimons, Jacqueline!*" an exuberant voice called brawnily from the third snowplow.

More single-minded and also less interested in what they were trotting past, N'Koda's northern tribal kinsfolk began a steady chant of "*À bas M'Lawa! Vive le Nagon libre.*" Even so, Hopsie couldn't resist teasing Goliadkin. "Such a pity Chairman Kruschev married so young," he said, stuffing a pipe that told me he was convinced we were safe.

"We still don't know what's happening in Ouibomey," Goliadkin reminded him. "There, I'm sure the Nagonese people's expressions of devotion to the Chairman and his impressive wife are extraordinary."

"Yes, they would be. Nan! *Stay* on the porch, please."

"Sorry!"

"Well, *I* think he's full of shit, Mr. Ambassador. Excuse my French," Virgil Scoleri unexpectedly took it upon himself to bellow. "Those goddam snowplows! Goliadkin, do you think we're stupid?"

"Can you rephrase that in the first person singular? I'm a guest here, Mr., ah—"

"Virgil Scoleri!" our Admin guy thundered, shoving out a paw. "Pleased to meet you! Put 'er there. Take a pew."

"Virgil," said Cadwaller quietly. "Go to the Embassy. Wait to see if anything comes in by teletype. Short of our death *en masse*, under no circumstances are you to compose or send a cable of your own to the Department. You must have one like him," he added to Goliadkin once Virgil's bull neck and sweat-palimpsested white shirt were stalking Embassyward.

After a hesitation, Goliadkin held up three fingers. He didn't need to say a word.

We heard the rest later. How the fifty or so Presidential Guards who didn't decamp tried desperately to get the sixth snowplow off its plinth to barricade the Palais's main gate; of course its engine hadn't tasted gas since it rolled off the jetty. How the lead rebel snowplow smashed through, spilling soldiers off its flanks who didn't need to do too much shooting before forty-seven or so Presidential guards realized that losing your life for Jean-Baptiste M'Lawa was one moronic way to go.

How the radio station followed the announcement of the Provisional Government—"when that term's not a lie, it's redundant," Cadwaller said—with West Africa's hit Francophone version of "Blowin' in the Wind": *"Combien de routes doit le Nagon marcher/Avant qu'on l'appelle un pays?/Et combien de voûtes doit le Togo chercher/Avant qu'on récolte le maïs?"* After a baffled pause—what now?—it was followed by "Dominique."

How M'Lawa and Mme M'Lawa were intercepted by the fourth snowplow as they drove on a back road to the Plon-Plon-Ville airport and brought back to the Palais du Président under arrest. That wasn't because N'Koda didn't want them gone; they were in Nice a week later. He just wanted the Nagonese left in no doubt that they were going into exile on his orders, not escaping.

Besides, even if M'Lawa had talked the pilot into it, the Nagonese Air Force couldn't have withstood the departure of its only plane. So he and Celeste ended up journeying to their new life on the Riviera on first Air Afrique, then Air France. Economy class, to punish his excesses—not that the distinction was an especially vivid one to most of their former compatriots.

We heard a lot of it from N'Koda himself before sunset. By late afternoon, it was obvious the shooting had mostly stopped. It's not wholly unlike listening for the rate of popping popcorn to slow. Most of the diplomats at our Fourth of July reception and cookout had gone back to their Embassies to start cabling.

Released from the Residence, though not yet the compound, the kids on the post were vying to outdo each other's confused shouts of *"À bas Jacqueline!"* and *"Pan, pan."* Then at twilight the vast Presidential convertible, sans blatting cat's cradle of motorcyclists, pulled up once again at our reopened gate.

"General N'Koda," Hopsie said, extending his hand. "We worried we wouldn't see you today."

"I'm a respecter of custom, Mr. Ambassador. Nagon's head of state arrives last."

Once we'd assembled our info, Hopsie gave Ned Finn the job of writing the cable. It spent a few months as a C Street legend, rivaled only by Ehud Tabor's light-hearted report to Tel Aviv recommending that the Israelis look into the uses of converted snowplows as terror weapons. Of course that was the idea he revived in earnest as Defense Minister thirty years later, to no end of suffering on the West Bank.

Ned's cable had no such consequences. Yet from its opening words ("STAFF was celebrating Independence with dependents") to its repeated identifications of the trotting northern tribesmen as "General N'KODA's *force de frappe*"—as in, "The *force de frappe*'s bows and arrows demonstrated to M'LAWA that the ball was now in the other Agincourt"—it was generally reckoned to be one of his triumphs. Even glum Dean Rusk was alleged to have cracked a smile at the coda: "NO AMCITS OR AMGOVS OR USGOV PROPERTY HARMED, THOUGH HUMAN ELEMENTS OF FOREGOING MUCH BEMUSED. WE'RE ALL RIGHT, JACK. YOURS TRULY FINN, U.S. EMBASSY, PLON-PLON-VILLE, NAGON."

It won him his dearest wish, too. When Andy Pond's final message on the subject from the Secretariat reached us a week later—YOUR CABLE OF 5/7/63 READ ALOUD IN OVAL OFFICE TO MUCH HILARITY. CONGRATULATIONS NED WE KNEW YOU COULD DO IT—Ned Finn walked on air until August.

Nan Finn told me years later that despite knowing better, Ned couldn't help nursing a fantasy that the Oval Office's occupant would request a meeting with that clever cable's witty author on the Finns' next home leave. They were due to head back to the States for six weeks' R&R in mid-December 1963.

POSTED BY: *Pam*   I saw Ned Finn get blubbery in his cups a number of times. I heard him cry sober just once, and I had no option but to retreat from the Residence's porch without a word. That kind of loneliness can't be cured by companions—male, female, or child.

I too was in shock, of course. We all were for a week. The welcome exception was Virgil Scoleri: our Admin guy's lack of any imagination had its plus side for once. Less welcome was Dunc McCork's blitheness. But my shock stayed dry-eyed until the ultimate triumph of the art of Nagon.

The first dislocation is that to us it was night. The cable from Washington clicked over the teletype in an empty Embassy, wasn't read 'til the following day. We had no TV, as I've said. Instead, we nearly all listened to the BBC World Service in the evenings, and that was the reason that first Ned and Nan Finn, then the Sawyers—the Warrens were in Greece by then—stumbled on foot in the dark to the Residence, children still dressed for bedtime in tow. We were expecting them too, with no need for acknowledgment. I'd made coffee by then in the big urn for parties, not the old percolator we used when alone.

The second dislocation is that we were an American handful abroad, surrounded not by compatriots but foreigners. Over the next few days, that was both a reprieve and a burden, for we were suddenly magical. People looked at us as if there were something wondrous in the fact that we were still in Nagon, moving around and speaking as if we were still real.

I've never had so many strangers, European and African, invent reasons to touch me. I've still never forgotten that after the Finns and the Sawyers, the third and last knock on our door was Ehud Tabor's. If it was policy, I'd rather not know.

Because we were so few and so far from home, we felt one added incredulity. The thing was, we'd *had* our death on the post for the year. Faddle had been pulled down by her shark just weeks earlier, and if you're wondering, yes: we'd gone right on swimming. What were the odds of its happening twice?

Nagon's climate and lack of facilities had left us no choice except to seal Faddle's remains in the biggest of our Sears-consignment coolers, in which I'm afraid they fit comfortably. It was the same one she'd stocked with Coke on the Fourth of July, wearing Bermuda shorts and popping her bubble gum. Awaiting her last plane home, she'd lain in state for three days in the Residence's big freezer, and I was enough of a coward that I couldn't bring myself to fetch anything out of it for weeks even after Faddle's Sears cooler went back Stateside for burial. It seemed preposterously excessive to lose another member of our tiny Embassy so soon afterward, even though his only job there had been as a portrait in the reception area.

Unbelievably, none of us—not even Ned Finn, or perhaps him especially—had a drink for a week. That was among the reversions to normal life that would've seemed sacrilegious, and we had so little control of our emotions on coffee that one gin and tonic could have triggered delirium. Ned even tried to quit smoking, but he was only human and that bobbing Marlboro stayed his equivalent of our Checker limo's tin flag. The dazed kids on the post agreed to have their toy guns locked away until Christmas, since we couldn't bear the sight of them or a shout of *"Pan, pan."*

Nell Finn learned to sew by helping the post's wives stitch black mourning bunting on the Embassy flags. Carol Sawyer was in charge of that, since she was the seamstress among us. Reducing our wardrobes considerably, none of us women could stand to wear anything alluding to Jackiehood. When grabby short curly-haired Beth McCork turned up at the Residence in a white A-line dress two days into it, we had such trouble speaking to her that she went home and changed.

That same evening, I was on about my twentieth cup of coffee—and smoking one of Ned's cigarettes too, for all that I'd mostly quit a year earlier—when Nell Finn, sucking her thumb (not regression: no thimbles), came to stand in front of me. Taking advantage of a private new license she'd adopted since my forty-second birthday, she said, "Pamela, how come everything's *staying* so strange? Is this just what we're like from now on?"

"Oh, no, honey. It's just—well, right now *we* don't know what's expected of us, either." It was the only time I'd alluded to our strange dialogue as snowplows clanked toward us on the day of the coup. "All in the same boat at last," I tried to smile.

Naturally, that week was also bereft of music. Our Scandinavian hi-fi sets gathered dust. Neither Hopsie's *Victory at Sea* nor Ned Finn's "Seventy-Six Trombones" nor the one the kids loved—"Dis-donc, dis-donc" from *Irma la Douce*—broke the silence of our American camp. But soon after Nell went out on the Residence's porch and sat down fists to chin to gaze at and inhale the redolent Nagonese night, I heard her quietly singing, *"Il était un petit navire, il était un petit navire…"*

Somehow I knew she meant the *Pélérin*, which indeed we didn't take out again for two months. Too reminiscent of a PT boat or a Cape Cod pleasure skiff, even after Christmas came and we let the boys have their toy guns back. They even got some new ones, but of course that Sears consignment had been ordered months ago.

Installed in the Palais du Président since July and busy merging the Presidential Guard with the Army, N'Koda pulled up in his inherited Presidential convertible the first morning to pay a formal condolence call to the Embassy with his wife, an upcountry woman as bulky and tribally scarred on both cheeks as Celeste M'Lawa had been sleek and cheek-pecking. Once they'd gone, Hopsie came over to the Residence with a peculiar expression. "N'Koda's going to give him a state funeral."

"A memorial service, you mean."

"No, that's just it. A funeral. It seems… well! It seems that was the custom in *mission civilisatrice* days when French heads of state died. Binding the colonies to the mother country, and not at all stupid when you think about it. They haven't done it since Independence, nor ever for a foreign one. But he wants one for Jack."

"Hopsie!" I said. "You never called him that in your life."

"No, and wouldn't have dreamed of it," Cadwaller agreed. Then he got a look on his face I'd never seen before. "Now I can," my husband said softly, knocking the ash from his pipe.

POSTED BY: *Pam* The funeral was in the grim Catholic church from *mission civilisatrice* days, flinty and gray as a Breton squall made of stone. It stood on Plon-Plon-Ville's erratically paved, bicycle-rattling main east-west road, which our Yankee Doodley picnic convoys drove down less often now that the Warrens were gone. Officially the Boulevard du Quatre Juillet since N'Koda's coup, it was still known to all of us, Nagonese and foreigners alike, by its traditional name: the rue d'Écu.

Thanks to its respelling once the church had been consecrated, that was a bowdlerization of its rough-and-ready monicker when the *mission civilisatrice* was no more than a French Army outpost. Back then it was the road where African girls in lantern-lit cribs had serviced the garrison for a few grubby francs at a time, presumably gratified by their introduction to Western economics and also relieved that they got to do so on Nagonese soil rather than in Haiti, Brazil, or Alabama. Plon-Plon-Ville's own name was another memento, some sergeant's satiric mess-hall tribute to the newly departed Napoleon III's most blackguardy cousin.

Checking the protocol, we learned I needed a mourning veil, something I despaired of finding on either short or long notice in Nagon or even Lagos. Carol Sawyer sewed me one, not that I wanted to know where our seamstress had gotten its filmy black gauze and lace trimming or cared to think about where it might've been before landing in front of my nose.

Hopsie'd said "funeral," Hopsie'd said "state." The coffin was alarming anyway. Covered by a taut and immaculate Stars and Stripes on loan from the Embassy, it stood just feet away from the front pew where we sat. Beside us was N'Koda in full uniform, his medals from Vichy, the Free French, and M'Lawa now augmented by those of the new Ordre des Compagnons du Quatre Juillet. Mme N'Koda's yards of black silk and black kerchief kept looking like a trick of photography, since the tribal costumes her mourning garb mimicked were always of cotton and festively colored.

Dank as a laundry, the church's interior was as grim as its outside. Grim rough-chinked stone walls, dark banquettes, no stained glass or saints' statues at all. Over the altar, the Christ on the cross—the work of the grandfathers of Ouibomey's woodcarvers—may have been unique in all Christendom. That's because he was nude, his never used (so they say) dowsing rod projecting down toward the coffin. As the Church often did elsewhere, the *mission civilisatrice*'s French Catholic priests had amalgamated local cults' customs into their liturgy, and an uncocked Christ made no sense in Nagon.

Gazing up at dowsing-rod Jesus through a mourning veil made of Carol Sawyer's old lingerie, irreligious Pam found herself recalling a line from Sinclair St. Clair's least favorite poet, apt here for the only time in my experience: *Polyphiloprogenitive, the sapient sutlers of the Lord.* The church's only other decoration was the portrait placed on the altar, which we'd also loaned from the Embassy; which indeed we had given, since we had no further official use for it. That's unless you consider the empty coffin decorative, which I might've been able to from the back row but peculiarly couldn't when sitting this close.

The Mass was obviously in Latin. We were in pre-Vatican II days, the detail more than any other that brings back to me how long ago this was. Not having sat through one since Chignonne's, I relearned how they do go on. We had it easy compared to the two Nagonese soldiers on vigil to either side of the altar, who stayed at a stiff-armed *garde-à-vous* the whole time.

Then the Bishop of Ouibomey—"Bishop of Plon-Plon-Ville" had been too much for Rome—turned to our pew. *"Le Président du Nagon,"* he said, ceding the stage.

Grizzled, sashed, and bemedaled, N'Koda stood stiffly and walked to the coffin. Resting one hand on the flag, he stood there a moment before he about-faced. *"Puisque ce sont nos amis d'Amérique qui sont le plus durement frappés par ce deuil, je demande à Mme Cadwaller, la femme de l'ambassadeur des États-Unis, de traduire mes paroles en anglais."*

Nobody'd warned me I'd be asked to translate his eulogy, and N'Koda later apologized. He hadn't thought of doing it until he turned around and saw our white-faced American crew dotting the congregation. As he gestured to me to rise, I sat paralyzed until Hopsie's nudge: "Dammit, Pam. Go."

Standing, I walked to the other side of the coffin. At least now I faced away from the portrait. My tense nod answered N'Koda's discreetly raised eyebrows.

"Le Président Kennedy était un bon ami de l'Afrique."

"President Kennedy was a good friend to Africa," I said as loudly as I could manage.

"Il a encouragé le peuple nagonais à devenir fièrement indépendant."

"He encouraged the Nagonese people in their proud independence."

"Il a créé le Peace Corps."

"He created the Peace Corps," I said and the two goofy kids from upcountry nobody much liked sat up straighter in their denim cut-offs and boots.

"Il m'a envoyé ses meilleurs voeux quand j'ai moi-même pris la responsabilité de poursuivre notre Révolution."

"He sent me his best wishes when I myself took responsibility for continuing our Revolution," I said, stammering a bit. Helpless not to recall a merry telegram sent the week *Glory Be* nosed out *Profiles in Courage* on the *Times* bestseller list: "I'M JUST GLAD YOU'RE NOT A POLITICIAN. BEST WISHES JACK KENNEDY."

"Il nous a envoyé son frère unique en mission de paix."

"He sent us his only brother on a mission of peace," I said and started bawling. Felt my chin go, yanking around without my brain's say-so. Then the most awful blubbering came up out of my lungs. Sucked onto my face by my gaping mouth's first intake of breath, my veil was soaked in three seconds. The horrible weeping of the Ambassador's wife was the only sound anywhere in Nagon.

"Pardon, pardon," I gasped between sobs. *"Un moment, s'il vous plaît."* I think N'Koda might've waited an hour, but then Nell Finn stood up and came

forward in the little banana-colored party dress from her most recent birthday. Discounting Tommie Sawyer, already destined for Harvard in his parents' eyes by his first black suit, the kids on the post had no appropriate togs for a funeral.

She took my hand. *"Continuez, Monsieur le Président,"* she said firmly.

"Nos pensées vont aujourd'hui à sa belle épouse Jacqueline, que nous invitons à venir en Afrique afin de se remettre."

"Today we are thinking more than usual of Jackie," said Nell in her now ten-year-old voice. "We want her to come here to Africa to—"

"Recuperate," I murmured.

"Recuperate."

"Elle pourrait constater par elle-même à quel point son mari était aimé, ainsi que ses enfants d'ailleurs, le petit Jean-Jean et Caroline."

"She would see for herself how her husband was loved. And the children too, John-John and Caroline."

If you're wondering, N'Koda's written invitation went out with Hopsie's endorsement in our Embassy's diplomatic bag a week later. He got a short but nice note back from Jacqueline Kennedy—*en Français, bien sûr.* Gist: not now, perhaps someday.

"Et aux Américains présents parmi nous aujourd'hui, le peuple nagonais offre sa sympathie la plus vive et l'expression de son amitié la plus chaleureuse."

"And to all us Americans, the Nagonais people offer their—"

"Keenest," I murmured.

"Keenest sympathies. And their most warmest friendship."

Pivoting smartly, N'Koda saluted the coffin. Turning herself, only briefly uncertain and well trained by the boys on the post—and I swear, we hadn't yet seen That Photograph—Nell saluted him back. Then N'Koda returned to our pew.

"Come on, Pam," Nell whispered. *"Ça va."*

She got me sat down again, a hand still childishly moist from her grip now held by Cadwaller's. Then Rich Warren's prize English speaker—the same one who'd gotten halfway through "Hiawatha" before Bobby Kennedy said "Please tell him we have another event"—sang "The Star-Spangled Banner" to us. I later wrote Rich and Laurel that I wished Rich could have been there to hear him.

Then the Bishop of Ouibomey pronounced a benediction. Then great hoary brown doors flung us out into African sun, everyday rattling bicycles, everyday stench of diesel and cow pies, everyday honks of ancient Citroëns and even older Renaults.

"Wasn't that something?" said Dunc McCork, hefting a camera. "One for the kids down the road—right, Beth?"

Even if you dislike him or her, everyone deserves at least one chance to speak for the community. "You asshole," Carol Sawyer spat. "It's one for ours *now*."

"Dunc! You took pictures?" Nan Finn gasped, revulsed.

"McCork, hand me that film."

Dunc looked startled. "Are you serious, Ambassador?"

"I'm not an Ambassador," Hopsie said. "I am bigger than you are, however, and in fairly good shape for my age."

POSTED BY: *Pam*   As I've said more than once, Panama, Nagon no longer exists. It's as absent from any Rand McNally globe you'll spin as Constantinople or Leningrad. At around the same time the Congo metamorphosed into Zaïre and Upper Volta renamed itself Burkina Faso—and Dahomey, of course, became the République du Benin—it turned into an entirely different country known as Djedjia.

Plon-Plon-Ville was replaced by a city on the identical spot that calls itself Djedjiamey. Oh, no doubt, if you visited, you'd see beaches whose waves boom in all the way from Brazil and fishermen hauling long nets full of still living silver out of the sea. No doubt the Catholic church from *mission civilisatrice* days and the Portuguese fort at Ouibomey both still stand, maybe even the Hôtel de la Plage and the Israeli Embassy. I'll bet my bottom dollar they've kept the Palais du Président's sugar-cube box looking grand. But the Nagon where Ned Finn boffed Carol Sawyer, American boys ran around shouting *"Pan, Pan"* and mimicked Mark Twain for Nan's Kodak on a raft made from the lids of USAID packing crates, 1962 was so happy to be here it lasted twenty-three months, Nell Finn and I translated Etiènne Maurice N'Koda's eulogy to John Fitzgerald Kennedy into English, snowplows thundered by in hundred-degree heat, and

Pam accepted her own middle age and her mother's Charybdeanism on some faraway beach is now gone.

Djedjia is a dictatorship, no great surprise there. N'Koda hung on until '65 before the Palais's revolving door did its thing. He and his wife wound up in Antibes, not too far down the Côte d'Azur from M'Lawa and Celeste. I'm told they used to socialize.

By the late Seventies, before Cadwaller's long dying began, I noticed I no longer felt the special State Department sharpening of alumna interest when I spotted stories about the former Nagon in the papers. That was soon after the onetime Minister of Education, Culture, and Tourism got his turn in the revolving door and spent a year slaughtering some ten thousand of his compatriots and raping three hundred more, mostly schoolgirls, until they killed him too. Since *La Terreur P'kapa*, the tale's been monotonous, just decades of suffering without respite. Sometimes I wonder whether modern Africa became a tragedy not least because tragedy felt more indigenous and peculiarly nobler than farce.

The Finns left in early '64, not long before Hopsie and I were transferred ourselves. When we saw them off at the airport, of course they were dressed to the nines, because that's how the Foreign Service did it. Our DCM was wearing a black wool suit that would be far more comfortable where they landed than where they were leaving from, Nan her nicest maternity dress. Nell had on the same banana-colored dress she'd worn at JFK's Plon-Plon-Ville funeral, matched now by the ribbon the same color in her hair.

Sean was in a white linen suit with short pants. As they mounted the Air Afrique ramp, he turned and looked back at me in perplexity, as if he'd only now grasped that all this could be snatched away forever by jet engines and his clutching eyes had decided the Ambassador's wife was the creature who made the rest verbiage. What had I come out of to be holding my hat on as we waved goodbye?

I'd never know if he was one of the kids who used to call me Cruella DeVil. But he was clutching a signed hardcover copy of *The Longest Day*. Now that I'd crossed out "Pammie Buchanan," the inscription read "To Sean-pronounced-*Seen*"—that's so he'd know it could only mean him—"with all good hopes for your own future work. Yours, Cornelius Ryan."

He left with the book but without his cannon. The birthday gift from Oui-bomey his mother had wangled through Portugal's consul never saw another country unless Djedjia counts. Virgil Scoleri flatly refused to spend taxpayer dough on shipping it Stateside, even though the Finns' storage allotment came in under the weight limit. Nan hasn't forgiven him, one reason I was surprised the year he showed up at her Christmas party. Rules are rules, and judgment calls based on taste weren't Virgil's to make. I still can't help thinking it may've been for the best.

As for the glorious girl, she was six months pregnant when they ascended the ramp. Believe me, I'd more than understand if she and Ned never considered "Carol" as a name for their lastborn, but would've been giving credit where credit was due. Back then, we could bet on the reason when couples had a belated new baby.

That was the future Stacy Finn, today over forty and diagnosed with pretty bad mental problems some years ago. Nan goes out to the West Coast to visit her often, not having much choice if she wants to see her youngest child. Not one of the chemical combos they've tried out has cured Stacy's terror of airplanes.

She was born in West Berlin, the Finns' next post after Nagon. Strangely enough, it too no longer exists.

At least here in the District, the only evidence Nagon ever did is a store near the upper limit of Georgetown on Wisconsin Avenue whose name may not surprise you: The Art of Nagon. One of its curiosities is that State Department families are seldom affected enough by a given post to alter their lives in its wake. Neither Nan Finn nor I has ever bought anything there; God knows we've got plenty of African tchotchkes, and ours were acquired at the source. Since we like Rich and Laurel, though, we both stop in every so often. They own it.

3. Esau

POSTED BY: *Pam*   Andy Pond had him later in Lisbon. Like me, if more amiably, Andy's flummoxed by fate's sense of humor in a game Pam once named American roulette. Neither of us could've guessed on a dare which dim name from our past would end up making us champions of Potusville's dinner-party quiz show.

Cadwaller's gone, Ned Finn preceded him. Andy himself is retired and unknown. Now pushing seventy, little Duncan McCork is one of the architects of this awful war.

Of course today no one knows him as Dunc. He's been Mack McCork since Nixon's second term, bobbing up in the cesspool of one American foreign-policy disaster after another. While a man who gets and keeps a new nickname in his thirties can safely be described as ambitious, even Hopsie had to admit the switch improved our former econ attaché's jawline.

Fools that we were, Andy and I thought we were shut of him twenty years ago. Not long after Cadwaller died, Duncan "Mack" McCork nearly got indicted for perjury after grinding the skeletons in the Reagan White House's closet down to pumice in his Congressional testimony over the Iran-Contra thing. To those of us who'd known him when, the hearings' real surrealism was the flashed title we kept having to blink at under his microphone and impossibly fierce new teeth.

Assistant *Secretary* McCork? Maybe it's for the best that Hopsie'd been too ill to pay much attention to appointments by the time that one got made. Yet his listlessness in following them was one of the dozen things that told me his long dying had begun in earnest.

Until Potus brought the former Dunc McCork back into the Department, I'd honestly thought he was either safely parked in a think tank's gunless turret or dead. I'd barely opened that morning's *WashPost* when the phone rang: "You know, Pam, those guys in the Econ cone always did have a lean and hungry look," said Andy. Like Cadwaller, like Ned Finn, Andy belonged to the Foreign Service's crème de la paper airplane: the political section.

In the flesh, albeit from a safe distance—Nan and I were under JFK's bust with our intermission wine, they far down the red carpet as Mack greeted Elliott Abrams and Jerry Bremer—I last laid mimsy borogoves on the McCorks two years ago at the Kennedy Center. The short grabby curly-haired Beth we knew in Nagon has grown quite grand and glassy-eyed, the default expression of someone who ignores twenty faces for each one she bares a smile at in public. She's the chairwoman of the National Endowment for the Humanities, goddessed here and lambasted there for her scourgings of left-wing bias in academia.

In the *WashPost*'s Style section, which could find strained whimsy in an outbreak of bubonic plague, they're often cutely hailed as the MackBeths. You'll never understand Potusville if you don't grasp it's meant as flattery—and taken that way, too.

I know I shouldn't waste ink on them here on daisysdaughter.com. I've got better things than Mack McCork to blog about as the light begins to change at last on Pam Buchanan's longest day.

POSTED BY: *Pam*   And—*oh, et puis zut*, as Celeste M'Lawa would say. The little shithead just exasperates me.

Like all Potus eaters, Mack McCork does the bad-penny routine on the Murphy Channel pretty regularly. Since this awful war began, I've seen him pontificate many a time to the lip-licking nods of one or another of my first husband's three heads. Call it Foreign Service snobbery or just Hopsie's widow's, but I can't help feeling the only relic of Cadwaller's time who's still active is letting us all down.

That's not only because he's swallowed Potus's view of the world and can be counted on to regurgitate it with the glee of a bulimic, whose faces are conspiracies with only one member. Whenever he's not the only guest, he's also got his fat nose up the crack of intellectual sock puppets thirty years his junior: Potusville's neocon Richelieus. Dunc was no heavyweight on either character or brains, but he'd still belonged to the old gang.

Since he was on hand the last time we got ourselves into this kind of mess, how could he not recognize the rerun's familiar lurch to disaster? Among ourselves, we mostly knew by 1966. That spring at an Annandale dinner party, Carl [Last Name Redacted] looked fatigued by his two years in Saigon.

"I guess you could say the python's out of the snake house for real," he said with a wince, recalling Pam's old warning about Ouibomey. "Even we can't build a cage big enough to talk it back in."

"Can't say I'd have picked you out to be Mr. Metaphor, Carl," I said, honestly trying to cheer him up. We were all so compassionate to fellow members of the insiders' club that I hadn't even reproached him for calling Eddie Whitling's brain aneurysm—"What that pompous bastard called reportage was giving aid and comfort, Pam"—a blessing in disguise.

"I'd like to think you didn't know me completely. I did want to tell you I was sorry to hear about that girl of yours—the goofy Embassy secretary who got pulled down by a shark. What was her name again?"

Perhaps it was thoughtless, but I'd always been curious. "Carl, did you ever—?"

He turned dark raging eyes on me. "No, Pam. I never *fucked* her. I *fucked* the other one, all right? And I can't remember her name either."

That was how people were suddenly talking then, with flare-ups of bitterness no one tried or needed to explain. Later that night I saw Carl [Last Name Redacted] impatiently reach a paper napkin out to a candle down the table and pull it back past three other guests' faces in flames to light someone's cigarette.

Buzz Sawyer's USAID tour in Phuoc Tuy province left even that drowsy man apprehensive. "Early on, I learned I couldn't argue with lieutenant colonels. By the end I couldn't argue with captains," he told us at a pool party in Falls Church that summer. "One more year and I'd have been dodging sergeants with my little trowel."

"Oh, hell, Buzz. *Plus ça change*," I said. "I've never heard you argue with anybody."

He gave me a defeated smile. "It wasn't my personality, Pam. It's because I was wearing a white shirt and they weren't."

At the brunch we threw in our Georgetown house to welcome the Warrens back from Athens that fall, Rich told us he was leaving USIS. "When a library's just one more American thing for kids to throw rocks at, and you can't blame them either? Well then."

"But what will you and Laurel do?"

"Play our Coltrane and remember, what else?" he said. "All the same, we didn't think we'd get old this young."

Ned Finn unexpectedly stayed hawkish longest, but he had the disease. He'd spent three years as chief of political section in Berlin, where we were probably more unequivocally—and thanks to the Wall, literally—on the side of the right than anywhere else. Besides, the Ned Finnish drug of JFK's *"Ich bin ein Berliner"* still lingered. Long-haired German students parading against our Asian war in streets protected by our troops had him gnashing his teeth and wanting a drink with Jayne Mansfield or somebody.

Knowing his vanities, I expect his only alternative would've been to eye braless Berlin girls bouncing alongside leonine-haired Berlin boys and feel help-lessly past his prime. Once he was back at the Department, boozing hard even for him, the bunker mindset claimed another victim of the fallacy that knowing our government's side of the story meant not knowing half but more.

Political romanticism takes many forms, Panama, and one of them is dog-gedness in the face of public incomprehension. Ned was plainly looking for the Galahad he'd left behind him, the reason I wonder how much headway Nan might have made if she'd just reminded him Jack Kennedy hardly drank at all and only smoked occasional cigars.

The future Mack McCork got off scot-free, since after Lisbon the nearest he came to Southeast Asia was a cushy posting in Tokyo. It was bound to give the worst of his temperament the upper hand, since men like him are all too apt to take Japanese decorum as reflecting a high estimate of them personally. The experience probably stood him in good stead when he came back to join Kissinger's NSC staff, recently depleted by resignations over the invasion of Cambodia. A working knowledge of Japanese decorum has always been useful to anyone eager to express a high personal estimate of Henry.

When he left government after Carter's election to take a job with Kiss-inger's new consulting firm, old hands were disgusted. If acting the toady to Kissinger at the Department was something too many FSOs had to endure, vol-unteering for the same chore in the private sector declared preference rather than duty. Even though he only spent a few years in New York before Reagan's inaugural pulled him back into the District's web, none of us ever really considered him a career man after that. He was just a political appointee who'd spent a while trapped in a career man's body.

As your dad knows even if you don't, bikini girl, every last one of Mack McCork's contributions to what even the Murphy Channel no longer calls a crusade has been dunderheaded. Putting him in charge of reconstruction over there made Katrina's aftermath look like the Kirov's *Swan Lake*, and when they brought him back to NSC afterward, even courteous Andy Pond said, "Shi-*ite*. Let's fold old Mack five ways and put him where the Sunnis don't shine."

He has the military expertise of a snowball, a grip of the region surpassed only by those who've watched *Lawrence of Arabia* even more times than he has—not that I'd bet Mack gets many chances to relish hearing himself called "McCork of Arabia" nowadays except when he's shaving—and a gift of command shared only by the NO SMOKING sign at an orgy. Somehow, in Potusville, that added up to an impressive range of knowledge. Only a man who didn't have a clue about such a *lot* of tricky things was up to the job of masterminding our Iraq venture.

Nonetheless, Mack will end up in the history books. Not so your great-grandfather, Ned Finn, Andy, and too many others who spent half a century doing their best to uphold what he's helped Potus blacken: the United States' good name abroad. Discounting some academic studies so unreadably desiccated you'd swear they were written by mummies, Cadwaller never shows up even in the ones about Vietnam, despite his three years as head of the Department's Policy Planning Staff.

One day in India, I asked if it bothered him that he hadn't appeared in any so far. While mostly futile (python, snake house, etc.), Hopsie's role hadn't been dishonorable. Looking quizzical, he only said, "What are you talking about? I'm in all of them, dear."

"You sure aren't in this one," I said, tossing whatever it was—Neil Halberd's *Brightest in the Fire?* Gerald Francis Sheehan's *Lake of Shining Lies?*—over to his end of the couch. Picking it up with a hum-what-have-we-here look, he wandered off to his study. Came back all of a minute later.

"Sometimes I don't understand you, Pam. I'm right where I belong, as usual. I'm sure you'll find me eventually."

When I did, I laughed. "Hopsie, you mean sometimes I still don't understand *you*," I called to his closed door. In the margin of a random page, my husband had drawn a small top hat.

POSTED BY: *Pam*   When Cadwaller and I came back from Nagon to Washington in 1964, far from spotting anyone on the lookout for pythons, we were brushed and gilded on all sides by our sunny country's belief the worst was over. We'd *had* our shock for the decade—Kennedy—but birds still sang and so, for children, did the Beatles. To us oldsters, the retrospective melancholy of that post-assassination reprise of optimism is that it didn't feel naive but earned. We'd taken the worst punch fate could throw, yet here we were on our feet. Still in the ring when the next bell's round rang, still America. Lyndon Johnson was popular *in New York City.*

That was when the District first became my home. *Regent's* reporter Pam Buchanan had done her stints there back in the war, staying with Jake Cohnstein in his Kalorama apartment. Eyeing its kitchenette as you might eye Grendel's cave, Pam Cadwaller had spent three months in drab Arlington housing while Hopsie prepared (Andy Pond's Checker limo!) for his new Ambassadorship in West Africa. I'd never experienced the city as much more than a motel with monuments. Aside from India and our foreign trips later, I've now lived here forty-two years.

It was different in the way-back-when. The Kennedy Center was a hole in the ground, not the glowing white Gitmo of the arts it can feel like today when the opera's too long and Roosevelt Island looks murkily worth swimming to over intermission wine. From just past the Treasury Building all the way to the base of Capitol Hill, the downtown streets off Pennsylvania Avenue were a clutter of clothing stores with prices on view in the window displays as if they'd been supermarkets, decrepit row houses, and a muzzy strew of bars no woman, black or white, would risk entering alone even in daytime—all swept away now by more commanding, squeaky-clean, safer but less flavorful renovation. The Metro only got built under Nixon and Ford, and we had a hard time believing as we made endless detours around the construction sites that *those* holes in the ground would ever amount to much.

Most blessedly of all, nothing was named for Ronald Reagan. Until I stopped flying, Pam made a point of growling "*National* Airport" at the necks of cabdrivers used to much worse. My prejudices on that score are nondenominational. As late as the Seventies, whenever I flew in or out of JFK, I'd be bothered that Jackie—of all people!—hadn't been sensitive to the loss of the Clio Airways poetry of "Pan Am from Idlewild," so truer to the tang of Jack's manner. But like Constantinople, Leningrad, Nagon, West Berlin, and Stacy Finn's mental health, Pan American Airlines no longer exists.

The now forgotten Thomas Wolfe to the contrary, I'm not sure only the dead know Brooklyn. Their inability or unwillingness to give street directions keeps the whole claim more or less moot. The only way to know Washington, D.C., is to roost here through multiple Presidencies, seven of them in my case before the final squalor of Chad Diebold renamed it Potusville. Old bags like me alternate between watching new productions of the same warhorse musical and madcap seasons when the latest artistic director smacks us out of the blue with Beckett, Pinter, or one of Sondheim's more eccentric ones.

Over lunches at Martin's or La Chaumière, we compare notes. The ingenue playing First Daughter this year has promise, but the Nixon staging's swordfight was better. It stayed fun for a long time.

Literalizing the conceit, people actually sang "Hello, Lyndon" to the tune of "Hello, Dolly." Herblock's LBJ cartoons in the *WashPost* favored Ned Finn's old standby *The Music Man*. Oh, it was definitely a musical, was 1964—not just for the Beatles fans, but for us stodgier wights too. Driving the George Washington Parkway as the leaves turned, we'd hear our inner radios playing *The Fantasticks'* "Try to Remember." Bliss it was to be alive, but to be middle-aged was very heaven.

Since Hopsie was now going to be singing the State Department equivalent of "Hello, Lyndon" to the President in person, I did feel obliged to confess to twenty-two-year-old Pam's knee-trembler with then Congressman Johnson in his Capitol Hill office in 1942. In our few back-and-forths about earlier innings, the quickest lay of the 20th century hadn't made the cut. I swear the reason was forgetfulness rather than shame or guile.

Cadwaller was never any damn good at getting perturbed about my doings before our marriage. "You'll never stop delighting me. I never know how or when." Then he frowned in the way I knew meant he was tickled. "You know, on the subject, I'm not sure I ever mentioned my other Pamela."

"Other what, mister?"

"I was in England that same year. You never *saw* me in my Lieutenant Commander's uniform, you know. I was reasonably dashing in a bald American way."

"So what was the story with your other Pamela?"

"Once or twice she saw me out of it. Not much more to add."

The pert Royal Navy Wren or fetching girl in Portsmouth I conjured up from the stereotype bin only gave way years later to someone less vague and more immediate. *"Hopsie!"* I boomed like a ceremonial cannon, turning to point one finger out our bay window *à la* Zola in the direction of a by then renowned Georgetown address. "You didn't mean Pamela *Harrima—*"

"Oh, Pam, don't be absurd. How could it have been? No woman by that name was known to anyone. Of course young Pamela Churchill was quite prominent."

"Cadwaller, tell me!"

"Whoever she was, it was only a weekend. I don't think she remembers. All I really got from it was a new word for the lexicon."

"Well?"

His eyes crinkled. "Funsy."

POSTED BY: *Not Pamela Harriman* Before his final months in office—of which more later, as the trad novelists say; sundown may keep me from describing the Taj Mahal's increasingly inert grandeur on one's twentieth trip there with a Congressional delegation, but only Potus on the elephone will stop *l'équipe* from getting to my White House *Piétas* here on plucky little daisysdaughter.com—I saw Lyndon Johnson only for a series of reception-line handshakes. If he recalled our encounter in the fall of '42, those weren't the occasions to reminisce about it. Anyhow, he always looked pretty glum in white tie. Texan enough to mistrust formal wear's designs on him, he was nonetheless Promethean enough that his only yardstick for success would've been Fred Astaire.

What may surprise my readers (if any, if any! Can't *somebody* post a comment? I've been at this since dawn, you bastards!) is that, with the retrospective exception of Franklin Roosevelt, LBJ was the only President of Pam's lifetime whom I revered. Spare me your whimpers about that crisply jaunty Kennedy élan.

Some fools out there may think I favor style over substance. Prose and social life—my specialties—are two arenas where they're Siamese twins, not Black Bart at odds with Sheriff Truegood. Not so American government, at least most of the time. Shove suave demeanor, say I. Get things done! Get things done!

Did he ever, and in the teeth of Washington's Camelotic court in exile. The bitterest courtiers would've rather seen Saint Jack's legacy wither on the Congressional vine than watch it rammed through into law with no elegance. East Coasters mocked him for his cottonmouth Hill Country accent, but which would you rather have, a President who prevented a new-kew-lear war? Or a dapper chap who called it "nucleah" and decided to start one?

In any case, to pretend that a man as volcanic, shrewd, alarmingly fragrant, opportunistically idealistic, holy and awful, vindictively generous and generously vindictive as Lyndon Johnson was *cornpone* just mixed spite with ignorance. It's true I was never subjected to an LBJ tonguelashing, just quickly why-Henry'd once in my youth and then plunked down in front of Cronkite over twenty years later to enjoy legislation's post-coital glow. But in '64 and '65, and even a lot of '66, you may as well know I idolized him.

That made Cadwaller snort, not because he didn't like Johnson. At the very least, Hopsie found him, let's say, funsy, and he saw far more of the man than I did. He simply thought idolatry was a self-indulgence to wait on until someone was dead or at least out of office. Till then, he'd stay alert to contingencies.

While he was obviously right in the not-so-long run, I still think I got the better end of the deal. LBJ was my Beatles, and the (internally) squealing thrills of Pam's two years of Lyndomania her most ecstatic experience of fandom. Previously not high on the to-do list outside marriage, as you may've noticed.

Callie Sherman disapproved, but hardly from Camelotic mopery. From her point of view, the *Kennedys* had been a bit common, with all that roughhouse touch football and wisecracking in public about their own gelt. Right she was too if you care, since all that kept her gimcrack American aristocracy able to believe it was one was agreement about the rules of engagement—or not—

with the great unwashed. Her grudge at the voters after LBJ's landslide election in his own right was that they'd retained a stablehand, understandably summoned in an emergency but nonetheless reeking of paddocks, to do the job of a butler.

At least the Shermans' farmhouse out near Middleburg didn't have one. Yes, that same equine spill of Virginia where Eileen Downslow still put the purr back in jodhpurs, though I never met her there or anywhere. We did see other horsewomen and horsemen here and there as we drove, but they weren't playing polo and Tom Buchanan had been dead since 1925. I doubt I even thought of him.

Anyhow, Callie and Cy knew a Jeeves wouldn't hit the right rustic note, so they settled for a handyman and a housekeeper. The handyman had the easiest job on the planet, since all he mostly had to do when they were there was wash their Cadillac in a rustic-looking way.

Cy was Deputy Under Secretary for something by then. Not yet transferred to Policy Planning, Hopsie was an Assistant Secretary, lower designation, in charge of the West African desk. Senior Department titles did have their Kabuki side; I'd tell you all about Assistant *Deputy* Under Secretaries if *l'équipe* had time.

Try to remember the kind of November. "Callie, don't be ridiculous." I knew I might as well be telling the farmhouse to grow wings and try to find Baltimore, but still. "Honestly, would you rather have Goldwater?"

"Of course! Say what you will, at least he's an idiot. Wiser heads would have prevailed and the like. We just couldn't come out and explain that, unfortunately."

"Why not?" The place honestly wasn't so bad, with the big stone fireplace near the throw rug I sat on and the wrought-iron weathervane over the mantel wondering what in God's name it was doing indoors. "It would've been charming."

"Oh, Pam, please! His supporters would've felt insulted and cranky. Everyone else would've thought we were *warning* them, or some such nonsense. Our people will just have to get better at fibbing for the good of the country, that's all."

"I'll tell the voters you said so."

"You would, wouldn't you?" Then her eyes turned ostentatiously wicked, indicating I was about to get zinged by Callie's odd humor. "I could swear they all think they're picking who owns the dealership, not who's selling the car."

"At least this one's not used," I laughed at her. (Nixon joke, bikini girl. Just Google and leave me alone.)

"Oh, drat! I was sure you'd rise to the bait. Hopsie, what's become of your wife and who is this?"

"Katharine Hepburn," said Cadwaller calmly. "Our secret's out, dear. Cy, you must've guessed all along she's who I wanted."

"Oh, Callie, stop pouting!" I told her. "I do know that deep down you mean every word. I'm just not going to get angry."

"But why not? It's your entertainment value."

"This week I'm on vacation. My guy won forty-four states."

POSTED BY: *Pam*   By early 1966, Panama—yes, we're now a mere twenty-four years from your birth—your great-grandfather was keenly anticipating another posting abroad. Temperamentally, Cy was more suited to representing Washington in Washington, since the Sherman grand manner went over better with foreign diplomats here than it might've with foreign populaces there. Hopsie was fundamentally nautical, and the point was a ship, large or small, to command.

On that count, you could say the Department misused him: just two Ambassadorships where lesser men racked up three or four. He'd have been ideal for Paris, but we both knew better than to so much as mention it. Like London and Rome, that was a prize denied the career service. It always went instead to a political ringer with a name, deep pockets or both—including, in later years, our deliciously Googlable Georgetown neighbor Pamela (Churchill, Hayward) Harriman, who got the gold cup when the Clintons were in.

Because of how the Department works, Cadwaller's knowledge of France, NATO, and de Gaulle ended up keeping us in Washington instead. Once you've worked up to Assistant Secretary for This and Deputy Under Secretary for That level in C Street's big aircraft carrier for paper planes, all the old hands know each other and there's a lot of mix-and-match spitballing in a crisis. Though

Africa was Hopsie's portfolio, he got pulled into the meetings after *le Géné-ral* pulled out of the alliance that spring. Nobody else on the fifth floor knew whether to shit on de Gaulle or go blind.

Apparently, Rusk was impressed by Cadwaller's appraisal. (Briefly: "You're looking for a practical gain to him when there is none. This is about uniqueness, which is obviously crucial to his famous 'certain idea of France.' If and when he's got to be practical about defense from a Soviet invasion, I'm sure he'll do what needs to be done in an eyeblink. But not without reason, his concept of a real emergency is different from ours," etc.) So when he needed to put in a new head of the Policy Planning Staff some months later, Cadwaller was one of the candidates whose file he asked for.

Having seen him in action during the Fourth Republic's long death throes, Pam herself was less bowled over, which pleased Hopsie no end. "Wait, wait! Twenty-two fucking years they've dealt with de Gaulle—and they still hear these as *insights?* Aw, Hopsie, you mean Rusk actually wondered, out *loud*, if the General was being *impulsive?* Don't they know impulsive and peremptory are two different things? Did you explain about drama, and timetables, and—?"

"Do you think there's a chance you've been married to me too long?" your great-grandfather asked kindly.

"Ask me in the next century," I said, which we both found humorous. Remember, 2001 wasn't even the name of a movie to us. In the way-back-when, the next century didn't seem to be thirty-four years off; it seemed to be, well, a century off. That I've now seen six years of the stupid post-millennial business— and had a full twenty sans Cadwaller, not to mention two missing Kelquen—is the sort of Methuselan slapstick that can make an old bag's mimsies gaze a beat too long at her own Rheumas' bickering writhe in her lap.

POSTED BY: *Pam* I don't claim any of us grasped the full implications. But 1967 was when it all went bad for my generation. So long as they were under draft age or had college deferments, it went great for the kids: they had *Sgt. Pepper.* No more able to avoid being surrounded by the thing than we could extinguish that same June's fireflies, we new-minted oldsters were beguiled by it too, perhaps for its strangely charming awareness of death.

Try to remember that kind Sergeant Pepper. As we weren't far from Georgetown University's campus, "A Day in the Life" was playing from two separate houses and one passing VW the day I Smith-Coronated the closing words of *Lucky for the Sun*: "And of course, we were loved." I hadn't expected to end on a note that puzzled and mournful, but writers never know what they know. That's what makes us different from scientists.

As I've explained more than once, the book came out a year later. Too soon after King's assassination and too soon before the murder in Los Angeles of the man who one hot day in West Africa had drilled me with eyes like a blue planet's twin Arctics and said, "I know where I am, Mrs. Cadwaller." We hadn't enjoyed each other's company much, but if you clip my name there may be worse last words.

Amused as he was by "When I'm Sixty-Four," particularly when sung by a quartet of English ragamuffins thirty years younger than he, Hopsie was immune to *neiges d'antan* melancholy. His passion was the art of the possible, mine for impossible art: that was our union, as sacred to us as the capitalized one was to Lincoln. But Policy Planning was hell on my husband, above all because he had a rare gift for it; as a very junior officer, he'd been trained by the section's founding director. The world, life, and Washington didn't and hadn't, and Cadwaller was smart enough to know going in who would win.

They'd asked him, though, and he persevered. "I think LBJ's gotten a bit fond of me," he drawled on the phone from C Street one night that year. Seldom used, even Cadwaller's drawl was on the terse side.

"Cadwaller!" I was perplexed by his tone. "Is that *bad?*"

"Who can say? Problem is, it's got nothing to do with affection as the rest of us know it. Combination of antagonism, yearning, craving for ownership, sense of loss we don't understand and can't share. Well, maybe that's not so far from how the rest of us know it! But with him, it's all on display."

"What are you going to do, Hopsie?"

"Oh, my job."

POSTED BY: *Sgt. Pam's Lonely Hearts Club Band* Halloween came a week early in the District that year. It wouldn't really go away until Cadwaller's fellow pipe-smoker Gerald Ford had bumbled and burbled his way through imitating Ike redux. Reassuring the hinterlands, Manhattan included, that life in our neck of the woods really was fairly dull and no cause for alarm.

By fall '67, of course we'd had the kids awhile. Our local Sgt. Peppers, trying to turn what bits they could of the District into sham San Franciscos. Because of the campus or under the impression it was our bohemian quarter, they congregated in Hopsie's and my Georgetown. Wisconsin Avenue's downhill amble past O Street acquired a head shop squeezed into a former blind alley, a proudly slovenly record store that didn't stock *Victory at Sea, The Music Man,* or even Callie Sherman's beloved *Turandot,* and a used-denim emporium across from Martin's.

All gone now *sauf* the good old neighborhood restaurant I'd first eaten in with Jake Cohnstein as the *WashPost* headlined Bataan and Corrigedor and ate in last with Andy Pond and Nan Finn only weeks ago. The District's ability to quietly stay itself here and there—cf. Dixie Liquor; cf., for that matter, my falcon roost here at the good old Rochambeau—remained my city's great talent even after its mutation into Potusville.

Even so, Cadwaller and I had never seen what Washington could look like when a hundred thousand protesters crowded into it. We'd still been in Nagon when King gave his "I have a dream" speech; Hopsie and Ned Finn'd had to rely on *Time, Newsweek,* and the Department's own obtuse official cable to brief the Palais du Président's new occupant. They did a good enough job that N'Koda greeted his people next Independence Day—theirs, not ours—with *"Moi aussi, j'ai un rêve."*

Try to remember the kind of October. VWs with New Hampshire and Massachusetts plates trolling in vain for parking spaces under oranging and lemoning leaves. Buses whose banners boasted they'd rolled in all the way from Chicago and Ann Arbor to give LBJ what for about Vietnam. Sleeping bags tossed from highway-grimed vans up to blue-jeaned girls on front stoops. Under the old Riggs Bank's gold dome at the corner of Wisconsin and M, an Uncle Sam on stilts walked around wearing a sandwich board: "I Want *You* to Burn Your Draft Card."

And yes, Tim: I know you've explained to me more than once that getting New Leftists and hippies mixed up is ahistorical. Hell, I'm not writing a book about them! I was a fifty-six-year-old American diplomat's forty-seven-year-old wife, just trying without too much hassle to get down M Street to La Chaumière for lunch with Laurel Warren, the new co-proprietor of The Art of Nagon. The antiwar hoopla reminded me fondly of the liberation of Paris turned freakshow until I caught on with a start that they thought Hopsie and I were the Germans.

Pam hadn't yet started writing checks to Gene McCarthy's Presidential campaign, since as yet there wasn't a Gene McCarthy Presidential campaign to write checks to. But I'd turned against the war soon after Cadwaller changed jobs. Primarily conversationally and only among friends, since being married to Hopsie limited my options. He might've been more than a top hat in the margin of the *WashPost*'s news section if it came out that the impetuous wife of Policy Planning's head had gotten herself arrested at a rally.

Even over a decade after *Glory Be*, I wasn't wholly anonymous in my own right. I fully expected the big demonstration all the out-of-towners were piling in for would be something I'd read about in the papers and watch on TV, and in literal terms that was the case. My bit part in what historians now know as the March on the Pentagon came two evenings earlier.

Blame the District's never overstocked pond of local parties who could pass for literary in visiting New Yorkers' eyes for the frazzled phone call I got from a woman I barely knew. Some Georgetown prof's wife, most likely met through the Warrens. Now that they were no longer in government, Rich and Laurel kept surprising us with the other crags and gullies of District life they found every bit as interesting as our eternal shop talk.

"Pam, I'm sorry," she said rapidly. "I don't know where to turn. Do I remember you saying you know Dwight Macdonald?"

"I'm not really sure if I do or just did. We haven't bumped into each other for nigh on twenty years." I saw no point in adding he'd given *Glory Be* its single most withering review: "It's a mug's game," and so on.

"Well! I don't know how we got talked into it. You sign one little petition too many, and boom! All *hell* breaks loose. I mean, of course [husband's name lost to Pink Thing's archives] and I are against the war. We want to do what we can, but you don't expect *social* pressure to be *your* pound of flesh. Is that a mixed metaphor?"

"Not quite, but keep at it. What can I do to help?"

"So help me, we're hosting a *party*. I mean!, did Rosa *Luxembourg* have days like this? And all these Manhattan *people* are coming. Macdonald, and I think Robert *Lowell*." Her voice trembled: "And *Mailer*."

"Sorry, I can't stand Lowell's poetry. Some men write with their penises, he writes with his nose."

"Pam, *please!* Now isn't the *time*."

"For literary criticism? It's always the time. I wouldn't give a rap if he's opposed the war in Vietnam since 1620."

"Can't you at least stop by? You know how they'll act! 'Oh, it's just a modest little Our Nation's Capital with no breeding, but I think you'll be amused by its presumption.' And then they *aren't*, even. Amused, for God's sake! Amused." Then a fresh horror scuttled into her voice: "And *Pam!* What if one of them *writes* about it? About *us*, about *me*? And our *place*, and my *food*, and—"

"Really, lassie! Calm down. I'm sure preservation in our literature is one thing you don't need to worry about. It might be nice to see Norman, though."

"Oh! I didn't know you knew *him*," she squeaked, half relieved and half dubious.

"We spent a few months in '48 waving at each other across the bestseller list. Him on his way up, me on my way down. It's social life of a sort."

Only as I hung up did I realize one oddity. Even if C Street's aircraft carrier for paper planes hadn't been detaining him deep past dark on most days, Hopsie obviously couldn't come to a protesters' buffet. Since my hostess knew that, I was being invited somewhere in Washington for the first time as Pamela Buchanan. It felt a bit like trying on a nine-year-old cocktail dress and seeing whether I could still scoot the zipper past that tricky sixth vertebra.

In my hostess's defense, I'll swear on a stack of vintage *Harper's* magazines that I've been to many parties worse than hers. It just didn't matter; her dread was well founded. Even far grander District gals than she quail at hosting Manhattan's self-impressed fire brigade.

If we behave like Washingtonians and discuss what interests us, they're incredulous at not being the center of attention—particularly when, say, Bob Dole's maneuver in the Senate that day gets the nod over their luster. If we nervously slip into trying to please them by acting like would-be or exiled New Yorkers, they turn derisive at a fraud that can be authenticated only by skyscrapers outside the window. A few salient points in our favor—e.g., our city's different purpose than theirs, its not colorless history (*we* saved the Union; *they* just had draft riots), its vastly greater access to new-kew-lear, nucleah, and nuclear weapons—don't make much impression on their eggy noggins.

Since her local crowd wasn't mine either, I felt dismayed on confronting her ululant living room once my coat had been shed and she'd carried it off to mate it to some unknown bedspread. Saw our surrounded out-of-town ring-ers right off, of course, along with some girls I knew had to be imports. Neither flower chickies nor *Vogue* models, they were synthesizing the two in a way on which New York had all but the patent that year. Our local edition would've been either scragglier or more Republican.

Then Dwight, as I think *l'équipe* has reported in some long-ago posting on Pam's longest day, hurried over to greet me with the arms of a bear snuffing a forest fire. Understand, he wasn't asking forgiveness for scorching *Glory Be's* hash. I was *being* forgiven for sharing a name with the stranger whose book had provoked him.

"PAM!" he explained. (Cribbed from Ring Lardner, and sorry.) "What was the last thing I saw you at? That sad Buñuel screening at MoMA?"

"Yes, and my God, what a memory."

"He's doing better these days. Have you seen *Belle du Jour*?"

"No, and don't torture me, monster. The last I heard, us poor Americans won't get our chance for months. I damn near hopped over to Paris when I saw that pic of Deneuve in her bra."

Fortunately, Dwight never noticed confessions. I suspect Mrs. Macdon-ald could've remarked she'd just murdered a lover and gotten an hour's cheery thoughts on Julien Sorel. Still, his next question did make me miss Manhattan: "You working on something these days?"

"Little itsy-bitsy something." Fair description in prepublication preview of *Lucky for the Sun,* mere plankton in the mouth of Dwight's whale. "I know what you've been up to, though, and Dwight! I don't see how you do it."

"Don't see how I do what?" he asked with a conjuror's combined pleasure and wariness.

"Well, think how it looks from the outside. Here you spent the Forties trying rather heroically to keep us all reminded of radical politics. Now the revolution's here, the barricades are going up as we speak—and you're off in dark rooms reviewing movies for *Esquire.* I swear if you tried climbing Everest, you'd be on top of Mt. Kilimanjaro by sunset. Looking around in an interested way."

"Let the last part be my epitaph, then." And it should be: Dwight Macdonald, 1906–1982, mountaineer. "Pam, do you know—sorry, wrong pecking order. Norman, do you know Pam Buchanan?"

Wearing a three-piece pinstripe suit—not what I'd've picked to storm the Pentagon in, but I believe it's the same one he has on in the photographs of his arrest two days later—he was nipping bourbon the way dogs only wish they could car tires. But his eyes were most blue and his handshake was pleasant: "No, I don't think we've met."

"I do know a friend of yours, though."

"Oh, who?"

"Doc Selzer." He was the Holt editor who'd proposed placing the Webster's definition of "incongruous" in front of "The Gates of Hell" in *Nothing Like a Dame* days. Then he'd moved on to Putnam's, where I'd gotten some funny letters from him about watching a bleary Norman show up with more revisions of *The Deer Park.*

"Oh, Doc! Of course. Wonderful guy. Really fabulous, super. How is he these days?"

"I thought you'd know better than me," I admitted. "But I heard the booze got him."

"Selzer's an alkie? That's not the destiny I'd have picked out for him."

I decided against saying that from an existentialist—Norman's chapeau of choice when mounting a hobbyhorse—talk of people's destinies is an oxymoron. Of course they don't think twice about that when it's someone else. Before

I could find a new topic, his eyes—not at all Bobby Kennedy's Arctics, more the color of bourbon if bourbon were blue and had interested ice floating in it— grew alert and then pleased with themselves.

"Wait, wait. *Pamela* Buchanan, yes? Now I've got it. The *Dame*."

"Yup. The naked, dead dame, you could say."

He laughed. "Maybe I should've read it."

"Well, maybe I shouldn't have read *An American Dream*. Honestly, Norman—I've got to ask, since I bet nobody else has the guts. What do you think your biographers'll make of your mother being named Fanny?"

The joke's too long to explain to a bikini girl, but it won me a real look of evaluation. I might be one of those ladies he loved to call "wicked"—not to mention "ladies"—and hence worthy of Normanic interest.

Or I might be a Washington broad with more frenzy than manners, and my guess why I got bumped to the lesser pigeonhole was the old brindle mop, now all gray. A wicked lady would've dyed hers. Callie Sherman's is jet black at ninety.

"Oh, probably no more than they would've made of your mother being named whatever she was." While there was no cruelty in the delivery, I knew I was being dismissed, and so what? There was always Vidal. But Dwight's hand restrained me—or rather, since I hadn't turned yet, vouched for me.

"Now, *Lyndon's* mother," he said, and believe me the way people said "Lyndon" by then was the opposite of singing "Hello, Lyndon" back in 1964, "was or is named Rebekah. In the Old Testament, that would make him Esau, who sold his birthright for a mess of pottage. Norman, don't you think 'Esau Baines Johnson' has a touch of dark majesty?"

"Not for me. Maybe I just can't picture him coming from any womb," Norman said in a revving staccato. "Honestly, Dwight, I think it's missing the boat to see a man like Johnson as altogether human. I think at some level he's some kind of energumen, some frightening force glued together out of our darkest impulses in the shape of a President."

"Oh, Norman," Dwight said, but stouter critics than he had failed to play brakeman to the Mailer locomotive.

"Without any forethought! Be it said. Be it said," he went on, free hand raised and voice now so far past staccato I swear Cagney would've sounded like

NPR's Diane Rehm next to it. "Try this, try this: the way you might idly mold bits of soap in the shower, mmm?" [Free hand twisting to demonstrate, bourbon glass in the other looking up sadly for Pop's lost attention.] "We don't want to step out, grab a towel, and hunt up a fresh bar. Too much bother, the hell with it. Gang, we're in the shower already! Let's *make* one."

"Norman, what you do in the shower and what I do in the shower—"

"Ah! Ah. But you play God with soap at your peril, Dwight. Don't you see? As we lathered and hummed one fine morning, scrubbing off—what? Ah, of course: Dallas—you could say some dark need had just made us produce an avatar of the national beast at its most demented, when the rider and bronco are one." As he lowered his soap hand and refound his bourbon glass, its blue twins in his eyes waited for the Nobel or the hook.

"Holy shit, Norman," I brayed. "You *talk* that way, too?"

He grinned like one of Rafael Sabatini's pirates, plainly having heard that one before from Mailer virgins. "It's called value for money, Buchanan, and my *father's* an accountant with gambling debts. Make of that what you will."

"Well, just for the hell of it, you might try a *leedle* bit of compassion for the President of these Yew-nited States." A Lyndomaniac no more, I still missed my two years of inner squealing at the Great Society. "Don't you realize how many people—not me, but many—would call 'the rider and bronco are one' a description of you?"

It was the second time I'd interested him. "Oh, I like that," he congratulated us both. "It's not too often I hear a theory of me I haven't already tested out and discarded. Oh, yes! That's good, Dwight, don't you think? Lyndon and Norman. Two riders fused with two horses, galloping at cross purposes in the American night. We're each trying to warn our fellow citizens the other is coming."

And I might've been forty-seven, but for a lively bourbon-blue moment only undyed gray hair spared my haggard plum from prospective service to American literature. It passed; our hostess hovered. Trying to locate not only podium but tone.

"Can I *possibly* talk you two literary giants into tasting some of my food?" she said, resting her hands in the air above Dwight's and Norman's forearms. "Oh! And Pam, you too of course."

"I'm afraid we dwarves need to go. All that kneeling around the glass coffin is just hell on our short little legs. No, I'm teasing you, silly! I've had a lovely time, but I've got to get home. Cadwaller's waiting." (I'm not sure what prompted that fib.) "Just tell me where you put my coat."

"Oh, the back bedroom. I'll—"

"Not at all. This place can't be so big I won't find it," I said, since she was clearly pained by the thought of leaving her two Manhattan sequoias to go help a pine tree glue on some needles. "Thataway?"

The Picasso Quixote was on inevitable display midway down the hall. The Ben Shahn was a bit out of date, though. Then I came to what must be the right door, pushed it open, and stopped. Even to oldsters like me, that sweet smell needed no introduction. And no by-your-leave either, given place and occasion.

On the bed heaped with coats, mine included, knelt two of the flowerized *Vogue* models or *Vogue*-ified flower chickies I'd seen in the living room earlier. The one with the joint pooching her lips and her knee on my coat was nude to the waist with her arms framing her head. The other, bent with hair canted in a Kirstenish spill—not that her *semblable* had even been born yet, but memory plays hopscotch sometimes—was painting a daisy's petals around the first one's left nipple, having already finished her right.

"Oh, hi!" said the done and budding daisies' new owner, lazily smiling. "I'm Claire. Are you doing yours too? She's good at this, trust me. She does bullseyes too, but heck, at a protest I think that's just asking for it."

First thought, appallingly bourgeois: *my* coat. A knee not mine held my coat pinned. With one done and one budding daisy eyeing me like two periscopes, I could no more have gone in to retrieve my usurped coat than I could've accepted an invitation to shoot up.

To stand in the doorway explaining and pointing would've been not only humiliating but an insult to two girls who were fellow guests and not maidservants. Besides, Claire as my coat's pinner would no doubt be its fetcher, one done and one budding daisy miming a waltz as she moved her knee, dipped, straightened back up, skipped off the bed, and came toward me with my coat held out and the waltz not yet done, and thank you but no.

Mumbling a handy Goldwynism—"Oh, no. Include me out"—I backed instead until I found the doorknob and pulled. Had an unpleasant memory of the Lotus Eater leaving her clothes and suitcases as she fled Provincetown forty years earlier. Heard a syrupy gurgle of giggles before Kirsten and Claire began quietly singing, but I'm fairly sure they weren't singing "All You Need Is Love" to me.

The proof poor Pam was now antediluvian was that it hadn't been dramatic to them. No panic at all at what they evidently didn't see—but how could they not?—as an even faintly sexualized, even mildly compromising situation. True, I was female, but their age combined and a stranger. Yet they'd just been happy with what they were doing, saw no need to explain it wasn't what it looked like or even *was* what it looked like. Claire hadn't shifted her knee and clapped on Pam's coat, which would've been the coat's former owner's first instinct.

I'd liked that coat a lot. To my fleeting panic, so'd Hopsie, but I was calmed by one of the few ways my husband resembled most men. He'd be no more likely to ask what had become of it than I'd be to willingly dawdle in Georgetown Pipe and Tobacco, the one place in Washington where I was often reminded my Cadwaller'd told me that as a boy he'd loved train sets.

Knowing our hostess as slightly as I did, I'd have been reluctant to phone up next day with inquiries. My missing coat might have forced us to turn italicized friends. Since I couldn't be there myself, something in me liked the idea of Claire going to the March on the Pentagon with one done and one budding daisy hidden in Pam Cadwaller's hairy old coat. Rather liked the idea of swaying, enjambed, with arms framing my head as Kirsten gave me two bullseyes, too, but from anywhere but inside my mind it would've looked like farce and not *neiges d'antan* poetry.

Keen observer of humanity that he was, Norman made nothing of the fact that I'd vanished to retrieve a coat and reemerged coatless. Hell, he'd probably had to leave his *shoes* behind more than once. A fresh glass of bourbon nearby, he hailed me.

"Buchanan, you're leaving us?" he called, handing off pen and a copy of that bum new novel of his to our hurt (she'd done the stuffed cream-cheese tomatoes herself) but bribable hostess. "Will you be marching on Saturday?"

This wasn't the time, place, or man to explain about Cadwaller's job. "I couldn't for love or money."

"Anyone can. LBJ could. Isn't that the point of this insane country?"

"Once upon a time I would've. But these days for me it's all Matthew Arnold."

"I'm sorry?"

"Oh, Norman! You must know: 'Now I only hear its melancholy, long, withdrawing roar retreating.' And so on and whatever."

Even though I hadn't planned to advertise myself on my way out, I'd interested him a third time. "What is that from?"

"Mr. Mailer, do you mean to say you've never read 'Dover Beach'?"

"Maybe in college. You know what they say, we all had a first wife."

"I didn't. Not really."

POSTED BY: *Pam*   When the Finns came back from Germany, I saw first that Sean-pronounced-Seen now wore glasses redoodling him as less spooky than spooked, next that Nell had grown gawky and uncomfortably pubescent. A Berlin-born wiggle named Stacy had eyes too young to grasp the perils of augmenting a family we'd all thought was complete. There were times when the State Department's magic carpet seemed to get stuck in the revolving door of Nagon's Palais du Président.

Nan hadn't changed much, since the whole point of being the glorious girl was to see how much life she could leap at without changing much. But Ned was forty and hated it, rabbit-punched by a clerical error at odds with Ned Finnness. Nan told me that when they last got invited to a costume party—waning custom in our crowd—he'd been eager to give himself Beatle bangs. Of course the Beatles themselves no longer had any.

"Oh, his work is still good. No doubt about that," Cadwaller reported a month or so later. He didn't have Ned in Policy Planning, but the Department wasn't that huge. "But some cog's getting stuck there. He'd still rather be promising: someone's clever lieutenant. Not so happy when he's where the buck stops on that part of the corridor."

That winter on C Street, so many lights stayed on most nights that our big aircraft carrier for paper planes looked like the *Titanic* to Capitol Hill's distant iceberg. Even on our way somewhere else, we'd all automatically check our husband's floor. Night protests terrified Nan when she had to drive the Finns' down-at-heels Fiat to collect hers, since even a few minutes' delay might inspire restless, ruddy forty-year-old Ned to nip out for a drink.

Then a taxi the Finns couldn't afford would lug the half burst suitcase he often resembled back from the District at some ungodly hour, and she had a hard time not blaming the caveman-haired wraiths in field jackets holding candlelight vigils when she was just trying to get across Memorial Bridge. Didn't they know how all the bills scared her, didn't they understand she hadn't started this war? She told me long afterward that fighting down the impulse to honk sometimes drove her to tears.

As for me, it must've been soon after New Year's that a call came I'd somehow expected since I laughed at Callie Sherman in Middleburg and said, "My guy won forty-four states." Licking and sealing Pam's first contribution to Gene McCarthy's Presidential campaign, I picked up.

"I'm at the Mansion," Cadwaller said a tad grimly. "You're invited for dinner."

"Hopsie, what are you talking about?" Not only were the formal White House events I'd gone to on his arm, seeing LBJ only in the receiving line, laid on months in advance, but there hadn't been many of *those* in a while. "When?"

"Now. The meeting went late—three or four of us here from State and Defense. He wants company."

"Can you talk? Are you trapped? Is it bad?"

"It could be," he said with false casualness. "The First Lady's in Texas, of course."

"And *that's* bad?"

He kept his voice light. "I've been told it can be very."

POSTED BY: *Pam*   In spite of the protesters who by then scruffily gathered in Lafayette Square nearly at random to heckle its occupant, the Executive Mansion's security was much less imposing in those days. Traffic flowed freely on Pennsylvania Avenue past a sidewalk as yet unridged by concrete dragon's teeth to guard against truck bombs. Even so, to avoid inciting the demonstrators, I was told to park off the Ellipse and present myself at the South Gate instead.

Which I did, feeling uncomely. Hopsie hadn't had time to give me advice on what I should wear, so I'd tried to approximate formality without ostentation in a high-collared blouse and long wool winter skirt. By good luck the gray brindle mop had recently been on a trip to the hairdresser's—yes, I'd tagged along too—and looked decent enough in a back knot. All the same, I'd only been to the White House before in white gloves, a full evening gown, and a silk shawl I liked. Wearing wool gloves instead gave me pause, and in spite of the cold I tucked them into my purse before giving my name.

Escorted up the South Portico's steps by a crisp Marine in dress blues— he was the one in white gloves tonight, and at least he wouldn't die in Hué tonight—I got handed off to an usher in the icy blast that swerved around the large door as he opened it. He took me by elevator to the second floor of the East Wing, which I'd obviously never laid eyes on: never seen more than the big reception rooms downstairs. These were the family quarters, if not for too much of a family since Lynda and Luci both opted for matrimony. *The First Lady's in Texas, of course.*

It looked almost ablaze, since they kept all the lights on in every room until the President retired for the night. I had no clue what to expect. This was Lyndon Baines Johnson, whom I'd once heard relieving himself noisily in a Congressional office's washbasin. Hopsie had been in the Cabinet Room the day LBJ stunned a visitor by standing, unzipping, hefting, and bellowing, "Tell me, does Ho Chi Minh have anything like *this?*"

My usher led me to the small family room off the Truman Balcony. Yes, past the chappie no doubt well versed in American dialects whose lap braced the briefcase containing new-kew-lear, nucleah, and nuclear codes. Of the five men and two other stunned wives seated on the three uncomfortably close striped couches that boxed in one big armchair at the far end, of course for me there were only two faces at first.

Cadwaller's looked strained. Johnson's looked, well, amazingly like Lyndon Johnson's, rather more so than it ever had in receiving lines. Tieless and jacket-less, shirtcuffs turned back on his arms and shirt's pale nether billows leaking all over his beltline—four sartorial details distinguishing him from the other men in the room—he set down his glass and looked up. Though his eyes were as incapable of widening as those of any man's I've known, their dark-lidded cavelets showed more of a brightening chink than I'd have expected.

"Well, now! This must be Mrs. Hopsie. Isn't that what they call you, Cadwaller?"

Hopsie gave a tired smile. "Well, some do, sir, yes."

"Think I'll appoint myself one of 'em. Mrs. Cadwaller, you come give your Hopsie a nice kiss on the cheek. You other folks introduce yourselves, will you?"

The only unwifed man present aside from the President didn't need to. "Why, hello, Carl!" I said.

Nodding exhaustedly, Carl [Last Name Redacted] shifted farther down on the couch to give me more room on its stripes next to Cadwaller. Sitting, I squeezed Hopsie's arm briefly. Completing the usual extent of our greetings in public, he patted my hand.

"Aw, hell. I said a kiss, didn't I?" LBJ grunted. "Are you another of these women who's plumb forgotten how to treat a good man, Mrs. Cadwaller? Your Hopsie's been at it all *day*."

I felt like a seal being trained and my lipstick was fresh, redaubed by yellow light in the car's rearview mirror before I got out. Puckering up like Fran Kukla in *Hamlet*, I quickly smooched your great-grandfather's cheek, atypically peppered since he'd shaved before dawn and it was past ten at night.

"Now that's better," LBJ said. "None of you knows just how hard your men work, but I do."

I couldn't help wondering if the other two couples had been put through the same performance, and as you may have noticed, we hadn't obeyed LBJ's other instruction. I never did learn their names. The Army bird colonel's lady had streaked blonde hair and about eight or nine cheekbones before I quit counting: the Fort Bragg version of a fashion plate. Measuring everyone's hemlines and then glancing down at her pumpkin knees, the Pentagon civilian's wife was not only as chubby as Judy Agnew but shared her simpleton gift for beaming into the abyss with as much paralyzed joy as if it were a vanity mirror. You won't know who that is and won't ever need to, bikini girl, but for reference, the

Second Lady of the as yet unborn Nixon Administration spent most of it looking like she'd missed her calling as some better carnival's dunking clown.

Fumbling a bit, LBJ pressed a button. Kaboom? Clearly not, as here I sit
inputting almost forty years later in a world more or less in one piece. The mess
steward's time matched any mushroom cloud's, though.

"Felix," said LBJ, "you can go tell the kitchen we're about ready to eat."

"Right away, Mr. President. What would you like to have?"

"God *damn* it! Do I have to make every puny decision in this damn mouse-
trap? I do not give a plug damn. Food! Just so long as it's meat. Burgers, sirloin,
buffalo for all I care. Cut Hubert's leg off, you jackass. Oh, and find out what
Mrs. Hopsie here might care to drink."

"If I could just have a club soda with lemon, that's fine," I squeaked. Not
Pam's usual register or cocktail request, but there's a first time for everything.

"No, no, no, no, no," warned LBJ, a Presidential finger instantly waggling.
"Both these other damozels tried that one too. My God, doesn't anyone know
how to unwind anymore? Scotch or bourbon?"

"Scotch. Water and ice," I told Felix faintly. It came in under a minute.

"There now. That's better," LBJ told us. "You know, I always like spending
time with young folks, I do. Ask my old Congressional staff. 'Course back then
they more or less had to be young, considering what I could pay 'em and how
hard I worked 'em."

If a single one of us there wasn't past forty, I don't know wrinkles and
creased necks from holes in the ground. And of course, thanks to the hour and
their jobs, the men looked even older than they probably were: Cadwaller's
age in advance, you could say. By then all the real youngsters were in Lafayette Square, or holding teach-ins at Columbia or Berkeley, or being inducted,
or dead.

"Mrs. Cadwaller, your husband plays it pretty close to the vest. I wasn't sure
I believed you even really existed and that is a fact. But now I can see why he's
kept you away from the White House."

This wasn't the moment to explain he'd met me four or five times at receptions—differently dressed, to be sure. With any President, there is no such
thing as that moment. You take your lumps.

"Why, thank you, Mr. President," I said, no doubt sounding perplexed. Even the Buchanan gams weren't what they had been, one reason my hemline made Judy Agnew's look like a miniskirt.

He leaned in like my confessor. I could smell his breath, which was loamy. I could practically smell his deodorant souring in its two crinkled Alamos. "So tell me," he said. "What's Cadwaller's secret?"

Recall, Hopsie was sitting right next to me. On the facing couch, poor Judy Agnew's eyes had just glazed with fear. She'd glanced at her husband to recall whether he had a secret and she knew it.

Startled enough to put a hand to my high-collared blouse, I laughed nervously. "I'm sorry! I don't have a clue."

"'Course you do. What makes your Hopsie tick? You can trust me."

"I'm afraid there's no secret at all, Mr. President," I floundered as best I could. "As the kids say these days, 'What you see is—'"

I suspect mentioning the kids was what did it. When addressing the man for whose public pronouncements the term "credibility gap" was invented, quoting "What you see is what you get" might not've been stellar either.

"Balls. Harvard men," LBJ roared, "*always* have secrets. They damn sure have 'em from me! And *West* Pointers, now," he went on, making the Army bird colonel's fidgety hands nearly do something West Pointers never do—hide the ring—"are just a bunch of smug Freemasons dressed up as soldiers, you know that, Mrs. Cadwaller? By God, if Congress would let me, I'd let ROTC take over the works and have you gold-ring nuggeted bastards put under arrest as an illegal cult. How'd it come 'Country' comes *third* in your book? I went to Southwest State Teachers' College, San Marcos! Where in hell'd you say you went to school, son?"

The Pentagon civilian not only hadn't but clearly didn't want to: "Rensselaer."

"Mm-hm. Another bright fellow who's had all the answers since he was in didies. Sonny, do you know the one thing you have not said to your President since four goddam p.m.? 'I don't know, Mr. President.' 'I'm just not sure, Mr. President.' Good goddam Christ. If McNamara just once, just once in his sanctified life, had said 'I don't know, Mr. President'—'I'm not sure, Mr. President'—'No goddam craphouse idea, Mr. President! We're as slaphappy as poontang from Pyongyang and you'd do better not counting on us. This thing could go either way or somewhere else or nowhere or Jupiter or all up in smoke, but we can't say which for pigeon shit in an envelope and the Lord sure does work in mysterious ways.' Had you said that just once to me or to God knows Jack Kennedy, why then *maybe!* Just maybe. But no, damn it, you don't—"

He'd heaved to his feet, one forefinger sweeping north. "You don't, you won't ever, sonny, even in your worst nightmares, won't hear all of them in the park shouting, 'Hey, hey—*Rensselaer Institute!* How many—how many—did you—did you'—*fuck!*"

Quaking, he dropped back in his chair. Passed a weary hand over his face before squeezing the bridge of his nose. "What about you, Carl?" he asked quietly.

"I don't tick anymore, Mr. President," said Carl [Last Name Redacted]. "I did once, but no more. Just not worth it."

"Moot question, you mean?"

"Yes, sir. Moot question."

"I stuck it out two years at Barnard before quitting," I said brightly. "I just couldn't see much point—not with that great big wonderful world waiting out there."

Johnson's big grateful paws clamped on Pam's future Rheumas. "Then, little missy, you just may be the smartest woman—smartest *person*, hell—in this room. I remember that great big wonderful world awful well."

Not as well as he thought he did, but it *had* been the quickest lay of the 20th century. "Well, I don't have so much to show for it," I apologized.

"Hell, look at me," LBJ said. "Come on, let's get something to eat."

POSTED BY: *Pam*   We all rose as he did. Then the President led us out into the hall and through a portico into the family dining room, where places had been set for nine. Only Mrs. [Last Name Redacted] was either unavailable or nonexistent. "Felix! Where in hell is our food?"

"Coming right away, Mr. President."

"Well, get us all another round while we're waiting. Make mine double."

The drinks beat the food by about thirty seconds. But the food took three mess stewards to bring. So far as I could tell, they'd emptied the larder: plates of steaks, ribs, and burgers with and sans cheese. No rump roast of Vice-President Humphrey, but I could see how you'd want to baste that a bit. We each had individual bottles of ketchup, mustard, Worcestershire, A-1 steak and hot pepper sauce at our place settings.

"Anybody here got a cigarette?" LBJ asked and the table froze.

With one possible exception—Judy Agnew, who'd started fumbling in her lap with a beatific peer into the good old vanity-mirror abyss before she recalled that she'd left her handbag back in the sitting room and didn't smoke anyhow—everyone at that table must've known the man asking had quit a three-or-four-pack-a-day habit after a near fatal heart attack in summer '55. Bull market in those too that year: President Eisenhower's, which very nearly let us enjoy President Nixon much earlier in life, came along under three months after Senate Majority Leader Johnson's.

Heart attacks were to the Fifties what shootings were to the Sixties. I'd even used to worry about Gerson, though not because of undue tobacco or boozing—just because he was under such pressure to be Gerson, Gerson, Gerson all the time. Try to remember the kind of Ike era.

"Oh, give me a break," LBJ wearily told our still faces. "One to be sociable now and again ain't going to kill me. And say it did? Say it did. Let's all *reason* together over just how real a heartbreaker that'd be by now to my fellow Americans except Lady Bird and our girls. I can't even be sure about my goddam sons-in-law. Now, Hopsie! Don't you think those kids out in the park would finally learn just how good marijuana tastes with champagne?"

"Mr. President," Cadwaller protested.

"Mmm. I'm not done yet. Let's see. Now, Bobby Kennedy and old Gene McCarthy would be waltzing arm and arm around a maypole—trying to trip each other up the while, of course, but that's politics and boys will be boys. Hubert's whole fat Woody Woodpecker trip would go into overdrive as he leapt nimbly over my body to take the damn oath. A few of the servants down at the ranch might feel bad, but Hill Country people are no strangers to death and they'll still be on the payroll. I don't think I've left anyone out. Now will somebody please give me a cigarette?"

"Mr. President," said Cadwaller again. LBJ held up a hand.

"No, no, no. As you can all hear from my tone of voice, I, Lyndon Johnson, am not being one bit sorry for myself. I'm only trying to analyze a situation cogently, just what the four of you bored me half stupid by not managing to do all afternoon after years of *assessing* this crap. Your C Street striped-pants crowd won't be weeping much either, *Hopsie*, if one lonesome old cigarette does kill me bang, dead, just like that right in front of your eyes like you're all worried it will. Well, then turn your backs on me, damn it! Let me have my one little smoke to be sociable. You know the funny thing, *Hopsie*, is I always say State's the one that never let me down. That because I never gave 'em much say to begin with, but neither did Jack and you all loved his ass."

"Mr. President, you know that's not fair."

"I agree, Hopsie. But you know what Jack said about fairness. That's why I don't let it get to me much. Now, would you happen to have a cigarette on you, Mrs. Cadwaller? Do you smoke at all?"

"Not in years."

"Well, I am glad to hear that. My mother never touched one in her life. I wouldn't want my death on her conscience anyhow. And Hopsie, I know you're a pipe man, which of course is no help to me right now at all. Pipes are for serene Harvard men with a secret and white-haired old coots sitting out front of country gas stations and counting and naming each other's nose hairs. Plus Jerry Ford, who can't count and just calls his 'My fellow guests here.' But can you see me with one? No, I don't think a pipe would suit me at all. I need a cigarette."

"Mr. President? I could run out to a People's or Dart Drug," volunteered Judy Agnew, faltering as the idea's absurdity hit even her. There must be cigarettes everywhere in the Mansion, summonable by pressing a button to make Felix materialize. I do like to think the rest of us had a bit more notion something else was afoot.

"Why, Carl!" LBJ said with a snicker. "Mr. Central Intelligence. Thought you said you don't tick anymore, but what makes you tick is right in your shirt pocket. Now, why wouldn't you give your Commander in Chief just one cigarette?"

"I'm sorry, sir," said Carl [Last Name Redacted], fumbling the pack out. "I didn't think you liked menthol."

"Never did in my prime. But if Salem's what's here, why, I've got no choice. So give over."

Extracting one, he half palmed then half tossed it into his mouth with an addict's finesse. An ex-smoker myself with occasional relapses, I knew it was like riding a bicycle.

"*Carl,*" said our President witheringly. "Now what am I supposed to do, breathe on it? I know the 'Hey, hey' kids in the park would believe that."

"Sir, forgive me." Carl patted for matches. But the Army bird colonel had just flicked open a Zippo.

"Well, well!" said LBJ shrewdly as he leaned in for the light. "Another county heard from. Colonel."

"Sorry, Mr. President. It's not for me. The General does like his cigar."

"Yes, he does." After one deeply satisfied inhale—*the First Lady's in Texas, of course*—Johnson held up his Salem for our inspection.

"Well, now! I think we can agree that this is *my* cigarette. My saliva is on it and its smoke's in my lungs. Doesn't matter anymore who gave it to me. Doesn't matter anymore who lit it. Doesn't matter I never liked menthol much in my prime. Nobody else is going to smoke it. No one'll take it away from me. If it does kill me bang, dead, right in front of your eyes, you all have my permission to tell them I asked for it."

"Mr. President!" all the men said. Yes, even Cadwaller.

"Oh, don't worry, Carl. Don't worry, Colonel. Don't worry, Rensselaer. Don't worry, Hopsie. Felix Culpa has orders from me to swear an affidavit saying just that if he finds me dead from this cigarette I only lit to be sociable. Now, if you boys want to work out my next step in *Vietnam*"—he took a deep drag, then switched back from his aggressive thumb-and-forefinger pinch to two-fingered equanimity—"you go on ahead. Have something to eat while you're at it. That is an order from your Commander in Chief. Dear Mrs. Cadwaller, come take a walk with me."

POSTED BY: *Dear Mrs. Cadwaller* His shirt baggy and yanked at the waistline, he'd stood. Indeed he'd stalked out, trailing twin contrails of smoke. Not feeling I had much say, I pushed my own chair back, blinking at the untasted plates of ribs, sirloin, and burgers before us. Then I found myself looking uncertainly at the most difficult moment of your great-grandfather's professional life.

Sweat on his forehead and said forehead pale, as was his usually immaculate jaw with its faint grit of stubble—oh, Hopsie! How I loved you just then— he made himself honor the noblest traditions of the Department of State. He accepted the prospect of cuckoldry for our nation's sake.

"Go, Pam," he said. "Calm him down if you can. Dear God, I've got to see him *tomorrow*."

"Tomorrow is another day!" Judy Agnew reassured him inanely. Or maybe not so inanely, not that she knew it, since I couldn't help hearing Nachum Unger's voice call, "Margaret *Mit*-chell." I felt no less inadequate this time.

"Not these days, it's not," said Carl [Last Name Redacted]. "Cadwaller, you in that briefing too? I thought it was only the toyshop."

"Please excuse me," I said. "The President's waiting."

In the hall, having just handed over his highball glass—"Right away, Mr. President," said Felix Culpa as he melted away—he was grinding his cigarette out in a sand-filled metal ashtray stand. Yes, the White House still had them then. Even though few people smoked in the President's presence, they all did the second his back was turned and nobody found that objectionable. If you're incredulous, these were dinosaur days: before our homemade, as you might say, Vatican III.

By then it must've been well past eleven. The East Wing's main hallway was still blazing with light, as were the empty rooms I could see. The President hadn't retired yet. "Ever been up here before, ma'am?" LBJ asked.

"No."

"I wouldn't say so in front of Cadwaller, but I thought maybe you might've in Jack's time. It was cooze Grand Central Station anytime Jackie hopped up to New York. Weren't you some kind of stewardess before you got married?"

Since *l'équipe* has no time to ransack my reception-line prattle, let alone scroll back to our first encounter in 1942, I can't guess from what mislaid

Johnsonian dossier that illusory Pam—not the last, daisysdaughter.com read-ers—had popped up tonight. I suspect learning I'd been a stewardess was the germ of what I've come to call Clio Airways.

"Oh, hell, Mr. President, don't you have eyes to see?" I said with a chuckle. "I was too old to be cooze in Jack's time."

"Sorry. When it's this late at night, I sometimes think it was all twenty years ago. Don't you too, Mrs. Cadwaller?"

"We all do, I think. Anyhow, Hopsie and I were in Africa."

"Oh, whereabouts?"

"Nagon. Djedjia now," I corrected myself.

"Hellhole?"

"Heaven back then if you were us."

He pondered his bourbon. "Too bad Jack never sent me."

"He sent Bobby," I said.

"Yeah, he would," LBJ grumbled. Once his next sip had cued us to start strolling, he stopped almost immediately to coach the man with the briefcase containing new-kew-lear, nucleah, and nuclear codes. "We ain't going far, so sit tight, son. Hope you've got a copy of *Playboy* in there."

"No, sir, Mr. President," came the prim reply. As we walked on, LBJ sighed.

"I keep trying to get them to smile," he confided. "Hell, in their shoes I'd be grinning like some damn Cheshire cat." Then we passed into a large oval room done in yellow.

"This one's still all Jackie," LBJ said, meaning the décor. "Only room on this floor that still is, just in case she ever decides to come back and visit."

"She hasn't?"

"No, never. Of course Mrs. Johnson and I have invited her a number of times. Her refusals have been mighty gracious, and I can't say as I blame her. I don't think Mrs. Lincoln ever came back either. I doubt Lady Bird will," which had me catching my breath as he shoved his glass in the far door's direction. "This next one's the Treaty Room. Jack named it, I didn't."

There are paintings you don't really think of as having originals, since they aren't reproduced in art tomes but history books. "My God! Forgive me, but I'm a historian," I said. As LBJ flinched, I swiftly added, "Retired."

We gazed at George P.A. Healy's *The Peacemakers*, showing Lincoln conferring with Generals Sherman and Grant and Admiral Porter soon after Richmond had fell. Though it was far outside *Glory Be's* time frame, I'd always quite liked it. Suiting how I imagine him, rough red-headed Sherman is doing the talking.

"Yeah," said LBJ softly. Newly close, newly redolent, newly Lyndonian with his shirttail out next to me. "I used to come in and look at this one a lot. Don't so much anymore."

"I'm sorry," I said. And believe me, I was.

"Well, they sure as hell aren't going to hang one of me chewing the fat with McNamara, Rusk, and Westmoreland. We've got plenty of photographs. A painting like this would be tits on a bull even if—*fuck!* Fuck, fuck, fuck. Never mind."

To have looked at him then would have invaded his privacy. Miming the scamp I so definitely wasn't by then and never really had been, I took a few steps and peered through the next door. "Lincoln Bedroom?" I guessed once he'd had a few seconds.

"Yep," came his voice from behind me, now more under control. "Of course, it warn't ever his bedroom."

POSTED BY: *Pam*   That's going to stay my one exception to a rule I've been quietly following here on daisysdaughter.com. Because laughter at this man's expense still revolts me—I can understand loathing, but *laughter?*—I've made no attempt to facsimilize Lyndon's cottonmouth accent. But that word could only be spelled the way Huck did.

"It was really the Cabinet room," he explained, recovered enough to come up alongside me. "He signed the Emancipation Proclamation on a desk right about where that pillow is now. Valenti had the numbskull idea I should sign the '65 Voting Rights Act in here, but I said piss on that noise. Hell, all I could picture was me on the bed in a stovepipe hat and fake whiskers."

"I'm surprised they didn't keep the original furnishings." Recall that in Beverly Hills I'd put in some time as an amateur decorator.

"Hell," Lyndon said. "Don't you know this whole building is bullshit? All renovations. They gutted the place stem to stern back when old Harry Truman was inventing the cold war. The layout's the same, but Abraham Lincoln never once put his hand to this wall." His own was pressed to it.

"Mr. President, did you say inventing?"

"Come now, Mrs. Cadwaller. You never once heard that word pass your President's lips. He had to scare hell out of the Congress to get done a few things that needed doing, was all. I've never asked him; we aren't any too close. Harry doesn't take kindly to *anyone* who sits at the desk where he used to, the more so when it's a fellow Democrat. Anyhow, I guess he got away with it and I didn't."

"Got away with what, pray?"

"How in hell would I know or care what I mean, Pam? He's Give-'em-Hell Harry and Jack is Saint Jack, but me? There's a goddam *play* running Off Broadway *right now* about how I *murdered* Jack to make myself President, you know that? The woman who wrote it says she don't really believe I did, but it would have been, quote, 'the least of my crimes.'"

"I know," I said.

"Did you see it?"

"I'd never," I said, for some loyalties outlast the end of a love affair. Not that Lyndon knew the only real one we'd had dated to 1965, when I'd watched on TV as he quoted "We Shall Overcome" in a speech to Congress urging passage of the Civil Rights Act and made 'em like it. So help me, I'd thought of my old *Regent's* colleague Jim Bond nattily quoting "Face of a Gauguin" back at me in 1943 and felt the mimsies go from half empty to half full. While Hopsie was no weeper, which is putting it mildly, he'd stuffed his pipe very slowly and said, "Pam, we don't often talk this way. But my favorite ancestor commanded a colored regiment in the Civil War, and I've always been fairly pleased I was named for him."

I digress, though. "Bless you," Lyndon muttered.

POSTED BY: *Pam* My guardian in Midwestern days—the future Brother Nicholas, *dans les grand blés sanglotants*—was fond of insisting that you can't repeat the past. I agree that it's stupid to try to on purpose, and I hope daisysdaughter.com proves I'm not prone to the fallacy. That's why it drives me bughouse when the past has its own ideas on that score. We now come to the *second* time I heard Lyndon Johnson make water.

"I'll just be a minute," he said as we stepped into a startlingly futuristic bathroom. Actually only contemporary, but a shock after our progress through Jackieland's facsimilized Lincolnisms. In a symptom of drunkenness or just Lyndonian prerogative, he was already fumbling with the front of his pants through his shirttails.

"You go on in the sitting room," he added over his shoulder, nodding toward another chamber off to my right. "But leave the door open so I can talk."

Note choice of pronoun. Note that Lyndon even deep in the bag, unlike his successor (oh, *Nixon*, Panama! Honestly, bikini girl), was no believer in soliloquizing just to fixtures or paintings.

Stepping into the doorway as per instructions, I found myself transomed between contradictions. In the smallest room I'd yet seen, its only seating a couch underneath a tall window, I was once more in Jackieland, the work of an eighteenth-century temperament recreating the nineteenth midway through the twentieth. Yet the President's voice came to me from white light and tiled glare.

"You're in the old White House telegraph room," he called over a stream of Johnsonian puissance. "Lincoln spent the whole war having to walk over to the damn War Department when he wanted news from the battlefields. Sure as shit not my problem, and sometimes I envy him. Never crossed anyone's mind to put a telegraph *here* until '65."

"Eighteen- or nineteen?" I asked the doorway's tiled glare. At which point it loomed large with Lyndon in disarrayed silhouette.

"Eighteen, Mrs. Cadwaller. As if you didn't know."

"I honestly didn't," I gasped. Then his arms curled around me.

A quarter century after the first time, here we bloody went again. But President Johnson didn't know what he wanted as surely as Congressman Johnson had.

"Please, ma'am, I'm your President. Hold me," he moaned brokenly. "Hold me, that's all I ask. Please just come sit and hold me a spell."

By then, we'd already launched a bear's waltz—hopping, ungainly, and in my case blind—toward the couch under the window. As my wool-covered calves got backed into it, my eyes clawed for directions, fell on a side cabinet crowned by a few family photographs. But I got plastered to the settee by John-sonian bulk before I'd more than glimpsed the most striking, boldly lit by the wedge of glare from the bathroom.

"Hold me," he begged again.

"You're holding *me*, Mr. President. There's not much I can do about it."

"I know that feeling," he muttered thickly. "And you *know* I know. That's all I was trying to tell them back there. *It was not my idea.* Never, never, never, never, never! By God, I wanted to finish what Franklin Roosevelt started. No more kids with hungry bellies. No more Negroes and Mexicans in shacks they'd never own. *And I could have done it, and I was so close*—and then this. I don't know how in hell I got in this mess. Please undo this button."

"Jesus Christ! I don't know how I got in it either," I muttered thinly right back, pushing my fist between squirreling fingers and my blouse's top pearl. Cadwaller! Insanely, I wondered if they'd finished eating. Or started.

"Ma'am, all I'm asking is a little sympathy. A little sympathy for the only President you've got. Courtesy and taste can go hang. I thought I saw some sympathy in your eyes in the Treaty Room."

"You've got it," I swore, meanwhile shifting my hand to brawl for my hem-line. "Just not with its skirts up. Lyndon, one or the other! Not both."

He drew his head back above me. Two wet scoops showed in his berry-dark eyes.

"Why the hell," he asked, "why the hell has every last mother one of you been telling me that since the day I was born?"

Until he drew back, I hadn't seen what his other hand was up to. Hadn't heard a zipper's tattletale noise either, but most likely he just hadn't bothered to do it back up. Yet his other hand's labors had all been for nothing. Far from becoming a python or even a cottonmouth, what his grip was attacking was a pale small uncooperative dove.

He toppled onto me sobbing. "Oh, damn! Oh, damn. Damn you, Ho Chi Minh. Damn you to hell, Jack. *Oh!* Too bad. Oh! Too bad."

POSTED BY: *A Mother* Not long after I mailed my second check to Gene McCarthy's campaign—as I'd been *planning* to do, children; do you really think my feelings were hurt or that would've mattered?—that eremite Mighty Mouse made headlines and then some by getting forty-two percent of the vote in the New Hampshire primary. A day later came a call from the White House switchboard asking Pam Cadwaller to visit the President that same afternoon. Alone.

Cadwaller nearly had apoplexy along with his eggs. Given my wrenched clothes and Flying Dutchmanized back knot, only Pam's urgent headshake had stopped him from rising and socking his President's jaw when LBJ and I returned to the family dining room in the East Wing.

"Yes, Pam, I know," he told his breakfast in a rare fury. "A man who's in torment, a man who's in agony. No arguments there. A man who's confused because he's all he ever aimed to be and now it's aimed at him. Granted. More *discussion* of that will cause me no pain. But there are limits. Sorry to sound incoherent, but I think you'll forgive me if I'm only human."

"Forgive you? I love it and you both," I told him. "But trust me. This time it'll be all right."

"How can you know?" Hopsie cried.

"I just do," I said, since it would take too long to explain and my husband's gifts stopped short of being female. "If I'm wrong, you've got my blessing to use that dandy little gun of yours we keep behind *Glory Be*."

Yes, daisysdaughter.com readers: the same one I've got in my lap now. Behind *Glory Be* was its home at every house throughout my third marriage. I doubt I need to go into my reasons to move it somewhere less impulsively convenient after Cadwaller's death.

"That's appalling to say under any circumstances. Even these," Cadwaller told me. "Anyhow, they'd never let me bring it into the White House."

"I meant on me, Hopsie, not him."

Was I sure? Pretty nearly. I chose my wardrobe with care. When I was shown into the Lincoln Sitting Room, LBJ stood. Full suit and tie now, but slippers. His shoes stood nearby.

"Ma'am, it's good to see you again."

"I can't quite call it a pleasure, Mr. President. But if ever a man needed comfort, it's you. What on earth are these?"

On the side cabinet where the family photos had been were a pair of stuffed eagles on stands. Their wild eyes, hiked wings, and every-which-way feathers left one unclear whether they were meant to look demented or the taxidermist was.

"From an admirer somewhere out West. They tell me I've got a few left here and there. Damn, but I wish even I didn't think they were kooks. If these are somebody's idea of a joke, at least I'll never know. The Secret Service can check this crap for bombs but not humor."

"What became of the picture?"

"Oh, it's here on the couch. I was holding it."

"May I?" I asked, reaching out. "I didn't get much of a look."

"Of course." As we shared it, he murmured, "You do look a fair amount like her, Mrs. Cadwaller."

"Mr. President, I don't want to insult her memory. But fashions have changed and I hope you'll tell me that at least my arms are much slimmer. I'm pretty sure I smile lots more often than it looks like she ever did, too."

"Most likely. Now I'll never know," he said dolefully and also inaccurately. "I didn't give you too many reasons to smile that other night."

"No, sir, not many. But some."

In 1917, when the picture was taken, Rebekah Baines Johnson was younger but more used by life than was Pam half a century later. And don't misunderstand: it was just a resemblance, not a Hollywoodish miracle on a par with Kirsten Dunst looking breathtakingly like Kirsten Dunst's long-lost twin sister. Luckily for me, not to mention 1956 readers of book features in *Vogue*, my jaw though no prize was far less problematic. It was mostly the eyes, the nose to an extent, the high forehead, along with the hair in a back knot and the clothes I'd happened to wear on my previous visit here.

"You do understand, though," said LBJ with some awkwardness.

"Yes, Mr. President, I think so. Would you like to come sit on the couch with me for a spell?"

When I sat with arm crooked for company, he huddled into my collarbone. His slippered feet were up on the couch right away. Once I'd squeezed his shoulder, though, I felt at sea. Not only wasn't I his mother, I'd never been anyone's—something I'm not sure Lyndon knew. He had his reasons not to inquire about Pam's real children if any.

"Mr. President, can I tell you a story?"

"Yes, do."

"It's really a scene from a play about Danton. He quotes the New Testament: 'It must needs be that offenses come! But—'"

"'Woe to him by whom the offense cometh,'" said a muffled voice in my shoulder. "Matthew Eighteen: Seven."

Though he favored Isaiah when speaking to Congress, a Texan raised Baptist like Lyndon naturally knew both Testaments backward and forward. If I hadn't liked Georg Büchner, most likely secular Pam would've thought Mr. Lincoln had just made the italicized bits of the Second Inaugural up.

"Yes, exactly. And then Danton says with a terrible cry, 'That *must* was mine.'"

"Thank you," he muttered. Then I think he fell asleep for a while.

Just as my arm started cramping like the blazes, a voice said, "Did you have a mother?"

"Of course I did, sil—oh, sorry. Mr. President."

"Silly's all right. Silly sure beats 'Hey, hey.' Tell me what she was like."

"Well, her name was Daisy Buchanan," I said and waited. But they clearly hadn't spent much time following moneyed Long Island love triangles in the Hill Country in the *Nine*-teen *Twen*-ties.

"Daisy," his voice said. "That's a nice old name. You know, I wish to hell everyone hadn't called that ad of mine that. I always did like that song."

My turn to flinch, since it may go without saying I didn't. Its lyric's first line after "Daisy, Daisy" would always appear in my mind engraved on a gold syringe that lay next to a silver one in the Paris footlocker. Something I'd quietly accepted on some faraway beach didn't really make that less painful.

"Could you sing it for me?" the muffled voice said.

"Mr. President, I've got the singing voice of an aardvark."

"Hell, I never even sang 'The Yellow Rose of Texas' into a microphone unless I had a big hat to wave and a goddam big crowd singing with me. But who cares? Please. I think we're alone now, Mrs. Cadwaller. Except Felix Culpa and the kids in the park, there doesn't seem to be anyone around."

I hadn't sung it since I was a child. I'd sung it a lot during the interlude when my father was gone and it'd been just my mother and me until the Lotus Eater showed up. Clearing a throat blocked by difficulties he needn't know about, I falteringly sang "A Bicycle Built for Two" to Lyndon Johnson the day after the 1968 New Hampshire primary.

Daisy, Daisy—give me your answer, do…

POSTED BY: *Pam* That's how my White House *Piétas* began. As best I remember, I was summoned back to the Mansion some six or eight times during the final months of LBJ's Presidency. I strained your great-grandfather's patience—though not, I'm proud to say, his credulity—with my remonstrations that a) I couldn't really explain what went on but b) no hanky-panky was involved.

Since I never asked him or saw her, I don't know if Lady Bird heard similar explanations or was kept in the dark. Because Lyndon told me, I do know my visits aren't in the logs, the reason even Lyndon Baines Johnson's most obsessive biographer has no idea they occurred. Of course he'll be welcome to read and reread daisysdaughter.com with tweezers, but there are things that were said between Lyndon and me I'll never repeat even here.

I do recall the dates of some of my *Piétas* quite well. The switchboard's call on the morning of March 31 was the biggest surprise, since the whole country knew he was set to deliver a speech on Vietnam that night. Hopsie and Ned Finn had burnt two a.m. oil preparing Policy Planning and Secretariat's comments on its early drafts, and Lyndon was scanning the latest one when Felix Culpa escorted me into the Lincoln Sitting Room.

"Mr. President," I said once the door closed, "it's not up to me what you do. But if I can make one suggestion, don't bring work here."

He rubbed a gray death mask: his own. "In this house, it's everywhere. Sometimes I wonder if the telegraph operators' desks faced the window or the wall."

"Come sit beside me a spell, Mr. President…"

"Ma'am, all things considered, you could call me Lyndon," he told my skirted lap some minutes later.

I had once in extremis; no doubt he didn't remember. "No, sir, I couldn't," I said, stroking his hair.

He still had those huge ears a young Pam Buchanan once seen swimmingly hung to either side of his oncoming nose like an elephant hunter's trophies. As for me, it's lucky I was still five foot ten and hadn't yet turned pretzel. Even in approximate repose, the wrinkled sixty-year-old leader of the free world who curled his slippered feet to nestle against my collarbone or lap had the frame of a lapsed Texas oil derrick. Cologne and hair cream never stood a chance against his Johnsonian pungency, which addled them into a redolence my nostrils could only call Presidential. Long after his death, I could smell him when someone was burning leaves outside as I stepped from the shower.

"Then I dare you to call me by one name nobody's ever called me to my face," the muffled voice said.

"I don't see your face a whole lot, Mr. President."

"Even so. Even better. Just try, Rebekah"—a first and only, if you're curious. "Just try."

"Mr. President, should I call you Esau?"

"I do," he said and wept. Of course that was the night he finished his speech on Vietnam in the Oval Office and then nodded to Lady Bird off camera before his announcement: "I shall not seek, and will not accept, the nomination of my party for another term as your President." One of the banners the kids in the park held up afterward read "THANKS LBJ," the zinger being that eyes that had long gone hungry for any such message might well grasp at it gratefully before their owner deduced he was still being given the finger.

No, he didn't tell me he was contemplating it. Any confidences between us—and yes, they were mutual—were of another sort. But the speech lay scattered around us, and by then I knew how to soothe Esau Baines Johnson.

> *I'm half crazy, all for the love of you…*

It wasn't all "Daisy, Daisy." Once when my aardvark voice had already sung it to him, he asked for another, and call me unimaginative: my brain seized the only other I knew whose lyric had the word "carriage" in it. But I thought it might make him laugh and it did.

BEE-cause I would not stop for death,
He kindly stopped for MEEE!
The carriage held but just ourselves
And immor-TAL-li-tee…

Maybe unsurprisingly, Lyndon loved that one. Though the tune was familiar to him and then some, I doubt he knew its lyric's unexpected provenance, and I didn't want to burden him by explaining it. Once he'd learned the words, we used to sing it together, and he was as right about his voice as I'd been about mine. One time we even danced as we sang, him shuffling in his slippered feet.

He hooked my elbow for a do-si-do and I flourished my long skirt in the best mimicry Daisy Buchanan's daughter could manage of a hoedown. Lord knows what Felix Culpa thought if he heard us performing Emily Dickinson's "Because I Would Not Stop for Death" to the tune of "The Yellow Rose of Texas" through the Lincoln Sitting Room's closed door.

As should go without saying, he didn't request and I didn't perform it when the switchboard summoned me on my forty-eighth birthday. By then, Nan Finn, Laurel Warren, and I had already agreed by phone to cancel Pam's celebratory lunch at La Chaumière, which would've somewhat awkwardly doubled as our de facto wake for Fiddle. Trying to be the first U.S. Embassy secretary to summit Everest, she'd been killed by an avalanche back in April.

"You know I never liked him," Esau whispered to my collarbone, not that Pam saw fit to say she hadn't much either during our seven hours. "He never liked me. But he'd made up his mind not to by the first time we shook hands, and I've never understood people like that. I've hated many a man but I always had reasons. The other is a luxury I couldn't afford."

Then he wept again on my shoulder and I sang to him in my aardvark voice the day Bobby Kennedy died.

It won't be a stylish marriage! I can't afford a carriage…

My one White House summons at night was on August 29, and by then I was more than sure enough of my man to overrule Cadwaller's objections when the call came at dinner. In synch for once with the country at large, Hopsie and I were eating ours in front of the TV in the den of our Georgetown house. Google "1968 Democratic Convention, Chicago" and you'll know why in a jiffy.

Ignoring my advice back in March, Lyndon had had a TV set installed in the Lincoln Sitting Room. Ignoring our usual practice, we sat bolt upright and side by side on the couch to watch Hubert Humphrey's acceptance speech. For once we were as much at a loss for words as the mad taxidermist's two stuffed eagles.

Then Lyndon rose to kill the set. "Do you know who else was on the short list to be my Vice President in '64, Mrs. Cadwaller? Gene McCarthy."

"Come sit beside me a spell, Mr. President…"

I think it was after I'd sung "A Bicycle Built for Two" to him that time that the muffled voice said, "I don't really know anything about you at all, do I?"

"What would you like to?"

He turned his face to mine. "Hell, I don't know. For instance, where'd you get that little scar over your left eyebrow?"

"Dachau," I said witlessly. His eyes and nose came up like tethered zeppelins.

"Good God, ma'am! Do you know your English is damn near perfect? I had no idea. I told you your husband had a secret—"

"No, no," I said and explained I'd only been there for the day.

"What was it like?" his remuffled voice asked. "I never much cared to know."

"Not in here, Mr. President. Not in here. There, there. There, there."

As I patted him and remembered "The Gates of Hell," I realized with some bewilderment that I'd become a nurse at last. Also that my one experience of mothering tallied with my one experience of being successfully mothered: Daisy stroking a budding pudding's hair on a Provincetown couch as the Lotus Eater hurled shoes around before making her escape. Anyhow, it sure beat Daisy inviting Pam to join her in the tub as a substitute for the runaway L.E., but we all improvise in emergencies and it had been a long time ago.

My final summons by the White House switchboard came on November 6, 1968. Squeaking past squeaky Hubert and foiling foul George Wallace, Nixon had just been elected. When Felix Culpa showed me into the Lincoln Sitting Room, Lyndon was not only slippered but in dressing gown and pajamas, a first. It might've alarmed me if I hadn't known my Esau so well by then.

"Go home soon," he explained, meaning not me but himself. "I might as well get used to this."

"Yes, Mr. President. Come sit beside me a spell…"

> *… but you'll look sweet—upon the seat—*
> *of a bicycle built for two!*

"Thank you," he mumbled into my shoulder, as he always did. "Thank you, Mrs. Cadwaller. I don't suppose we'll see each other again."

"You won't come back to Washington, Mr. President?"

"No," he mumbled. "I can't stand it. I been there before."

4. Dottie from Kansas and Dolly from Gray Star

POSTED BY: *Pam*   After his retirement, Lyndon Johnson returned to his ranch in Texas with his patient Lady Bird. He not only went back to chain smoking but, in the single best joke of the Sixties, grew his hair long.

Fortunately, if only from a selfish point of view—as Cadwaller said, there are limits—I bore no resemblance to Hannah Milhous Nixon. It's still a matter of record that her son's favorite White House lair was the Lincoln Sitting Room. Come Washington's car-exhaust Augusts, he used to command his own Felix Culpa to turn the air conditioning up full blast so that he could enjoy a fire in the fireplace while listening to Richard Rodgers's—sorry, Hopsie, it's true— *Victory at Sea.*

Once again fortunately, aside from the fact that we're both in our eighties, I don't look at all like Potus's mother either. As I've mentioned, instead her son resembles my father—long dead Tom Buchanan, barely known to a budding pudding named Pammie at the very beginning of my way-back-when.

The way-back-when! For people my age and even somewhat younger, it ended on August 9, 1974. In the real coda to my generation's Clio Airways ride, that's when Nixon resigned. All the push and bother since then strikes the likes of us as something else: either the past tense of the present or the present tense of the past.

Nonetheless, *l'équipe* does realize some things may need glossing to make sense to Panama and her fellow bikini girls. Here you go, Gidget's granddaughters:

One. Robert Strange McNamara—yes, that was and as of 6/6/06 is his middle name—served as Secretary of Defense in the Kennedy and Johnson Administrations from 1961 to 1968. He left once Vietnam became an undeniable disaster to head the World Bank. As I write, his successor there is a man named Paul Wolfowitz. During his own stint as Deputy Secretary of Defense, he rejoiced in the title of "Wolfowitz of Arabia," but there were and are competitors.

Two. Pam sometimes wondered if her *Piétas* with Esau Baines Johnson had been a delusion until she read Doris Kearns Goodwin's descriptions in *Lyndon Johnson and the American Dream* of LBJ huddling with her in bed for comfort. While I don't know what my fellow historian's singing voice is like, I did feel caught between relief that I hadn't imagined it and annoyance I wasn't the only one.

Three. In case you've forgotten, the chant from the kids in Lafayette Square that Johnson hated so much he couldn't bring himself to repeat it went like this: "Hey, hey, LBJ! How many kids did you kill today?"

Four. The most notorious commercial of the 1964 contest between Johnson and Senator Barry Goldwater was an LBJ ad so inflammatory it only aired once. It showed a girl not unlike a very young Kirsten Dunst pulling the petals off a flower and counting aloud. Then an announcer reversed her lisping "Six, seven, eight" with "Eight, seven, six" and so on, ending in a mushroom cloud. The implication was that LBJ would be far less likely than Goldwater to start a new-kew-lear, nucleah, or nuclear war. Nothing was said pro or con about escalating a conventional one, but the commercial has been known ever since as the Daisy spot.

Five. Gene McCarthy, whose showing in the 1968 New Hampshire primary helped prompt LBJ's decision not to seek another term, was an amateur poet. His best-known collection is called *Other Things and the Aardvark.*

Six. At a considerably higher level of prosody, "Never, never, never, never, never!" is Lear's most famous groan. By coincidence, in the same speech Lear also says "Please undo this button."

Seven. Unless Google lies, George P.A. Healy's *The Peacemakers* hangs to this day in the White House Treaty Room. Since it's a painting and not one more TV set permanently tuned to the Murphy Channel, I assume William T. Sherman is now and forever saying, "War is cruelty and you cannot refine it." Of course no one can hear him or ever will.

Eight. While we're on the Civil War, "Oh! Too bad. Oh! Too bad," is Robert E. Lee's recorded reaction after Pickett's charge failed on the third day at Gettysburg. Don't blame me for feeling just a bit flattered on the forty-seven-year-old Buchanan bod's behalf.

Nine. In pained hindsight, "All you need is love" is about the dumbest nostrum I've ever heard. The Beatles were carried away by the moment. Imagine a moment that could carry *them* away.

Ten. Apropos of nothing particular, Tim Cadwaller told me once that Sean Finn's favorite childhood quotation was from *The Jungle Book*: "They have cast me out from the Man-Pack, Mother! But I come with the hide of Shere Khan." His favorite line in *The Longest Day* was Brigadier Norman Cota's farewell to the beach: "Run me up the hill, son."

POSTED BY: *A Voyager*   And yes, Tim: I do see it now. Congratulations for outfoxing me. It never crossed my mind that you named my website daisysdaughter.com because mygeneration.com was taken.

Think of my vanity, after all! Your Gramela is much too proud of her life's peculiarity in the way-back-when to consider being *representative* of much as anything but a demotion. It's ridiculous to imagine that everyone my age had a vaguely notorious, bewitchingly selfish Jazz Age mother—let alone one who ended up in dull, dumb, puzzled exile during the Depression before dying too young of lollipow. Yet perhaps we all did in one way or another.

In one way or another, everyone my age got to hear "Happy Birthday" sung to us on D-Day. In one way or another, we all ended up trapped into crooning "Daisy, Daisy" to our broken last President—*our* last one, I mean, not the country's—as choppers hovered, Cronkite mulched the ink and chalk he hoped to alchemize, the kids in the park chanted their baiting slogans, and B-52s turned Southeast Asia into the land of a thousand napalm suns.

Dear, I suppose I'd better wrap this thing up. Aside from one or maybe two exceptions, though I'm only guessing about the one in 1920—an embryo with just seconds of pure happiness left, I was never told later whether my birth had been easy or difficult—this has been the longest goddam June 6 of my life. Now that the sky outside my window at the Rochambeau has turned Omaha indigo at last, I must admit I'm damned tired.

I see I never quite got to India here on daisysdaughter.com. I've got some fairly distinguished nautical company on that score, and they say the land he reached instead was something to see in its salad days. May I take it upon myself to report back to Admiral Columbus that India was very nice? Hopsie was sixty when he presented his credentials to Mrs. Gandhi.

Of course, half the reason he'd been appointed was that he'd rubbed Kissinger the wrong way a few too many times in Policy Planning once the Nixon crowd came in. It may say something about both Kissinger's and Nixon's priorities that India was their idea of the back burner, meant to leave Cadwaller feeling why-Henry'd. Half my husband's happiness at the posting was that he knew career Ambassadors only get a fighting chance to do the diplomatic job they're trained for in countries Washington isn't obsessed with.

Predictably, in that Kissingerian *Et in Arcadia Ergo* way of his, Henry—always the kind of cook who never tasted soup 'til it was burning—leapt in with glasses aglow the minute the '71 India-Pakistan war began. Not only undoing all Cadwaller's work during our first year but depriving the United States of a prize opportunity to improve our always persnickety relations with Delhi, he made it our policy to tilt in Pakistan's favor. When I see Potus praising Musharraf, I don't know whether to mutter *"Plus ça change"* or hum "A Bicycle Built for Two."

Hopsie's cables explaining the stark idiocy of our choice of favorites may've been the hardest test of your great-grandfather's adherence to one basic rule of decorum in diplomatic cables, namely that they include no cursing. He was later briefed that the tilt's indirect value had been in helping to orchestrate Nixon's opening to China, but that smugly invented bank shot was just more of Kissinger's bullshit. Luckily, though, Henry's eagle eye soon spotted even hairier bouillabaisses to stick a talon into—as Ned Finn used to sing in the corridors of our big aircraft carrier for paper planes, "I Wonder Where's Kissinger Now?"—and that left Cadwaller free to try repairing the damage without too much interference.

Also luckily, despite the fact that most human emotions were at best intermittently interesting hobbies to her rather than the point of much, Indira Gandhi liked him. While Hopsie couldn't quite return the favor, the weak spot that always left my husband most tempted to explain away people's faults was the pleasure he took in braininess, of which she obviously had a cartload. We were also gone before the Emergency, as she cleverly styled her suspension of civil liberties during the crackdown of '75. From a distance, Cadwaller had no trouble conceding that intelligence shouldn't be a leader's only virtue.

Albeit mostly enjoyably, India kept me terrifically busy myself. Since Nagon was my main point of comparison, the biggest adjustment was in scale. Paying lip service to India's importance while vaunting our own, our sparkling sugar-cube Embassy was damn near the size of M'Lawa's old Palais du Président. I was directing a large staff at the Residence—our entertainments were to scale too—and playing Mrs. Cadwaller on a much more high-stakes diplomatic circuit than Plon-Plon-Ville's had been.

There, my motley past proved surprisingly useful. The ashes of the Jazz Age as widowed Daisy's luggage, a Midwestern adolescence in the Depression with an increasingly religious-minded Nick Carraway for a Scarecrow, New York's pre–Pearl Harbor glitter and glow, World War Two, the voluptuous allure of Hollywood, and encounters with both Jack and Bobby Kennedy, *among other things*, should never be mistaken for the careening whole of American experience in what we had enough hubris to name the American century. They just made lively stations of the conversational cross when I'd be asked about the imaginary nation other countries love most in us and Pam could confirm or deny its points of contact with reality.

As the Ambassador's wife, I was also the frequent escort—hell, the local equivalent of a *bateau-mouche* Marianne—to junketeering Congressmen's wives and other American dames of stature on their India splashdowns, not only giving them rides on Delhi's touristic merry-go-round (I did love the Red Fort every time) but taking them to Jaipur, Agra, Calcutta, and the rest: destinations as inevitable in their way as Jazz Age, *grands blés sanglotants*, Omaha, Dachau, etc. I boned up on reincarnation so as to be able to explain that the quality of your next life depended on your actions in the previous one, which oddly or not neither Mrs. Cadwaller nor most Americans I explained it to had any trouble nodding at a bit wearily. Only the idea that we had to die to face the music was a sticking point.

My favorite was always Bombay, where the erotic sculptures at Elephanta put a wry grin on a now considerably less uptight Ethel Kennedy's face and the British Raj's pomp was on its mightiest display in Ozymandian stone. Like Constantinople, Leningrad, West Berlin, and Plon-Plon-Ville, Bombay no longer exists, but I wouldn't mind seeing Mumbai someday.

Oh, yes: Ethel. I forget which year she showed up, and she didn't return my sunglasses—the gesture of gestures that would've redefined us as a couple of merry Clio Airways stewardesses *sans peur et sans reproche*. On the contrary, I couldn't tell if she'd forgotten our first meeting or was just hoping I wouldn't bring it up. Since I had no idea how she played the compartmentalization game to keep "When Bobby was alive" at bay, I didn't.

Perhaps because this was India, where immunity to experience isn't in the cards, she was much pleasanter company. I had a hard time of it all the same to keep from goggling when she started to talk eagerly about her oldest son's Presidential prospects. Not only were we riding back to Delhi as roadside entertainers, hoping for a penny from the caravan, hiked dancing bears to their feet—the stick that gets them up on their hind legs is thrust through a ring in their noses—but I'd just recalled a day at Ouibomey when the Warren and Sawyer kids had been chasing each other around with toy six-guns, yelling *"Pan, Pan."*

I think it was after Ethel's visit that Cadwaller looked up to see me drooping dramatically in the doorway of our private quarters at the Residence. Not Mrs. Kennedy's fault, but it *had* been about my twentieth trip to Agra.

"How'd it go, dear?"

"Oh, Hopsie," I groaned. "When you've seen one Taj Mahal, you've seen 'em all." Not having seen it as often as I had, he chuckled.

To my disappointment, our tour didn't overlap with that of Nan Finn, who came out to Delhi soon afterward in her hopeful, nervous new guise as a junior consular officer. After Ned's too early death—proving what a crapshoot the whole thing is, neither cigarettes nor booze was to blame—Andy Pond had arranged to bring her into the Department, since the glorious girl had been part of our world too long for us to lose her. You'd better believe we took care of our own when we could.

More peculiarly, by the time I reached India and saw the Pink City, my old champion Celia Brady—then White, then Singh—had just left Jaipur for good. Once things went sour with her maharajah, she'd married an eccentric DNA researcher and moved to Scotland. That turned out to be among the few places Hopsie and I never got to during your great-grandfather's final State Department job, in some ways his true calling all along.

In others, he was being put out to pasture and knew it. By then Kissinger was Secretary of State *en titre* as well as in influence, and Cadwaller spent a few months walking the halls—old-hand jargon for a senior officer without an assignment—before Henry punched his ticket: Director General of the Foreign Service. The Kissingerian diminution in that promotion was that he was cut out of policy, but Hopsie was the kind of man whose love of country, unlike his wife's haywire version, was most fiercely projected through devotion to the one of its institutions that best expressed his idealism. The appointment was as popular within the Department as Kissinger himself wasn't.

That's when our greatest travels together took place. In Leningrad, not yet restored to its identity as St. Petersburg, I laid eyes at last on Falconet's equestrian statue of Peter the Great, the surreally active protagonist of Pushkin's great "The Bronze Horseman." In Moscow, I surprised our guide—and given our official status, mildly nettled Cadwaller—by choking up at John Reed's burial spot in the Kremlin's wall.

I didn't think he'd been anything but deluded. I'd still known a number of his co-delusionists, and it seemed right that one of them had made it to Churchill Downs. Bran was gone by then, but otherwise I might've broken our long silence by sending him a not wholly unaffectionate postcard.

I sent Jake Cohnstein one instead, but it wasn't quite the same. I'm still glad we were in touch right up until Jake's death just months before Hopsie's; he was the same age I am now. The last time we saw each other, he introduced me to the much younger man who lived with him—a first.

We saw Asia, though naturally not Vietnam (drat!). Saw Central and South America, though naturally not Cuba (double drat). Saw Africa, though not the former Nagon: it was the time of *la Terreur P'Kapa*, and Hopsie himself had given the order to withdraw all but our most essential personnel. So we never revisited the beach where he'd worn swim trunks and a top hat, but his favorite picture of *me* in later years was taken in Sydney, Australia. By a fluke of the breeze, the big bonnet I'm clutching to my gray mop simultaneously mimics and quarrels with the swoop of the opera house behind me.

Determined to be as hands-on as he could—monitoring resources and morale, reassuring himself that every Ambassador who was a political appointee had a good career DCM, learning where CIA or the Pentagon was playing hardball in the endless turf wars, taking care to meet every junior officer who'd been described as a thorn in people's sides and often coming away as his advocate—Hopsie wanted to see every U.S. Embassy and mission worldwide. We didn't fall far short of it. Some of our dearest friends during his too short retirement were people we'd met in Cairo or Manila for a week.

Trailing a step or two behind him and getting my first whiff of whatever the local climate's cinders had just sparked, I watched my husband step forward at airport after airport, the remaining close-cropped hair around his ears now snow white and his pipe lit on landing, hand outthrust as he said "Cadwaller" to the young FSO sent to collect us. It was at those moments I most often decided he'd been too modest, no great surprise there, in front of St. Sulpice.

Panama, it isn't only that other human impulses beside religion deserve commemorating in architecture more poetic than C Street aircraft carriers for paper planes. Nobody proved better than your great-grandfather—who'd have crinkled his eyes in amused dismay had I ever teased him with the notion—that other vocations earn the right to be called priesthoods. Especially dogged ones to which the world pays little heed unless you're bad at them, something he never was. Of course he'd have said that the American St. Sulpice wasn't C Street but a few pieces of faded eighteenth-century paper under glass in the Archives.

Hopsie's retirement bash at the DACOR Bacon House on F Street would've been the greatest night of Nan Finn's shutterbug career if the glorious girl hadn't been interviewing visa applicants in New Delhi. Kennan only sent a telegram from Princeton, but Cadwaller's earliest Department mentor was too well on in years to travel much by then and everyone else came: Nick Veliotes and his wonderful Pat, Brandon Grove. Even McIlvaine and his wife, and I was as happy as always to see her: Alice and I were the two tallest women in the world of the Foreign Service. Because Pauls Valley, Oklahoma, is a long way from Washington, Cadwaller himself was most touched when John Burns put in an appearance. Names unknown to you, known to too few, unmentioned until now even on daisysdaughter.com. But they were the best of the best in our lot's glory days.

We had a few good years then, entertaining other District geezers for whom the State Department's magic carpet now stood framed in bits and pieces on their walls. That's when we got our weekend place outside Culpeper, Virginia, first seen by Pam in the *Nine*-teen *Fif*-ties when I was hoping to surprise Martha Shelton's pregnant ghost around a corner of "Saltsbury." Then Cadwaller's long dying began.

He was diagnosed in late October of '83. Both when alone and out in public, always our marriage's version of *mens sano in corpore sano*, we kept up not what you children call appearances but our life's staunchest, most valued realities for another year or so. My husband's Vietnam-era stint as head of Policy Planning had made him more expert than I'd ever be at finding real pleasure and intellectual stimulation in objective considerations of a situation for which no good outcome existed.

Even by 1985, however, he was too sick for me to ask if he wanted to come downstairs to watch Reagan's State of the Union Speech. In former times, so much as imagining skipping it would have struck us as absurd no matter who was President. As it was, Pam felt selfish and guilty when she devoured the *WashPost*'s transcript of his callous *niaiseries* the next morning while Cadwaller still dozed after a restless night.

Your great-grandfather went into the ICU in early October of '86, deliriously muttering about the idiocy of people who took rabbit's feet on airplane trips. By mid-November, his pain was so awful that I realized at his bedside I'd only make it worse by chatting about the news, normally as nourishing to Hopsie as the glucose dripping from an IV into his now Cape Codified arm. He died late in the evening of November 25, 1986, and Andy Pond drove me home from Bethesda Naval Hospital for the last time soon before he left himself to take up his final post in Berlin.

Today my deepest regret, bikini girl, is that your great-grandfather never knew you. Because Cadwaller understood the difference between values and priggishness—the latter consisting entirely of the belief that anything *you* wouldn't do is something no one else should do either—I think he'd have enjoyed your grandpa Chris's picture of you last summer on the dunes near Provincetown's Pilgrim Monument. As you stand with bare legs planted in surf and Goya-dark hair tumbling, a Spandex oyster footnotes your black T-shirt's defiant and eternal NEW YORK FUCKIN' CITY.

That's about all I can manage for now. Though the bookshelves, neighborhood, and millennium are new, Cadwaller's gun has been tucked not back into the Paris footlocker but its old post of honor behind *Glory Be*. Andy is due any minute, bearing his dubious gifts on DVD of *The Gal I Left Behind Me* and—what was the other?—*Meet Pamela*, a forgotten Franco-American romp chosen solely for its title. Those are always such fun to actually sit through, but I'm rather hoping that's the one he chooses. I'll have a better excuse to start snoring early.

Oh! If you're wondering what's going on, I should probably explain I'm now convinced Potus won't call. In fact, I guarantee it.

That's because he did around seven-fifteen. Oh, yes, the elephone rang. We spoke.

7:15 p.m., June 6, 2006: around when the first trucks went lumbering up the bluffs beyond Omaha. Around when that lone Spandau stopped hammering, probably done in by a grenade. Around when those dazed boys barnacled to the Vierville sea wall got done singing *"Happy birthday, Miss Buchanan— happy birthday to you."* That's when Eddie and I knew we had to say goodbye to this bloody beach and go inland.

Dear me, what sloppy habits I've gotten into on daisysdaughter.com! And me a writer, too. I should probably have mentioned Potus's call earlier, shouldn't I?

POSTED BY: *A Caddy* "Mrs. Cadwaller? This is the White House call-ing," said a decorous but understandably brisk female voice. "Please hold for the President."

I seized Cadwaller's gun. "I'm here," I pointlessly told limbo.

"Hello?" he said when he came on the line. "Caddy?"

"This is Mrs. Pamela Cadwaller, yes."

"Don't they call you Caddy?" he asked pleasantly. "They ought to."

"Whatever you say, Mr. President." It was out before I knew it; I'd spent too many years as a diplomat's wife. No, not enough of them, Hopsie!

"You know I asked my mom about you," he confided. "Want to know what she said? 'Why, George. I don't recall you calling me on *my* last birthday.' Heh, heh. I had to say, 'Well, Mom, I had the Turkish Prime Minister in here and I had Tony Blair the day before. I had to work.'"

"Yes, I remember Mr. Blair's visit."

"Well, we get along. I like to tease him, you know: 'How can you call your-self an Oxford man? You're wearing a pink shirt.' But once a Mom always a Mom, what I say. Isn't that so, Caddy?"

"I guess so, Mr. President." In my lap, the Rheumas curled around my ord-nance.

"No guessing allowed! That's our rule in this White House. You've got to be a mother yourself, I imagine."

"I'm afraid not, Mr. President. Only a writer."

"That's right and I want to tell you, Caddy. The First Lady is a big admirer of, uh"—check your notes, Potus—"*The Gory Bee.*"

He may have thought I wrote children's books. "Well, I know it's no *The Pet Goat*, Mr. Pres—"

But he hadn't stopped talking. "I know you had one, though." He meant mother. "They tell me she was somebody, too."

"Everyone is, sir," I said, which may have been the closest I came to succeeding at elephonic terrorism.

"Sorry, what's that you say, Caddy?"

"Nothing, Mr. President. Just clearing my throat. Please excuse me."

"Well, I'm glad we got this chance to talk. You know the Senator"—that would be dear Bob, of course—"must think awful highly of you. He came down here, showing everyone his gun."

I had no idea what that meant. Don't blame me if I felt stuck inside, immobile, with the Potus blues again.

"Mr. President," I said and suddenly didn't know what to accuse him of. Where would *you* have begun?

"Anyhow, Caddy. You keep well, you hear? Be careful blowing out those"— did he use index cards or a PC?—"eighty-six candles. We want you with us for a good long while yet. Well, good—"

"*AGH!*" I screamed. Shakily hoisting Cadwaller's gun and putting its barrel to my temple, I pulled the trigger.

POSTED BY: *A Failure*   Mission accomplished? Plainly no. What's Denmark *coming* to?

In Pam's defense, my "*AGH!*"—though no pistol shot at a concert—did rattle Potus somewhat. "Hey, Caddy! You all right there?" he said. ("I think she's having a heart attack," I heard him murmur swiftly to someone in the pause.)

"Oh, my! Dear me. Oh, sorry, Mr. President. Just a cat jumping in my lap. Kelquen, how you startled me."

"You ought to try it with daughters," he advised. "Anyhow, happy birthday again, old Caddy. Keep well. Anything at all we can do for you down here, just let us know."

"Well, Mr. President, for Bob's and my sake, you could try attending at least one soldier's funer—" But he was already gone.

Once the line went dead and I realized Pam wasn't, I gazed in a Lex Luthor stupor at Cadwaller's gun, now relowered to my ancient snatch. Hopsie, what—?

Your dandy little gun, so handleable and light even in your eighty-six-year-old widow's uncertain grip. Your nifty nickel-plated pistol, so near to weightless every time I'd hefted it since dawn. Your damned unloaded gun whose ammo clip Pam Buchanan, onetime ETO war correspondent, had never thought to check once I'd fetched it from the Paris footlocker.

I knew it was always loaded in your lifetime and I hadn't touched it since. So who—? And when? And why?

"Heck of a job, Pammie," I muttered, staring at a rug obstinately unspattered by pink and gray things. "Heck of a job."

Then my fat-lunetted mimsies wandered to my Mac's screen and the Rheumas feebly homepaged as I wondered if I could possibly eradicate daisysdaughter.com's flood of posts from human memory. But my God! That little dialogue box I'd given up on must have been glowing for hours as my Mac docilely updated the numbers.

You have 18 comments pending, it read. When I tremblingly clicked on it, I saw that the first was a mildly sick joke. But I won't deny it came from a shrewd reader.

POSTED BY: DOTTIE FROM KANSAS   Hello, Pamique! What's cooking? It was a lovely oyster stew, too. Adieu, lover, adieu.

P.S. Toto says woof!

POSTED BY: MAISIE   I really liked what you wrote about that summer in Provincetown! I've never been there, but now I feel like I have been.

POSTED BY: SCOUT FROM MILLEDGEVILLE   I think you have a very firm sense of Right and Wrong. My question is, Where did it come from? Mine came from my Father. This doesn't seem to be your situation.

POSTED BY: MADELINE   Ram-Pam-Pam, so you and pauvre petite Gigi didn't like me? Boo hoo. Having my appendix out wasn't my idea. Saying *"je t'emmerde"* to you is.

POSTED BY: DOOM   Dear Mrs. Cadwaller, I run an online support group for daughters of oblivious mothers. Would you care to join? Please let me know. Topsy Diver, Laura Wingfield, and Caddy Compson are already on board.

Best wishes,

Pearl Prynne Dimmesdale, founder of DOOM

POSTED BY: Bonnie Blue Butler   Sorry, I can't link to DOOM. Can anyone out there help me?

POSTED BY: Eve in Topanga   Pam, don't you know the kids love *The Gal* nowadays? You should come to my next filmcon—last time I signed autographs for two hours. Or maybe you shouldn't, since you know what I'm like. It's always been all about me.

POSTED BY: Sabra in Passaic   Thank you so much for writing about my late husband. Nachum and myself as well greatly enjoyed our times with you on your and Ambassador Cadwaller's visits to Jerusalem. And yes, I'm afraid what's happened to Israel today is depressing.

Best always,

Sascha ben Zion (had you forgotten my name? I didn't forget yours.)

POSTED BY: A Psychiatrist   Dear Mrs. Cadwaller, I believe you would benefit from a consultation and I am a professional. My rates are quite low.

Yours,

Lucy Schroeder, Las Vegas

POSTED BY: Diva in Brussels   *Ah! Je ris de me voir si belle en ce miroir.*
Meilleurs souhaits,
Bianca Castafiore-Hergé, rue Rémi

POSTED BY: Une Dame Parisienne   *Je n'avais que sept ans le 25 août 1944, mais je me souviens très bien de vous agitant votre "cunt cap" pour amuser une petite fille ahurie qui vous regardait d'un balcon alors que vous rouliez vers la place*

Saint-Sulpice dans votre "jeep" avec M. Whitling. Je n'aurais pas su comment vous répondre mais je serais enchantée d'enfin faire votre connaissance. J'habite toujours le même immeuble.

    Fifi Rol-Tanguy

POSTED BY: PROF IN BIRMINGHAM, AL   Pam, I can't believe I'm inheriting "The African Queen"! But I don't want to for years and years yet. Many happy returns,

    Professor Helen F. Eichler, University of Alabama

POSTED BY: THE MERMAIDS   Hi, Pam! And we were singing to you. So there.

    Love, love, love

    Claire and Emily (a "Kirsten" to you)

POSTED BY: ERNEST WARNING, ESQ.   Ms. Buchanan, please cease and desist or we'll be forced to take action. You may be an old lady without even a cat, but a stalker's a stalker and we can't be too careful these days.

    Yours,

    Ernest Warning (attorney for Ms. Kirsten Dunst)

POSTED BY: CRAZY/BEAUTIFUL   Oh, come off it, Mac. I'm charmed. And Pam, I really am awfully good in *Interview with the Vampire*. Tom and Brad, not so much, but go figure. I knew what I was doing and they didn't.

POSTED BY: C   Pam, you honestly didn't know it was me at the beach house that day in 1951? Oh, well. *Honi soit qui Malibu*, as Dad used to say. If you aren't going to shoot yourself, why don't you come visit Edinburgh? J.K. Rowling lives nearby.

    Your warm admirer,

    Celia Brady (White, Singh, O'Grady)

POSTED BY: FSF   LOL

POSTED BY: DOLLY FROM GRAY STAR   I AM ALIVE I DID NOT DIE I AM A GRAND-
MOTHER TODAY IN GRAY STAR ALASKA

LOLITA

Dolores Haze Schiller

POSTED BY: *A Friend of Andy Pond's*   I'd just gotten through mumbling "Well, hello, Dolly" when I heard a key in my door at the Rochambeau
and clicked my Mac's screen off. "Pam, what on earth does this mean?" Andy
called, half amused but half worried.

As he stepped into my living room past the African Adam and Eve, he was
holding Kelquen's collar and a sheet of paper warning him in 72-point boldface
type: **ANDY—DON'T COME IN. CALL THE POLICE.** (Had you forgotten? So
had *l'équipe.* That was well before noon on Pam's longest day.)

"Oh, Andy! I'm so sorry to scare you. But my hair was just a wreck, and—
oh, I don't know what I was thinking. Give it here."

He did and I crumpled the message. Laid Kelquen's collar next to my Mac
before closing it down. With an octogenarian's careful if whistling (in truth,
carefully whistling—we geezers are awfully brittle even as flutes) version of
litheness, Andy returned to the foyer to collect the other burdens he'd set down:
a grocery bag loaded with my birthday dinner's makings and two DVDs, along
with a desiccated cardboard box whose inexplicability alarmed me.

He deposited the groceries in my kitchen and put *Meet Pamela* and *The Gal
I Left Behind Me* next to my TV. Then he rehefted the box, clearly the unadver-
tised *pièce de résistance* of the whole business, and presented it to me.

It was the size of a child's coffin. And the weight too, as I learned when he
laid it across the arms of Pam's wheelchair. "Andy, what is this?" I said.

He glowed with self-pleasure. "Oh, how I planned it! I planned it for
months. I first e-mailed Nenuphar back in November."

"Nenuphar?" Then I grew more incredulous: "Nenuphar has e-mail, for
Lord's sake? Some bloody monastery."

"I think they have to for the bread. You know, 'Flour of the Lily.' I've got a
loaf of their sourdough in the groceries too. It's said to be, well, heavenly."

"Then is this what I think it is?"

"Brother Nicholas's earthly possessions," Andy confirmed. "They turn everything in when they enter the order. But what they want preserved after they're gone gets put in a locker—like street clothes when you go swimming. This is all that your guardian asked them to keep, but no relative ever came forward to claim it."

"But how did you get it? You aren't a relative."

"That's where you're wrong," said Andy triumphantly. "Andrew Carraway Pond, at your service. Cadet branch of the family on my mother's side."

"Why didn't you ever tell me that?" I demanded, glancing up with some reluctance. All the mimsies wanted to do was stare stunned at what I'd never guessed might still exist: the Paris footlocker's missing twin.

"You never said 'Carraway' once until you mentioned his old agency last fall at the Kennedy Center. He doesn't come up all that often, and when he does, it's always been 'Nick,' 'Uncle Nick,' 'Brother Nicholas,' or just 'my old guardian.' That's when I got curious and checked."

"And then never told me," I protested.

"I wanted it to be a surprise. Isn't that what birthdays are for?"

"Are they ever," I grumbled through my dentition. Of course Andy knew nothing of Pam's longest day.

"Well!" he said, still beaming over his hat trick or tricks. "I know very well you can't wait to look inside. But I also doubt you want an onlooker while you do, since it's not really the same as cooing at the brand-new scarf Panama will probably give you. Why don't I go absent myself in the kitchen and start prepping dinner? I'm no Dottie Crozdetti, but I hope I'll do."

POSTED BY: *A Ward*   Once I got the thing open, inhaling its twice cloistered smell of *grands blés desséchés depuis longtemps*, the mimsies were greeted by a framed photo I'd studied many a time in my adolescence. Nick, Daisy, and Father stood in summer whites on a dim dock whose white lightpole a budding pudding had often done her pudgy solo best to turn into a maypole soon after I learned to walk.

Underneath it were a dozen or so unframed others in an envelope, including one that showed a surprisingly saturnine young Nick chatting with a Twenties dandy who had one white-shod foot balanced on the wide running board of an over-ornamented *nouveau riche* touring car. While I'd never laid eyes on him in the flesh that I knew of, I guessed his identity and instantly disliked him. The humorless self-love, the pompous narcissism of that superficially "sensitive," not unhandsome face had the power to appall me over eighty years later. It was true the former James Gatz had died young and by violence, but still.

Next came a manuscript carefully typed on an old typewriter, no doubt the same austere Olivetti I'd often seen parked on his desk's side table in the back room of the Carraway Agency's office. While I knew it could only be the memoir of my mother he'd claimed he'd destroyed, the title puzzled me. Beneath a crossed-out *Trimalchio in West Egg*, the top page advised that this was *Under the Red, White, and Blue* by Nicholas Carraway.

I read the opening paragraph, smiled reminiscently. Nick, your younger and *more* vulnerable years? And just how did those differ from your later ones?

I didn't want to grow absorbed, as Daisy's daughter and Nick's ward was reasonably sure she might be, and then get interrupted. While my practiced riffling of pages told me the thing was probably under 50,000 words long—bad for its commercial prospects had he ever considered publishing it—that was still far too much to get through while Andy mimicked *The Good Life with Dottie Crozdetti* in my kitchen, making just enough noise to confirm his lack of proximity for my benefit.

So I put *Under the Red, White, and Blue* aside and promptly regretted doing so more than I ever had not drinking the Great Unknown's sun tea, which is saying something. The final item in the Nenupharcophagus was something I dreaded seeing.

Unlike one of the contributors to it, the Fall 1934 edition of *Pink Rosebuds* hadn't changed a great deal. Same inept drawing of a nude screened by flowers as she gazed at a unicorn on the duly pink cover, same dutiful if sneakily brutal dedication "To Miss Hormel, Our Onlie Begetter." And above all, as the Rheumas turned now dully age-grayed pages the mimsies didn't want turned, the same long mentally suppressed poemess: "Chanson d'automne," by new girl Pamela Buchanan.

One minute later, an aproned Andy rushed to my side with an octogenarian's careful version of urgency. "Pam, my God, my God! What is it?"

Wrapping my ribcage for protection, I was keeling and keening in my wheelchair. Jaw blindly agape and fat-lunetted mimsies groping like unfed mouths, I was begging somebody, something's, anything's mercy.

Cast away violently, the Fall 1934 edition of the Literary Magazine of Purcey's Girls' Academy of St. Paul was a mess of pink and gray things on the rug.

POSTED BY: *Our Newest Pink Rosebud*   Even as five clawing Rheumas waved Andy away, the mimsies turned wild Civil War memorials on him. Desperate for concealment, what little was left of my unsplattered but still shipwrecked brain grabbed *petit-navire*-style at a straw. As I'd told a jumpy Georgetown faculty wife once long ago, it's always the time for literary criticism.

"Oh, my God, Andy! It was just, well, it's just. It's just, you see! I always thought my French was so good back then—and it wasn't. Honestly, how could I—could I of all people!—have used '*arrachent*' as an *intransitive* verb? At that age? That's the sort of mistake Tim would make. He was out of that bloody country by the age of seven."

"Come on now, Pam. We know each other," Andy gently reminded me. "Just try to regroup a bit first. I'll wait."

"I'm perfectly all right. But Andy, the *tense change!* From the conditional! It's so awful, so awful. My God, even you would know better! And Hormel— poor Hormel—poor Hormel didn't. Her and her Bawdyleer! Oh, we were made for each other, that's obvious. *C'est le bal de la comtesse Hormel!*"

Delicately stooping in lunette-befogged triplicate, Andy collected *Pink Rosebuds* from the rug. "Forgive me, honey," he said. "I'm just not going to be a lot of help if I don't know what's upset you."

"Go on, then! Go on. You'll laugh 'til your sides split, I swear," I cawed at him. "Christ, in all these years I never knew how lucky I was to be at stupid Purcey's by then. At Chignonne's, they'd have laughed at me more! Hated me, hated me, made fun of me more—and for better reasons, too. They can do without honor, but grammar's the last line of defense."

Unlike his role in my life as Cadwaller's proxy, Andy's own French wasn't Proustian. But it hardly had to be to decipher my mess of a poemess. As its sole virtue was brevity, he didn't need long.

And was unfooled. "Pam, I'm so sorry. I had no idea. What an awful mistake this was. I should have gone through the box first and then asked what you wanted to see."

"No, no. I'm honestly fine now," I shakily said, reaching for Kleenex. Tried to smile: "My God, what came over me? Andy, forgive me. No excuse at my age. It was seventy-two years ago."

For one minute it hadn't been. For that one minute, flitting, mincing, and sauntering around me, Purcey's Girls' Academy had once again snared gawky boat-footed Pam in its corridors.

The burlesque declamations of "Chanson d'automne" as I crept by to beg Hormel to let me drop French class. The jokes: "Guess we know now why Buchanan's mom did it. God, Harmony, could *you* have stood that sniffling one more second?" (*"May nawn,* Sigourney," Harmony Preston snickered.) And worse yet, since Daisy was at least dead but I wasn't and didn't know how to be, the lowing greeting that stopped me in doorways, sent me hastening down hallways, kept me blubbering in bathrooms: "Moo! ... Moo, big Sandy, here comes Buchanan! ... *Moo!*"

"Sure you're okay now?" Andy asked. "Glass of water?"

"Scotch. A bloody great big one," I said and wondered why I was quoting John le Carré. If *anyone'*d earned a drink at the end of the day, you must agree *l'équipe* here at daisysdaughter.com had.

"Water and ice?"

"Do I look like I've changed? And oh! Andy, of course get whatever you like for yourself. I should've said so earlier."

"Pam, I'm your cook! I did feel entitled to pour a glass of red wine in the kitchen."

"Then bring that too. At least it's good for your heart," I told his back as he went.

"Oh? It is, really? Good news."

POSTED BY: *A Blushing (I'll Say) Bride*   After we'd let our drinks do the talking for a bit, Andy steepled his fingers. "As your birthday chef, I'm at your disposal. I'm also damned if I'm going to make another decision tonight without getting your input first. Would you rather eat now or watch one of your movies?"

"Oh, eat, eat. I'm starving. Nothing but nibbles all day."

"Why didn't you say so?"

"It didn't seem all that interesting."

"Sometimes I wonder why I put up with this crap," Andy muttered. He'd already restowed *Pink Rosebuds* and Nick's other mementos in the Nenupharcophagus, tactfully placing it in the foyer so that I could nudge it out into the hall with no trouble if that's what I wanted. As he moved to clear my living room table, he looked puzzled at the battlements I'd stacked against my ruins: everything from Murphy's *Collected Plays* and *The Pilgrim Lands at Malibu* to a picture of Noah Gerson exiting a jeep at the Wailing Wall and another of Hopsie in his topper and swim trunks.

"Pam, what've you been up to?"

"All that? Oh, nothing. Just a few things Tim Cadwaller—you know him, our Cadwaller's grandson—asked me to sort for him. Something to do with a book, I believe. That's why I got out his last one, see what I'd be in for."

Andy was holding Nan's snapshot of Cadwaller. "I've always liked this one," he said with Pondian fondness. "You know I regret missing out on Nagon."

"Someone had to hold the fort at the Department. You had Paris and none of the others did. But how do you know the photo?"

"Pam, I've met Nan Finn once or twice in my life," Andy said patiently. "She sent me one afterward too."

"I thought it was just me." (I did feel a bit trespassed on.)

"As I remember, there were fifty or sixty of us. Nan's idea of a gesture is just quieter than yours. But ours were smaller."

As Andy restored *You Must Remember This: The Posthumous Career of World War Two* to its spot in the trophy bookcase, his eye fell on the hastily replaced and damnably protruding copy of *by Pamela Buchanan's* second book above it. He'd known since Paris days what had nestled behind *Glory Be* throughout Hopsie's and my marriage, and one push of the book's spine told him it was again. Cadwaller's gun was in his hand before I could protest.

"Now I'm *really* getting curious," he said. "I thought this had been exiled to the Paris footlocker with the other private souvenirs. What's going on?"

"Aren't I allowed to make one sentimental gesture on my birthday?" I croaked. "Anyhow, it's not loaded."

He looked so infuriatingly amused that I'd have shot him with it if it had been and I could've wheeled over to wrestle it from his grip. "How long ago did you find out?"

"Some time ago. But the question, dear Andy, is how you know to begin with."

"Cadwaller asked me to do it before he went into Bethesda," Andy explained, ejecting the empty ammo clip with an octogenarian's careful version of cockiness. His mimicry of Hopsie was convincing mostly because it was affectionate: "'Andy,' said he, 'I'm not a vain man. But I worry our Pam cares about me a good deal, and under the circumstances I can't count on her intelligence to choose the best way of demonstrating it after I'm gone.' So, yes—I've got the bullets." He displayed their former home on his extended palm. "Which, yes, I've been sentimental enough to keep. In my *Berlin* footlocker."

So naturally, once the table was cleared and then set—oysters brought out on the half shell, then replaced by crab cakes, salad, and sourdough bread baked in Brother Nicholas Carraway's old kiln as Andy's red and my white wine (one Scotch had been more than enough to make an invisible Hardy Boys doctor gibber in distress) flowed—we talked about my and our Cadwaller. Then we talked about Nan and *A Midsummer Night's Dream*, the last play we'd attended with her at the Folger: a marvelous Oberon, a miscast but often delightful Titania.

Then, as we always did, we turned to Potus and Potusville and the war and the rest of the mess he'd made of our now ancient lives. "Yes, and then they started calling French fries freedom fries," Andy said, twinkling.

When that didn't provoke me to a fresh Pamamiad, he looked mildly quizzical. He knew nothing of Pam's longest day. Nor had I told him of my White House phone call, since I knew I'd have to rehash it at length and it had turned out in the end to be so negligible.

That wasn't the only reason I was distracted. By the time Andy cleared our plates and went to get us our coffee, Pam's awareness that she had one more chore to perform had the Rheumas twisting my napkin. He came back with two cups, set them down next to our respective medicinal Rubicon cubes.

"Andy," I said. "Not without some surprise, I've got to admit this has been really lovely. What I've got to say now is rotten thanks, but I've made up my mind. You need to know I can't marry you."

The milk he was pouring didn't even break stride. "Well! I'm glad that's been settled," he said cheerfully. "Of course I have no idea what you're talking about."

POSTED BY: *Meet Pamela* "Andy Pond, you've got nerve! You've spent three or four years trying to talk me into moving in with you," I accused him. "'Why don't we play out the string under the same roof? Wouldn't it be easier to quit kidding ourselves?' Yes, and then you even said, 'Pam, you can't cook and I can. Why don't I do it for both of us every day? I'm not Dottie but I'll do and so on and so forth.'" Speaking of cooking, I'm afraid Pam's humble pie came straight from literature's Automat: "Have you met someone else, for God's sake?"

"Yes, quite a while ago." He'd gone from perplexed to concerned to affectionate as I spoke. "Pam, I'm sorry, but I wasn't proposing. I was just being practical. You live alone, so do I, and we're ancient."

"So a little rash senile groping in our old age might do us in and good riddance?"

"No, not at all. I worry about you. So does Nan, for that matter. I can't tell you how often we've talked about it."

"Oh boo fucking hoo," I snapped at him. "If you two are my friends, I am not to be worried about. I forbid it. I'll shoot you both."

"With what? I told you I've got the bullets. Pam, listen. You can't walk half a block without needing your wheelchair. If those fat glasses of yours broke, you'd be as lost as a mole at the Ice Capades. Apparently, looking out for you also runs in my family. What if there's a fire in the Rochambeau, what if you break your hip in the shower? I'm not saying I'm robust. I'm just betting against you falling down in the bathtub at exactly the moment the kitchen stove blows up in my face."

"Oh, what horseshit. Alone we could die game. Who's the somebody else?"

"Pam, you're joking."

"Often. Not right now. Who is she?"

Andy sighed and then smiled. "I've been in love with Nan Finn since the week *Breathless* came out in Paris," he said, and I *did* feel a bit slow on the uptake. "You and Hopsie didn't know them yet then, but I did. They were over from Frankfurt and we saw the odd little movie everybody was talking about."

"And?"

"And nothing. And everything, at least for young Andy. Afterward we went to a café and Nan started prattling about how mean she thought Godard had been to poor Jean Seberg—you know, the same way she still does at her Christmas party. All of three sentences in I was praying my face wouldn't give me away."

"Why not? I know Nan. She'd have been flattered."

"You knew Ned too. He was watching. He always did most men. Like a hawk, drunk or sober."

"Why didn't you ever do anything about it? I mean once he was no longer with us. It has been a while."

"Love's love," Andy shrugged. "It's an emotion, Pam, not a directive. Nothing in any law says you've got to do something about it. I didn't, I haven't. I was and am pretty sure Nan wouldn't want me to."

"Does she know?"

"Oh, I think so by now. That's why I'm pretty sure she doesn't want me to do something about it."

"But then—oh, for God's sake, Andy. What about bloody *me*?"

"What about you? You're the wife of the man I admired more than any I've known. You're my dearest old friend. I've never regretted a moment I've spent with you no matter how hard you tried. But romance? No, never. That's the whole story."

"Romance, my ass," I reproached him. "I'm just being practical too. You could've at least groped me a few times before we got senile. As I recall, I was still up for boinky-boink as late as Clinton's reelection. Hell, I'd've let you call me Nan if you wanted. Or *needed* to, Andy. So there."

Instead of fading, Andy's smile took an odd turn. "Pam, let's be honest. Don't you think that shoe might belong on the other foot?" he asked mildly.

"And what does that mean?"

"Oh, Pam, please."

"Oh Pam please what?"

"Oh Pam please," said Andy as if to a child, "we knew even in Paris that you were a lesbian."

Such a long day I'd had. Would it ever end?

"Well, Mr. Pond. You *do* have the bullets," I told him.

"That's not how I thought of it."

"God, how I do loathe that word," I said, an aversion daisysdaughter.com readers have presumably noticed by now. "The only word in the language I hate more is 'orphan.'"

"Pam, I'm sorry."

Then my head jerked back up. "'*We*'? Who in hell is this 'we,' may I ask? Oh do tell," I drawled.

But that only tickled him. "To be honest, my hunch is a fair number of people. But I was mainly thinking of Cadwaller."

5. Carole Lombard's Plane

POSTED BY: *Pamus*   Sorry, daisysdaughter.com readers. Which I now know I do have, however scattered or odd or disguised or perverse. I didn't mean to leave you hanging.

If you must know I passed out at midnight. Then I dragged the old pretzel I live in to bed with no recollection of what I'd been doing at my computer. May I remind you I turned eighty-six yesterday.

It's now afternoon on June 7. D Plus One, as we called it in Normandy. What the D might stand for here is of course up to you.

Nonetheless, I'm a believer in courtesy where courtesy's due. That's why the first thing I did this morning was to pick up the telephone—no longer the elephone; that was yesterday too—and call dear Bob's office. "This is Pamela Cadwaller. Is the Senator in?"

True, he's been out of the Senate since '96. His wife's now the one whose office is on Capitol Hill. But beside the Potomac, your last title's permanent. Hopsie was "Mr. Ambassador" even in the ICU.

"I'm sorry, no, Mrs. Cadwaller. Would you like to leave a message?"

"Yes. I just wanted to thank him for arranging my birthday call yesterday. It made for an interesting day and I do so like those. Don't you?"

"I'm sorry, I'm new. Will the Senator know what you're talking about?"

"Oh, yes, dear, I think so. But if not, he'll know how to fake it. We're old."

I left my number in case. Then out of the blue I plucked the likely significance of my Oval Office interlocutor's most peculiar remark: "He came down here, showing everyone his gun." Must've meant Bob did a little reminding he's got a bit of standing as a World War Two vet—as also, by attachment, do I.

The second thing I did was to open the Nenupharcophagus and retrieve Nicholas Carraway's *Under the Red, White, and Blue*. Spent a couple of hours with the only eyewitness account of the Scandal and could see why he'd fibbed to Pammie about burning the typescript. Almost involuntarily, he'd kept painting my mother in hues less than lovely.

Nick's ridiculous infatuation with her pigheaded Narcissus of a bootlegger suitor had me more than once rolling the mimsies behind my fat lunettes. When I got to some guff about the fellow's "Platonic ideal of himself," I snorted "Forty-nine cents for *cabbage*? Cripes! What's Denmark coming to?" But I must say that in every gesture and sneer, Father lives and breathes like a lab rat under cold light. As for the budding pudding who was to become me, she only trots in and out once or twice, a child of no particular interest or importance except as a refraction of Daisy's mentality.

Was I hurt? Oh, hell no. Children that young don't interest me either. What charmed and engrossed me was the discovery that my diffident guardian, the modest Chicago ad man who'd coined "WE KEEP YOU CLEAN IN MUSCATINE," was an astonishing writer. His perceptions of romance remain immature: picture Daisy's dim life at forty with her bootlegger suitor and you'll see what a crock the whole thing is. Yet the verbal music, knit of detail, and compact choice of incident were all breathtaking. As you may've noticed, achieving compactness has not been daisysdaughter.com's best event.

I honestly think that if *Under the Red, White, and Blue* had been published as fiction—perhaps under some better, more compact title in an alternative funhouse America I sometimes like to imagine—it'd be seen today as some sort of small classic. Knowing my compatriots, of course they'd swoon at the drivel instead of admiring the prose and planning.

Then just for the fuck of it I watched *The Gal I Left Behind Me* for the first time since Glendale, and guess what? Tim was right. Now that Bill M.'s long gone, I can better appreciate Hal Lime's skill at miming chipper but unreliable callowness. Eve is yummy, and of course there's no pretense that she's playing me. As for Pam's own mute cameo—as "Peg Kimball" enters what I think is supposed to be Claridge's in her bouncy new war-reporter togs to taunt Eddie "Harting," I come out the revolving door's other side, dressed as a nurse—it's fairly funny if you're in the know. They cut away just as I start to glance behind me.

Those two seconds of film are also the only photographic record of Pam as she was then in motion. Gerson and I took no home movies, that being too much of a busman's holiday for my second husband. I admit to reprogramming that DVD chapter more than once.

After I'd watched myself exit a soundstage revolving door multiple times, the next thing I did was to retrieve yesterday's Metro section from its June 6 seagull skate under my table. Smoothed it out and reread the story the mimsies had read at a quarter past six the morning of my longest day. That was mere minutes before I fetched Cadwaller's gun and daisysdaughter.com first Lindberghized cyberspace: "As of now, my name is" and so on and on.

What was it? Why, Dottie Idell's obituary, of course. I did keep saying "recently," didn't I?

POSTED BY: *I'll Be Damned*   Sorry again, daisysdaughter.com readers. I've just realized I never did get around to wrapping up my conversation with Andy Pond about me being a lesbian. No doubt you could script Pam's next line yourself:

"Cadwaller?" I repeated with some consternation.

"Oh, sure," Andy said. "Some days in Paris, he'd come into my office if you were meeting him, pop his pipe out, and say, 'Where's that big dyke wife of mine gotten to? Do you know, Andy?' with the happiest grin on his face. But never in front of someone who might take it the wrong way, of course."

"Then he was joking."

"Oh, Pam! I don't know how many times when we three were out some-where we'd both catch you eyeing the girls through the window or getting all flustered if the waitress was pretty. He'd look at me, I'd look at him, and we'd smile. He wasn't a winker, though—hated that kind of redundancy and knew the difference between affection and insult. So did I."

"But then why," I stammered idiotically, wringing Pam's third and last wedding band on my left Rheuma Three, "if Hopsie thought so all along—"

"He was Cadwaller. A man who'd spent his career counseling people against thinking in categories," Andy reminded me. "You could say he had 'a certain idea of Pam.' He loved you and he knew you adored him. He knew all that was a longing, not an imperative. He knew you'd never do anything about it."

"And I didn't."

"I know, but come on. At some level you must've realized he was tolerant instead of oblivious. The day you dropped your oyster fork at La Coupole, the look on your face when our little Brigitte knelt down was so lovely that we both had to fight not to start laughing like two Yuletide revelers."

"He never once hinted he knew," I marveled. "Even in private, when we talked about everything. Not once in twenty-eight years."

"Of course not," said Andy. "You'd have been devastated, and then—what next? Not Cadwaller's way, Pam. He liked having a what next well in hand."

"Yes, he did," I said and we looked at his bulletless gun. Then a fresh panic welled, cued by I knew not what: "Andy, you said lots of people! Does *Nan*—"

"Dear Lord, no," he laughed. "You know our glorious girl. I guarantee she'd never wonder or guess in a century," which relieved me immensely. I couldn't have faced her next Christmas party otherwise.

"Listen, this is so wonderful," Andy went on. "You know Nan's been crazy for Sondheim for years. But I swear just last month she suddenly blurted, 'And what's funny is I don't know *anything* about his personal life. Andy, do you?

Marriages, children, divorces?' We're just lucky she did visas, not Army recruitment centers."

"Or unlucky." My sharp tone was only a baby step, Panama. But mine own.

"Or unlucky," he agreed. Then his face took on the look of compassion I'd found unforgivable when I saw it on Gerson's, but up to then Noah had been a husband and not an old friend. "Pam, if you don't mind me asking—did you ever do anything about it? Not during Cadwaller. Even once in your whole blessed life?"

"If you must know, just once. A very long time ago. And I can't say *I did*, only that I was there. She was braver. And now if you don't mind, Andy, can you let yourself out? You've been very kind, but I've had a rough day. Didn't sleep much at all."

POSTED BY: *Alfred J. Pamfrock*   She was Dorothy Idell on our Bank Street lease, Dottie Crozdetti to fans of her roistering laugh and way with a chicken on *The Good Life*... many years later. She was, uneuphoniously, "Dottie I. Crozdetti" in the headline of yesterday's obit, suggesting some excessive minding of p's and q's. But in my arms, she was always—oh, good God, what am I quoting? While I rue Pam's cowardice, which I've broadcast quite some time ago was splendid, I hardly think I in any way was Dottie's monster.

She may've been the love of my life. Or perhaps I mean could've been, but what I won't say is *was*. Not only do I mistrust *love of my life* as a category—how can we be positive until we've laid eyes on the last stranger we'll meet?—but I don't see how it has much meaning when it's not acted on. And obviously, Panama, if anyone does fit the bill in the life I did have, it was your great-grandfather.

But for a few precious months of 1940 and '41, in our little nook of West Village bliss, she was so lovely and I loved her so: my Dottie, my Dottie, my Dottie Idell. And I loved her dotties and I loved her idell. Lovers' talk, dating to when few people knew where Pearl Harbor was! No doubt she didn't mean to be prescient when with a grin, elbow to saucily nippled pillow and bare hip a crescent of down playing dawn, she laid a finger on my nose and named me Pamique.

I made just one contribution to *The Good Life with Dottie Crozdetti*. In Bank Street days, as I've mentioned, she was still caught between cooking and acting, a choice no one could've guessed she'd solve by combining them in a medium then embryonic. As I think I've also mentioned, she loved giving burlesque poetry recitals in our apartment, and one sweet afternoon (how I lived to win my Dottie's glee, when she'd flash her small teeth with delight and toss up her sunset-colored hair!) I taught her Sinclair St. Clair's old Provincetown jingle. When I watched her recite it in triumph on television half a century later—it was her farewell show, meaning she'd saved it up—I burst into tears. Except for a beaming "You heard me. Now good luck to you all!," the last words spoken by Dottie Crozdetti on her old TV show were ones daisysdaughter.com readers well know:

> To eat an oyster
> You crack it foister.
> This part is moister!
> Oh, drat—I loyst her.

And it was a poem that ended it; it was a poem that triggered Pam's fear. Oh, Dottie! We could've had weeks, months, a whole Bank Street year more together. Why did you have to turn on one heel in my oversized shoe, arms raised, and gloriously starkers with our windowed June at your back, just as you hit that point of "Dover Beach"—the first line and a half of its final stanza, if anyone out there is reaching for Bartlett's—and your eyes and your dotties and your lovely blonde idell all stared in Pamique's just-turned-twenty-one face? That evening was when Brannigan Murphy crashed through the commode door at the Commodore, two Pulitzer Prizes to the wind.

And oh. Are you out there, Miss Dunst? If so, please forgive me. I don't know if the comment from "Crazy/Beautiful" came from you or some cyber-masked prankster, but I do hope you were charmed.

I do think you're a wonderful actress, Miss Dunst. But dear God, oh, God—the *resemblance!* Face, voice, manner, and all. Everything, everything, unless loving me counts. When I first blinked at you, never once having heard of you—not in one of your movies, but on TV red-carpeting it at some awards show—I thought I'd gone out of my mind and then that I wished so. Wept, stroked puzzled Kelquen an hour. Then Andy Pond, who I now realize had more than an inkling we weren't just movie fans but still can't have guessed the whole truth, became my tolerant escort at film after film where we were sixty or seventy years older than most.

If you care, the one in which you most resemble her is, of course, *Bring It On*. Fans of *The Good Life with…* don't suspect not only because Dottie's show had been off the air for some years before you began acting but because Dottie was past fifty, hearty, and as big as a barrel by the time it premiered.

Miss Dunst, perhaps now you can see why the prospect of seeing you as Marie Antoinette first bewitched and then terrorized me yesterday. For the gallant girl who so closely resembles my Dottie—my Dottie, my Dottie, my Dottie Idell—to play the queen I most equate with Daisy Buchanan was too much crossed circuitry for one old bag to bear. Now that I think of it, daisysdaughter.com may owe Lady Antonia Fraser a mild apology too.

Dottie was three years my senior, which I agree ought to've made seeing her *WashPost* obituary painful but highly unremarkable. At my age, so many contemporaries have shuffled off to that big Buffalo in the sky that even the dearest don't rate much more than a twinge of affection for our days flying Clio together. Even Bill M.'s adios didn't tempt me to say the hell with it and end the whole shebang, and my District was Potusville by then. It may strike you as preposterous that even my old Bank Street lover's obit could drive me to Lindberghize cyberspace with Cadwaller's gun in my lap.

True. But what I couldn't understand was why someone would murder her: my Dottie, my Dottie, my Dottie Idell. I couldn't imagine a housebreaker vicious or panicked enough to shoot a woman that old as she and her walker shuffled out of her kitchen—my Dottie, my Dottie, my Dottie Idell.

The obituary was in the Metro section, but the box was on Page A1: "Host Slain." When I lifted the gun out of the Paris footlocker, what overcame seven decades of dread that I'd end up making a "Like mother, like daughter" exit was Pam's thought that my Dottie and I would at least both die by violence.

Anyhow, once I'd got done rereading the obit today—not much on Crozdetti except that he'd been a French-born banker, unless that "n" was a typo, and

had long predeceased her, giving me a pang I soon stifled at our lost merry widowhood in a small house in Provence or Providence—I slid out the full page
(four in all, really: newsprint seagull-wings fluttered) of the Metro section that
included it to refold and then place in the Paris footlocker. Then I opened the
footlocker and set Dottie Idell next to Cadwaller's gun.

Before I closed the lid, though, I realized I had two more mementos I ought
to make amends or just understanding's belated concession to. Fishing past
Dottie's obit and Hopsie's last gift to me—life—the Rheumas found and with-
drew two old velvet cases. For the first time in six decades (Paris, 1944, briefly),
I opened them and took out the two syringes inside.

Gold and silver, silver and gold! You can get Daisy Buchanan addicted to
morphine, but you can't make her stop being Daisy Buchanan. The gold one a
gift from her to the Lotus Eater, coyly inscribed *Give me your answer do* by some
patient, devoted, bribable jeweler.

From her to the Lotus Eater? Oh, hell yes. One thing a child's photograph-
ing eyes very seldom get wrong is colors, particularly those featured in fairy
tales. Roseately glowing, the gold one had been in the L.E.'s soft paw when that
fabled bathroom door creaked open in Provincetown. Knowing my mother,
swapping works wouldn't have been Daisy's thing. Too inelegant.

In a tiny casket I'd dropped deep down a well and made haste to cover with
all manner of rubbish, I'd always secreted the knowledge that my mother had
been wooer, not prey. On the beach that night in 1927, she'd gaily said "Lech"
in order to sexualize the instantly sulky L.E.'s quite mild comment about the
actress in the movie we'd seen. The L.E. had fled Provincetown the next day
because Daisy was getting as obsessively proprietary as her own bootlegger
suitor had been in the year of the Scandal. If you thought my narration was, as
they say, reliable, congratulations: you got fooled by a traumatized seven-year-
old.

My guess is the Lotus Eater was only in it for the morphine. When I came
upon her having sex behind a dune with the wristwatched man Pink Thing
needed many years to concede was probably the young Brannigan Murphy—
Jesus, you did get *that*, didn't you?—her eyes were hoping that what Pammie
knew would provoke a rupture. But I'll never know whether my mother's pas-

sion in widowhood to get her dazzling gold Daisy-head between the L.E.'s thighs was an individual case, as Cadwaller would put it, or the lifelong and generic yearning it had been for her daughter. Certainly in Belgium she hadn't shown tendencies. Just got fat, moody, depressed, and then suicidal, despite the best efforts of a Swiss sanatorium.

In that same tiny casket was the secret that, other than suicide, turning greedily, insanely, lickingly, ceiling-kickingly, joyously lesbian was the "Like mother, like daughter" I'd most feared and quaked at all my life. Only Dottie won out because she was Dottie, even if Celia Brady—assuming that comment too wasn't a cybermasked joker's—came awfully close one day at Malibu. My cruelty to Hormel was in taunting her after that poor woman's sheer unattractiveness had made her too bloody easy to dismiss as a freak.

As for me, don't you see I was too strange already? With both parents dead by inordinate means, the Scandal still fresh, my European schooling, my impoverished bust, and my five foot ten? Even between L.E. thighs, my mother's gold head was at least pert and comely. She was Daisy Buchanan, lovely and rich enough to make her own rules. But her ungainly daughter? My God, bikini girl, I had to hope or pretend that *something* about me was normal—as we called it then.

I never told Andy Pond last night that Pam's only other confessor had been the thirty-sixth President of the United States. Can't remember which of my White House *Piétas* it was, but he looked up from my lap after I'd sung "A Bicycle Built for Two."

"You're a big ol' dyke somewhere in there behind those eyes. Ain't you, Mrs. Cadwaller?" he asked thoughtfully.

My head dipped. "Yes, Esau," I said. "How did you know?"

"Oh, hell. I've been mighty used my whole life to women acting like they know something I don't know. The ones who act like they know something I *do* know always kind of jump out at me."

Yet the other "Like mother, like daughter"—suicide—was the one I had acted on. What may surprise you is that I'm not referring to pulling the trigger of Cadwaller's (blessedly) unloaded gun yesterday. I mean my suicide in self-defense at the age of fourteen at Purcey's Girls' Academy after "Chanson d'automne" made me a laughingstock.

Surrounded by jokes at my dead mother's expense and cries of "Moo! Moo!," I'd not only sworn I'd never write another goddam poemess so long as I lived. I'd vowed I'd never again let the world see Pam's unguarded heart.

I kept that vow seventy-two years. That was why hearing Dottie peal "Ah, love, let us be true to one another!" as she turned to me in our Bank Street apartment had panicked Pamique into bolting to Bran Murphy's arms, hairy reputation and Murphine avoirdupois. The only other *what next* would have been to find out whether she meant it or was just cutting one of her dottily idyllic capers.

What if it turned out my naked roommate was not only goofing around but her pirouette's golden prisoner and hadn't especially meant to address Pam face to face at that moment? Then the only *what next* for me would've been to like-mother-like-daughter it right off the Brooklyn Bridge. Or if I had subway fare (only a nickel then!), off the top of the Empire State Building.

So tell me, tireless daisysdaughter.com readers: are you blubbering yet? Are you getting misty at the dismal old lady finally spilling the torments that warped, scarred, and blighted her life—the situation, incidentally, of Bran's rotten-sounding unwritten play, *The Other Eye of the Newt*? Are you getting ready to gasp at the Miss Havisham wedding cake my dead Dottie baked for me in 1941 as I suddenly produce it from the Paris footlocker? (Shit, it's not *that* big.) Are you waiting for the Fall 1934 edition of *Pink Rosebuds* to start charring in the Rochambeau's incinerator as dark music swells? Are you, children? Are you? *Are you?*

Well, the hell with that noise.

POSTED BY: *Pamerica*   I daresay by now we've met a few times. The odd mermaid joke aside, does the voice of daisysdaughter.com strike you as Prufrockian? Is my vibe *plaintive* to you? Sorry, but I'm an old e.e. gal from way back on the beach.

You've read the tale of my life and you don't know the half of it: countless glimmers of fun and moments of radiance from Washington, India, Hopsie's and my later travels. A thousand jokes, four hundred friends, Istanbul and Jakarta. Our Culpeper getaway, where we two old hands at it made love dozens of times after his diagnosis.

I wrote three books, saw a war, rode an elephant through the Pink City. I got briskly why-Henry'd by Lyndon Johnson and gave him some comfort in belated return. I shared a few laughs with Jack Kennedy after he'd beaten me out for the Pulitzer. I fell in love with the best war cartoonist in American history in a villa at Anzio, got introduced to my third husband by Art Buchwald dressed as a Pilgrim. I lit a Lucky Strike on Dog Green at sunset of D-Day and answered a voice calling "Margaret Mitchell" in a concentration camp.

I had three marriages I wouldn't give up for anything. Not even the first one, messy portage to the rest. After all, no Murphy and no *Clock with Twisted Hands* premiere, no *by Pamela Buchanan* in *Regent's*. No Viv, Tess, Josie, and Babe in a Tennessee coal mine, no Lieutenant Connie Ostrica snapping off a salute, no Jessie Auster becoming a dot in the sky over Avenger Field, Sweetwater, Texas. And no ETO: no Anzio or Omaha, no Eddie Whitling or Bill M.

No Anzio, Omaha, Eddie Whitling, or Bill M., no Dame and no Gerson. No *Dame* and no Gerson, no voluptuous allure of Hollywood: Pam's gams flashing sly lilac bloomers to tarmac and sportcoats as I got into my studio car, Myrna Loy sipping tea amid bougainvillea and chatter about Truman's chances. No Eve and Addison in their garden paradise in the hills above Malibu, where the Great Unknown might've gotten me not only sipping sun tea but sunbathing next to or even on top of her if she'd only told me she was—great Scott!—Celia Brady.

No Fran Kukla's *Hamlet* and no *Glory Be*. No visit to Israel when it was still Panavision. No Nachum (and Sascha!) ben Zion.

Also no painful breakup with Gerson, true. But no breakup with Gerson, no retreat to Paris to paste it together. And no retreat to Paris to paste it together—here comes the big one, bikini girl—no U.S. Ambassador Richard Anson "Hopsie" Cadwaller. He was dressed as John Paul Jones, too.

Who cares if I still occasionally had dotty reveries of parting an idell's emjambments as my Hopsie tongued me? If there's a woman alive, closeted dyke or frustrated *pétroleuse*, who'd pass up the chance to spend twenty-eight years with that man, I wouldn't stop running after him long enough to piss on her if she were on fire. What I would've gained had I stayed on my own and kept calling "Red rover," I can't say. But I know what I'd have lost. It's no contest.

Recall what I said to Andy quite late last night: "If you two are my friends, I am not to be worried about. I'll shoot you both." So listen up, all my new friends in Lindberghized cyberspace. If you ever have the gall to shed a single tear in my case for what might've been, *I'll shoot you all.* Dottie Idell or no Dottie Idell, Great Unknown or no Great Unknown, do I look that damned greedy to you?

Honestly, what's wrong with you people? What is all this American gibbering about lost sleds and such? Or a green light that blinked from some future morphine junkie's dock on Long Island? Oh boo fucking hoo. I know better than anyone what a sweet man and fine writer Nick Carraway was, but that boats-against-the-current hogwash of his just makes me upchuck. Something I did not do on the run-in to D-Day as German shells turned the ocean into gray pine trees.

So shove the Miss Havisham wedding cake that my Dottie—my Dottie, my Dottie, my Dottie Idell—never baked. For Christ's sake, she might've moved out a month later. We only roomed together because neither one could afford a place of her own.

And yes, darling: I miss you anyway. I dab your nose back, my love, and I remember. But imagination makes up for a lot in Pam's skyborne and vaulting view through a thick window. I'm a writer, you see.

Oh, I was no Mary McCarthy, Martha Gellhorn, Marguerite Higgins, Janet Flanner, Lillian Ross, Pauline Kael, Barbara Tuchman, or even Susan Mary Alsop. Just as my Dottie was not only no Kirsten Dunst but no Julia Child, whose kitchen is in the Smithsonian and should be. As should the *Spirit of St. Louis*, which preceded it there. On my favorite imaginary airline—Clio Airways, of course—I was only a passenger and at best sometime stewardess. How we flew.

POSTED BY: *Pan Am for Paname*   I can't help being smitten with the notion that Pam's longest day gave dead Daisy something she never expected. Or wanted, since she'd have just felt old. She nonetheless deserved a grandchild from her ungainly dyke daughter, even if a misshapen one made only of words.

Maternity at my age is no bowl of cherries, so you'll have to forgive me if I take it easy for the next day or so. Among other chores, I've got a trip to get ready for.

Where am I going? Why, Provincetown! Two visits eighty years apart hardly qualify as a return to the scene of the crime. Other than the Pilgrim Monument and possibly a shack or two, I doubt I'll see a single thing there I've ever laid eyes on.

That's unless I bump into Norman, a monument of a different color, out walking on his two canes. Then maybe, from my wheelchair—I've got a cane too, just don't use it for much except poking people—I'll tease him about borrowing a garbled phrase from "Dover Beach" for the title of *The Armies of the Night*. Or maybe not, since we all know how lesbians unnerve him. I'm a wicked lady now, Mr. Mailer, aren't I?

And yes, Panama: of course I'll see you. I'll see your foxy grandpa too, along with his Renée. Plus your old dad and mom. How odd I've hardly mentioned Concepción! Tim married his Nicaraguan bride the year my Cadwaller died. You came along four years later, and so far as I can tell your parents are still very much in love. I'm sure Tim's never looked at another woman since—not one available to him, anyhow.

I do feel a tad apprehensive about my first plane trip in two years. It'll be my first with this damned wheelchair, which'll look bloody silly at the end of a parachute if we have to bail out. But does it really matter?

Even here on the ground, I'm already riding. I'm already riding, riding. (Good lyric for Pink, bikini girl—yes, no?) I'm already riding Carole Lombard's plane.

So are you, Panama. So are we all from the day of our birth. We could all smack into a mountain tomorrow, and so what? Crammed with people not too different than we were, other aircraft that took off the same morning will land safely. Whatever else we were that day, we were a minority.

I don't know about the rest of you, but I've always liked it here on Carole Lombard's plane. Good drinks, marvelous company, interesting chat about art and the news of the day as we ride. That glorious girl Nan Finn once made my favorite comment about death, perhaps understandable only to old District hands: "Of course, what I'm really going to hate is never knowing how all the politics came out."

Music of our choice on the earphones. Pretty stewardesses I can imagine newly naked as Eve—as in Genesis or African, not Harrington—as they bend to retrieve a fork I've dropped and smilingly promise to bring me another. They're used to that betingled look from their elderly passengers and we're all wearing seatbelts anyhow, so no danger.

Nonetheless I feel reasonably sure I'll get to Provincetown in one piece. The Cape can get windy: I know I'll need a scarf. Can't shake an idea one will be waiting for me when I get there, along with the helpmeet Chris said he'd hired to keep Gramela's wheelchair and grumpy dentition in line.

I'll ask Moesha Kendricks to park me on the dunes. Then I'll give her the rest of the afternoon off, let her bulky but resourceful pink-swimsuited body challenge the up-and-down waves' great unknowns just for the fun of it: something her ten thousand unknown Nagonese relatives never got to do in my day. The sea wasn't for pleasure unless you were us.

I do so like her! She's awfully enchanting, and I seem to amuse her when my odd tales falter in a mist of the mimsies' fat-lunetted charmed gaze at her shrewd jokes in reply. Who knows, I may even ask Moesha if she'd be willing to undertake a move to Washington and a full-time job as Pam's caregiver back at the old Rochambeau, since after all Andy's right about my debility.

Then the African Adam and Eve will finally have someone to honor for a year or a few. Not only are Moesha's hips a song that's meant for better things than dirges, but she's got the face of a Gauguin.

There I'll watch you too, Panama. As you decide we're being boring and scamper uphill, Tim will say, "Pam, I'm thinking of showing her Paris and vice versa next year. Do you think they're ready for each other?"

And I'll probably answer, "Tim, why not? I'd say it's about time she met her real namesake."

Then we'll smile. Of course your old dad and I both know the ancient French slang for Paris—the city where good Americans get to go when they die—is *Paname*.

Turn and wave, bikini girl! Turn and wave at me once before you run on up the hill. Since I can't follow, I'll just sit here next to history's ocean and watch. Scarf hugging my neck.

I shall be nothing like a dame. I shall feel lucky for the sun.

Glory, be.

In Memoriam

A.   From the *Owl Creek News*, June 5, 2006

[Versions of Pam's obit appeared in any number of print and online venues. This was the mildly peculiar one most likely to have been read by Dottie Idell Crozdetti at her vacation home in Colorado just before, clumping forth on her walker from her heretofore cheerful kitchen to call "Who's there?," she encountered a burglar and died game herself. Unless it was her cat's name, no one has ever explained Dottie's final remark to her murderer: "Thomasina Jefferson still lives. Buck, buck, buck!"]

Daisy Buchanan's Daughter Dies

WASHINGTON, D.C. (wire services) Pamela Buchanan, only child of legendary Jazz Age figure Daisy Fay Buchanan and her husband, polo player Tom Buchanan, died quietly in her sleep on Sunday, it has been learned. She was two days short of her 86th birthday.

In her own right, Ms. Bookman was best known as a writer. She wrote "Nothing Like the Sun," a novel, and "Glory Be," a history of the American Revolution. Her mother committed suicide in Brussels in 1934.

At different times, she was married to playwright Brannigan Murphy, Hollywood producer Noah Gerson, and U.S. diplomat Richard Anson Cadwaller. She had no known blood relatives.

Despite repeated threats to do so, she never wrote her autobiography. However, according to her literary executors—Tim Cadwaller, writer; Sean (pronounced "Seen") Finn, artist—plans for a memorial volume are already underway.

B.   A Very Partial Bibliography

1.   Books by Pamela Buchanan

Nothing Like a Dame, Henry Holt, 1947.
Glory Be, Random House, 1956.
Lucky for the Sun, Simon & Schuster, 1968.

2.   Selected Articles by Pamela Buchanan

"Spare the Ambassador," Los Angeles Times, June 6, 2004.
"Omaha at Fifty," *Hemispheres* [United Airlines in-flight magazine], June 1994.
"Remembering Jake Cohnstein," contribution to *Biquarterly*, Fall 1986.
"Come Back to the Raft Again, Pauline, Honey" [review of Pauline Kael's *When the Lights Go Down*], *Washington Post Book World*, April 20, 1986.

"Nagon, Dahomey, Upper Volta, Congo: So What's in a Name? Lots," *Foreign Service Journal* [as "Pamela B. Cadwaller"], October 1969.

"Marianne's Shotgun Wedding to Charles de Gaulle," *Regent's*, June 11, 1958.

"Juliette Greco on the Left Bank: *Allons, les Enfants du* Paradise Lost," *Regent's*, August 28, 1957.

"It's Called 'Glory Be.' Not Glory Me," *Vogue* [interview], November 1956.

"Poolside at the Beverly Hills Hotel: Gadzooks and Vaudeville Hooks," *Regent's*, March 16, 1949.

"The Gates of Hell," *Regent's*, May 17, 1945.

"Tiger! Tiger!" *Regent's*, January 3, 1945.

"Allo, 2ième D.B.? Ici Paname. Our Gal Gets the First Interview with Dronne, the Man Who Liberated Paris," *Regent's*, September 6, 1944.

"The Day the Tide Ran Red," *Regent's*, June 28, 1944.

"'Dear God, Miss Buchanan! You're Holding the Only Salami in London,'" *Regent's*, May 24, 1944.

"Bacchanapoli," *Regent's*, April 12, 1944.

"A Thousand Words About Bill Mauldin," *Regent's*, March 30, 1944.

"The Angel of Anzio," *Regent's*, March 1, 1944.

"The View from Ward Three," *Regent's*, April 28, 1943.

"Finding Mr. Wright," *Regent's*, February 17, 1943.

"To the Ends of the Earth," *Regent's*, January 14, 1943.

"Every Woman Needs a Hobby" [profile of Oveta Culp Hobby], *Regent's*, November 11, 1942.

"Liberty Belles," *Regent's*, October 21, 1942.

"The Mighty Flowers," *Regent's*, September 23, 1942.

"Gold Bars for a Redhead," *Regent's*, September 9, 1942.

"Adios, Adolf. Tojo Too? Tojo Too," *Regent's*, August 5, 1942.

"She-Worthy," *Regent's*, June 17, 1942.

"Brides without Grooms," *Regent's*, April 29, 1942.

"Skirting the Issue?," *Regent's*, February 18, 1942.

"Che Te Dice La Patria?," *Regent's*, January 21, 1942.

"A Cross with Many Roots," *Regent's*, December 31, 1941.

"Silent Knight, Lonely Knight" [review of *A Sebastian Knight Omnibus*], *Our Chains*, December 24, 1941.

"She Thought of Bunny" [review of Rita Cavanagh's *Sybil Choate*], the old *Republic*, November 17, 1941.

"Ma Semblable, Ma Soeur!" [review of Celia Brady's *The Producer's Daughter*], the old *Republic*, April 1, 1941.

"Isn't It Pretty to Think So?" [review of Lady Brett Ashley's *Farewell the Sun*], the old *Republic*, June 3, 1940.

"Chanson d'automne" [poem], *Pink Rosebuds,* the Literary Magazine of Purcey's Girls' Academy of St. Paul, Fall 1934.

3. Other Sources

May or Mayn't. By Chris Cadwaller [photographs]. Kaylie & Gallagher, 1969.

You Must Remember This: The Posthumous Career of World War Two. By Tim Cadwaller. First Cold Press, 2005.

The Mountain and the Stream: Letters from Nenuphar. By Brother Nicholas (Nicholas Carraway). Vaughn Trapp & Co., 1969.

It Was All Theater: From Brannigan Murphy to the Moscow Show Trials. By Jake Cohnstein. Sadder, Weiser & Sons, 1954.

Hello, Dottie. Omnibus edition of *The Pearl I Left Behind Me: Dottie Crozdetti on Shellfish* and *Cast a Cold Pie: Dottie Crozdetti on Baking.* Introduction by Sebastian Knight Jr. Paris & Bogey, 1999.

The Pilgrim Lands at Malibu. By Addison DeWitt. George Sanders Press, 1956.

An Apple for My Eve. Also by Addison DeWitt. Mankiewicz & Co., 1970.

The Collected Plays of Brannigan Murphy. Edited by Ernest Hemingway. Hofstra University Press, 1981.

How the Red Faded Out of Old Glory. By Alisteir Malcolm. Cowley & Crowley, 1965.

"My Anzio Bobbsey Twin." By Bill M____. Canceled MS. chapter of *Up Front.* Unknown to Pam and available only to qualified researchers at UT Austin, Texas, but it seems he loved her too.

Les problèmes de l'Afrique moderne. By Jean-Baptiste M'Lawa. Petit Navire, 1957.

Dat Dead Man Dere: Brannigan Murphy, 1899–1964. By Garth Vader. Odets & Sting, 1990.

The Rough Draft of History. By Edmond Whitling. Murrow, Smoke & Mirror, 1946.

The Gal I Left Behind Me [DVD]. Cast: Eve Harrington (Peg Kimball), Walt Wanks (Eddie Harting), Hal Lime (Chet Dooley). Screenplay: Bettina Hecuba & Claude Estee and Wylie White & Pamela Buchanan, based on *Nothing Like a Dame* by Pamela Buchanan. Producer: Noah Gerson. Director: Tod Paspartu. Metro, 1949.

Fran Kukla's Hamlet: The Legendary 1956 Broadcast. Cast: Frank Ukla (Sarah Bernhardt/Hamlet), Dorothy Kirsten (Ophelia), James W. Dean (Laertes), etc. Director: Ike Nixon. Incidental music, not counting "Love for Sale": Adlai Kefauver. Criterion, 2002.

Exodus. Cast: Paul Newman (Ari ben Canaan), Eva Marie Saint (Kitty Fremont), Sal Mineo (Dov Landau), etc. Director: Otto Preminger. United Artists, 1960. Panavision.

The Longest Day. Cast: Robert Mitchum (Brigadier Norman Cota) and many, many others. Rumored scene featuring Paula Prentiss as Pam and George Peppard as Eddie Whitling on run-in to Dog Green apparently cut before release and now lost. Producer: Darryl F. Zanuck. 20th Century Fox, 1962.

Gatsby le magnifique. Par F. Scott Fitzgerald, traduit de l'américain par Jacques Tournier [only version obtainable in Cannes in May of 2006]. Livres de Poche, *passim.*

C.   From *Pink Rosebuds*, the Literary Magazine of Purcey's Girls' Academy of St. Paul, Fall 1934

CHANSON D'AUTOMNE

Où est-tu, Maman? Tu sais, je t'ai cherchée,
Ici, aux États-Unis, parmi les grands blés
Inconnus dans ce Mid-West étranger.
Tu n'as les jamais vus. Mais quand même,
Quand je suis seule—pas grand problème,
Maman!—je pense que tu y es.

Ou êtes-vous, mon père? Sale lâche,
Je sais quand-même que c'est ma tâche
De vous trouver dans les sanglots qui m'arrachent.
Et si on se rencontrait maintenant,
Dans les grands blés sanglotants,
Vais-je vous reconnaître, Papa? Signé, votre vache.

English translation by Panama's dad:

[Note: the "game of nonperpendicular pronouns" Pam mentions can't be reproduced in English. Otherwise, one or two inevitable liberties aside, the sense is exact.—T.C.]

Where are you, mother? I wish that I could greet
You here, in the United States, amid the rye and wheat
So new to me, in a Midwest still so strange under my feet.
You never saw it. Even so, when I'm
Alone—which would be all the time,
My Ma!—I hope someday we'll meet.

Where are you, Daddy? Cruel coward, you
Made it my job to find you too
As I sobbed in the fourth-form loo.
And if we do meet by and bye,
In the weeping wheat and rye,
Will I know you, father? Moo.

by Pamela Buchanan

(our newest Pink Rosebud — be nice to her, girls!)